CROWN OF RENEWAL

The cloth over his father's body quivered like the candle flames. It lifted over his mouth, and Ferran quickly folded back the cloth. Out of Jeddrin's mouth came the spirit, a pale wraith of Jeddrin, shivering, trembling . . . and then it steadied.

"Son?" The voice was softer than a whisper, the merest touch of sound on Ferran's ear.

"Ferran, Father. Death came suddenly, but not from an enemy."

"I choose light." The wraith leaned to a candle flame, and at once the candle burned brighter, a clear white light bright as summer sun, and the wraith was gone. But in the silence, inside Ferran's head, his father's voice said one more thing:

"I leave you my magery."

"What magery?"

No answer came.

CROWN OF RENEWAL

ELIZABETH MOON

PALADIN'S LEGACY

BOOK 5

www.orbitbooks.net

ORBIT

First published in Great Britain in 2014 by Orbit

Printed and bound in Great Britain by
Clays Ltd, St Ives plc

Papers used by Orbit are from well-managed forests
and other responsible sources.

MIX
Paper from
responsible sources
FSC® C104740

Orbit
An imprint of
Little, Brown Book Group
100 Victoria Embankment
London EC4Y 0DY

An Hachette UK Company
www.hachette.co.uk

www.orbitbooks.net

For Sgt. Nicholas M. Dickhut, killed in action, Afghanistan, a long-time reader of the Paks books, and for all the other readers, who have made this journey both possible and worthwhile

Dramatis Personae

Fox Company

Jandelir Arcolin, Commander of Fox Company, Duke Arcolin of Tsaia, and
   Prince of Arcolinfulk tribe of gnomes
   Calla, his wife
   Jamis, his adopted son
Burek, junior captain of first cohort
Selfer, captain of second cohort
Cracolnya, captain of third (mixed/archery) cohort
Andreson, captain of recruit cohort

Tsaia

Mikeli Vostan Kieriel Mahieran, king of Tsaia
   Camwyn, his younger brother
Sonder Amrothlin Mahieran, Duke Mahieran, king's uncle
Selis Jostin Marrakai, Duke Marrakai
   Gwennothlin, his daughter and Duke Verrakai's squire
   Aris, his son and Prince Camwyn's friend
Galyan Selis Serrostin, Duke Serrostin
   Daryan, youngest son and Duke Verrakai's squire
Dorrin Verrakai, Duke Verrakai, formerly a senior captain in Phelan's company,
   now Constable for the kingdom
Beclan, Kirgan Verrakai, formerly Beclan Mahieran
Oktar, Marshal-Judicar of Tsaia
Seklis, High Marshal of Gird

Lyonya

Kieri Phelan, king of Lyonya, former mercenary commander and duke in Tsaia,
   half-elven grandson of the Lady of the Ladysforest
Arian, Kieri's wife, queen of Lyonya, half-elven granddaughter of the elven
   ruler of the Lordsforest
Aliam Halveric, Kieri Phelan's mentor and friend
   Estil Halveric, his wife

Elves

Amrothlin, the Lady's son and Kieri's uncle, elven ruler of the Lordsforest

Fintha

Arianya, Marshal-General of Gird
Arvid Semminson, former thief-enforcer, now Girdish
Camwynya, paladin of Gird
Paksenarrion, paladin of Gird

Aarenis

Jeddrin, Count of Andressat
   Ferran, his son and heir
   Meddthal, his second son
Visla Vaskronin, Duke of Immer (formerly Alured the Black)
Aesil M'dierra, commander of Golden Company
   Poldin, her nephew and squire
Count Vladi (the Cold Count), commander of Count's Company
Kaim, Arcolin's squire this campaign season

Kuakkgani

Sprucewind, itinerant Kuakgan

Gnomes

Dattur, Arcolin's hesktak (advisor of Law)
Faksutterk, envoy of Aldonfulk Prince

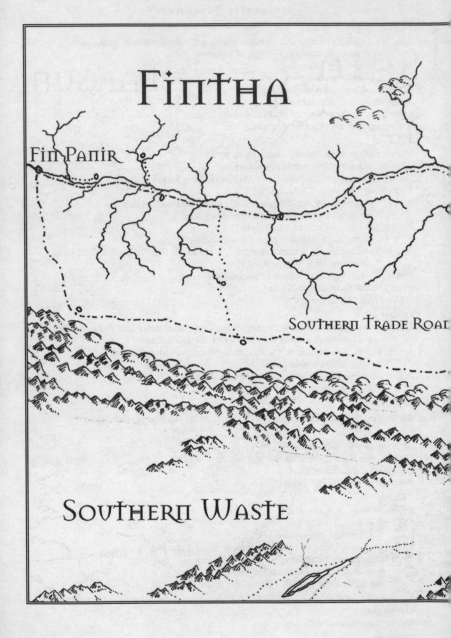

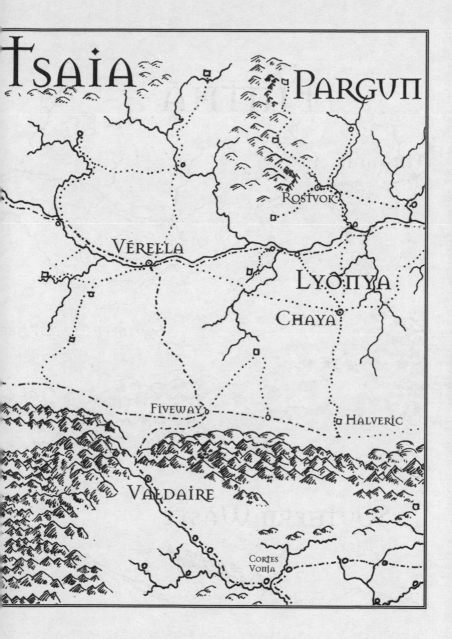

Author's Note

Crown of Renewal is the fifth and final volume of Paladin's Legacy, and not an entry point for new readers. *Oath of Fealty* is first.

This book presented some challenges in chronology. First, and simplest, readers need to know that *Crown of Renewal* begins a quarter-year before the end of *Limits of Power,* at Midwinter in Aarenis. This allows the viewpoints of characters who were out of contact to catch up. Timelines converge as communication resumes.

The other chronological challenge most affects those who have read *Surrender None, Liar's Oath,* or the omnibus version of these two, *The Legacy of Gird,* which are otherwise very helpful to the readers of *Crown.* The end of *Liar's Oath* will not match exactly certain scenes in *Crown.* Assume an unreliable narrator.

Finally, this final volume of Paladin's Legacy pulls together those prequel books—the history of Gird and Luap from their own viewpoints—and connects them to present events. The flaws and the strengths in the Fellowship of Gird shown in the original Paks books began with Gird and his followers, fault lines that cause the schisms appearing in the books' present time.

So those who have never read either *Liar's Oath* or *Surrender None* will benefit from reading them—they enrich understanding of the new books. *Liar's Oath* is the book almost no one likes, but it's more palatable if read as a gloss on *Crown*—as a dry history. If you don't want to do that, there are some take-home things I can offer from the earlier books.

1. Luap is a classic tragic protagonist—a man of talents ruined by a fatal flaw: his inability to accept the truth of his faults. He lied, re-

peatedly. To himself and to others, about himself and others. He made up stories he thought were better than reality, including those about Gird's life and death. Gird's daughter managed to suppress that once, but as people died who had been there, Luap renewed his effort to tell the story his way. *Surrender None* (Gird's book) has the accurate version.

Luap could not accept Gird's judgment of him—that he was unfit for command—or that of the wise old magelady who knew his parentage. Because he was a king's bastard, he thought he had inherited the ability and the right to rule *somewhere*. Like so many, he told himself that lies didn't matter if (a) he meant well (and he always did) and (b) the truth would bother somebody (him, for instance).

Those lies led to disaster for those who followed him and to schism and confusion over the centuries. Knowing himself so little, he was a poor judge of character in others, so he was unable to determine whether the magelords who came with him to Kolobia were coming in good faith or not. Some weren't. And for the same reason, he was easy prey for iynisin, who convinced him that he was so important to the colony that he must not age. This led to his stealing life force (and age) from those around him and making it possible for the iynisin to escape their old imprisonment in the stone. When they felt strong enough, iynisin attacked Luap's magelords openly.

2. The last chapters of *Liar's Oath* (Luap's book) gives the viewpoint of Luap and some of his followers at the time the magelords in Kolobia were attacked and then put into enchanted sleep. None of the participants—enchanters or enchanted—had full understanding of the situation on either side. Luap himself was stunned by both iynisin attacks and the sudden demands of the Elder Races that he and his people leave at once, without the benefit of the magic transfer patterns. In the chaos of that day, he prayed for help and had a vision that resulted in the situation the much later Girdish expedition (including Paksenarrion) found: a great stronghold hollowed out of a mountain, with a large group of men and women in armor kneeling in its main hall. In *Liar's Oath*, events are seen from Luap's POV; in *Crown of Renewal*, from the enchanter's POV.

CHAPTER ONE

Andressat, winter of the previous year

Winter storms, one after another, cut off the high plateau of Andressat from the lowlands around it as Midwinter Feast neared. On the morning before the nightlong vigil, Meddthal Andressat, the Count of Andressat's second son and present commander in the north, woke to hear the thud of the inner door closing, then voices in the tower's main hall: exclamations, then quieter tones.

Someone, he gathered, had sent something to someone as a gift. Found it by the door. Sighing, he pushed back the covers, dressed quickly, and went out to see what was going on. Families did not normally come to the towers to leave gifts for their kin on duty, especially not during winter storms. Especially not without pounding on the door and coming inside. He thought immediately of treachery, poisoned food, perhaps, sent by an enemy.

"Whatever it is, don't eat it," he said, coming into the mess, then stopped short as he saw the wide eyes and horrified expressions turned toward him and the quick movement of men hiding something from their commander. "What?" he demanded. "Show me."

The sergeant who had served with him since Meddthal first gained command shook his head. "Sir, you don't want to see this."

"Of course I do. Stand aside."

"Sir, please. It's . . . it's horrible . . ."

Meddthal could feel the hairs on his arms rising; cold foreboding struck like a blow. His younger brother Filis had been missing since the previous summer, disappearing on a routine trip from Andressat to Cortes Cilwan. Almost certainly Filis had been captured by the one man in Aarenis who would want an Andressat son in his hands: Alured the Black, self-styled Duke of Immer.

"It's Filis," he said. "Isn't it?"

"There's a letter, sir. To Count Andressat."

Meddthal moved forward. "It's more than that by the way you're all acting. Stand aside. I must see to report to my father." He braced himself for horrors: Filis's head, Filis's body. Then he saw it, and his breath came short, his vision darkened.

The box had been made with great skill, leather laid over a framework of wood. Filis's face formed the top—skillfully padded enough to show the contours, like a mask, though much flattened, the ears—those distinctive ears—forming a hideously decorative border to left and right. Meddthal struggled to think about that, not that it was *Filis's* face, the familiar face of a brother he had loved and quarreled with. Not—absolutely *not*—about how it had been taken from Filis, whether Filis had been skinned before or after death.

He struggled to stay upright, to breathe, to hold back the nausea that threatened to shame him in front of all. He became aware gradually that the sergeant's arm was around him, steadying him—a strong, warm arm, and most of all a *live* arm. That his men were looking away from him, giving him time to recover, stirring about as if it were a normal morning and they were getting ready for another day. He dragged in one lungful after another of the chill air—air that would never be warm after this. And looked again.

He could not unsee what he had seen. He could not unthink the thoughts that raced through his mind, deadly as a flight of arrows. He had known—they had all known—that Filis was likely dead, killed by Alured or at his command. They had told themselves that; they had even—as his father had said aloud first—hoped he was dead and past suffering. Had it been Filis's severed head . . . even a body bearing marks of torture . . . it would not have been so bad.

Filis's hair fell over the back of the box, carefully braided with ribbons in Immer's colors and formed into a decorative knot. On one corner was a scar Meddthal recognized from Filis's shoulder . . . then he saw the fine stitching that had attached that piece of Filis's skin to the others. A tube—it must be the message tube with the letter to Count Andressat—protruded obscenely from Filis's mouth.

Rage shook him as suddenly as horror had. That scum had planned all this to the last detail . . . to foul one of the year's holiest days, Sunreturn, with such horror . . . to make of it not the day of hope and joy Midwinter Feast had always been but to stain it with the memory of Filis's death.

"It was in a sack, tied with a green ribbon," one of the men said. "There was a message: Send it to Count Andressat as a Midwinter gift from his liege, it said." He pointed to the sack, crumpled on the floor, coarsely woven, and the ribbon with a wooden tag still attached.

Meddthal shook his head. "He has no liege, and it would kill him." To his surprise, his voice sounded almost normal.

"You're never going to hide it from him—"

"No. I'm not going to hide it. But he will have word from me, to blunt the blade, before I send it. Now, however, I will open Immer's letter. Simthal, is the food ready?"

"For Midwinter, sir? I thought—"

"We have much to do, and days are short. We will eat, and we will prepare for the attack that is surely coming." Already his mind was working again, offering alternatives and the problems with each. In Midwinter, no one could ride from this tower to Cortes Andres in one day's light . . . but had Alured's men sent a message directly to the Count? No . . . they wanted to unnerve the border guards first. "Tell the cooks: breakfast now. And we will observe most parts of the Midwinter ceremony, though we will not be fools and exhaust ourselves in games this day. We will honor Filis's memory best by saving Andressat from the same fate."

They nodded. Someone handed him a mug of sib, and he sipped cautiously . . . his stomach kept it down. The tears burning his eyes did not overflow. He took the tube from between the lips, leaving a gaping hole in the face, and untied the green and black ribbons.

It was written in blood; the rusty color could be nothing else. "Brother," he murmured, and kissed it. Filis had died, no doubt a terrible death, but this was proof he was no traitor, as some had thought. The words made it clear what had been done and when and how. A terrible death indeed. The box had not required all of Filis's skin . . . the rest had been made into a rug for Alured's bedside—"and as I stand on it each day, so will I stand on Andressat: master of all." "The best parts" of Filis's broken body had been cooked and force-fed to the Count of Cilwan and his wife before they were killed and their bodies fed to dogs, their skins added to the rug.

So Alured had killed not only Filis but their sister, and his father had lost two children. Thank the gods their child, the count's grandson, was safe in Cortes Andres. A few tears slipped from Meddthal's eyes. Nerinth had been married to Cilwan young, unwillingly and had endured years with that—Meddthal cut off the thought. It would do no good now to despise Cilwan's timidity and avarice. He blinked back more tears and read on.

The rest was yet more boasts and threats. Meddthal thought of burning it, saving his father that knowledge, but the old man would not thank him. He rolled the letter once more and put it back in the tube, then put the tube into his belt pouch.

Cooks had brought in bread, porridge, pastries, roasts; for a moment his stomach turned again. But vengeance required nourishment. Starving himself, heaving his food out: neither one would help him defeat Alured. He forced down a bowl of porridge and a slab of bacon. Others ate after seeing him eat. He went to the door and opened it, shut it behind him, then opened the outer door. A gray day, just enough light to see, barely past dawn. Low clouds like a lid shut them away from the sun. Wind cut through his clothes like a knife. He went back into the vestibule when the wind had frozen the tears on his face, and brushed the tiny ice chips away.

Kolfin was his best rider, and his own horse the fastest. Meddthal wanted to go himself, but if Alured did plan to attack—and he himself would have—in the next few days, he needed to be here to command the defense. He went back inside. "Kolfin."

Kolfin stood up from the table. "Sir?"

"Finish quickly. Take two days' ration, and you'll ride my horse to Cortes Andres with my letter. Be ready to ride when I've written it."

"Sir."

He sat down with pen and ink, and his mind blanked again. Filis. This . . . this abomination . . . but his father must know something, and as soon as possible. He wrote quickly, plainly.

Father. Bad news. Filis's death proved; Alured has sent—

He paused. He could not say it all, not like this . . .

—proof of what he did to Filis. It is beyond my words to say. Laid on our doorstep here last night; no doubt it is Filis. I ex-pect attack when he thinks we are unmanned by grief; I remain here to command defense but will come at your command, bringing what was sent. I send also the letter he wrote you, written in what I am sure is Filis's blood, admitting he killed the Count of Cilwan and your daughter as well.

He sealed that, put it and the letter from Alured in a message bag, and gave it to Kolfin, who had already saddled Meddthal's horse. "Take a spare horse," Meddthal said. "Ride fast but warily. Those who did this may be looking to intercept any messenger."

"Yes, sir." Kolfin took the message bag; another soldier brought out another of the horses, saddled it, and transferred Kolfin's saddle-bags to the second horse.

When Kolfin had ridden away, Meddthal set about readying for attack. By midday, he had completed that chore as well as sending couriers to the two nearest towers to warn them. "Half of you must rest this afternoon," he said. "If they attack, it will be when they think we have all spent a sleepless night in the dark after a day of grief and worry or perhaps drunken rage. Tomorrow—or even the day after—is when they will come."

"What about tonight, sir?"

"Tonight we will do as we always do. Today and tomorrow, how-ever, we will rest as much as we can, to be fresh when they attack."

"And . . . that? Him?"

Meddthal looked at the table, at Filis's face staring upward from the top of the box. It felt—it was—indecent to leave it there like any other box. But he could not close it into the storeroom . . . or put it outside . . .

One of the youngest men, Dannrith, spoke up. "Sir, someone dyin' or dead should have a candle and someone by. They wouldn't of give him a candle . . . We should."

A scrape of boots on the floor as others considered that, and a low murmur, then they all looked at Meddthal. The silence lengthened as Meddthal tried to think, in a mind suddenly fuzzy, whether to say yes or no, where to put the thing, in here or in his quarters or . . .

"I'll stay with 'im," said another. And then a chorus of offers.

That settled it. "In here, then," Meddthal said. "Bring a trestle and a blanket. We'll do this right."

Very shortly the grisly box had been placed at one end of a plank, with a blanket laid flat below it and Meddthal's best cloak spread over it, hiding the face and making, with the blanket, a pretense of a body laid straight for burial. Though it was not yet sundown, they lit a candle, and one at a time, as if for a new death, each spoke a word about Filis, for all had at least seen him, if they had not known him.

Then Meddthal sent half of them to bed, to be wakened at full dark, and the rest took up their duties except for the watcher. At each turn of the glass another took his place. At full dark, when all assembled, the hearth had been swept clean and a new fire laid but not lit. Only the feeble glow of one candle outlined the shape on the board and the face of the one who sat beside him. The others turned their faces from the light and began the long night's watch for Sun-return.

When it was Meddthal's turn to sit beside his brother's remains, he wondered if his father would send for him or for the box alone.

Jeddrin, Count of Andressat, looked at the face of his dead son and wept. Rage burned in his heart, but grief drowned it for the moment, and he made no attempt to hold back the tears. Let them fall;

let them flow; let them be emptied like a bronze bowl so the flame of vengeance could burn higher.

When the tears ended, he looked more closely. Honoring the dead, especially those who died in war, required the mourners to see and respect every mark life had made on them. "We'll give him his rightful colors," he said, and began unwinding the complex knot that the braided hair had been coiled into. "He'll not go under earth wearing that scum's." After the knot came the braids themselves. Three braids; his sons Narits and Tamir, Narits recalled from Cha earlier in the year and Tamir recalled from the south ward, each took one, and he took the last. Deft fingers unbraided the hair, pulled out the black and green ribbons.

Narits finished first. "You'll want just one braid, won't you, Father?" he asked.

"Yes—we'll have to comb it all."

Narits took up the comb. "There's blood," he said.

"Of course there is," Tamir said. Next to Filis, he had been the hothead of the sons. "What did you expect—"

"The hair's clean," Narits said. "They must have washed it, or this didn't bleed much—" He had parted the hair and was peering closely at the scalp. "It looks . . . almost like . . . fingernails dug in. Not scratches."

The others had finished now and leaned over to look.

"Let me finish," Narits said. "I think there are more marks . . ."

"Of pain," Tamir said, turning away. "What does it matter?"

Narits ignored him and ran the comb through the hair, parting it every half fingerwidth to look for marks. "It's code," he said finally. "Like the old scrolls. Father, can you read it?"

Andressat looked. "Not like this. Can you copy it, Narits, one mark at a time, onto paper?"

"Yes, Father."

When he had done that, it was clear that the marks—each a slightly curved line—formed a definite design. "Alured's work," Tamir said. "Maybe an evil spell?"

"No," Andressat said. "No, it's Filis's." His voice wavered. "He . . . managed to give us warning. He must have known—" He cleared his throat and went on. "Filis knew what was coming. With only his fingernails to use—knowing Alured was going to send me his skin—he used them where Alured would not see. Under his hair. Perhaps Alured told him he would leave the hair to make sure we recognized him. This—in the old language of Aare, the old writing—tells us that Alured is controlled by a demon inside him, a demon who looks out his eyes at times and has a different voice. That is like the stories from the north of the Verrakaien who stole bodies."

He looked around at his family and his most trusted servants. "Think on this, any of you who thought Filis might be a traitor. Captive, alone, tormented, yet he thought of us—of saving us—and tore his own skin to warn us. Think what courage that took." He bent down and kissed the hair, then the forehead, and finally the lips. "My son, you deserve every honor that we can bestow on you. You will be remembered as long as our lives endure. And you will not go under the earth but be borne aloft in Camwyn's Fire, as if with a dragon for your mount. From Esea came all life; back to Esea you shall go."

"By Camwyn's Claw," everyone responded. "It shall be done."

"Though first I must write to the north," Andressat said. "Lord Arcolin must know of this, and his king. Perhaps his captains in Valdaire can get word to the north even in winter."

Two days later, the funeral pyre stood ready on the cliff just outside the walls of Cortes Andres. On it lay the box, now drenched in oil, and in the box was Filis's badge. "If it is Camwyn's will that this fire may send every bit of Filis left below, wherever it may be, on the same smoke rising to the sky, then I invoke Camwyn's Curse," Andressat said. "By the Claw and the dragon who bore it, and by the power of Camwyn and the dragon together, I invoke it."

When they lit the fire, the flames roared up to the sky as if drawn by the air itself and burned the pyre completely; white ash lifted and swirled like snowflakes. Then far, far above, a white line of fire raced across the sky, from above Cortes Andres to the east, and vanished.

"Camwyn consented," Andressat said. He felt hollow of a sudden, and then a pain as if a horse had kicked him in the chest took all his breath, and he knew he was falling.

Cortes Immer

A servant's screams brought the Duke of Immer from his study to his bedroom to find the bedside rug—patched together of skin from Filis Andressat, the Count of Cilwan, Cilwan's wife, and several other people he'd had flayed—in flames, flames that quickly spread to the bedclothes. More servants ran in with pitchers of water, but the flames could not be stopped until every flammable thing in the room had burnt to ash: stinking, black, oily ash that clung to and dirtied whatever it touched.

"How did you start the fire?" he asked the servant.

"I—I didn't, lord. I swear—I was sweeping when it—it burst into flames. Then I screamed."

"Nonsense. Leather doesn't burst into flames by itself. You dropped a lighted spill if you didn't start it by intention. And the way the bed burned—what did you do, splash oil on the bed?"

"No! I didn't!"

He made a gesture, and one of the guards ran her through. Even as she fell, a commotion broke out in the courtyard below. Immer looked out the window to see a fire in the kennels. He looked back at the guards. "It seems we have more than one firestarter. See to it."

Some time later the guard reported that the dogs in question had been seen to burst into flame while in the dog yard. Nothing burned but the dogs . . . and not all the dogs. Only the dogs that had been fed human flesh. Immer shrugged. Someone had thrown a curse at him, clearly. Given the time of year—could it have been the old man, Andressat? He hadn't thought the man had that much power—any power at all, in fact. He'd never been spoken of as a mage. But he claimed to be bred of Old Aare, a true line, so perhaps—perhaps he had been hiding it all these years.

F erran Andressat, heir to the title, stood watch over his father's body turn and turn with the others. No attack had come after all, and he had called Meddthal in from his guard post for the mourning.

They must all be there; in the absence of a king to confirm any of them in the title, they used a ceremony passed down in the family for generations. But that would come after placing Jeddrin's body in the appointed cave. Until then . . . they stood watch.

While he watched, each of his brothers had other chores to complete. Narits received visitors, then ushered them one by one into the chamber where Jeddrin's body lay. Meddthal organized the household for the reception that would follow the funeral, and Tamir organized the funeral itself. Ferran had given them those assignments. No one had argued.

As the day wore on and he took his turn at his own assignment— reviewing the status of his father's governance—servants brought meals he ate, out of necessity, but did not really taste. He knew his father had insisted on the need for nobles to work, but he had not realized how much of the work of managing Andressat and its outlying lands his father had done personally.

He ate the last meal of the day with his brothers in the room where the body lay—it could not be left alone—and nodded his approval of what they had accomplished. "We are ready for the burial, then, thanks to you. How one manages alone—how our father managed—I do not know."

"And how stands Andressat as a whole?" asked Narits. "I know he had been concerned about the costs of governing the South Marches."

"Solvent and whole, thanks to him, and may we do as well now that it is up to us."

"Indeed," Narits said.

"Do you remember, Ferran, the time you told him you were not going to spend one more morning in the library? You must have been ten or so."

Ferran grinned. "I do indeed. As I recall, I spent that entire day copying lists and wishing I could do it standing up."

"I was in awe," Meddthal said. "Arguing with *him*? Amazing. But seeing the result saved me the trouble of trying it myself."

They shared memories for a while . . . times with their father, with their mother, with both. The candles around Jeddrin's body burned bright, flames standing up straight, without a flutter. At last Ferran said, "I need to stay with him tonight—go, sleep, and I'll sleep tomorrow, after—after it's done."

When they had left, he sat by the body and began the old Song of Death his father had taught him. It was in the language of Aare, which he had been forced to learn, as had they all, though none could speak it but themselves.

The candle flames stirred. He sang on, the near drone of the song fitting his mood, fitting death itself.

> There is a lord above all lords
> And a death below all deaths
> Go to the highest lord, to the court of that one
> And be free of death, but never return,
> Or lie in restful sleep, safe from harm
> Far below, below the deepest death
> And never return.
> This night decide, before the death is done,
> While still the spirit has will enough
> Make that choice, make it soon,
> For the sand runs through the glass
> And candles shorten and daylight ends the night
> Come, spirit, make that choice
> So this body may be laid in honor
> Where it should be laid
> Then never return.

The cloth over his father's body quivered like the candle flames. It lifted over his mouth, and Ferran quickly folded back the cloth. Out of Jeddrin's mouth came the spirit, a pale wraith of Jeddrin, shivering, trembling . . . and then it steadied.

"Son?" The voice was softer than a whisper, the merest touch of sound on Ferran's ear.

"Ferran, Father. Death came suddenly, but not from an enemy."

"I choose light." The wraith leaned to a candle flame, and at once the candle burned brighter, a clear white light bright as summer sun, and the wraith was gone. But in the silence, inside Ferran's head, his father's voice said one more thing:

"I leave you my magery."

"What magery?"

No answer came.

CHAPTER TWO

Valdaire, Aarenis

Aesil M'dierra's nephew Poldin, beginning his second year as a squire in that company, rode over to the Fox Company winter quarters at least thrice in a fiveday. Everyone in Valdaire knew the boy had spent more than a quarter year with Fox Company. Golden Company and Fox Company had long been strong supporters of the Mercenary Guild Agreement, and their commanders were friends. This explained the trips back and forth.

So though the omnipresent spies noted the boy making yet another trip to Fox Company, this time on one of his aunt's chargers, it meant nothing more to any of them than that Aesil M'dierra's horse needed exercise and the boy was thought skilled enough to ride it in city traffic. Poldin, for his part, paid attention to other horsemen and pedestrians both, alert for someone who might want to grab a rein or cut it. He found the potential for danger exciting.

"Morning, Squire," the Fox Company gate guard said. "That's your commander's horse, isn't it?"

"Yes," Poldin said. "It's the first time I've ridden him in the city. Is Captain Selfer here?" The stallion fidgeted under him.

"Yes, he is." The guard turned his head. "Tamis, hold the squire's mount while he speaks with our captain. Walk him up and down in the courtyard."

Poldin dismounted and handed the reins to the soldier who had come to take them.

"I swear you've grown a hand this quarter," the guard said.

Poldin grinned. "That's what my aunt—Commander M'dierra says. She threatened to put a rock on my head and hold me down."

"Well, you know where the captain's office is."

Poldin nodded and jogged quickly along the near side of the courtyard. He felt relieved to be in this safe place again, though when it had become "safe" he could not determine. Valdaire itself was more dangerous than when he'd first arrived, his aunt insisted. He could see some signs of that himself.

He knocked at the closed door of the captain's office and heard Selfer's familiar voice. "Come in."

"Squire M'dierra with a message from Commander M'dierra," he said as he opened the door and saluted properly.

"You grow a finger a day," Captain Selfer said. "Any news?"

Poldin closed the door. "Yes, Captain. A message from Count Andressat, very urgent my—Commander M'dierra says. And she asks when Duke Arcolin will be coming, if you are permitted to say."

"Immer's on the move?"

"I don't know what the message is, Captain," Poldin said. "It's for the north."

"The pass isn't open yet," Captain Selfer said. "Though I hear it may open in the next hand of days. Let's see."

Poldin put the leather message case into Selfer's hand, then stood back.

"Sit down, lad. I may have an answer to return." Selfer untied the strings and lifted the flap. Inside were two scrolls and a folded sheet, the sheet marked with M'dierra's sigil. He unfolded that. "So," he said aloud without looking at Poldin. "She worries for your safety, Poldin—and for the safety of the message. Andressat declares it most secret and most urgent, and she advises me to find you something to do that will take a half-day and look as if you're idling. She will send a few men to escort you back later."

"I'm careful!" Poldin said, stung.

"I'm sure you are, but these are chancy times. The worst since Siniava. She says to tell you to expect an undeserved scolding—it's all for a reason."

"Yes, Captain," Poldin said. Would Captain Selfer open the other scrolls or wait until he was out of the room?

"I'll tell you what," Selfer said. "You rode her chestnut stallion over here, she says. Why not show him off to the troops—exactly what you wouldn't dare on your own. Have you practiced any fighting on horseback?"

"Only a little," Poldin said.

"Captain Burek's out with a troop at our practice ground—you know where it is. I'll write him a note for you to take, and then you dawdle about showing the horse off. That's something a boy your age with less sense than you have might do." Selfer scrawled a note and handed it to him. "Then you'll eat midday with us, and by the time the escort arrives to scold you for not returning right away, everyone will have seen a safe reason why."

Poldin reclaimed his mount, told the gate guard he had a message from Captain Selfer to Captain Burek, and—feeling very daring despite the permission—touched the stallion with his spurs. The horse was more than ready to prance along, in full view of the main road down the hill, to the east side of the compound, where Captain Burek and his cohort were doing mounted exercises.

"That's a fancy fellow you're on, Squire," Captain Burek said. "Your commander's favorite, isn't it?"

"Yes, Captain; here's a note from Captain Selfer."

Burek halted, waved the troops on to continue their exercise, and took the note, nodding as he read it. "Well, then, your riding's improved a lot—let's see how you do with our formations. Unless you have to get back."

"I can't stay too long," Poldin said.

"Join up with that third group," Burek said, pointing. "See if you can keep an even line."

Jumping low obstacles—a row of rocks, a log—followed formation riding. Poldin had been through that with Golden Company, though not on this mount. The stallion had his own idea of the pace they should take and bucked after some of the jumps, apparently just for fun.

"Enough," Burek called, and the troop halted. "Our former

squire's doing so well, I think we can risk a little weapons practice—if he wants to."

Poldin nodded. Soldiers fetched odd-shaped lumps—balls made of rag strips, he saw—and put them on top of poles standing along one long side of the exercise area.

"You'll start with a wooden waster," Burek said. "We don't want to risk a cut on Commander M'dierra's favorite mount. Start out at a walk, knock off two, then pick up a slow trot for the rest of the line."

The stallion was jigging before Poldin even got lined up and would not walk composedly along the line. Poldin missed the first rag ball, knocked off the second. When he lifted the reins slightly, the horse charged forward, straight along the line but so fast that Poldin missed all but two of the balls and almost fell off when the horse skidded to a halt, wheeled, and charged back down the wrong side of the line at full tilt. Poldin reached across and caught two more balls, then concentrated on stopping his mount, this time managing a straight stop.

No one said anything. No one laughed. Captain Burek rode over, close enough to speak quietly. "I gather you didn't plan that."

"No . . . sir." He had a stitch in his side.

"I saw that horse pull the same trick on your commander three years ago. I thought he'd have calmed down by now or she wouldn't have let you ride across the city on him. You did well to stay on and take down four heads."

"Thank you, sir."

"Take him across the field and walk him dry. I'm going to have one of the others walk with you."

Poldin could feel the flush rising to his ears.

"Nothing to be ashamed of, Squire. That's a top commander's battle mount, and they do sometimes take over."

"Yes, sir. Thank you."

Kerin rode beside him as he guided the stallion across the field to the far side. "That's some horse," Kerin said. Poldin remembered him from his time with Fox Company. "Glad I wasn't on him when he pulled that stunt. These fellows—" He patted his horse's neck. "—are just transportation for the most part. Officers' mounts learn that kind of thing."

"Commander M'dierra will be angry with me," Poldin said. "I didn't touch him too hard with the spur, did I?"

Kerin looked down. "Not a scratch, not a rumple. Didn't look like you used the spur at all. He's just a warhorse, that's all. Give him a bit more rein now; see if he'll relax."

They rode up and down the length of the practice field; Poldin relaxed enough to watch the others. Walk, trot, swiping at the rag-ball heads. Some missed even at the walk. He felt better. By the time the stallion was cooled out, the rest had finished, and they all rode back into the compound together. Kerin took Poldin's horse as well as his own to the stables, and Poldin followed Captain Burek into the captains' office.

Captain Selfer nodded to them both. "Squire, I have a message for you to take back when it's time—two, in fact, one to be sent on to Count Andressat. For now, though, get yourself over to the mess hall. I need to talk to Burek in private."

Poldin found the mess hall busy but sat down at the nearest table and helped himself to slabs of beef, redroots, and steamed grain.

"Growing lads," someone said down the table.

"Did well staying on that horse," said another.

He was watching unarmed practice in the courtyard when he heard the hail from the gate. He looked over his shoulder and gulped. His aunt had sent a sergeant and a full tensquad for him.

The scolding began right then, in front of all the others. "You knew you were supposed to come straight back! What do you mean spending the better part of the day over here when there's work to do with Commander M'dierra?"

"I just—"

"He was showin' off that big stallion," one of the men said. "Should've seen him ride—squire's damn good. Even took off some heads in the weapons exercise."

"You were riding *her* horse in a *weapons* exercise?" Sergeant Valud's tone cut like a blade. "Boy, she's going to take the hide off you, and you won't sit down for a week, let alone ride. If he's got a mark on him—"

"He don't," Kerin said. "Squire rode him easy; horse just took off."

"Well, of course he took off: it's how he's trained. You know that," he added to Poldin.

The scolding continued as he got the stallion out of the stable and mounted and as they rode out the gate, down into the city and across it. Boxed in on all sides by the tensquad, Poldin could do nothing but sit there, ears burning, as Sergeant Valud let all Valdaire know what he thought of spoiled boys taking advantage of their relationship to their commander, showing off when given the privilege of riding a high-bred, well-trained battle mount. One of Clart's troopers, reining his own mount aside to let the tensquad pass, called, "Bet it was fun, though, wasn't it, lad?" and Sergeant Valud yelled, "Don't encourage him. He's for punishment drill, he is."

Despite all that and his fear that his aunt really would take it out of his hide, when he was in her office with the door closed and had handed over the messages from Captain Selfer, she read through them then gave him one of her rare smiles. "You stayed on—that's well done, Poldin; he's unseated more experienced riders with that maneuver. I really thought Stony would behave better for you."

"You're not angry?"

"Not with you. You won't get to ride him again for a while— you're being punished, after all—but you did exactly what I hoped you'd do. Gave people plenty to talk about other than why you might have gone over there again today when you'd been yesterday."

"Do you really think it was too dangerous for me to ride back alone?"

She clasped her hands on her desk. "You know what happened to Andressat's son."

He shuddered; he couldn't help it. "He . . . his . . . skin was sent to his father."

"Yes. I don't want such a package coming to me or to my sister, your mother. War is never safe, but this is more than ordinary war. Our enemy is a mage; he has powers I do not understand. Tell me what you saw on the way over and back."

"On the way over, three thieves near an alley this side of the horse market—that one that angles off from the little fountain. Just standing there in those black clothes. A scuffle in the far corner of the main market, where the fruit sellers are, but I couldn't see what, exactly. I watched for anyone coming too close." Poldin scowled, trying to remember every detail he'd noted on the way over and back: known thieves, soldierly-looking men not in a recognized uniform, the city militia, down to the fellow peering out an upper window and then flipping a bit of cloth twice. "And the smell is worse this afternoon, on the way back, and I heard one woman complain that the well in the fruit market square was low, two turns low."

"A good report," his aunt said. "And yes, there is danger, and danger to you more than to someone not related to me."

When she said nothing more for a moment, Poldin said, "I understand."

"That's why I can't tell you what Andressat sent me or what Captain Selfer wants taken to Andressat. We're fairly sure Immer's spies suspect you of carrying messages of more import than a joint training exercise or a social engagement between captains. If you're captured—and I pray Camwyn's Claw that you're not—you will not know anything that can harm the Company. I thought of sending you home until this is over with—"

"Please don't—"

She shook her head. "I won't, because I don't think you'll be any safer there and because this is the life you wanted—you saw last campaign season what it's like, and you said you wanted to stay."

"I do!"

"You'll spend a fiveday in camp, ostensibly punishment for your escapades today. The next time I send you out will be with a small escort, again on the grounds I need to make sure you don't stray. Be especially careful any time you eat or drink away from camp, Poldin. Food and drink can be drugged, and a 'helpful' person helps the victim into an alley or a small room . . . I don't want to lose you."

"I will eat here, then," Poldin said. "But what about water—are the public fountains drugged?"

"No. That should be safe enough if you use your own mug. Don't let anyone draw the water from a well for you. Do it yourself."

"Do . . . do we have spies?"

Aesil grinned. "Indeed we do, and very busy they are right now. But again—I cannot tell you who or what they're doing."

〜❦〜

Six days later, one of Valdaire's outbound scouts came back from the pass to report that it was open enough for foot and horse travelers, still not passable for wagons. A stream of couriers and scouts rode out at once, Fox Company's official couriers among them.

"Wherever you meet Duke Arcolin," Selfer told the couriers, "let him know the situation here, but be sure he understands this one—" He tapped the packet. "—is for King Mikeli and has not been opened. It must go on at once; Andressat thinks it's urgent to the welfare of the Crown."

"Yes, Captain."

Selfer tapped the courier's knee, and the man nudged his horse into a trot. The courier did not know—no one knew, he believed—that a gnomish courier had taken Andressat's letter on to the north the very night it arrived. Having a commander who was also a gnome prince had many advantages, though it added complications.

Back in the stronghold, Selfer met Burek. "I have a word for you, Captain, now that the courier is off."

"Yes, sir?"

"I have another letter from the new Count Andressat, to be handed to you once the pass is open, he said in his note to me. He says he is your father."

Burek nodded. "He told me that when I was coming back from Cortes Andres."

"He may want you to come there—to stay, I mean. I would, if I were . . . he has to recognize your ability."

"This Company is my home—"

"Forever? I doubt that. But read your letter and see what he says."

Selfer went into his office. He liked Burek—his good sense, his steady personality, his courage—and hated the thought of losing him. This close to the new campaign season, he would wait until Arcolin arrived and let him hire a new captain if Burek left.

The list of soldiers due punishment for various misdeeds lay precisely in the middle of his desk. One of his least favorite duties and one that grew more common as winter waned. No matter how they trained, in this season troops grew bored and stale, tired of winter quarters, bored by Valdaire. The list lengthened every tenday until the recruit cohort arrived, and this year was made worse by unseasonably warm, sunny weather and the increasingly bad stench near the bridges in the city.

He sighed, looking at today's list: two repeat offenders, both for drunkenness. One for brawling with a Golden Company soldier; as a first-time offender, still a worse offense than simple drunkenness. A first-term had wandered away from a work detail and come back late . . . a girl, of course, was his excuse. Another had been found asleep in the storeroom he'd been assigned to clean. Then there were the problems found at inspection: uniforms and weapons not cared for, missing items, and so on. He jotted down the punishment by each name, then called in the senior sergeant for each cohort and had them assemble their troops in the main courtyard, with the miscreants to one side, in a separate formation.

After the regular daily inspection of the rest, Selfer called each of those on the list forward with the sergeant for that cohort. One by one he assigned punishments, and when it was done, he went back to his office to file the list. Burek was waiting.

"He does want me to come back," Burek said, his expression sober. "I am his oldest son by several years, and I have more experience, he says."

"Does that mean he's naming you his heir?"

"He offers that. I wish you'd met him. He's a good man, I think."

"Who let you grow up without his name," Selfer said, and then disliked the edge in his own tone. "I'm sorry," he said then. "It's not fair when I haven't met him. And I suppose he was young."

"Yes. And he makes no excuses for how it happened. What he says is that since his father died, he must stay in Cortes Andres most of the time, as the Count. He has three brothers to help, but in the present threat he thinks it is not enough."

"He's hiring Golden Company again this year, isn't he?" Selfer noticed he was tapping his fingers and quit.

"Yes. But he still wants me . . . When we rode together, when he escorted me back to the border, we found we liked each other. More than blood relation; Filis did not like me, or I him, for that matter."

"So . . . you want to go?" Selfer forced back what he wanted to say about Andressat's family, about how hard it would be for Burek, how resentful the new count's other sons would be.

"I said I would stay here. Yet—he is my father by blood. Yet again—the man who raised me, the only father I knew—is also a good man. If I went back—he would be someone I gave orders to. It could not be the same." Burek met Selfer's gaze. "And I am needed here, as well. I know that. I owe Lord Arcolin a lot, and you and I are friends. I feel a responsibility for the troops. I know them, and they know me—"

"You said you would stay here until you were needed there . . . maybe you will know when you feel the need there more than the need here. But you must tell Lord Arcolin when he comes."

"Of course."

"And for my part, Burek, I hope you stay. We do not want another Harnik."

"Gods, no!"

"And you may have noticed we're getting more misbehavior now. We need to get them out of the city and then back in time for Lord Arcolin and the recruits. A five-day march will do no harm and show up anything we need to work on."

"Agreed. And if it rains or we get a late snow, all the better to cool the hotheads among them."

❧

By the third day of the march, Selfer had a long list of what must be done when they got back to Valdaire. They were more than a day from the city, in the rough outbounds that belonged to Foss Council, working their way along the foothills of the Dwarfmounts, where rotten snow lay in shaded hollows. No rain had come; the sky was summer-blue, and the wind from the south blew warm.

They had seen few people the day before, and Selfer did not expect to see many until they were nearer the cities again. Besides keeping the Company busy, he had wanted to look for the old north track Arcolin had mentioned. So far he'd seen nothing but narrow trails. He rode with a wax tablet on his thigh, sketching the route they were taking and trusting his horse to pick its way on the trail.

"Captain!"

That cry brought his head up. He shut the cover on his tablet and shoved it and the stylus into the bag hanging from the front of his saddle as he looked around.

And there, off to his left, was the evidence that someone intended to use a northern route. Below the hilltop route he'd chosen, on the north side of the hill, trees covered the slope . . . but a line divided them, running back to the east. It was clearly a new-cut track, straight and wide enough for a cohort in marching order and for the largest wagons. Selfer was sure it connected with the north road that ran from Pler Vonja to Sorellin and then on to the Copper Hills.

The line stopped almost below their present position. He could not see the road itself . . . but with the company halted, he could hear the chunk and ring of axes biting into wood. Whoever was down there had not heard them . . . yet.

Quick hand signals for silence, for change of direction. No movement of so many could be truly silent, but they came down from the ridgeline and into the upper trees, scouts deployed ahead of them, with as little noise as possible. Selfer had sent ten hands back, to descend well behind the sound of axes, and four hands ahead. The officers' horses had been sent, with the pack animals, down the south side of the ridge, where they would not be seen or heard. When they were in position, he signaled all to descend, still as quietly as possible.

He estimated they were halfway to the line itself when the sound of axes stopped. He halted the advance. Voices . . . he could not tell how many. It was nearing midday; were they stopping for a meal, or had they realized they were being stalked? Moments passed like days. Then he heard someone walking in the woods, grunting a little as he moved uphill. They had sent their own scout; some noise had alerted them.

The enemy scout looked like a brigand, very like the brigands who infested Vonja outbounds. He passed the first line of troops without noticing them—and two, rising behind him, threw him down and gagged him before he could yell, trussing him thoroughly. It had taken no time; it had caused no noise. But, Selfer thought, it was time to move quickly. He still had no idea exactly what they faced below.

As they neared the clear-cut trace, Selfer could see that those actually doing the work were gaunt, dressed in little more than rags, shackled together in pairs and trios. Twenty . . . thirty . . . as many as forty of them, some harnessed to a stoneboat, struggling to move rocks others loaded on. Some struggled to hack branches off newly felled trees and drag logs to the side of the track. Perhaps a dozen or so well-fed men in rough clothes with whips and clubs yelled orders.

Selfer did not wait to find out who the workers were; he signaled for the attack. As his men charged from the trees, the guards turned on the workers, clearly intent on killing them. Only a few faced the soldiers to hold them back. These were overrun almost at once, and the rest of the fight was short and bloody as the troops tried to kill the guards while protecting the men in chains.

When it was over, all the brigand-looking men were dead but for the scout they'd captured and left trussed up the slope. So were fourteen of those they had supervised, for some of the prisoners, unarmed as they were, had fought back rather than wait for Fox Company to finish the job.

"Who are you?" Selfer asked. Those who were left looked as if they could scarcely stand, but they had lined up in rows.

"Corporal Nannsir, sir. We're what's left of Sobanai Company, sir, and we surrender to the Duke's Company under the Mercenary Code." Blood ran down his arm and dripped off his hand, but he stood stiffly upright. "They thought it was a patrol from Foss—never come this far before, he said, but it couldn't be let go back, and they must not know about us."

"Sobanai! We heard in Valdaire that the entire company perished of disease. Yes—of course you are under our protection, under the Mercenary Code." He turned to his nearest sergeant. "Feed these people, patch them up. We'll camp here—bring the supplies down—and start back tomorrow."

"Thank you, sir," Nannsir said. "I—I don't know your right name, but—but you carry the Fox's mark. I thought then we might be saved."

The rest of that day, Fox Company set up camp, and took care of the former prisoners.

"Most died," the corporal told Selfer after his arm was bandaged and while he was eating, he said, the first hot meal in two tendays. "There was fever, right enough, all through the city, but Commander Sobanai, he didn't let us drink the well water wi'out boilin' it, didn't trust it. But then assassins killed him and his son and his captains— all in one night, that was, and before we knew what was what, cohorts of the Duke of Immer was all over us. We fought hard, but—there was too many."

"Are there any of you besides these?" Selfer asked.

"Was some still in Rotengre when we marched out. Doubt they're still alive. I'm surprised I am." He took a swallow of sib, then grimaced. "We got nobody to ransom us, Captain Selfer. But I beg you, sir, don't turn the lads over to the Debtor's Court. I know we owe you for rescue and our keep, but—"

"You owe *nothing*," Selfer said. "You were in Siniava's War, just like me—I'm not going to mistreat a comrade, and that includes you. All of you."

The man's eyes glittered; he sniffed back tears. "Thank you, sir. But you can't—"

"Duke Arcolin left me in charge. I can. Come now—I see the washpots are steaming. Let's get you lot cleaned up and some clothes on and then some rest. We've a long march back to the city, though we'll take it as slow as we can."

Early the next morning, Selfer sent a mounted courier to Foss to request assistance and supplies for the Sobanai survivors. Fox Company had not brought more provisions than they needed for their own march. Despite their best efforts, it was a day and a half before they met the Foss Council militia, who had brought wagons as far as they could and then come on with loaded pack animals. Everyone was hungry, and the Sobanai men were exhausted despite everything the others could do to help them.

"They skirted Sorellin and Pler Vonja," Selfer told the militia captain. "There's an old drover's track along the foothills out of Pler Vonja . . . that's where they started cutting the new road, but they were headed straight west, not so far north as that track. There are—or were—more Sobanai prisoners in Rotengre, and if they send another group to work on the road, be ready for a dozen or more well-armed nasty characters with them."

"What about your prisoner?"

Selfer glanced at the man, now wearing the same shackles the Sobanai men had worn and burdened with a pack from one of the mules so that an injured man could ride.

"He's in your jurisdiction," Selfer said. "I doubt he can tell you more than the Sobanai had told me, but he's yours."

"I doubt they'll waste time on him," the militia captain said. "But he can carry that load a ways."

Once they reached the wagon the Foss militia had left—another day and a half—Selfer put the Sobanai survivors in the wagon, loaded pack animals with the supplies, and headed back to Foss and then Valdaire. He had been gone days longer than planned; he knew those left behind would be worried.

They were. Fox Company's courier had ridden out to see where the company was and met them between Foss and Valdaire.

"The pass wasn't open, after all. Clear enough on this side, but the gnomes say it's closed on their side and will be at least another three hands of days. They'll send a messenger down to Valdaire, they say, to prevent what they call too much traffic on mud."

Selfer nodded. On the north side of the pass, the road ran across gnome territory; humans could use it only with gnomish permission. "We ran into—not exactly trouble—but what could be. Clandestine road from Pler Vonja west, up in the foothills . . . and the survivors of Sobanai Company, who were prisoner labor on it. Foss Council is not happy."

"I wouldn't think so."

"Go back to Valdaire, set up a separate area for the Sobanai—"

"You didn't take them prisoner—"

"No, they're under our protection. Mercenary Code, remember? Immer's agents in Valdaire will want them dead. Send out one of our wagons; tell any who ask we have some injured soldiers."

CHAPTER THREE

Duke's Stronghold, North Marches, Tsaia

The half-Evener storms arrived early, piling snowdrifts as high as the north wall of the stronghold and giving recruits plenty of exercise keeping pathways open from barracks to mess to stables and the main gate. The half-Evener itself dawned clear, the wind no more than an icy whisper across the expanse of white outside the walls.

Jandelir, Duke Arcolin, looked out the window. Below, one of the cook's assistants hammered on the thick ice of the inner court's well with an iron bar. When the ice finally shattered, the water looked black against the white. Smoke rose from the mess hall chimney. Arcolin raked at the coals in the bedroom fireplace and put on more wood. Behind him, Calla stirred in the bed, then yawned.

"It's brighter," she said. Arcolin grinned at her and handed her the robe hung on a peg beside the bed.

"Not snowing," he said. "We may get the courtyards completely clear today. I should ride over to Duke's West."

She was out of bed now, shrugging into the thick robe and then padding to the door. "I'll get Jamis up."

Arcolin dressed and went downstairs, eager to see how deep the snow was. Through the gate to the main court, he saw a line of recruits heading to breakfast. Knee deep at least; the recruits would have plenty of healthy exercise today and half tomorrow, he estimated. The inner, smaller court had been partially sheltered by the surrounding buildings, though snow lay waist-high against the downwind wall.

He went back in, meeting Arneson, his one-eyed recruit captain, in the hall near the dining room, and his foster son, Jamis, coming down the stairs with Calla. "Your recruits are headed to breakfast," he said to Arneson. "They'll have a job getting the courtyard emptied out."

"Better outside than in," Arneson said. They all sat around one end of the big table while the cooks brought in a hearty breakfast: porridge, slices of fried ham, hot bread, butter, and honey.

"Da, may I go outside today, please?"

Arcolin looked at Calla. "What do you think?"

"I think he needs a good run around the court if he won't be in the way," she said. "Once before lessons and again after." She turned to Arneson. "Are you taking the troops outside?"

"Not today, milady," Arneson said. "We'll want the courtyard clear of snow as soon as may be, and it's not going to warm up enough to melt off. But it won't bother me if the lad's there as long as he stays clear of the shovels."

"I can shovel," Jamis said. "I shoveled snow on the walkway in Vérella."

Arcolin thought back to the previous winter, when gnomes had been living in the cellars. "We have a couple of short-handled shovels, Jamis—it would be a help if you'd shovel in the inner courtyard. A clear path from the door to the well, for instance."

"I can do that, Da. Promise." The boy squared narrow shoulders and nodded formally.

"Finish your breakfast, then, and be sure you wear your mitts."

Soon the recruits were busy in the main courtyard, and Jamis, furnished with a short-handled shovel cut down for the gnomes, had started a path to the well. Arcolin went through to the main court, skirting the busy recruits on his way to the stables. Here the stablemaster had a string of horses ready for exercise.

"I thought I'd lead 'em down the road, see how it is, just to get 'em out of the stalls and loosen 'em up. Anything we need to take to Duke's East or back from there in case I make it that far?"

"No, but I was going to ride that way myself—both vills if I could make it."

"Is Captain Arneson coming with you?"

"I hadn't thought to ask. Just a moment." Arcolin went out to the court and called Arneson over. Arneson shook his head.

"Not unless you need me, my lord. I've plenty to do here."

"That's fine," Arcolin said. He saddled his roan ambler, and he and the stablemaster rode out together, a string of horses trailing behind. Once out the gate, the string swung wide, lunging at the snow.

"Race you?" the stablemaster said. "A short run won't hurt 'em."

Arcolin grinned and closed his legs on the roan. Off they went, not particularly fast in the snow. The stablemaster had veered wide of the road to be sure none of the string stumbled into the ditch. Arcolin stayed on the road, and the roan plunged on. About halfway, the roan slowed, and Arcolin let it continue at a slow pace. He was almost to Duke's East when he saw a small figure emerge from between the buildings and walk toward him over the snow. A child, he thought at first. One of the boys Jamis played with when he brought Jamis into the vills with him. But something . . . As he came closer, he saw that it was a gnome, and not one of his gnomes. Aldonfulk by the braid on his jacket. What was an Aldonfulk gnome doing this far north in winter?

He dismounted and walked forward, pulling the ends of his gnomish scarf loose. His gnomes had insisted he should wear or carry it always, in case he met gnomes, so they would know who he was and treat him "in the Law." The gnome stopped at what he now knew was the appropriate distance away and bowed.

"It is that you are prince of Arcolinfulk?"

"It is," Arcolin replied in his increasingly fluent gnomish. "And it is that you are of Aldonfulk."

"My prince sends you greetings and news he considers urgent. I am called Faksutterk. Where is the hall of Arcolinfulk?"

Properly, the "hall" was that still being excavated by his tribe of gnomes, but Arcolin was of no mind to ride there today in the snow. As well, he knew that his tribe needed more time to make what they considered a proper hall. On the other hand, gnome protocol insisted that a gnome hall was the proper place to discuss business.

"It is that I must speak to the mayor of this vill today," Arcolin said. "You are welcome in my stronghold as envoy of Aldonfulk, incurring no obligation."

Faksutterk bowed. "It must ask: Stronghold is Arcolinfulk hall?"

"No," Arcolin said. "Arcolinfulk hall is in hills to west." He pointed. "Stronghold is for human troops in training." He wondered how much Faksutterk understood of his situation.

"It is that all is aboveground?"

"No," Arcolin said. "Stone below as well, chambers for kapristi visitors, where Arcolinfulk dwelt until they had excavated enough of the tribe's stone right."

Faksutterk bowed again. "I will go and await Prince Arcolin's return if that please the prince."

"It pleases the prince," Arcolin said. "Go in Law, carrying Law."

Faksutterk's eyes gleamed. "Law is life."

"Law is life." Then, to the stablemaster, Arcolin said, "Go swiftly back to the stronghold and tell Captain Arneson to expect this gnome and be sure all is prepared for him in the best cellar. I must speak to Mayor Fontaine and will then return. I had hoped to make it to Duke's West today as well, but courtesy for the guest must come first unless there is an emergency."

The stablemaster saluted, turned the exercise string—now much more docile—and picked up a trot along the road back to the stronghold. With a last bow to Arcolin, Faksutterk followed the horses.

Mayor Fontaine wasn't at his house but with a half dozen men at the mill, clearing the drifts from the mill lane. "My lord Duke!" Fontaine said. "How fares the stronghold?"

"Recruits are busy clearing the courtyard," Arcolin said. "And my stepson is doing his best to clear a path to the well in the little court."

Fontaine grinned. "My lord, you're fortunate in that lad. And his mother, of course, but I must say . . . the lad should make a fine officer some day."

"And a fine heir, perhaps?" Arcolin said. "I'm pleased with him, I admit. Started calling me 'Da' sooner than I expected, and he's cheerful and active. Tries to be helpful, as today."

"Village likes him," Fontaine said. "He gets along with the childer when you bring him in, speaks polite to adults." He chewed his mustache a moment. "If you chose, m'lord, to adopt him as your heir, wouldn't anyone here mind, I'm thinking, assuming he grows as he started." He yanked his shovel out of the snow. "Most do."

"Anything in the vill I need to know about?"

"Savin' that gnome passed through this morning? But you met him already—no, nothing once we get the mill going again. You might drop in on Kolya; she's had a bit of fever. M'wife's checked on her 'most every day but not yet today."

"I'll do that." Arcolin mounted again and rode over the bridge to Kolya's house. Smoke rose straight into the sky, but he saw no marks in the snow from a visitor that day. He hitched his horse, took the shovel from its mount over the door, and cleared the doorstep and then the path to the gate. The latchstring hung outside, coated with snow; he brushed it free, knocked twice, then opened the door.

Kolya, bundled in blankets, half lay on a chair with a footstool placed near the fire. She turned her head, then threw back one blanket. "My lord—" A cough racked her.

"Don't get up," Arcolin said, closing the door behind him. "Fontaine said you had a fever."

She nodded and lay back in the chair, her hand plucking at the blanket. Arcolin looked around the neat front room, then opened curtains to let in the sunlight before approaching her. She looked tired and sick, her lips more gray than pink. He spotted a copper can set near the fire—sib, probably—and an empty mug on the table at her side and poured a mug for her. She sipped it but put it down still more than half full.

"Fontaine said his wife checked on you daily—but Kolya, you need more care than that."

A shrug; she looked away.

"Kolya . . . is it just the fever? What else is wrong?"

"He's never coming back," she said.

"Who—oh. Stammel." Who had died far away in the South.

"He had friends here," Kolya said. "We would have helped—"

"And he chose to go—and did not say a word to you." Arcolin

had known that she and Stammel were friends, but . . . had they been more? He tried to think back to the days before her injury and retirement or even the years she had lived in Duke's East.

"No. I hoped he . . . but he didn't. And now he's gone."

"You have friends here," Arcolin said. "And away, as well. Your Kuakgan, who sends you apples."

"The trees are old enough now," Kolya said. "And I have trained others to trim them. They don't need me."

That sounded ominous. Arcolin had seen sick people give up before; fighting a fever could be exhausting. But Kolya had always been a fighter. Was all this about Stammel, or was there something else? He went into the back room and found a hotpot, now cold, with a meal the mayor's wife must have brought the day before. A loaf of bread with one slice cut off was wrapped in a cloth next to an overturned bowl—he lifted it. A mound of butter on a plate. Bread knife, spoons, and small bowls lay nearby. He found a tray, loaded all this onto it, and carried it back into the front room. He set the hotpot in the fire and set about slicing bread.

"I'm not hungry," Kolya said.

"I am," Arcolin said. The little iron pot heated quickly; he stirred the stew of meat, barley, onions, and redroots as it warmed and put slices of bread into the toasting rack that sat near the hearth. The smell of toasted bread mingled with that of the stew; he buttered the toast and set it near Kolya. "And you aren't drinking enough. Finish your sib."

"I . . . I'll need to go—" She moved her head to the side.

"I'll help." Before she could protest, he had an arm behind her back, helping her up. She paled; he held her upright until she could stand on her own, then helped her to the jacks in the back of the cottage, wishing he'd thought to light the brazier there beforehand. The small room was as cold as outdoors. He left her there and went to get a small shovel of coals for the brazier.

Once reinstalled in the chair, wrapped again in shawls and blankets, she seemed a little more comfortable. Arcolin urged her to drink the rest of the sib, then poured water for her and handed her a slice of buttered toast.

"I'm not really—"

"You need food," he said firmly, the voice of captain to soldier, and she ate, though slowly. He put a little stew in the bowl for her and took more for himself, carrying another chair across the room from the table. She ate one spoonful, then another.

"She's a good cook," Kolya said. "I just . . . I didn't feel like eating."

"A bad storm . . . and being sick . . ."

"She brought wood, too, for the fire."

"Good," Arcolin said. He watched as she ate several spoonfuls more. Then he said, "You're on the village council, Kolya. You're important to us. I think you should have someone here until you're well again."

"I don't want to trouble anyone—"

"It's my responsibility. If you were still active in the Company, I wouldn't leave you alone when you're sick. Same with this."

She nodded slowly. "I didn't want to ask the mayor—"

She and the mayor got along well enough these days but had never been friends.

Just then a knock came at the door. "Kolya?"

"That's Seri," Kolya said.

"Good," Arcolin said. He went to the door. Fontaine's wife nodded to him. She had another hotpot, wrapped in cloths, in a basket, and behind her was a girl with an armload of folded linens.

"My lord," she said. "I'm glad you're here." Arcolin stepped back, and she bustled in. "Kolya—glad to see you're eating, m'dear. We were that worried yesterday, but we couldn't get out." She turned back to Arcolin. "My lord, it's to my mind Kolya should not be here alone. Now, our house has room—it's only having the lads share a bed—and if the weather turns bad again, no worry that someone can't come and check on her."

"I don't want—" Kolya began, but Arcolin looked at her and she fell silent.

"I think that's most generous," Arcolin said. "I was thinking of hiring someone to stay here with her—an older girl, perhaps—"

"I could, Ma," Fontaine's daughter said. "Then the councilwoman wouldn't have to move—though if she wanted, she could have my room."

Arcolin looked at Kolya. "Would you rather stay here or be with a family for a few days?"

Kolya looked at the girl, then her mother. "It's very kind of you," she said to Seri, "but I'd rather stay here. If you'll allow—"

It was all settled in a half-glass. Arcolin made sure the girl knew enough about nursing; her mother promised to come by once a day as well except in the worst weather. Arcolin insisted on the duke's duty to pay for a veteran's care. "Tomorrow I must visit the gnomes' hall—an envoy from the Aldonfulk prince came today—and Duke's West if I can. But I will be back the day after—or perhaps another day, but not more than three."

He rode away, still worried about Kolya, but not as much—the girl, Caelin, seemed delighted to have her first job outside the home, and Kolya had plenty of supplies in the house. Still, when the roads cleared, he would send for a Kuakgan for her.

When he reached the stronghold, Arneson told him that they had lighted a fire in the cellar chamber before the gnome arrived, and the gnome seemed satisfied to be under stone. Arcolin went through into the inner courtyard, where he found a narrow, slightly crooked—but complete—path from the door to the well. One of the kitchen helpers hoisting a bucket grinned at him.

"Your lad begged us to leave the path as he'd dug it until you arrived, my lord. Says he'll widen it this afternoon."

"I think Calla will want him indoors this afternoon," Arcolin said. "But I'm impressed. That's quite a job for a lad his size." He went on in, stripping off his cloak, scarf, and gloves. Jamis and Calla were in the dining room, near the fireplace; the boy turned quickly to look at him.

"Da?"

"A fine job you did," Arcolin said.

"I can work more—" Jamis began; Calla gave Arcolin a look.

"No," Arcolin said. "There's others would like to get some exercise outside. I'm proud of you, working so hard, but there's more than one kind of work, and the weather's holding, so you can go out again tomorrow."

Jamis nodded. "Yes, Da. Did you know there's a gnome, Da? And not one of yours?"

"Yes. An envoy from the Aldonfulk prince. I must meet with him. I don't know if he will eat with us or not—if he does, we must all be very careful not to stare or chatter." He looked at Calla then. "Kolya Ministiera's been sick during the storm and isn't well yet. I've hired Fontaine's daughter to stay with her for a few days. When the road's clearer—"

"Of course I'll go," Calla said. "Sick and alone in the storm—and with only one arm—and of course she misses Stammel—"

"She told you?"

Calla smiled. "People do tell me things, you know. She hoped he'd settle down and retire here eventually. When he left so suddenly, she was afraid he'd never return. And then—he was gone." She shook her head. "I can hardly believe it is really spring where he was, and here we have snow drifted halfway up the north wall of the stronghold."

Arcolin thought back to springs in Valdaire. "The dragon said so . . . he was far south of where I've ever been." He sighed, thinking of Stammel's death. "But I must go meet with the prince's envoy." He made his way down to the cellars, now bright with the decoration the gnomes had added during their stay.

Faksutterk answered to his knock on the door of the cellar chamber. He bowed, and Arcolin inclined his own head in return. In gnomish, he said, "It is my wish that the envoy of your prince be comfortable."

"It is comfortable," Faksutterk said. "Will the prince enter?"

"It is the guest's choice, to go upstairs to my office or to speak here. This is guest space." Arcolin's tribe had all preferred to meet humans out of their own space once they were settled into it.

"The prince's office," Faksutterk said. He closed the door behind him, and Arcolin led the way upstairs.

In the office, Arcolin sat first, as gnome protocol demanded, and then waved Faksutterk to a chair. The gnome did not sit immediately but pulled out of his tunic a gray leather tube and handed it over, then climbed into a chair. "My prince has word beyond writing," he said. "When the prince has read it."

Unlike the stone-etched invitation he had received the previous summer, this was written on a cream-colored material—coated fabric, he thought—in Common, not gnomish. The first section, in fact, was in Selfer's familiar hand and revealed that the situation in Aarenis had worsened faster than he had imagined possible.

> . . . the Count died shortly after; his eldest son, Ferran, inherited the title. Lûn and Immervale have both certainly fallen, and I believe Cortes Cilwan is certain to follow, if it has not already. Though there is little travel on the great road in winter, Cortes Vonja reports refugees from downriver. I have that from a reliable source. Foss Council offered a winter-season contract at one-third pay, with immediate increase to last year's, to remain in readiness in case of attack. I agreed in your name. I have urged Valdaire's Council to ally with Foss and have been assured all reliable mercenary companies will be contracted soon. Aesil M'dierra has contracted with Andressat and has moved a cohort of mounted infantry . . .

In another hand and less easy Common, Arcolin read the Aldonfulk prince's assessment.

> Though we meddle not in human affairs and wish no meddling in our own, yet in fair exchange for information received and as Law requires between princes, I say thus. It would be well if you gave your command to your captains in Valdaire, which should make contract and set them free to act until you return. By kapristi, word of this mad duke comes from east: from the Takkinfulk, the Varonfulk of the Eastbight, and the Kastinfulk of the Copper Hills.

Arcolin had heard of none of those gnome tribes; the prince had included a map. Gnome tribes inhabited many hills he had not known about, both north and south of the Dwarfmounts, excepting the area of Lyonya labeled Sinyi.

The prince's letter went on, giving information from other tribes and the latest information available on the whereabouts of the Duke of Immer and his resources.

"Extraordinary," he said aloud, then looked up at the gnome sitting patiently in a chair too large for it. Faksutterk nodded. "And your prince has more, by word?"

Faksutterk spoke in rapid gnomish, taxing Arcolin's ability to follow. Time and again he held up his hand, asking Faksutterk to repeat something. The Aldonfulk prince, he understood finally, proposed a regular courier service between them, including carrying messages to and from Fox Company when Arcolin was not there. The gnomes were positive that the necklace—Arcolin could not help thinking of it as "Paks's necklace"—was now in the Duke of Immer's possession and that it posed a special threat. The prince also asked questions about the organization of Arcolin's tribe "that their names may be written."

"Is there then a single list of gnomes?" Arcolin asked. "All the gnomes in all the princedoms?" As far as he knew, only granges, in Tsaia, tried to keep count of everyone. Towns and nobles reported only certain categories to the king.

"Yes. Is most secret; only for prince to know." Faksutterk stared at Arcolin without saying more.

The next morning, Dattur appeared at the front gate even as Arcolin and Faksutterk were emerging from the inner court on their way to Arcolinfulk stone-right. Arcolin greeted him in gnomish and introduced Faksutterk.

Dattur bowed; Faksutterk returned his bow. Dattur said nothing; his expression offered Arcolin no clue.

"Faksutterk brought news from the South," Arcolin said. "And word from his prince."

Still Dattur said nothing. Arcolin sensed a resistance to . . . something . . . a resistance like that of a mountain of rock. "You had a message for me?" he asked Dattur directly.

"It is invitation for *prince*—" The word was accented heavily, "—to visit and see what has been wrought since Midwinter." He spoke in Common, not gnomish; his gaze held Arcolin's, conveying more than the words themselves.

"I see," Arcolin said, trying to decipher that message. Surely the gnome wanted a fellow gnome to come to the stone-right . . . or did he? What if he didn't? Why wouldn't he?

"It is Law to speak tongue of Law to speak Law! It is to speak kapristi!" Faksutterk said to Dattur in gnomish. "Human speak kapristinya—no need talk man-talk."

"It is Law to speak as other understands best," Dattur said, this time in gnomish and slowly. "It is to speak to one spoken to and not to one overhearing."

Faksutterk turned a darker gray and said, *"Kteknik!"*

"It is your prince gifted this Law-teacher correct attire," Dattur said. His eyes glittered. "It is that you argue with your prince?"

This would not do; three recruits had turned to stare at the quarreling gnomes, and Arcolin was sure those on watch on the parapet were watching as well.

"It is not Law for kapristi to argue in front of all," Arcolin said in gnomish. "If words must be said say them indoors: come to my office, both of you."

Silence. Two pairs of shiny black gnome eyes stared at him.

"My prince speaks Law," Dattur said, and threw himself down to kiss Arcolin's boot. Faksutterk bowed very low, and the two gnomes followed Arcolin back through the courtyard. Cobin, one of the recruit sergeants, had already yelled at the curious recruits, and no one stared as they passed.

In his office, he sat down but did not offer either of them a seat. A gnome prince, he thought, might well have chewed them out, but he knew no gnomish curse-words, if they even had such things. He let the silence lengthen as he might for soldiers in trouble, but unlike soldiers, they did not fidget. Rockfolk. Silence and waiting would be no problem for them. He pinched the bridge of his nose, trying to gather his thoughts and his still shaky grasp of their language.

"Very well," he said in slow gnomish. "Faksutterk, you are your prince's envoy. I gave you welcome. I gave you place to stay. You said it was Lawful."

"It is Lawful," Faksutterk said.

"Dattur, you are my hesktak—" Faksutterk shifted as if about to speak; Arcolin stared him into immobility and then went on. "Is it Law that the envoy of another prince be granted guest-space?"

"Yes, my prince."

"Is it Law that the envoy of another prince be granted food and drink?"

"Yes, my prince."

"Is it Law that the envoy of another prince be granted all freedom of a stone-right, to go where he will?"

Dattur hesitated. "It is that some princes send same envoy to a prince once and again, and that prince grants them freedom of stone-right. But not all. It is not that Law requires. It is custom under Law."

"Lord Prince Arcolin." Faksutterk bowed again. His face had paled to its former level of gray.

"It is permitted to speak," Arcolin said.

"It is Law Dattur speaks. It is that Lord Prince Aldon would have report of Arcolinfulk gnomes to know health. It is not that Lord Prince Aldon has no trust of Lord Prince Arcolin, but only . . ." He paused a moment, then went on. "Lord Prince Arcolin is not kapristi in birth and blood. Lord Prince Arcolin has . . . human knowledge and perhaps has not all knowledge to know . . . to judge . . . health of kapristin."

"This says not about that," Arcolin said, stumbling among the gnomish for a moment. Dattur opened his mouth, and Arcolin turned his command gaze on Dattur, who subsided.

"Is it that Lord Prince Aldon has said 'Go see' or that a report from hesktak is sufficient?"

"Lord Prince Aldon said, 'Learn if it is that they prosper and if it is not, then if it is that Lord Prince Arcolin, as human, has need of service of instruction.' It is not said how to learn."

"Dattur," Arcolin said in gnomish, "it is that you came to bring word from my kapristin?"

"Yes, my prince." He glanced aside at the other gnome. "It is word should come to my prince first, but . . . then share as the prince wills."

"Excellent." Arcolin bowed to Faksutterk. "Honor to Lord Prince Aldon for concern for kapristin who should not suffer because a human prince knows too little. Will you wait while Dattur gives me his report?"

"I will." Faksutterk bowed and withdrew to the hall.

Dattur took a scroll from under his jacket and handed it over. Sure enough, it was a list of the gnomes in the stone-right: age, sex, names. "Five more births since Midwinter," he said, not waiting for Arcolin to read it.

"So soon?" Arcolin asked. The list was many more than he had expected.

"When kapristin few and work large, then . . . quicker."

"All healthy?" Arcolin asked, scanning the document. His mind had difficulty wrapping itself around all the names. Why were some so short—like Lord Prince Aldon—and some so long and hard to say—or hear in the mind, reading silently?

"Very healthy," Dattur said, dropping now into Common. "Once planted, the misiljit grows rapidly and so food is abundant, and more food makes more . . . but we do not talk about it." He shook his head. "But you are my prince, and you need to know. When the kapristi-nya eat misiljit untainted and abundant, then they can . . . childer. Many."

"It is in my heart that Law does not require me to know all about that," Arcolin said. Arvid had told him one night, late over wine, that he had tried to unremember his one sight of Dattur naked. He would not explain it and the next day claimed not to remember the conversation at all. "But to know that my people gain in number and health pleases me greatly."

Dattur bowed. "My prince will see that those who came here have a mark by their names. Those names may be known to Faksutterk and Lord Prince Aldon if my—if those once known as Kargin-fulk sent their report as they should. I had been gone, as my prince knows, for several winters."

"Should I show this to him? Let him take it to Lord Prince Aldon?"

"Show it to him, yes. Allow him to make a copy—or ask your hesktak to make the copy and stamp it with your seal." He nodded to the desk, where the seal of Arcolin's gnome tribe lay, the first gift of his people, carved from stone of the hills.

"And should he see the Hall, or is it not ready for visitors?"

"We would prefer not, my prince. It is . . . the kapristinya are at work there, and also . . . childer . . . and it will be more fitting later."

"Then so it will be. And should I write to Aldonfulk prince, as he wrote to me?"

"As my prince wishes. A prince may thank a prince, and ask help of a prince, where one kaprist may not. This list will make exchange for what he told you."

"Add to the list, then, a letter of thanks for his information and due respect, and say that I concur in the need for us to exchange information. I will also write to my captains in Aarenis and ask that he pass that letter to them, at his convenience. Will that do?"

"Yes, my prince."

"Ask him to return, please."

Faksutterk came in and bowed again.

"My hesktak came with word of the health and names, and here is the list," Arcolin said in gnomish, handing it across the desk. "If it is that Lord Prince Aldon needs a copy, it would be my desire for my hesktak to make that copy for you. And I would ask that you take a letter to Lord Prince Aldon and carry one I am asking him to give to my captains in Valdaire, to do as he suggested."

"It is marks here?" Faksutterk said. He used his right little finger to point.

"Those who came from where Dragon cast them out."

"It is so few."

"Yes."

"It is that so many now means health," Faksutterk said. "Lord Prince Aldon glad of copy."

"Dattur—"

"It is done at command," Dattur said, and then in Common, "If I may have use of paper, less time."

"Of course. In the clerk's office; you know where that is." He turned to Faksutterk. "It is that Dattur will write list on paper from here. It is that you go with him."

"Lord Prince, I go with him." Faksutterk bowed, Dattur bowed, and both gnomes left the office.

While they were gone, Arcolin drafted a letter to Selfer, briefly explaining what the gnome prince had told him and giving him authority to issue what orders seemed best until Arcolin returned. He sealed that with wax and his ducal seal, then mixed the ink he would need for the gnomish seal. When the gnomes returned, Dattur handed Arcolin the original and the copy of the list and a short letter in gnomish to the Aldonfulk prince. Arcolin looked them over carefully, then inked his seal and set it on the page with the list while he pricked his thumb with the stone knife used only for this purpose. He lifted the seal and squeezed one drop of blood onto the circle to one side of the seal design. As Dattur had taught him, he said in gnomish: "With this life under Law, it is done." When the blood and ink dried, he handed the paper copy to Faksutterk, who bowed low. Then he did the same with the letter to the Aldonfulk prince and handed that and his letter to Captain Selfer to Faksutterk.

"Lord Prince, it is that I return to my prince now."

"I offer welcome to Lord Prince Aldon's envoy, Faksutterk," Arcolin said. "Guesting as long as desired, and no exchange."

"It is that I return quickly, my prince says, when I know. Now I know. Now I go."

"It is that supplies for journey—"

The merest hint of a smile lit Faksutterk's face. "It is not need, Lord Prince Arcolin. It is good offer. It is that this one excused?"

Arcolin nodded. "It is so. Travel in Law, arrive in Law, be held in Law."

"It is Law," Faksutterk said. Arcolin rose and went with Dattur to the inner courtyard gate while Faksutterk fetched whatever he had left in his guest quarters. When he came out, they all bowed, one to another, and Faksutterk headed back down the road to Duke's East.

CHAPTER FOUR

"You had things to tell me when you came," Arcolin said to Dattur. "You wanted me to visit the stone-right, but it is too late in the day. Will you stay here overnight and we will go in the morning?"

Dattur bowed. "That is well, my prince."

"Under stone, you may choose your chamber," Arcolin said. "But for now, tell me more details of my kapristin."

"My prince has names and ages—what more to know?"

He would have known how to ask another military commander whose company had been near-destroyed—indeed, people had asked him about his cohort's recovery after Dwarfwatch. But he still had no idea how gnome society was organized and thus could not find the words for the questions. He tried to explain that to Dattur.

"I would understand more . . . more how you live, what tasks are appointed, and to whom. Not because I want to interfere but to find out so if the prince needs to aid, aid will be given in Law."

Dattur nodded. "My prince asks about the paths of power. It is . . . like your army. For each task, one in command and those who obey commands."

Arcolin opened his mouth to explain that the Company wasn't organized like that but then listened instead.

"When a princedom is large enough, tasks change with seasons above: on the year turnings, the tasks change. When yet small, a princedom must assign several tasks to each. The kapristinya delve—"

"But—they have childer—" Surely working rock was not compatible with bearing children.

"Kapristinya strong in rock . . . All have rock-power, but kapristinya have most. Though now no elder kapristin, so work goes more slowly." Dattur paused; Arcolin said nothing, his mind stuck on the image of a grandmother gnome cutting rock. "Estvin as you say is local . . . captain. Those he tells do or tell others to do. Most spend time seeding new delvings with misiljit and making cloth. All now but childer have proper cloth. Until child speaks Law, no matter. And my prince named me hesktak, teacher of Law to prince."

Dattur ate dinner that night with Arcolin, his family, and the resident captains before retiring to the cellar guest room. In the morning, he walked on top of the snow while Arcolin rode, and they reached the gnomes' new home by midmorning.

Arcolin already knew gnomes worked hard and tirelessly—but the change to the hall entrance amazed him. Now the entire entrance bore an elaborate interlacing design of gnomish writing; he paused to read it, and Dattur murmured a translation he now scarcely needed:

> Here Arcolinfulk dwell. Law is Law. Lord gives Law.
> Enter in Law, Dwell in Law, Depart in Law.

His estvin and four other gnomes came into the light to greet him. The four carried a roll of cloth. The estvin bowed, then came forward to kiss Arcolin's boots. "Lord Prince, welcome to your hall. We bring at last a prince's robe for our prince, grown here for you. Will you accept it?"

"I will accept it," he said. "It is in Law."

Unrolled, the robe resembled in style, though not in size, the one worn by Lord Prince Aldon. The tribal name, Arcolinfulk, ran around the neck and down the front; on the back, the weavers had worked in his blazon, a foxhead, in a lighter, more silvery gray. Arcolin put off his winter cloak and thick tunic, then put on the robe. It felt more comfortable than he expected, cutting the chill wind better than his heavy cloak, though much lighter.

"It is very good," he said, bowing to the estvin. He pulled his stole out from under the robe and laid it around his shoulders. "Your prince is pleased and honored by this gift."

The estvin led the way into the entrance hall and then to what would be, Arcolin learned, the hall of judgment, where the prince might receive visitors and give judgment on cases of Law. Arcolin could see that it had the same shape and style as that in the Aldonfulk hall: a carved screen, a dais with a throne in front of it, a broad floor on which visitors could wait and chairs might (or might not) be placed.

"Beyond the screen?" he asked.

The estvin bowed and led him onward through an entrance invisible until he was only a few paces away. Behind the screen was a shape like the inside of a shell, curved and arched, and facing it was a dais matching that on the other side, with another seat.

"So prince's voice is heard," the estvin said. "The prince would hear?"

"Yes," Arcolin said.

"My prince will sit in his seat and speak Law. Any true Law."

Arcolin climbed up and sat in the stone seat; it fit him perfectly. "The Lord spoke Law," he said in gnomish, no louder than he would have said it to one beside him at a meal in a quiet place. His voice rang out, much louder, it seemed to him.

"Good work," the estvin said. He did not smile in the human sense, but Arcolin could tell he was pleased. "We were not sure of height of human mouth."

"Why this way?"

"Always this way. Prince speaks Law, not seen, as High Lord not seen speaks Law to prince."

By the time Arcolin returned to the stronghold, he knew a lot more about gnome society, enough to know he was the most ignorant prince a gnome tribe ever had. He had met the gnome women—only they weren't like any women he'd ever known, even leaving aside the gray skin and black beady eyes. They came to be introduced, to kiss not his boots, like the male gnomes, but his fore-head. The ritual kiss was dry, almost like the touch of a stick or, more likely, a rock.

They brought their children, from the tiny ones wrapped in a gray cocoon of the gnomish fabric to the ones able to walk, now for a time clothed in the maroon and brown of Fox Company wool. Those little faces, a gray so pale it almost looked white, filled Arcolin's heart with gratitude for Gird's guidance in saving them.

Then the women and children withdrew deeper into the stone-right, and the others showed him what was finished enough to show: halls and passages and rooms whose purpose he could not yet guess, though some were lined with misiljit. To Arcolin it looked like gray-blue moss, and it scented the air with a peculiar smell that made his nose itch. Certainly there was a lot of it.

One chamber had rows of narrow shelves packed on every wall with little round bundles and what looked like very complicated looms in the center. He looked up. Long threads hung from the ceiling. "Make clothing here," Dattur said. He touched Arcolin's robe. "This . . . grows. And see here—"

He led Arcolin across the room to a passage that glowed brighter than the rest. All over the walls and ceiling, moving lights edged along, a peculiar greenish yellow. Arcolin leaned closer to see what they were. Dattur pulled him back. "Stone-moth lights," he said. "First egg, no use. Then lights, no use. But then . . . sleepers make thread for bed. We use thread from some, leave others to free stone-moth. Stone-moth lays eggs. Then we eat. Only us. Not kapristinya."

After that, they led Arcolin back to the main reception area. Ten of the senior gnomes stayed as the others vanished into the corridors.

"Have questions for Prince Arcolin," the estvin said. "Please to sit there." He gestured to the dais with its seat.

Arcolin climbed up and sat. All ten gnomes bowed. He nodded back. In his formal robe and stole, sitting on an elevated throne, he knew he was indeed a gnome prince and had best speak like one.

"Your prince awaits to answer questions with words of Law," he said.

"The stone-right pleases, Lord Prince. The stone-right is generous. It is only . . . the near boundary is set and that to the south toward the running water, but no boundary set for north or west. If it please the Lord Prince, boundaries are Law."

"Boundaries are Law," Arcolin said. "When all questions asked, we will look at maps and define boundaries."

Another bow, another nod.

"Westward are humans, Lord Prince. A long way westward, but . . . the hills go beyond. Houses and walls mean humans claim—is that within the Lord Prince's gift?"

"No," Arcolin said. The hills ran into the westernmost baronies in Tsaia on another tributary of the Honnorgat. Neither Kieri nor he had ever ridden that far to see if proper boundary stones had been set. That would be unthinkable to gnomes, for whom everything had a thick black line between categories: mine, yours, gnome, human, Law, and Lawlessness. "It is matter for king in Vérella," he said. "Land grants of long ago. And beyond the king's realm is Fintha, all Girdish."

"This stone-right." It was the estvin this time, eyes cast down. "Lord Prince, forgive, but perhaps the Lord Prince being human does not know how large a stone-right . . . usually . . . is . . . ?"

"The estvin is correct. Is the stone-right too small?"

"We will look at maps."

Maps were in the chamber set up as a library. He had not realized that the gnomes had saved and brought with them most of the records in their home. He had seen only that one map, showing only the area of their former stone-right and the land the dragon had said must be ceded. Now, on a stone table, they spread out another, larger, covering the whole table. As before, when he looked closely at any one area of the map, it enlarged, showing more detail. None of that detail to the west included human names or boundaries; the gnomes had not known them.

Arcolin quickly found the tributaries he knew, following them upstream to the area in question.

"A prince may give only that land he holds," Arcolin said.

"That is Law," the gnomes agreed in a chorus.

"This is mine," Arcolin said, drawing the border line of south, east, north. "From this, I granted stone-right here."

He defined the eastern boundary again and then the northern and southern. "I have not yet visited my western land to see that the boundary stones are properly set. When I gained this land-right from the king, after its former lord, the former lord had told me he had no vassals from here—" He pointed to the map at the edge of the stone-right. "—to the western border. He told me the border ran along a high place, not quite a ridge, from here to here." Once again he pointed to the map. "Duke Phelan was in peace with his neighbors there and did not patrol."

Ten pairs of eyes stared at him. He wondered if he would ever learn to interpret that gaze. Finally Dattur said, "There are stones of Law?"

"There should be. Your prince does not know if such stones were set."

"If no human dwellings are built there . . . or if stones not set . . . is that stone-right?"

"Your prince must learn the truth: what is there, what is not there—stones, walls, buildings. Do you have witnesses to that?"

"No, Lord Prince."

"Then your prince must find out. I am certain no steading was granted within this line . . ." Arcolin ran his finger along the map. "Until I know truth, let this be the west margin of the stone-right, but if you find an intruder has built a home, do not attack but tell me—or if I am gone, my recruit captain. Since I must fulfill a contract far from here, as you know, I will not have time to see for myself where the stones are. I will tell the king when I go through Vérella, and I will send messages to the barons as well. Now on the north, here is the line that must not be crossed."

The gnomes nodded. Then one said, "Lord Prince, if wanderers come into the stone-right, what is your command?"

"Bring them to Duke's Court for judgment. Have any of my people violated your boundary lines?"

"No, Lord Prince. But humans do, and those who do not expect a gnome stone-right here—"

"I will think on this," Arcolin said. "I will talk with the barons."

Finally he was done—all but his estvin and his hesktak had returned to other duties. He took off the robe, which would be kept for him to wear whenever he visited, and put on the tunic and cloak of a human instead. It felt a little strange. He bowed to the estvin and to Dattur. "I will return several times before I leave for the south in the spring. You may come to me anytime you have need, as well. Law is Law."

"Law is Law," they both said.

All the way back to the stronghold he wondered how Gird had endured all that time—seasons long, the tales said—underground, without sunlight. Surely he hadn't eaten misiljit. The gnomes would have brought him human food—bread and cheese maybe. Probably not ale.

They had changed Gird, made him capable of fighting a real army, capable of inventing a legal code unlike any seen in human lands before. And they were changing him, Arcolin realized.

He had wondered if a bastard from Horngard could possibly take over Duke Phelan's company and lands—surely, like the taunts he had heard in his youth, he must fail and bring all to ruin. Now he was a duke in his own right, a mercenary commander respected in the south, a married man with a stepson who called him "Da," and the prince of a gnome tribe, something no human had ever been before. Once he would have felt overwhelmed by all that responsibility. Now it felt natural—a burden entirely bearable. Failure and ruin lurked around the edges of his world—always had—but he had not failed yet.

CHAPTER FIVE

Back at the stronghold, Arcolin dove into preparations for the coming campaign season. He was happy to give permission for Jamis to go on a series of short outings with Dattur as escort.

"It will help him to learn gnomish," he explained to Calla when she asked. "Dattur is a formidable guard, for that matter. He drilled with the Company in Aarenis, and I saw him knock down men twice his size. Jamis will be safe with Dattur."

"But that stuff they eat—"

"Jamis won't eat it—he takes his own food from the recruit mess."

Jamis set off one morning with Dattur when the ground had frozen hard again after the snowmelt and days of mud.

"To the stone-right?" Arcolin asked as they left.

"No, my prince," Dattur said. "North along the hills."

"There were orc lairs up there, too," Arcolin said. "Do you want an escort?"

"No need," Dattur said. "I have weapons. Jamis can ride pony. Today for practice, learning to recognize gnome border on different surface."

Arcolin watched Jamis, well bundled up, ride out the gate, Dattur walking beside him, and went back to his work. Near midday, he was talking to the quartermaster about supplies for the next season's recruits—what he, Arcolin, would send back north from Vérella on his way south—when he heard the light clatter of the pony's hooves gallop into the forecourt. He frowned. Jamis knew better than to gallop the pony toward the stables.

A shout brought him to the door of the quartermaster's office, and an instant later he was running. The pony was alone and scared, sides heaving, curds of sweat on its neck, skittering aside from the groom who tried to catch it. Arcolin felt his heart stutter and then race. Instantly he thought of the day Kieri's first wife and children had been killed.

"Close the gate," he said to the gate watch; to the groom he said, "Don't chase—he'll settle in a bit." The gate creaked shut. The groom went into the stable and came out with a few oats in a bucket. The pony stared, ears pricked, and then took one step toward the groom. Arcolin noted that the reins were not loose but tied up neatly so they could not dangle and trip the pony; the lead rope was looped and wound in the military fashion. So . . . the boy hadn't been thrown. Maybe. The saddlebags weren't on the saddle—had the pony escaped while Dattur and the boy were eating lunch? Why hadn't they tethered the pony?

The groom finally got a hand on the bridle and led the pony—its nose in the bucket—into the stable. Arcolin looked at the gate guard. "Signal Assembly," he said. He went into the stable as the horn blew its long three-note call. The stablemaster had anticipated his orders; he had the chestnut out of the stall, almost ready to go. Arcolin went to the pony, checking the tack for any message that Dattur might have sent. Nothing. He frowned at the knotted reins—neat, but not a knot he recognized.

He came out of the stable, heading for the officers' court to get his helmet, when he saw Calla in the archway.

"Jandelir . . . ?" she began, then paled. *"Jamis?"*

"Dattur's with him," he said. "He'll be all right, I'm sure. But the pony came home. I'm going to find him." She stared at him, eyes wide, but did not try to stop him as he jogged across the inner court, took his helmet off its hook just inside the door, caught up his heavier cloak, and came back toward the main courtyard. He gave her a quick hug as he passed. "I will find him, Calla." *I will not let him be killed; not my son.*

Cracolnya's cohort was just outside the gate—open now to let Arneson bring the recruits in. Cracolnya's unit was mounted. Arcolin swung up onto the chestnut and said to Arneson, "Jamis is missing—the pony came in without him. I'll take a tensquad from Cracolnya; you organize things here."

"We'll all come," Cracolnya said. "We don't know what the problem is."

They rode north into a biting north breeze, veering westerly to pick up the line of the gnome boundary. Cracolnya's face showed nothing but a tightness around the eyes that might have been from the sharp wind. Arcolin knew he would be thinking about the same thing: Kieri's wife and children, killed on an outing into the hills. Arcolin held the chestnut to a strong trot, trying to figure out how far the pony would have gone at Dattur's pace . . . and had it galloped all the way back or only partway?

His eyes watered from the wind; he blinked repeatedly, trying to see everywhere at once. Then he saw the gnome boundary off to his heart-hand, the thin line surprisingly clear, for the melting snow had frozen again to ice, reflecting the sun. It ran straight toward horse nomad country, and they rode along it on the human side.

The ground rose under them, dropped again; when he looked back, Arcolin could not see the stronghold. Ahead was another rise; they were into the tumble of hills that would end with the steep lift to the steppes beyond. Orc country, in Kieri's day, though no trouble lately. Surely Dattur would have known, and told him, about any orcs on the border of the stone-right. Patches of brush and stunted trees grew in some of the hollows, pickoaks, bird plums, sourberries, chainvine, brambleberries, still leafless and bleak in this season though the bare stems showed some color. The gnome line still ran straight on up the next slope.

They climbed that and had just topped it when the chestnut threw up its head and snorted, ears pricked sharp forward. Cracolnya's chunky dun stopped, too, looking the same direction, toward the cluster of pickoaks and bird plums at the bottom of the hill. The wind was right to have brought them scent, or perhaps they had seen movement. Arcolin could see nothing, but he could not ignore such a warning. He studied the terrain. "See anything?" he asked.

"No. Three tensquads each side, four with us down the middle?"

"Yes." Arcolin drew his sword; Cracolnya signaled the cohort, and they started down the north slope of the hill at a walk, allowing the two wings time to swing out and pull ahead a little. They picked up speed as the others moved into place.

They were almost to the flatter slope near the pickoaks when eerie screams raised the hairs on his arms and dark figures emerged from the trees, long black cloaks flapping in the wind. All the horses shied, including Arcolin's veteran battle mount. Neat formations dissolved into chaos as the horses bolted, bucked, swerved, even collided; some riders fell off; many dropped their weapons and grabbed for mane. And the tall, thin, graceful dark figures came on, faces now seen clearly. Blackcloaks. Kuaknomi. Iynisin. By any name feared, and rightfully so. Arcolin felt a chill colder than the wind seize his body. He had not imagined these ancient dangers here, in his domain. They had had orcs before but not these . . .

The high voices screamed again; the sound tore at his concentration. One of the figures laughed aloud, a jagged spike of sound that almost loosened his fingers from the reins as the chestnut jigged and half-reared under him.

"Mortal fools . . . did you really think your charge would break us?" The voice had somewhat the silvery quality of elves' voices, but edged with cruelty and spite. "We will feast well tonight on your horses . . . and you we will torment without mercy."

"Tir's bones, but you're an ugly bunch," Cracolnya said. He sounded more annoyed than frightened. Despite his dun horse's antics, he sat as firm in the saddle as if he were straddling a quiet log. "It's no wonder your cousins don't want to admit you exist."

"You will die this day," one of the blackcloaks said, and hissed what must have been a command, for they ran forward, striking at the horses' legs and screaming their unnerving screams.

"Not without a few of you," Cracolnya said. He leaned forward and said something to the dun that sent it straight at the one who had threatened; Arcolin spurred toward another, and the chestnut obeyed. It was foolhardy with the cohort in disarray, but running would be no better. A few of the cohort now had their horses under control and converged on the captains. Those who had been thrown picked up fallen weapons and came on foot.

Arcolin took his first target in the throat, a sword thrust that killed iynisin as easily as humans. He fended off a swing by another, and one of the dismounted soldiers put a bolt in the iynisin's side and then another, just as Arcolin managed a thrust into the iynisin's shoulder.

More of the cohort were on foot now, gathering into squads, running quickly toward the fight. There were fewer iynisin than Arcolin had feared when he first saw them—perhaps fifteen or sixteen in all—and Cracolnya's cohort now outnumbered them. The iynisin screeched again; this time it had no effect, and they began to retreat, edging toward one end of the trees.

Cracolnya yelled something Arcolin could not understand, pointing across at the facing slope. Arcolin glanced upward just as he caught the sound of hooves and the first birdlike ululation. A loose crowd of small horses ridden by . . . he blinked . . . riders with lances. Who were *they*? Cracolnya yelled again, and the other group charged down the slope, riders in outlandish clothing on horses hardly larger than Jamis's pony. Horse nomads—they had to be horse nomads—

Arcolin's horse leapt suddenly, and only his years of experience kept him in the saddle as the horse evaded what he'd missed: an iynisin whose sword would have killed him if the horse hadn't been more alert. That one was running now, running fast to its companions as they all turned, running faster than any human afoot.

Beyond the pickoak tangle, the oncoming horse nomads whooped and cheered, swerving to cut off the iynisin's attempt to escape. Cracolnya spurred his mount to meet them, giving the same whoops and yodels as the nomads. Arcolin started to follow, then checked; the cohort needed him. A few were down, injured in falls from horses or wounded by iynisin, he could not yet tell. The others, under the orders of the cohort sergeants, had re-formed and rearmed themselves from dropped crossbows.

Arcolin stood in his stirrups for a better view. If the iynisin got into the pickoak thickets, where horses and formations couldn't go, they'd be more dangerous, so cutting them off, or at least establishing a line in the thickets they could not pass, would be best.

"A hand to check our wounded and make sure the blackcloaks are dead. Half to the thicket; cut them off inside it, work toward that end, but stay in touch. All should have bows. Half with me."

"Yes, my lord."

He led the half-cohort toward the end of the thicket where the iynisin still seemed bent on escape, Cracolnya close behind them but out of sword range. The nomads, still whooping, galloped straight for the iynisin, waving their lances.

The iynisin swerved, running hard now, trying to cut between Arcolin's half-cohort and the oncoming nomads. But the nomad horses, small as they were, flattened out in a burst of speed. Lances flashed as the horsemen reached the laggards.

In moments it was over: all the iynisin dead before Arcolin's group could close with them. Now the nomads swung back to ride toward them. Arcolin urged his mount forward, and Cracolnya let out a warbling call that brought the nomads to him instead. Arcolin rode that way, signaling the troops to stand where they were.

He had known for years that Cracolnya was part nomad but not that he could have been brother to any of those in this group, barring the lack of the intricate tattoos most of them wore down the heart-side of their faces. Now Cracolnya jabbered away in a language Arcolin didn't know, and this gave Arcolin a chance to observe the nomads, most of whom were staring at him. Short, broad-faced, cheeks bright red from wind and sun. Their clothes, heavily embroidered with brilliant colors, looked to be various kinds of leather and fur. They rode small rough-coated horses with stiff upstanding manes and bushy tails, and, Arcolin saw with astonishment, they did not use stirrups. Their boots had embroidery all over the soles, and they sat with the soles pointed at him, as if to make sure he saw them.

Cracolnya turned in the saddle and pointed to Arcolin, saying something else Arcolin didn't understand. Laughter broke out. Arcolin nudged his mount and moved closer to Cracolnya.

"Care to explain?" he asked.

"It's your horse," Cracolnya said. "He's . . . showing interest. I'm trying to negotiate for the loose horses."

Arcolin blinked. "They're ours," he said. "Besides, we need to keep moving—find Dattur and Jamis." Or their bodies, but he didn't want to think that, let alone say it.

"Loose horses up here are theirs, they say. And the lad's fine, they told me. They thought you'd know—they tied the reins with one of their knots before sending the pony home with a whispered spell. If I'd seen it, I'd have told you."

"Where are they?"

"On the way here."

"I'll go—"

"No. Just wait. You must meet their leader."

Arcolin struggled for patience and courtesy as he was introduced to the nomad leader, Vastolnya, in some way a distant cousin of Cracolnya's, when all he wanted was to go and see for himself that Jamis was safe.

A new thunder of hooves and high yipping cries brought his head around. Down the slope came another group of nomads, many of them women with small children on their backs or on the fleece in front of them. Some children rode alone . . . and one of these, he saw, was Jamis, a wide grin on his face as the horses galloped down the slope faster than Jamis's pony ever went. Dattur ran down the slope on his own legs.

As soon as he was close enough, Jamis said, "Da! I knew you'd come!"

Arcolin's heart swelled. "You're all right," he said. He took another breath, and another, each one easier than the last.

They did not get back to the stronghold until near dawn the next day. Negotiations with Vastolnya for the loose horses his people rounded up, for the use of the chestnut stallion on their mares, for the information the nomads had about iynisin numbers on the steppe to the north, lasted until sundown, along with the miserable business of gathering up the dead—eight had died of injuries from a fall or from iynisin blades. Two more had injuries but would live, one with a broken leg and the other with a sword wound.

Vastolnya shook his head over the wound and insisted that Arcolin let one of the nomad women pack it with a special poultice of herbs. "Otherwise more sick, die," he said in barely understandable Common, then spoke rapidly to Cracolnya, who translated.

"Iynisin wounds fester and eventually drive men mad, he says. This will heal him if there's no metal left. He doesn't smell any. And he says the bodies must burn. The iynisin dead, he means."

The bargain finally struck for the horses saw ten of the animals— the smallest and scrubbiest—traded to the nomads and a promise that the chestnut stallion he rode could run with the nomad mares the next year, when Arcolin had had time to buy a replacement. The nomads had not known about the gift of stone-right to gnomes or that Arcolin was the new lord of the North Marches, but they approved of Jamis. In the end, they approved of Arcolin.

The ride back was slow, paced for the wounded, with scouts out all around in case of another iynisin attack. Jamis rode with Arcolin and fell asleep, the small body warm against him in the cold night wind. They could see torches flaring from the wall of the stronghold from a distance, and a small troop came out to meet them.

Calla waited for them at the gate, lips pressed tight and shawls wound around her. When she saw Jamis and Arcolin passed him down from the saddle, she did not cry but held the boy close.

"He's not hurt," Arcolin said. "Just tired. Get him to bed and back to sleep. I'll come to you as soon as I can."

CHAPTER SIX

After breakfast, Arcolin returned to the complicated task of readying recruits and supplies for the campaign season and readying the stronghold to receive a new cohort of recruits. He and the quartermaster discussed supplies needed for the next season's recruits. Winter weather closed in again, and when it cleared, Selfer's junior captain, Garralt, arrived from Fiveway to report on the gossip along the trade route north of the mountains. He and Arcolin would take the recruits south; Arneson would accompany them as far as Vérella with enough of the permanent garrison to escort a supply train back north. Arcolin considered what use to make of Count Halar's son. Arneson had given him a glowing report, and the boy had matured a lot since the previous spring. He called Kaim in and asked him.

"Yes, my lord, I do want to go south."

"I must have your father's permission," Arcolin said. He didn't bother to point out that it was dangerous; Kaim knew that. He just didn't know what real danger was like. "We had no formal contract. I'll send a courier to him."

The answer came back quickly.

If you think he's ready, I have no objection. Send word when you're on the road; I'll meet you as before, unless you have time to stay a night or so with us.

"Would you like some time with your family?" Arcolin asked Kaim, showing him his father's letter.

Kaim fidgeted. "No, my lord. My mother and sisters will make a fuss. Easier for all if I don't."

"Your father will meet us on the road, then, with the contract." And he had better see that Kaim was safe after the history with Count Halar's father.

Days passed quickly, each one longer as spring advanced. He took the recruits' oaths, signing them into the Company book. No Paksenarrions in this lot that he could see, just the usual mix of youngsters looking for something other than a quiet life at home. He held his last Duke's Court of the season at Duke's East and Duke's West and made his last visit to the stone-right to ensure his gnomes knew his plans and how to communicate with him. Only a few days before he would leave . . . he felt the familiar excitement that came before every journey, along with a reluctance to leave he knew would disappear once he was out of sight of Duke's East.

"Before you leave . . ." Calla stepped into Arcolin's office, hands folded before her.

"Yes?"

"I have news I believe you will welcome."

He understood in a moment from the joy in her eyes, the pink of her cheeks.

"You . . . are bearing?"

"I believe so. It is early; things happen sometimes. But the count of days suggests I am."

He was out of his chair and around the desk before he realized it. "You—you are a wonder. A child! I never thought I would have a child of my own—" A movement in the open door caught his eye; he turned. There stood Jamis, paler than usual. Calla turned as well.

"Jamis! Did you follow me?"

"I wanted to ask Da if I could ride to Duke's East with him—" He paused. "Am I—are you—will I have a brother, then? Or a sister?"

The look the boy gave Arcolin pierced his heart. He knew instantly that the boy knew too much and not enough. He remembered and knew the fear the boy felt. Jamis had never known his own father—he'd died when Jamis was not even one winter old. He had called Arcolin "Da" almost from the first; he had been everything a father could want in a boy that age. And now . . . the shadow in his eyes showed that he knew what this could mean. He had heard the joy in Arcolin's words; he had probably heard comments about his status from others in the towns and even here in the stronghold. He expected to be shunted aside for Arcolin's own child. As Arcolin himself had been the one shunted aside, though for a different reason.

"We hope you will," Arcolin said. How could he mend this? "Come here, my lad. When I leave, you must be your mother's comfort, and if your brother or sister should be born before I return— though I think that unlikely—it will be yours to protect and guide them. You are the eldest, after all."

"I am . . . not really yours, am I?"

Arcolin went down on one knee, meeting those guileless eyes on the level. "You *are* my son, Jamis. You have had two fathers—your father who died and now me. You are the blood-son of an honorable man, your mother's first love, and it is clear what a man he was from your mother's telling and from you yourself."

"But you—but the blood tie—I heard men talking . . ."

"Men talk. Men always talk. I am your father now and proud to be so. I am a duke; I can choose my heir as I will." Arcolin laid his hand on the boy's head. "I choose you, Jamis, so long as you do not disgrace yourself—and that would be the same if you were child of my seed." He looked up at Calla. "We have had no formal ceremony because Jamis is so young yet, but if it will ease your mind and his, I will have it done."

"Jamis?" Calla said. "What do you think?" She sank down to the floor in a rustle of skirts.

"Will it make trouble with other nobles if your heir is not your son by blood?" Jamis asked, a question far too mature for a lad his age.

"No," Arcolin said. "Duke Verrakai's heir is not her son by blood nor any relative of hers."

Jamis flushed. "I just . . . I just want to have a da. And I try—I would try, truly—to be the son you want."

"You already are," Arcolin said. "But I think it is time we put something in writing so the king will know." Inspiration struck. "Calla, it is early for you—what do you think of a visit to Vérella to see your parents and give them the news? You and Jamis could come to court with me."

Calla looked startled, as well she might. "But you're leaving in two days."

"Yes. But traveling with the recruits, we'll be going at a wagon's pace—it won't slow us down to have you riding in comfort. What do you need but clothes?"

She frowned, thinking, and then said, "What about our journey back? You'll be going on, won't you?"

"Yes, most likely . . . though that depends on the king. With the unrest in Fintha, he might want me to stay here. In either case, you'll have an escort back, the same as when you came north at first."

"Well . . . yes, then."

"Good. I'll leave you to pack. Jamis, come with me to Duke's East; we'll talk on the way."

The boy still seemed subdued, but perhaps he was just thinking hard. Arcolin told a groom to saddle his horse and Jamis's pony, then led the way to the mess hall. "We might as well have something in our saddlebags," he said. "I'd like to go on to Duke's West, and it's always wise to carry a meal with you." The cook, as he expected, offered Jamis a honey roll and gave Arcolin three cheese rolls.

They were halfway back to the stable, where a groom held their mounts at the entrance, when Jamis spoke. "Da . . . you don't have to make me your heir if . . . if it's better for your own blood to inherit. For the king and all."

Arcolin stopped short. "Jamis. It's true I don't have to make you my heir. But I *want* to make you my heir. And the king will not mind, and you will make a fine duke someday."

"But if I'm not a good enough soldier? Captains have to be better than other soldiers, don't they? And commanders better than captains?"

"There's no reason to think you won't be, and even so—by then the dukedom may be able to support itself in other ways than by war in the south." He started to say "Don't worry about it," but the boy was already worrying about it, and he knew from experience that a boy Jamis's age could not stop worrying by trying.

When they reached the horse and pony, Arcolin picked Jamis up and set him in the saddle, then mounted. "When I was your age," he said as they rode out the gate, "I did not think about heirs and things—and I should have, perhaps. I spent my time with half brothers and others like me—bastards."

Jamis frowned. "No fathers?"

"No. Our mothers were not married to our father. He was a king. My half brothers included both princes of the realm and other bastards. We were . . . security." Jamis merely looked thoughtful, so Arcolin went on. "If the princes got sick, or were killed, or even died later, one of us might be made a prince and then a king. But when we were very young, we didn't know that. We all lived together in the boys' hall and trained together in the salle and the soldiers' court. We all thought—we young ones—that we were princes, all alike."

"When did you find out?"

"When I was a few years older than you. I had a brother, as I thought—a half brother, in reality a true prince—who began ordering me about and hitting me. I complained about it to the boys' hall steward, who gave me a smack that near knocked me down. He told me what I was and that I would be the other's servant as I grew up and it was time I learned my place and stayed in it."

"What did your father say?"

"I knew better than to complain to the king. I saw then that some of the others were clearly like me and some were not. Some became friends with those they served—not all the princes were as mean as mine. It was my destiny, as everyone there saw it, to come to manhood as the other's servant, to do his work, endure his mistreatment. So . . . when I was old enough . . . I left."

"Did they chase you?"

"No. By then I knew enough of the king to tell him I was leaving and make no complaint. He was not a bad man; he wished me well and gave me a ring—a royal ring—to wear if ever I wished to return or to show if they came searching for me, to prove who I was. Enough money for a start. 'You might still be king someday,' he said."

"Do you still have the ring?"

"No," Arcolin said. "I gave it to the dragon."

"What did you do after you left?"

"Went to Valdaire—well, I started for Pliuni, the nearest city, but I met people on the road who said Valdaire was the place for a youth who knew what to do with a sword. And there I was lucky enough to join Halveric Company, and from there I was able to join the Guard in Tsaia and then this company. I'd met Kieri Phelan when he was with Halveric."

"My . . . how do I know what to call my first father?"

"First father sounds good to me. Or first-da."

"He was from Vérella and never anywhere else. Wasn't it hard, leaving home by yourself?"

"Yes . . . but not as hard as staying would have been."

※

Arcolin finished his business with the mayor and walked over to Kolya's house. He had visited often since her illness; she seemed to have recovered completely. He found her supervising two of the town boys, who were digging her garden.

"I'm not supposed to do heavy work yet," she said to Arcolin.

"Can I help?" Jamis asked.

"We can't stay long," Arcolin said. "Don't get too muddy."

"Tell you what," Kolya said to Jamis, leaning down. "I need more kindling in the front room: These boys stacked branches beside the woodpile—could you take two armloads inside for me? They're busy."

"Yes, sera," Jamis said.

When he was far enough away, Kolya said, "That's a good lad you have there. Very good."

"He's supposed to be on best behavior in town," Arcolin said. "But I promise you, there's a little mischief from time to time out at the stronghold."

"He'd make a good heir, unless Calla bears a son—"

"She's expecting—just told me. But he's my heir anyway; they're coming with me to Vérella, and I'll make it formal with the king."

"Good." She nodded. "I was hoping you would. So are others."

"Need anything from Vérella? Or—do you want to come down with the troops and witness the ceremony for the council? You could come back with Calla and her escort. And it would give her a woman companion to chat with when Jamis is riding with me."

She looked surprised, then nodded slowly. "I could do that. Belan took over the pruning for me; we'd be back in plenty of time to thin the fruit. Thank you." She looked at the boys now making furrows in her garden. "I wish it would rain. We haven't had that much since the half-Evener storm. And last summer was drier than usual."

Arcolin remembered reading that in the year rolls, but the harvest had been down only a little. "As long as it rains this year," he said. "I expect it will."

On the ride to Duke's West, Arcolin told Jamis what to expect in the ceremony. "You won't need court clothes at your age, but your best clothes certainly. Your mother will probably insist on a lace collar—"

"Lace is *itchy*."

"Yes, but this is at the king's court, where everyone wears lace and itchy clothes. It helps us remember we're in a special place, very formal. I will wear lace, too, and so will your mother." Jamis nodded. "Now," Arcolin went on, "our king here in Tsaia isn't an old man, as my father was, but a young man. Older than you but scarcely half my age. His younger brother, Camwyn, is his heir. The king isn't married yet and has no son to follow him."

"But he must marry, mustn't he?"

"He will, I'm sure. When you meet him, you must bow very low—I'll show you when we get back this evening so you can practice. And you say 'Yes, sir king,' and 'No, sir king.'"

When they returned to the stronghold, they found Calla already packing and also planning Jamis's clothes for the ceremony. "We don't have the right cloth here," she said. "It's all good wool, but for this he will need velvet in your colors, and he will need new shoes. We can get those in Vérella, but it will take me several days to have his clothes made up. I'm sure it will take several days to set up the audience, so that should not be a problem."

"I'm sending a courier to the king to ask him to arrange it as soon as possible after we arrive; the courier will be in Vérella at least three days before we are, more if we get much rain on the way. You could send word to your parents to prepare clothes, couldn't you?"

"Indeed I could. I'll just measure him—Jamis, come here. By the time you've written your letter, Jandelir, I'll have mine ready." She pulled a length of cord from her pocket

Arcolin went to his study to write the king about both his new-named heir and the gnomes' questions about boundaries, then letters to the barons whose lands bordered his to the west. He had met Dortlin once at court, a tall man, younger than himself, with thinning hair and a thick north-country accent, the southern of the two. Kieri had mentioned Masagar, whose very small holding was north of Dortlin's. Arcolin had never met him and had no idea how far north he claimed.

Next morning the couriers set out, and the day after, Arcolin, Captain Arneson, and Captain Garralt led out the recruit cohort and the supply wagons. Jamis rode beside Arcolin's roan ambler.

The journey to Vérella, so familiar to Arcolin, was exciting to Jamis. Arcolin was glad to see that his new status as Arcolin's heir had not changed his behavior for the worse. Calla asked that he spend part of each day in the wagon with her "for company," she said, but Arcolin knew it was to keep the boy from exhausting himself or bothering the captains and his stepfather with his endless questions.

When they came to the border with Halar's lands, the Count waited there, his tent set up so they had a dry place (it was one of the rainy days) to talk and then sign Kaim's squire contract. Jamis came, too, watching the proceedings with obvious interest. Count Halar, Arcolin noticed, did not protest his son's decision or show much emotion; it was evident only in the glitter of tears in the man's eyes at the end, when he gave his son a man's arm clasp and a thump on the shoulder. He looked past Kaim at Arcolin, a long measuring look that said everything he felt about sending his son into battle.

Arcolin bowed. "As my own son, I will care for him."

"That is your wife's son, is it not?"

"He is *my* son and my heir now," Arcolin said. "We go to the king when we reach Vérella."

"Ah. Then you understand." Halar's expression softened, and he bowed.

❧

As they came into the city, Jamis wrinkled his nose. "I didn't know it smelled like this when I lived here."

Arcolin laughed. "Cities do smell very different from open land," he said. "You lived in it all your life; of course you wouldn't notice. But remember when you came north last fall, you told me about the smells on the way, and when we got to the stronghold?"

"Yes . . . I like *some* of the smells here. More bakers. When will we see Grandda and Gramma?"

"Very soon now. Your mother wants to visit them before coming to the palace. You'll go with her; I must report to the king first, and then I'll join you."

Arcolin spoke to Captain Gerralt, then turned his horse aside on the broad street that led to the palace gates; behind him, he heard the steady tread of the recruits continue across the city. Calla, he knew, would turn the wagon down the street leading to her parents' house.

Mikeli greeted him at the palace entrance; he was just in from a ride, Arcolin could see by his boots. "So—your courier says you're ready to declare your heir. He looked a fine boy last fall, but are you sure he is old enough?"

"Not really, but it's the right time for other reasons." Arcolin explained the situation on the way to the king's office.

Mikeli nodded. "That's a good decision. We arranged a time day after tomorrow, when Marrakai and Serrostin would both be back in the city. The way things are, with the trouble in Fintha, I'd like to see every succession settled as soon as possible and without regard to magery—your lad hasn't shown it, has he?"

"Not a bit, but it doesn't always show at his age, as you know. We've three in my domain that I know of. A girl of ten winters and boys of five winters and eleven. Came suddenly in the past winter, without warning, in families—veterans' families—with no known mage blood."

"Any trouble?"

"No, and I think that's because my people are mostly veterans. First, they're not all Girdish. Second, they've seen more on campaigns, and they don't think magery is inherently evil even if some magelords were. Are you having trouble elsewhere?"

"Not as much as Fintha, but some. A few Marshals don't want to obey my prohibition against punishing children for it; they seem to think I've influenced the Marshal-Judicar and even the Marshal-General. Clearly they don't know Oktar . . . or the Marshal-General. High Marshal Seklis mutters about their attitude but hasn't been able to change it yet. Have you heard about Gird's Cow?"

"Gird's Cow? What cow?"

Mikeli chuckled. "It seems some Girdish farmer in Fintha got the idea that a stuffed cow would convince those most angry at magery to change their minds. So he draped a cowhide over a framework of wood, put it on a cart, and dragged it all the way to Fin Panir, gathering some followers—and many hecklers—along the way." His expression hardened. "It's not funny, really. The situation worsens with every tale I hear; Fintha is coming apart, and I don't know what to do. We've had people coming in—mostly to escape the mage-hunters, but a few hunting mages here. I sent those packing with a stern warning. Marrakai's taking the brunt of that, but all the barons on the border north of the river have had some incursions. They're letting the fugitives stay, with my permission. I can't see sending children back to be killed."

"I should talk to those barons," Arcolin said. "I'm not even sure of my western border . . . and I didn't give the gnomes a map. I didn't think . . ."

"Dortlin's domain would border the southern third of yours. Masagar's, north of that, but he doesn't claim all the way to horse nomad country. How far did you tell the gnomes they could have?"

"The hills west of the stronghold—but I didn't tell them who owned beyond that. I need maps, sir king—"

"Indeed you do. I'll tell the librarian to have them copied for you. I'm surprised Kieri didn't have some. But on another topic . . . I need your advice and Duke Verrakai's on how best to secure our west border. We've had no serious trouble there since Gird's War, but I fear that with trouble in the South, we might also face more trouble there."

"We might indeed," Arcolin said. "I'm certain the Marshal-General won't mount an attack as long as she's in control, but if the Fellowship in Fintha splits or if the other faction takes control, then Tsaia's stand on magery will be seen as a threat."

"And we could be attacked on two fronts."

"We could . . . but I don't see any alliance between our southern enemies and the Finthans."

"Does it matter whether they're allied or not? Either way, it splits our forces, doesn't it?"

"You're right, sir king, though I have trouble believing that Fintha will attack—that the unrest will go that far. A few border skirmishes, maybe, but—"

"You have not heard the latest news," the king said. "Yesterday's courier—so you could not have heard it. The Marshal-General was badly wounded in an attempt to unseat a Marshal who had supported killing any and all with mage talent, and they believe the weapon used was of kuaknom manufacture. Cursed to kill slowly while infecting the mind, like Paksenarrion's wounds in Kolobia."

"Kuaknomi—" Arcolin's mind raced. "We had a band of them not three hands of days past, up near the border of nomad country. It was a shock; I thought they had been driven out long since."

"So I was told as a child." The king sighed and pushed papers around. "Many changes have come upon us, upsetting what I was told then—and you, too, I have no doubt. Magery manifesting in those who never had it before, a dragon seen in these lands—even in Gird's day no one had seen a dragon—treachery in the heart of every one of the Eight Kingdoms whose stories we know, treachery even among elves."

"And gnomes," Arcolin said before he could stop himself, remembering Dattur's story. "But that was corruption spread by Achrya, or so I believe."

"And Achrya, too, is supposed to be vanquished, by the dragon, but the treachery did not disappear with one evil power. King Kieri has informed me that an elf of the far west has demanded that he wake the sleeping magelords Paksenarrion told of—a tale confirmed from Fintha. Supposedly that is necessary to stem a great evil arising from Luap's Stronghold. The Marshal-General had a similar visit seasons before, with the same demand, but insisted she lacked the ability to do so. It makes no sense to me: Why would enchanted magelords spawn evil? But that, King Kieri tells me, is supposed to be the origin of the kuaknomi's return to these lands."

"Are the western baronies seeing them?"

"There are suggestions—night-walkers, poisoned wells, dead trees. But few sightings that I'm sure are kuaknomi. People—including the worst of Fintha—are moving, some begging refuge from the mage-haters and some threatening to test children. That we cannot allow. I wanted to ask your advice about moving some of the Royal Guard west to assist the smaller domains. Marrakai assures me he has troops enough to guard his."

"Yes," Arcolin said. "There are enough troops—mine included—in the northwest of Aarenis to slow down any attack that might head over the pass, and I have the Aldonfulk prince's assurance that a large force will not be able to penetrate the gnome rockways. You—or Duke Verrakai—would have ample time to move troops back to this side of the pass from the Finthan border if Immer's troops invade from the south."

"Duke Verrakai." Mikeli tapped the pen on his desk. "I do not doubt her loyalty, but . . . the regalia still troubles me. I almost wish—she would take it home with her. Get it out of here."

"Have you told her that?"

"No. Do you think she would?"

"Sir king, I think she will do whatever you command. But although I know Immer wants that crown, I don't think sending it away will keep him from attempting the north. From what Andressat wrote me, I believe he is inhabited—the way some Verrakaien took over others, including that groom at your coronation. And the ambitions of whoever inhabits him seem fixed on the North. Kieri has had warning from Kostandan."

"I wish you were not leaving the realm this season. If anything happens—if she must leave—I have no experienced military commander for our defense."

Arcolin bit his tongue. He knew Dorrin had tried to push the peers to do better training—and to improve their own skills in warfare. But not even the king's uncle had done more than individual weapons practice. The peers with an interest in military matters still studied the battles Kieri had been involved in a generation before without really understanding them. Most thought they were doing well if they led a few hands of yeomen up and down a road twice a year and ended with a mock battle between—at most—eight hands of them.

"I suppose you must go . . ." the king said.

"I must, yes, but I will be near enough the pass to return quickly if you need me. Having my force there ensures at least a delaying action, with time to send word to you. Dorrin—"

"Will be here in the meantime. Yes. There's something else. I have a letter from the king of Kostandan, speaking of a relative of his in Aarenis."

Arcolin frowned. "Kostandanyans . . . that would be Count Vladiorhynsich? Or Sofi Ganarrion?"

"You know them?"

"Both have mercenary companies; both fought with us against Siniava. Vladi said once they'd both come from Kostandan."

"It's Ganarrion he speaks of. A cousin, if I understand the term he uses, and his daughter married down there."

"Married the Duke of Fall's son, sir king. This is widely known in the South." Arcolin saw in memory the rich farmlands of Fallo, north and east of the once-ruined fortress of Cortes Immer that Alured now occupied. If the old rumors about Sofi Ganarrion were true, then of course the Kostandanyan king would be watching events over the mountains.

"He is concerned, the king of Kostandan, that they may fall into the hands of that Alured the Black you told me of, and he asks passage for troops under one of his sagons across Tsaia, to the pass at Valdaire, to go aid his cousin. Where is the Duke of Fall's domain? I thought all Aarenis was Guild League cities."

"Not all, sir king." Arcolin explained. "We should send for maps or go to the library—Alured's ignored Fallo so far, but if he took it, it would protect his rear as he moved west."

"Then . . . the Kostandanyans could get to Fallo by crossing Lyonya or Prealíth and go straight over the mountains there, I'd think. This request must be a ruse, because I have not accepted his suggestion of taking Ganlin as my wife and he would bring force—"

"No, sir king. There are no passes over the Dwarfmounts where an army and supplies might cross other than Valdaire. That's why Lord Halveric traveled through Tsaia on the South Trade Road to bring new recruits from Lyonya in years past. That was before you were crowned; did your regency council not tell you?" Arcolin saw from Mikeli's expression that they had not.

"But Kostandanyans are Seafolk," Mikeli said. "They trade by ship with the Immerhoft ports; surely they could take troops south that way—"

"They could not land an army at the Immer ports," Arcolin said. "And if they did, they'd be fighting Alured's forces all the way upriver from the coast; Alured commands all that country. The east coast—they might be able to outface pirates and the scum of Slavers' Bay, but that's a dangerous coast even without pirates." Even as he said it, he wondered . . . had the Kostandanyans ever traded there? Kieri had written that the Sea-Prince of Prealíth reminded him a little of Alured, but without the cruelty. Yet if they were moving troops by sea, why would they ask permission to bring them to Tsaia?

The idea came to him in a flash: to confuse Alured's spies, lead him to think it was safe to attack Fallo—because the Kostandanyans are taking the long road. He explained that quickly to the king.

"So, sir king, a cohort or two of Kostandanyan pikes marching through Tsaia would be enough to prove to spies that they're allied with you, and rumors about the princess make that even more believable."

"But I'm not marrying Ganlin. Roth, maybe . . ."

"And he's still in the succession, right? As good a reason, or near it. Their king won't tell you if he's sending troops by sea, but at the least I would advise agreeing to some coming through here. Or if it's quicker and King Kieri agrees, it would be simple for them to go through Lyonya to pick up the South Trade Road as Halveric Company did. From Valdaire they could move east along the northern route. And that would help us if Alured moves faster than expected. If they're anything like Vladi's pikes . . . well, I'd be glad of them."

"But how can I be sure they don't really intend an invasion?"

"Kostandan's never been as aggressive as Pargun," Arcolin said. "Besides—they don't know the terrain, and we can protect against them."

Mikeli finally agreed and called in the Kostandanyan ambassador. The ambassador nodded on hearing Arcolin's suggestion that they seek King Kieri's approval for troops to march across Lyonya and use the South Trade Road. Arcolin did not mention his suspicion that some Kostandanyan troops were also being sent by sea to Slavers' Bay.

"Looks like trying to hide plans," the man said, grinning. "March along river, obvious. This, not so. King will like. King Kieri called Fox for good reason; he will like, too. Must be force big enough. Rumor say advance of more."

"Have you already talked to King Kieri?" Mikeli asked.

The ambassador raised his brows. "Is not me. With pardon, lord King, is considering our beloved and admired Princess Ganlin still?"

Mikeli turned red. Arcolin intervened.

"The Royal Council has concerns, milord. Not about the lady but about other factors concerning our traditions here. For instance, she is with the Company of Falk, quite honorable, yes, but untutored in the Company of Gird and the Code of Gird."

The man scowled. "What matters what wife knows or does not know other than obedience and pleasing king? It is not wife who rules."

Arcolin shook his head. "Tradition here, milord, is that wives be capable of taking on a husband's duties if necessary. King Mikeli's mother was his regent after his father died, until she also died. She had been schooled here; she grew up with our laws, our customs. The Council feels that the king's wife, the mother and guide of his children to be, should be familiar with the Code of Gird and be herself Girdish. The matter is still under discussion."

"There is no more princesses. That Pargunese one will never marry."

"We have no tradition of the king marrying princesses," Arcolin said.

"There is another factor," Mikeli said, having recovered himself. "My cousin Rothlin, who met the princess in Lyonya, is much taken with her. Should I come to agree with my Council, he may well seek your king's permission to wed her."

The ambassador pressed his lips together and then nodded. "He is in succession to you, is right? What number? Is mage or not?"

"Not a mage," Mikeli said. "And presently third, after my brother and my uncle."

The ambassador nodded again and then turned to Arcolin. "But would Council object, so close to throne?"

"I suspect not," Arcolin said. "I would not object. Rothlin will not be so close to the throne when the king begins his own family, and that would give time for the princess to learn more in case . . ." He stopped there. One did not discuss a king's possible death or failure to sire children in front of him. "At any rate, the important thing is to ensure that Alured—the Duke of Immer—does not succeed in his plans."

"Yes." The ambassador bowed to both of them. "If the lord King will send a short word over his hand, I will send courier to my king at once."

Mikeli looked at Arcolin, then nodded. "I will do so." He opened a drawer in his desk and pulled out an inkstick, the mixing bowl, and other writing materials. In less than a half-glass, he handed the ambassador the letter, sealed with the Tsaian Rose, tied with the formal rose and white ribbons, enclosed in its tube, also tied with formal ribbons and then in a small rose velvet pouch. "Duke Arcolin already has his company on the march south; I suppose your king will send his quickly."

"Very quickly," the ambassador said. He bowed and withdrew.

"I hope that was wise," Mikeli said. "And now—we shall go look at those maps in the library and settle the issues with your gnomes." He led the way out of his office, and two of the guards fell in behind them. "Tell me, do you have to speak gnomish to them?"

Arcolin answered in gnomish and then translated. "That was the proper greeting from a gnome prince to his own gnomes. I have had to learn gnomish, yes. I suspect my accent is very bad, but they understand me, mostly, and I'm much better with gnomish than I ever expected to be." He pulled out the stole he wore. "I wear this always now, so if I meet a gnome I can identify myself and we are within Law."

"Girdish law?"

Arcolin shook his head. "According to gnomes, there is but one Law, that handed to them by the High Lord. They taught Gird what they could but say that no human legal system is truly Law. We are, they say, not precise enough. Where there is only the light of Law and the darkness of un-Law, we see shades between, which they do not think are real but only our blindness of mind. As the eyes of the old become clouded, they say, so are the minds of humans."

"What are they like, really?"

"Much as you see them in the outside world: hardworking, honest, tough, skillful in their crafts."

"The . . . uh . . . gnome women? You mentioned children last time—"

"Very reserved. Seldom seen; some, I'm told, never leave the stone-right. All we see in our travels are males." He was not going to tell Mikeli more than Mikeli needed to know.

"Don't they mind?"

"No. For them it is home and perfectly comfortable."

"Dark inside?"

"No . . . and I do not know if the light is by gnomish magery or something they grow on the walls. They do cultivate things that glow."

"I was wondering if they could help protect our western border. How many do you have?"

Arcolin explained how few. "Supposedly all gnomes are trained in basic weapons skills, but these were evicted from their former home. They came without weapons, and I have no idea if they're able to fight. However—" He paused a moment. He had written Mikeli about the Aldonfulk prince's communication. "I think all gnomes would be appalled by the mage-hunters, though they were not fond of the old magelords. They value children highly, and child killers of any kind would be considered outside Law. There are other princedoms—"

"How many? Where?"

"I may not know them all," Arcolin said. "Lord Prince Aldon told me of those he thought I might meet in Aarenis, but I'm sure you've heard of Gnarrinfulk, west of the pass to Valdaire."

"I'm not sure where they are," Mikeli said. They were at the library now, and he entered. One of the librarians came forward. "We need maps of northern Tsaia," he said. "Especially from the Finthan border to the North Marches."

"At once, sir king." The librarian went to a rack of map sticks, checked labels, and plucked out two. He hung each from a separate frame. "This one's the most current."

His neighbors' boundaries—both with Fintha and with the North Marches—were clearly marked. "When the trouble in Fintha began," Mikeli said, "I asked all the holders who bordered Fintha to look to their boundaries, make sure the markers—fence or wall or stones, whatever they might be—were clear and firmly set."

"Thank you," Arcolin said. "I will send word to my gnomes of their limits of stone-right and to my neighbors, confirming the existing boundaries."

The ceremony of Jamis's investment as Arcolin's kirgan did not take long. Dukes Mahieran, Marrakai, and Serrostin stood as witnesses for the Council; Kolya Ministiera, on the village council in

Duke's East, and Captain Arneson, as Arcolin's military liaison, stood as witnesses for Arcolin's realm. Calla's parents and Arcolin's squire Kaim were the only guests.

Jamis, wide-eyed and subdued at his first visit to the palace, wore the lace collar without commenting on the itchiness, along with a new maroon velvet tunic with silver buttons, a snowy white shirt with a frill of lace at the wrists, maroon velvet short trews buckled at the knee, black hose, and new shoes adorned with silver buckles. The shoes, a little too big and stuffed with tags of wool, clumped when he walked.

Calla and her parents stood on one side; Kolya, Captain Arneson, and Kaim stood on the other, forming an aisle. Arcolin and Jamis walked up the middle of the room and bowed to the king.

Mikeli questioned Jamis a little, questions Arcolin had anticipated and explained to Jamis, but then nodded decisively. "Duke Arcolin, I approve your choice of heir. Jamis Arcolin, kneel and place your hands in mine."

Jamis knelt and held out his hands. Mikeli took them between his own.

"You are too young for the oath of fealty a man gives, Jamis, but here is an oath for a boy. Repeat after me: I promise to obey my lord, my father, and obey the king's command—"

Jamis repeated this in a voice that shook only a little.

"I promise to tell the truth and to deal honestly and fairly with all. I promise to obey the Code of Gird in Tsaia."

Jamis's voice steadied as he repeated that as well.

"I promise that when I come to manhood, I will take a man's oath of fealty. By Gird's Cudgel and the High Lord and the grace of Alyanya."

Jamis repeated all that.

"Then rise, Jamis Kirgan Arcolin, and take from my hand this gift of your king."

Jamis came to his feet; the king held out a dagger in a sheath with the tooled design of a foxhead, the Mahieran rose, and Gird's initial on it, already fitted to a belt with "Jamis Arcolin" carved into it. "Take this blade, Jamis, as a sign of my favor, but draw blood with it only as your duke commands—and I am sure that command will be only to save a life, yours or another's."

"Thank you, sir king," Jamis said. He was struggling not to grin, Arcolin saw.

"Let your father, your duke, put it on you—for a liegeman receives his weapons from his liege."

Arcolin leaned down and helped Jamis put it on.

"Thank you," Jamis said again with a jerky bow.

Arcolin also bowed. "Sir king, this was very kind."

The king chuckled. "A soldier's son should be recognized with a soldier's tools," he said, getting up from his seat. "And now—Lady Calla, I am pleased to see you again, and your parents as well. And you, Captain, and Councilwoman Ministiera. Let us see what the kitchen has prepared to celebrate this occasion and make plans for the kirgan's future."

The party lasted longer than the ceremony, but Arcolin left before it was over, riding out of Vérella with Kaim, eager to catch up with his troops.

CHAPTER SEVEN

Cortes Immer, Aarenis

Alured the Black could not help thinking of himself as Alured, the name he had been called almost all his life. Alured the Black, Terror of the Seas, the pirate other pirates admired and obeyed. Alured the Black, leading his troops through the southern forests, allying with the mercenaries and Guild League cities against Siniava. Strong, brave, visionary Alured, seizing the opportunity at the end of that war to take up the abandoned title of Duke of Immer and control the entire lower Immer River, from the sea to Cortes Immer. The man who had risen from impoverished boyhood to wealthy, powerful maturity . . . that was Alured.

He had difficulty thinking of himself as Visli Vaskronin, even though his advisor insisted it was a more suitable name for a duke who would soon be king. Insisted that he must force everyone to use it. But in these moments alone, looking out over the ramparts of his stronghold, the name Visli fit him ill, and he was, in his own mind, always Alured. Alured the boy, the boy captive, then the favorite of his master, then his master's ally and secret weapon, then the pirate, then the brigand. Alured the Duke, yes, he could feel himself a duke; he would feel himself a king: King Alured sounded well, he thought. But that name had been changed *for his own good,* his advisor had said.

It did not suit your station.

Alured sighed. The advisor, who had once been his master and thought he was master still, chose his own time to come into consciousness. His advisor did not approve what he called Alured's nostalgia or his attachment to his own name.

A slave's name. You are a slave no longer.

That was true. He had slaves of his own now, and servants who might as well be slaves, and soldiers who accepted him as their commander, and vassals to whom he was unquestioned lord.

There will be more.

That promise—always more: more wealth, more power, more admiration, more pleasure—drew him on, as it had drawn him in that first time, so long ago.

You give up little to gain so much.

Indeed. Only his name and the sense that the connection to himself—the connection running back through a life from now to then, to earliest memory—frayed with every passing day. Yet his advisor had explained, and he understood, that to be what he would become—the great ruler of all, the crowned king of all the lands he knew, master of water and fire and blood—to become *that,* what he wanted more than anything, some price must be paid. The boy Alured, the youth Alured, must be banished from the man's life. What belonged only to the name Alured—even the name—must go. And he had agreed.

"I am Visli Vaskronin," he murmured, looking out over the lush green of the Immervale. "I am Duke of Immer, and I will be king." In his mind, he heard the trumpets, saw the cheering crowds, felt the flowers thrown touch his face.

You will be king if you heed my advice. Let me take those memories from you so they will not trouble you again.

"No," he said aloud, as if to someone standing beside him and not the being that coinhabited his body. "They fade quickly enough." The oldest of the memories now . . . all earlier had faded . . . was of himself at perhaps eleven or twelve, his defiance of his master. It is not fair, he had yelled . . . actually yelled, outrage overwhelming fear for the moment. He liked remembering himself as brave. And his master had laughed and patted his shoulder, approving.

You were always brave. That is why I chose you.

Warmth spread through his body. Praise always did that, and his advisor's praise most of all. In time he would feel like a Visli—his advisor insisted the name was appropriate, and after all, he had given Alur—*Visli*—so much.

That is better. You are growing more powerful every day.

His advisor said that many times; Alur—*Visli*—had the same warm feeling every time. More powerful. That's what he wanted. Power, strength, long life, never to be cold or hungry or alone or hurt or frightened ever again. It felt so good to be clothed in soft garments, to have a full belly, to have water or wine at his side and never know thirst, to feel the brimming health, the supple strength of body, to see men rush to serve him, obey him.

But Siniava had had powers he still lacked. Siniava had been able to change shapes, to appear like someone else.

You do not need that. Your face brings terror to your enemies and respect to those who serve you.

Still . . . it would have been nice to be able to change.

A lesser power. Great powers become greater by being more themselves.

That made sense. He sighed once more and took a last look to the north, where the height on which Cortes Immer stood trailed away as a descending ridge into the lowlands along the eastern branch of the Immer, the Imefal.

Sunlight glinted on something—something moving. He squinted. No dust rose behind it—rain had fallen the day before. A shout rose from the lookout's post just below. He heard the clatter of feet, of weapons, from the lower levels and then, leaning over, saw his men running to the walls. A mounted troop was already at the gate.

Fallo. The Duke of Fall, like Andressat, had not been receptive to his demand for obeisance. But the Duke of Fall was old and would die soon, and his son might be more malleable. His son had a taste for luxury, it seemed. He had dealt with those who traded in and out of Slavers' Bay to the east, bypassing—as he thought—the Duke of Immer's control of the Immer ports. But in his pirate days, Alured—the right name for that time—had made contacts he'd never lost. So he knew what Fall's son desired and made sure he got it in more quantity and better quality and at a lower price than before.

True, Fall's daughter-in-law was the child of Sofi Ganarrion, whose mercenary company had, despite flamboyant uniforms, fought extremely well against Siniava and now had joined with Fallo's own troops to guard that dukedom. And Ganarrion was northern—from some northern kingdom—

Kostandan. Like her father, of royal blood. Seafolk, originally.

His advisor's annoyance edged the information; he had been told that before. Seafolk . . . who might know that he himself still had connections in Slavers' Bay. But probably not a girl.

He headed down the stairs to the lookout's post. The man bowed as deeply as Alur-*Visli* wished. Yes, he thought he could see that it was a horseman coming along the Fallo–Immer road. A messenger from the Duke, perhaps?

He said nothing but continued on to his chambers. If it was a messenger, he should appear to be what he was: the most powerful lord in Aarenis. He changed his shirt, his doublet, shrugged into a new capelet, lifted his chin while his servant adjusted the fall of lace at his throat. He always wore his sword—a sword now, not a seaman's cutlass—and the various knives he had found useful over the years. He hesitated, once his servant had left him, over the casket where the necklace lay. Rumor said everyone knew he had it—must have it—but he had shown it only to a few trusted men. Was it time to wear it openly?

Yes. But with the chain of office.

The chain of office, made to his order in Immerdzan, downriver, with the medallion of the Duke of Immer, copied from a design found in the ruins before he rebuilt Cortes Immer. He took the chain of office from its velvet-lined box and put it over his head to lie smoothly on his shoulders. Then, anticipating the beauty within, he opened the casket. It always took his breath away. The stones were flawless, radiant with their perfection. His. His forever. And someday . . . soon . . . he would have the rest of the set. The crown, the rings, the goblet . . . all would be his, and the power they held as well.

The necklace settled around his neck, inside the chain of office. The image in his expensive polished mirror looked . . . exactly as a powerful duke—even a king—should look. It lacked only the crown.

In his office, he spread maps on his map table . . . He already knew his plans for this year's campaigns, but the maps would make it clear, if the messenger was from Fallo's court, that he had yet more plans. His advisor had taught him how to look impressive—his clothes, his demeanor, his actions.

The messenger, escorted into his office still mud-spattered, was in fact one of his own spies, not from the Duke of Fall at all.

"My lord, Fallo gathers an army—"

"An army? All he has is that excuse for a militia and Ganarrion's cavalry that everyone jokes about."

"My lord, no . . . I mean, there's more, my lord. The Cold Count—his polearms company has been reinforced, from the north I hear."

Count Vladiorhynsich. In Siniava's War, the commander who had held Rotengre in siege while Kieri Phelan had taken over half the rest of the besiegers north to free Dwarfwatch from Siniava. Brutally effective, his troops. Alur-*Visli* had seen them at work, had been glad not to face them. But now he had more . . . he was sure he had more. And he had magery to strengthen his troops and weaken his opponents.

"They're moving, my lord. And the farmers say that Fallo is reinforcing the border."

"Market gossip?"

"Some, my lord. And some say . . . what happened to Count Andressat's son . . . it's made Fall angry."

Let the old man be angry; he had no teeth to bite. But the Cold Count might, if he had enough troops. Surely he did not. Five hundred at the start of Siniava's War and fewer later. Even if he'd been training Fall's lax militia . . . but if the northerners got involved here, in eastern Aarenis . . . he'd counted on them coming in from Valdaire only. Kostandanyans . . . yes, there'd been some going in and out of Slavers' Bay in his pirate days, and from there . . . not so far across the Copper Hills to the North Trade Road.

He'd intended to take Fallo eventually, but maybe he should do that first, to have security at his back when he pressed west to Valdaire. The Guild League cities were already frightened, already distrusting one another's commitment to the League. Very little interference would keep them stirred up. One campaign season should be enough to conquer Fallo; it would be over by Midwinter Feast.

His advisor was silent but aware—he had learned to tell. Silence usually meant agreement.

"You will speak to no one of your message," he said, putting power into it.

The man's face paled. "No, my lord, to no one."

"You will not go back to Fallo; you might be recognized. You will stay here, with other duties, for the time being." The man bowed, even paler now. "Other duties" had, for some, meant a cell in the dungeon and long interrogations. "You are excused," Visli said. The name draped his shoulders with power; he could feel it.

Now for the planning. The maps, arranged for show, held his attention as he considered how many troops, what kind, how long to gather them, move them . . . He looked up as sunlight lay a bright hand on the maps. So long? But he had his plan. He sent for the captains resident in Cortes Immer.

"A change in plans," he said when they stood before him.

"My lord."

"Fall is our new target. I would not have that fool at my back as we move west." He looked with particular intensity at the captain who had dared suggest, the year before, controlling Fallo first. The man showed no expression, no flicker of eyelid, no traitorous wish to claim that idea for himself. "We have word of an attempt by northerners to infiltrate from Slavers' Bay and suspect an attempt to take over the Immervale while we are far to the west. Instead, we will take Fallo and gain control of Slavers' Bay. I will send word to my sea force today."

"Yes, my lord."

"I have decided what troops we need. Each of you, with a suitable escort, will ride west and north to bring back those units, except for you, Captain Gedarnt." This time the man's eyelids did flicker in surprise.

Send Gedarnt north.

That had not been his idea. Why that?

I have a reason he should not hear. Do it.

He gave the orders as smoothly as if he'd thought them over for days. "You will take your troops to the Northern Trade Road, ready to attack Fall's forces in the rear, should they retreat, and to interdict any reinforcements that might come by that way. You will note all trails that might lead over the mountains and note signs of usage. Though it is unlikely, we know small groups have used at least two such in the past. You will have all my forces now at Rotengre, including the raiders harrying Sorellin's fields. That should reach near four hundred."

Gedarnt bowed low. "Yes, my lord. As my lord commands."

He looked at each face intently, allowing his advisor to see with those eyes, so much more penetrating than his own. "One campaign season," he said. "One will see it done. Come to the maps and see how it will be done."

They came, and he showed them—step by step, march by march. "The forces opposing us are the Fallo militia, whose qualities we know—they may have had more training with Ganarrion there, but Ganarrion was never known as a strict disciplinarian. Count Vladi was, but he is older now, and his force somewhat reduced. So a cavalry company who have seen no combat for these several years while their commander played courtly games, a polearms company of good quality, but again out of practice, and the militia. An unknown number of Kostandanyan troops brought in by sea . . . possibly good soldiers but possibly those thought least useful at home. We cannot know that yet."

"My lord—" That was Captain Tikart. "Will not the Guild League sense a weakness and attack?"

"No. They will have rumors enough of why we delay even as they try to adjust their trade routes to avoid Lûn and Cortes Cilwan. They will be glad of a respite but not trust it. And next year . . . next campaign season or before . . . we will be on the move west again." He cast a look at Captain Gedarnt. "Had we moved against Fall first, it would have given them warning of our initial attack on them and they might well have combined against us—but now they're paralyzed by fear, and the corruption of their currency has made them distrust one another. Now we can attack Fall without worrying that they will attack us."

The discussion went on; Alured-*Visli* allowed his captains to ask questions for a while, then told them to return after dinner for their written orders and bring their own estimates of troop strength and supplies. When they'd left, he went to the window and held up the necklace of blue and white jewels, watching them catch the light just like ripples of the sea.

He knew. His advisor had told him what they were, what power they held, what power the crown held, the crown that someday would be his. He would command an element, and the very element so important to him for so long as a pirate captain. He would command water. He would never be thirsty, never lack for water to float his ships or fill his wells.

Light danced on the walls of his office, as if from moving water; he smiled and tucked the necklace under his shirt.

Y ou must go with your troops.

Alured-*Visli* had not expected that. When he'd sent agents and then troops west and northwest, his advisor had forbidden him to go, had insisted he must stay in Cortes Immer. This was just a small campaign, nothing like as complicated, and if he hadn't been needed on the field there, why now?

I must see with my own eyes what resources the Duke of Fall has.

His second woman would birth her child in the next hand or two of days. He wanted to know if this would be another son or a daughter. His first son was just standing now, wobbly and unable so far to take a step without holding on to something.

But if he must go, he must.

B y the time his troops from downriver, Lûn, and Cortes Cilwan had gathered, Visli Vaskronin, Duke of Immer, was more than ready to leave. His concubine had birthed a daughter three days before, a child he had ordered killed for the horror of that cleft lip running right up into her nose and the disfiguring birthmark across half her face. The concubine as well: the curse must have come through her side, not his; his son by his first concubine had grown into a handsome shirtling. It had not escaped his notice that the birthmark was shaped like a dismasted ship. When he found that the family from which he'd taken her had disappeared in the last twelve hands of days, he was sure they'd done it.

You must find and punish them. His advisor had taught him the uses of punishment long ago but still insisted he was not hard enough. *Take your vengeance; never let an enemy escape; never give one ease. Else they will see weakness and make alliances against you.*

Two other women were pregnant by him. He had their families under guard now, but . . . what if those children, too, were cursed? He knew gossip raged in his stronghold; he could not help but know. Best to be on the road to battle with men—*men,* not gossiping women and boys—around him.

He rode the handsome black bay his agents had brought from Valdaire's horse market. A thief's horse, it had been; that pleased him. Market talk his agent had brought back with the horse suggested that the Thieves' Guild in Valdaire wanted it out of the city, far to the east if possible, before some legendary master thief from whom it had been stolen returned. Well. He understood thieves' politics. The loser in this game would never find his horse. So far, Vaskronin had not been able to discover what thief-taught tricks the horse knew. Perhaps he would on this journey.

From his scouts he had an accurate idea of the land ahead. Immervale, the rich lowlands between the Imefal and the middle branch of the Immer . . . slow going, with the inferior road deep in mud in places. Ahead were the rounded hills and fertile valleys of Fallo itself, and finally the estate—hardly a stronghold—of the Duke of Fall. No grim gray stone walls too high to scale with ladders here but a wall intended more to train flowers against and hold out cattle from the house gardens than a defense against invasion.

A few days on the road and he'd almost succeeded in putting the frightening mask of that dead infant behind him. Here he might also see infants dead, but they would not be of his breeding and therefore of no concern. His scouts reported Fall's troops moving, but not all were headed south, toward him. He hoped that meant Fall had a report of troops coming along the North Trade Road. Surprise would have been good, but dividing troops was also good. With luck—and with the winds this time of year it would take luck—his ships would be approaching Slavers' Bay and he could frighten Fall from three directions.

They were yet days from the Duke's estate when his scouts reported a force blocking the road ahead, a hundred or so of Fall's militia and less than that of cavalry in Ganarrion's colors. That would be only what showed, he was sure. A cavalry reserve, perhaps among trees on the slopes of a hill. A militia reserve. Some kind of archers. Even a half-hundred of Count Vladi's pikes.

Sitting on his black horse, two names for himself competing in his head, listening to reports, Alured-*Visli* considered how best to attack, drawing on what he had learned from his onetime allies in Siniava's War: expect reserves, expect a unit you did not know was there, with weapons those in sight have not shown. His advisor stirred in his head but for once did not interfere. His advisor, he'd been told, had never fought this kind of war.

It would be a test battle, this first one. He had brought six hundred with him, a mix of weapons—he would see what worked. Every other consideration vanished as he made his decisions, ordered his troops, and advanced.

T he Fallo contingents stood firm, though they were visibly outnumbered. So—they thought their reinforcements were larger than his. Larger they might be; harder they could not be, especially the veterans of the battle for Cortes Cilwan. Nor were they better equipped. In the first sandglass of the battle, his troops pushed back the Fallo infantry and his cavalry swept Ganarrion's riders aside time and again. The Fallo reserves—poised, he was sure, on the slopes of the hills—did nothing.

That worried him. They should have—they must have—some point at which they would come charging down. He would have put his reserves in by now if his troops had been pushed back so far.

Now the Fallo front line appeared to waver, and in the rear some turned to run. His own troops pressed forward, his captains glancing back at him for an order to advance, pursue . . . but it did not feel right. So short a battle, given up so easily? He gave the order to halt; his flagmen flipped the flags back and forth at once, and his captains yelled at their men. His troops halted, shifted to a tighter formation.

Even as they did, the woods to either side gave back the sound of men running headlong through the trees, and Fallo's reserves poured out into the open. All the reserves? They had seemed to lack discipline before, and now again they had not waited to be sure they had his flanks.

He signaled advance, and once more his troops pressed forward. The lines stiffened on Fallo's side; the noise intensified. Slowly, bloodily, his troops made headway, pushing Fallo's troops back step by step, death by death. He had the advantage; he had the numbers and the right weapons, and it worked as he had planned.

Because you knew to halt. How did you know?

He did not have time now. His advisor could see what he had seen only if he spoke the words to explain in his mind or let his advisor take over. The battle could still be lost if he did not stay alert. He said those words aloud as well as in his mind: "Not now. Later."

Silence from his advisor. He rode his horse a little way up the slope of the hill on his sword-hand to get a better view of what lay ahead. Fields, a few simple farmhouses, a vill in the distance. A narrow bridge over a small creek, the line of the creek winding between him and the vill. And between him and the vill, what looked like a long mound casting a shadow—with no hedge on top. Black dirt against the green of young grain. It ringed the vill.

Fall's troops must have come from there, must have tried to fortify the vill and then decided to march out to meet him. That could have worked if he'd had fewer troops or fallen for that ambush. But he had enough men to kill them all, given time.

He pushed them back almost to the creek, which seemed sunk deep in the rich soil. Then, to his surprise, a line of soldiers rose from the creek, coalesced into four cohorts of pikes, and—fresh and eager—plowed into his front lines. At the same time, cavalry in Ganarrion's colors galloped out from the vill, jumped the creek upstream and down of the battle, and fell upon his flanks.

Vaskronin disappeared from his mind, leaving Alured, survivor of many desperate times. He called on the magery his advisor had given him, clutching the red jewel on a chain around his neck. His troops roared and held their ground; he cast a dark cloud laden with fear at the enemy. For a moment the massed pikes faltered; the cavalry horses shied, bucked, bolted out of control. His troops advanced again, pushing the enemy back toward the creek while Alured aimed the fear and anguish trapped in the advisor's jewel.

Finally the enemy broke and ran. He held his troops back from pursuit and pressed on to the vill. That fortified vill would make an excellent camp, a base from which to advance again.

He had won. He could conquer Fallo, and next year—next year he would take the rest of Aarenis. The year after that, the north. King. King of all.

You are strong and brave; you deserve to be king.

Familiar warmth spread through his body, this time more flame than warmth along his bones. He felt more alive than ever, filled with strength, power, the wild joy of victory. In that moment of exultation, he had no thought of the disfigured child, of Andressat's curse, of possible treachery. He dropped the reins, raised both hands high— sword and jewel symbols of his power—and spurred his mount toward the vill with the others, yelling in triumph.

And in that moment, the horse—the thief's horse—squealed and twisted like a snake, fastening its teeth in his left leg, crushing his boot, grinding, yanking at his leg with all the strength of its powerful jaws and neck, pulling him out of the saddle. He dropped both jewel and sword, grabbing for the saddle, the mane, trying to stay on, but the horse shook his leg like a rag, kicking out behind. His own soldiers, aghast, could do nothing before he finally fell hard on the ground. The horse dropped his leg and bolted back the way they had come. No one pursued it.

He knew as he fell that he must get up at once and take control; without the jewel-caused terror, the enemy forces would return to the fight. His own forces might break. But the fall stunned him for a moment, and he heard a low moan from those nearest. He struggled up, mouth too dry to yell over the noise, but as soon as he put weight on his left leg, pain lanced through his twisted knee, and his leg gave way. He lurched but managed to hop on one foot. He felt for the red jewel on its chain but found neither chain nor jewel. He saw his sword at a little distance . . . then one of his men was there with a horse, and another on foot. Together, they boosted him onto that horse; one of them handed up his own sword for Alured to use as the Fallo troops closed in.

His left leg dangled, painful and useless; he struggled to say atop the horse, let alone use the sword he'd been given. His troops, surprised by the turn of fortune, looked to him, expecting the familiar magery. The enemy, heartened, closed again; arrows flew from their bows. Even as he shouted orders—close up, hold the ground—he wondered where the jewel was. What if the enemy found it?

The battle now going on had a different feel to it; his troops were giving way—stubborn in their resistance but outnumbered. A fighting retreat was still possible—was necessary; Alured gathered his wits and gave the orders. Movement between the horses caught his eye. The man who had given up his horse and sword looked around— bent down and came up with Alured's sword . . . and then, backing up two steps, stooped again, with a handful of chain and the red jewel glowing in the light.

Kill him!

His advisor was back, angry as his master had ever been at seeing the jewel in a stranger's hand. The pressure of that other mind filled Alured's head, punishing: the pain in his leg was as nothing to the agony in his head.

Kill him! Take the jewel! Hurry!

The man had turned toward him, his mouth open, calling something, but Alured could hear nothing over the voice inside. The man held up the jewel even as battle raged around them . . . he was coming to give it back.

KILL! He knows too much!

They were too close to the roiling edge of battle; Alured could see Ganarrion's troopers only a few horse-lengths away now. The man on the ground ran the last few steps, holding up the necklace. "My lord—I found it! Here it is!" Alured reached out for it, overbalancing as his injured leg could not grip the horse's side; the man pushed the jewel into his hand and then pushed Alured back upright. "My lord—you're hurt—you must retreat. I'll lead your horse."

The jewel warmed in Alured's hand; strength flowed back into him as the pain in his head receded. Even his injured leg obeyed his command; his foot found the stirrup, and the leg snugged against the horse's side. By then the man had caught hold of the reins and turned the horse, leading it toward the safer interior of his troops. Though his advisor still told him to kill the man, Alured-not-Visli felt relief. The man had saved his life; the man was not a thief but had given back the jewel. He did not want to kill the man; if enemies should be punished, surely those who gave good service should be rewarded.

Fool! He knows too much; he must die.

They might all die if he did not concentrate on the battle and drive back the enemy once again. Yet he knew the jewel offered only one power at a time—he could not use it for strength for himself and at the same time send terror to his enemies. Had enough healing already occurred that he could use his leg without the jewel's help?

He shifted his concentration, ignoring the pain that gripped his leg, and felt once more his own troops' renewed confidence and the enemy's loss of it. But this time the effect was not so powerful, and he could not maintain that concentration—and his balance in the saddle—very long. By worse mischance, an arrow struck his injured leg.

All that day the battle wavered back and forth, but by nightfall they were farther from the village, with the enemy testing their camp's defenses.

The surgeon who attended him insisted he must not ride again until the leg healed—if it did. "The bite of a horse is a crushing wound, my lord. And the fever demons delight in a crushing wound. And your knee, my lord, was wrenched, I suppose when you fell. This is a serious wound, my lord—"

"From a *horse*." That was humiliating, to be felled by a horse bite. "And then the arrow, my lord. It struck the bone." He made himself look at the wound. They had cut off his boot; the horse's teeth had gone through the leather and into his flesh. His leg was swollen, purple and red, with blood oozing from the teeth-marks and the slice the surgeon had made to extract the arrowhead. His knee was swollen to twice its size. The surgeon laid a poultice of healing herbs on it and bound the leg in splints. "Stay off it or it might never heal."

The next day began the miserable retreat; he lay in a wagon, using the jewel as much as he could to hold off the most dangerous attacks, but he was soon exhausted and feverish. Every jolt of the wagon sent waves of pain through his leg and his ribs; the surgeon told him now they were likely broken. Daily his advisor told him to find and kill the man who had saved him, but he had no energy to spare for that.

By the time the army reached Cortes Immer, his leg was obviously infected, swollen almost to the groin. His surgeon had cut it open again to drain the stinking pus and pack the wound with healing herbs, but Alured—never thinking of himself as Visli now—was sure he would lose his leg or die. How could a one-legged man become king?

You can still be whole and a king. Do what I tell you.

CHAPTER EIGHT

Gird's Hall, Fin Panir

Her shoulder ached; she could not sleep. Arianya, Marshal-General of Gird, squirmed higher against her pillows, trying not to make a noise. If she couldn't sleep, at least she could think, and she thought better sitting up. She hoped.

The past half-year had been the worst of her life as the Fellowship splintered on the matter of magery. She blamed herself for not anticipating the degree of resistance—the resurgence of the same hatred and resentment of magery that had in the end cost Gird's life even as it gave peace for a time to the Fellowship and allowed Luap to get the surviving magelords to Kolobia.

Where they had died, most of them, through Luap's stupidity. She shifted, clenching her teeth at the pain as she thought of it. Only a few scraps gave clues to exactly what Luap had done . . . and so he offered her nothing to learn from. She would have to figure this out for herself. The only thing she could think of that might work was having everyone—every single yeoman, from birth to old age—cursed or gifted with mage-powers at once. And even that might not work. And even if it did, she had no way to accomplish it.

Down the hall she heard footsteps . . . boots, not soft indoor shoes as most wore at night. Her breath caught; her pulse quickened. Another assassin? Moving openly because he had already killed the guards—or the guards had proved disloyal? A firm tap on her door and a voice she knew: "Marshal-General? Are you awake?"

"Come in," she said. Arvid Semminson was an assassin—or had

been—but she hoped he was now Gird's true yeoman, surprising as the transformation had been. He smelled of the outdoors: horse, leather, sweat, and a breath of night's coolness clung to him. "What news?"

"How's that wound?" he asked. He tucked his gloves into his belt, doffed his cloak, and hung it on a peg across the room. "You're not sleeping, and you look like someone in pain. Should've healed by now with all the Marshals around to give it a nudge."

She shook her head. "Too many others in the city needed them. I'm not that—"

"You are," he said across her words. "You are that important. Who's going to take over if you die?"

He had once seemed suave, tactful, but since the troubles started, he had shed his smooth manner for directness.

"The Marshalate would vote," she said. "It might be Donag."

"Or it might be some idiot," Arvid said.

"How's your boy?" she asked, hoping to divert him.

"He's fine. Growing, learning . . . and not, so far, showing a speck of mage talent, Gird be thanked." He shook his head at her. "It's you, Marshal-General, we have to worry about. The Fellowship needs you, and you're not healing as you should. Was the weapon poisoned?"

He'd asked that before. So had others. Her memory of the attack was blurred, more than any other memory in her life, and she did not understand it. Several dark figures—she could not say how many— and though she had fought them off until approaching help sent them fleeing into the night, one had pierced her shoulder, the tip grating on bone.

"Let me see," he said now. "But I still think—"

"Oh, very well." She moved, and the pain wrenched her again.

"Soon," he said. This time she did not hear his boots on the floor, but before she could wonder why not, he was back with one of the yeoman-marshals, Lia. To her he said, "I had a report to give the Marshal-General, but she looks no better than when I left—I believe the weapon must have been poisoned. Has no one seen it?"

Lia frowned. "Marshal-General—who's been binding it up for you?" She turned to Arvid. "She's been at her desk half-days; we thought it was fine. But she does look bad tonight."

"Others needed help more," Arianya said. "I could do it—" But the pain worsened as if to mock her, and she sagged back against the pillows. "Sorry . . ."

"Let's get her shirt off," Arvid said.

"I can . . ." she began, but sitting up wrenched a groan from her, and Lia quickly moved to support her back.

"She's hot," Lia said.

"Fever, most like," Arvid said. Arianya wanted to protest, but she could scarcely keep from crying out as they lifted the shirt. She heard Lia's sharp intake of breath at whatever it looked like. "And that's more than one wound," Arvid went on. "I would wager you told no one about the others, did you?" He sounded angry.

Arianya summoned the last of her strength. "They were scarcely more than scratches. I put herbs on them."

His hand touched her shoulder lightly; she tensed, expecting the pain again, but instead felt the warmth of his breath. "I'm smelling— some poisons have a strong scent . . ." His voice trailed away.

"What?" Arianya said.

Instead of answering her, he said, "Lia, she needs healing—find any Marshals or paladins; bring them here."

"Now?"

"Now. We do not have much time."

The girl's footsteps clattered away. Arianya opened her eyes; Arvid was beside her, staring down at the wound.

"What is it?" she asked again. This time he met her gaze.

"It's definitely poisoned," he said. "And by something we in the Guild believed was an elven poison. Could your attackers have been elves?"

She tried to force her memories to clarity, but the attackers remained shadows. "They were tall," she said. "They wore dark clothes, like . . . thieves—"

"The Guild never contemplated killing a Marshal-General," Arvid said. "It would cause too much trouble. If elves attacked you, though—you had that visit from elves—"

"The kuaknomi," Arianya said. "Those elves were worried about the kuaknomi in the western stronghold, where Luap was. Said he's let them out—"

"They're just elves, aren't they? Another tribe?"

"More than that," she said. All at once she felt strength flowing out of her, as if even mentioning kuaknomi harmed her. She could scarcely keep her eyes open.

"No!" Arvid's voice was loud, painfully loud. "Open your eyes—look at this!"

She struggled and managed to open her eyes enough to see what he held. Her Girdish medallion, with a candle held close so it glittered in that light.

"Gird does not want you to die now," Arvid said in a quieter voice.

She wanted to laugh but lacked the strength. "You're sure of that?"

"Yes. You know Gird . . . speaks to me."

"And he spoke to you about me?" She could not really believe that. Everyone knew the gods and heroes of old spoke to some but not to most.

"Sometimes people don't listen," Arvid said. "Sometimes they're doing well enough and nothing needs to be said." A pause, then he added, as if prompted, "He doesn't want you to die now. I'm sure."

She heard voices outside her rooms, echoing in the stairwell. Too many voices—Lia must have roused more than a couple of Marshals. First in the room was High Marshal Donag.

"You!" he said to Arvid. "What are you doing here?"

"I came to report to the Marshal-General and found her wounds had not been properly treated," Arvid said.

"You accuse us—!"

"Of nothing," Arvid said. "But it is a fact. There's poison—possibly even a remnant of the blade that made the wound."

"She didn't say—"

"Marshal-General—" Camwynya, one of the paladins now resident in Fin Panir, ignored the High Marshal and threaded her way through the others to the bed. "May I see?"

Arianya nodded. Several were talking now, some arguing with the High Marshal and some agreeing with him. She wished they would all be quiet and go away, but she could not summon the energy to tell them so.

Camwynya's face showed her shock when she uncovered the wound. "It's not healed at all—who looked at it first?"

Arianya could not remember. Someone, she thought, had helped her stanch the bleeding, laid folded cloth on it, wrapped the bandages around, but all she clearly remembered was struggling to replace them . . . when? The next morning, surely, but she could not remember that, either. She murmured that. Camwynya's eyes narrowed.

"It's definitely poison, and one I don't know. Arvid, do you?"

Arvid moved closer to the bed. "We thought it was elven in the Guild. Marshal-General mentioned kuaknomi."

Arianya looked up—the other faces seemed strange—still talking, some looking at her, some at one another, all shadowed, this cheekbone and that brow picked out in yellow candlelight.

"Kuaknomi." Camwynya leaned over her. "Marshal-General, we must probe the wound, see if anything's left inside. You know how often their weapons are designed to leave a fragment in the wound. I fear the effect of numbwine, as weak as you are."

"Light," Arianya said. "Need light."

Light blazed in the room—Camwynya's light, Gird's light. She blinked against it. She felt the bed move as several dragged it out into the room and then hands on her shoulders. Camwynya laid one hand over Arianya's heart and the other on the wound itself. Pain stabbed deep—deeper than the wound itself, it felt like. Arianya closed her eyes, trying not to struggle against it . . . and still there was light, shadowless, pure, unending.

And another face, the one she had imagined so often but never seen, emerged from the light, looking at her . . . steady gray eyes, endurance and compassion in the lines of his face.

In the haze of light and pain, Arianya murmured, "I'm sorry."

The brows went up, and the mouth quirked. "For others' misdeeds?"

"For my mistakes." She was aware that she was not speaking aloud, that somewhere else others were working on her body, but the pain had eased . . . had vanished . . . leaving her here in the light with the old, stoop-shouldered balding man in his faded blue shirt.

He shrugged. "Everyone makes mistakes. I made mistakes. Are you leaving my service?"

"Leaving . . ."

"You allowed none to care for you. Why?"

"I did not deserve—"

He grunted. "What you deserve is not at issue. Others deserve a good Marshal-General."

"A good Marshal-General would have found more paladin candidates . . . would have foreseen this trouble . . . would have . . ."

"Been a god?" A bite of sarcasm in that. "Neither of us, Arianya Girdsdotter, is a god. I was a good-enough leader when I lived in that room; I am a good-enough messenger now. Make up your mind: Will you leave my service, or will you stay?"

Faced with that face, she had only one answer. "I will stay."

"Good. We must talk again another time. You do not always listen well, Arianya. Be well." She felt the touch of a hand on her forehead—his?—and the brilliant light slowly dimmed. She felt pain again and heard other voices.

"It's stuck in the bone—I can't get a grip."

"Try this."

"It's so small—"

She heard the gritty sound of something being pulled from bone and a gasp from someone nearby.

"What is that? Black—"

A door banged, and other footsteps came closer, running. Through her closed eyelids light glowed red. "Who is it—ahhh."

"Paks." That was Camwynya . . . and Paks was here? Here? She had been gone . . . a long time, Arianya thought. "We think it was an iynisin attack. I just pulled this from the bone—and look."

"I see. If they used what they did on me, then the only healing I know is Kuakkgani . . . and there's no Kuakgan nearer than the southern mountains . . . perhaps in western Tsaia."

"Surely we can do something."

"We will do our best."

Paks leaned closer; Arianya could smell horse, leather, dust, and then as suddenly as before she slid into another place . . . this time not white light but green.

A green glade, spattered with sunlight piercing the tree canopy overhead. Purple flowers gave off a fragrance spicier than violets; a bright-colored bird flew past, a winged jewel when the sunlight touched it: glittering green, red, blue, purple. Out from the forest shade came a strange cat—gray spots on a snow-white coat, eyes of palest blue. It paced up to her, rose on its hind legs and set its forepaws gently on her shoulders, extended a pink tongue and licked her across the face.

Across the glade, a pile of pillows and coverlets appeared, inviting her to lie down. The cat returned to four feet and butted her gently toward the pillows. She took a step, then another; the cat walked beside her, and when she faltered, she found its back under her hand, warm beneath the soft fur, a firm support.

She sank onto the pillows; the cat lifted one paw and gently pushed her down, then drew the coverlets up. With her last sight, she saw the impossible . . . the purple petals of the flowers rose up and flew to her, covering her with purple. When two petals touched her eyelids, she fell asleep in that instant.

Waking again was strange. For an instant, the forest glade overlaid the familiar room, as if the walls were draped in embroidered veils. Then the veils faded away, and she saw whitewashed walls and heard someone snoring across the room. The light coming in the window was dim, blue-gray . . . predawn? Near nightfall? She lay still, not wanting to wake the pain, listening to the snores. The wall seemed more distinct moment by moment; the air moving into the window carried a tinge of woodsmoke. A rooster crowed; a mule brayed. Morning, then. She moved one leg, then the other, then turned her head to see who was in the room with her. Slumped in a chair, feet up on a stool, Paks slept with one arm dangling, the other hand on her Girdish medallion.

In the passage outside, the *slap-slap* of light shoes came nearer. Then a knock on the door. Paks woke at once, the way a cat wakes, and turned to the door.

"Sib, lady. Cook says bread'll be out in a half-glass, and porridge in less."

"Thank you," Paks said. She came back into the room with a tray and met Arianya's gaze. "You're awake—how do you feel?"

"What happened?" Arianya asked.

"That's a story with two sides," Paks said. "I know what we tried to do; you alone know what it was like for you."

Arianya moved her left arm a little. Her shoulder was stiff but not painful. "It doesn't hurt. And I—it's clearer."

"Want some sib?"

"Yes." She tried to hitch herself up in the bed but achieved only a fingerwidth.

Paks came to the bed. "Let me help."

With her help, Arianya was able to sit up against the pillows. Paks handed her a mug of sib. She sniffed—the familiar fragrance seemed even sharper than usual. She sipped; the slightly bitter, earthy flavors cleared her head.

Paks leaned on the table, drinking from her own mug and watching. She put it down when she'd drained it. "Marshal-General, you must be careful. We are not sure we got everything."

"Two paladins of Gird? I'm sure you did."

Paks shook her head. "No. It's like what happened to me. Whatever it is they use . . . well, you know about me. That must not happen to you. I think you need a Kuakgan."

"But I'm Girdish!"

"Yes. But the Kuakkgani have special skills. They were never enemies of the Girdish. You surely know many Girdish in Tsaia visit Kuakkgani—"

"They do?"

"Yes. Some ills the farm wife treats with sweetherb, some with tongue-bite, some with fever-bark. So with Marshals and Kuakkgani: Marshals have their skills, and the Kuakkgani have other skills. I am no less Gird's because Master Oakhallow knew how to draw iynisin poison from my flesh and my spirit."

"We should learn that," Arianya said.

"If we could, yes. I suspect it would take a lifetime and maybe more to learn all the green blood can teach. You know the stories about how they become Kuakkgani . . ."

Yes, she knew the stories. She did not believe the stories, but then, she had never met a Kuakgan, only the occasional remote family who declared they were Kuakgannir. Simpletons, she thought them. Had thought them until she heard Paksenarrion's story, and even now . . . "Are there any Kuakkgani in Fintha?" she asked.

"I don't know. I know there are some in Tsaia. If you ask for that help, I can bring one."

Marshal-Generals should not need help from anyone but Gird. Something in her head snorted derision. Abruptly, she remembered the conversation she'd had with . . . someone.

Someone?

She looked at Paks, and Paks looked back at her—that same friendly face, that same apparent naivete. Yet Paks had seen, had experienced, the worst of both mortal and immortal viciousness. If Paks thought she needed a Kuakgan's care . . . then it would be stupid to refuse it.

She pushed herself higher against her pillows, and this time her body responded almost normally. Surely, then, she was normal and needed no healing . . . yet Paks had thought the same.

"You think I should . . ." she began.

Paks interrupted. "I can't forget how it was for me. That must not happen to you, Marshal-General, or anyone else if I can prevent it. I'm not a Kuakgan; their powers come from the health of living things. Even the touch of iynisin blood can be fatal; their malice infuses it with evil. King Kieri, remember, had but a scratch . . . and it was a Kuakgan who healed him."

Arianya took a deep breath and nodded. "Well, then. If I need a Kuakgan, I'd best find one." She pushed away from the pillow and swung her legs over the side of the bed; dizziness blurred her vision. Paks's arm steadied her.

"Not you—one of us. You lost more blood than you know."

B y the next day, Arianya was back at work, accompanied always by a High Marshal or one of the paladins, while somewhere— she did not know where—someone, almost certainly Paks, sought a

Kuakgan willing to help her. She felt better, though still weak, and dug through the paperwork that had accumulated during her illness. Arvid had organized it for her and explained his reasons when she asked.

"I never expected a thief-assassin to be this good at organization," she said on the third day, leaning back and shaking out a hand cramp.

Arvid ducked his head. "If I were good at organization, I would be head of the Guild in Vérella," he said.

Arianya looked at him. "Do you wish you were?"

"No . . . not now. But it still gripes me that I was fooled—"

"And it gripes me that I was fool enough not to anticipate the attack that left me flat for hands of days. I must let that go—and so must you."

"Speaking as the Marshal-General," he said, this time with a tinge of humor.

"Yes. Precisely. Arvid, you're now in the Fellowship of Gird, and though we value your knowledge of the Guild, we value *you*—you as a yeoman of Gird—more. If I fix my mind on my failure . . . I will fail again. The same with you."

"I am well rebuked," Arvid said, though the glint in his eye left her in doubt about the depth of his contrition. "But I prefer not to fail."

"I, also. You do realize that you have gone far beyond your duties as one of the scribes?"

"Yes, Marshal-General."

"In another quarter-year—no, it's less now—your candidate year will be completed. Have you thought what you will do when you are no longer a yeoman-candidate and under your Marshal's direct command? You have not missed a drill night but one; isn't that right?"

"Saving the time on the journey north, Marshal-General."

"And honest as well. Arvid . . . Gird speaks to you. You have some purpose here, more than just one letter in a page of writing. Has Gird given you any hints lately?"

Arvid scowled, staring at the floor, and rocked backward and forward on his heels. "Marshal-General, Gird is . . . hard to understand sometimes. There are hints . . . but I do not know how to interpret them."

"Tell me." When he said nothing, she waited until finally his head came up and he met her gaze. She nodded.

"It cannot be . . . what I understood," Arvid said. "I am not shy of my past, Marshal-General, as you know. I was what I was; it made me what I am; it is . . . real. But it is not the life that leads . . . anywhere . . . in the Fellowship, I mean."

"Gird was a peasant," Arianya said. "Luap was a bastard, and I know your opinion of him. So what impediment is there for you in any position Gird might suggest?"

"I'm starting late," Arvid said.

She sighed.

Daughter, do not waver.

"Arvid, you have done all you could to *become* a good yeoman . . . you have observed the duties, you have said the words. By that measure, you *are* a good yeoman. But I cannot see you working the rest of your life among the scribes, copying out one document after another. You are not that kind of man—you know that."

Now it was his turn to sigh. "I cannot leave my son," he said. "Until he is grown—"

"He fares well," Arianya said, "Both in the grange and with his fellow junior yeomen. He is happy—or so the yeoman-marshal for juniors reports."

Arvid nodded. "He is indeed happy and healthy, and I intend to keep him so."

"So do we all," Arianya said. His eyes widened briefly, then narrowed.

"You would take me from him?"

"No. You are his father. But you need to know, and accept, that you are not the only one wishing him well and happy. Should you fall—and that may happen to anyone by a strike of lightning from the sky, by a fall, by someone's carelessness with a horse and cart, as well as by malice—you should know that others will care for your son."

His eyes glistened. "So Marshal Steralt said in Valdaire. But I—he is *my* son."

"Yes. But what is it Gird has said to you that you think rises above your abilities?"

"Not exactly my abilities," Arvid said with a touch of his old arrogance. "But my due—"

"Just say it, Arvid!"

He flushed, then answered. "It's the Code, Marshal-General. It's . . . what we know now of what Luap wrote means that the Code itself should be changed. You've already said that—"

"And what has that to do with you? Come, Arvid; you're shying around the matter like a colt afraid of a saddle on the ground in a training pen."

"Gird . . . thinks I should . . . speak out about such things."

"And so you should. And—?"

"And . . . not just as a very junior yeoman or scribe. As . . ."

"A judicar?" His jaw dropped; Arianya could not help laughing. "Come, Arvid; that makes sense. Someone who has been outside the law sees the law more clearly—and yes—" She held up her hand to forestall him. "Yes, I know you consider the Thieves' Guild to have had a law of its own. So you are doubly qualified, are you not? And you learned something of southern law in Vérella and military law from your time with Fox Company."

"Um . . . judicar, yes, Marshal-General, but also . . . um . . ."

"Gird's right arm, Arvid, just tell me what he said. Marshal-Judicar of Gird, was it?" She tossed it out like a jest.

For a moment she thought he would literally fall over even as her own thought caught up to the idea seriously. A thief as a Marshal? A Marshal-Judicar? Well . . . why not?

"I can't—I haven't—I don't let myself—"

"You'd better," Arianya said, her voice now steady. "Because if Gird has that in mind for you—or anything else, including heading the Fellowship—then you'd best be about learning what you need to know to do a good job of it." He still said nothing, breathing too fast. "You don't want someone like you, two hundred winters from now, saying you were a second Luap, do you?"

"I'm not!" That in a voice absolutely devoid of jest, boast, or anything but determination.

"Indeed, you are not anything like the Luap we now know. You are a far better man, in my estimation, and that's a judgment I made before the attack." She gave him a long, considering look. "It will be a difficult trail to follow, Arvid, and would have been so even without this turmoil over magery. But if this is Gird's charge to you—and I think it is—then we need you. *I* need you."

He nodded finally, a decisive nod. "So—now what?"

"Now I will have one of the senior judicars review your knowledge of the Code as it is. Then we will see." She called in the guard at the door and sent word to the head scribe and the Judicariate that she requested a conference.

Removing Arvid from the scribes took only a moment. "Gird requires him elsewhere" got a bow and a respectful "Yes, Marshal-General."

The judicar who came, however, was a different matter, Deinar being one of those who held strictly to the Code and had argued already that magery could not be made legal. He looked at Arvid with disfavor. "This is the thief?"

"This is the *former* thief," Arianya said with all the patience she could muster. "Now a yeoman of Gird—"

"A provisional yeoman still in his first year of service and having missed drill-night attendance at a grange for—"

"For the time it took him to travel from Valdaire to here, as commanded by his Marshal in the south. I am aware of that, Judicar Deinar."

"Hmmph. And what do you want me to do, Marshal-General?"

"Arvid has a broad background in several legal systems—"

"Thwarting them, no doubt," Deinar said.

"Hear me out, Judicar." Arianya allowed her voice to acquire a bite, and Deinar stiffened.

"Yes, Marshal-General."

"Arvid will be studying the Code more deeply than his Marshal can supervise—on my behalf—and you will need to examine him and determine what his current level is. Are you able to do that, or does your bias against him prevent it?"

"Bias? I'm a judicar; I am perfectly impartial. I adhere to the Code." From his tone, no one could possibly doubt that.

"We shall see," she said. "Arvid, you will spend four glasses a day with Deinar, and Deinar, I expect a daily report from you on which parts of the Code you have covered that day and how Arvid's understanding fares."

The two men glared at each other. "Yes, Marshal-General," Arvid said barely a moment before Deinar said the same.

"When must I start?" Deinar said.

"Now," Arianya said. "And Arvid, I have a few trivial questions about these papers, so check with me before you leave for home."

CHAPTER NINE

D einar's first daily report, delivered with a scowl that evening, was that Arvid Semminson's knowledge and understanding of the Ten Fingers and the Ten Toes was entirely adequate.

"Is that as far as you got?" Arianya asked. Though she felt no pain, she was tired and noticed that her voice sounded peevish. She hoped that meant nothing, that the Kuakgan Paks had gone to find would not be needed, but she would not ignore any symptom.

"Yes, Marshal-General. If the foundation is not sound, the building will not stand. The thief—the yeoman must fully understand the foundations of the Code, not merely recite them as any youngling can do."

"Good, then," she said. "I expect he will wish to continue the same schedule he had as a scribe, four glasses' work in the morning and the afternoon to care for his son."

Deinar nodded. "He seems to care for his son, Marshal-General, more than I expected."

"It is a long story," Arianya said. "And one I would rather tell another day, if you do not mind. It is my first full day of work after they took a kuaknomi blade from my bone."

"Of course, Marshal-General." For just a moment his expression softened. "We in the Judicariate are most pleased you have recovered."

"Thank you," she said, somewhat surprised. Given his views on magery, she would have expected him to wish her dead.

"I disagree with you about magery," Deinar said. "And possibly about the conversion of a lifelong thief. But I respect you as Marshal-General."

"Thank you," she said again. He bowed and withdrew. Arianya leaned back in her chair and sighed. She felt bone-deep weariness and was just about to call for sib when Marshal Vesk came in with a tray heaped with dishes and mugs.

"You don't need to be wasting your energy going down to the kitchen for supper, since you insisted on working today."

Arianya opened her mouth to protest and found herself thanking him instead.

"By your leave, Marshal-General, I'll eat with you. I've got the early shift on guard in the hall, and this saves me steps, too."

"Suits me," Arianya said, setting the papers aside. "Here—what are we having?"

"Beef-barley soup for you, which is what the cooks think you need, and sausage and beans for me, which they insisted was too spicy for someone just out of bed. I could be bribed to share. Your soup smells good."

Arianya laughed. "They know I love that spiced sausage. Let's both share—surely if most of what I eat is the soup, all will be well." She picked up one of the small loaves on the tray, broke it, and he sprinkled salt on both halves.

Partway through the meal, Marshal Vesk said, "I wonder how long it will take Paksenarrion to find a Kuakgan."

Arianya swallowed the bite of sausage—it was spicier than she remembered—and said, "I suppose it depends on how near one is to Fintha. Although some wander—she might meet a wandering Kuakgan."

"We . . . worry a little."

"As do I. A lot, in fact. Was my moment of temper this afternoon a sign of some evil influence or just the way I've been for years? Am I tired because of blood loss and spending too many days in bed, or . . . again . . . evil influence? If it is that, then I'm the last person to detect it."

"You seem yourself to me, but everyone knows about Paksenarrion."

"Yes. However, thanks to her, I will not have to endure what she did. I still think about that—"

"You know the Marshalate agreed with you. Well, except for those like Haran."

"Yes, but the Marshalate was as ignorant as I was. And as for Haran, it's her views we're now faced with." She sighed. "Though had I known all I needed to about Paksenarrion and had I found her a Kuakgan, Haran would still have felt aggrieved . . . Why was a Marshal-General consulting a Kuakgan? she would have asked. And those of her mind now would still oppose any acceptance of magery." She looked at the rest of the sausage and decided to finish the beef-barley soup instead.

Several days later, Deinar's report on Arvid's progress was accompanied by a scowl that the report itself did nothing to explain. He had examined Arvid on the first section beyond the fingers and toes, something taught to yeoman-marshals. Arvid had mastered the material and was able to apply it to the standard situations yeoman-marshals were expected to face.

"I spoke to Marshal Cedlin," he said, "and asked if he had thought of making Arvid a yeoman-marshal. He said he had not, but Arvid was outpacing the other yeomen, so he allowed him to read deeper into the Code." Deinar looked hard at Arianya. "I would like to be able to say that this is unwise in all cases, but Arvid seems to have an unusual ability to absorb the meat of the matter. Although he often seems glib in his speech, there is nothing superficial about his understanding."

"Have you an explanation for his progress?" Arianya asked.

"He is unusually intelligent, obviously. Quick to learn, Marshal Cedlin says, and says he was so informed by Arvid's former Marshal in Aarenis." Deinar tipped his head. "Have you considered, Marshal-General, that he was, before becoming a thief, a defrocked judicar, perhaps in Tsaia?"

"No," she said. "That never occurred to me. It is my understanding he was born into a thief family and brought up as one."

"I have not known many thieves—we do not have the Guild here, as you know, so our thieves are not so organized. But this man—

truly, Marshal-General, he is in some way not . . . not what I expected. I still do not understand his motives . . ."

"I'm sure you will," Arianya said. "You are perceptive; I believe
all judicars are."

"Perhaps. We try to be. Mostly we try to be very precise and
very clear." A long pause as Deinar looked out the window. Finally
he turned back to her and said, "I suppose there's no possibility that
he's half-elven . . ."

"Arvid? Not so far as I know, and I myself have seen nothing
elven about him."

"It is his way of speaking, at times," Deinar said. "Very . . . elaborate."

"He is from Tsaia," Arianya said. "And I know he spent much
time in Vérella. So perhaps he picked up that way of speaking from
the court." She wondered why she had never thought about that before. Arvid had been a thief—why would he speak with such sophis-
tication?

"Perhaps." Deinar sighed. "But at any rate, Marshal-General, I
must say . . . he is far more interesting a pupil than I expected, and so
far I would judge that he will master the entire Code fairly quickly.
What then? Surely you have plans for him."

"Not precisely," Arianya said, folding her hands. "I feel he has
great potential, and I feel Gird's own hand pushing me to see that he
learns to use it. But as what exactly—that I do not know."

"You are sure it's Gird—" Deinar stopped and shook his head.
"Of course you are. You would not say it if you weren't."

"Excuse me, Marshal-General, but there's a man—"

Arianya and Deinar both turned. A young yeoman-marshal stood
in the doorway, looking worried.

"A man," Arianya said. "What kind of man?"

"A Girdish yeoman from someplace I never heard of. He wants to
put a cow—I mean a . . . a sort of statue of a cow, though it isn't really
a statue, exactly, but the skin and the head and bones, and all that,
over some kind of frame—"

"Come now, Yeoman-Marshal," Deinar said as Arianya was trying
to imagine a cowhide draped over sticks tied together to make a cow

shape. The head would surely stink. "Do you mean a cow statue or not?"

"It's supposed to look like a cow, but it isn't a cow, it's got the hide and all, but it's not alive and it's not made of stone or wood," the yeoman-marshal said in a rush, her ears bright red with embarrassment. "He wants to put it in the High Lord's Hall."

"He can't—" began Deinar.

"Why does he want to?" asked Arianya, cutting across Deinar.

"He says it's because Gird loved cows. And if there's a cow to remind people, then they'll think about Gird instead of magelords."

Arianya looked at Deinar. He shrugged, eyebrows raised. "It has a certain logic," he said. "The original Gird, his known fondness for cows . . . but I don't think it would work."

Rapid boot steps rang down the corridor, more than one pair, and loud voices with them.

"I don't care—nobody is taking that stinking thing—"

"You can't just—it's up to the Marshal-General—"

"No, it's not—it's up to the Marshal-Judicar-General."

Voices arrived at the door simultaneously—High Marshal Bradlin and High Marshal Celis, both ready to leap into argument. Arianya held up her hand.

"If it's about the cow, I'm about to go see it."

⁂

Arianya ignored the peculiar object on the wagon at first and concentrated on the people. Beside the wagon stood a short, stocky man with weathered skin and callused hands. He whipped off a shapeless hat, revealing a freckled bald pate, and his gap-toothed grin expressed both a sunny good nature and absolute confidence in his mission. Behind the wagon a small group of dusty, trail-worn travelers clumped together, looking wide-eyed at the High Lord's Hall on one side and then the old palace on the other. All looked like country folk, all wore blue shirts, and all wore little wooden cow shapes dangling from strings around their necks.

She looked back at the first man. "I'm Marshal-General Arianya," she said. "What's this about?"

He bobbed his head, still grinning. "I'm Salis, Marshal-General, from Tillock-Uphill. And this is Gird's Cow."

"Go on," Arianya said.

"It's this, Marshal-General." He took a long breath and started into what was clearly a memorized spiel. "Gird was a cowman. We know that; m'Marshal told us it says the same in the new things that's been found. We call him Gird Strongarm, and I don't doubt he was, but he was also a cowman, and it's my thought that's a better way to think of him. Now, a cowman cares for cows, be they spotted or solid, fawn or black, even if they got one crooked horn or wry tail or hoof-rot. Even if a cow has a two-headed calf, he don't kill that calf for having two heads. And he don't cut off one head." He paused.

Arianya looked at the thing in the wagon. It was vaguely animal-shaped, four-legged at least, and the wrapping was clearly cowhide. The head had cow ears, and holes where the cow's eyes had been, but below the recognizable part of a cow face was a bulbous lump, also covered with cowhide.

"I built it on a frame," Salis explained. "It's not that heavy, really—I stuffed it with straw to make it lighter and round—"

It *was* very round, like a giant pillow, and not at all cowlike except for the hide and the ridgepole that would have been a spine in a cow, but here was clearly—even through the hide—a not quite straight tree branch or possibly the trunk of a sapling with a couple of sticks—or maybe branches—poking out of the hide where a cow's hip bones would be. Instead of hooves, the postlegs ended in wooden wheels. Each leg was lashed fore and aft and sideways to the cart.

Arianya knew she must not laugh. The man was completely serious, convinced in his own mind. Yet it was ridiculous. This—this *thing*—was not a cow, and though Gird had loved cows, she could not see any connection between Gird's love of cows and Gird's admonitions to his followers on the subject of magelords. And she had important problems to deal with—this was a distraction just when she didn't need it.

"As Gird he loved his cows so much . . ." The little group began to sing in the wavering, nearly tuneless voices of those who aren't sure what will happen.

As Gird he loved his cows so much,
so we should love our yeoman friends.
And this here cow she stands as such,
to show Gird's care it never ends.

"Hideous!" muttered High Marshal Bradlin.

O Gird, O Gird, your cow we bring to you!
O Gird, O Gird, you wear a shirt of summer blue.

As they sang, the tune they were trying for became clearer. " 'Run Fox Run,' " High Marshal Celis said. "The northern version. 'As fox runs through the summer grass, the farmer's home he will not pass . . .' "

"They're singing it *wrong*." High Marshal Bradlin sniffed as the yeomen continued with another verse. "And they all stink of cow."

O Gird, O Gird, your cow we bring to you!
O Gird, O Gird, you wear a shirrrt—of summer blue!

The group finished with enthusiasm and stood staring at the Marshals so much like cows over a fence that Arianya had to grin at them. Their leader grinned back, clearly pleased at what he saw as approval.

"So now," he said, "we want to put Gird's Cow in the High Lord's Hall."

"Why there?" Arianya asked.

"So everyone will see it," he said, as if that were obvious. "People come here, don't they? And they come see the High Lord's Hall—"

"Have you ever seen it?" Arianya asked.

"No, not until now, but I heard of it. Our Marshal, that's Marshal Tam, he told us about it. Bigger than three granges end to end, he said, and colored windows, and was there before Gird. I can see it's big—" He glanced toward the Hall.

"You all come with me," Arianya said. "You and your followers. Leave the . . . leave Gird's Cow here; High Marshal Celis will take care of it." She gestured and noticed that the group did not move until Salis nodded and took a step. Devout followers already.

She led them into the High Lord's Hall; they stopped, once inside, and gaped at the colored light, the height of the interior.

"It's . . . really big," Salis said. "And beautiful. And to think Gird was here. Himself."

"Yes," Arianya said. "Come see where he was buried."

They stared at the stone she pointed out, the letters blurred with all the hands that had touched them. After a long silence, one of the women sighed.

"An' he had no childer . . ."

"He had one who lived," Arianya said. "His daughter, Rahel."

"But no one after."

"No. She could not have children; she had been hurt by the magelords."

" 'Tis sadder that way," the woman said. "Marshal says we're all Gird's childer in a way, but I wish . . . it doesn't feel the same."

"There's a scroll Paksenarrion brought us," Arianya said. "It records a dream Gird said he had before the Battle of Greenfields. He thought he was being told he would die in that battle but it would bring peace for his people . . . and he accepted that. But he did not die then. He felt he'd done something wrong. Dreams are not always about what we think they're about. I believe his dream was about what was coming later, not what came then. He gave his life to bring peace to his people, and for a time it did. But people do not always want peace as much as they want their own way."

"That be true, Marshal-General," Salis said. "And that's why I made Gird's Cow to remind them. Quarrelin' and hatin' don't help none, but carin' for a cow or a person's much alike." He looked around. "But . . . tell you true, I didn't imagine this . . . Would Gird's Cow be better outside?"

It would be better unmade and something more cowlike made instead, Arianya thought, but Salis's earnest goodwill kept her from saying that. The thought lingered—she'd never seen a life-size statue, but *could* someone make a cow? Of what—of clay? Carved in a block of stone? Something more like a cow? Would Salis mind?

"I think this may not be the best place for it," she said. "We should pray about that, don't you think?"

He nodded. "That be right, Marshal-General. That's what we should do."

Together, the little group moved to the far end of the Hall, where light shone through the round window. Arianya knelt, as she had so often. In the still air, the smell of sweaty human and cow grew stronger . . . the cow smell gradually predominating. What could that mean? The smell diminished, vanished, replaced by the fragrance of a forest. She didn't understand that, either. But questions she could ask Salis rose in her mind and some ideas about Gird's Cow—in this or another form.

When she stood, the forest scent vanished. In silence, she led Salis and his followers back outside. The cowhide-covered shape on the wagon looked even more ridiculous now. Salis stopped, staring at it. "Marshal-General . . . it's not right."

"Salis?"

He shook his head. "I'm sorry. I'm just an old farmer . . . I was stupid."

"No," she said. "You were not, and are not, stupid. Please tell me what troubles you."

"That's . . . I wanted it to be Gird's Cow, but it's not. That—in there—praying—I saw it."

"What?"

"I saw Gird's Cow. A dun cow, just like I always heard, and there was Gird, plain as day, with his hand on her neck."

The hair stood up on Arianya's arms. "You . . . saw Gird?"

"Yes." The battered hat came off again, and he rubbed his head with his other hand. "Didn't you?"

"Not like that," Arianya said. Should she say she smelled it? Probably not.

"So this—" Salis gestured at his wagon. "This is just a cowhide over some sticks and straw." He paused, glaring at it. "I thought it was enough—but I kept having to tell people what it was. If it was really Gird's Cow, they'd know right off, wouldn't they?"

There was no other way; she had to tell him. "I smelled Gird's

Cow," Arianya said. She tried not to see the look on Marshal Celis's face. "In the High Lord's Hall, just now—that's what I was granted, to smell it and know that Gird approved."

Salis looked worried. "You're sure it wasn't just us?"

"Yes," Arianya said. "And I think your idea—of reminding people that Gird was about caring for people first, not hating and killing—was good. I think your idea of an image that would remind them of that was good. We have so many stories of Gird fighting— Gird Strongarm, Gird's Club, and so on—that the Gird who loved cows and cared for cows and his family—isn't that much in mind."

"But—but that—" Another look at the wagon and the cowish shape.

"It was the best you could do, wasn't it?" Arianya said. He nodded. "Then it was a gift that Gird accepted. I think that's what your vision of him meant. With maybe a suggestion to let others help you do better."

"But who—" He looked at her. "You? You would help?"

"We need something," Arianya said. "I've been praying since the troubles started for something, anything, that might unite the people in peace. I never thought of a cow, but *you* did. And look— people who agreed with you already." She waved an arm at his followers.

"But I told them—"

"And they believed you were right. Salis—you may well be the answer I asked the gods to bring. You and your—Gird's—cow."

The look on High Marshal Celis's face offered no encouragement; Arianya looked at the stuffed shape again. "Your wooden medallions— who whittled those?"

"Benis," Salis said. Arianya looked at the group; one of the younger men nodded, blushing. "Benis whittles the bowls and spoons in our vill, as well as pegs and such, Marshal-General. He can whittle most anything."

"They look very cowlike," Arianya said. "Benis, would you whittle one for me?"

He turned redder. "Yes'm. Be glad to."

"Salis, let's move your wagon into one of the stables for safety.

And then let's talk about how to make Gird's Cow and your ideas do Gird's work."

"Marshal-General—could we come back after eating . . . we didn't stop on the way up the hill—"

"Come to the kitchens," Arianya said. She led them through the small garden, where they stopped to wash in the fountain, and then directly into the kitchens. Soon they were all seated at one of the tables, tearing open loaves of fresh bread as the cooks sliced cheese and meat.

Arianya watched as they ate. All of them but three came from the same vill. "Dakin's from Rosehedge," Salis said through a mouthful of bread and cheese, waving at the darkest of the lot. "Married in, didn't you, Daki?"

"My grandda's from east somewhere," Dakin said.

"Clothi's from Sheepwalk," Salis went on. "And her cousin Gadin as well." Those two nodded at Arianya.

Arianya nodded back, thinking hard. Could the idea of Gird's Cow help stop the violence? Maybe. She couldn't be sure.

Arvid came into the kitchen—an unusual time for him—and held up his hand. A note, probably from his Marshal. Arianya smiled and waved him over to the table. "Have you eaten, Arvid?"

"Marshal-General, I've brought you a message and am expected to bring one back. There's a situation."

Arianya glanced at the others. Salis was staring at Arvid, a spoon halfway to his mouth.

"Excuse me," she said. "I must answer Arvid's Marshal." She hoped it was his Marshal. "Come along, Arvid."

Behind them, as Arvid led the way out of the kitchen, she heard, "It *is* him. Him and that gnome—"

"What's the problem?" she asked on the way to the stairs.

Arvid handed her the note but spoke as she opened it. "Group of rowdies went through Marshal Hudder's grange and took the children to test for magery. They're holed up in Master Talin's wool warehouse and say they're not coming out until they've—" His voice changed to a snarl. "—'dealt with what the Marshal-General got no guts for.'" In his own tones again, he said, "They claim they've got a perfect test for magery."

"Where's Marshal Hudder?"

"They attacked him and his yeoman-marshals, beat them badly, and left them tied up in his office with the door barred on the outside. Mador may die—head wound. Hudder's got broken ribs and an arm, and Nadin's got two broken arms."

"Who's with them?"

"Marshal Gantol and an herbwoman. Rivergate Grange's yeomen are guarding the grange."

The smell of cow—the cow and cow manure both—overwhelmed her for a moment. No cows here . . . Why couldn't Gird just say what he wanted?

Arvid had a faraway look.

"Arvid?"

"It's him," he said. "Gird. And he says bring the cow."

"Bring—"

"The cow. And he's smiling."

Arianya turned back to the kitchen. The little group was still eating, though more slowly. To Salis she said, "I need you. All of you. We need to take Gird's Cow with us."

"Now?"

"Now."

Marshal Hudder's grange was one of the lowest in the city, backing onto the remains of the old city wall. The wagon with Gird's Cow had to be held back by ropes on its way down through the streets but arrived safely, the cow figure still intact. A crowd surrounded the grange, many of them parents of the children who had been taken. Some of the women were wailing, arms around one another's shoulders. Men muttered; most held staves.

"Marshal-General!" That was Marshal Stoll. "You've come!"

"As soon as I heard," Arianya said. "How's Hudder? And Mador?"

"Bad," he said. "Marshal Gantol is praying a healing, but you know when the headbone's split—"

"Where are the child thieves?" she asked. "I heard in a woolhouse?"

"Talin's. They broke in, knocked down t'old man and his daughter, pushed 'em out, and barred the door. You know where 'tis?"

"Yes. How many children?"

"All that was in school here, like every morning. That would be fifteen or so. And they say they'll fire the woolhouse if we try to break in."

Around the tall blank front of the woolhouse—its door shut, the windows shuttered—surged an angry, frightened crowd, growing larger by the moment. Gird's Cow was a momentary distraction— enough to quiet them so Arianya could hear a ranting voice berating the crowd through the door's peephole. Whoever that was caught sight of her.

"There's the problem, yeomen! Calls herself Marshal-General but lets evil mages live. Gird wouldn't a done that! Gird knew magery's evil. She's weak; Gird was strong!"

Behind and around her the crowd growled, a sound that raised the hair on her neck.

"Gird wouldn't hurt children!" she yelled. "Hurting children is evil."

"*Magery* is evil. Child mages is evil. Like rats—kill'm young!"

The crowd heaved itself forward a little. A screech from nearby: "My Suli's not evil! She never done nothin' mean!"

"You come too close, we burn the house and all in it!"

The pressure of bodies, the smell of rage and terror mixed . . . and no way at all to break into the woolhouse that Arianya could see.

"I can get in without their knowing," Arvid said quietly. She hadn't noticed that he'd come that close; he spoke practically in her ear. "But I'll need my cloak." He glanced at the cow. "And a distraction. Can you have them sing about Gird's Cow? Over and over?"

She looked at him. That narrow handsome face did not look like the Arvid she'd known these past quarters, the peaceful scribe, but even more dangerous than she'd seen the night he had stood between her and her attackers. The way he must have looked in his days as a thief-enforcer. But she had no one else. "How long to get your cloak?"

He flicked fingers where she alone could see them.

"Go, then."

CHAPTER TEN

A wool warehouse was nothing like so difficult a target as a thieves' Guildhouse . . . except it was broad daylight, the streets full of alert and angry citizens. Arvid began three buildings away in an alley no one seemed to be watching. Buildings here were old and had once been barracks for magelord troops or warehouses for their stores, then merchants' homes and stores. A staircase, built later, led up to the roof, but he preferred a less obvious way up in case the child stealers had a lookout up there.

Arvid slid into a narrow crevice and went up the angle of two walls to the roof and eased over, staying back near the city wall, where he could not be seen easily from the street. A cautious look . . . he saw no one on any of the roofs. He picked his way over mossy slates to the next building—only a long step across from one to the other—and then with more care approached the wool warehouse. It was taller than the one he was on, but they shared a wall. At the back of the warehouse, he spotted a gap between it and the city wall, about a man-length wide. A ledge ran across from the roof he was on to a small arched opening in the back wall of the warehouse. He considered the ledge and its inviting approach to the warehouse interior. Above it, a beam projected, just like the one in the front of the warehouse, but without the block and tackle. Why was it even there?

Then he grinned. A bolt-hole, a way out . . . and a way to remove goods, if necessary. In the old days, a way for smugglers to move goods over the wall without being noticed. Surely magelord troops had lived in the woolhouse once. He looked down; a long drop, but the building did extend to the wall below, leaving a blind space wide enough to fall into and no way to climb out. And—since it was on the highest floor of the warehouse, a warehouse that most people thought backed up right onto the wall—not an exit the mage-hunters were likely to know.

Still, he approached the opening with caution. Street noise now included the toneless loud singing of "Gird's Cow" along with the angry shouts and wailing of forlorn parents. He could hear nothing when he put one of his "donkey's ears" to the planks that filled the opening. The wood was weathered but solid, oak by the grain, clearly an actual door, though small: it had hinges on one side and a lock-plate on the other.

Not, as it happened, a very good lock. A few moments with his picks, and he felt the lock give. Was there an interior bar as well? He paused to pour oil from his flask onto the hinges and then pushed. Slowly—for it was thick and heavy—the old half door moved. Arvid clambered over the tall sill into a long, high room that ran the full length of the building from street to wall. High round windows let in dim light along the left side, and a single tall window at the front let in more. Toward the front, sacks that smelled like wool formed an irregular mound, but much of the floor was covered with a jumble of old furniture, boxes broken and whole, and a layer of thick dust. To his right, the floor slanted down abruptly . . . a ramp that led down into dimness.

Arvid chose the ramp; he suspected that the front had either a staircase beyond the wool sacks or a crane arrangement over that window for lifting heavy loads. The window would be visible from the street below—someone might look up, then they all would, and watchers within the warehouse would guess someone was above.

The ramp, dust-covered and unobstructed, revealed to his sensitive feet linear gouges . . . tracks? Wheel marks? They might have used a cart or barrow to move things up and down. A single thin rail marked the inside of the ramp; Arvid stayed near the back wall.

The ramp ended a scant two armswidths from a wall. Around the turn, the floor was flat . . . but he suspected another ramp led down another level. The space he came into was darker than that above . . . it would have, he recalled, common walls on both sides. Two small narrow windows at the back, opening into that shaded space between the back wall and the city wall, gave little light, just enough for dark-adapted eyes to see that a cross-wall closed off any view to the front. In this space, he saw more sacks of wool and also stacks of hides with cropped fleece still on. He could smell both distinctly.

"Mmrow?"

Arvid started, almost allowing a gasp to escape, before he realized it was a cat. Of course a warehouse would have a cat to keep down mice and rats . . . but a cat might reveal him to those he wished to evade. He felt the cat—a dim shadow—swipe against his legs. He reached down; a damp nose touched his hand, then withdrew.

He had killed cats to prevent discovery in his days as a thief, but he had no desire to kill an animal now just for his own convenience. Experience told him, however, that finding a sack or box to shut the cat into would only increase its noise and lead to investigation by those holding the children. That might be useful if he had a way to set up a trap for them . . . but at the moment he was simply exploring, learning what was and was not possible.

The cat moved away—dimness moving in dimness, more visible when it crossed the paler dimness of the two small windows, then jumped up onto a stack of hides and down onto whatever lay behind them.

What lay behind them let out a gasp, then a small sound more like a tiny moan or whimper. Soft-footed, Arvid eased across the floor to the same stack of hides. That did not sound like someone left to guard this floor but like . . . a child?

He leaned on the stack of hides and pitched his voice to carry no more than a handlength or two. "Are you hurt?"

Nothing but a silence so full of meaning it could not be anything but a person in hiding, trying not to breathe or move.

"I am not one of those below," Arvid said. "I came by roof, hoping to keep children safe. Can you help me?"

A shaky whisper then, more carrying than his own practiced voice: "They'll kill me! Da said run hide."

"Quiet voice," Arvid said. The cat jumped back up, landing on the hides with a tiny thump, and rubbed itself on Arvid's arm. "I am Arvid. You hurt?"

"N-n-o."

"Good. Tell me where in the building they are."

A rustle of clothing, of someone uncoiling . . . the faint scrape of a shoe on wood as the child stood—hardly as tall as the stack of hides. Arvid could make out nothing of the face except the smudge of eyes, nose, mouth, and a shock of dark hair.

"I—think—in our—where we live."

"You are?"

"Cedi." The voice was steadier answering a familiar question.

"Your da's the wool merchant?"

"Yes, and Grandda." A faint glow appeared; the boy gasped. "No!"

"Quiet voice," Arvid said. His skin prickled; two of the boy's fingers gave off a rosy glow even as the boy shoved them into a pocket. A mage child; no wonder his father had sent him to hide. "Don't burn yourself," Arvid said. "I won't hurt you." But why would the boy believe him?

"I can't stop it," Cedi said. "I try—"

He needed to get the boy to safety . . . that light would show almost anywhere in this room. Up the ramp? It might not show in that top room, but could the boy hide there? Get out the little door and over to the other building? At least in daylight, in the back of the building, no one would see his glowing fingers.

"You need to be where it doesn't show," Arvid said. "Can you go very, very quietly up the ramp to the top floor? There are wool sacks there to hide between and more light from the windows. Or there's the door out onto a ledge."

"Da said that door don't work."

"It does now," Arvid said. "If you could wait in that top room . . . maybe I could free the other children and they could come up—you could let them out, lead them across the roofs to where they can climb down."

The child blinked. He was younger than Arvid's son, a head shorter at least. "Da said don't move, stay hid."

"Your hand betrays you," Arvid said. "Even down there behind the hides. If someone comes up here—"

"They did. Didn't see me."

"But your hand wasn't glowing, was it?" This was taking too long; he could feel time passing. What was happening to the other children? What was happening outside? And yet this child was no less valuable . . . Arvid argued with himself. Of course the child wanted to do what his father said . . .

"I have a fleece down there—I put my hand under—and then it went out for a while."

So maybe he would be safe, with the glow hidden. "How old are you?"

"Seven winters."

Seven winters . . . for some, old enough to have sense and accomplish a lot . . . for others, not. Too young, Arvid finally decided, to be expected to go out alone and make his way across the roofs.

"Stay hidden, then. If your hand lights, be sure it's under the fleece, but don't start a fire. Now tell me how the rooms are arranged—and what's behind the wall to the front on this floor."

The boy was able to do that in a controlled quiet voice. Arvid started down the next ramp, directly under the first, knowing he would emerge in another such room, with a hall extending forward through a wall that cut off the front—that hall opened into the family apartments on either side. He was just starting down the ramp when he heard the slam of a door and voices coming toward the foot of the ramp.

"We can't go anywhere as long as they're there," said one.

"Well, we can't stay here forever. There's got to be a back door."

"There's not. Back wall's solid to the city wall."

"Donag said there was a window up the next floor—so it can't be solid, really. I'll show you."

The sounds of two men walking . . . shoes, not boots. Were they armed? Where best to meet them? If someone had already been up this ramp, then his own foot marks wouldn't draw attention.

He chose his place, shielded from immediate view by a stack of wool sacks, readied his materials, and listened to the footsteps com-

ing up. The men continued to talk; Arvid hoped they'd say something he could use.

"You think that red-haired girl is one of 'em?"

"We'll find out when Goram tests her. Admit I'm surprised we
only found three so far . . . I thought sure there'd be more of 'em here
in the city."

"Goram—you see the look on his face when he killed that third
one?"

"Bin—you can't let it bother you. They're mages. Doesn't matter
how Goram looks—"

"Does to me. There's killin' evil and there's evil killin'—"

"You want to be careful, Bin—that's soundin' a bit too much like
the old lady."

The Marshal-General, that must be. The footsteps came on, slower
now up the ramp.

"Lighter up there," said one.

"Windows in the wall got to mean there's an outside."

"Did Donag go all the way up?"

"Dunno. Just said windows but no door."

"Well—I can see those is too high to get out of . . . and there'd be
a drop."

"We should go all the way up—maybe the top one has a bigger
window or something."

Arvid wished he'd gone back up—ambushing these two would
be easier up there and quieter, too. But he would not have left the
child behind.

Now the footsteps were loud, on the same floor; they did not immediately head for the next ramp but approached the south wall . . .
and he had to make his move.

A bolt from his crossbow took the first one in the neck; before he
hit the floor, Arvid was on the second, a choke hold and the tip of a
dagger laid under the man's nose. "Come quietly," he said. "Or die."

"Grrhgh—"

"Quietly." He let the dagger tip dig into the sensitive point under
the nose, and the man made no more noise. Arvid manhandled him
around the corner, into the angle of the wool sacks, and shoved him

facedown into the sacks, where any cries would be muffled. He moved the knife point to below the man's ear "Quiet and still," he said again. The man obeyed, but his muscles were stiff with either fear or anger.

No matter. Arvid had dealt with such men before. Soon he had the man trussed so he could not kick the floor and gagged so he could not yell, braced in a cradle of wool sacks, held down by more, but with a small space for air . . . if he did not move and tumble another sack down to close it. Arvid explained this quietly, watching the eye he could see go from terror to fury to terror and, finally, to resignation.

The other man's body presented a dilemma. Hide it? Drag it to the top floor? Surely someone would come to find out where those two had gone, why they had not returned. He pulled the bolt free of the neck, swiping blood from the grooved shaft thieves used for inside work instead of fletching. He stripped the man's pockets and pouches, looking for anything that might help him, then lifted the corpse, grunting at the man's weight, and carried it carefully around the piles of wool sacks to lay it out of sight; he pulled another wool sack down on top of it.

Now. Up or down? If he could get the child killers to come to him in ones and twos, it would be easier, but his stomach churned at the thought of three children already dead and a man—Goram—who seemed to enjoy killing them. The longer he waited . . . the more children would die.

You know what to do.

"Gird . . . Father Gird . . . help the children." A pause in which he felt pressure like a weather change. "And me."

He had to go down. If he could identify Goram . . . kill the one who wanted to kill children, because clearly some of them weren't that eager . . .

He paused a moment to tell Cedi what he'd done, wondering as he did why he hadn't killed the second man—once, he would have, without a doubt or a thought—then went down the ramp, silent as the thief he had been.

Down there, he could see the door into the hall the boy had spoken of, shut as he'd expected, and the room off to his heart-hand, much like the one above but even darker. Another ramp continued down to the ground floor, and he heard voices from there, men's voices, and vague distant noise that might be the crowd outside.

He moved to the door of the hall, standing to one side, and applied a donkey's ear. No sound . . . then a thin wail, as of a child. He eased the door open; it swung silently. No one was in the passage, much lighter from a window at the front, and showing two doors to one side and one to the other, just as Cedi had said.

Arvid moved through, closing the door behind him. It would not be just one person in the room with the children . . . not merely the killer . . . they would need another one, at least. But two had left . . . and a lot of scared children, maybe tied up or shut in a closet . . .

Go on.

That voice. It steadied him now instead of shaking him to the core as it had at first. He reached for the bow to span it, and something pinched his arm. Gird? Probably. Maybe. He hoped. He reached for his throwing knife instead and felt a little warmth on the back of his neck.

A burly man with thinning dark hair held a child down on a table, his hands around the child's throat, squeezing. To one side, another man watched, lips pressed tight. Arvid's throwing knife took the first man in the face, just missing his eye; the man gasped, letting go of the child's neck, and grabbed for the knife hanging from his cheekbone. Arvid's edged disk took the second in the neck with a left-hand throw; he was across the room to finish that one with a slash of his dagger, and then, as the man near the child turned with Arvid's knife in his hand, Arvid moved in, grabbed the man's elbow, and twisted, forcing him down and into the point of his dagger.

He had expected the third man but not that he'd have a crossbow; the bolt sliced his ear and thunked into the wall behind him. He had nothing left to throw but a chair, and grabbed it up. Another bolt split the chair seat; Arvid rushed the man, pinning him against the far wall before he could span the bow a third time. All he could think—as the man whacked his ribs with the crossbow stock and opened his mouth to yell, and Arvid stuck the dagger in it, but the man didn't die, not then—was how much noise they were making and how long it would be before the men downstairs noticed. Finally he wrestled the crossbow away from the man and hit him over the head with the stock, then yanked his dagger free and cut the man's throat.

The child. He whirled and saw a gaggle of children—all in blue shirts, barefoot, all wide-eyed but silent, watching him. One, sitting up on the table, had darkening bruises on his throat. Another was the red-haired girl the men upstairs had mentioned, the mark of a hand clear on her pale skin where someone had slapped her.

"All of you?" Arvid asked. He felt breathless and off balance, and the stench of blood and death seemed unnaturally strong. He looked around the room. A pile of children's shoes, of children's small daggers. One of the children pointed down, under the table. Arvid leaned over to look and almost gagged. Three children lay there, obviously dead.

"We have to go now," he said. "Quiet and fast. Up the ramps to the top floor—there's a way out."

"Can't leave Gan and Suli and Tam," one boy said. His brow wrinkled. "They need buryin'. Tam's my brother."

"We don't have time," Arvid said. The sounds below had changed; they had to get away. "I can't carry them and fight, and I can't fight all those below by myself."

"We can take 'em," the red-haired girl said.

Arvid opened his mouth to protest but remembered—these were Girdish children. Brought up in the grange. Organized. "Who's senior?" he asked.

They all looked at one boy, the one who had already spoken. "Me, sir. I'm Vol. We can use the cloaks."

"Hurry," Arvid said. "We need to move fast."

Faster than he thought, the children took cloaks off pegs on the wall, wrapped the bodies, and lifted them—two to each—and followed Arvid out of the room, down the hall. He opened the door; now he could hear the argument at the foot of the downward ramp.

"Somethin's happened up there."

"Goram found another one—maybe kid fought back—"

"But it went on—"

A loud boom. Thank Gird, the Girdish outside must have decided to ram the door. Yells from below; Arvid hoped all those men would move to defend the door.

"I still say we should check on 'em—"

"Come quietly," Arvid said to the children behind him. They were quieter than he'd expected, moving across to the upward ramp and starting up; Arvid waved them on. To Vol he said, "I'm rear guard. You send them all the way up—the back window opens on a ledge—"

Vol nodded. Arvid waited until all the children were past him, his crossbow spanned and a bolt in the groove. He closed the door behind him, then moved across to the ramp and backed up it slowly, listening. Definitely footsteps from below: the stubborn careful person he was going to have to kill. Maybe he'd go look in the front room first.

On the next floor, the children clustered near the foot of the next upward ramp, waiting for him. He walked over to them. "Go on," he said. "They're following, but if you're quick, you can make it. Window's like a small door in the back wall. Climb out onto the ledge, follow it to the next roof—keep going until you find the outside steps down to an alley."

"By ourselves? What about you?"

"You're junior yeomen," Arvid said. "You'll do fine." It was then he remembered the child—the younger child—hidden here on this floor. "There's a child hidden here—I have to find him, bring him—"

He turned away, back the way he'd come, listening to the voices below, now louder.

"I don't hear anything—"

"Goram! Selis! What's going on up here?" The footsteps diminished, heading down the hall, Arvid thought. He found the pile of sheepskins and leaned over. "Child? You need to come right now. They're coming to search."

No answer. Had the child fallen asleep? He reached, and the pain in his side stabbed him. He felt something hot trickling down his side. "Damn." He did not have time for this. He climbed over the stack and found the space behind empty. No child. No fleece to hide the child's mage-bright hand. He felt around . . . only stacks of sheep-skins or wool sacks.

A yell from below—he couldn't make out the words, but he understood the urgency. They'd found the dead men. They'd seen that the captive children were gone, and the only way out was up. And he was hurt and couldn't find the other child.

He could still make it out. He could help those children, hold back pursuit—but what about the scared younger child he'd left behind? Surely the child had just found himself another hiding place . . . and the pursuers would take the obvious route, up and out the window.

With no one to guard those children's backs . . . he could imagine the mage-hunters hurrying across the roofs after the children, catching up, maybe even pushing the children off, dropping them like sacks of wool onto the alley below . . .

He had to move. The pain in his side was worse now, but he ignored it and rolled back out of the hole, over the fleeces. The yelling below intensified, but he heard no feet on the ramp yet. "Boy," Arvid said in close to his normal voice. He could not remember the name. "*Boy*—"

Cedi.

"Cedi—listen—bad men are coming. I can get you out the top—with the other children—please, come out right now, come with me."

Silence in the loft, and below, voices arguing. "Them mages—"

"That weren't mages; that were knives. Some men—"

"How'd they get in? There's no way out—"

"Broke through t'roof, maybe. Blood's still wet; we can catch 'em—"

"How many men? I'm not goin' up there with nothing but a hauk and a dagger, and it might be a dozen—"

"And where's Bin and Fenis?"

"Just one couldn't have taken five men out—must be a lot of 'em—go down and get the others, Jamis."

"What about the door?"

"Damn the stupid door—some gang's already got the childer, and we need a way out ourselves! We can set a fire behind us."

Footsteps ran downward, and the muttering below continued.

Arvid drew a breath that hurt more than the previous, and said again, "Cedi, please—let me help you out. The bad men will hunt for you and then burn the warehouse—"

And if they burned the warehouse, the man he'd made a prisoner would burn to death in it, helpless under that wool sack. He should've killed him first.

No.

Have sense, Gird, Arvid thought. *He'd have died fast and easy, and I wouldn't have to worry about him now.*

Free him. Find the boy.

Right. Before the men below came up all in a bunch, free one of them, find the boy, make it to the top floor and out the window and along the ledge and over the roofs . . .

You're wasting time.

Arvid pressed a hand to his side and found the little hole in his leather jerkin where something narrow had gone in. He walked around the end of the wool-sack piles, past the dead body, toward what he hoped was the right canted pile under which he'd stowed a prisoner. Had he really put the wool sack on top of the man that crookedly?

And something landed on his head and skidded down his front, claws pricking through his clothes. That damned cat! It hit the floor with a slight thump. Arvid grabbed the end of the wool sack and pulled . . . something tugged back. He gave a strong yank, gasping as the pain hit him again, and uncovered not only his prisoner but the boy Cedi.

"What—never mind. Cedi, come on. Help me get him out."

"Bad man!" Cedi said. "Want Da!" In better light here, he looked less like an innocent, scared child and more like a boy who would pull cats' tails and lie about it.

"Cedi, more bad men will be coming upstairs any minute. We need to go up and get out and across the roof."

"You could kill him." The boy's eyes gleamed.

"I could, but I won't." Arvid leaned over and pulled the man onto his back. "You—don't even try to talk. You're alive by Gird's direct command." He cut the thongs binding the man's feet. "Get up." He yanked on the man's shoulder.

"Don't want him!" Cedi said, pushing the man back down. "He wants me dead."

"Stop that," Arvid said, yanking on the man's shoulder again. Cedi's hand, he saw, was now glowing brightly, and the man's eyes widened. "Gird wants him alive for no reason I can understand, but we have to give him a chance to get away when his friends start the fire."

The man stood now, a little unsteadily at first, looking back and forth from Arvid's face to the boy's hand.

"Walk," Arvid said. "That way—" He pushed; the man stumbled forward. "Come along, Cedi." The boy reached up and grabbed his cloak. The cat, he was not happy to see, marched in front of them, tail high.

They made it to the upward ramp; the man stopped, shook his head. Arvid pushed him. "Walk or I'll stick you. I don't trust your killer friends to set you free in time to escape the fire they're planning—" A faint smell of smoke came from below, followed by the sound of running feet. "Hurry!" Arvid said. "Cedi—let go of my cloak and run up!" The boy took off up the ramp; the cat ran after him. The man resisted. "Have it your way, blockhead," Arvid said. He kicked the man behind the knee and swung him around at the same time; the man fell full length and rolled down the ramp. Arvid hurried up to the top floor, the pain in his side growing with every step. Once there, he found the little door open and the older boy, Vol, helping Cedi through. The other children were already well away.

"Go!" Arvid said. "I'll try to hold them back as long as I can."

Vol nodded, and both boys started along the ledge to the next-door roof. Arvid looked at the ledge. Not wide enough to stand and fight on. Could he wedge the door shut from outside? Would the lock catch if he shut it partway? He spanned his crossbow while thinking about it and set one of the grooved bolts ready. He could hear the men coming up the stairs—not running, but in a group.

He dragged some of the broken chairs and other debris over to the head of the ramp, forming a partial barricade, and threw everything he could grab down the ramp. Maybe they'd think a group of men were still up here from the noise.

The smoke smell intensified; the ramps were a giant chimney.

Arvid coughed and realized he couldn't make a stand there. He clambered out the low door onto the ledge and edged carefully along to the neighboring roof, then climbed to its peak and lay down on the far slope, resting the crossbow on the ridge. He hadn't seen the children on roofs anywhere; he hoped they'd made it to the stairway several buildings away. He took in lungfuls of fresh air; he hadn't been able to wedge the door, and smoke oozed out around the edges.

He heard yells and thumps from inside the warehouse, and then the door opened. Arvid planted a bolt in the first man onto the ledge; the man staggered and fell off into the gap between the warehouse and the old wall. Two men tried to push through the door at once, coughing violently; one shoved the other hard, and that man fell crookedly onto the ledge and rolled off. Arvid saw no reason to reward selfishness and shot the one who'd pushed when he was halfway out. One of those inside pushed the body the rest of the way out.

How many were there? The report they'd gotten said only "a gang of men" had attacked the grange. Arvid felt in his cloak pockets—he had only three bolts left. He glanced behind. Could he make it over the next roof before they got to him? Maybe.

He slithered down the slope, pushed himself up, and hopped to the next roof—with a fast glance at the one he'd just left—and went up the slope at an angle. As he neared the top, a bolt skittered on the roof slates, just missing his foot. Once over the ridge, he crawled along then back up to the ridgeline. Nothing on his roof. Nothing showing on the other . . . no, a head, but looking back, not toward him. He ducked, waited, dared another look. A man crawling awkwardly over the ridgeline of that roof, an unspanned crossbow in one hand. Arvid waited until the man looked up, saw him, and opened his mouth, then put a bolt in his neck. The man dropped; his hand convulsed on the crossbow but then opened, and the crossbow rattled down the slates to the gutter between the buildings.

Two more crossbows appeared, and blind-aimed bolts whizzed past Arvid. Next were three dropping shots he could avoid only by looking up and moving quickly to one side. Not safe at all.

Fire bells were ringing now, and the noise in the market square grew. Fire crews would try to save the adjoining buildings . . . which meant someone would be coming up to the roofs, Arvid hoped.

Except—they would not expect armed enemies . . . would they? He pulled out his next to last bolt. It felt sticky. He looked at the tip— red, sticky blood.

Arvid laughed to himself. He'd been wounded with his own bolt—it must have been when the man hit him with the crossbow stock, and the bolt had cut a hole in its pocket, then his clothes, and . . . hadn't penetrated very far. Knowing the pain wasn't a deep wound cheered him up even as another bolt dropped onto the slates less than an armspan from his face, bounced up and then off his back. He dared a look over . . . Sure enough, someone was on the near side of the next roof. Arvid shot him, then quickly spanned the bow and set his last bolt in. The bolts shot at him had all rolled down the roof, and he slithered down to see if he they were still useful. Crawling along the valley, however, left him unable to watch for more trouble and in a bad position—he grabbed two bolts and scuttled up to cross the next roof.

He was almost to the ridgeline when a bolt struck the back of his thigh. He knew at once that it was deep and dangerous; the pain made him gasp, and his leg didn't function. He dragged it upward, got his hands onto the ridge, and pulled himself over even as another bolt grazed his hip. Though he tried to hold himself to the ridge, he lost his grip and slid down to the trough between the buildings. One of the bolts lay in the gutter; he wondered if he'd have time to use it.

At least the children had gotten away. Surely by now they were safe, with adults to defend them. He hoped.

Arvid had time to question his own intelligence—he could have brought a helper along, at least as far as the roofs, and he could have brought more crossbow bolts. He lay awkwardly on his side, braced on an elbow to shoot the first one who appeared.

Then he heard someone coming up the roof behind him. They couldn't have gotten around him in that brief time he was tumbling, could they? And why would they bother? They would have seen the bolt hit; they'd have known he was disabled.

"Gird's COW!" came the cry, along with the sound of more feet on the slates.

"They've got crossbows!," Arvid yelled. "Beware!"

"So do we! Yeomen! Volley!"

That had to be a Marshal. Which Marshal? Arvid tried to think whose voice that was. Cedfer? Machlin? Dimod? One of his pursuers showed a head; bolts from behind him whizzed toward it. He saved his last bolt, thinking this could not possibly end well.

Then three yeomen with crossbows rolled over the ridge behind him and down into the valley between the roofs. "You're hurt," one said. Arvid recognized him as from his own grange but another drill group. He could not think of the man's name.

"Yes," Arvid said. "I can't pull the bolt out."

"And you're pale as new cheese."

"Probably." Arvid refrained from suggesting that telling a wounded person he looked bled out was no help. His vision was blurring now; he blinked hard twice and told himself to wake up and stay alert.

"We'll get this sorted," the man said. More supporters now rolled or slid gracelessly down the near slope of the roof and into the valley; a Marshal came over to Arvid.

"How bad?"

"Bolt in the thigh," Arvid said. "The children—?"

"All safe." The Marshal's expression was grim. "How many of *them*?"

"I'm not sure," Arvid said. "I killed four—no, more than that, but I never saw them all together."

"Perrin—go back and fetch us blankets and ropes. We'll need that to move Arvid." To Arvid he said, "I'll be back. Don't die yet."

The Marshal and the others scrambled up the roof, crouching low near the top, and then rolled over the ridge again and down to the next valley. After a short while, Arvid heard shouts, thuds, more shouts, and finally the sound of men coming back.

"Now let's see," the Marshal said.

Arvid passed out before the Marshal had done more than cut open his trousers to expose the wound. He roused briefly to hear someone say, "Not *that* way, you idiot!" and realized he was being carried down something—roof slope? stairs?—bundled up in a blanket like a corpse. On that thought he passed out again.

CHAPTER ELEVEN

He woke slowly, first aware of dull pain and lassitude, then light beyond his closed eyelids, and finally—when he opened his eyes—he realized he was in bed in a room full of people, one of whom was his son, white-faced and tense with worry, at the foot of the bed.

"The children?" he asked. He thought he'd asked that before, but he couldn't remember the answer.

"Well, and with their parents, but for the three who'd been killed," Marshal Cedlin said. "The child-thieves are all dead—there's still some unrest, as some of them were locals and their families are upset." He cleared his throat. "Arvid . . . are you able to tell us how you got the children out? And did you hear anything while you were in there to help us prevent more such?"

They could have waited until morning, surely. Arvid blinked and realized that the light in the room came from the window and most resembled afternoon light. He had a vague memory of waking once before.

He nodded, tried to clear his throat, and coughed instead. Pia put a mug to his lips, cool water with mint in it. When she took the mug away, he began, giving as clear a report as he could.

"You're sure the one killing the childer was Goram?" Marshal Cedlin asked.

"That's what one of the others said. There were two—one named

Bin. I think he's the one who said Goram enjoyed killing them. It bothered him. The other—um . . . I think someone mentioned Bin and . . . Fenis, it was . . . later. If that was the same man, he's the one said it didn't matter if Goram enjoyed it or not, mages were evil."

"Bin—that'd be the journeyman woodwright in Emon's shop," one of the other Marshals said. "A local . . . Fenis I don't know. The other might have been Donag—"

"No, because they mentioned Donag." Arvid could not stop looking at his son; the boy's eyes were glittering now with unshed tears. He lifted his hand. "Come sit with me, lad." Instead, the boy hurled himself on the bed, burying his face in Arvid's shirt.

"Da! Don't die!"

"I have no intention of dying," Arvid said, putting an edge of humor in his voice. He looked around at the others. "But grateful as I am for the rescue, I wouldn't mind a little time with my son. Would that be possible?"

"Are you hungry?" Pia asked.

He was, he realized. "Yes—and I'll bet this lad is, too."

Most of the others left the room, boots loud on the floor, with smiles and murmured good wishes. Pia, Marshal Cedlin, and the Marshal-General stayed.

They pulled a table Arvid had not seen before out of a corner and set chairs by it. Pia spoke to the boy.

"Come now, lad; help me bring the food up, won't you? He's not going to die if he's hungry, and the Marshal-General and Marshal Cedlin can help him wash up. You could do with a wash yourself."

Slowly, the boy unpeeled himself from Arvid and stood, tear tracks down his face. "Da?"

"I'll be fine, Arvi. We can eat together in a bit, all right?"

The boy nodded and with a last look back followed Pia out of the room. Marshal Cedlin helped Arvid sit up and use the pot, then washed him down with cool water from a jug. "A clean shirt—where?"

"In the press," Arvid said. He felt a little dizzy, but his leg didn't hurt the way he expected. "You—healed me?"

"Gird did," Cedlin said, bringing a blue shirt from the press.

"Nasty thing—hit the bone, but you won't have bone fever from it. Now, that hole in your side—that wouldn't heal. Any idea why?"

"To teach me to be more careful," Arvid said. He tried to sit up straighter as Cedlin put the shirt over his head and then wriggled one arm at a time into a sleeve. His left side twinged when he moved that arm. "It was my own bolt. When the fellow hit me with the stock of his crossbow, it hammered the point into me. Right through the leather."

"Lucky it didn't go deeper," Cedlin said. "Here—lie down again. You lost a lot of blood from the leg."

"He has a habit of that," the Marshal-General said. She shook her head at him. "Remember last year?"

"Wasn't my plan," Arvid said. He felt worse briefly, lying down, but then his stomach settled. He heard feet coming up the inn stairs. Cedlin lifted his shoulders and packed more pillows behind him. "Just in time."

"Well, now," Pia said, coming in with a tray. "That's more like it." She put the tray on the table. "I brought enough for everyone, I think. A bowl of beef broth and barley for you, Arvid, and for you Marshals, bread and cheese and a pitcher of ale. Arvi, your da will like what's in that jug, I expect. Honeyed sib. Pour him a mug."

Arvid had not felt particularly hungry, but the honeyed sib woke him enough that the beef broth with barley went down smoothly. Arvi finally relaxed enough to eat a slab of bread spread with soft cheese.

"We have a problem," the Marshal-General said when Arvid quit eating. He merely looked at her, then at Marshal Cedlin. "More than one," she said. She looked at Marshal Cedlin.

"You've done well, Arvid, as you must know," Cedlin said. "You've learned everything and more I ask of new yeomen. You get along with the others; your section leader says you take on every task he asks of you. Gird knows you're beyond yeoman level in your knowledge of the Code. You're skilled with weapons, and you've been patient and effective teaching longsword to those who want to learn." He shot a glance at the Marshal-General, who nodded for him to go on. "I hear from up the hill that you've almost qualified as a judicar in that regard—and could easily in another half-year of study. And as you told me, and the Marshal-General, and your Marshal in Aarenis, you hear Gird directly."

Arvid still said nothing. He began to guess where this might lead, and he was not—absolutely not—ready to hear what was coming.

"You've been loyal to me, Arvid," the Marshal-General said then. "You gave us warning that night last fall; you fought for me. You are . . . well, I can't say exactly . . . but unexpected is the least of it. You aren't afraid of those different from you, and you seem—amazing for a man with your background—to have almost an instinct for justice."

Arvid tried to laugh, and his side stabbed him. "I—think thieves understand justice, just from the other side."

"That may be. But Arvid, I must know: In this matter, did you call on Gird, and did you hear Gird speak?"

Had he? He thought through the slight haze that blood loss and a good supper had given him. He used the pause to take another sip of honeyed sib before he answered.

"Yes. I asked Gird's help for the children—and myself. And he sent a cat—"

"A cat?"

"Well . . . perhaps it was just there, but it helped me find Cedi—the boy—twice, when he had hidden. And yes, Gird spoke to me, in my head . . . several times."

Marshal Cedlin nodded. "I thought so. Arvid, you are just what we need."

"Me?" That came out in a squeak that annoyed him. He swallowed and tried again. "Marshal, I was lucky—"

"Not lucky. Gods-guided. Lucky to meet Paks, perhaps, in Brewersbridge that time, but even that—I dare not say it wasn't Gird's doing, for both of you. Who else here could have done what you did?"

He wanted to say *Anyone who thought of it,* but he knew that wasn't true. Fin Panir was woefully short of thief-assassins trained to climb sheer walls, infiltrate buildings, and carry out such missions as rescuing captives . . . or killing the Master of a Guildhouse. His breath caught, remembering the Master in Valdaire and the child in his bed. He looked at his son, who looked back at him, eyes wide this time with wonder and hope, not fear.

"They . . . might have."

No.

Arvid shook his head. Gird would not let him alone, and . . . truth be told in his own head . . . at this time he did not want him to. "No," he said then. "You're right. I don't know everyone in the city, but I doubt there's another with my training. A retired mercenary specialist, maybe. So . . . what are you creeping toward here? Surely not that you want me to be Marshal-General?"

A look passed between them that he could not quite read, but they did not laugh.

"No," said the Marshal-General. "Not yet, anyway. But we are short good Marshals now since some have left the Fellowship. They claim I had no authority to prohibit killing children who showed mage power. And few—if any—hear Gird's voice clear. Or are now being hailed as heroes by those whose children they saved. The children were able to give a good account of what happened from the moment the child-killers came into the grange. You can expect to be showered with gifts—"

"But—it was only what I should do," Arvid said.

"Yes, I thought you'd say that." She sighed. "Arvid, I know you're abiding by the Code. Girdish do not accept gifts for doing their duty. And you saw rescuing those children as your duty and talked me into letting you try. Honestly, I thought it was hopeless. One man alone against those child-killers, and no one even knew if there was a way in. But you did it—"

"It would have been better if I'd taken one other up to the roof, with another crossbow," Arvid said.

She shook her head at him. "Quit trying to put me off my topic, Arvid. I want you to be a Marshal—and before you start, no, you're not quite ready, much as I need more Marshals. But Marshal Hudder needs a yeoman-marshal now—Mador died. Marshal Cedlin and I both think you're suited for that. I'll appoint you Marshal as soon as you're ready, which we all suspect will be sooner than you think."

"But—but—I'm not—"

"Arvid, we need you. If Gird doesn't care what you were before, why should I? Why should anyone? It's time you gave over defining yourself by your past."

It wasn't that easy. But even as he thought that, he remembered what else he'd done. It had not been easy to get Paks out of the Thieves' Hall in Vérella, to protect her from Barranyi's malice . . . or anything since.

"Marshal Arvid," he said, testing the sound of it. No sillier than Marshal Hudder or Marshal Donag. He looked at his son. "What do you think, Arvi?"

"It's . . . it's what you are, Da." The boy's face held no doubt at all.

"Well, then, I'd better start living up to it," he said. "But first— yeoman-marshal. And more study, I assume?"

"Yes, quite a lot. Marshal Hudder will be glad to tutor you in grange organization and record keeping."

"Will I need to move there?"

"No, because you have a family and I think Arvi will be happier staying with his friends in Marshal Cedlin's grange for another year or so. My suggestion is that you continue to live here—Marshal Hudder has agreed that you will have night duty only every third night." She turned to the boy. "Arvi, will you be afraid to stay here the night your da is down the city? If so, we can find you someone to stay with."

"He could stay at the grange," Cedlin said.

"I won't be afraid," Arvi said. "I will do as Sera Pia says, and she will tell me to go up to bed and bar the door, and I will."

"Good, then. Is it settled, Arvid? As soon as you're able."

"Yes," he said. His head was swimming again, and he closed his eyes for a moment. Clear as a painted picture, the broad face and graying yellow hair of Gird looked back at him and nodded.

You'll do. Good lad.

Arvid woke hours later in the first light of dawn. The shutters were open; he heard a rooster crow in the courtyard below and Arvi's breathing in the room. He looked around. Arvi slept on a pallet near the bed instead of in his own bed at the far end. Arvid was suddenly thirsty, hungry, and restless all at once. He sat up cautiously; his side twinged, but not badly. He put his feet on the floor, fitting them between the bed and Arvi's pallet, and made his way to the table. Pia had left a pitcher of water there and a clean mug. He drank and walked a little unsteadily to the window.

Everything that had happened ran through his mind as if written on a strip of ribbon pulled through his hands. He felt all the emotions he had felt—the alarm, the anger, the urgency, the need to convince others, the pity, the anger again . . . and finally, the acceptance. Marshal. It was ludicrous. It was inevitable. It was . . . "How did I not know?" he asked the lightening sky, speaking softly not to wake his son. No answer this time. He didn't really need one. It didn't matter anymore.

Across the room Arvi woke with a little snort, sat up, and stared wildly at the empty bed before seeing him. "I'm fine," Arvid said.

"Da?"

"Really. Come, let's get dressed, see if I can manage the stairs, and then the jacks and the bathhouse. We both have work to do."

Arvi leaned into him. Arvid put an arm around those shoulders, not now so thin—or so far down: the child had grown fast once freed from the thieves. "It's all right, Son. Gird healed the bad wound; the other one's hardly a wound at all."

After Arvi had gone off to class with the other youngsters, Arvid made his way down the city to meet Marshal Hudder. Unusually for this time of day, a dozen adults were there: guards, he realized, to prevent another attack. All had the sullen expressions of deeply angry men. Marshal Hudder, a short square-built man with graying black hair, came out to greet him.

"I didn't expect to see you for several more days, but I can't think of anyone I'd rather have, Arvid. Nobody can replace Mador, o' course, not really, but everyone in the grange wants to thank you. Marshal-General's told me what she wants and what you already know. I'd like you to take over the adult sword-side drill groups and the records keeping that Mador did."

"Certainly, Marshal," Arvid said.

"We think the children would be too likely to spend their lesson time asking you questions until they get used to you—but our yeomen, right now, are eager to work on their fighting skills." He gestured. "Come on in and I'll show you the offices."

By the end of that day, Arvid had met the parents of the children he'd rescued and seen the children themselves at study in the barton with the other yeoman-marshal, Nadin. Nadin's arms were still wrapped in bandages—though the Marshals had been able to start the bones healing with the help of a herbwoman, his arms were still painful and not strong enough for drill.

Arvid took the drill sections, one after another, and trudged back up to the Loaf as tired as he'd ever been. But—he'd done it. He'd remembered all the drill commands; he'd learned all the names. He could do this. The knights going off-duty for the night walked with him, then waved and walked on up to their quarters.

Arvi woke when he came into the room, quiet as he'd tried to be. "Da?"

"Here. Tired. Go back to sleep, lad." He laid his hand on the boy's head for a moment. His lad. Safe. The three who'd been killed had been buried while he recovered; he'd missed that.

CHAPTER TWELVE

Chaya, Lyonya

She had changed again, Kieri thought, watching the tall yellow-haired paladin dismount in the courtyard. He wasn't certain yet what the change was and hoped it would not alter the Paks he had known beyond his recognition. Foolish thought, he knew. With a dragon loose in the world again, they were all being changed.

By the time he reached the palace entrance she was there, chatting with one of the doorwards about—of all things—darning. The doorward had his shoe off, showing a hole in the heel of his left sock, and Paks was explaining, in exactly Stammel's words, why everyone in any uniform, anywhere, any time, should be able to mend and maintain his or her own uniform.

"But it's just a sock," the doorward said, as Kieri had heard many recruits say. He waited, just in earshot, and sure enough, Paks said it just as Stammel had.

"It's not just a sock. It's a sore heel, a blister, a gods-ratted hole in your skin, and the fever will come into it, and you'll be lame and someone else dead because of it." And then, quite unlike Stammel, Paks laughed. "That's what my sergeant always said. I came into the Company already knowing how to knit, sew a plain seam, and darn socks: it's not hard if you catch the hole early. I'll show you later, but now I must see the king."

"I'm here," Kieri said. She looked up at him and grinned; he felt his own smile widen. "Paks—how are you?"

"Fine," she said. He could see a few silver strands in amongst the yellow of her hair now, and the silver circle on her brow still made him uneasy, but she looked healthy. "I was sent," she said. "And I have word."

Word. He did not quite shiver. "Arian has had her babes," he said. "Both healthy. Come and meet them."

Inside, he led her first to his office. "How long can you stay?"

"I don't know . . . longer than one day or two, I think."

"Sit down," he said, and nodded to one of his Squires. "Varne, bring refreshments, please." When the Squire had left, he said, "What word?"

"My lord—sir king—Sergeant Stammel is dead. He had left the Company—"

"Stammel?"

"With a dragon and then asked leave to stay away and live apart, where he was not known, because of his blindness. He made a life there, among villagers on an island, and he died there, defending them."

"As he would," Kieri said. "You heard this from—?"

"Captain—Duke Arcolin as he is now. I arrived in time for the burial."

"Thank you for coming to tell me," Kieri said. In the years since he had seen Stammel last, he had never been able to imagine him blind—he knew, but his mind refused to see anything but the same steady, tough, capable sergeant, brown eyes clear and keen. Now he thought back to the young Stammel, the Stammel of his recruit cohort. "I can't . . . I can't imagine him dying any other way than that."

A servant knocked then and brought in a tray with a pitcher and glasses and a plate of pastries. Kieri poured and handed a glass to Paks, then took one himself and a pastry.

"So is that why you come?"

"Not only that." She looked at him. "I am in search of a Kuakgan; the Marshal-General was attacked by iynisin and suffers wounds that do not heal properly. Marshals and paladins have tried, but it is with her as it was with me. We know of no healing but through a Kuakgan, but there are none in Fintha. Most in Tsaia are bound to their Grove and do not travel far or long. Master Oakhallow will have her, if she will come there, but says he cannot go so far. He has asked some who wander to come to me here—it was the closest way."

"So it is not our need for a paladin? Glad as I am to see you again, Paks, it's a relief to know it's not our problem."

"No . . . but you seem especially happy. Is it the children? How old are they?"

"Twins," Kieri said. "Born today. You will have to see them, but not this moment. I hope Arian's gone to sleep." He took another swallow of sib. "Tell me, what does Gird think of the Marshal-General's injuries?"

"I cannot tell." Her nose wrinkled. "It's complicated. When I was a recruit, I had to learn to obey orders I did not understand, but Stammel taught us ways to understand them—the why of things we had to do. Now—I am sometimes given orders, very clear, and sometimes know why and sometimes do not. I know Gird wants me to find a Kuakgan, but it's not in words. Just . . . feeling. And at times, I have nothing to do but . . . be."

"Hmm. As a king, I am supposed to know why I give the orders I do . . . I certainly did know, when I was a mercenary captain."

Paks looked at him, a penetrating look from those gray eyes; he wondered how far in she could see.

"You have changed," she said. "The seeming younger—that's the elven blood, of course—but now there's . . . it's almost like . . . the Lady."

"You do know she died—"

"I heard," Paks said. "And how. But—are you then her heir? Is that what I sense?"

"That is a very long story, but in short—yes, in a way that confounds both elves and humans. Not so much of the ability to form an elvenhome as my grandmother—the Lady—had. More than any human should have as far as elves are concerned, but since the choice was the complete loss of it or my lesser version, there are still elves in Lyonya."

"And the Lady had taught you how to do whatever it is?"

"No," Kieri said. "My mother wished me to have the elvenhome talent, and the Lady—did not. They quarreled, over that and other things. I discovered the talent last summer in the very place my mother died and I was taken."

"You found *that* place?"

"Yes, by accident or the gods' design." Kieri took another pastry; he was suddenly ravenous. Through a mouthful, he said, "You did know that Arian's father was a western elf, and his father the elf-lord somewhere near Kolobia?"

"No!" Paks stared. "I knew such an elf had come to the Marshal-General and ordered her to remove the enchanted magelords from the hall there, but she did not know how. The iynisin who captured me had once been captive in solid rock, but the elf told the Marshal-General they escaped because of the magelords coming to Kolobia, mostly Luap. When whoever enchanted the magelords was done, the elves thought the chamber sealed—but it opened again when the expedition I was on went there to search for the place. We were able to use the elven transfer patterns, and that let the iynisin free again." She stopped for a moment, her brow furrowed. "Do you mean the elf who came to the Marshal-General is actually Queen Arian's grandfather?"

"Yes. There's a very long, tangled tale involving my grandmother and her grandfather—not a tale to tell on a happy occasion, as there was no happy outcome. But he came to me and told me that I am the one who must remove the magelords, supposedly because the elves can tell that the magery used to enchant them contained elven, magelord, and Old Human components. How I am to do that, I have no idea. I'd studied elven magery before the Lady was killed, and Dorrin Verrakai has agreed I have some magelord talent, but . . . I don't even know what spells were used." He shook his head, running his hands through his hair. "Arian's grandfather—privately we call him Grandda Elf, though I suspect he would not like that—agreed I should not do any great magicks around her while she was expecting or while they were too young. He did not define 'too young,' and I hope he doesn't come back for years and gives us some peace."

"But more and more iynisin are emerging," Paks said. "Something must be done."

"We had them here; that's how the Lady died," Kieri said, nodding. "I agree it's important to do something, but first I must learn how. Without endangering Arian or the babies. And while doing everything else I need to do as king of Lyonya."

"When I was a girl in Three Firs—" Paks began.

Kieri interrupted. "Have you ever gone back to see your family, Paks? I know you wanted to."

"I did want to. Sometimes now I want to. But . . . I don't know why, but I know I mustn't go until I'm told to go." She looked sad for a moment, then brightened. "It's for their safety, I think. My being there would bring trouble to them."

"You started to say something else," Kieri said.

"Oh. Yes. Well, when I was a girl in Three Firs and heard the old tales about kings and queens and elves and witches and such things, I thought kings sat on a golden throne and did nothing all day but give orders."

"What did you think of that?"

"It sounded boring. Sit all day and tell people what to do? I would rather do things myself. You do, don't you?"

"Indeed. Ride, fence in the salle, hold Council with the Siers . . . though that is sitting and talking, I admit."

"Sir king?" That was one of the Queen's Squires at the door.

"Yes—is Arian all right?"

"Oh, yes. She wants you to bring the guest up to see the babies."

※

Paks greeted Arian and looked closely at the two sleeping babies. "They're twins, but they're not alike."

"No. The dark-haired one's the boy. We named him Falkieri, for Kieri's father, and Dameroth, for my father. The girl's name is Estil for Estil Halveric and Merrandlyn for my mother and Kieri's—the names combine well."

"Will they have Kieri's talent?"

"Perhaps," Arian said. "We hope so."

"Though I don't think the western elves have that hope," Kieri said. "Perhaps they'll get used to it." He touched Arian's cheek. "Shouldn't you be sleeping?"

"That's what everyone says. And I'm wide awake. The midwife and Estil Halveric tiptoed away thinking I was asleep . . . but I'm not." She looked at Paks. "Did you come just to see the babies?"

Paks explained her errand.

"Good," Arian said. "I'd like to see a Kuakgan again myself. Last year, when we were trying to find the source of the poison, I was so upset—I would like to learn more about them. Maybe we could do something to heal the enmity between elves and Kuakkgani."

"I don't think that's likely," Kieri said. "Lessen it, maybe—with my elves—but ending it would require them to change long-held notions about the proper way to interact with the taig."

"Maybe that's not the only proper way to interact with the taig," Arian said.

"If it was, elves could heal iynisin wounds," Paks said. "And they can't, can they?"

"No."

"Yet what Master Oakhallow did for me, besides removing the bit of iynisin weapon left in me, all involved the taig. I don't understand it; I was asleep for some of it."

"Dorrin told me about the Kuakgan healing one of her squires' injuries," Kieri said. "The lad's father had the same objection to that healing as the elves: mixing the natures of plants and other living things. And from what I hear, the boy's thumbs did look woody at first. But the tendons healed in his legs, and he has thumbs. Finally his father accepted it . . . what else could he do? Cut the lad's thumbs off again?"

"What was the poison?" Paks asked.

"Last year? Melfar, hidden in a cake of farran. It was a wedding gift; cooks had used it to flavor pastries for the feast." Arian's head drooped. "Every pregnant woman who ate it lost the child." When she looked up again, her expression was angry. "It was an elf who did it. An elf who tried to kill Kieri later."

"And who, I'm certain, arranged my mother's death and my capture," Kieri said. "But she is dead now, and we are here with two healthy babies and a paladin. Who should not be hearing such dark things." The babies had waked, their little faces contracting into a mass of red furrows.

"Ah, youngling." Paks scooped up the girl, who was nearer her side of the bed. She nuzzled the baby's hair. "You, littling, you are so lucky." To Kieri's surprise, the baby's face relaxed, and Paks began to sing softly. "Sweet one, little one, your mama's a queen, sweet one, little one . . ."

Kieri picked up his son, then sat on the edge of the bed. "All's well, lad," he said, and yawned deliberately. "Oh, we're sleepy, all of us, aren't we . . . or are you hungry?"

"They're probably hungry." That was the midwife in the doorway, hands on her hips. "I came up to wake the queen and find a roomful of chatter—"

"I wasn't asleep," Arian said. "And *I'm* hungry."

"I'll tell them to send something up," Kieri said, handing his armful to the midwife. "Come on, Paks." Paks grinned and laid the girl in Arian's arms.

"Has anything been found in Kolobia to explain how the magelords were enchanted or by whom?" Kieri asked as they made their way downstairs.

"Not that I know," Paks said. "But I haven't looked at everything. I would expect the elves to know. You said they talked about three kinds of magery."

"They don't know who, or how, but the magery—I suppose they can sense it. I can tell if magery's being used." He told the first servant he saw to send a meal up to Arian's chamber and another to prepare a room for Paks.

Near sundown, a man in a Kuakgan's dark green leaf-patterned robe came to the palace gate while Kieri was on his way back from a trip to the King's Grove to give thanks for the births.

"It is not more poison, is it?" he asked Kieri. "You must be the king, with this retinue." He glanced at the King's Squires.

"I am the king," Kieri said. "Kieri is my name. And no, it is not more poison. The paladin Paksenarrion asked Master Oakhallow to find a Kuakgan who could travel to meet her here. The Marshal-General of Gird has been wounded by iynisin. Come inside; Paks will be glad to see you."

"I was not sure how hard it would be," the Kuakgan said. "Usually the elvenhome repels us."

"I have no quarrel with Kuakkgani," Kieri said.

The Kuakgan looked at him, brows raised. "You—but it's not your elvenhome; you're but half-elf—"

"Yes, it is, now," Kieri said. "It is complicated and I will be glad to tell you about it later, but you need to talk to Paksenarrion first."

They went inside together and found Paks sitting with the same doorward, demonstrating how to darn holes in the man's socks. He was barefoot, working on one sock while she did the other. "Now if you reinforce the heels when you knit them—"

"I don't knit my own socks," the doorward said. "I don't have time."

"Do you have time to darn? It takes longer than knitting something the same size."

The doorward caught sight of Kieri and the Kuakgan and jumped up, dropping the sock. Paks reached out and caught it. "Sir king, I'm sorry—"

"Finish your darning lesson," Kieri said. "Paks, here is a Kuakgan come looking for you. Master—?"

"Sprucewind. Like Master Elmholt, from whom I heard about the poisoning done here, I am a wanderer, not having bonded to a Grove. I had word by root from Oakhallow that I was needed here." He turned to Paks. "And I am told you come on behalf of the Girdish Marshal-General, wounded by iynisin."

"Indeed," Paks said. She had given one sock back to the doorward and still worked on the other. She told him what she had told Kieri. "It happened to me, as well. Wounds that faded and then flared, exhaustion and weakness, and no other healing seemed to work. I remembered Oakhallow and what he did for me, but he does not travel so far."

"Hmmm." A hum like a hive of bees trembled on the air. "Are you sure all the fragments of the weapon are out of the wound?"

"We think so, sir, but one was stuck right in the bone, high on her arm. We could not tell if all came out or if it broke off."

"And where is she?"

"In Fin Panir. Do you know where that is?"

"West of Tsaia, in Fintha . . . Tell me, what trees are there?"

"Not many. Pickoak, a scrubby ash, juniper . . . it's dry there, you see." Then, to the doorward, "No, pull that back out—it goes in the other way . . . yes . . . and then out there. Now another one."

"No stretches of forest? No spruce?"

"None."

"Then she will have to come nearer or I must find a spruce—at least a fir—willing to come with me. My powers of healing depend on the trees. It is so with all of us. How bad are her wounds? Can she travel at all?"

"Not when I left," Paks said. "But if hers are like mine were, her strength will vary—she will grow stronger again and then weaker. I think she will not travel this far, sir. She has duties there; she will stay."

"Then I must find a tree," Sprucewind said. "It will take some time. I will go to Fin Panir as soon as I find one."

"Wait," Kieri said. "Will you not stay the night at least?"

"I travel mostly at night," Sprucewind said. "It is cooler then." He smiled at both of them. "Fare well, king of Lyonya, and thank you for the welcome of your elvenhome. Paksenarrion, I smell fir upon you, a gracious scent and kin to my birth-tree. May the firs you left behind grow tall and straight." Then he turned and walked out into the dusk.

"There are firs in Three Firs," Paks called after him. She was not sure he heard.

"You will stay a night or two at least, won't you?" Kieri asked.

"Until I'm called away," Paks said. "It feels peaceful here. I think it's your magery."

"Elvenhomes are supposed to be peaceful," Kieri said. "But I'm not sure about one with a soldier for a lord."

CHAPTER THIRTEEN

A day or so later, Paks asked Kieri about how he had come to create an elvenhome. He told her in more detail about finding the place where his mother had died, the relics risen from the ground, and all the elven woman, the traitor, had told him. "That night she used elven magery to lure me away from the others and would have killed me if I had not killed her."

"You killed a full elf? In spite of her magery?"

"Yes. And after that, I realized that the taig recognized me. I was surrounded with elvenhome light. When I collected the branches to lay on her, they fell into my hands." He sighed. "And with that death ended the mystery that has haunted my life. A waste, all around. But I need not fear anything like that again. The taig itself tells me that none of the other clvcs here are traitors. My children will never be in such danger as I was."

"So—the man who tormented you is dead?"

"He must be," Kieri said. "He was not young when I was his captive, and he was human, not even part-elven. He boasted of that."

"But he was a mage—you said he had great powers—"

"Yes, but not immortality. Why do you ask?" His heart began to pound, and suddenly he remembered. "You think he—he might be one who could—transfer bodies?" The very thought made him sick; his stomach churned.

"Is it not possible?"

He didn't want to imagine it. Sekkady alive? In a body he would not even recognize? His children, those sweet infants, stolen to become slaves, tormented as he had been? He struggled to find an objection. "Why would he come here? He had . . . I heard him say . . . he had never traveled over the sea and never meant to."

"Perhaps he had not . . . perhaps he would not . . . but you escaped him. He must have been angry when he found you gone. Are you certain he never looked for you?"

"No." He had not thought about it once safe in the great forest; he had known somehow that it would protect him. Now he knew that was because of his elven heritage; the taig knew him for the Lady's grandson. And once he reached Halveric Steading, and Estil took him in, and then Aliam taught him to fight . . . he had known he would never again cross the sea, and he had believed Sekkady would never come.

"If he is alive, if he knows that you are now a king, and a father—" Paks went on,

He started to say Sekkady would have no way to learn either, but the sea trade the Pargunese and Kostandanyans carried on had brought him to this safety and could as easily carry word back. A cold chill ran up his spine, born of the old terror and pain.

"It was not my intent to upset you," Paks said, leaning forward. "You are not a child now; you are a seasoned warrior, and you have elven magery and the elvenhome's protection."

"No—no, you did right to mention it. I should have thought—" But his eyes were shut tight, and the images that filled his mind were all horror and despair. The elvenhome had not protected his mother, a full elf, the day she died or the Lady herself from iynisin attack. "I will take . . . precautions," he said at last. He forced himself to look up into those candid gray eyes and smile at Paks. "But for tonight, I think it's time we both sought our beds."

"Of course," she said.

Paks did not bring up the subject again, to Kieri's relief, and he buried himself in his duties as king and his study of elven magery as the days passed. He was uneasily aware that he was still expected to wake the sleeping magelords in Kolobia, and he still had no idea how he was going to accomplish that.

A bout half-Summer, as leaves lost their first freshness, she asked how his studies in the various mageries were coming along.

"Dorrin is helping me with the magelord part," he said. "And the western elves their king sent have taught me much about elven magery. But the real problem I see is that Kolobia is so far away. I can't imagine it—either the distance or what it's like. Magery at a distance requires the ability to focus, to see, at least in the mind, what is there. I can now direct my magery to something I cannot touch—I could set a flame to that kindling in the fireplace, for instance, from another room. But I can imagine the kindling. I cannot imagine Kolobia."

"I see it in *my* mind," Paks said. "Is there no way to send the image from one of us to the other?"

"Not that I know," Kieri said. "Can you draw it?"

Paks could not. Her attempts to draw either a map of the route to Kolobia or an image of the underground chamber looked like a child's first attempt to make marks with a stick in the dirt, Kieri thought. He did not tell her that; her expression told him she knew it. "I'm sorry," she said. "I can see it . . . I just don't know how to show it."

"Never mind," he said. "I still need to find a way to access the Old Human magery they said was latent in me."

"Couldn't you use the transfer pattern you said was here and come out there?"

"No," he said. "I'm oathbound to this land, and since I made the elvenhome here, leaving might damage it. The elves tell me it might disappear and leave here—the land I gave my oath to—without its protection. Whatever I do in Kolobia must be done at a distance, from here. I suppose that's why I need all three mageries to do it."

Paks brightened. "I'm all Old Human as far as I know; our family's lived up on the edge of the moor forever. And I have paladin's magery. Maybe that will work. If I focus on what I remember seeing and we try to merge your magery and my memory . . ." Her voice trailed away.

Kieri thought about that. "Suppose we tried that just to give me an image to work from later. After all, I don't have the Old Human magery working at all yet, nor can I work at greater distances than from one room to the next. So it would be less magery, less disturbance . . . and might not affect the babies at all."

"Will you ask the elves about it?"

"No," Kieri said. "They will expect me to do it all at once, and I can't."

"So . . . when?"

"Why not now?"

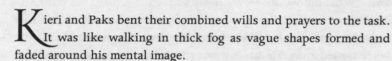

Kieri and Paks bent their combined wills and prayers to the task. It was like walking in thick fog as vague shapes formed and faded around his mental image.

"I should know the way," Paks said. "I have been there; I have seen the mountains, the great clefts in the rock. I saw the shape of Luap—I think it was Luap—on the rock arch. If I can just see it again—or the chamber inside, where the sleepers were—if Gird will guide me—"

All at once Kieri felt his will touch another's . . . like a hand brushing his in the fog, then tightening to a grip, a sense of someone in peril begging for help. Did the sleepers dream? Did they yearn to awake?

"Paks . . ." he said, and glanced at her. She nodded, and now he felt, along the strand of his thought, something he could define only as an essence of her being as he had known it. He himself had never been Girdish; he had not fully grasped what Gird might be like, but now beside her he could sense a burly broad-shouldered figure, oak-sturdy, stubborn.

Abruptly, as if a curtain shifted aside, he saw a handsome dark-haired, dark-eyed man of apparent early middle age staring at him. Wide awake, not kneeling in enchanted sleep as Paks had described. The man was handsome, and yet . . . spoiled by something. Petulance marked his mouth, and yearning shaped his gaze. He wore a belted gown of what looked like embroidered white silk and a blue overrobe with silver embroidery marking out an entwined G and L. Beside and behind him were others, also awake: an older woman, dark hair heavily streaked with gray, in a rose-colored surcoat over mail, her expression grim and angry; two middle-aged warriors, man and woman, the man more slightly built and somewhat pale, as if from a wound. In the background, others, men and women and children, milled around, clearly frightened. What was this? Had the sleepers wakened already? But there were far more than Paks had told him of.

"That's Luap," Paks murmured. "In the blue and silver. He's . . . he's *alive*. This isn't what I saw. This is . . . it can't be before, can it?"

"Before?"

"Gird's time . . . when Luap was still alive . . ." Her voice faded in awe. "What did we *do*? How did we do it?"

"I have no idea. But we must do whatever we do quickly. If this is the past and they are awake before the sleep, then we must . . ." His voice trailed away. He had no more idea how to put them to sleep than to waken them, but he knew he could not transport them as they were now. "The world would break," he said finally. "And it must not."

Kieri concentrated on the man staring at him—Luap, if Paks was right—and wondered how Gird could have been blind enough to trust someone so obviously flawed. Kieri felt, through Paks, the sorrow of that person—Gird, perhaps—at what had become of him. Kieri himself felt only anger, remembering what he had learned from the western elves. How dare the man abuse his people so? Leave them unprotected in the face of harm? Indulge himself at their expense? And he thought himself a prince? He would have blasted the man to nothingness if he'd known how, but Paks and Gird would not let him.

I knew his flaws. I had flaws myself.

That had to be Gird's voice, as blunt and uncompromising as his appearance. So something—some worth—was there, some chance for—a use, a purpose?—was still in Luap, and without him this would fail. The man still had power, Kieri could tell, though he had no will to use it rightly.

And he looked at Kieri as if Kieri could save him, pleading in his eyes, in what was left of himself. Remorse, shallow as it was, in the thin shell of a self that allowed nothing deeper.

Kieri leashed his anger for the moment and concentrated on what he could discern of the situation. Where were the magelords he was supposed to waken . . . after they slept? But Luap's silent pleading, the touches of power he kept using, broke his concentration again and again. It was like wounded soldiers who kept grabbing at a surgeon's arm while the surgeon tried to work . . . he would have to find a way to hold Luap down, contain his panic, as men had to hold soldiers still for the surgeon to work on them.

It seemed to take longer than it should, speaking to the man, asking the questions he must ask, getting answers that only emphasized what was wrong. Kieri had to restrain himself, control his own anger, and in so doing he returned to his earlier thought, that with the magelords he could undo some of the damage he'd done by trusting Alured the Black in Siniava's War. That seemed to make an impression on Luap; Kieri pushed aside for the moment his knowledge that his place was here—even more now that he was lord of an elvenhome. But still . . . perhaps the magelords could do it instead of him.

The face before him wavered, Luap's unstable will as obvious as a flame in a gust of wind. Then Paks spoke, and Luap's expression changed again, this time to awe. Kieri waited, watching that conversation and glancing beyond her to notice again the two, man and woman, who stood near Luap. One, the woman, gave him the same feeling Paks gave him. She met his gaze as frankly, then turned hers to Paks. The man looked at Luap and then directly at Kieri and gave a little nod.

"Don't worry," Paks said. Kieri focused on her words again. "Gird will help you."

Luap flinched. "Not me," he said. The words seemed dragged out of him. "I erred. Stupidly." He said more, but sounds seemed to blur; Kieri poured more of his own power into the connection. "I could read, you see. I was smarter," came through clearly. Luap blinked and looked down.

"Smart enough to cut yourself with your own sword?" Kieri felt compassion for the broken man for the first time. "I did that, too."

From the corner of his eye he saw that Paks was looking at him. "We kings' sons have much to learn from peasants, Luap."

Luap's laugh was harsh, followed by a rush of tears. "So Gird said. And Rahi."

Kieri quirked an eyebrow. Who was Rahi, and why was he or she important in this crisis?

"Gird's daughter."

"You knew his daughter?" Paks said, shooting a worried look at Kieri. "I thought all his children died young." She looked back at Luap. "You're afraid. What is it?"

"Iynisin," Luap said, and then, as if capable of a final burst of resolution, even honesty, he told the tale in a hurried monotone, from moving the mageborn to the canyon to actions that made Kieri's blood freeze. Stealing life from a mageborn healer? How could anyone—? "We will die," Luap said at last. "All of us—"

And they *had* all died. That much was clear from what the expeditions from Fintha had found. No sign of mageborn life in that wild land, only things left behind in the stronghold under the mountain. Far too like the elfane taig his grandmother had created and in which she had been trapped for a time.

"Can you help us escape?"

"No." Not this way, not this man, not even the two who seemed to glow with a power similar to Paks's. He could not, because he had not, because they were out there now, enchanted. But how could he tell Luap that? He had to try, and he began, thinking it out as he went.

Paks interrupted, eyes bright with an idea. He let her talk, let her push past Luap's objections, instead concentrating on what they might do—how they might do it. Then his ear snagged on something Luap said, and he interrupted. "You? Oathbreaker? You seized command against your oath to Gird?"

Another rush of excuses followed, layer after layer of them, onionlike, explaining what Luap had thought and why breaking his oath was right. Kieri's brief sympathy waned. At last, Luap fell silent and the silence lengthened. "I was wrong," Luap said. "I thought I would be better than my ancestors."

Kieri thought of Dorrin, working so hard to be better than hers when she had been better from the beginning.

Luap gulped and went on. "I was worse. And I don't know what to do. Aris and Seri—" He glanced at the two Kieri had noted. "—told me to pray, and when I prayed, I saw you."

So the gods—or a god—were in this with him? Had they sent Gird to help? For the first time Kieri felt certain this impossible situation, magery worked across time, had a real purpose, that he was meant to be part of it. In fact, he knew what he had to do: just what he had done so often as commander, as duke, and now as king. Take command from someone who was incapable and straighten things out.

Luap had power, though without character or strength of will. So little was left of the Luap Gird had known and loved, so much alien in the dark hollow of his core.

"Yield to me," Kieri said, heart to that feeble heart. "Let me do what can be done." Little as it was, and deep as his own grief at it.

"Please," Luap said.

Kieri reached into that dark center of Luap's self, that hollow some evil had eaten out and nestled in. He plucked out the thing—he had no word for it but the elven *banast,* "cursed"—and squeezed it, feeling something like hands around his own will, helping him, until it was nothing, a spot of slime that vanished.

Luap looked different—but weaker, not stronger as Kieri had hoped. He would, Kieri realized, waste precious time wallowing in guilt if allowed, but Kieri had no intention of letting him indulge himself in anything, not if any could be saved. He pressed deeper into Luap's self, taking over his mouth to give the orders that—to a man of his experience—were so obvious. His meaning came out in Luap's words—words his ears could not quite understand. The woman beside Luap nodded, her intelligent face showing determination now more than anger, and she turned to others. The man behind Luap, the healer-mage, frowned, then nodded and turned away; the woman protested, by her expression, but finally followed the man. All three moved into the crowd; it quieted; he could see clumps appearing that fit his orders—children and parents, adults bearing arms—until all had chosen a group.

"Take them now," he said to the group with the children, speaking in Luap's voice. "At once, with what you can carry. You know where." He hoped they did. He hoped the legend Paks had heard of survivors riding in from the west to Fin Panir was true. That group, the larger, moved out of the great chamber. At the far end, he saw a dais where Paks had reported a transfer pattern—but it had been blocked. Why had the Elders not let the innocents leave?

He put that aside for the moment, focusing once more on Luap, that shell of a prince. Luap stared at him, still expressing nothing but fear and pleading.

Let me. Gird again.

Kieri dared not glance aside, but in his mind he argued: *Wait. One more command.*

The pressure eased. Once more he seized Luap and through him gave more orders. Slowly the group of armed men and women arranged themselves on one side of the chamber, row on row, still talking, a few looking back at Luap. They knelt, and he pressed with all he knew of his magery, feeling Paks and Gird doing the same. *Sleep. Rest. Wake later at need.* Slowly now, the heads all turned to face the dais. Silence grew. No more fidgeting, no more movement at all: they knelt motionless, silent, in their formation.

Luap alone remained upright, the look on his face something Kieri did not want to see or remember, though he knew he would not forget it. Grief, fear, pleading . . . If he had been a child, Kieri would have gathered him up, hugged him—but this was a man, or what should have been a man. "It wasn't *all* my fault," Luap said, heart to heart. Kieri's sympathy vanished in a wave of contempt.

Now. Let me.

Gladly. Gladly he would let anyone else deal with that thing he could not call a man. He still gave power to the link but let Gird and Paks—or Gird through Paks—do what they would with Luap. The man's shape enlarged and faded until it was a huge misty figure that then rose through the air—and as it passed into the rock, all at once Kieri saw the outside of the place and that shape wavering on a fin of rock sticking out from a big red block of it. So alien was the place compared with anything he'd seen that he could hardly take it in.

Took me that way, too.

Gird. When had *he* been there in life?

Tell him to stand guard. You are a king; it will mean something to him.

The wraith or phantom bothered him less than the human man had; Kieri gave his orders crisply, precisely, and the wraith bowed, then stood upright again. For a moment more his awareness held the place—he was seeing what had been, tiny planted fields in the canyon, now trampled and blighted by iynisin as they neared the block of rock on which the wraith stood. And far down the canyon—had it really been that long?—the cluster of refugees, hurrying along a thread of trail.

Then it was all gone; he was falling, falling, and hit the floor of his study, its familiarity like a blow, like waking from a nightmare.

He lay a moment, gathering his wits, and looked over to see Paks also lying still, eyes closed. Then, as he watched, her eyes opened. "Are you all right?" she asked.

"I could ask the same question," he said. The fall had been but a jolt; the whole experience still roiled his mind.

"Kieri!" Arian's voice. "What happened? I felt—"

He pushed himself up to sitting; his head swam. He felt as exhausted as if he'd gone three nights without sleep. Arian, still in her dressing gown, stared at him, then looked at Paks.

"Did you try—?" she began, her tone accusing.

"We did . . . something," Kieri said. "At least, now we know who put them to sleep. At least we think we did that."

"We did," Paks said. "Gird was there," she said to Arian.

"I thought you were going to wait until I could help," Arian said in a tone so like a mother to an errant child that Kieri could not help grinning.

"You were sleeping soundly," he said. "The babes were quiet for once. All we hoped to do was have Paks show me what the place looked like now so I could focus on it later. I thought, if it worked, it would be such a small magery it would not bother you or the babes. But some power—"

"Gird," Paks said.

"—sent us earlier, in Luap's own time, when the iynisin attacked and the Elders closed the transfer pattern there, trapping the mage-lords. There was nothing to do but figure out how to put them—some of them—into enchanted sleep."

"So I wake thinking you're under attack and falling? That's *better*?" She shook her head at them. "You look half dead, the pair of you. I'll get food and drink; don't bother to get up."

Kieri wasn't sure he *could* get up; even sitting, he felt unsteady. He lay down again.

"I suppose we did ask a lot of the gods," Paks said. "That was a long way—time and space both."

"I still think it's impossible," Kieri said. "All I wanted to do was see the place. But then, I was told having the elvenhome magery was impossible." And meeting the Old Human dead and alive returning from it that Midwinter night had seemed impossible. He shivered, suddenly cold with all the impossibilities.

"In here," he heard Arian say. King's Squires brought blankets and trays of food and drink.

Very shortly, he and Paks lay wrapped in blankets and propped up on pillows; a fire crackled on the hearth. Arian sat in his usual chair, now set between them. A mug of sib spiked with honey and a pastry cleared his mind, though he still felt tired and sore.

"You are both reckless fools," Arian said when Kieri had finished the first mug of sib. "You had no one with you—not even one King's Squire—you might both have broken your heads falling down—and what if an iynisin had come through?"

"I didn't think of that," Kieri said, startled. Why had he not thought of that? The use of magery could be sensed by others who used it. As for no one around . . . "I did not want to expose anyone else to whatever danger there might be."

Arian heaved a sigh of the kind that conveys entire paragraphs. Kieri winced. "Fools," she said again. "A king—the only king we have, the only lord of an elvenhome we have, the only father our children have—and you still think you should face danger alone? Yes, you had a paladin with you—" The glance she sent Paks could have pierced steel, Kieri thought. "And I do not doubt, had it come to that, she would have warded you as much as she was able. But she, too, was bound into the magery. A paladin is not immortal; she could have died of it for all you knew and been no help at all."

"Gird was there," Paks offered.

Arian's snort was eloquent. "Gird is *your* patron, Paks. Not Kieri's. Gird is always with you, yes. But did Gird save you from falling on the floor like a sack of rocks?"

"I admit we should have had someone on guard," Kieri said. "I did not think of iynisin, and I do not know why, since I know they were involved." He took a deep breath. The lethargy was fading now—how long had it been? He realized he had no idea. One glass? Two?

"Your eyes have gone blank again," Arian said. "Drink more sib."

Partway through the next mug, he fell asleep and woke in his own bed to the sound of babies nearby, not crying but making other baby sounds and . . . splashing? Sunlight streamed in the window. He sat up. Arian and one of the nursery maids were bathing the babies; as he watched, Arian lifted Falki, laid him on the towel in her lap, and rolled him up like a cheese roll. Tilla kicked a final time as the nursery maid lifted her.

"I'll take them, my lady," the nursery maid said after bundling Tilla in another towel. She went out with a babe in each arm.

Kieri looked at Arian; she tried to keep a serious face but then grinned. "I'm fine," he said. "I don't even ache where I hit the floor."

"You scared me," she said. "If—"

He was up and by her side and laid a finger on her lips. "I'm sorry I scared you. The worst didn't happen, thank Falk and Gird and all the gods, and I won't be that careless again. I will try to understand the compulsion that made it seem reasonable. No one was there—"

"But Paksenarrion."

Kieri shook his head. "It wasn't Paks. I'm sure of that, because—now that I can remember it all—she asked if we should have someone in the room."

"Gird, then?"

"I don't think Gird could affect me. Falk might, but I didn't sense

Falk there. But something . . . I can't believe the danger from iynisin never occurred to me." He stretched, then started dressing. "I can't believe we did what we did—what I think we did—and I can't believe your grandfather didn't know it. If he could tell it was a mix of elven and human mageries, why couldn't he tell it was me?"

"Would that have made more sense to you? That you were going to travel back in time to enchant them?"

"I suppose not," Kieri said. "I would have thought it even more impossible." He pulled on one sock, then another. "Where is Paks?"

"I don't know. I had Queen's Squires carry her to her room; I haven't seen her since. She has the freedom of the palace."

Kieri finished dressing and belted on his sword. "Someone should check on her. She looked worse than I felt."

"I'll come with you," Arian said. She picked up the sword that had lain by her chair and hung it to the baldric she still wore. "I'll be glad when I fit back into my proper gear."

Kieri touched her shoulder. "It won't be long."

Upstairs, outside Paks's chamber, they heard nothing at first. Arian tapped on the door. A peculiar noise, like a truncated snore mixed with a gulp, came from the room. Then a yawn. "Uh?"

"Paks, it's Arian and Kieri. We were worried."

The thud of bare feet on the floor, then another yawn, and finally the door opened. Paks had color in her face again, and after a few more blinks, her eyes brightened. "I haven't slept this late in years," she said.

"I'm glad to see you upright," Arian said. "Kieri woke less than a half-glass ago. Do you remember what happened?"

"We worked magery," Paks said. "And—" She grimaced. "We're going to have to work it again."

"Not today you're not," Arian said. "And not alone, either."

CHAPTER FOURTEEN

Paks left the next day as suddenly as she had come. "I must be back in Fin Panir for Midsummer," she said.

"A rule for paladins?" Kieri asked, smiling.

"No . . . just . . . I must go."

"Go with our prayers, then. Come again—we still have to wake those magelords, you know." She waved, already moving away. Kieri sighed. Her Old Human magery had helped him, but what if she did not return? Supposedly he had it, but he felt nothing when he tried to imagine what it might be like.

The western elves, who had left immediately after the twins were born to take word to their king in the west, had not yet returned. Elves' sense of time again . . . He had expected them back by now, since travel by their patterns seemed instantaneous, but to them it might be no time at all since they left.

On second thought, that might be convenient in this instance. He did not know how to explain to them what he and Paks had done. He was sure they would have questions he could not answer. How had he imposed enchantment on the past? He had no idea. Why had he not then broken the enchantment? And so on. It would be simpler not to tell them: in this day, the magelords were there, silent and motionless, and if the elves hadn't known who put them there, they did not need to know now.

On that thought, he set to work in his office, reading through reports from supervisors of various projects he had put under way. Every time his thoughts veered to what Paks had brought up—the possibility that Sekkady still lived, perhaps in another body, and might still be a menace—he pushed it away and forced himself into the details of the day.

Later, he tried twice—very carefully, with a King's Squire sworn to secrecy at hand, and sitting down—to reach with his magery to Kolobia and do something—anything—that might wake those he had enchanted. He was sure he found the place again—he felt it the same way he felt his former stronghold, or Vérella, or the winter quarters in Valdaire. But that was the most he could do, lacking Paks and Gird. And though he asked Gird for help, nothing more happened.

Except that night after night, he remembered what Paks had said and could not push aside the thought of Sekkady still alive, in another body, searching for him, threatening his children. His dreams were troubled. He did not want to bother Arian while she was so busy with the babies. He would try something else.

Arian was asleep; the babies were asleep. Kieri sat by the window in his own chamber, the box of selani tiles open before him. He took one without looking and then read the rune. *Sorrow.* He took another. *Loss.* Another and another and another: *pain, rage, distance, death,* each one drawing a fine line of pain on his heart as Sekkady had long ago used a stone blade on his skin to draw a fine line of blood. And then, with the bloodstone he always had with him, Sekkady had sorcelled that blood into the stone and murmured to Kieri as he did so.

Even if you escaped this place—but you will never escape—you could not escape me, for your blood is with me, and with it your fear and your submission. By this stone I command you. Here you are, held motionless and silent, even when you know what I will do to you. So will you be always, everywhere and anywhere, every time and any time. And someday, I will let you have something precious to you, and you will think you are safe, but I will come, and you will kneel before me, helpless as you are now. And I may let you beg for mercy, but you know now as you will then that my will is greatest, and you will surely suffer all I desire.

He had heard that voice in dreams even after escaping; he had forgotten those dreams, the words that once more caught him, held him motionless, his throat clogged with fear. Cold sweat ran down his back, he could scarcely breathe, he scarcely knew where he was or when—

At the screams, he fell back into the present. A baby crying, screaming—and now two of them, loud enough to hear through the closed doors and the passage between. Shaking, he stood up, staggered a few steps before he caught his balance, and went quickly through the passage to the queen's suite. Arian was awake, sitting up in bed; nursemaids had already picked up the twins from their cradle. Wide-eyed, Arian stared at him. "Kieri! What's wrong? What's happening?"

He could not answer. He stood there, his ears almost shattered by the volume of the babies' cries, desperate and helpless. Arian looked back and forth from him to the babies and pushed herself out of bed. She went first to the nursery maids. "Are they injured?"

"No—they just woke suddenly, screaming—"

"Take them down the passage, all the way to the back of the palace—you—" She spoke to the Queen's Squires who had looked in to see what the commotion was. "—go with them. Walk them up and down; it will soothe them. I will deal with the king."

The nursemaids carried the babies out; Arian came to Kieri. He could not look directly at her. Tears blurred his vision. Her hands on his were warm, firm but gentle. "Kieri . . . you are in some evil enchantment. Let me help."

He shook his head. She must not come closer—what if it caught her, too? But she was already there, her grip now commanding, pushing him toward one of the chairs set near the fireplace. "Sit—you are trembling enough to fall."

He sat as if his legs had failed. She sat across from him, holding his hands . . . he looked down at hers, such strong, competent hands,

only to see them change, broken, twisted, bleeding, and hear Sekkady's triumphant, gloating laugh as he had heard it the very night
he escaped while the man who freed him suffered.

A groan burst from him, and a fresh flood of tears. He clung to
Arian's hands until finally he could breathe again. She pulled one
hand free and wiped his face with one of the towels laid by the fire
for the nursemaids to use. He reached for it and began mopping his
face himself.

"I—I'm sorry—"

"Shhh. You have done nothing wrong—"

"Nothing but put you in mortal danger, you and our children
both—"

"What? How?" She sounded far too calm, he thought.

"The selani tiles . . . I was looking . . . thinking . . ."

"Thinking what?"

"Something Caernith said about them and something Paks said—I
can't say it, Arian. I *can't*."

"Don't, then." She got up, dipped another towel in the can of
warm water on the hearth, and wiped his face, then his hands. "I
remember what Caernith said. What memories prompted your
thoughts?"

"I was . . . hoping . . . that something horrible could not be true,"
he said. He looked at her then; she showed no fear, nothing but concern for him. He took a breath; his voice steadied. "But the tiles gave
me no hope."

"You know the tiles do not show an immutable future," Arian
said. "If they warn of danger, we will meet it. If they promise doom,
we will defeat it." She put out her hand; he took it automatically.
"Whatever it is . . . we have already defeated the Pargunese, the iynisin who sought our deaths and dishonor, that one who poisoned me
and betrayed you . . . We will prevail."

His breath eased. "Arian—there are things I never told you—"

"Of course there are. We both have fifty years and more behind
us, and we have been together only two winters: we have not begun
to tell each other everything."

"But this is important. The man who . . . who owned me for most
of my childhood—"

She put her hand on his lips. "Kieri . . . is this a tale best told late at night? I can see you need to tell it, but should it not be told by day, in clean sunlight?"

"I do not know," he said. "Memories, bad memories . . . I had forgotten, meant to forget forever, but they have come now—"

"We have two problems," she said. "A daughter and a son who woke screaming, I think from their link to you—for when I woke, the entire taig was roused. If it can wait until daylight, if you can be calm and let the children rest—"

"It is for the children I fear," he said.

She sighed. "Well, then. One night without sleep will not kill any of us, even the babes. Come—we will go back to your chamber and see those tiles, and you can tell me all."

He began with what she already knew and then with what he had not told her before, and what he now feared. "He said I would always be commanded by his magery because my blood was in his stone. But after all the years, I was sure he must be dead. When Tamarrion and the children were killed, I wondered if he might have done it. But that was orcs, and how could he have commanded orcs from so far away?"

Arian said nothing, just held his hands, strength and clarity in her grip. Was it her own elven magery? Or just her character? He went on, more slowly now. "When I first heard of the Verrakaien changing bodies, it did not occur to me—it should have—that he might have done the same. I didn't ask Dorrin. I didn't think . . ."

Arian glanced at the selani tiles still on the table. "Perhaps this is your thought rising again in the wake of the magery you did with Paks. Seeing those old magelords—perhaps they reminded you of Sekkady."

Kieri took a long breath. "Perhaps. I didn't think of that . . . they were from a time when he could not have been alive. Unless . . . *could* someone really live so long?"

"I doubt it," Arian said. Her brow furrowed in thought. "Surely the mind wears out. We must ask the elves."

"Not elves," Kieri said. "They do not pay enough attention—or not always. They might not recognize someone in a different body." He looked over at the tiles, each rune clear in the lamplight. "If it was my hidden thought coming forth that moved the tiles . . . then I should be grateful . . . but I cannot."

"I can," Arian said. "For if we know a danger is possible, we can think how to meet it. It is the unknown danger that defeats forethought."

Kieri felt his heart lift at her confidence. "There are always unknown dangers, but you're right."

"Well, then. Do you think any of those old magelords you propose to wake from enchantment knew a version of Sekkady? They certainly cannot know you were his . . ." Her voice faltered.

"His *slave*," Kieri said firmly. "No. Even if he was alive then, in an earlier body—and they knew him—I was not yet born, so they could not have known about his use of me. But if his powers are from those days, which *is* likely, then any of those magelords could pose a similar threat once awakened."

"And that is good to know," Arian said. "We will be alert to such dangers."

"But how will we know? How do we know he's not here now? It could be anyone." Fear gripped him again.

"Let me try the selani tiles," Arian said. She moved to the other side of the table, and—looking Kieri in the eye—picked up the tiles on the table, dropped them back in the box, stirred all with a finger, and then drew one out. "Ah. The one we've picked so many times: *Awake*. So we shall be, awake, alert, and . . . let's see." She drew another one. "Joy."

Kieri shook his head. "Your skills exceed mine when it comes to finding good outcomes."

"I have not endured what you have. That cruelty would leave darkness in anyone it touched." Her expression hardened. "I would gladly kill him if he is not dead. Not only for your sake, though that is enough, but for the sake of all he tormented."

Kieri shook his head. "No—it is my past and mine to solve."

"If he threatens our children and you are not near—I will kill him. Do not say no."

Kieri nodded. "I would never ask you to let harm come to our children—for any reason. If—if the worst comes and he overpowers me . . . if I stand between him and you, if I become a danger to them . . . kill *me* if you must."

"Kieri! NO!"

"Can I be certain I will not yield to his magery? Suppose he was right and implanted something in me—or the stone really does control me—" Panic rose again; he heard it in his voice.

"It won't. I'm certain it won't. You were not controlled by elven magery—not even an iynisin. And you escaped him when you were but a boy."

"With another's help." He had told her that before; now the details seemed important. "We must face the possibility that I am not really free of him."

"And this is what kept you up so late?"

"I . . . think so. Yes. The selani tiles seemed to . . . to threaten me with that." He shook his head sharply. "It is being a father again, Arian, that frightens me most. That children of mine could suffer as I suffered. Sekkady . . . if he lives, if he comes, *that* is what he would want to do. Make them suffer. Make me see it and be unable to stop it."

"Then you will stop it," Arian said. "Having thought now it might happen, you will think how—and you will stop it."

"How can I know—?" That came out in a rush, and grief cut it off.

"Ahead of time? You can't. I didn't know I could ride in a dragon's mouth. I didn't imagine I would ever need to. But I did—and you will do whatever you need to protect the children—all the children—and so will I."

***

"My lord." Caernith, one of the western elves, bowed from the doorway. "We are returned from the west."

Kieri looked up; more than a hand of days had passed since that terrible night. He was still shaken, but calmer and glad he had not needed to cope with the elves immediately. In the meantime he had changed his mind: they needed to know what he and Paks had done. "Welcome back," he said.

"I bring a message from our king to you, my lord, and another for the queen. Our king rejoices in the birth of your heirs and in the queen's health. He is concerned, however, that you are no closer to knowing how to awaken the sleepers under stone."

Kieri nodded. "It is true; I am not any closer to that. I have asked all I know what they know, and what they know is nothing . . . There are no records, or even stories, about waking someone from a long enchantment. But on another matter——"

Caernith bowed again as he interrupted. "Please. I bring other messages from our king, written in our language as the king cannot write in yours. For this reason I must be privy to what he said, to translate for you. Your elvish is not yet advanced enough, and mistakes are easy to make."

"Very well," Kieri said. Best to let Caernith have his way, though he could now read elvish tolerably well, he was sure. He could surprise Caernith afterward.

Caernith pulled a scroll case from his doublet and then a scroll, bound with ribbons, as Kieri's own letters were, but with braided grass, still fresh and green by elven magery, and with a sprig of some conifer tucked into it.

"Yew," Caernith said, pulling it out. He sniffed it and gave it to Kieri. "The choice of a sprig carries part of the message. In this case, warning." He slid the grass ring from the scroll, and—as Kieri had noticed before—the scroll unrolled itself, the graceful elvish writing clear against its creamy smooth surface. "By your leave——" he said, and gestured.

"Of course. Bring a chair." He glanced at the scroll while Caernith fetched a chair, pleased to find that he could read all of the salutation and much of the first three lines, though he came to a word he suspected of complicated meaning.

"This message," Caernith said as he sat down, "is longer than it seems." He put a finger on the scroll. "It is in what I believe you call a code, a way of saying more than is said on the surface." He moved his finger in a pattern, and new smaller lines appeared, seeming to stack behind and between the those Kieri had seen. "When I put my finger on this——" He touched one of the lines, and it grew in size, seeming to come forward. "—I can read it easily and know its correct place in the sequence. I will begin now."

"Will you teach me that?" Kieri asked.

"Yes, but not at the moment. There is urgency."

Kieri nodded, then watched and listened as Caernith read something far longer than he would have thought could fit on a single sheet that did not even cover his desk.

Iynisin leak from the stone like poison from a wound. Many were imprisoned there in ancient times, and that false prince's alliance with them set them free again.

"Alliance? Luap was their ally?"

"It is possible he did not know what he did, but he offered no resistance to them," Caernith said before reading on.

We cannot stop their emergence until the stone can be remade in soundness. Dragon has granted us the boon of transforming fire, but Dragon cannot or will not undo the magery that holds the sleepers safe. The iynisin have some purpose in the east— in my granddaughter's land and yours, Lyonya's king, or in the lands nearby—and they will come, with all their malice. We think their purpose is magery they shared with humans before we left the land you call Aare; we think they seek remnants of that magery with which to destroy the north, as they did the south. We are not certain what that magery was; we moved our elvenhome to the north before others and rarely met with other Sinyi.

Kieri's mind leapt at once to Dorrin's discovery of a mysterious crown and other royal regalia. But elves at Mikeli's court had seen the jewels—he was sure he remembered being told that—and had not recognized them. *Which elves?* "Did your elves—those from the far west—ever come to Tsaia's court?"

Caernith nodded. "The Bells at Vérella—they rang when you drew your sword, did they not?"

"Yes . . . and they're said to be of elven make."

"Indeed. They were given by those of an elvenhome destroyed long since to the magelords when those came over the mountains and the elves moved away. With goodwill then, for there was no enmity between those elves and those magelords, and the sound of those bells repels iynisin."

Kieri blinked. He had heard many tales of the mysterious Bells of Vérella in their sealed tower but not that one.

"Let me read on," Caernith said. His clear, pleasant voice made the words he read even more ominous. Iynisin in numbers moving east, more than had been seen since before Gird's day, since before the magelords came, iynisin accompanied by their constructs and lending them more power than they'd had when left behind in earlier times.

What we believe is that either healing or great harm will come upon the world in less than four cycles of the sun. The rock-brothers speak of spreading evil in the rock, making it nedross as the dwarves say. We have known of daskdraudigs; we see more of them here and rumors of them moving along the flanks of the great mountains, opening the way of iynisin trapped there in old times. We would send you what was our greatest treasure, the Elvenhorn, but it was used before and vanished as they do for a time after use.

"Elvenhorn?" Kieri murmured.

"Ardhiel used it when the Girdish expedition was beset near the stronghold, and I cannot say he was wrong to do so. It was before the paladin Paksenarrion was taken; she would have been killed with the rest if he had not used it. But he did not know how sorely it would be needed later."

"Perhaps he knew how badly we would all fare if it fell into the enemy's hands," Kieri said.

"Perhaps. But you see, my lord, how urgent is the need for you to wake the sleepers. Until the Father of Dragons can transform the stone, iynisin and their evil threaten all."

Kieri bit back the answer, which Caernith knew as well as he did.

No searching he had done, nothing the elves knew of their own magery, had given him a way to do what they demanded. But he had changed his mind and decided he must tell Caernith what he and Paks had accomplished.

"I have my own tale to tell you: I now know who set the enchantment that binds the magelords there, though I still do not know how to free them." Caernith stiffened and started to speak, but Kieri waved him to silence and quickly told what he and Paks had done and what he now understood of the situation there at the time.

"You—and a Girdish paladin?" Shock and disdain combined in that.

"Yes. I could not see the place, make a mental picture of it, myself. Though you taught me how to perform small acts at a distance, it was always someplace I knew and could imagine clearly. Paks, because she had been there, remembered it clearly enough to imagine."

"*You* worked magery across that span of time?" Caernith's expression was one Kieri had never seen on an elf's face—complete astonishment. "Indeed—you are the king we hoped for. And you enchanted them—so surely it is your enchantment to break."

"Except I cannot. I can now imagine the scene as I last saw it—but I cannot reach it. Paks was involved in that magery, and Gird himself, I believe. But I am not Girdish, and my calls on him have gone unanswered. Paks had to leave at his call; I do not know where she is. If I am to accomplish it, I must gain access to all my own magery."

"No age is easy," Caernith said. "But this one seems like to be exceptionally hard. It is our shame that we cannot help you learn what you need to know. If there were Old Humans yet in this world—"

We are not gone. We do not talk with elf-kind.

The words, blunt as hauks, came from a voice Kieri had heard before. The Old One, as he thought of that skull, now on its plinth of stone in the bone-house where the hill had been. Would that one talk to him, teach him Old Human magery? Help him wake the sleepers out west? Because those sleepers were magelords . . .

Humans. Not elves.

And magelords killed Old Humans or enslaved them.

Sometimes. Here it was elves that destroyed our power and took our home.

So . . . would the Old One help him wake the magelords?

Yes. Come at midnight. And before Kieri could open his mouth: *Do not tell the elf. Do not tell any elf.*

That was clear enough. He looked up at Caernith. "I will try again; I have not asked others here with Old Human blood if they know aught. I will ask them now."

"Do so, my lord, with what urgency you can. As well, given the situation in which the magelords were enchanted, we cannot guarantee their character."

Kieri agreed with that but said nothing. Caernith went on. "We met none but the prince himself, Selamis Luap, and thus know little of the others except that at the very end, we felt both good and evil in the crowd around the prince."

Kieri still did not grasp how elves sensed time passing. "You speak of a year or more to wait—"

"What cycle it is, I leave to you, my lord; you and your queen know best how long the babes remain so closely linked that any magery your lady makes will pass through them—"

That, too, was news to Kieri, though he well knew their sensitivity to himself. He said nothing, and Caernith went on. "We of the King's Guard remain at your service, my lord, and are vigilant against any return of iynisin. Though I believe your own powers have grown and you as well as I would sense their presence."

"They—or that one—broke in while the Lady was yet alive," Kieri said.

"The Lady . . . was not all of herself," Caernith said.

"So I was told."

"Did her son—what you call your uncle, I suppose—tell you why? What happened?"

"Some of it," Kieri said. He wanted to know more—but not now. Not when he was going to have to spend however long it took in the bone-house discussing Old Human magery with the dead. "But if you will excuse me for this time, the queen and I have things to discuss."

"Of course." Caernith bowed. "If you need to leave the palace later, merely call."

Kieri nodded and left the room. He'd forgotten that Caernith would expect to accompany him if he went out, as protection from iynisin. How was he going to evade an elf? Caernith did not come into the ossuary with him, so perhaps he could leave Caernith outside the King's Grove. But no—Caernith would see danger in that.

When he came to Arian's room, she was on the floor with the babies, holding a ball on a string for them to bat at. She looked up. "What disturbed you this time?"

"It shows that clearly?" Kieri let himself down onto the floor, and Falki turned, reaching. Kieri put his finger into that grip and stroked his son's head with the other hand. "Hello, bright one."

His daughter turned her head and gave him a toothless grin, waving a hand vaguely.

"You, too," he said to her. "Arian, are these two approaching readiness for bed?"

"You need to talk to me?"

"Yes. And not something I want to discuss around them; they're too tuned to our emotions."

"Ah. Well, it's time anyway."

In a shorter time than usual, the twins were sleeping in their cradle. "Now—what is it?"

"A message from your grandfather." Kieri took a swallow of sib. "I wish for once someone would send a message that everything's all right and there's nothing to worry about."

"What is the worry?"

"Iynisin. Their movement from Kolobia eastward. I think it's the regalia Dorrin found, myself. Iynisin and magery both appeared in the world shortly after the regalia were brought to Vérella."

"Could be Dragon," Arian said.

"So it could, but I think Dragon would tell us. I think it's the regalia. Your grandfather urges me to hurry and find a way to wake the magelords in Kolobia. Yet no one can tell me how."

"But—?"

He grinned at her. "But . . . I may have found a way to gain access to the Old Human magery that the elves say is necessary. The Old

One's skull spoke to me again. It won't have anything to do with elves, but it will help me. It said. The only thing is—"

"How to evade your elven bodyguard?"

"Exactly. Ideas?"

Arian smiled, a singularly smug smile. "I need him."

"What?" That was the last thing he'd expected; Arian had been no more than coolly polite to the western elves.

"I need him. I need to consult him about the babes and about any limitations on their exposure to magery, as well as their education as . . . what they are. The nursery maids as well as I have noticed how quickly they advance." She stretched, then gave a sharp sigh. "I'm not inventing a need, Kieri. I should have done it before, because we have no other I trust to teach me to mother children who will rule an elvenhome. So, when does the skull want you to come?"

"Midnight."

She grimaced. "It would. Hard to explain why I need to meet with an elf at midnight without you present. Does it have to be to-night?"

"I don't know . . . I don't think so."

"Good. Tomorrow night, then. I'll talk to Caernith."

K ieri left his King's Squires at the dike around the bone-house. Starlight showed him the path down; the roof of the bone-house sparkled with dew. He bowed before entering and felt his way to the Oathstone. Faint sounds of clicking and rustling raised the hairs on his neck, but he ignored that and bowed again.

"Elder, I am here," he said.

A vague glow appeared in the dark, then strengthened until the skull on the Oathstone was outlined in green light. By that light Kieri now saw two skeletons standing, bone on bone, one to either side of him.

You are not of this tribe. The skull's voice in his head was clear, but his outward ears heard nothing. *To learn the magery of which you ask, you must be adopted. Give your hands to your father and your mother; they have agreed to sponsor you.*

Kieri reached out, and the cold bones of the skeletons clasped his hands as if he were a child between parents.

They will lead you where you must go.

They were already moving, their grip on his hands inflexible as the bones, powerful as stone; he had no choice but to follow. Out of the bone-house and then to the heart-hand . . . then an intricate dance he could not understand, stumbling now and then as he was pushed and pulled through the pattern. Darkness rose around him; the starlight disappeared; under his feet he felt earth, not grass: damp, yielding, slippery.

You must be born, child of Alyanya, child of Sian and Olath. That was a different voice, softer yet more powerful than the old skull's. Kieri stared into dark nothing, hearing a rhythmic sound, and realized that the bones no longer held his hands and he was curled into a ball, hands fisted. What was this? He tried to take a calming breath—and could not. He struggled, and whatever was around him squeezed, pushed at him; he felt himself sliding . . . where? He was a grown man; he could not be birthed . . . but he could not stop what was happening, compressed as he was. Whatever it was would happen. *Do not fear, child. You must be born in love and joy.* Love poured from that voice; he relaxed in spite of his confusion.

In that moment, he was once more able to breathe, the moist night air clean and fragrant on his face. Once more he was clasped in bony hands, as if he were in truth a tiny child.

Alyanya's Grace. A child is born to the tribe. May he grow in peace and share in the parrion of power. The skull again. *Sian. Olath. Name this child before the tribe.*

The skeleton holding his heart-hand raised it high. *I, Sian, mother of fathers, new-birthed this child and name him Palan, for his parrion's use, in Alyanya's honor. Let the child bear this name with other names, and let it be known to him and the dead alone.*

The skeleton holding his sword-hand then raised it high. *I, Olath, father of mothers, engendered this child anew and name him Oathkeeper, for his guidance, in Alyanya's honor. Let the child bear this name before all.*

Kieri shivered; had it been Alyanya, then, who spoke while he was helpless? And where was he now, besides in the air, standing, able to breathe? The bony hands tugged again at his, and again he followed some pattern they walked or danced, confused but willing.

When they stopped, he could see more clearly: the bone-house, the glowing skull within, the other skeletons now standing in rows to either side of the aisle to the Oathstone.

Bring him.

They led him forward.

Palan Oathkeeper, kiss my brow.

Kieri, hands now free, lifted the skull and kissed it.

You are one of us. For Alyanya's sake, I will share what you would know.

Power poured into him, dark as dirt, rich with life. The Old Human magery reminded Kieri of both elven and Kuakkgani magery, based as it was on the life that flowed through the world. And yet it was different at root from the elven, for the Old Humans did not use it to force even beauty or growth from plants. Their magery was based on giving, not taking . . . on asking, not commanding.

Alyanya gives life, and so this magery gives blood and breath.

The Kuakkgani, Kieri knew, gave a limb to their host tree . . . and the tree gave a limb to them . . . each kind to the other kind. But the Old Humans had given season by season, act by act—blooding their tools before cutting the soil and the cornerstone of a new building, burying the birthsack of each child in the corner of a field to be planted, giving the land back the flesh of each who died, and then raising the bones for their spirits. They gave breath—days of their lives—for the magery that saved others from dying of fevers or injuries.

Giving is power.

The techniques, the rituals, poured into his mind. At last, when he felt stuffed with the new knowledge, the skull released him.

Go in Alyanya's peace, Palan Oathkeeper. We do not forget.

Kieri returned from the King's Grove to his own chamber in the first soft predawn light; he was, he realized, streaked with mud and other substances he didn't want to think about. He took the back way and made it into the bathing room without seeing either of his elven bodyguards. Water for his bath after morning exercise in the salle had just been put on the hearth; he poured it into the tub over the servant's objections.

"I need to get this mud off, and I'll need another bath later. Doesn't matter if it's cold; I've bathed in colder."

It was more cool than cold, refreshing, and he came out of his bath wide awake and ready for drill. Arian was in his room when he entered, in exercise gear with the glint of mail under it. She grinned at him. "Get any sleep?"

"No, but I'm fine." He dressed quickly. "You're going to the salle? Are you sure?"

"I'm sure. They've had their first breakfast, and I'm too restless to sit around."

"Half speed," Kieri said, wriggling into his own mail. "No accidents."

"Half speed," she said.

They went down together and met Caernith in the lower hall. "My lady," he said to Arian. "Are you quite sure you should—?"

"Yes," Arian said. "What you told me about the children—I need to be fit just to keep up with them, and sitting around will not do."

"You have servants," Caernith said.

"And I am their mother for both body and magery," Arian said. She glanced at Kieri. "Besides, I have the king's leave."

Kieri chuckled. "As if you needed it. Come now: a short workout for you today and then you can laugh at me for staying up far too late with that research. Carlion will probably leave bruises."

They came into a salle already echoing with the sound of steel on steel, but Carlion called a hold as the king entered.

"My queen," Carlion said, coming to Arian. "Are you certain—?"

"Yes!" Kieri and Arian spoke together, and then Arian laughed. "Yes, Carlion, I am certain. I am wearing mail. I have done the preliminary exercises. I know I must not go full speed yet, but I need to get started. Do not treat me like a crystal goblet; I am not so easy to break."

"Yes, my queen. I just . . . we all just . . ."

"I know." She laid a hand on his arm. "I am not angry, just determined. I would like you to closely supervise my exercises the first tenday or so."

"Well, then . . . no banda for you today; you're not going to touch a blade. Let's see you stretch. And you, sir king—" He turned to Kieri. "Usual stretches, then go to the middle with any two of your Squires. One to watch, since I'll be busy with the queen, and one to engage. Take turns."

Kieri picked up one of the practice blades and absently, without thinking, ran his thumb down the sharpened edge above the slightly bated tip. A bead of blood smeared the blade.

"What did you do?" Carlion said sharply.

The answer came before he could stop it. "Blooded the blade."

Caernith looked at him. "Why? That's—"

"An Old Human tradition, yes. If I'm to find out about my Old Human heritage, I should be using some of their rituals, don't you think?"

Caernith stared, then said, "Blood magery is . . . wrong."

"It's not the same as taking blood," Kieri said. "Old Humans blooded the blade to give of their own life."

"It's . . ."

Kieri could almost see the words running through the elf's mind. "It's . . . primitive."

"But not selfish or cruel," Kieri said. He walked on to the middle section of the salle.

Kieri sat in the rose garden, as usual once in the day, fingering the selani tiles for the first time since . . . that night . . . letting their runes and their arrangement lead his thoughts. Today, tiles and thoughts seemed scattered. The opposites of *wound* and *heal* were obvious, but what did they refer to? And how could that fit with *seek* and *find,* another pair of opposites, and *truth* and *consent,* which were not opposites? Elves, Kieri knew, hated seeing his scars, even faded from what they had been. Unlike his King's Squires, they avoided seeing him partly dressed, let alone unclothed.

They had offered to erase the scars, as the Lady had offered to erase Paks's scars—but not his, he thought suddenly, spun out of a consideration of bodyguards who couldn't look at his body to another of his grandmother's oddities. Had she lacked that gift? No, because she had offered healing to Paks. Why not to him? Perhaps she could not do it always? He himself had been able to heal Torfinn's poisoned wound once but not his injured leg later.

He fingered the torc he now wore, invisible under his mail and gorget. Thinking of his grandmother led inevitably to his mother and the gifts that had risen from the ground to become his at last. He had shown elves the selani tiles; he now knew all the runes and some of what the tiles were for—not so much foretelling as remembering and connecting memories into patterns that allowed deeper understanding. They knew about his sword and dagger, about the ring he wore on his heart-hand and the belt buckle. But he had not shown them the torc. Every time he'd thought to do so, he had been distracted by something else. That brief glimpse of something inside the golden twist . . . what was it, and what did it mean?

He scooped up the tiles, glanced at the angle of the sun, and decided he had time for one more meditation with them. He let a few slide through his fingers, landing on the table as they would. *Wound. Heal. Choice. Protect.*

Sun blazed down on him; the scent of roses became overpowering. He felt a pressure, as if someone tried to force his understanding. Whose choice? It must be his. A choice to protect or heal or wound? He would choose to protect and heal whenever he could.

Whom?

Whom? Heal whom? Anyone hurt, was his immediate thought. Immediately the patterns he had just learned from the Old Humans rose in his mind.

For them, healing was the most delicate, intricate of gifts, one requiring full understanding of the situation, not just the injury. Just to lay pain on a stone—a traditional remedy for pains that did not respond to an infusion of feverbane, bruisebane, or goodweed—

depended on the pain and its cause, the parrion of the one in pain, and the stone's own nature and its function. Casting sleep on an adult or waking one out of cast sleep was even more complicated.

Kieri talked all this over with Arian when they met later that day.

"My mother had what we called good hands," Arian said. "I don't know if that's the same."

"What do you mean? Healed people?"

Arian shook her head. "Not exactly. But if you were sick or hurt, when she touched you, or laid her hand on it, it felt better. Not just for me, but for others in the household. And I remember as a child, being restless and unable to sleep. Her hand on my forehead would be so gentle, so soothing . . . I'd wake up the next morning and never have noticed going to sleep."

"What about waking you?"

Arian laughed. "That was a wet cloth dropped on my feet if I didn't come when called," she said.

Kieri tried out the magery on Arian, at her suggestion. At first he followed her mother's example: a hand on her forehead, along with what he understood of the magery itself. He had to find peace and rest in himself and give that to her . . . and the second time he tried it, she fell asleep in an instant, a smile on her face. Within days, he could cast sleep on her from a distance. Waking her gently was more difficult; her memories of cold wet feet interfered with his intent and woke her with a jerk. Finally he found a way to do it—and give her sleep again—and do it from the other side of the room.

"Almost there," he said, yawning. "But I need to sleep myself. By Midsummer I might have this figured out. Surely nothing will happen between now and then."

CHAPTER FIFTEEN

Vérella, Tsaia

Unseen, unheard, the shadows entered the palace gate past guards who stood open-eyed, staring at nothing. Unseen, unheard, the shadows moved across the courtyard, up the stairs, where the great doors swung open for them, and the guards posted there stood as motionless as the others, eyes open, seeing nothing.

Within the palace they moved in a body along corridors dimly lit, past the occasional guard, up stairs, around turns, unerring in their search . . . and still unseen and unheard. At the last door, the one that guarded the treasury, two guards stood, the whites of their eyes gleaming a little in the faint light. The shadows paused; the guards saw nothing, heard nothing. The shadows touched the door; it did not open to them at first, but the locks yielded at last to slender wands and wires of steel.

Prince Camwyn woke with a start and stared at his hands. Both were alight; his room showed clear in every detail. He scowled. This had not happened for a quarter-year; he had finally learned, he thought, how to control this part of his magery. He stood up and padded barefoot across the carpet to the candle holders always ready for such a situation. Candle after candle flared; his hands did not dim.

Come!

His hand jerked away from the candle he intended to light. The crown again. He had given up hoping it would not talk to him; it talked to Duke Verrakai and Mikeli as well, and its intrusions had grown more frequent of late. But why did it command him to come now, in the middle of the night?

Come! Come now! Danger!

His skin prickled with sudden excitement. Danger? Here in the palace, surrounded by guards? His first thought was for Mikeli, and he took three steps before his mind caught up. Running to face danger in his nightshirt, barefoot and unarmed, was . . . stupid. He had been stupid before; he was older now.

His clothes for morning weapons practice lay ready, as always. He put them on, trying to think clearly through the pounding of his heart. Mail? Should he wear mail? What kind of danger?

Danger. Evil. Come!

Evil. He should rouse the Marshal-Judicar, the Knight-Commander, any Girdish at all. He wriggled into the mail shirt—it no longer felt so heavy though it struck chill through his arming shirt—fastened the gorget around his neck, and set the helmet on his head. His sword—a gift from Mikeli this last name day—a check to be sure his dagger and saveblade were in place, and he went out the door to the anteroom where his guards should be. And where they stood stiff and still, eyes open, staring at nothing.

He touched them, spoke to them. No reaction. He shivered, suddenly cold. A spell . . . an evil spell. It must be another renegade Verrakai. One? More? He should find someone to help him—but if he could not rouse his guards, and if it took too long—

Light spread down his sword from his sword-hand. "Holy Gird and Camwyn," he murmured. "Help me now." It was not a magic sword, not that he knew; Mikeli had said nothing of it . . . it must be his own magery . . .

As if his sword were alive, it tugged him down the passage, turned him away from Mikeli's quarters—he saw nothing that way but the motionless guards in their places—and up another flight of stairs, another turn. He knew now where they were going, the treasury, and what the attack must be.

The Verrakaien wanted the crown back. One at least had been in league with that pirate in the south who had the necklace; another must be stealing the rest to take to him. He rounded the corner. In the light of his sword, he saw the guards by the treasury door—the *open* treasury door—and with belated caution flattened to the wall, rather than charging through.

He heard voices like no voices he had heard before. Silvery, musical, cold as snowflakes, patterning sound into what was nearly song but . . . not. He had heard elves speaking elvish once or twice—similar to this but not quite the same.

Danger!

Elves? Danger?

Iynisin! Danger!

He stood, listening. What were "iynisin"?

Not elves! Elves no more! Danger!

Kuaknomi. For a moment his skin crawled with horror. Kuaknomi, blackcloaks, dark cousins . . . creatures of the Severance . . . they had cursed Gird and his line; none of Gird's line survived. And here he was alone—the only one awake to them in the whole palace? His knees weakened; he clenched his teeth and through that fence muttered, "Gird! Camwyn!"

Warmth returned. He hurtled into the room, light blazing from his sword, to see five dark shapes crouched around the chest, chanting. The chest itself trembled.

Faster than he had imagined, the iynisin spun to face him; in an instant all held blades, two already slashing at him. He ducked, shifted, blocked one, the other, and felt the tip of his blade caught for an instant as the other's blade squealed on his, sliding toward him. *Disengage and refuse!* He remembered the armsmaster's words barely in time; the iynisin's blade missed him by a finger's breadth.

He yelled, "Gird and Camwyn, Falk and the High Lord!" hoping that someone would wake, break whatever enchantment, and come to aid him. He could not face five alone—but Beclan had, he remembered. Beclan had called on Gird—and indeed, in that instant, as one of the iynisin blades screeched on his mail shirt, his own pierced one of the shadows and he felt the familiar resistance of muscle. The creature hissed, spat, and spun away. That left four, and one . . . yes . . . was edging around to get behind him.

Camwyn retreated toward the door—he could back into a corner there—and continued to fend off his attackers. He heard a yell from the distance—far down the corridor by the sound. Footsteps, running. Help? And for whom? Another near miss—and then a spike of pain in his knee. He'd never seen the blade that stabbed him; he tried to limp back another step—and another blow took him in the side, throwing him off balance. He missed a parry; the thrust at his chest was hard enough to force him back. His injured knee gave way, and he fell, rolling to avoid two more thrusts.

He caught one of the iynisin in the body when it leaned over him to finish him; another in the thigh; another in the calf. But they were too many, and he was only one; he took wound after wound to his legs, though the mail protected his body. Finally he saw—too late to dodge it—the foot aimed at his head.

Aris Marrakai woke in the pages' quarters as if someone had stabbed him with a hot needle—all in one instant, he was out of bed, standing, heart pounding. The room was almost dark, the single tiny lamp burning in its niche, just enough to help the younger boys find their way to the jacks. The flame was steady—it had not been any gust of wind. As a senior now, on duty with the younger boys, he usually slept clothed and needed only to put on the low boots he wore in the palace. He did that and hesitated before pulling a short blade from the rack and hooking it to his belt.

Outside, all was still. He knew something had wakened him— what? Then he heard a faint cry . . . from . . . where? He went toward the sound and came to the guard station where corridors crossed. The guards said nothing. He cleared his throat. Still nothing. He risked touching one on the shoulder. No reaction.

It was a dream. It had to be a dream. He pinched himself hard, and that hurt. Another faint sound that brought his heart into his throat—the screech of metal on mail.

He was moving before he thought, running toward the stairs; he was sure the sound had come from above. He passed guards who did not move or speak; he yelled "GIRD!" "HELP!" No one answered. Up the stairs, grunting a cry at each step in the hope that someone would wake. Was it Camwyn the attackers had come for? No, surely the king. And some enchantment held all in thrall. He made it to the floor with the royal apartments—Camwyn that way, the king the other—and now he could tell the yells, the clash of arms, came from higher yet, up where the treasury was.

And here, nearby, was the bell pull that went, he'd been told, to no bell but summoned—if anyone—immortal aid. Unused for centuries, collector of legends no one could prove. But it was all he could think of, and he pulled it hard, then charged up the last flight of steps.

Outside, over his head, a great clangor rang out, bells upon bells, louder than he'd ever heard bells while inside the palace. A waterfall of sound it felt like, shimmering and dancing around him as he went up. He reached the top, and sight of the treasury door, where two guards changed from rigid immobility to startled alertness. Dark shadows rushed from the treasury; one guard fell before he could draw a weapon, throat slashed by one of the shadows. The other tried to stab another shadow, but it evaded him. For a moment, the dark figures loomed over Aris, staring at him; his tongue blocked his mouth; he could not make a sound.

Then, with a single word in a voice cold as Midwinter night, they turned and ran the other way, the bells' clangor following them like hounds.

Now, as the bell sound followed the intruders, Aris could hear noise from below. Booted feet running, voices shouting questions. Help, if they thought to come here. He worked his tongue in his mouth, tried to swallow, and yelled down the stairs: "Up here! The treasury!!"

Flickering light approached the foot of the stairs.

"Here!" he yelled again.

"Gird's blood—it's the prince!" the remaining guard called from inside the room. "Get help, lad! Quickly!"

"The prince is hurt!" Aris called down the stairs; torches lit hel-mets and drawn swords, the soldiers blurry below the light, and he waved, then turned and ran into the treasury.

Camwyn lay sprawled in a welter of blood. In the light of the torch the guard held, his face was pale as beeswax, his blood shock-ingly red. Like horse blood, Aris thought for a moment. Camwyn's helmet had a deep dent in one side that connected with a purpling bruise on the side of his face. Aris took out his dagger and slashed at his own sleeve.

"What happened?" the first guard asked. "Did you—" He looked again at Aris and shook his head.

"Shadows," Aris said. "I saw them—five in dark cloaks. They made a spell." He had a length of sleeve off now and tried to stanch the wound in Camwyn's thigh; blood soaked through almost at once. "Bandages," he said, ripping at his other sleeve one-handed. "Quick!"

"Yes . . ." One of the guards hurried out, calling for a Marshal, bandages, more help.

Others pushed into the room; more noise outside . . . the bells had quit, Aris realized. He used his teeth to rip loose part of his heart-hand sleeve, balled it up in his sword-hand, and pushed it down on top of the red sodden lump of the first.

"Let me through!" That was Master Plostanyi, one of the palace physicians; Aris knew his voice. "Have none of you any sense? Why are you standing around doing nothing, and only this lad trying to keep the prince alive?" He knelt beside Aris, unrolling his case with-out regard to the blood on the floor. "Lean on that," he said to Aris. To the guards he said, "Get me sheets; rip them in strips. Now!" That last at a bellow.

"I was too late," Aris said. Tears filled his eyes and dripped onto his arm; he couldn't help it.

"You may have saved him," Plostanyi said. "Were you the one pulled the bell cord?"

"Y-yes."

"Thank Gird for your good sense." Plostanyi's hands were busy, feeling for Camwyn's throat-pulse, ripping Camwyn's trews, exposing the wounds. He pulled wads of washed fleece from his kit, stuffed one into a bleeding wound, and pointed to one of the circle of guards. "You! Push down on this, here!"

In the corridor outside, Aris heard his brother's voice and then the king's. "I don't care!" the king said. "Let me through!"

"Not yet, sir king," Plostanyi said without pausing in his work. "This may be iynisin work; I see the telltale sparkle in the blood. Their blood's poison to us."

Aris had not noticed it, but now, in the greater light of many torches, he could see something odd about some of the blood on the floor. "It's not all Camwyn's?" he said.

"No. Too much of it is, but not all. He wounded at least one of them. You'll need care yourself when this is over." Plostanyi handed him another wad of cloth.

"Will he live? Tell me he will live!" That was the king's voice from just outside the door.

"If the gods will," Plostanyi said. And then muttered under his breath, "If I can stop the bleeding, if the iynisin poison has not gone too far, if his brain is not reft . . . The gods have their work cut out for them this night."

Aris struggled with an urge to giggle or scream.

"Steady, young Marrakai," Plostanyi said, as if he knew that. "You've done well so far, but your work is not over."

Aris clenched his teeth and through the next turns of the glass did whatever Plostanyi told him, trying not to think about any of it—Camwyn, kuaknomi, the contamination of their blood, the cramp in his back from crouching over Camwyn, the king's mounting anger until at last he was allowed in to see Camwyn, and the king's grief when he saw the prince looking as near to dead, Aris thought, as a live person could look.

"He yet breathes," Plostanyi said to the king. "That is all we know now." Plostanyi directed the guards, who shifted Camwyn onto a litter and carried him out. He made them hand off the litter to four more who had not entered the treasury and had no blood on their boots, pulled off his own boots, and padded sock-footed ahead. The king pulled off the cloths wrapped over his own boots; a physician checked to be sure he had no blood on him, and then he followed the procession with Camwyn.

Aris started to follow, but one of the other physicians stopped him. "No—you're bloody all over, the prince's and the kuaknomi's. No farther than the door for you. Strip and bathe." In the time he'd been with Camwyn, a tub and buckets of water had been carried to the corridor outside.

Aris stripped to the skin, surprised to find out how much blood had soaked through his clothes. One physician hovered by him, pointing out or scrubbing off spots he hadn't noticed and looking for any injury that might need treatment. Only when he was pronounced clean enough did a palace servant hand him a length of cloth to dry himself on and another hand him a robe far too long for him.

He heard steps coming up the stairs and turned to see his brother Juris. "They're cleaning all the blood off the prince," he said. "The king asked me to check on you, Aris. Are you all right?"

"He's fine," said the nearest physician—now supervising one of the guards who had helped Plostanyi. "No cuts, no wounds of any kind."

"Let's get you some clothes, then," Juris said. "Back in the pages' quarters?"

Aris nodded. "How is he?"

"Still breathing, Master Plostanyi says. He's worried about the wounds—if they're poisoned—and the effect of iynisin blood in the wounds as well. And that knock to the head. Did you see any of the fight?"

"No . . . I heard something . . ." Aris stumbled on the robe, going down the stairs, and Juris caught him.

"Kilt that up before you take a tumble," he said. "Or—I know—Camwyn's rooms are only one flight down—do you still keep your roof-climbing clothes there?"

"Y-yes." He did not want to go into Camwyn's room and rummage for clothes with Camwyn near death. But Juris led him there, and once he was in his old knee-patched climbing trews and his soft faded shirt, he felt better. "What about the shadows—the kuaknomi? Iynisin?"

"The king sent guards after them, searching—the bell sound followed them, I think. I don't know—he sent me to you. But Aris, how did you know? Everyone else was caught by their glamour."

"I don't know . . . Gird maybe?" Aris shivered, and Juris put an arm around him. "I was asleep and then I was awake, and I went to see what had waked me . . . and the palace guards were all just standing there. Then I heard a cry."

"And the prince is lucky you did. We're all lucky. You, that they didn't kill you—did you even have a weapon?"

"One of the uniform blades pages carry, my dagger—"

"Gird's blood, Aris, you'd have been killed if they'd attacked you—"

"Yes . . . I kept thinking someone would wake up."

"The Bells must have recognized iynisin," Juris said as they walked down the passage together. "I wonder why not sooner. Maybe when Camwyn wounded one and the blood spilled . . ."

"Ummm . . . I think it was the bell pull."

Juris stopped short and grabbed Aris by the arm. "The bell pull? *What* bell pull?"

"That old one in the passage between the king's rooms and the prince's. The one everybody knows doesn't work . . . the one with the stories about it . . . but it was all I could think of."

"You . . ." Juris shook his head. "I would never have thought of that. Never. When I was a page, I yanked it once, just to see, and nothing happened. Didn't you, your first year?"

"Yes. And it was like yanking a rope tied to a rock. I thought it was tied off somewhere up in the ceiling. But no one was answering me, and I heard Camwyn up there, yelling, and blades . . . I had to do *something*."

"You woke the Bells in the tower, and how that happened I do not know. Some elven magery, I suppose."

They met a palace servant hurrying toward them. "The king wants you," he said. "Down in the scullery."

The first words Aris heard the king say, to the captain of the palace guard, were "Where are the other iynisin, then?"

"They fled somewhere—the bell sound followed them, but the palace guard did not pursue past the gates."

The king, clearly furious, opened his mouth then shut it again, shook his head, and said, "And your task, as you understood it, was to protect me and the prince."

"Yes, sir king. I'm sorry, sir king . . ."

"You did what you thought was your duty. No one can ask more." He caught sight of Aris. "And you, Aris Marrakai—if he lives, it is you who saved him. You alone broke the spell laid on all the rest of us. Do you know how?"

"No, sir king." Aris's throat had closed again, seeing Camwyn lying so pale, so still, blood seeping through the many bandages. The dented helmet still covered his head; the physicians argued over how best to remove it without causing more harm. "But . . . we're friends."

"So you are. And it was you who pulled the rope, I understand, and woke the Bells of Vérella. How did you know to do that?"

"It was all I could think of, sir king. I could not wake the guards. I didn't know it would wake the Bells, only that someone had said they'd heard it could bring the gods' help."

"And so it did. Aris, you have my thanks for this, and another day I will thank you properly. Stay watchful; those who did this may hold a grudge against you for it."

"Yes, sir king." He wanted to ask Mikeli if Camwyn would live, but he knew he should not.

"King of Tsaia, a word." The speaker, a dark figure by the door, took everyone by surprise. Several drew blades; Mikeli whirled, scowling.

"I am no iynisin," the figure said. Aris stared at him, the dark leather clothing faintly patterned like scales, the dark-skinned face and startling golden eyes like flames. "And you, King, have met me before, when I was sent by Lord Arcolin in company with his sergeant, Stammel."

"Put up your blades," Mikeli said. "I do indeed remember Sir Camwyn."

"Your brother the prince fares ill," the man said.

"He does. He was attacked."

"We must talk, King. Step aside with me."

The king's guards protested, but the king and the strange man went into the kitchen, the king gesturing for the servants there to leave.

❧

"Why are you here?" Mikeli asked the man who was not a man.

"I came too late for another; I may have come too late for my namesake."

"Your . . . name really is Camwyn?"

"No. I am Dragon; that is all the name I need. But your brother—he has a touch of dragonfire, and he loves me. I felt that before. So I came at once."

"The physicians will not tell me . . . I know by their looks . . . and already a High Marshal has prayed for Gird's healing and it has not come. I laid my hands on him—some kings in the past could heal, it is said. Kieri of Lyonya healed the king of Pargun. But when I tried, nothing happened." Mikeli fought back the tears rising in his eyes. "What kind of king am I, if I cannot heal my own brother? Was it to murder him that I prayed I might have no magery, in order to keep the throne?"

"You love your brother," the dragon said.

"Of course I love my brother," Mikeli said. "And he . . . he may die. They think he will die. And that if he does not die, his mind . . . it is like the kick of a horse that splits a skull, they said. A few live, but not as themselves . . . a broken life."

"Do you love your brother enough to lose him?" The dark man kept his eyes fixed on Mikeli's.

"To . . . to let him die, you mean?"

"Would it not be better than living as a mindless body?"

"No . . . yes . . . but is his mind then destroyed?"

"Perhaps not. But *here* it cannot heal. There is a place . . . You surely know, King, that there are places of power as well as powers embodied."

Mikeli wept. "If there is a place of healing for him, then . . . then yes, I will take him there, leave him there, if that is what it takes." He struggled to keep speaking. "But . . . but our physicians say he will surely die if he is moved."

"If you moved him, the way you travel, he would die. He will not die if I take him."

Mikeli stared. "You? You would take him? In your . . . in your *mouth*?"

"Where all who fly with me must ride, yes. Half-Song, Lyonya's queen, has ridden so, and the Blind Archer has ridden so. Your brother for a short time, as you know."

"And . . . you can heal him?" The thought of Camwyn alive, Camwyn beside him again, almost stopped his breath.

"I am certain he can be healed. But I tell you this truth: he may not be as he was—as you know him. Alive, well, in a good place, and yet changed."

Mikeli struggled with his grief for himself at losing his brother and his joy if Camwyn could live. "I love him," he said, hating the shakiness of his voice. "The last thing both my father and my mother said to me was 'Take care of your brother, Miki . . . he needs you.' If he must leave, to live, then . . . then I must let him go . . . but not to *know* . . ."

The man's impossible tongue came out, shimmering with heat, and touched Mikeli's forehead, a touch no warmer than his father's hand had been and as comforting. "You will know how he fares in healing, for I will tell you. I promise that, though I cannot promise his return." He looked aside at Camwyn for a moment. "It would be best if I took him now, sir king. He is sinking."

Mikeli noticed, even in his grief, that the dragon had addressed him formally for the first time. He went back into the scullery and waved the others away, ignoring their protests. They would think he had given up, that he knew Camwyn was dying and wanted to mourn, and that much was true.

He sat down again on the stool by the table on which Camwyn had been laid and touched Camwyn's forehead. "Brother, heart-kin more than blood-kin, if you can hear me at all, know I love you and always will. You wanted to fly with the dragon; the dragon offers a chance at healing for you, and so I send you in the best and only care

I can find. If I never see you again, I pray you know in your heart your brother loved you and for nothing less than saving your life would have sent you away." He looked at the dragon. "Can you take him here, or shall I carry him to the courtyard for you to change?"

"I must change," the man said. "For the shape of this body will not encompass him as he is now. But I can carry him more safely than you; for what lesser magery this body can do will keep him safer."

Together they walked through the palace, the dragon man cradling Camwyn like a small child. Camwyn never stirred. In the courtyard, the man handed Camwyn to Mikeli. Once again Mikeli saw the transformation of a man's shape to a dragon's. When the last scales rattled a little on the pavement, the mouth opened, and the long red tongue slid out, hissing a little on the dew that slicked the stones.

"Lay him there," the dragon said in Mikeli's mind. "His head to the outer world."

Mikeli bent with difficulty and laid Camwyn on the tongue, then kissed his brow.

"Touch your tongue to mine again," the dragon said. "For this is a vow between us."

The dragon's tongue tasted, impossibly, of Camwyn's favorite food.

"So you know that I know him, and care for him," the dragon said.

Mikeli stood and backed away. The tongue, with Camwyn upon it, slid into the dragon's mouth. Mikeli saw no movement of the dragon's throat, nothing at all but that great yellow eye gazing steadily at him. Then the lid of that eye blinked over it once, and the dragon rose into the air, still with its tail coiled to avoid the wall of the court. When it rose above the palace, it stretched, opened wings so wide they shadowed the entire palace, and sped into the sky, vanishing into the blue.

Mikeli stood a long moment in the courtyard, then turned and bypassed the turn to the kitchen wing, instead climbing up the stairs and turning to Camwyn's room . . . the room his brother might never see again. He had thought he was over the worst, calm again after his decision, but the empty bed, covers still rumpled where Camwyn had been sleeping earlier, struck him to the heart with grief and guilt. He collapsed onto it, smothering his sobs in Camwyn's pillow.

"Sir king . . ."

He did not recognize the voice at first; he wiped his face on his sleeve and turned around. It was Rothlin, his cousin. A coolness had come between them after he'd forced Beclan's exclusion from the family, and a little more when he'd realized that Rothlin really was interested in the Kostandanyan princess and was afraid Mikeli would offer for her.

"Is he . . . did he die?" Rothlin asked.

"No. Not yet." Mikeli took a deep breath and let it out slowly. "He was failing so fast . . . we could all see it; you saw it. And the dragon came."

"Dragon? The same one who—"

"Yes. The dragon said Cam could find no healing here, but only in a magical place the dragon knew of. But that he might never return . . . I suppose that means his memory . . . he might have none."

"I'm sorry," Rothlin said. "Cousin . . . I am sorry for it all."

"And so am I, Roth. You love Beclan as I love Cam. *Damn* this stupid prejudice against magery! If we had magery, we might have saved Camwyn from the beginning, and more besides."

"You are making changes," Rothlin said. "There's been no mob violence here, as in Fintha."

"But too many deaths, and deaths from lack of magery as well." Mikeli reached out, and his cousin took his hand. In a moment they were hugging, pounding each other's back.

"We will survive this," Rothlin said. "You will, as king, and—in case no one has told you during this mess—you're being a good king."

"And so will you be," Mikeli said.

Rothlin looked shocked.

"I have no heir of the body; you just moved from third to second in line."

"But you will marry—"

"If I have time." Mikeli walked around the room, picked up Camwyn's dagger, wishing he'd thought to send some of Camwyn's favorite things, then realizing the dragon might not have agreed to take them. And if Cam had no memory, how could these things remind him of home? He put down the dagger, touched the stone in its hilt, and turned away. "What if the iynisin come again? What if they are able to take the regalia?"

"It's still there, isn't it?"

"Yes. For now. But it's a danger to us all, just being here and wanting—wanting to be somewhere else."

"How do you know that?"

"Duke Verrakai. It speaks to her—she told me it wants her, thinks it belongs to her. And she alone can open the chest now." He glanced at Rothlin, who had raised one arched brow. "Yes. And . . . it has begun speaking to me. In my head."

"Does that mean you're a mage, too?"

"No. Or Camwyn would be here, healed, and not wherever the dragon's taken him." Yet even as he said that, he felt something deep inside himself, something he could not define . . . but knew, with terrifying certainty, was his own magery. He turned to Roth. "We must send the regalia away with Duke Verrakai."

"It's not her fault—"

"I know. But it is the lure that brought the iynisin, the lure that drives the Duke of Immer's ambition. Better that it be somewhere else. Duke Verrakai believes it may be from Old Aare and wants to return there. I do not see any other course than to send her with it, since she alone can move the chest."

"Will she be a queen in Aare?"

Mikeli shook his head. "I have no idea . . . but she will be gone, and the regalia with her, and that may save us from invasion from the south or more of those—things—that attacked Camwyn."

"We will get through this, Mikeli," Rothlin said.

"We had better," Mikeli said. "Because, feeble as I often feel as a king, I can't think of another family that would do as well."

CHAPTER SIXTEEN

Dorrin Verrakai looked out the entrance of her home—and how strange to feel that it was indeed hers, and a home—down the grassy slope between the house and the river. The cattle had been up by the house overnight, leaving their mark, but now grazed a comfortable distance away. On the front steps, the children clustered around their tutor, who sat on the bottom step with a book in hand. Soon their shrill voices were chanting sums; Dorrin went back inside and then through the kitchen.

"Morning, my lord." Farin Cook glanced up with a smile, both hands deep in a bowl, mixing something that smelled delicious. "Your saddlebag's full. Fresh pastries cooling over there." She pointed with her elbow. "And this mince will make a nice meal for you this evening."

"Thank you," Dorrin said. "I'll have a pastry later; it's too soon after breakfast." She picked up her saddlebags—enough lunch for two, she was sure—and went on through the kitchen, down into the scullery, and then out into the stableyard. One of the grooms, Hath, was walking her horse around.

Once mounted, she rode out the gate and turned south. She took no escort for the first time in several years now they were sure they'd scoured all the old Verrakai from nearby vills. On this bright day, it was hard to believe how much evil had stained this land. The guilt that weighted her shoulders—the burden of her family's crimes—seemed less now as the land and the people recovered from it.

Where a small creek ran across the track to the river, once a mud-hole, now water ran through a wood conduit wide enough for wagon wheels. Another such culvert kept the track firm near the turn onto the old west trace that would someday—maybe even this year—be a road again, allowing trade to flow through from the Vérella–Valdaire road. She turned onto it, riding west, noting where wagon ruts bit deep to bring rock from a quarry she'd authorized.

By midday, she had found the working end of the road crew at the top of a ridge: two score men, four ox teams, one heavy horse team, and her kirgan, Beclan. They had been eating, she saw; they all rose as she rode up. By then she was hungry and ready for a rest.

"Not as far as I'd hoped, my lord," said Niart, an experienced road builder hired from Serrostin for this job. "Ran into some problems down the west slope. Want to see?"

"Yes," said Dorrin, "but I'll have a bite of lunch first." Beclan had come to hold her horse and untied the saddlebags, brought them to the rock she chose to sit on, then took her horse to the water barrel and scooped up a bucketful for it to drink. The workmen sat back down as she untied the thongs and opened it. Cheese rolls and meat rolls both and two of the pastries, only slightly squashed from their trip. The other saddlebag held a stone jug of water and another of berry juice. Dorrin looked around as she bit into a cheese roll. Across the hollow between this ridge and the next, the gap for the road was clearly visible, and the road itself climbed up the ridge without a turn.

"That one's not as steep," Niart said. "Different rock—rockfolk'd call it nedross, so it's weathered different, rounder. This one . . . we had to build turns into it. You'll see, if you've time."

Dorrin nodded. Beclan came and sat beside her; his blue shirt was sweat-stained and smudged, and his boots were mud at the bottom and dirt on top. He said nothing, but Dorrin held out a meat roll and he took it. Then he paused and looked at the workers.

Niart shook his head. "You're that age, lad—go on, eat up. We're not hurtin'."

Dorrin certainly hoped not, since she'd sent food to the site. After years with mercenaries, she knew how much hardworking men needed. Beclan finished both the meat roll and one of cheese before she finished hers. Dorrin finished her roll and stood up; Niart stood waiting for her. She patted the saddlebag. "Beclan, there's a couple of pastries, and I don't dare let Cook know they weren't eaten. Best take care of them for me."

Niart grinned at her and turned away; she followed him until she could see down the track coming up the ridge.

"Without them ox teams, we'd have been in a bad way," he said. "See the way those rocks stick out? Was trees all in there, roots dug in between rocks, under rocks. Not good ground for loggers or horse teams."

Dorrin looked at the jumble of logs at the base of the slope; Niart nodded at her when she glanced at him. "Rolled 'em down there— we'll need a bridge there. Little bit of a creek it looks like, but trash either side shows it gets up a lot, come hard rain. But what I really wanted you to see—that slowed us down most—is the turns. See, got to have room to turn teams and wagons, if you want traders, and the turns do best with flat places."

Niart's crew had carved out a turning space at each of the turns, cutting into the slope and piling rock on the outer edge.

"Will that hold in a rain?" Dorrin asked.

"Aye . . . well, maybe. Should. Old track ran straight, but was a gully down it deep as to here—" He gestured at his chest. "Naught but packhorses could use it, I'd think." He spat, politely to the side. "Ask me, I'd say it's been hundreds of winters since wagons made it through. Come you down here a bit."

Dorrin followed him a short distance down the new road, skin pricking a warning. She checked her blade; he'd been Serrostin's road builder for a decade, but still. He glanced back up the road and then said, "This was found, my lord. Lucky by me; the lads is honest for the price of a mug, but this—" He pulled out of his pocket something that gleamed . . . a gold chain with a mud-crusted lump attached that Niart brushed at with his callused thumb until a gleam of blue showed. "Your land, m'lord, so it's yours, whatever it is." He held it out.

She knew the instant the blue showed what it must be . . . but she didn't remember a place for this in the box. Were there more stones scattered about? In her hands it warmed a little.

"I thank you, Niart. It must have been dropped by someone on the road—"

"Long ago," he said. "And maybe hid, not dropped. Was under a rock we moved, right down there." He pointed. "I'd say it had been there a long time—rock had moss, lichens, fern, all the things you find on a rock's been just as you find it. I'm thinkin' some magelady, in Gird's War maybe, hidin' her jewels and never made it back."

"Could be," Dorrin said. She brushed away more of the dried mud; the stone gleamed in the noonday light, the same clear blue as the others, just the one stone, held in a plain gold oval hung from the gold chain. "Master Niart, you deserve a reward for this find—and any others—but I have nothing with me of enough value. But surely you will receive a personal bonus to the contract."

His face darkened. "M'lord, I'm an honest yeoman and a master of my craft. I don't ask—"

"You didn't ask, but I'm not going to ignore your skill and your caution, either," Dorrin said. "Shall I then add it to the contract as a whole, and you can do what you like with it?"

After a moment he nodded. "That's fair. Share with the crew; that's the best. And since I don't want 'em shirking the roadwork to go hunting baubles, I'd ask you to say nothin' about it. I'll keep an eye out, and if someone finds somethin', I'll see it gets to you."

"Thank you," Dorrin said. Movement caught her eye; she turned in time to see travelers on foot coming down the opposite hill toward the creek. "Early merchants?" she asked.

"Don't look like it," Niart said. "They's childer with 'em. My duke said you'd been asking about settlin' newcomers, fillin' out this land a little. Might be some."

Dorrin nodded, watching the travelers, who had now spotted her and straggled to a halt. She'd expected to get a list from the lords who might send her some of their excess families, not have people just walking in . . . but roads invited travelers. And here it was midday past, and those five—no, nine, counting the children—four adults, three older children, two younger—would never make it on foot to the next vill.

"Niart, I'm sorry, but you and your crew will have to let them camp with you tonight. I'll send another wagon of supplies as soon as

I get back to the house." She looked back up the road; two of the road workers had come nearer and now stared at the travelers. The workers looked enough like brigands in their rough work clothes to scare any families. The men, she noticed, now had their staves held in front of them, and the young children, in the care of the older, were being herded into the woods. She explained that to Niart, then headed back upslope, calling for Beclan to bring her horse. Only a ducal appearance would reassure them.

Once mounted, she bade Beclan put his kirgan's cloak over his dirty shirt and ride with her. Together they rode down the new road at a foot pace. By the time they reached the bottom of the slope, the adults and one older boy were in a tight cluster, all armed with staves, doing their best to look impregnable.

"Ho, travelers," Dorrin said. "I am Duke Verrakai, and this is my domain. You have come upon my road builders, who are just up there." She pointed behind and up the slope. "Who are you, and where from? This road is not finished yet, and you are a long way from the nearest steading."

The little group lowered their staves and glanced at one another. One of the men stepped forward. "We be from Duke Elorran's lands . . . we heared was land here and a new lord."

"I have had no word from Duke Elorran," Dorrin said.

"We has word," one of the women said. She pulled from her pocket a message tube, crumpled in the middle, and held it out.

"Kirgan," Dorrin said. "Bring me that message." To the group she said. "This is Kirgan Verrakai, my heir."

"My lord," Beclan said, dismounting. He put his horse's rein in her hand, then walked across the stones of the little creek. The woman took a step forward to meet him, and he took the message tube.

Elorran's man of business had written the message, saying they could well spare two families at once, good workers with nothing against them but the poverty of Elorran's land. "We can spare more if you have the room, but these two brothers and their wives are ambitious and eager to begin." He had listed the names, including the children.

"Which of you is Tamis?" Dorrin asked when she finished.

"Me, my lord," one of the men said. He was the shorter of the two, with sandy hair and blue eyes; by Elorran's account, the elder.

"And you must be Derstan," Dorrin said, nodding to the other man. "And your wives—"

The women announced themselves, Erdin and Medlin.

"Call your children," Dorrin said. "For I must see all of you."

Another doubtful look, then the boy went into the woods. Dorrin dismounted, and Beclan took the reins of both horses. "I sense nothing evil," she said softly to Beclan. "But if you do, call a warning."

"Yes, my lord. Do you really think—"

"It never hurts to be wary," Dorrin said. She walked forward, down to the creek bed where water gurgled softly among the stones the road builders had laid down. From back up the slope, she could now hear the ox teams lowing, the cart and wagon wheels squeaking, and Niart's voice yelling something blurred by distance. The little group had spread out, staves now held more like walking sticks, and the voices of children came through the trees. When they came out on the road, she saw that three of the children were girls, though dressed in boys' clothes, a sensible precaution while traveling.

Three went to one woman, two to the other. Dorrin waited while their mothers named them, then smiled at the group. "I have read your duke's letter, and he names you good workers who wanted a better chance. I have land to be worked—your duke or his steward may have told you that too many of the people here died, thanks to the previous duke. But did he also tell you that the king allows me and my kirgan to be mages? Will that frighten you?"

Tamis answered. "No, my lord. I mean, yes, my lord, we knew you's a magelord; everybody in t'kingdom knows that, I'd say. But if t'king says you're not evil, then—that's good enough. But—ye're not Girdish?"

"No," Dorrin said. She touched her ruby. "Falkian. But we do have Girdish granges here and hope to have more when we have enough people." Now there were smiles and nods from them, but the younger children looked tired and footsore. "There's no vill nearby," she said. "You'll camp with the road builders tonight—they're at the top of that hill there, and they know you're coming. Kirgan, let's give these littles a ride up the hill, shall we? Your mount's fresher, I think—will he carry three if you lead him?"

"Yes, my lord," Beclan said.

The adults led the children across the creek and helped Dorrin settle them on the horses. The oldest boy refused a ride, so each carried two, one child in the saddle and one behind, holding on tightly. Dorrin set off leading her mount, Tamis coming up alongside the horse in case one of the children grew unsteady.

"They never been on a horse before," he said.

Once they reached the road builders, Tamis and his brother volunteered to help the rest of the day, and the women said they'd cook supper that night for the whole crew.

"I must take Beclan back with me," Dorrin told Niart. "I will need him on the way back to let the nearest vill know someone is coming. They have five cottages empty; they can ready two of them."

"Very well, my lord," Niart said.

As she left, she saw Tamis driving an oxcart with an empty water barrel back down the hill to fetch water from the creek and Derstan cutting brush with two of the road builders halfway down the slope toward home.

"How many new folk will you accept?" Beclan asked when they were well away.

"We could use three times what we have now," Dorrin said. "But I don't want to bring in that many at once. For one thing, they'll multiply, and for another, those native here need to know they're valued, too. If we had time, it would be better to site the newcomers in new vills, but for this group—can't be done. They can't build homes, clear fields, plant, and harvest all starting this late in the year."

Beclan nodded. "I see that. My father said—I mean, Duke Mahieran said—that Duke Elorran was . . . was strange. Do you trust the letter?"

"Very straightforward and signed by his man of business and his steward both. I've never met Duke Elorran, but I heard he was unwell."

"Crazy, my mother—Lady Mahieran—said."

"Beclan, you need not use formal titles for your parents here, you know."

"Thank you, my lord, but . . . if I do not, it will be the old habit. Like a child's shoe on a man's foot."

"Wisdom indeed, Kirgan. You are right."

They picked up the pace where they could, and Dorrin left Beclan explaining to the first vill what they would need to do as she rode on to the house to arrange for more supplies. There she found a very grumpy royal courier stalking back and forth in the stableyard.

"Duke Verrakai! I have a summons from the king!"

"Just a moment," Dorrin said as a groom came forward to take her horse. To the groom, she said, "Squire Beclan will be coming in tonight, probably very late; be sure someone is ready to meet him."

"Yes, my lord," the groom said. She dismounted, ignoring the fuming courier as she untied the strings and lifted off her saddlebags, slinging them over her shoulder. The groom led the horse away; she turned to the courier. "You have a message?"

"It is of the utmost urgency; I was supposed to give it into your hands as soon as I arrived—"

"The king knows I am not always in the house," Dorrin said. She held out her hand. "The message?"

"It is in the house."

"You left a royal courier bag unguarded?" Dorrin aimed her haughtiest look at him and had the wicked satisfaction of seeing his own hauteur dissolve into panic. "I'm sure you won't want the king to hear about that." She stalked past him toward the scullery, then turned and headed for the front of the house. He scuttled along behind, spouting apologies and excuses. Dorrin ignored them.

The velvet bag lay—untouched she was sure—on the table in the front hall, and Grekkan, her steward, sat at another with account books open in front of him, busy but within sight of the courier bag.

"You didn't—" began the courier, but Dorrin held up her hand, and he stopped short.

Grekkan looked up and pushed back his chair, bowing slightly. "My lord."

"Squire Beclan may be in late tonight with information about our new tenants," Dorrin said.

"We have new tenants?"

"Duke Elorran sent them. Here is the letter from his man of business." He took the message tube. "Two related families, five children in all. Met them on the new road. They'll stay the night with the road crew, and Beclan's arranging housing in the nearest vill. As we discussed, they'll take the oath when they've been here a quarter and we see how they do. But I'm sure these will work out; the men were already at work with the road crew as I left, and the women were taking over the cooking. They're Girdish; we should send word to the Marshal nearest that vill."

"Yes, my lord. I'll add them to the rolls at once. Do you think there'll be more coming that way?"

"Almost certainly, and equally certainly, some will be problems. But we knew the risk when we chose to start the road at the other end. I'll change the militia patrols to give better coverage there."

"My lord—the king's message—" The courier now stood by the table with the bag.

"Whatever it is," Dorrin said, "I'm not riding more tonight." She picked up the bag. "Grekkan, find quarters for tonight for—" She looked at the courier, whose insignia did not indicate any family connection, just that he was a courier.

"Jostin Hamilson, my lord," he said almost meekly.

"Thank you," she said. "For Jostin, then, and see that he has whatever he needs. I'll be in my office with this—" She lifted the pouch. "We're expecting the headmen of Kindle, Rushmarsh, and New Quarry this evening, are we not?"

"They're here already, my lord. I suggested they walk in the garden."

"Very well. When you've arranged Jostin's situation, send them to me in the office, please, and bring your notation book."

"Yes, my lord."

Dorrin nodded to both of them and headed for her office; on the way she passed the kitchen, and Farin waved. "Supper late, my lord?"

"Yes—but a snack now. Pastry and sib, please."

In her office, she emptied the courier's pouch onto her desk, finding the expected scroll case tied with ribbons in the royal colors. By the time she'd picked apart the elaborate knot and settled into her chair, a kitchen maid had brought a pot of sib and two pastries.

The letter Mikeli had sent was startling—Prince Camwyn, attacked by what everyone had decided must be kuaknomi trying to steal the regalia, had nearly died, only to be whisked away by the same mysterious dragon as the only way of saving his life.

We most earnestly beseech you, whatever cost it may be, to come at once and remove these things from the treasury. That it is not your fault, the Crown knows, and yet you are the only one who can remove them. We can no longer risk their presence here. The dragon has said Camwyn may never return.

Dorrin shuddered, imagining the prince—scapegrace as he was—facing those kuaknomi and their poisoned blades. The king was right. She must take the regalia away—

Home. Go home.

She could bring it here. If done in secrecy, who would know? She considered how that might be done . . . It could not travel in the large chest she'd put it in when she gave it to the king. At that moment she remembered the jewel found earlier in the day and pulled it from the pocket of her doublet. It flashed in the lamplight. How many such, she wondered, were lost under a rock or in the soft remains of a rotted hollow tree? As she closed her hand around it, she felt a pulse of something like joy, but a knock on the door interrupted her.

"My lord—the villagers to see you."

Dorrin slipped the jewel into her pocket. She had begun the meetings with villagers before the end of her first year as duke. The former duke had never conferred with village councils, but after the first few meetings, the villagers had become used to the routine. The meeting did not last long, and when it was over, Dorrin began packing for her journey to Vérella, considering what to tell her heir, her squires, and her staff.

The king wanted her to take the regalia away . . . and the crown wanted her to go to Aare. She knew only one way to go—through Valdaire, down to the south coast of Aarenis—but that was madness in the face of Alured's army. She could not go west even had she known a way over the Dwarfmounts and west of the Westmounts, with Fintha in turmoil over magery. North—going to Arcolin's domain might make Vérella safer but got her no closer to Aare. East— she had never been deeper in Lyonya than Chaya, let alone to Prealíth. How long would it take to cross Lyonya and Prealíth? She would have to take ship from Prealíth—they had ports; she knew that. She would have to sail—and she had never been on a ship—all the way around the Eastbight, down the coast of Aarenis, and then—what? Alured held the Immer river ports. Pirates infested the whole Immerhoft Sea.

She tried to estimate the time it might take. Ships traded from the Immerhoft to the north, but she had paid no attention to their schedules the one time she'd been in the Immer ports. Did they make one voyage a year? Two? And did any of them go to Aare itself? All legends claimed it was barren, uninhabited. Could she just land there, set the regalia down, and walk away?

No. Find the home. Another vision rose in her mind: three white towers, all broken but still taller than the dunes of red sand, and a cliff above a vast chasm. Not a tree or bush or blade of grass showed in the vision, only wind-sculpted sand and the empty towers.

Dorrin paused in her packing to look around her bedroom with its bed, its chairs, the inlaid table, the sword rack and stand for her mail—mail she had not worn for a quarter-year now—the fireplace, the window open to the garden and orchard below. Here in this room was the most comfort she had ever had; here she had allowed herself to enjoy the beauty, even some of the luxury, she had inherited.

Would she ever come back? A lifetime spent traveling back and forth from Aarenis to northern Tsaia, from place to place in Aarenis . . . a count of days rose in her mind as she estimated the distance across Lyonya, across Prealíth . . . She had no idea how long a trip by sea would be, but surely the distance was longer than from Vérella to Valdaire. A quarter-year, perhaps, to reach the south coast of Aarenis. How long to sail across the Immerhoft? She had no idea. Hands of days, certainly. And then, once in Aare—without a guide, without a map—she must go some undetermined distance inland to find a place that matched the vision. If she could do that—without being robbed or killed on the way—then she must find her way back. Twice the time, if no ill befell her, but traveling alone—with a treasure—she could not expect to escape danger.

She would be gone at least a year. Perhaps more. Perhaps never—but she pushed the thought of death away.

She walked to the window, breathing in the cool night air. She did not want to go. She was through with adventure, with travel; this was her place; these were her people.

Mikeli was her king, to whom she had sworn her oath. If he told her to go, she must go. If he told her to go forever, give up her rank, her holdings . . . Would he? He wanted her to take the regalia away from Vérella. She could keep it here for a time—perhaps. But in the end—and she could not hide this from herself—she must take it where its destiny—and hers—lay. She turned away from the window, back to her packing.

Beclan arrived just as she finished; she went downstairs to meet him. Farin Cook had left dinner in the warming oven for him, and they sat at the kitchen table while he ate. "I'm leaving you here," she said after telling Beclan about the king's letter. "I'm not risking my heir's life on this journey, and besides, you're my legal representative."

He frowned. "I won't abuse the power."

"I know that. You've matured a lot, Beclan; I trust you for everything but the experience you cannot yet have. Should anything befall me, I know you will have the sense to make use of the experience of others."

"You really think it's dangerous? I mean—so soon after the attack on Prince Camwyn?"

"Yes. I don't know whether the kuaknomi are allied with Alured—hard to believe they'd bother—but they held the entire palace in a glamour except for the prince and Aris Marrakai. They want the regalia; Alured wants the regalia. And worst, I have no idea how to hide it again other than blood magery, which I will not use."

"Of course not," he said in a tone that revealed the very lack of experience she'd mentioned.

"I expect—and hope—to return here, though only briefly, using speed to foil enemies. But if something happens . . ."

"What about the new settlers? If more come, I mean. Where do you want them put?"

Dorrin stared; she had forgotten them and the strong possibility that more were already on the road, headed to Verrakai holdings. "Most important is that they have written permission from their lords to come here. If they're farmers, we want them in vills with more tillable land than they're using. Though if some are foresters, we'll settle them near useful forest land. Stoneworkers—doubt we'll get many, but if we do, New Quarry has room for more families. New settlers don't give oaths for a full quarter after they come; we want to know if they're the kind of tenants we want."

"What about Gwenno and Daryan? What if something delays you and you can't make it back?"

"Send word to their families and suggest an escort be sent for them. Their contracts cannot transfer to you. I will confer with the dukes when I reach Vérella; they may prefer to terminate those contracts at once."

Beclan looked stricken.

"I know," Dorrin said, softening her tone. "It will be a hardship on you if—when—they must go. You will have no companion your age here. But you will soon be of age to begin your knight's training, anyway. Grekkan can manage for a time; that's what stewards do." And a guardian—how could that be arranged if she had to leave the kingdom? She left that for the moment and went back to the other squires' situations. "They should not travel alone, and you should not disperse Verrakai armsmen. I suppose I must write something—" She was tired; her head hurt from trying to think of everything at once, but Beclan was right. At the end of squires' terms, their families were due a formal report, including, if warranted, a recommendation that the squire was now ready for knight's training.

"My lord—*must* you leave tomorrow? It's late; you were riding most of today . . ."

"I should; the king said it was urgent——" But was that true? Her duty to the king required all possible haste, but her duty to her own land and people also mattered. She must write to the squires' fathers—including, in the peculiar situation still existing, Beclan's father. She must write to the training halls for the knights, as well. She could not write that many messages tonight and then ride at dawn for Vérella; she was simply too tired.

"You're right, Beclan," she said finally. "Given the danger—though I believe I can escape it—I must make better preparation here. I will need you here tomorrow, though I may send you out to the nearer vills. In the morning I'll send word to Gwenno and Daryan; they may be close enough to arrive before I leave. Tonight I'll write the king and let his courier take that." She headed back to the office with him. "I was very pleased to see how well you're getting along with the road workers, Beclan. And the way you were able to present yourself as kirgan so quickly today."

"Thank you, my lord." He yawned. "I could copy messages for you if that would be helpful."

"Bring the rest of your supper into the office and keep me company while I write to the king," Dorrin said. "And bring sib and an extra pastry if you see one."

"Yes, my lord," Beclan said.

She had just rubbed the inkstick in water when he arrived with a tray of food, dishes, and a pot of sib. It smelled so good Dorrin's stomach rumbled. She unwrapped the writing paper and pulled a sheet from the top of the stack, covering the rest and retying the ribbon, then dipped her quill in the ink and began her letter to the king.

"My lord." Beclan set a mug of sib and a plate on the desk.

"Thank you." She glanced up and realized he'd piled the plate with slices of roast lamb, redroots, steamed barley.

"Cook left a plate for you, too, my lord. And you did not eat when I did."

Dorrin grinned. "Thank you, Beclan. I forgot supper in my haste to pack and then tell you what the situation was. I'll eat when I've finished this." A short letter was all Mikeli needed; she finished it, blotted it, and set it safely aside before eating. She was aware of the silence in the old house—not ominous, just . . . still. Children asleep upstairs; servants gone to their beds. The chink of knife on plate seemed loud.

When they'd finished, Beclan took the tray back to the kitchen. Dorrin let her hand take light and went to the front of the house, opening the heavy front door to the night air. A breeze brought the scents of a spring night leaning to summer—and the moo of a startled cow grazing near the steps. Several loud plops—more than one cow, then—and hooves thudded away. Dorrin laughed. It was a clear night, the stars softened by moist air but spangled across the sky. Cows grazing quietly were proof nothing was outside but the night itself.

She stood in the cool air, listening to Beclan walking back to the stairs, up them to his own room. She had been so determined to get away from this place as a girl; she had never expected to become fond of it, let alone so quickly. Again she felt a pang at the thought of leaving, going somewhere strange.

Come, Queen, and claim your crown before it is too late.

And there was the challenge. A crown she must now wear, sworn as she was to Mikeli as his vassal. And why too late? Too late for what?

The vision assailed her even as she stood there: waves of sand rolling across the fields and forests she knew, scorching heat, the great river drying in the sun until all lay barren.

CHAPTER SEVENTEEN

ext morning before dawn, she handed the courier the message bag. "The king will understand," she said. "I will make all haste, but must ensure the security of the border."

Much less arrogant than he had been the night before, he bowed and said, "Yes, my lord. Of course." He rode off at first light, and Dorrin started in on what promised to be a very busy day.

Grekkan was not surprised when she told him she must leave and for an indefinite period.

"War, my lord?"

"I don't know," Dorrin said. "If it were an invasion, I'm certain he would have said so, telling me to bring what troops I could, but it's some matter of great importance. I will learn more when I reach Vérella." Not exactly a lie, as Alured's known desire for the regalia posed a military threat. "I'm leaving Beclan here; I hope he will rely on your advice, but he is staying as my kirgan."

Grekkan's brows went up. "My lord—"

"He's underage, I know. But should the king's command lead me into a prolonged absence or . . . or danger, then he *is* my heir, and the circumstances have not permitted me to name guardians. I intend to do that in Vérella. I am taking Gwenno Marrakai with me but leaving Daryan Serrostin as companion to Beclan; I will speak to both their families about canceling their contracts if, again, the king's commands require a long absence. Beclan won't hold their contracts no matter what happens to me."

"Yes, my lord. Do you . . . do you foresee any difficulty should there be a . . . ummm . . . gap?"

"I think Beclan has more sense now than to push his authority, if that's what you're asking. They should not be sent on the road alone, is my concern."

She left Grekkan with a list of things to be done and not done. Messengers had already gone out to find Gwenno and Daryan, who should be on their way back from patrol. Farin had the kitchen staff at work preparing food for the journey.

Around midday, Gwenno and her patrol rode in; they had scarcely dismounted when Daryan's arrived. Dorrin looked out on the stable-yard full of horses and watched the two squires properly organize their patrols for dismissal. They had both come a long way. Gwenno was certainly ready to enter the Bells if her family could persuade the Bells to admit a female member—and they might even send her to Fin Panir. Daryan needed another year as a squire.

They appeared at her office door shortly. "My lord duke, what service?"

"I have been summoned to Vérella by the king," Dorrin said. "From the tenor of his message, I may be absent for some time—longer than you should be left here without my presence. If the king needs his Constable's presence in Vérella, you might stay with me there and continue as squires, but with the threat of war from Aarenis, his need may be other. It might be something dangerous enough that neither I nor your families would choose to risk you with me. I will not know the extent of the duties he requires until I am there—"

"We could stay here," Daryan said. "Beclan's not so bad."

Yes, Daryan was still too young for the Bells. Dorrin shook her head. "If I must be gone for a long time, you cannot. Your family's contract is with me, not with my heir. I do not deny you would be helpful about the estate, as you have been, but that makes no matter."

Gwenno opened her mouth and shut it again; Dorrin nodded at her. "You may speak, Gwenno."

"I just thought . . . if you might be kept in Vérella, should we go with you? Or would you rather we stayed here until you sent word?"

"I was coming to that," Dorrin said. "The situation is slightly different for each of you. Beclan and you, Gwenno, are now old enough to begin training as knights, even though your squire terms are not over. Ideally, you would continue as squires another year, but you have both had more responsibility than many squires outside of active military units. It's my understanding that novices are inducted into the Bells around Midsummer. If you, Gwenno, were to come to Vérella with me, your family might be able to arrange your entrance."

Gwenno grinned, then sobered, with a glance at Daryan, who looked stricken. "Daryan?"

Dorrin looked at him. "You're still too young, Daryan. You have made remarkable progress, as I will tell your family, but you are still shooting up in height, and that—as I'm sure our armsmaster has told you—means you should wait at least a year before entering the Bells. In addition, your second thumb is budding; you should not be in heavy training until it is full-grown and you can use it as easily as the other. If I am able to return quickly, I will be glad to continue training you as squire and then present you to the Bells myself." She paused; he said nothing. She went on. "There is another possibility. Duke Arcolin, I hear from him, has a squire with the recruits in the north, a lad about your age. Duke Arcolin has married, and his lady and his adopted son, a boy scarce learning his letters, are staying north while he's campaigning. I know of my own experience how useful another squire might be up there."

The two of them looked at her, now both wide-eyed. "Or you may stay here and await the news."

"What about Beclan? Are you sending him away?"

"Not yet. All will depend on what the king tells me when I get to Vérella. Now: this is my decision to make, but I want to hear *your* reasons for coming with me or staying here. Gwenno, you first."

"For staying: I would be a help here. Continuing the patrols as usual would give me more experience, and there's still much to learn. I could also be a support to Daryan and Beclan, and as the only girl, I could continue to show the little girls that a girl can be strong without being mean." She paused. Dorrin nodded, and she went on. "But if I went with you, then if you had to end my contract with you, I would be near my family. I hope they would send me to the Bells or perhaps to Fin Panir if the Bells will not take a girl."

"Have they ever?" Dorrin asked.

"Yes, my lord, but not every year, and not very many. Not very many apply, I think. At any rate, if I were in Vérella already, my family would not worry that I might travel alone from Verrakai Steading."

"Daryan?"

"Yes, my lord. I think much the same as Gwenno about staying here. I am learning so much in all those things you told us to study and master. So I can be useful here, and I feel—I feel more at home with Beclan and Gwenno than with my own brothers and sisters. I like the country more than the city—though I never did spend much time there, except at the quarter-courts. I'm not—I would trust Beclan, my lord, to be fair, if he were in charge."

"I'm glad of that," Dorrin said. "I, too, feel that he is much more mature and reliable now. But the fact is that he's not a knight or a lord himself yet, and he's underage to hold your oaths in contract. So— your thoughts about coming with me?"

"It would please my father," Daryan said. "He might find me another squire's place, if that's necessary, but—my lord, I want to be *your* squire."

Kieri had had squires who needed a firm nudge to go when their time was up, caught in their admiration for their commander. Dorrin glanced at Gwenno, who stirred as if to speak and then said nothing. "I think it best if Gwenno comes with me when I go. Daryan, you will stay here with Beclan. If it is necessary, your family will send an escort for you. I will speak to your father while I'm in Vérella and suggest Duke Arcolin as another place you might find squire experience."

The rest of the afternoon Dorrin spent writing letters—to the squires' parents, to King Kieri, to Arcolin, to her banker. She spoke to Natzlin about security; now that Natzlin was no longer riding out on patrols every few days, she seemed more energetic, though she still limped at the end of the day. At dinner, Gwenno reported herself ready to ride: packed, her horses and Dorrin's shod and fit for the journey.

Next morning, they rode out toward the new-made road: Dorrin, Gwenno, and a guard of six. No one, Dorrin thought, would expect her to go to Vérella this way. Clouds obscured sunrise, and it smelled like rain. They made good time to the road builders' camp; Dorrin stopped to congratulate the foreman and handed him a pouch. "I've been called to the king," she said. "I may be gone on the half-day—" The traditional payday for such workers, every quarter and half-quarter day. "—so I'm giving you this now."

"It's not done yet. Still rough. Won't get the permanent bridges in this year, most like."

"I know. But you've made good progress; I'm very pleased."

"Found another," he said in a low voice as his crew went back to work. "Two." He slipped a hand into a pocket and gave them to her. One blue, one clear. She put them away in her own pocket and nodded.

"My thanks."

"Gird go with you, my lord."

"And Gird strengthen your arm," she replied.

Beyond that, the road was amply wide enough for two abreast without clashing spurs. Rain began, first a drizzle, then a steady light rain. Soon they could hear water trickling down the slopes, and the horses' hooves sucked holes in the road that filled quickly. Where possible, they rode off the road's surface, but this end of the steading was thickly forested, and most of it on a slope.

They made what speed they could without straining the horses or the pack mules and camped on a terrace above one of the creeks that crossed the road. Here the road builders had used timber they'd cleared for the road to make one of the bridges the foreman insisted were not permanent. It wasn't very high above the water, but it was strong enough for one horse at a time to cross at a foot pace and saved fording the creek.

"It would be worse mud on the River Road," Dorrin said to Gwenno as the escort set up tents. "The courier's horse came in splashed above the knees and hocks, though it hadn't rained for days."

"Does the Duke—did the Duke set up tents each night on the way to Aarenis?" Gwenno asked.

"No. We camped in the open or used barns he'd paid to have reserved for our use. As he grew richer, he had some built—leased to the local vill for them to use except when we were heading south. But they were a good day's march apart, and if the weather was bad and the road hadn't been maintained, a cohort might not make it all the way. That could be miserable."

Gwenno looked at the rain, the soggy ground. Though she said nothing, it was easy to see what she was imagining.

"Yes. I have slept on wet ground. And so could you if you had to, but I prefer to have a tent. Someday I'll have way shelters built—or Beclan will."

"Do you really think you'll be gone so long?"

"I might be. Come, let's take another look at this bridge. I think it might be stronger than I thought at first." She led Gwenno to the middle of the bridge, stamped on it, leaned over the railing to look at the supports beneath. Speaking softly, she said, "The king's worried about the regalia; he wants it out of the palace, and I'm the only one who can move it. It's a danger wherever it is, because our enemies in Aarenis are not the only ones who want it."

"Take it to Fin Panir," Gwenno said. "They'll keep it safe."

"They didn't keep the necklace safe. And they won't want it and the trouble it might bring. They have problems enough already."

"Oh." Gwenno leaned over, elbows on the railing. "So . . . will you bring it back to Verrakai Steading?"

"At first. But I may have to leave Tsaia entirely." Dorrin leaned over, tapped the railing, then stood up again. "The regalia sings to me of a distant land. I think it wants to go there. I don't know if it's wise."

Gwenno said nothing and at Dorrin's nod turned and walked back to the camp. Dorrin followed.

Near the Vérella–Valdaire road, they met another family coming from Duke Elorran's domain. Dorrin sent them on after reading the letter of introduction from Elorran's steward. Once they turned onto the road to Vérella, traffic thickened. Gwenno had never seen this road before, and Dorrin explained all she remembered from years of traveling back and forth. They made good speed, though Dorrin was uneasily aware that a spy hiring fast horses could outstrip them.

In Vérella itself, Dorrin stopped at Verrakai House just as if it were an ordinary visit to the city. Her housewards knew which of the peers were in residence in the city and which had left for their country estates. Everyone, they said, had heard about the terrible attack on Prince Camwyn and seen the dragon fly down and then away, carrying Prince Camwyn to his only hope of recovery. No one would be surprised that she had come to offer advice to the king in such an emergency.

Dorrin sent a messenger to the king, telling him that she had one urgent errand, for the welfare of her squire Gwenno Marrakai, and would come to the palace as soon as she had been to Marrakai House.

Dorrin rode to the Marrakai residence with Gwenno beside her. Lady Marrakai welcomed her in, eyeing Gwenno with evident approval. "You want to speak with Selis, I'm sure. He should be back in a few days. He's gone to fetch a mare for Aris—the lad's in need of something after Camwyn. Well. What can I do for you and your squire?"

"I'm here at the king's command," Dorrin said. "What little I know of the matter I should not discuss until I have talked to the king, but I may be required to be absent from my domain—possibly from the realm—for a considerable time. Squire Gwenno's term is not yet up, but she is, in my opinion, advanced enough to qualify for knightly training, which she desires . . . and that is a matter for her parents to decide."

"The Bells?" Lady Marrakai said, looking at Gwenno. "Are you sure, Daughter?"

"I am," Gwenno said. "I have learned so much, and it is the life I would lead—"

"Never to marry or have children?"

Gwenno grinned. "I would not say 'never,' but not any time soon. Besides, knights may marry—most of them do. What if trouble comes to Tsaia—even an invasion? I want to defend it—"

Dorrin stirred; Lady Marrakai looked at her. "The king, during his visit, mentioned the possibility. I've told her—all of them—that war is nothing like a simple ride out with a patrol, but I commend her courage and sense of duty."

"Well, then. It will be for Selis—for the Duke—to decide finally, Gwenno. You know that."

"And I know you will have some weight in that decision," Gwenno said.

"Indeed. So you and I will talk. Duke Verrakai," Lady Marrakai said, her voice now formal, "will you grant your squire a few days' leave to spend with her family, or do you need her services?"

"I can spare her while I talk to the king," Dorrin said. "Indeed, I cannot stay and must to the palace quickly. I brought her with me in the hopes that the Duke and I might amend the contract and allow her to begin knightly training or . . . whatever you choose."

"Very well, then. I hope you will find time to dine with us while you are in Vérella. Tomorrow, perhaps?"

"I would be glad to," Dorrin said. "If the king does not command me elsewhere."

"I understand. Gwenno, you are travel-stained; let someone take your horse, and I'll have a bath prepared for you."

Dorrin rode away wishing she had time for a bath and a rest before seeing the king—the no doubt distraught king—but she knew he would be waiting impatiently.

At the palace, she was ushered up to his office immediately. "My lord Duke," he said. "How is your squire? Has she been injured?"

"No, she is well and with her mother," Dorrin said. "I brought her here, hoping her family would sponsor her for knighthood . . . I did not wish to leave her at my domain without a proper chaperone in case I had to be away long."

"Did you tell them what the problem was?"

"At my domain? No, sir king. There's been talk enough of possible invasion, as you know, and I used that and my position as Constable to explain your call. Beclan can remain, as my kirgan; I need to appoint guardians for him. I will suggest to Duke Serrostin that Daryan needs another year as squire, perhaps two, before he is ready for the Bells. It might be that Arcolin will want another squire to be with his wife while he is in Aarenis."

"That's sensible." He stood and paced back and forth. "I won't try to hide from you that I'm . . . I'm unsettled. A tyrant in Aarenis possibly planning invasion was bad enough, but the emergence of magery here, the unrest in Fintha, and then the kuaknomi—iynisin—whatever they really are—coming into the palace, laying a glamour on the guards—"

"Enough to unsettle anyone, sir king," Dorrin said. He looked to have lost weight; his face had little boyishness about it now, strained as it was, the bones prominent. "I know what I have been told about the attack here at the palace, but—would you tell me more?"

He nodded and began at once. "I was asleep—or under the kuaknomi spell, I know not which. The Bells woke me—thanks to Aris Marrakai, who had the wit to try the old bell pull we thought connected to nothing. We do not know who woke first, Camwyn or Aris, but apparently Camwyn confronted the kuaknomi in the treasury—fought them, killed one, and wounded at least one other—before being sore wounded and suffering an injury to his head—the skull fairly crushed in. Aris had been in the pages' dormitory, near the kitchens, and came near the treasury in time to hear the swords clashing and Cam crying out. He pulled the old rope—then the Bells rang out and I woke, along with everyone else. When I reached the treasury, Aris was trying to stanch Camwyn's wound with cloth torn from his own shirt. The kuaknomi had fled."

Dorrin tried to imagine the scene in the treasury . . . the prince in a welter of blood, the Marrakai boy—

"There was a legend," the king went on, frowning. "At great need the Bells could be summoned by that one bell pull. Aris thought the Bells frightened the kuaknomi away, but perhaps they simply realized their spell was broken."

"Do you think the kuaknomi could have taken the regalia?" Dorrin asked.

"They didn't," the king said. "I don't think the chest was moved at all, though it was damaged, as if by fire."

"If the iynisin had the entire palace—but for Camwyn and Aris—spelled into immobility, they had more magery than I have or anyone I've heard of but elves. You do know I fought one in Lyonya after King Kieri's wedding—?"

"I forgot about that." Mikeli rubbed his forehead.

"It was but one iynisin and its ephemes—apparent selves split from the first—"

"They can do that?" Mikeli's eyes widened.

"Yes. And those ephemes, as the elves call them, can fight individually. Kieri, two Kings' Squires, and the Lady and another elf—and then Queen Arian and I—all fought that one and managed to kill only several of the ephemes, not the original. One or two of the ephemes rejoined it before it vanished."

"So . . . what attacked here might have been only one?" The king's eyes showed white, and his breath quickened.

"I doubt it. Kieri said the iynisin did not separate into ephemes until hard-pressed, then used blood magery by killing one of Kieri's Siers to create them. To put the entire palace complex under a spell—surely that must have taken more than one. If they did not move the box the regalia is in or break it open, then—"

"It looks scorched," the king said. He shuddered. "You must take it away, out of the kingdom; it is too dangerous here."

Though she had considered this, Mikeli's vehemence surprised her. "Take it where?" Dorrin asked.

"I don't care," the king said. "It tells me it wants you; even Camwyn heard it. Maybe it will tell you what it wants with you. Have you any idea at all?"

Dorrin said, "Perhaps. I have had strange dreams, which I think may be of Aare."

"Aare?"

"Yes. And Ibbirun's attack on Aare. Of Ibbirun coming here, even drying up the river—"

"It has been drier this winter and spring," Mikeli said. "Another reason to take it away if that's what it's saying. Back to Aare will surely be far enough." He leaned forward. "Duke Verrakai, I am sorry to demand this of you, but I must. I pray you, believe that my distrust of you is all past and what I say comes from present threat to the realm, not only to me."

Dorrin started to say that the spring had not been dry on her own lands, but he was already talking. "You are my Constable, but Duke Arcolin can take on that role. You have been a good lord for your domain, but others can do that as well. You are the only one who can move the regalia, and in my judgment that threat must leave the realm forever. If there is a hope of forestalling such ruin as came there by returning it as it asks, I beg you to take it there."

Dorrin could not answer for a moment. Lifelong exile from here? From even Aarenis? Was it even possible to live in Aare? She nodded without speaking.

"You understand that whatever route you take, the journey will be long to Aare," he said. "If this were a time of peace and tranquility all around us, I might risk releasing you from attendance at court and trust in your timely return. But it is not, and—unfair though it be—I must have my realm in order."

Dorrin nodded again. "You want me to vacate my oath and rank and confirm my heir?"

"Yes. Should you return before his majority, I would be pleased to restore you to your rank and holdings—after that, I would want his consent as well, but you could be dowager duke, though I do not think anyone has ever held that position."

She knew return was unlikely. Despite having come and gone to Aarenis and war year after year—perhaps because of that—she was aware of the many hazards facing a lone traveler, and she could not justify risking a companion.

"Will you call Beclan here to renew his oath?"

"No; I will take his earlier oath as valid."

"Sir king, he gave that oath as Beclan Mahieran, not as Beclan Verrakai—you should ask the Marshal-Judicar if that is sufficient."

He looked startled. "I had not thought of that. But he is the same person—"

"In a different name and status. I am no judicar, sir king, but I would recommend having him renew that oath. You should also know I consider him ready for knight's training now and like to be a good lord for Verrakai holdings. He would prefer to train with the Bells if you permit."

The king nodded. "I think I must make that possible. What about your folk there on Verrakai lands?"

"I am sure they will pledge to Beclan. My steward is reliable, as well."

"Excellent. But how will you get to Aare with Vaskronin's force so powerful in Aarenis? Can you slip past in the west of Aarenis?"

"I would not dare to try that road," Dorrin said. "It would be impossible to conceal from him, if indeed he has the necklace and the necklace wants to reunite with the rest. And it may be better if you do not know what route I take. I do not know that the iynisin can snatch thoughts from human minds, but it is not a chance to take if it can be avoided. I have not yet decided on my route—and try not to think of it overmuch."

"I wish," the king began, then stopped and sat silent for a time. "I wish," he said again, "that I need not send you away. But wishes are not enough."

"I understand," Dorrin said. "I am glad to have served you here and will serve you best by leaving now. I need a few days here in Vérella to settle affairs with my squires' families."

"You may have some little time," the king said, "but my heart tells me it cannot be long."

"By your leave, I will take the regalia to Verrakai House today. That will at least remove the worst immediate danger from the palace and yourself."

He waved his hand. "Do so. Find a way to conceal it if you can. We can go into the treasury without an attendant; I persuaded the Seneschal that I needed access to the treasury."

In the treasury, Dorrin eyed the now-scorched chest with dismay. It looked a little smaller than it had been, but perhaps that was the effect of the charred surface.

When she put her hand on it, the crown spoke to her: *Take me.*

"I have come to take you home," Dorrin said aloud. The box trembled under her hand; the wood groaned, then splintered—a more violent opening than ever before. The king flinched and jumped back. Not only the surface had charred; the black penetrated to within a finger's thickness of the interior. The regalia, in the jeweled casket and various wrappings, floated into her hands.

Dorrin glanced toward the door; she hoped the guards had not heard. How was she supposed to get all this out of the treasury and the palace and through the public streets of the city unseen? She could stuff her pockets with the smaller pieces in the casket, but the crown and chalice were too big for that. As well, the jewels of the casket might be important.

Yes. Bring it.

And what about the half-burnt chest? It looked as if thieves had hacked at it, splinters sticking out of the opening. Someone would surely notice that.

The king raised his brows. "I should have thought of bringing a traveling container."

"If you want my taking it to be secret, we'll need more than my cloak to wrap it in. But if the point is to end the threat of thieves coming here to steal them, why make it a secret that I'm taking them?"

"I . . . thought only to make your departure with them less perilous for you. I was going to let it be known later that the jewels had been moved to someplace remote."

"Perhaps say for now that you asked me, as the only one who could, to remove the jewels from an insecure container, perhaps to find one more secure."

"I suppose."

"Or—what about a double switch? Think of something other than these I might take from here at your behest. Something your Constable would have reason to use. References relating to the Crown levies, for instance, or military engagements."

"The library," he said. "I know just the thing. Duke Elorran's reports from the time of the first to seventh dukes. The seventh was killed in the Girdish War. I've been looking at them because of their location."

"Good," Dorrin said. "We'll need a box or bag that can be left here, supposedly containing these . . . and then something to carry them—and those reports."

"I'll send for them both," the king said, and went to the door. Dorrin set the elements of the regalia down on the one table, unfolded her cloak, and set them on it. The crown rose a little; she pushed it down. "Patience," she said to it. "Not long—we leave this place soon."

Light poured from the crown for an instant. She folded her cloak over it.

The king came back to her. "I've sent for a box to rehouse the jewels," he said, making no effort to lower his voice. "And while we wait, I sent to the librarians for those documents I spoke of. I'm particularly interested in your opinion of the archery formerly practiced here."

Just then the a palace functionary—the Seneschal's assistant, she remembered—bustled in, holding a box, a small hammer, and a sack. "Sir king! You wanted a box? Is this the right size? And Duke Verrakai! You as well? Oh—the chest—! It's open!"

"Quietly," the king said. "What are you doing here, Porchal?"

"The Seneschal sent me. One of the guards came to him for a box, and the Seneschal sent me—" Porchal frowned. "I don't understand—why is Duke Verrakai hiding something under her cloak? How did she open the chest? Was she stealing them back?"

"No, she is not a thief," the king said, his voice edged. "I brought her here. I felt those things were not safe in a damaged chest and asked her to open it for me, since no one here could."

Porchal still scowled. "Well, but—what will you do with them? She can't take them away; they're Crown property now."

"What do you think I needed a box for?" the king asked. "She will repack them. Meanwhile, I had also sent to the library for some documents I wish the Duke to take with her this evening and examine at length. Go to the library and find out the delay. Oh—and the Duke will need something to carry the documents in to and from her residence. Bring some of the large courier bags."

Porchal's mouth hung open, then closed with a snap. "So . . . the box with the regalia will be kept here?"

"Yes, of course," the king said. "You are excused—I want those documents; the day wanes."

"Yes, sir king." Porchal bustled away, reminding Dorrin of a beetle.

"Now," the king said. He opened the box Porchal had brought; it had hinges and a hasp for its lid. Inside the box was a lock with its key inserted. In the sack were nails.

Quickly, he and Dorrin found another box—small and heavy—and put it in the one Porchal had brought. Dorrin nailed down the lid; the king snapped the lock into the hasp, and they carried it to a back corner, surrounded by boxes of exotic spices and woods. When Porchal returned with one of the librarians, both laden with documents and a courier bag, the regalia were tucked within a furl of rose brocade, and Dorrin's cloak, clearly not hiding anything, was spread flat on the table to protect the documents.

The king took one of the old books and opened it, turning a few pages until he found what he wanted. "Ah. Here. You'll want to compare with your records, but see the troop components in the third duke's time . . . That would be about a hundred years—maybe more—after the first duke was established."

Dorrin leaned over to look. Mikeli stepped back, then said to the librarian, "The duke will need to remove these from the palace tonight; she has other documents at Verrakai House. She will return them before leaving the city."

The librarian looked doubtful, but under the king's gaze she said nothing and finally bowed and backed away.

"Longbows," Dorrin said, aware of Porchal still standing there watching. "That's surprising." Instead of writing, she saw a row of sketched figures, all with drawn bows. She hadn't looked at other records that old except in Verrakai's own archives. "I wonder what they used for bowstaves."

"Exactly," Mikeli said. "Now here—in the next one—" He reached past her to close the volume she had just seen and opened another. Dorrin glanced over and saw that the librarian had already left the room. Porchal, however, was all too interested. She looked back at the book the king had opened. "This is a generation or two later. Crossbows, you see. That implies to me that Tsaia used to have a quantity of bow wood. Duke Arcolin told me the Aarenisians use only crossbows, so these would not have been made in the south and brought north. You're sure you have no blackwood trees in your domain?"

"I haven't seen every single tree," Dorrin said, "but I don't know of any. And on the trail through western Lyonya that I've ridden, I saw no blackwood trees near the border."

The king looked at Porchal. "Are you still here? We have no more need of you, Porchal. Return to the Seneschal and your other duties."

He turned back to Dorrin. "We need more archers," Mikeli said, "if an invasion comes. King Kieri has told me of the greater rate of fire of longbows. With that mess in Fintha——" He shook his head, making it easy for him to see Porchal, who was moving only slowly toward the door. "So I want you to compare your records and see if you can figure out what they used for longbow staves and if there's enough to fit out a longbow unit."

"Do you have forestry reports from other domains?"

"Yes. That's how I got this from Elorran. You're taking some of his excess farmers, aren't you?"

"Indeed. The first ones are already settled; I passed more on the way here."

"Good. And now I know you are road-weary, so I'll let you take these things and get some rest. You said you had business in Vérella as well, so shall we say day after tomorrow? I don't expect you to have answers by then, but we have other things to discuss." He grinned at her; Porchal had started down the stairs across the passage from the treasury.

"Certainly, sir king," Dorrin said. She retrieved the regalia from between the folds of brocade and slid them and the books into the leather bags. She put on her cloak and slung a courier bag from each shoulder. Mikeli led the way out and assigned one of his guard to escort her down to the palace entrance. "Carry that for you, m'lord?" the young man asked when the king had turned one way and they another.

"No, thank you," Dorrin said. "I've got them balanced now." At the palace entrance, Dorrin tied the bags to her saddle, mounted, and rode out into the street.

The cloudy day had darkened early; torches burned bright at the palace entrance and the gate to the street. Dorrin rode back to Verrakai House, but instead of going to the front door, where torches also burned, she turned down the dark, narrow lane to the stable gate. Once in the stableyard she could carry the bags into the house without being observed. Busy with her thoughts, she did not see the attackers until her horse flung up its head and snorted. One grabbed for the reins; the other tried to push her off the horse with a pole.

Dorrin leaned back, shoved the pole upright with one hand, and drew her sword. Her horse, battle-trained, crouched and jumped forward; she heard the crack of a breaking bone and a cry as it landed. The one with the pole tried again, but Dorrin ducked, thrust under the pole, and the attacker dropped the pole and fell. She heard footsteps coming into the lane behind her; she lifted the reins, clucked, and her horse reared, turned, and charged toward the street, knocking down the third attacker.

The noise had attracted a city watchman and two Royal Guardsmen riding back to their own stable from the palace. The watchman broke into a run, calling for aid; the Guardsmen reined their horses toward her. "Halt!" one of them cried. "Stop, thief!"

"I'm Verrakai!" Dorrin said. "Give aid!"

"My lord Duke! Pardon, my lord. What happened?"

"I was attacked in that lane," Dorrin said. "Three of them."

"Bring torches!" one of the Royal Guards called to the watch.

Dorrin rode to her own front door, where her housewards and escort now peered out to see what was happening. "Secure the stableyard," she said to her escort. "Who was on watch out there?"

"Meldall, my lord."

"Find him. He may be hurt. And one of you hold my horse here until the lane is clear." She dismounted.

"What happened, my lord?"

"Later." She had the courier bags in her arms now. "I must get these upstairs; when the watch or the Royal Guard ask for me, tell them I'll be down again shortly."

She paused on the upper landing of the stairs. Blood magery had been done in this house; despite having cleared out all the traps, all the signs of Liartian practice she knew about . . . could she have missed something? Would the regalia be safe?

Yes.

That was clear enough. She laid the bags on the worktable in what had been her uncle's study, pulled the books out, and left the bags in an untidy pile with the regalia still inside.

Downstairs, a Royal Guard officer awaited her. "My lord Duke, we need to inspect your stables—I know you have your own men there, but we found thief marks on the gate and signs of someone having been in the stable itself."

"The house door was locked, my lord, as you said it should always be," one of her escort said. "We heard nothing inside."

"Did you find the thieves?" Dorrin asked the Guard captain.

"Yes, my lord. One dead—your mount trampled him—and one near dead from a sword thrust and a third caught as he tried to run."

"My lord—" One of her people interrupted. "Meldall—we found him in the feed room—"

"Alive?"

"Yes, my lord. A big lump on his head, but he's breathing, and since we soused him with cold water he's waked."

At least none of her people had died. She clung to that through the turmoil of the Guard's search of the stable and yard, the questions from watch and Guard captains, the arrival of a messenger from the king wanting to know if she was safe, and the questions from her own people.

By the time she finally finished with the Guard captain, the city watch, her own escort . . . she was exhausted and hungry and very glad she'd left Gwenno at Marrakai House. She put the regalia in its bag under her bed that night and slept uneasily, waking every time a board creaked.

CHAPTER EIGHTEEN

Next day, Dorrin set about the legal formalities of transferring her property to her heir and releasing her two squires from the agreements that bound them. She was uneasily aware that doing so admitted more and more people to the very secret she and the king wanted to keep: that she was leaving the kingdom on a long journey.

Of course her man of business was supposed to be discreet, but how discreet was he, really? Some of the necessary documents required witnesses. Then there was her banker. And her housewards and the servants. And the witnesses to the events of the previous evening. All the palace staff, for that matter. Once it became known she was leaving the kingdom, anyone with sense would suspect she had come for the crown and other jewels and was taking them somewhere.

She sent a note to the Serrostin town house before going to meet with her man of business; a Serrostin servant came to her there with a note from the Duke. Dorrin looked at it and scribbled another, accepting an invitation to lunch with the Duke and his lady.

"How is my scamp of a son?" Duke Serrostin asked as she came in the door. He had long since given over his anger about Daryan's Kuakkgani healing.

"He's doing very well," Dorrin said, handing her cloak to a servant. The Serrostin house was only a short distance from the Marrakai town residence. "He's still growing."

Lady Serrostin appeared from a back passage. "Come all the way through, Duke Verrakai. We usually have lunch in the back garden in fine weather like this."

Once they were seated in the small back garden, Lady Serrostin said, "Galyan tells me you want to talk about Daryan's squire contract. Is something wrong?"

"The king has given me a task that requires me to be away from my domain for a considerable time," Dorrin said. "I will not be able to fulfill my part of the contract. Daryan has done nothing wrong—he has, in fact, done everything asked of him."

"So—you think he should come home?"

"I think he needs another year or two as a squire before he enters knightly training," Dorrin said. "Though he has matured greatly since he came to me, he is still the youngest of the three and has not reached his full growth."

"Do you think he can make knight, with . . . with everything?" Serrostin asked.

"In time, certainly. His sword-hand has strength now to manage a light blade and in time will be stronger. As I wrote, his left hand has grown a thumb, though it is still rather sticklike and not as strong as the other. He walks, rides, and dances with grace and no pain. He wants to continue his training."

"I don't know," Serrostin said. He looked at his wife.

"I had an idea," Dorrin said. "Duke Arcolin might agree to take a squire who could serve under his recruit captain in the north. Daryan's not old enough to go to Aarenis—"

"Certainly not!"

"He could learn skills with Arcolin—or Arcolin's recruit cohort— that will serve him well as both a knight-candidate and a lord."

"Duke Arcolin had a squire with him when his son was confirmed as his heir," Serrostin said.

"His son?"

"His wife's son, really. She was a widow, you know," Lady Serrostin said. "Duke Arcolin adopted him and brought him down to be formally named his kirgan."

"So he has a squire already," Serrostin said. "Will he want another?"

"His lady might find one useful up at the stronghold," Dorrin said. "You might ask. I will be glad to give Daryan a good name."

"I like the woman he married," Lady Serrostin said. "Calla, her name is. Very sensible, very sociable. I might write her." She glanced at her husband.

"I suppose the Marrakai girl will go home," Serrostin said. "They'll send an escort for her."

"I brought her with me when the king summoned me," Dorrin said. "She is with her mother now; she wants to enter the Bells."

"Is she ready?"

"I think so. It will be up to her parents, of course, to decide. If the Bells won't take her, she could go to Fin Panir."

"Well," Serrostin said, leaning back. "I'm glad to hear the problem wasn't of Daryan's making. I don't suppose you can tell us what the king's task is . . ."

"Forgive me," Dorrin said. "I don't have his permission."

"Something to do with the war in Aarenis, no doubt," Serrostin said. "I suppose you heard about the Kostandanyan soldiers marching through here on their way to Valdaire?"

"No . . . I had not. Why did they want to come, and why did Mikeli let them?" And why had he not told her, his Constable? But it no longer mattered. She would not be Constable or duke by the time she left Vérella.

"We have your friend Arcolin to thank for Mikeli letting them come, though his reasoning made sense to me." Serrostin repeated what he had been told. "And now, it seems, Rothlin Mahieran and not the king will marry that Kostandanyan princess."

"Ganlin? She's . . ." Dorrin searched for the right words. "Very attractive. I met her in Lyonya when I went to King Kieri's wedding there."

"So I hear, through Roly. He says Roth talks about little else these days." Serrostin leaned forward again, elbows on the table. "But what will you do about Beclan? He'll need a guardian unless you're coming back fairly quickly."

"The king advised me to find a guardian," Dorrin said.

"Hmm. The king's given up that absurd notion of keeping Beclan from his family, hasn't he?"

"Yes. Though he doesn't want him at court yet." She hoped the king would change his mind on that, too.

"Well, then, why not ask his father to be his guardian?"

"The king will wish to decide; I'm supposed to find several possibilities. I was thinking of you."

"No," Serrostin said without hesitation. "I am not stepping in that wasp nest between Beclan and Lady Mahieran. I would not be able to keep my temper."

"He should go for knight's training soon," Dorrin said. "He would rather the Bells, and the king has said he'll think about it. There's always Falk's Hall. I have already spoken to the Knight-Commander."

"In Lyonya, that would be," Serrostin said. "If he's with the Bells, he'll be expected to visit his home."

Lady Serrostin shifted in her seat. "Parlan, if he's not with his mother—"

"Is she still so . . ." Dorrin let that trail off; she had no polite words to describe Lady Mahieran, now confined to the Mahieran country house.

"According to Sonder, she's a very angry, bitter, and confused woman," Serrostin said. "He thinks she will never recover. The younger children are still living here in Vérella, in the Mahieran house. Sonder says he's afraid to let them be around his wife unless he is there."

Dorrin left shortly after, and spent the afternoon in the same kind of tedious business as the morning. She was glad when it was time to go to the Marrakai house for dinner. The Duke had indeed arrived and explained to Dorrin about his errand.

"Aris and Camwyn were close friends, as Juris and the king are. He was first into the scene and did his best to treat Camwyn's wounds. Camwyn's injuries and then his absence have been hard for him. He's continued to do his duty as a senior page, but he's struggled. Juris suggested it was time to let Aris raise and train his own horse. I agreed. So I brought up a mare near foaling, and she's in the royal stables now. We Marrakai are all horse-mad. If anything can help Aris over this, it's a horse. But come into my study. What's this about Gwenno leaving your service?"

Dorrin explained again. Marrakai nodded.

"I understand. Yes, of course you can cancel the contract. And if you're sure she's ready for the Bells, I'll talk to the right people—though she would be the only girl at present."

"What about the Company of Gird in Fin Panir? Aris was there, wasn't he?"

"In the junior school, yes. But I'm not sending any of my family to Fintha. Too dangerous. I don't suppose you've seen any mage-hunters over where you are."

"No, none. But surely not in Fin Panir itself. The Marshal-General spoke out against it, didn't she?"

"She did. She's been physically attacked—seriously wounded is what I heard—in Fin Panir itself. Riots in the city. Children taken, tested for magery, and the ones that the mage-hunters believed are mages killed." He shook his head. "No, no daughter of mine is going to Fintha. It's the Bells or nothing. She won't like it if they refuse, but I can send her down to the country, where she can ride horses and play at being a soldier without causing talk."

Dorrin opened her mouth to say that Gwenno was far beyond "playing" at being a soldier, but . . . it was not her concern anymore. This was between Gwenno and her parents.

At dinner, Gwenno appeared in a dark green gown with her hair up: a proper daughter of the house. She did not look happy, but neither was she openly rebellious, as the Gwenno of two years before would have been. With none of the younger children there—all were at the country house for the season—the meal was quieter than the one Dorrin remembered so well, the day Gwenno had become her squire.

After dinner came the ceremony: the salt, the tearing of the original contract, the token gifts back and forth. "I have one gift I did not expect to give you at this time," Marrakai said. "But you say you are going a long journey. I have seen your horses, of course. Good horses, well-trained, useful mounts for an officer. But not Marrakai-bred. Next to the Windsteed's foals, I would place Marrakai horses best. Will you accept one? Not just for the care you have given my daughter while she was your squire but as a friend?"

"I may have to journey by sea," Dorrin said. "I cannot risk a Marrakai-bred on such a journey. But I thank you for the offer."

"Ah. I understand. If by chance you should travel by way of Lyonya, you might do me a favor, then. Kieri Phelan favors Marrakaibreds, as you know. He has with him two stallions, but he has bought a mare. I brought her along with the one in foal and was going to ask Juris to take her to the border at Harway. But if you are going that way, you could deliver her for me."

"That I could do, and gladly," Dorrin said.

"When are you leaving, do you know?"

"Tomorrow I have another meeting with the king, so at the earliest, day after tomorrow. Perhaps even a day or so longer."

"Good. Send me word tomorrow if I do not see you."

That night, Dorrin's ride back to her house was uneventful. The next day's conference with the king completed all the official business of transferring her title to Beclan and freeing her from her ducal oath to King Mikeli. On the matter of guardianship, the king surprised her with his decision: he would give Beclan the choice of returning to his own family name while remaining Dorrin's heir or staying a Verrakai, and in either case he would appoint Beclan's father, Duke Mahieran, and two other dukes as guardians of the estate until Beclan reached majority. They could not refuse him, he said with a smile.

When she left the palace at last, nothing now held her to Vérella—or Tsaia—but a lifetime of memories and the people she'd known.

She and her escort set out for the Verrakai estate the next morning. Nostalgia sat heavy on her shoulders, reminding her at every turn that she might never see the city again . . . the familiar inns on the road south . . . the houses, the fields. The young Marrakai-bred mare she rode, a handsome chestnut, and the regalia's palpable joy at being with her and on the way were all that kept her from an even darker mood. The mare was everything claimed about Marrakai-bred horses but inclined to spook at surprises for the first day or so.

Once back on her own land, the new-made road reminded Dorrin how much more she had planned to do. Even if Beclan chose to complete the work, she might never see it. Those fields and orchards would be his accomplishment, not hers. But it was a road where no road had been for generations. A road with the signs of travel on it—footprints, hoofprints, even cart tracks.

By the time she arrived back at the house, she was resigned to leaving and ready to explain to her people—including her remaining squires—what she could of what the king had said and what would happen next. She gathered the household in the front hall, the only room big enough for all of them.

"Grekkan will remain as steward here, and Master Feddrin will continue to supervise the children. The rest of you will retain your present positions. All the plans I had made, the works begun for roads, quarries, and so on, will continue." She paused; no one said anything, though Farin had gone red in the face, which meant she was about to explode into speech. Dorrin went on quickly. "The king felt it best, since the duration of the task he gave me is uncertain, to assume that my heir succeeds to the estate. I brought with me copies of the papers that complete this transaction."

"But—" Beclan had gone as white as salt. "I'm not ready—" He stopped as she held up her hand.

"As my heir is indeed underage to manage all affairs, the king appointed guardians to oversee its management. When Kirgan Verrakai is of age and has become a knight, he will then be invested with a title and the guardianship will end. In the meantime, as I said, the situation will remain as it is, including the plans for improvements and the settling of incomers." She took a deep breath. "I will speak to many of you individually. At this time, however, I will speak to my kirgan and to Daryan Serrostin in my office. Grekkan, please hold yourself in readiness. The rest of you should return to your duties."

In her office, she handed Daryan a letter from his father. "He's seeking another squire position for you, Daryan," she said.

Daryan held the unopened letter and said, "I could go with you—I could be a help."

"I cannot take you, Daryan. Nor would your father consent even if it were possible. Your father will send an escort for you in a few days, he told me. Go read your letter."

Daryan left the office. Beclan, still pale, said nothing. "Your situation is more complicated, Beclan. Two of the people approached as possible guardians suggested that Duke Mahieran should be named instead."

"They must know I'm not supposed to meet my father," Beclan said, shifting in his chair.

"They do. Not everyone was in favor of how your situation was handled, and after magery began to appear in others, including the king's brother, more took the position that you were being treated unfairly. The king . . . made two suggestions."

"You said he had decided—"

"He decided to make two suggestions. The most important, for you, is that you may choose to be restored to your family—and your name—"

"No!" Beclan jerked upright. "No, I will not!"

Dorrin stared. She had not expected this reaction whether he took that choice or not. "Why?" she said, folding her hands on her desk.

Beclan did not relax; he stood rigid, breathing hard. "They—he—threw me away. You saved me—*you* made my father bring you there the night they attacked; you saved my life. And then you accepted me as your kirgan and gave me your name. I could tell you didn't want to, but you did. You didn't hold it against me that the king forced you. You made it as easy for me as you could, and . . . I am *not* a Mahieran. I *am* a Verrakai. I am *proud* to be a Verrakai and your heir. You brought honor to this name, and I swear I will bring honor to this name."

"Beclan—" She paused. What could she say, in the face of such vehemence, that would make a difference? What would calm him and help him come to rational thought? "Sit down, Beclan," she said. "You're shouting."

"I am determined." Beclan sat down. "I'm sorry I shouted. But I am determined. Unless you tell me differently, that you don't want me as your heir now—or the king commands that I must not be—"

"You are my heir," Dorrin said, "as long as you want to be; the king did not command you to give it up. But I could wish you were less angry with your family. And the king."

His color had returned, and he no longer looked ready to leap on someone. "It is not so much—now—that they did what they did back then. I understood it then; the good of the realm comes first, and that seemed best, to prevent unrest. But to make that offer now— it's an insult. An insult to you, and an insult to me."

"It wasn't intended as one," Dorrin said. "Let me tell you of the other suggestion. All the dukes would be guardians to ensure that no one of them could take advantage of you in your minority and also because they are all busy and one—Arcolin—is also out of Tsaia and does not know about any of this yet. When you come of age and inherit the title, you must be at court, of course. The king agrees that you should no longer be isolated from the family of your birth, or from Vérella. There is still a question about admittance to the Bells, because the new commander is a very conservative Girdsman, somewhat at odds with the notion that mage talent does not necessarily mean a breach of the Code."

Beclan scowled at that. "When *is* the Marshal-General going to change the Code?"

"She's trying, but the Marshalate does not entirely agree with her. Unrest in Fintha has spread. So there's some opposition to your being in the training hall. The king is unwilling to allow you to go to Fin Panir because of the unrest there, with mage-hunters seeking out mages and killing them. That leaves Falk's Hall, but I know you would rather train with Girdsmen."

"I'm not sure," Beclan said. "I didn't know they could be like that . . . killing children just for making light. If that's their idea of Gird—" His voice rose again.

"Not all of them," Dorrin said. "The king's protecting them as best he can. Some Marshals agree with him . . . so do others. Even in Fintha. You've been Girdish all your life, and your family has been for generations—that's not something to give up easily."

"I gave up my name," Beclan said, but without heat.

"And perhaps you gave up enough and need not give up more," Dorrin said. "You said Gird helped you fight off those brigands—and I believe that he may well have, even if that meant giving you mage-powers."

"So you think I should wait until the Bells will accept a mage?"

"I think you should discuss it with your guardians," Dorrin said. "They need to know what you want and why you want it. They're all men you have known from childhood."

Beclan nodded. "I wish you weren't leaving."

"So do I. But I trust that you will be a good duke, a good lord for this domain, when you come of age. I will talk with you again before I leave, but now I need to talk to Grekkan, your steward."

Beclan stood and bowed. "Yes, my lord. I cannot yet think of Grekkan as *my* steward."

"You will," she said.

When he had left, Dorrin called Grekkan in and explained how the guardianship would work. "Duke Serrostin and the other guardians will come soon. Though I left them a general account of the estate, they must see for themselves. You should have a detailed account ready for them, a copy they can take back. You will contact the same man of business and banker, sending accounts there you have been accustomed to giving me directly. You can also contact the guardians—any one of them. I expect they will give Beclan some limited power to make decisions here, and I expect he will seek your guidance."

"Yes, my lord." Grekkan's expression was sober but not distressed. "When are you leaving?"

"In a few days. I will go east first, but though many may guess at that direction, no word should come from here."

"Of course not, my lord."

After Grekkan left, Dorrin went to the kitchen. As she expected, Farin and Natzlin were both there. Farin pounded a mound of dough as if it were an enemy; Natzlin perched on a stool and looked miserable.

"So you're deserting us," Farin said, shoving her fists deep into the dough. Before Dorrin could answer, she went on. "And I know you'll say it's the king's command, m'lord, but it's a *stupid* command. Best lord this place ever had and he's sending you away, and for what? To spy on some foreigner who might invade someday?"

That was an explanation Dorrin had not thought of. "It's not for me to discuss the king's command," she said.

"No, of course not." This time Farin smacked the dough with the flat of her hand. "You just obey it." She leaned on the table, a hand on either side of the dough. "I never thought I'd have a master of this house I could respect, and then you came, and now . . . am I to respect that pup Beclan?" Natzlin stirred, and Farin rounded on her. "He's a puppy, I say. Respect due to his breeding? Well, his breeding made him a mage, didn't it?"

"You will respect him," Dorrin said, "because although he is young, and although he has made mistakes, he has learned from them and he is, as you know well, my heir, who I tell you now will be a man who deserves that respect."

"And you're sure of that." Farin's tone was less angry but still challenging.

"I'm sure of that."

"Well." Farin rolled the dough around until it made a compact ball and covered it with a cloth. "Well, then. I suppose I must give the lad a chance to prove you right."

"Yes," Dorrin said. "You must."

"But I don't have to like your going away. Neither me nor Natzlin likes it."

"I understand," Dorrin said, glancing at Natzlin, whose eyes glittered with unshed tears. "But you two are pillars of this household. Food and safety. None more important. I trust you both to keep the household fed and safe and to teach others to do the same."

Natzlin's tears spilled over. "I—I gave my oath to *you*, m'lord."

"And I gave mine to the king, and he returned it to me. And the same with King Kieri, and it always hurts to have an oath returned. But you will manage, Natzlin, and so will you, Farin. Support each other. Commit yourselves to Beclan and this household."

Both of them nodded.

"And now," Dorrin said, "I'm more than a little hungry after all this emotion."

Farin chuckled. "Thought you might be." She went over to the warming oven and pulled out a platter. "Now, if your oath to the king is gone, does that mean you're not a duke?"

"Farin!" Natzlin stared at her.

"I suppose it does," Dorrin said.

"Then you can eat here in the kitchen if you'd like."

Dorrin sat down and grinned at Farin. "I'm merely a humble traveler passing through . . ."

Farin snorted. "Here you are, then."

Next day, Dorrin took Beclan with her to the nearest vills when she said goodbye to them. That was hard, but the hardest of all the farewells were those to the children she had orphaned, children who now called her "Auntie Dorrin" and were growing up without the fears that had controlled their lives before she came. They clung to her, and most of them cried. She blinked back her tears and hoped what she said to them—that they were safe, that they would be cared for and loved, that Beclan would be to them as an older brother, a protector—would eventually be a comfort.

It was easy to think of reasons to stay one more day . . . and then another. So many things she needed to tell Beclan, Grekkan, the house staff, the children. So many vills she could visit, so many people and places and projects. She knew she must not linger. On the third day, she set the day for departure and considered what she needed to take with her.

Not her court dress, not her ducal insignia, not her Verrakai-blue doublets or tabard. Her working clothes as a mercenary would be best. Plain shirts, plain trousers, leather doublet, a brown wool cloak. Mail? Yes, the same she had worn in the Duke's Company, for she might be attacked on the way. Her sword, her dagger, her kit for repairing clothing, her own eating utensils, her sharpening stone and oil, her firestarter—she laughed at that but kept it anyway. She might be places where lighting a fire with her finger would be unwise. She hesitated over her ducal ring. At Kieri's court, where she was known as Duke Verrakai, it would be noticed if she did not wear it. She did not want to explain to his Siers that she was no longer a duke. Kieri could send it back for Beclan.

Her own needs fit, as they always had, in two saddlebags and a roll behind the saddle. The regalia would travel on a packhorse, with supplies for the trip. And it was done. She looked around her room as if seeing it for the first time. The bed, the chairs, the table, the fireplace with its decorative screen in this season. She looked out the window at the garden, at the apple tree where Arian had first shown her how to reach the taig.

She turned away from that. Night had fallen; morning would come early. She undressed in that room for the last time, lay down, and in spite of all fell asleep at once.

CHAPTER NINETEEN

Chaya, Lyonya

The news of the enchantment laid on the Tsaian royal palace and the injuries suffered by Prince Camwyn arrived in Chaya by special courier. Kieri, reading King Mikeli's letter, felt a cold chill—this was worse than what had happened the previous spring, when the Lady was killed. Easy to imagine how Mikeli had felt, seeing his brother apparently dying, realizing that everyone had been helplessly trapped in an enchantment but the prince and the prince's best friend. All too easy to imagine such an enchantment here . . . Would his own elvenhome be any protection?

Mikeli had sent for Dorrin—of course—and of course wanted her to take the regalia away. By this time she was probably on her way to Vérella. He stopped reading and counted off days of travel in his mind. His couriers and Mikeli's now used relays of horses, thus making the journeys much faster. She would not be in Vérella yet.

He read on, brow furrowed. Mikeli's analysis of his kingdom's peril showed the experience the young king had gained from the many challenges of his reign. Asking Dorrin to leave the realm and resign her title and heritage: he might have done so himself in Mikeli's place. A king must consider his realm before his own feelings. Wherever she went, as long as she had the regalia with her, Dorrin would be a danger to anyone who sheltered her, attracting both common thieves and those with greater purpose.

"I believe she must go east, through your realm, to begin her journey. I ask that you give her what assistance you can to come safely to a destination she will tell you. You have powers I lack, and these items have a destiny Duke Verrakai discerns. You are better placed to help her than anyone else I know."

Kieri had duties Mikeli did not know and could not understand. Oaths to keep: to his dual realm, the people of Lyonya and the elves of his elvenhome, and the Old Humans into whose tribe he had been adopted. Magelords to release from old enchantment so that the dragon could remake the stone and end the irruption of iynisin. From everything Dorrin had told him, from everything Mikeli told him, she and those strange jewels threatened all he was sworn to protect. By any measure of common sense, he should ban her from his realm.

But he could not. He would not. Though she was not oathsworn to him now, their friendship was not a matter of mere oath. She, like Arcolin, had been the foundation of his domain in Tsaia. She wore Falk's ruby, even as he did, and never once wavered in her duty.

He wrote a short note to Mikeli, saying he would give Dorrin whatever help he could, and gave it to the courier, who mounted and rode away. One thing was clear to him. He must attempt to break the enchantment he and Paks had made and get the magelords out of the stronghold in Kolobia so that the dragon could do his work and once more lock iynisin into unyielding stone. He had thought to wait until he was certain of his magery; he had thought iynisin would attack him, not Tsaia. And certainly not the young prince. He would not wait any longer. If he succeeded, there would be fewer iynisin anywhere, less danger for all. If he failed? He would not fail. He must not fail.

He called Caernith and the King's Squires on duty into his office and read them Mikeli's message.

"You see, my lord, why you must hurry," Caernith said.

"Yes. I do. Delay will not serve any of us. And I will make the attempt today. I'm going now to tell the queen about this. Come."

"You should be dressed formally," Caernith said as they went upstairs.

Kieri glanced at him. It had grown hot a hand of days before, and he had been wearing only a light shirt over his mail. "Why?" he asked.

"You will try to bring them here, you said. They are used to formality in kings and will respect that. And where will they stay? You must have plans, my lord, even if it means a few days' delay."

"So I must." They had come to the royal apartments. Arian opened the door of her chamber.

"Am I late for luncheon?"

"No . . . I have had disturbing word from Mikeli, and I must talk to you about it." He told her the bare facts while she stood there. "And so," he said, "I will do my best to wake the magelords and bring them here. Today."

Her glance flicked to Caernith and back to him. "Today. You would like me to arrange . . . something . . . with the steward?"

His mind had caught up with his emotions now, and he nodded. "It will take both of us most of the day, I don't doubt. Possibly longer . . . though I feel strongly that every moment counts now. We need rooms for them—the palace will not hold so many. I'll send someone into the city to make arrangements at the inns. Food. A place to gather them as they come." He looked at Caernith. "How many can use the transfer pattern at once?"

"Only a few, my lord."

"And Caernith says I must change and show a king's appearance, something they will recognize."

Arian smiled. "I agree. I will see to the palace arrangements if you deal with the innkeepers and such. And you will rest, Kieri, before you begin the magery: this is not something to begin with your mind full of hurry and confusion."

Soon the palace was all in a bustle of preparation, and Kieri's messengers had found and secured every available room in Chaya for the guests they hoped would arrive. In late afternoon, Arian found Kieri trying to squeeze in a quick meeting unrelated to the immediate need and insisted he come upstairs instead.

When he came from the bath she'd arranged, she held out a nightshirt. "There's no time," he said.

"There is." Arian laid her hand on his brow, kissed him, and said, "I will not let you sleep too long," before she cast him into sleep in the old way. He woke refreshed, and as he dressed, this time in full formal style, Caernith came in, Kieri assumed, to give him more elven advice.

"Where did you get *that*?" Caernith asked. He sounded angry.

Kieri turned around, startled, his gorget in his hand. "What?"

"Around your neck."

Kieri's hand rose to the torc. "This was my mother's."

"No. It cannot have been hers."

"It was. She wore it the day I was taken." He bent his head a little to let one of the Squires fasten the gorget around his throat, hiding the torc.

"And how, then, did you get it? Have you always had it?"

"No—it was when I returned to the place where she was killed. I told you about that."

"You didn't mention this," Caernith said.

"No, I didn't," Kieri said as Squires eased the green, gold-bordered surcoat over his head. "What has it to do with the magelords I'm supposed to wake?" A hint, if Caernith took it, that he needed no distraction now.

"It is far older than your mother was. It is a great treasure of elvenkind, and your grandmother was its guardian. It belongs to *us*."

Kieri repressed a sigh. "What is it, then?"

"I . . . must not say. It is from the dawn of this world, like the Elvenhorn, but even older. Be sure those you bring from the west do not see it."

Caernith wouldn't have seen it if he hadn't come in while Kieri was dressing. Kieri did not say that, tipping his head a little so his Squires could place the crown on it. Then he straightened and looked at Caernith. "No one will see it. You haven't seen it in all the time you've been here. I am more concerned that it might have magical properties that affect what I'm about to attempt."

Caernith flushed a little. "It will not. Unless . . . no, I believe it will not."

"I trust you will tell me what I need to know if it should do whatever it does," Kieri said. He could hear the edge in his voice, and it annoyed him. He did not need to be worrying about what the torc was, or what it might do and under what circumstances, when preparing for magery he was not certain he could perform. And facing magelords who might have powers he could not match.

Then Arian came from her chamber in her own formal robes, and he forgot all about Caernith. She took his hand, and they went down together.

I n his office, the transfer pattern had been uncovered and all furniture moved well away.

"Are we ready?" Kieri looked around the room at those assembled for the attempt. To his sword-side, the elves—two from the west and four from his own elvenhome—murmured their assent. By the door, two King's Squires and two Queen's Squires; they bowed. Still others waited in the hall to escort any magelords brought successfully from Kolobia to the reception room prepared for them.

Kieri looked at Arian, standing beside him next to the transfer pattern on the floor. Arian had insisted, despite his continued protests, that she would not stay safely away. Now she met his gaze with such determination that he did not even try to protest again.

"Then let us begin," he said. He touched his magery—the elven, the mageborn, the Old Human—and braided them into one strand of power, then imagined the chamber he had seen before. It was easier this time. Almost immediately a wavering scene, as if painted on a veil of air, hung before them: the great hall partly filled with rows of kneeling figures. No sign of Luap. No turmoil in the background: just silence and stillness deeper than silence, the way Paks had described it. For a long moment he and Arian stared at the scene, unspeaking.

"This had better work," Kieri muttered finally. He raised his voice. "Awake! Awake: your rest is over; your time has come." It sounded silly to him, but what else could he say?

For a moment nothing happened. He was sure he had failed again.

Then a stir moved over the kneeling figures, as if they took a long breath in concert. More than half simply vanished, as if they had never been there. Slowly the others rose, row by row, their shining armor and colorful cloaks brilliant in the clear light, and slowly they turned, first to one another and then all around, as if searching for others.

"Too long," Arian said of those who vanished. "Nothing left but the semblance the enchantment held. Like the figure of Luap Paks saw, I suppose."

Light blossomed from one hand after another as the magelords greeted one another and then turned to face whatever it was they saw from their end.

Arian eyed Kieri. "You must come," Kieri said, staring at the image. The wavering image steadied as more and more of the faces looked toward him. "Now that you are awake, you must leave that place."

One, a gray-haired man with startling blue eyes, shook his head. "We cannot, mage-king. Outside is death. We were told . . ."

"On the mageroad," Kieri said. "Come to me."

"It is forbidden to us now. They said—"

"It was forbidden then," Kieri said. "Ages have passed, hundreds of winters, since you were cast into enchantment. Now it is time to go. I am King Kieri of Lyonya, half-elven and half human, of mage-born and Old Human blood both."

"You—I saw you before—" That was another man, younger, almost pushing the older one aside. "You talked to Lord Selamis the Luap. You are half-elf *and* mageborn? If it is so long—then is your elven blood why you live so long?"

Kieri had not realized any of them would recognize him from the first time. He'd thought no one but Luap and those standing near him could see him, and besides—all those years. But for them it had been no time at all since they slept. Thinking about it made his head hurt; he did not want to try to explain it to them.

"I am indeed half-elven and half human," Kieri said, not answering the rest. "And my queen, Arian, is also half-elven. We have spoken to the Lord of the Kingsforest, eldest of living elves, and by his permission, the mageroad is open to you." He paused for breath; the magelords stared at him, silent. "Take the mageroad now."

"But . . . but where will we go upon it?"

"You will come here," Kieri said. He hoped saying it would make it so. If any of them knew other destinations that had not been blocked, they might go . . . anywhere. But if he was firm enough, their bewilderment should lead them to where he wanted them.

"Here in Lyonya," Kieri went on. "Your old homeland is all Girdish now, and Tsaia's king does not want you there. Here none will harm you if you do no harm."

"We do not know Lyonya—it is for elves—" The older man looked worried; others nodded behind him.

"And for humans now. Come: fix your minds on this place and on us as your hosts. Come one or two together; those who arrive can then help bring the rest."

"I will go," said one woman, streaks of gray in her dark hair. "Derin—will you come with me?"

"Gladly," said another woman. The two of them walked to the dais at the end of the hall and stepped onto the pattern. They made gestures Kieri did not recognize and then, with a gust of air, appeared on the pattern in his chamber. One of the King's Squires quickly led them aside and offered a seat, but they turned back to the group by the pattern.

"Lord king," the first woman said with a bow. "Tell me true, what are you?"

Kieri felt the enchantment she tossed over him and shrugged it aside. "I am the king of this land, as I told you. Falkieri Artfiel Phelan, whose mother was an elf, daughter of the Lady of the Ladysforest, and whose father was a mix of mage and northern human. Bear in mind, Lady, that I am not easily enchanted, and in this day it is considered unmannerly to attempt to enchant one's host."

"My pardon." She bowed very low indeed this time. "I am called Meris, now a widow, for my husband was killed in Gird's War, and my children by iynisin there in the west."

"Be welcome, Meris," Arian said. "And also . . . Derin, is it?"

"Yes, lords," said the other woman, bowing low as well. Both wore mail and had swords belted at side. Derin carried a bow of a shape Kieri had not seen before. Neither had the calluses he would have expected from soldiers. Or farmers, for that matter.

"Come, reassure your comrades that you arrived safely," Kieri said. He gestured, and they came forward to the group.

"Can you see us?" the first woman asked the image in the air. "Here is real—and the people look as they should. No demons. It is a palace. There are elves here as well: it must be Lyonya."

"You must come now," Kieri said to those in the stronghold. "The Elders mean to close the stronghold, destroy it permanently, and needed only your long sleep broken to begin their work. If you stay, you, too, will be destroyed."

Some of those waiting looked around wildly, as if for friends or belongings.

"Nothing is left where you are." Kieri said. "While you slept for ages, others have visited from time to time. Come now." He held out his hand. The mageborn moved toward the dais and its pattern. He concentrated on keeping the connection open and knew Arian was helping.

By ones and twos, the magelords stepped onto the dais of that underground hall. As they emerged in the palace, King's Squires led them out into the hall to make room for more. Kieri could hear them behind him speaking softly, but he ignored that. Men and women both; most were somewhere in what seemed middle age. At last, he saw one final person step onto the dais and turn to face him . . . and shock held him. This was no magelord, this dark-skinned flame-eyed person. Out came the long tongue, flames flickering from its surface.

"That was well done, Sorrow-King and Half-Song. Let us seal this passage." And the tongue, glowing, slid through the veil while Kieri's mind seemed to stutter in its thoughts.

"As you will, Lord Dragon," he said, stepping forward onto the pattern with Arian at his side. As before, heat smote his face, but the dragon's tongue did not burn his own. Instead, he felt warmth spread through his body.

"Sorrow-King, I rejoice in your children."

Arian followed next, unhesitating. Kieri knew the dragon spoke to her but could not hear the words.

The tongue withdrew. In that distant chamber they could see but not touch, the man's shape transformed to Dragon's own shape, and the great eyes blinked at them. "Your honor is clear," the dragon said. "Release the bond, Sorrow-King, for what I do now must not be seen by mortals."

Kieri was not sure how to release it; his mind felt clenched on that connection, but he tried to visualize opening his hands and his mind . . . and it was gone, melting back into nothingness.

He looked at Arian; she was pale, and her hand trembled as she reached out to him. Squires helped them both to chairs; his knees gave way as he sat down, and his vision darkened for a moment.

"At least we didn't fall on the floor," he said. Arian smiled but did not answer; her eyes were closed. The Squires brought them sweet pastries and water, and in a short time Kieri saw that Arian was sitting upright, eyes bright and cheeks flushed.

"We did it," she said. "You woke them, and we brought them here."

"So we did," Kieri said. He looked over at Caernith, still in the room though the other elves had gone. "Your king will be pleased."

"Indeed so," Caernith said.

"I suppose you heard one of the magelords say he had seen me in that other time?"

"Yes . . . it is still hard to believe."

"I know," Kieri said, running a hand through his hair. "I do not understand it, and I prefer not to think hard about it—it hurts my head."

"Nor does that surprise me," Caernith said. "For such magery is too like that of Gitres Undoer, who would change the past."

"But we didn't change the past," Kieri said. "We made it as it was found."

"However it was done, it was done, and what was done made what was known before it was done, so it could not be undoing," Arian said. Caernith's brows went up. "Do not plague the king with it now, when he has other duties." To Kieri she said, "I will check on the twins and make sure none of this affected them, then join you and our guests."

Caernith bowed as she left. Kieri waited a moment, but the elf said no more, only gestured toward the door.

The mutter of magelord voices from the reception room sounded strange, and Kieri realized that without the magery he had used, he could scarcely understand them. What they spoke was not the Common tongue now so widely used but a dialect long since forgotten or their own language from Old Aare.

They fell silent as he entered, bowing courteously.

"Be welcome," Kieri said. From their expressions, he could tell that they, too, did not now understand him. He spoke very slowly, hoping that would help. "This is the city of Chaya, in Lyonya."

"Lyonya . . . Elfland?" one said. The accent was thick, but Kieri could understand it.

"Two kingdoms . . . elf . . . human . . . joined." He brought his hands together and intertwined his fingers. That they seemed to understand.

"Finyatha . . . Gird?" A gesture that must mean "all."

What was Finyatha? It must be Fintha.

"All Girdish," Kieri said. Except for the newly discovered mage talents . . . but that was too complicated to explain when they could not understand one another.

Puzzled looks that finally cleared. Several nodded. One gestured to the table, and a pastry rose from its tray and came to his fingers. Kieri stared for a moment, then decided that his own show of magery would do no harm and might be comforting. Or impressive. With a glance at Caernith, who had taught him, he lifted a jug on the table by magery, poured from it, and then brought the goblet to him and drank. Silence held the room a long moment, then more questions erupted.

He had expected the magelords to be confused, not knowing where they were or when. But he had thought, since they came from

Fintha and Tsaia and had lived for some years with Girdsmen, that they would speak Common fluently and already be familiar with customs and Girdish law. Their confusion and anxiety were obvious, but their difficulty with the language made his initial plans—to talk over what skills they had and how they might fit into Lyonyan society— impossible. Instead, with a mix of sign language and the few words they did seem to understand, he explained they would not stay in the palace but elsewhere in the city. They followed him, staring and pointing as they went from one lodging place to another.

By nightfall, Kieri had settled the magelords in their lodgings and explained their lack of local speech to the innkeepers. "See that they have food and drink; the Crown will pay for it, and I will be glad to hear what you think of them."

"Where are they from?"

"Far beyond Fintha. They came by magic, at the elves' behest, and they have magery not seen in lifetimes."

When all had been settled and he was back in the palace, Kieri conferred with his Council.

"So—these are the same bad magelords Gird fought against?" Sier Davonin asked.

"We believe these are the magelords who survived the war, tried to live in peace with Girdsmen in Fintha, and left because the others would not believe them changed."

"How do we know they are?"

Kieri had the same troubling thought. "We don't. If Duke Verrakai were here, she could detect those who have taken over others' bodies, but she is not. I must find out what they can do—what skills they have, how they can be useful here—and . . ." And what? he wondered. What could he do if they weren't suitable here? The magery he had already seen them use made them dangerous if they had ill will; he could not just turn them out on the world any more than a man would turn loose a vicious dog to harry his neighbor's flocks.

"Are they all soldiers? Would they help Aliam?" Sier Halveric had discovered more interest in military matters since Aliam had become commander of the Lyonyan military.

"I had hoped so from Paksenarrion's description, but I am not certain," Kieri said. "They wear mail and carry swords, but they do not have the look of soldiers. They do not move like soldiers." He considered pointing out the differences he had noticed, but his Council members were not soldiers either. "Aliam and I will learn more. I suspect they used magery instead of the weapons and tactics we know."

"What is their magery like?" Sier Belvarin asked.

"Not the same as mine," Kieri said. "When they make light, it is hot, like a flame. As you've seen, mine is elf-light, without heat. They move things by their will, but though I can do that, using elven magery, I suspect it's not quite the same. Supposedly they can cut rock by magery and multiply some nonliving things; it's in the old records the Girdish have. I have yet to verify that. They have some skills of enchantment, similar to that of elves, but not as strong as mine." For which he was profoundly grateful.

"Do they use blood magery for these powers?"

Kieri had hoped no one would ask that until he knew for certain himself. "Supposedly not, though some of the magelords of Gird's day certainly did."

"I think they're dangerous," Sier Davonin said, shaking her head. "I wish they were not here."

"If I had waked them and left them there, they would all have died," Kieri said. From the expression on Davonin's face, that would have been fine with her. He tried to explain. "The western elves and the dragon were going to remake that place—"

"How?"

"I have no idea." Kieri liked Sier Davonin, but once she took hold of an idea or a topic, she clung to it and more than once had shifted a discussion off its course. He brought the meeting to a close as soon as he could.

As Kieri learned more about the magelords, he found very little of it encouraging. "Once again," he said to Arian, "I was wrong. It's disappointing . . . I thought of them as a potential army to fight evil in Aarenis, but they are only a few and their experience in war is limited to losing the one against Gird. None of the women fought in it, nor did some of the men. None of them commanded regular military units. Siger and Carlion have watched a few of them in the salle—most ignored my invitation—and say their technique is mediocre."

She nodded. "I'm glad you've given up that notion. Your place is here—must be here."

"I know that. But what are they to do? It's understandable that they are confused by the changes since their day; none of them had visited Lyonya anyway. And I'm not sure how to make use of the considerable magery they have. Multiplying rocks, for instance, or splitting them . . . I can move stones, but it's very hard and feels peculiar. To some of them it's natural. At least they can multiply only nonliving things. They say their ancestors could do the same with plants or some animals."

Arian shuddered. "Or humans?"

"I don't know. I don't want to know." Kieri downed the last of the wine in his goblet. "If . . . if they could multiply living bodies, could they multiply the spirits in them, or would that give them bodies to transfer into? Is that like the iynisin multiplying themselves with ephemes?" He shook his head. "Let's not talk of that. Surely it is a great evil to multiply persons."

"What about skills?" Arian asked.

Kieri shook his head. "Until Gird's War, they seem to have lived off their holdings. Their peasants grew the crops, built whatever was built, prepared the food, wove the cloth, and so on. They used magery for personal pleasures and to enforce their rule, though by Gird's time they had trained nonmages as militia. In Kolobia, they used magery for those things we consider skills and trades as much as possible. They are quite proud of having done so. But no two have the same mage talents, and they show little respect for those who do things without magery."

"It's . . . sad," Arian said. "Elves use magery, but they also have skills of hand and eye . . . weaving, for instance, and carving."

"Exactly," Kieri said. "I asked those who lacked a mage talent for working wood, for instance, if they used tools instead, and they laughed and insisted they would not consider it. If a woman cannot magically make cloth, she leaves that to one who can, or to what they call a handworker. Apparently some of them in Kolobia were hand-workers, but none who survived." He sighed, considered pouring himself more wine, and then decided against it. "I could almost agree with Sier Davonin, annoying as she can be: it may have been a mistake to bring them here. Yet how could I not, with both elves and Dragon insisting I must?"

※

Trying to meet with most of the magelords every day added to Kieri's workload. He could not spend as much time with them as he needed—only a single glass—and the rest of the time they were free to wander about the city. Though they adapted to the modern forms of Common very quickly, Kieri could not understand their language.

"It is from Aare, as they told you," Amrothlin said when Kieri asked him. "It is nothing like the language of Old Humans here in the north."

"But you understand it," Kieri said. "Translate for me. Teach me some of it. What does this mean?" He recited a phrase he had heard often.

Amrothlin spoke in elven, a longer utterance that Kieri turned into Common: "It is sorrow to leave a land of power."

"Why don't you say it in Common?" he said. "Or why don't they speak elven? Then I could understand them myself."

"They never did," Amrothlin said, his lip slightly curled. "They said it was too elaborate." Kieri could have said the same but knew better. "I cannot say exactly what they say in Common; it is easy to put in elven."

With Amrothlin's help, Kieri made headway in the magelord language, but he had little time to spend on it and still needed an elf with him to understand an entire conversation.

A few days after their arrival, one of the magelords fell sick—Dualian, who woke with a fever and cough and became rapidly worse.

"She said she was tired yestereve," the innkeeper said. "She spent the afternoon in the garden with our youngest three . . . but she'd taken to them, and them to her, from the time she came. Like you said, I couldn't understand what she said, but she made signs . . . I think she lost her own children."

"Are they sick?" Kieri asked. "Do you think she brought an illness with her?"

"Oh, no. Cali was coughing before the magelords came, and of course Issa and Vorli caught it. Runny noses, all three, but they'll be fine. It's nothing serious, just the usual summer drip children get. No, the magelady is much sicker than that. It might even be lung fever."

Kieri sent his physician, who came back looking grave. "She's very sick. I looked at the others in that inn. Dualian shares a room with Tammar and a table with Derin and Meris. Tammar is sneezing and coughing; Meris has a headache and fever."

"I worry that they might have brought a sickness from Kolobia."

"From the past, you mean. I suppose, though if they were under a glamour for five hundred winters, anything they had should have worn itself out."

"No other travelers have been sick at that inn. Only the children—"

"And theirs started before the magelords came and thus cannot be the result of their coming. I don't know, sir king. I don't know what it is, but I gave the draught I would for lung fever. We can hope it's just traveler's ill. I expect you've had that."

"The flux once every year when I went south, those first years," Kieri said, nodding. "Then I got used to the water and food there. It's a long way from Kolobia to here; perhaps it is just the change of water."

"For some it's flux, for some it's coughing. Traveler's ill usually passes quickly," the physician said. "I did ask, and not just the innkeeper but no one else staying or eating there has been sick with the like, so it's not something wrong with the food."

Despite the physician's opinion, the other mages complained to Kieri, demanding to know what the sickness was and whether someone had tried to poison them. Kieri began to hear of quarrels among the mages and complaints from his own subjects about their behavior.

"I don't mind drinking," one innkeeper said. "I sell ale and beer and wine, after all. But there's drinking and drinking, and when I say a man's had enough and I'm not serving more, I expect him to go sleep it off. Not lift the pitcher out of my hands by magery and drink it dry."

Kieri nodded. "Quite right. I'll speak to them."

That was easier promised than done. That mage and a half dozen others had borrowed horses from the royal stables and ridden out somewhere. Meanwhile, another two women mages had fallen ill.

"They're not only useless, they're actively causing me problems," he said to Arian. "And when I said that to Caernith, all he said was, 'So we found when we allowed them into the rock.'"

Then High Marshal Seklis arrived from Vérella with two scribes. By then the oldest woman, Meris, had died, and another appeared near death. The High Marshal was another problem. He said he wanted to know more about Gird's time, which to these mages was their own and fresh in memory. But it was clear from the start that he was suspicious of them and looking for an excuse to condemn them.

For the magelords, the Girdish rebellion and Gird himself were only a few hands of years past. Though they knew nothing of the intervening hundreds of years, they knew their own time better than anyone else in the world, though their version of Gird's rebellion differed widely from Girdish dogma. Marshal Seklis immediately disputed their memories; tempers flared. Kieri found himself having to moderate words and actions on both sides of the table and finally dismissed them for the day.

"It would have been simpler, sir king, to have sent them to Fin Panir," High Marshal Seklis said later, when alone with Kieri.

"Into the turmoil there? They'd have been killed and made things worse for the Marshal-General. Besides, when I first heard from her about them, she was adamant she did not want them in Fintha. I'm surprised she didn't tell you."

Seklis flushed. "In fact . . . she said something like that. But it seemed to me if they came there and tried anything, they could be . . . well . . ."

"Killed?" Kieri said. "And if a mob killed them, so much the better?"

Seklis said nothing, but his face was dark red.

"I suspect the Marshal-General thought of that possibility and believed Gird would not approve."

"I suppose," Seklis said.

"You know she came to visit me when I was still a duke in Tsaia, don't you?"

"Yes." The flush had faded, but his face was still blotched and his expression dour.

"I respect the Marshal-General highly," Kieri said. "I would not cross her will without good reason—very good reason."

Seklis let out a gusty sigh. "Nor I, sir king. It's only—we know nothing about these magelords. Why were these chosen, out of all who were there, to be cast into enchantment? Or did they cast that magery on themselves? There are no records—there could be none, I suppose, to tell of the final time—however long it was—leading to that. I intend to find out, but can I trust their reports?"

"I don't know," Kieri said, skirting the question of how the magelords came to be enchanted in the first place. That was not something he wanted to discuss with Seklis; time enough if the magelords revealed it. "But don't Marshals have some ability to sense evil?"

"Paladins. Marshals can be fooled . . . We're supposed to use our wits, but—"

"Then you're where I am. I don't feel inclined to trust them fully, but I also don't have special knowledge of which ones are good and which ones bad—if any are." He shook his head. "If Dorrin—Duke Verrakai were here, she could at least determine if any were body changers."

Seklis scowled. "Blood mages."

"But she's not here, and neither of us is a paladin." Kieri placed both hands flat on his desk. "So we, High Marshal, must figure this out for ourselves. Try not to enrage them tomorrow and perhaps you'll learn something we can use."

"Perhaps." Another sigh, and Seklis pushed himself up from the chair.

"Do you have any feelings one way or the other about any in particular?" Kieri asked.

"I'm not sure, and that's the truth of it. They're so . . . so lordly. Yes, we have nobles in Tsaia, but they're not like this. This kind of glossy confidence. Doesn't that bother you?"

Kieri chuckled. "I've been living around elves several years now, High Marshal. You have not experienced real lordliness until you've been condescended to by the youngest of them, whom you find to be hundreds of years old though he looks like a youth."

"Well, that's natural for them—they're not human."

"True, but it's eroded my sensitivity to condescension. And that may be a bad thing," he added. "You're aware of it, and I'm not, and my lack of awareness is a blank spot, a blindness. I thought they were controlling the kind of fear I'd expect anyone to feel, yanked through five centuries. I expected self-control, as if they were soldiers. Yet it's clear they're not soldiers. So if they are confident because they have no anxiety . . . then—"

Seklis nodded sharply. "Yes, sir king. That is exactly what makes me uneasy. They should be struggling to adapt, but they seem perfectly at ease, as if they were the lords here and not you or the elves."

"One tried to lay a glamour on me, but I tossed it away," Kieri said.

"I will go softly tomorrow," Seklis said. "And what I hear, I will tell you. They will expect that, but still—you must know."

"I will sit with you until I am sure you are safe—"

"Me?"

"What if they try to enchant you?"

"I—?" Seklis stared, then recovered himself. "Gird will protect me."

"Will he? I have no doubt he could, High Marshal, but consider what happened to Paks. His protection is more distant and less sure than mine."

Seklis said nothing. Kieri got up and came out from behind his desk. "We will work together, High Marshal, and not at cross-purposes. They have enough of modern Common now—and should they talk among themselves in their own tongue, elves can understand it." At Seklis's look, he added, "It is the language they brought from Old Aare, and elves knew them there and learned their speech."

"Will elves be there, then?"

"Yes. I'll ask one of the western elves. They might actually have met some of these people back in Gird's day."

CHAPTER TWENTY

Dorrin's last view of Verrakai House, with the early sun shining on its face, the water meadows speckled with grazing cattle, tore at her heart. She had thought herself resigned to the necessity, but everything she saw reminded her of what she had hoped to accomplish. Though Beclan had promised to take care of it for her and clearly hoped she would return in a season or two, she did not expect it. She would die, she was sure, on this venture even if she was successful. Yet she had no choice. Not only her king's command but her own reason told her the regalia must go somewhere else. The coast of Old Aare? Perhaps.

All the way to the border she could not stop grieving for what she was losing . . . the first home of her own, the work she had started, the people she had come to love and care for. She would never see trade moving on the road she had begun; she would never see the children grown and know whether her intervention had done them good.

Her escort, silent out of respect, did nothing to distract her from her thoughts. Not until the border itself, where five Lyonyan rangers waited, did her escort speak. "My lord Duke—" That was Natzlin. Her voice sounded thick. "My lord—we will hope for your safe and soon return." The others murmured assent. Natzlin came forward and bent her knee; Dorrin clasped her shoulder.

"Natzlin, you will do well, and I know you will be a strength for my heir if I do not return. All of you—I believe your lives will continue to prosper. Beclan will have his father's advice and help; the king himself wants you to prosper."

"My lord—" Natzlin stepped nearer and lowered her voice. "*Will* you return? On your oath?"

"I don't know," Dorrin said. "I can't know. If I can, I will return. But if I cannot, then I believe you are in good hands."

"But not your hands," Natzlin said. "I will do my utmost for you, my lord, but I hope you do return."

They stood beside their horses as she remounted and rode forward to join the rangers, into the tall forest of Lyonya. Dorrin did not know these rangers. They greeted her politely but talked little. One handed her a letter from Kieri welcoming her to Lyonya but warning her about magelords . . . she read the rest of that with astonishment. She would not have believed the tale from anyone else. He and Paks had caused the enchantment the elves wanted him to break? He and Arian had then broken it? She looked at the rangers, but they showed no sign of knowing what she read.

When they stopped for the night at one of their way stations, Dorrin tucked away Kieri's letter and unloaded her packhorse herself. She set the pack saddle in the back corner of the three-sided shelter, in a row with the rangers' saddles. The rangers were busy with camp chores; she rested on one of the logs and watched them work until supper was ready.

"You were at the king's wedding last year, weren't you, lord Duke?"

"Yes, I was. And I was in Chaya still when the queen lost their child. I look forward to seeing the twins. I've known the king since he was at Falk's Hall . . . I'm sure you know I was one of his captains when he commanded his own mercenary company."

"Yes, lord Duke. He made sure we knew you were his friend of old. He also said you have mage-powers."

"Some, yes," Dorrin said. "Blocked for years by the Knight-Commander of Falk but released by the paladin Paksenarrion." She waited for someone to ask about the reason for her visit, but no one mentioned it. One of them turned the conversation to horses instead.

"That chestnut you're riding—is that a Marrakai-bred?"

"Yes, it is," Dorrin said. "Your king wanted a mare of that breeding, and Duke Marrakai asked me to bring her, since I was coming this way."

"I always thought Tsaia bred heavy horses, like Pargunese Blacks only not black."

"The royal stables breed a heavy gray," Dorrin said. "But they're too slow to be useful for a mercenary company or ordinary travel. Mahieran, the king's family, breed horses as well, but they're taller and leaner than the Marrakai."

The rest of the evening passed in horse talk—breeds, colors, stories of favorites—not a word about magelords from Kolobia who had lived in Gird's day. Well, if they weren't going to mention it, she would not ask. Dorrin slept soundly, to her surprise, and woke refreshed. She remembered that feeling from her travels with the Duke's Company—often a reluctance to leave, followed—once on the road—by an eagerness to reach a destination. Only then she had known the destination. This time . . .

She pushed herself out of her blankets and went to check on her horses. Soon they were riding again. At the next way shelter, they met four King's Squires, who took over as her escorts on the following day. From them, she heard a little about the magelords and about Kieri's concern for her and what she carried.

"They're not like anyone here," a young woman said. Dorrin had met Lieth the year before and remembered her. "And though you're a magelord, they're not like you, either. They thought if they ever wakened again, it would be a world where magelords ruled."

"How many are there?"

"Fewer than were enchanted. Some turned to dust when the king broke the enchantment. Eight hands, perhaps? More men than women, no children. The children were sent away. They were afraid of Lyonya, afraid of elves. And some of them are sickening—two have already died. The physicians suggest it is a form of traveler's ill but do not know for certain."

"What kind of magery do they have?"

"They can lift things—they don't walk across a room to get something; they make it come to them."

Others chimed in with more. "They can make two rocks from

one . . . they can cut rock without tools . . . grind grain by making a rock roll in a bowl . . ."

"Do they fly?" Dorrin asked, thinking of Camwyn's visit the year before.

"Not that I've seen or heard," Lieth said. "Do you?"

"No," Dorrin said. "But one of the younglings who came to magery unexpectedly could rise off the ground."

"We leave the main trail here," Lieth said, pointing ahead to where a narrow trail veered off to the sword-side. "We're circling around—the king said you would understand why. Tell us at once if you feel any danger."

"I will," Dorrin said. The crown in its wrappings had not spoken to her since she had left Verrakai House; she hoped that meant the magelords could not detect it. Kieri wrote that he had arranged a tour for them to get them out of Chaya for her arrival, but he did not know how far their perceptions could reach or if they could follow his directions.

The party finally emerged from the forest onto the Royal Ride, just out of sight of Chaya. There they met the queen and her Queen's Squires.

"Well met, sword-sister," Arian said, touching her ruby. Dorrin did the same. "You have read Kieri's letter, no doubt."

"Indeed. You think these magelords are evilly inclined?"

"We can't tell. They are different from anyone we've known, they speak archaic Common and the language of Old Aare, and one of them has asked about your family and some Finthan treasure sent to it for safekeeping in their time. Perhaps it is because they're so far out of their time, or perhaps it is because they have nothing to do, but they are not . . . easy guests. One of those who had left for the north came back this morning, claiming to feel unwell."

Dorrin's neck prickled. "Do you think he . . . she? . . . was faking?"

"Less now than when he arrived. He was pale then and now clearly has a fever. But the sooner we get your packages into the ossuary, the happier Kieri will be."

"Why does he think that's a good hiding place?"

"The bones. These magelords are afraid of the ossuary, disgusted by bone-houses. Kieri believes the bones will themselves protect the . . . whatever it is. Also . . . he has been adopted into a tribe of Old Humans."

"You have a tribe of them here?"

Arian shook her head. "No . . . not alive. But remember what I told you of Midsummer last year?"

Dorrin nodded.

"Since then, as he tried to find in himself some trace of the Old Human magery the elves told him was there, he asked those bones for help. And was adopted into their tribe. We haven't explained that to the elves; those bones and Kieri's elves do not get along."

Dorrin stared at her. "Kieri as half-elf I could believe. So when he seemed younger, I understood that as his elven heritage showing once he was here and around elves. Even what you wrote about him and the elvenhome. Kieri communing with his father's bones I could believe, with some difficulty. But—this?"

"That is not quite all," Arian said. She glanced around, then leaned a little closer to Dorrin. "Our children . . . have our magery."

Dorrin wanted to ask how she knew, but if the children's magery was secret . . . She nodded instead.

"Since you told us you are the only one who can handle your—what you brought—we had to find a way for you to get to the ossuary without any of the magelords seeing you. That's why Kieri sent them north."

"What about the sick one?"

"One of the elves is sitting with him in his room. This is the first of the men to get sick, and I hope it doesn't spread. All but one of the women are sick now, though the first may be recovering. The elves are sure none of them are iynisin in disguise—I am not—but they cannot tell if any of them are . . . Do you have a word for those who take another's body?"

"Evil," Dorrin said.

"I wondered if an iynisin could invade a magelord—and if that magelord then invades another—would that hide the iynisin from elves?"

"I have no idea," Dorrin said. "I thought iynisin sometimes tried to impersonate true elves—but why would they want to invade a human? They would gain no additional powers."

"Except the ability to fool humans and possibly conceal themselves from elves."

"I hope that is impossible," Dorrin said. "It sounds too much like one of those fancy dishes at feasts—the pigeon inside the chicken inside the ham, and everything stuffed with mushrooms. I cannot imagine an iynisin giving up an iynisin body—taller, stronger, and certainly longer-lived—for a human one. What made you think of it?"

Arian chuckled. "Probably my annoyance with the elf who told me. They complain of the arrogance of the magelords, but that is nothing to elven arrogance." They rode on. "And we have High Marshal Seklis from Tsaia—"

"I know him," Dorrin said. "He can be difficult."

"He is not," Arian said, "a congenial man. I will be glad when he has finished interrogating the magelords."

Dorrin nodded. "He wants to know everything they remember about Gird's time, am I right?"

"Yes, and he finds them insufficiently humble and apologetic for magelord misdeeds. Kieri has had to send both parties to their rooms more than once, like a parent with quarreling children."

"An uncomfortable situation," Dorrin said.

Arian changed the subject. "That's a Marrakai-bred you're riding, isn't it?"

"The mare Duke Marrakai sold Kieri, yes. He asked me to bring her."

"Kieri will be delighted. He's put Oak to good local mares, but he wants to breed the true strain. How does she ride?"

"I wish I'd followed his advice and bought one years ago," Dorrin said.

Once in the palace courtyard, amid the bustle of grooms and servants, Arian led Dorrin away to the ossuary, as if the bag slung over Dorrin's shoulder were nothing of importance. The Seneschal greeted Arian but ignored Dorrin, even turning slightly away from her.

"The matter we spoke of several days ago," Arian said.

"Yes, my queen. If the queen will ready herself."

Arian went to the bench beside a door with a green wreath above it, sat down, and took off her boots. With a finger to her lips, she pointed to Dorrin. The Seneschal, Dorrin noticed, had his back to her, humming a tune she did not recognize. She sat down and pulled off her boots, then her socks.

Arian rose, pushed open the door under the wreath, and Dorrin followed her into a room unlike any she had ever seen. Whitewashed stone walls, a stone floor, and rows of racks on which were laid brightly painted skeletons.

Arian closed the door and said softly. "The Seneschal did not see you. He will not speak to you. You were not here. Come, let me show you Kieri's father."

The decorated bones looked grotesque to Dorrin. She could not read the writing; Arian read a few of the things on Kieri's father's bones then said, "Choose a place for your treasures that you can find if we are busy distracting the magelords."

Dorrin untied the sack and pulled out the crown in its wrappings. "Do you want to see them?"

"No," Arian said. "Then I can truthfully say I have not seen them. King Mikeli described them for us. Do you know yet what they are?"

"I think so, but I think I should not say it aloud, even here. The dead do not talk, but—" Whispers rose in the room, a susurration as of crowds in the distance. Dorrin shuddered. "Pardon," she said. "I meant no disrespect." Silence again, heavy around her shoulders.

"Quickly," Arian said.

Dorrin felt no attraction to any part of the ossuary but the door out; she put the crown back in the sack and the sack itself under the table on which Kieri's father's bones lay. When Arian opened the door, the Seneschal still faced away from them, now near another door, and stayed there while they put their boots back on.

"Thank you, Seneschal," Arian said in a normal tone.

"My pleasure, my lady," he said without turning around. "I am always honored to see you." The faintest emphasis on "you." Arian led Dorrin up the steps to the courtyard and from there to the palace entrance.

"Your rooms are where they were before," she said. "I must go feed the twins . . . Come see them when you're refreshed."

Dorrin could have found the room, but servants led her anyway. She bathed, changed, and spent a pleasant hour with Arian and the twins before Kieri returned.

"How is Mikeli?" he asked after greeting her.

"Worried, grieving, and angry," Dorrin said. "He loves—loved—Camwyn dearly, scamp though the boy was."

"Any evidence that Mikeli himself has magery? With both a brother and a cousin—"

"I have felt nothing in him yet, though like you, I think it is certainly possible."

"And will tear Tsaia apart if he has and it's found out," Kieri said.

"If it manifests, he will confess it," Dorrin said. "You know how he is."

"I do indeed." Kieri leaned back in his chair. "You're looking well, Dorrin, but . . . this journey . . . do you know where you need to go?"

"South," she said. "That is all I know."

"Aare?"

"Yes," she said, not surprised he had guessed.

"I can help you—partly shield you—if you go across Lyonya to Prealíth and take ship from there."

"Is there a road?"

"Not exactly; you would travel with an escort who knows the way. I have met the Sea-Prince . . . You did, too, at the wedding, didn't you?"

"Yes, but just an introduction."

"Still. We have written back and forth. He gave me warnings about Alured, admitted he knew him well years ago. I believe he could arrange passage for you."

"Should I leave before the magelords return?"

"That is your decision. I wish—we cannot tell, you see, if they are what they claim, magelords who were driven out by Girdish hatred though they tried to fit in. We cannot tell if they were blood mages who took over others' bodies—if any of them are like that."

"You want me to—"

"It is your choice, Dorrin. You're not my captain; you're Mikeli's vassal, not mine—"

"He released me from that oath. He said I must be free of concern about him and his realm."

"Well, then. You are free of all oaths but Falk's." Kieri touched his own ruby. "I will not urge this on you. It would be a service to me, yes, but a danger to you and your mission. I cannot gauge how large that danger is, because I do not know enough about the things you brought. Mikeli described them but not their powers. I would ask—do you think you must try to get the necklace away from Alured?"

Dorrin shook her head. "No. The . . . the crown has said nothing about it. If it is part of the same set—and I think it is—then I believe Alured will find he cannot keep it from the rest. My task is to take the crown where it wants to go."

On your head. Together.

She stiffened. *Not here,* she thought back to it.

Safe now. No dangers near.

"What was that?" Kieri said.

"It told me something. I asked it not to talk to me here. Arian said one of the magelords was in the city. It thinks there's no danger."

Kieri gave a low whistle. "I'm glad my crown doesn't talk to me." Then he stood. "Time for dinner—I hear stirrings outside the door. I must go down; will you ladies come, or shall I have yours sent here?"

"Let's go down," Arian said.

Dinner reminded Dorrin of dinners at Kieri's old steading or her own at Verrakai House. Squires, the king and queen, and the other guests all talked freely, as if with equals. Kieri had invited two of his Siers, both women, and a couple of merchants. Dorrin had seen Lady—now Sier—Tolmaric before, but she was entirely different from the distraught and helpless widow Dorrin remembered. Confident, she discussed the progression of the river port constructed on land she had ceded and the revenues coming in from both the port and an inn she'd built. Sier Davonin, much older, spent most of her time in Chaya, where she also had commercial ventures. One of the merchants traveled regularly to Tsaia on the River Road and wanted to know from Dorrin when the Middle Road would be open. The other had come to the new port from Immer. Squires chimed in with their observations from their courier trips about the kingdom. Nobody mentioned the reason for Dorrin's visit except Sier Davonin.

"You were here last year, I remember, Duke Verrakai. So sad, that was, all those babes lost. I suppose you've come to see the twins."

"Yes," Dorrin said, grateful for an acceptable excuse. "They're a handsome pair."

"Falki is so like his father, spare the dark hair. Tilla's a beauty but not much like Arian," Sier Davonin went on. "But they'll be trouble once they're up on their legs, I've no doubt. Not to tell tales, Duke Verrakai, but our king, as a tiny lad, was too bold for his own good. If they have his bold ways, and two of them—!"

"We'll keep close watch, my lady," Kieri said. Sier Davonin raised her brows but said no more about it.

After dinner, the guests went back to the city. Kieri and Arian went upstairs with Dorrin. The twins were asleep, and they settled around the table in Kieri's room to talk. A King's Squire brought a pitcher and three fluted glasses, then left the room at Kieri's gesture.

"I noticed High Marshal Seklis wasn't at dinner—isn't he staying here?"

"He went with the magelords on their tour to keep an eye on them, he said."

"Tell me more about them—I know Seklis is suspicious of any mage-powers, but you and Arian seem uncertain as well. Why?"

"If you'll excuse the diversion," Kieri said, "I should start with something else—it explains some of the uncertainty."

"Of course," Dorrin said.

"You need to know about the elvenhome." Kieri poured for all three of them. Dorrin took a sip of cool water with a hint of tart fruit juice. "I wrote you, but none of the details, and I think they may be important." He began with his realization that he had come to the very place where his mother had been killed and he had been captured. After describing the relics that rose from the ground, he said, "I can only think that the taig itself took them . . . why not the sword, I can't imagine."

"Did you find out who had done it?"

"Yes. An elf who hated my mother—she said, for having married my father, but I suspect more than that." He related the story in detail. "So after I killed her, I realized that the light was coming from me. There'd been that incident with Torfinn—but I thought that was something else. And on the way back, from the way the taig reacted, I knew it was the elvenhome growing around me."

"You . . . it's yours now?"

"In some way, though I think Arian is also involved. We're both half-elven and both from royal lines. Her father had the gift from his father, though it was not known that it could be passed to a half-elven child." What Kieri told her seemed impossible—if very few elves could form an elvenhome, how could a half-elf? The Elders had always held themselves apart; she had always assumed they were infinitely more powerful.

"Is this something new or something they did not know?"

He nodded. "That is the exact question I want answered. Amrothlin—my elven uncle—and Arian's father both insist it's never been heard of before in all the vanryn of elvenlore. But—bearing on your mission from your king and what little he's told me about the regalia—I wonder the same thing. This resurgence of magery in Tsaia and Fintha—is it connected to the regalia or something else? Amrothlin wonders if the Singer is changing the song."

Dorrin frowned. "I don't understand what that has to do with your having—making?—an elvenhome."

"What if it's all connected somehow? Magery in Tsaia and Fintha, the regalia—clearly an ancient power of some kind—my ability to form an elvenhome, the iynisin, whom the elves here refused to admit existed for so long. And the dragon, too. What if it's all one story, begun long before us and continuing to an end we cannot see?"

"I can't see the pattern, Kieri. What do you think connects—oh." Power, of course. Magery—human, elven, iynisin, and probably gnomish and dwarven as well.

"You have your powers from mageborn who came from Aare. I

have some that way, though I never sought to use it, but my guess is that it's entwined with what I did inherit from my mother. Then there's the Old Human side."

Dorrin shivered. "What you found in the ossuary?"

"And under the mound in the King's Grove. I suspect it's why magery's recurring in Tsaia and Fintha . . . it's a mix of mageries, not the pure form of either."

"But why now?"

He cocked his head. "You really don't know?"

"No."

"Two things, I believe. Two old mageries were released when I became king of Lyonya and you became Duke Verrakai. And the same person wakened both—Paks. Everything's changed since she became a paladin. I became a king, you became a duke, Arcolin took over the Company and is now a duke."

Dorrin thought about that. "She's Girdish . . . so it's Gird behind it all?"

"More than that. Were you there when she said she wasn't *just* Girdish? I think the high gods also move her, and when she moves, change follows."

Dorrin nodded. "It certainly does. Paks told me I should take out what was in the vault and examine it. Then she told me I should take the crown to Mikeli to prove my loyalty."

"She is the flame that lights the candle," Kieri said, "and then the candle lights the oil. But her flame comes from the gods."

Dorrin drank off the rest of her glass and set it down firmly. "But now we come to my decision—to leave now and make all speed where the crown wants to go or stay and help you find out what these mage-lords really are. And I still do not have your full assessment of them."

"Pardon," Kieri said. "They are so unlike people I know today— and their language so strange, though it is easier now—that I have found it difficult. They are not comfortable people. They use their powers openly, easily, with no sign of effort. Granted, I had seen only wizards until I met elves—not true mages. They seem to test, constantly, the strength of one another's magery—and tried to test mine—by casting enchantments."

"How strong are they?"

Kieri shrugged. "I cannot tell. Not as strong as I am, and I have no tame mages with which to compare them."

"Except me," Dorrin said. She grinned at him. "As you tested me when we were young."

He grinned back. "So I did, young fool that I was myself. And I may be a fool now to ask you to risk yourself—"

"Oh, I would gladly risk *myself*. It is that other I must not risk. How sure are you that the ossuary is enough protection?"

"Very sure," Kieri said. "And certain that I can shield you, at least temporarily, when you take it away."

"We should ask Falk," Arian said. "Three Knights of Falk and we're talking about something that may affect the whole world—we should at least ask guidance."

Dorrin nodded. "We should indeed."

Silence followed in which Dorrin had a curious vision: she was surrounded by a curtain of falling water yet was dry. She reached out a hand to the water, and it avoided her hand. Through the opening she could see a vast barren plain of red sands and black rock, but out from the curtain of falling water flowed a stream of grass, the blades bending under the movement of the water. That vision changed, and instead she saw herself as she had been, ardent and young, receiving her ruby when she became a Knight of Falk.

She opened her eyes. "Well?" she said, as Kieri and Arian said nothing.

"It is up to you," he said. "That's all the answer I received."

"I will see your magelords," she said. "And I will be very wary."

CHAPTER TWENTY-ONE

Chaya, Lyonya

The magelords arrived back in Chaya two days later. Dorrin spent the intervening time making arrangements for her travel east. Kieri sent two Squires ahead of her with supplies and spare horses so that she could ride out in an ordinary way.

High Marshal Seklis came to the palace first; the magelords had returned to their lodgings in the city.

"Duke Verrakai!" he said. "I thought you would be . . . somewhere else by now."

"King Kieri thinks I might be useful in learning whether these magelords are like my father was."

"That's true," Seklis said. "But what about the regalia?"

"Safe," Kieri said.

"I'll be leaving soon," Dorrin said. "I stayed only to help, if I can, discern which of these magelords might be harboring another spirit."

Seklis took Dorrin to see the magelords at their lodgings. The first she met, though glad to see another magelord, one familiar with the present-day world, seemed more ordinary than she had expected. They had put off the clothes in which they'd arrived, trading them for local styles. "Even the mail," one said. "I hope no fighting here, ever."

"And I as well," Dorrin said. "Peace prospers lands and peoples."

At the next inn where magelords lodged, she felt something even as they entered, but when they asked the landlord which rooms the magelords had, he shook his head.

"They went out a glass ago at least. I don't know where—the market, maybe?"

Outside, Seklis said, "Those are the ones I most wanted you to see, Duke Verrakai. Something about them—it's as if they're laughing at us from behind a screen."

They found no magelords in the main market square, nor had anyone seen them.

"We should go back," Dorrin said. "If they're at the palace and I'm not—"

"Yes," Seklis said, the set of his mouth grim. "They will be snooping about again."

"Again?"

"Well, they say they only want to learn about this time so they will fit in. I don't believe it."

A small group of magelords were at the palace when Dorrin and Seklis arrived. Dorrin knew at once that several of them had changed bodies. Kieri was with them, looking annoyed.

"They came in search of you, Duke Verrakai," he said formally. "And somehow they did not find you on the way."

"Nor did we see them," Dorrin said. "But now we are met. Will you introduce us?"

Kieri nodded. "This is Duke Verrakai, of whom you have heard. She is an old friend and came here to visit the queen and our children." He paused, and one woman stepped forward. "This is Flannath, Duke Verrakai, who has been most anxious to make your acquaintance."

Flannath looked to be some years Dorrin's junior, dark hair braided in a coil on top of her head. She bowed politely to Dorrin. "My lady Duke . . . or is it my lord?"

"As you will," Dorrin said easily. The person within that younger body was older, and thus Flannath was someone to distrust. One after another the others came up, all polite, even cordial. Dualian, another woman. Matharin, a man in older middle age, and his son, Lethrin. Caldor and Norin, brothers. Fifteen in all, and every one of them in a body other than that of their birth.

Kieri, standing behind them now, raised his brows. Dorrin smiled and ran her hand through her hair, down to the ruby of her knighthood: a signal Kieri knew. He excused himself to the group and left the room with a hand signal to Dorrin that meant he was going for reinforcements.

Matharin spoke up. "There was a crown and other jewels in our day, sent to Verrakai for safekeeping, after Greenfields."

"A crown?" said Dorrin. "There is no crown there now."

"But you Verrakai, is?"

"Yes," Dorrin said.

"You know old words . . . power words?"

"Some," Dorrin said.

He uttered a string of words that Dorrin half understood, among them "speak" and "true" and "yield." The hairs rose on her neck as she felt power wrap around her. Without hesitation she responded with the command words Verrakai knew. Matharin stared, and his son's eyes widened.

"You great mage," he said. "You ruler! Why here? Why not you rule?"

"Tsaia has a king," Dorrin said. "I obey my king."

"He more mage?"

"He is the *king*," Dorrin said. She was not going to reveal what this man would think Mikeli's weakness. "A good king."

He shrugged. "Strong is good."

"He is not weak," Dorrin said.

"We go Tsaia, meet him."

"He says no," Dorrin said. "None of you will go to Tsaia."

"He afraid of trial of strength?" Without giving her time to answer he went on. "I go; I challenge him. King is strongest. Grahlin made mistake, follow weak king. I no make."

"You were at Greenfields?"

"No . . . that king weak. No follow weak king."

"You did not challenge him?"

"Grahlin said no. Grahlin stronger than me."

"Legends say he had great water magery," Dorrin said.

The man nodded. "He did. Nearly kill Gird once, did kill many. Water magery greatest of mageries. He last to have. He father-father make water shape. You know?"

YES.

She heard the regalia as clearly as ever and hoped the magelord did not. He narrowed his eyes at her but not, she thought, with that knowledge.

"Water shape?" she said.

"Solid. Like glass. Like . . . jewel."

The truth burst upon her. Jewels. Water. Regalia. Not magical jewels that might repel the sand and call water but water itself, the element. No wonder the rockfolk disclaimed knowledge of their origin.

"That's . . . impossible," she said. "Water can't be solid except as ice or snow. Magery can't change something's nature."

He grinned, more relaxed than he'd been before. "So much lost. You strong mage but not know. You have some water magery, yes?"

"Yes," Dorrin said. "I healed a cursed well, brought water."

"You broke mage curse? Very strong, you. Verrakaisti always strong. Cannot believe they lost crown."

Dorrin shrugged. "Maybe they took it somewhere else. It has been a long time."

"If you alive back in our time, your family teach more water magery. Make jewels, maybe." His look was challenging. "Would give much for such jewels. Have only this." He dipped into a pocket in his tunic and brought out a jewel the size of her little fingertip, red as blood and reeking with evil power. "Know what this is?"

"It looks like blood," Dorrin said. "Do you say it is made with blood as you say the others are with water?"

He nodded. "Yes. Much blood it takes. A hundred and a hundred died for this." He wrapped his hand around it quickly as if afraid she might take it from him. "You do magery with blood?"

"Never," Dorrin said. She could not keep the anger out of her voice. "Blood magery is evil."

He lifted one shoulder and let it fall. "So that peasant said. I not agree. What your king say? And this one?"

"Use blood magery here or in Tsaia and you will die." His brows went up: disbelief. "You know I am stronger than you; so is Lyonya's king. I will kill you if you use blood magery here."

"You would kill your own kind?"

"I have killed mages," Dorrin said. She did not elaborate.

His hands moved in a gesture she hoped meant submission. "It is good to know. No blood magery here. Over the sea is same?"

"Over the sea?"

"Esa-aare, sun-land, Esea Sunlord's home. Do you not know it?"

"I do not," Dorrin said. "The Seafolk trade there, I think. Pargunese and Kostandanyans."

"Seafolk . . . good fighters after they learned ships; we taught them that after taking land. What that red jewel you wear, if not blood jewel?"

"Falk's honor, a ruby," Dorrin said. "You know of Falk and the Knights of Falk?"

He sniffed. "King Cunias's youngest son, yes. Before our time, but heard story. He never amount to anything. When he came back that time, he crippled and scarred and no one marry him, so Cunias offered him a woodsman's house and a servant, but he went away. The Company of Falk just band of younger sons, not inheriting. Wander around with Falk, wear rags until tired of it. Went back to real clothes after Falk die. You are one?"

"Yes. I trained here in Lyonya, at Falk's Hall."

"All students mages?"

"No. Only some. But all well born. Girdish now have knightly orders, you know."

He laughed. "The peasants? Did they finally learn to ride horses and wear fancy clothes?"

"Indeed yes," Dorrin said.

His eyes narrowed. "It is hard to believe a Verrakai would not know about the crown even if it had been moved."

"I left home early," Dorrin said. "My father did not like me. He was angry that I wanted to be in the Company of Falk."

"Ah. Suspected you a bastard and did not wait to see that you had the water magery. Sorry later, no doubt."

"No doubt," Dorrin said. "But I came to the title and the estate. To my knowledge there is no crown as you describe anywhere in the house or on the estate."

"It may have been suspected and they moved it. Too bad you do not know."

Dorrin blessed the years of military service that gave her the control she needed now.

Finally he bowed and left her. The others followed, with polite excuses. Dorrin went immediately to Kieri's office, where a group of King's Squires, both western and local elves, and Aliam Halveric waited.

"What have you learned?" Kieri asked.

"Much to distress us," Dorrin said. "All in that group are indeed in others' bodies. Matharin, the oldest man, not only has shifted bodies at least once, he admits to having used blood magery. I warned him that use of blood magery here would mean his death. He confirms the story King Torfinn told you of how the Pargunese came here: the magelords invaded and stole their land across the ocean. I now know their name for that land; they think it's where Esea Sunlord came from. Matharin thinks Falk was a fool and his father reasonable to send him away."

"By my word, Dorrin, you could have killed him for being a blood mage—are you sure he is not one now? And how did he survive the Girdish Wars and make his way to Kolobia? I thought all those mages who left were thought to be of good character."

"He survived the war by not being at Greenfields," Dorrin said. She told him what Matharin had said. "I suspect he survived later by transferring to the body he now wears and pretending to be a peasant, but I did not ask him that."

"Faithless to his liege *and* a blood mage," Kieri said. Dorrin could feel his anger, see it in the tightening of his mouth. "I will not have him here. He must go or die. I wish—"

"I did not know what killing by magery would do to your elvenhome or the taig," Dorrin said.

"You could have used steel," Kieri said.

"He will fight with magery," Dorrin said. "He tried to dominate me and now considers me stronger, but he would use magery to defend himself. That's another of the things you must know. Will that destroy or harm the elvenhome, do you think?"

"I don't know," Kieri said. "Amrothlin?" He looked at one of the elves.

"No human magery can harm the elvenhome, sir king, but only injury to you."

"Do you think he sensed the regalia?" Kieri asked.

"No. He showed no sign of it, and he was not as careful of his face as I was of mine. I believe, too, that the regalia wants nothing to do with his kind. And I now know what the stones are."

"What?"

"At least what he thinks they are. Water, changed by magery to jewels. He showed me a bloodstone, made he said from the blood of a hundred men."

Kieri's face paled. "Bloodstone! Are you sure?"

"It felt evil to me, but I do not know more than he told me."

He looked at Arian. "Baron Sekkady, the magelord who held me captive all those years, had a bloodstone the size of my fist. He told me it held his power and the blood of ten thousand, drained one by one into it. He used it to control people; he said the spirits of those men were trapped in their blood."

"But the water . . ." Arian said, her hand on Kieri's arm. "Are *those* stones evil?"

NO.

"I am sure they're not," Dorrin said. "I think they're why the Sandlord came. I think the old magelords used up the water to make them."

"So few?"

"Who knows how many jugs of water it takes to make one of them? You say the blood of ten thousand went into the fist-sized stone—imagine if it were water—and we don't know if the amounts are the same. Or if the stones in the regalia are the only stones. Remember, I told you more were found on Verrakai land."

"It hardly seems possible . . ." Kieri said.

"I know. And yet . . . the regalia say that's what it is . . . they've been trying to tell me, but I didn't understand. That's why they want to go back to Old Aare, I'm sure. There's some way to undo the magery and restore the water."

"But the other magelords want the regalia and the power in the jewels to regain their power. Of course." He stroked his beard. "And we must not let them. This one you spoke with—is he the most dangerous, do you think?"

"I won't know without talking to the others. I suspect he's their leader—or the most powerful mage, which means the same to him. He wanted to go fight King Mikeli for the throne; he thinks only mage strength matters."

"We can't wait," Kieri said. "It will not be long before they do mischief, one way or another. I thought them stupid and harmless at first, so far out of their time, so ignorant of current happenings, but even one magelord determined to upset rule—Mikeli's, mine, the Marshal-General's—"

"Is too many. Yes."

Another King's Squire came to the door. "Sir king, a messenger arrived for Duke Verrakai; he will not say the cause—"

Dorrin's belly clenched again. "What colors?"

"Tsaian."

"Excuse me, then," she said.

The messenger, a royal courier, was still standing in the entrance hall, gulping down a mug of water, when she emerged and nearly dropped the mug in his haste to reach her. "My lord Duke, the king's word—" He held out the velvet pouch.

Dorrin took it. "I have received the king's word," she said formally. "You have witnessed it."

"I must start back," he said, taking another gulp from the mug.

"You must rest until the Master of Horse finds you a mount," Dorrin said. "And why not overnight?"

"King's orders," the man said. "Do not spend even the turn of a glass in that place with magelords, he said. Leave at once, ride back to the nearest relay station—"

"That's a half-day's ride," Dorrin said. "You won't be there until full dark, even riding fast."

"I must—the king said—"

"Did he not want an answer from me to whatever this is?" Dorrin asked.

"Yes, if you could, but he expected you'd send your own messenger."

"Come with me," Dorrin said, and led the way outside. To the doorward, she said, "Send for food and drink from the kitchen; I will be in the stables with this man."

She found the Master of Horse in his office looking at the list of mounts available for courier duty. "We have three lame and one that needs shoes," he said as he looked up. "The king's been lending mounts to these visiting magelords any time they want to ride, so the horses are out every day. I've only two in who are rested, besides the Squires' horses, which cannot be lent. Of those two, the gray knows that trail—are you comfortable with air and water horses?"

The courier looked confused.

"Elves prefer grays and blue roans," Dorrin murmured. "The color of air and water, they say. Humans here prefer earth and fire horses: bays, chestnuts, red roans."

"Oh . . . ah . . . I ride any color," the courier said.

"He's in the west paddock right now," the Master of Horse said. "I'll have him brought in and tacked up—say, a turn of the glass."

"I'm having a meal brought from the palace," Dorrin said. "It's crowded in there, and a bit of quiet won't do us any harm. I need to read the king's word that this courier brought me."

"Stable mess is quiet enough for another turn of the glass," the Master of Horse said. "Second door on the left. I'll send in the food when it comes."

The room—the size of a double box stall—had a table, six chairs, and a wall of cubbyholes. The courier sat down, leaning on the table. Dorrin untied the ribbons on the velvet pouch and pulled out the king's message.

The news, as she'd expected from its urgency, was not good.

*You must leave at once. We captured a spy who knew the re-
galia was with you and no longer in Our treasury; this spy revealed that others knew as well. You endanger Kieri of Lyonya
as well as Our own person and reign. Please—go quickly. Send
word if you can that you are gone, but if not, just go.*

Leaving at once would mean retrieving the regalia from the ossuary. If the magelords, especially Matharin, could sense the regalia
directly, then they, too, would know, and they were surely—she had
to believe—closer than any pursuit from Tsaia could be.

"Sometimes solutions lead only to new problems," she said aloud;
the courier stared at her. "I'm sorry," she said. "It's just—I dare not
give the king an answer lest you be beset on the road. He is right that
you must not linger here, tired as you are, but anything I send with
you might be intercepted."

A noise in the corridor alerted her; she stood and made for the
door. Servants with trays . . . and behind them, a sly look on his face,
Matharin.

Dorrin waved the servants into the room, where they set out
dishes and bowls of food on the table but stood in the doorway,
blocking Matharin.

"I thought you were busy with correspondence," Matharin said,
brow raised. "In the stable?"

"I had a new message," Dorrin said. "From my king, who bade
his courier return in haste. I came here with him to arrange for a fresh
horse and thought we might as well eat here. Why should that concern you?"

"Oh . . . so you *are* busy . . ." No relaxation in his stance, no re-
lenting in his gaze. "But I wonder if I might have just a moment—"

His gaze fogged; Dorrin felt a wave of enchantment. It did not affect her, but she heard noises in the room behind her—falling crockery, someone falling to the floor, followed by unnatural silence. She
did not turn to look; she met his gaze steadily, and her own power
rose within her. "You forget that you are merely a guest," she said.
"And a guest does not so abuse a host's servants. Not if the guest
wishes to remain within the protection of guest-right."

"I merely gave us a quiet place in which to talk," he said. "They take no harm, though the maid will have to wipe redroots off her face."

Falk, help me. Dorrin felt a surge in her own power and shaped it into a spear that pierced the bubble of silence he had wrought, and then—with no attempt at gentleness—she thrust him away with power alone. He staggered back and back again until he fell against a stall door across the aisle.

"You!" he snarled, pushing himself to his feet. Dorrin walked forward, and he stumbled sideways toward the stable opening. She walked with him, keeping the pressure on, noting as she went by that the Master of Horse was slumped over his desk and the palace courtyard empty of its usual traffic.

"You abused guest-right," Dorrin said. "And I, as the representative of Tsaia's king and the friend of Lyonya's, will not let you get away with it."

"What are you going to do, kill me?" he asked, all sarcasm now. He made a gesture with one hand, and Dorrin felt his power pushing against hers.

"I am going to present you to King Kieri for judgment," Dorrin said. "As I would do with any thief or liar or lurking menace I found in his palace."

"You can't—" He made more gestures, this time rubbing the bloodstone on his finger. Wind swirled in the courtyard, cold as Midwinter night.

Dorrin's gesture quieted the wind. "You are not the ruler here," she said. "Your day is done."

He opened his mouth again, but Dorrin saw Kieri coming across the courtyard, glowing in silvery elf-light, his sword already drawn, his Squires and some of the elves behind him.

"What has this fellow done?" Kieri asked.

"He laid silence on all in the stable, holding them in thrall, including your Master of Horse, and would have forced me to speak to him if he had been able. He has abused guest-right; I was bringing him to you for judgment."

"You dare not harm me," Matharin said. "I am greater than you know—"

"You are a blood mage," Kieri said, his voice cold as stone in winter. "You have taken body after body, killing the souls of those born to them. You believe that puts you beyond all law. You are wrong."

"I am—" Matharin's face shifted from anger to calm in a moment; his lips quirked in that false smile. "I am no danger to *you*, sir king— you are more powerful. And there is much I could teach you, ancient wisdom lost for centuries."

Kieri's answering smile held no mercy. "From my elven mother, I have ancient wisdom of vanyrin, not mere centuries, and from my years as a soldier, I have war's wisdom, which knows an enemy and the use of a sword."

Matharin's expression changed again from calm to exasperation to, finally, fear. "You cannot—you would not—it would be murder to kill an unarmed man—a guest—"

Kieri shook his head. "No mage is unarmed. I have seen and felt your magery, and I know you have used it to harm my people. Your life is forfeit."

Amrothlin now stood behind Kieri, his sword also drawn. "I am here," he said.

"Little you know." Matharin looked calm again, and as they watched, his human semblance darkened, blistered, and peeled away, leaving behind a dark-clothed shape Dorrin had seen—and fought— before. Iynisin . . . how had she not known that? How had the *elves* not known that?

The iynisin laughed as a sword grew from his hand, flickering with mage-light. With his other hand, he made a gesture and a dagger appeared in an instant. "You call us evil, you tree lovers who claim the name of singers. And you humans . . . blackcloaks, isn't it? Or tree haters, which is true in part, or unsingers? The names mean nothing. Your rules mean nothing."

Dorrin took a step toward him, pushing with all her power, but he did not retreat, and she could not advance. As she watched, his shape wavered, as if to disappear, then solidified again.

"That won't work now," Kieri said. He moved. "Dorrin—hold what you have and no more."

"She can't—"

From the corner of her eye, Dorrin saw other magelords in the palace entrance; Matharin's son, Lethrin, ran down the steps, both hands glowing with mage-light.

"Kieri! 'Ware behind!"

Two King's Squires turned, intercepted Lethrin, and—when he drew a dagger and lunged—spitted him on their blades. Kieri did not turn; Matharin's lunge toward him met steel—blade clashing against blade. Matharin's form wavered again, solidified again, as both Kieri and Amrothlin pressed in. Dorrin dared not look aside. She ignored the noise from the palace entrance—the magelords, Squires, palace staff yelling, struggling—as she would have noise on the battlefield, meaningful only if it suggested a reinforcement or a weakness. Instead, she concentrated on Matharin—now recognizable as iynisin—using her magery to hold him in that one form so that he could not be become invisible or divide into ephemes, as the other iynisin had done.

She did not see the blade wielded by one of the other mages until it was a handbreadth from her face, striking from the left side. She whirled, grabbed for her dagger—but it was in the other's hand. He lunged again. Dorrin retreated, drawing her sword, frantic to keep her power on what had been Matharin, but she could not ignore the attacker. At least he had no long blade—but the dagger was faster than her sword. Then he had two daggers, one in either hand . . . and then another danced in the air before her.

They could multiply things; she'd been told that. Including—she jerked her head aside—daggers. But how many could he control at once? And how experienced was he? She snapped her blade back and forth and charged him. One dagger rang against her blade and fell; the man jabbed at her with the daggers in his hands, a beginner's mistake—and her sword swept his arms aside, almost severing one. He dropped both daggers and screamed, stumbling backward. Dorrin rushed him before he could gather his wits and killed him quickly.

When she turned back to Kieri and Amrothlin, the iynisin was dead, a sprawled mess on the paving stones. Kieri shook the guts from his sword and looked at Dorrin. "Well done, my lord Duke. You gave us time."

"And you," she said.

The courtyard now was ringed with elves, the hand of surviving magelords huddled in a tight group at the foot of the stairs, under guard. Five more lay dead, sprawled between that group and Kieri. Dorrin spotted a stealthy movement along the wall behind the others, a hunched figure, almost invisible, heading for the passage between the main palace and the salle. "There!" she said, pointing. The figure tossed something at the nearest elf and then ran for the passage. The elf crumpled. Dorrin ran after the magelord, but he made it into the salle before she could stop him.

Except it was not "he" but a woman, Flannath. Dorrin caught a glimpse of Siger and Carlion turning from the rack of practice blades, then a gesture of Flannath's hand plunged the salle into darkness.

Dorrin called her own light, but only a dim glow came, just enough to see the blade that flew at her and evade it. Then light filled the salle again as elves came through the door, and the iynisin who had worn Flannath's skin hissed, then screamed in what Dorrin guessed was elvish. Together, Dorrin and the elves advanced, trapping the iynisin in the far end of the salle. An elf killed it; Dorrin turned to look for the armsmasters. Both were alive, unharmed.

Out in the courtyard, Dorrin found Kieri, looking as grim as she had ever seen him, staring at the bodies. All the magelords there were dead, not just the ones she had seen attacking. "What happened?" she asked. "Did these also join the fight?"

"They ran at us," one of the elves said. "They threw fire from their hands and dire spells."

"And they had all stolen the bodies they wore," Kieri said. "Murderers."

"What about the others?" Dorrin asked. "The ones in the city?"

"The others," Kieri said, "await my judgment. And I do not know what is best to do."

"I know you'll say the Girdish are unfair," Seklis said, "but while I'll agree a child who turns mage may be innocent, these are mages from the days when mages ruled and abused those they ruled. As long as they have mage-powers, they're a danger."

"What kind of king invites visitors and then condemns them to death when they have not yet offended?" Kieri asked. "The others have not stolen bodies, have they?" He looked at Dorrin.

"I know all of these had; I am not sure of the others—most have not. But they may have done other mischief."

"You can't trust them," Seklis said. "Not any of them. Not while they have magery and know how to misuse it."

"Sir king, what about the Knight-Commander—or the Captain-General of Falk?" Dorrin said. "Remember that my magery was locked for years; I had no use of it or even the knowledge that I had it. Perhaps the magery of those remaining could also be locked."

"Could you do it, Dorrin?" Kieri asked. "It would be days before either of those could come here."

"I don't know," Dorrin said. "I could try, but I've never done it."

"We will try it," Kieri said. "Come—before they do something."

"But magery can be unlocked again," Seklis said. "Sir king—it is not wise—"

"No paladin is going to unlock *their* magery," Kieri said. "Dorrin didn't recover hers by herself."

At the first inn, where the sick magewomen were staying, they found the innkeeper and several servants staring in consternation at the two dead magewomen on the stairs, blood pooled around them. "I swear, sir king, I did nothing to them. The one who got sick first ran down the stairs and out the door, and then, before I could even shout after her, these two come staggering and falling . . . they'd been stabbed. Stabbed!"

"Dualian," Kieri said. "The first to get sick and the one who didn't die of it."

"But—she—a woman killed them?"

"I think so," Kieri said. "And tried to kill others . . . but she's dead now."

"What about the sick woman upstairs—will she kill me?"

"No," Kieri said. He turned to two of his Squires. "Go up and make sure she's really sick—and then make sure she stays there."

Very shortly nearly all the remaining magelords were collected in the common room of one inn. One sat slumped in a corner with a jug of ale before him; the innkeeper said he spent every day drinking.

"I brought you here to save your lives," Kieri said. "I could have broken your enchantment and let the dragon melt you into the stone itself."

They stared at him but said nothing. Dorrin sensed nothing but shock and fear.

"I meant you no harm," Kieri went on. "But some of you meant harm to me and mine and broke the guest-truce. They used magery against me—against me, the rightful king. Against others as well."

"Who?" one of them asked.

"They died," Kieri said without answering that question. "They died at my hand and the hands of my people because they broke the guest-truce. These are their names . . ." He named them one by one. "And these are the women Dualian killed on the way to seeking my death. Mages like you."

Silence again.

"I welcomed you with an open mind," Kieri said. "You have eaten from my hand, been housed by my hand, and I had hoped to see you living and prospering. But now . . . now I know I cannot trust you. Not as you are. Not as mages."

"But we are—" one of the younger men said.

"Yes. You are mages, mages from old times, and I do not trust you. You have a choice. You can choose to give up your magery. Or you can die."

"But . . . but lord King . . . without magery how can we live?"

"I lived without magery for years," Dorrin said. "I was in Falk's Hall as a youth, and my magery was locked away because I was not trusted."

"But now?"

"Now," said Dorrin, "I have the same powers as you, and stronger. No harm came to me from learning to live without it. It can be so for you."

Disbelief on all the faces turned to her. The drunk in the corner giggled, pointed, and a jug on the bar across the room lifted and came to him. He took it, poured the contents down his throat, dropped the jug, and slumped over onto the table, mouth open.

"How can we not be mages?"

"I can lock your magery," Dorrin said. "But I will not do so unless you agree, each of you individually. Only understand: the king's command stands. Either you allow it or you will die this day."

"It would have been better if you had let us die out there!" one of them said.

"Is that your choice?" Kieri asked.

For answer, the man threw fire at Kieri; one of the elves speared the man as Kieri's gesture dispersed the fire. The others gaped.

"That solves one problem," Seklis said.

Kieri turned on him. "So might a magelord have said when killing a band of peasants in Gird's War. So might an iynisin have said, killing me. Are we no better than that, to think only of our convenience?"

Seklis flushed and bit his lip. "I'm sorry, sir king. It is unworthy of me. Unworthy of any follower of Gird, who did, we know, want mages and nonmages to live in peace."

The remaining mages looked at one another and back at Kieri.

"Fifteen of your number died at the palace," he said. "And two more of the malice of one of the fifteen. Decide." He pointed to one in the front. "You. Tell me now."

The man looked at Dorrin, then back to Kieri. "I . . . she may block my magery."

Dorrin felt her way into the core of his magery and found the same formation the Knight-Commander had found in her. She touched it, twisted . . . and it was done.

Two more agreed before one shook his head. "I don't care—I don't like it here, and I see nothing to gain in living longer. I will not resist, but there is no need to make more mess for the landlord. The stableyard will do."

In the end, fewer than two hands of them agreed to have their magery locked away. The forlorn little group straggled back to their lodgings, alone in a foreign land and foreign time.

"I don't think they'll live long," Dorrin said when she, Kieri, and Seklis had returned to the palace. In the meantime, the bodies had been taken away; no trace remained of the fight except in their memories.

"I hated it," Kieri said. "It wasn't fair—"

"You couldn't have done anything else, sir king," Seklis said. "Mages of old—"

"Enough," Kieri said through his teeth. Seklis stepped back. "You don't understand. You're Girdish." He took a long breath. "Good or evil, mage or not, they were guests. *Guests.* They had no choice; I broke the enchantment and brought them here; I was responsible for them—"

"Not for their choices," Dorrin said. "Falk's Rules."

"The king," Kieri said heavily, "is responsible for everything." He turned to Caernith. "Did you know all the time they were like this? That it would end like this for even the best of them?"

Caernith bowed. "Lord king, we did not know how it would end, only that without you it would end worse, with more and more iynisin emerging to spread their hatred and evil everywhere. If I may suggest . . ."

"Go ahead," Kieri said, still through clenched teeth.

"Honor those who chose death willingly, doing no harm. It will comfort those who chose life to know that both honorable choices are recognized."

Kieri's shoulders relaxed. "That is a good thought, Caernith. I will talk to those that remain and ask them to help plan a ceremony." He sighed. "Well. Not a day I ever wish to see again. But I suppose we must go on."

"And there is a meal waiting," Arian said from the foot of the stairs to the royal apartments.

Not even food could lighten the mood, though each of them tried. Exhaustion and disappointment lay over the party like fog. After the second course, Arian excused herself to see to the twins.

She came back a few minutes later with them and to everyone's surprise set them down on the table. Both could sit up now, though Arian set a rolled cloth behind them just in case. Dorrin and the others looked around and then at the babies.

"Falki and Tilla," Arian said. "Two happy, healthy children." As if on cue, they both grinned at the adults. "The gods granted us these children . . . and granted them Kieri and me for parents. Shall we make ourselves, and them, miserable for having had to face hard choices?"

A startled silence in which Falki let out a happy crow that brought a smile to Kieri's face. Dorrin felt her own face relax. Tilla copied him.

"We took a chance," Arian went on, "to save this time from more destruction by iynisin and to save those who had been enchanted into five hundred winters of stillness. It was only ever a chance, not a certainty, that they would live and thrive here. It was only ever a chance, not a certainty, that after losing my firstborn to poison, I would bear more children. And there they are. Look at them."

Dorrin looked. Everyone looked. The mood shifted; the babies grinned toothlessly from side to side.

"Arian," Kieri said, "you are very wise, and sometimes I am very foolish."

"More tired and worried than foolish, but this is a time to consider what was accomplished, not what was lost."

"Will you give them a bit of pastry since they're up so late?"

"No . . . or they will be up all night. But let's have no more gloom."

After taking the twins back upstairs, Arian came down again. The talk had strayed to safer topics. Kieri mentioned the Marrakai mare and his breeding plans. One of the King's Squires brought up the odd-shaped bow one of the magelords had carried and wondered how it was made. Finally Kieri said, "Will you stay another day or so, Dorrin, or will you leave tomorrow?"

"Tomorrow. I would leave tonight but that I am too weary to travel far. Mikeli bids me hurry; there are spies who spread the word that I have the regalia and travel east. I must reach Bannerlíth before them."

Kieri nodded. "You know I have sent supplies ahead of you. Rest a glass or two, bathe perhaps, while your things are packed, and you can ride a short way tonight with the King's Squires to guide you. It will be easier to bar the elvenhome forest to others if you are already within it."

Before the turn of night, Dorrin retrieved the crown and jewels from the royal ossuary and rode away into the elvenhome forest. She woke the next morning to peace and beauty such as she had never known before. Everything around—every tussock of moss, every leaf on every tree, every glittering dewdrop—glowed with life and beauty. She could have stayed in that one glade forever, she thought, without exhausting its beauty. The taig Arian had taught her to reach for here surrounded her, flowed into her and through her.

"It is the elvenhome," said one of the King's Squires with her. "And yes, it affects everyone like that at first."

She had slept late, so the first day they did not travel, but the next day they journeyed on. Dorrin could not keep track of the days they spent crossing Lyonya; the elvenhome's innate enchantment blurred her sense of time even as it sharpened her awareness of the taig and its beauty. They never rode above a foot pace; Dorrin's earlier urgency and worry had vanished. She and her escort talked little as they rode, for the elvenhome was a place of quiet and peace. The crown she carried was silent as well. When they came to the dell Kieri had told her about, still carpeted with violets as he had described, she saw the little white shrine to his mother and no other sign that tragedy had touched the place.

She would not pluck a flower in the elvenhome, but as she approached the shrine and knelt there, violets rose from the ground and lay on the stone, as if she had placed them. "All blessings," she murmured.

From there, the journey went on the same, day after day, in a land that seemed untouched by seasons—violets, this late in the year?—or storms. Dorrin began to wonder if they would ever reach Prealíth.

CHAPTER TWENTY-TWO

Vérella, Tsaia

Camwyn was gone. Lost forever, most likely. Aris Marrakai went about his duties in the palace, determined not to let anyone see how he felt. He stayed out of the king's way as much as he could: the king looked as grim as rock, and no wonder. Aris knew he could not have been faster. He knew pulling the old bell rope had been the exact right thing to do. But the great dragon had taken Camwyn away and had not said the prince would ever come back.

Not that Camwyn would want to if he could live with a dragon. If he lived at all.

"Fold those blankets properly," he said to the younger boys, startling himself with how harsh his voice sounded. They said nothing but refolded the blankets and then stood waiting for his morning inspection.

He didn't really care if their fingernails were clean, if their badges were on straight. The lump in his throat grew, and he swallowed it down again. "Very good," he said at last. "Remember to wash your hands after eating. And do not run in the Long Hall."

"Yes, Aris," they said in a chorus, and off they went to breakfast.

He looked around the room. Nothing out of place. His own uniform was as perfect as he could make it. If he skipped breakfast, he would just have time to visit the stable and see if the chestnut mare had foaled.

The mare was standing in the big corner stall, a spindly-legged foal nursing at her side. Aris caught his breath, forgetting Camwyn for the first time since the attack.

"Born just a turn ago," said the Master of Horse. "Skipped your breakfast, didn't you?"

"Yes—but everything's in order." The foal flipped a little brush of a tail, nursing. "I'm not due back in the palace for a half-glass. May I?"

"Go ahead. Your da the Duke said you knew how."

"Yes . . ." Aris slipped into the stall. The mare gave him a long look. He crooned to her. She knew him well; she was one of his father's mares, and he'd seen the foal before this one born. She ran her tongue in and out, and he moved slowly to her side and gave her a slice of the apple he'd saved from the day before. She bumped him with her nose, asking for more, and he gave it.

The foal pulled back, stumbled, and sat down in the straw, startled at its own clumsiness, then noticed Aris and stared.

"I help?" Aris asked the mare in the old language his father had taught him. She reached out and blew in his face, then looked at the foal. Aris turned to the foal. "So, little one, brave one," he said, still in the old language. "I help you." He leaned near, breathed gently into the foal's nostrils, breathed in its milk-smelling breath, scratched along the crest and that infant mane. The foal shook its head and lunged forward, trying to stand again. Aris reached quickly, an arm under the rump, and helped it up. The mare spoke to the foal, and it tottered a step forward.

Aris leaned close to the foal and spoke into its ear the secret name his father had suggested, then gently turned the head and spoke into its other ear. Now it was his and his alone, a naming even Juris would not know. "Must go now," he said in the old language to both foal and mare. "Will come again."

"You'd better run," the Master of Horse said, smiling. "The house bell's rung."

He'd never heard it. The foal . . . not a replacement for the horse Verrakai viciousness had killed but the first horse he would train himself, for himself, from the very first day. Sired, his father had said, by one of the Windsteed's own. He jogged across the stable court, through the gate, in through the scullery entrance, pausing at the well there to speak a word of thanks to the *merin*.

Lessons took forever, yet once he was back in the stable, time raced. He was sitting in the corner of the stall with the foal's head in his lap when Juris showed up, carrying a tray. "You skipped both breakfast and lunch," Juris said. "Starving yourself won't help you with the foal."

"I wasn't hungry," Aris said.

"You've lost weight since . . ." Juris's voice trailed away, then strengthened again. "If anyone can heal the prince, the dragon can."

"I know that," Aris said, his voice rising. The foal flicked an ear, opened its eyes, and lifted that heavy little head. "Saaaa . . ." he said to the foal, and it dropped its head onto his lap like a rock.

The mare, across the stall, gave them both a look.

"You know me, lady of grass," Juris said to the mare in the old language, and she waggled her ears. To Aris he said, "I brought you food, and I'm staying until you eat it." He uncovered the dishes on the tray.

The smell went straight to Aris's stomach. He was hungry all at once. A cheese roll disappeared, then another.

"You've handled it all over," Juris said, swallowing the last of his own roll as the mare took a step toward them.

"Of course," Aris said. "From nose to tail, ears to hooves."

"It's clear there's no fear," Juris said. He uncovered the last dish on the tray between them. "Look—apple custard." He dug a spoon from his pocket and handed it to Aris.

The mare whuffled. She had come closer, and her head dipped toward the custard.

"You can't have it all," Aris said. She blew on his hand. Juris laughed softly and reached out to stroke the mare's head. The foal woke up again and this time lifted its neck all the way up; the mare nuzzled it.

Aris dipped his finger in the custard and rubbed it on the foal's muzzle. Out came the pink tongue, licking. The mare made a noise;

Aris pulled an apple slice from the clinging custard and offered it; she pulled it in.

◈

Marrakai had no pastures near the city; their own were to the west. Aris knew the mare and foal must go now that the foal had been bonded . . . but not until the day before did his father tell him that he could come along.

"You've done very well, the Master of Pages tells me, and kept the younger ones in line without abusing them. If you'll stay in the palace over the winter rather than take Midwinter leave, you may come home now and only need to be back for Midsummer Court. How say you?"

Aris barely restrained himself from jumping up and down, something he was too old for. Next morning he mounted the mare, and with the foal ambling along at her heels, they rode west up the River Road, he and his father and five armed guards. They did not hurry, for the foal's sake, and it was four days before they reached Marrakai's green pastures. One of the mare bands trotted over to see them, but they rode past, the mares jogging alongside to the end of that field, and turned down the lane that led to the house.

It seemed forever since he'd seen it. The years in Fin Panir . . . a quick visit, then the trip to the palace where he was installed as page, almost the youngest. He turned his face away, riding on to the stables, then dismounted, untacked the mare, waited until his father had finished chatting with the senior groom, and then turned the mare and foal into a double stall for the night. He began cleaning the saddle, but his father interrupted him.

"Come, Aris; let one of the grooms finish that. Your mother will want to see you."

He bit his lip, set the bridle down carefully on a shelf, stoppered the bottle of oil, and followed his father up through the kitchen gardens, all the smells of home around him. Herbs, vegetables, the clucking of hens being urged into the coops for the night, and there, at the scullery door, the two old hounds, gray-muzzled now, which flattened their ears and grinned at his father and then at him.

"You've grown again," his mother said as she came into the scullery from the kitchen.

He had been sure he would not lose control, but the sight of her, the smell of her cooking wafting in from the kitchen, took him by surprise, and a sob caught in his throat before he realized it. She opened her arms, and he was in them, crying like a fool, he thought, but he could not stop. She said nothing but held him and stroked his hair. He felt his father's hand on his back, and shame flooded him, but his father's voice eased it.

"About time," he said. "You need to cry, Aris. No shame, lad, no shame at all. You loved the prince; everyone knew that, and he loved you."

The sobs went on a long time; he couldn't stop them. He heard his father's feet on the stone floor, water running from the spigot, then his father returning. Cool wet cloth wiped his hot face.

"I—I didn't stop them—"

"The iynisin? You could not. Even Mikeli could not have if he'd been there, and Gird's grace he wasn't. You did the one thing you could do, rouse the Bells, and that broke the spell. And then stanch the prince's wounds so there was a chance and time for that dragon to come. Nobody blames you, Ari . . . do you blame yourself for not doing the impossible?"

"He . . . *he* did the impossible."

"Fighting them, you mean?"

"N-no." Another round of sobs filled his throat. He'd never told his father or Juris about Camwyn saving his life on the roof. Even though his father knew about Cam's magery because Mikeli had told his Council, he hadn't . . . and now it came pouring out between sobs: ". . . saved me . . . on the roof . . ." His mother stiffened a little, and he raised his face to reassure her. "I just slipped, is all. And the prince—he was too far away to reach my hand—and he—he flew."

"Gird's Cudgel," his father said. "When was this? You didn't go up in winter, did you?"

"No, sir. In the spring, before the king's first progress. The prince had found a way . . . more than one . . . to the roof by finding where the roofers had left repair materials, and the king said he must not go alone, so he asked me."

"Where exactly did you go?"

"At first onto the roof that runs south, almost to the Bells' tower. The east side dried fast in the morning; we could go before lessons."

"Is that where you slipped?"

"No . . . we were on the north side that time." Aris tried to explain the complicated way they'd found.

"The north wing—with nothing down to King Street below?"

"It was my fault," Aris said. "The prince wanted me to wait by the chimney stack while he scooted along the roof peak to where there's a skylight."

"Gods!" his father said.

"And I thought he was teasing me for being afraid, so I got up and slipped on a bit of moss and slid—"

His mother's hands tightened on his shoulders.

"—and then the prince caught me, and then he landed on the roof, too, and we wiggled back up to the trapdoor, and when we got inside it was dark, and then his hand lit up."

"So . . . you knew he had magery before that trip?"

"Yes, sir."

"Did you tell the king?"

Of course not. "No, sir. The prince didn't want to."

"When did he find out?"

Aris told that, and what the king had said the next day, and the punishment he'd assigned both of them.

His father sighed. "Suitable," he said. "And I presume you don't keep secrets from the king now, do you?"

"No, sir."

"You haven't shown any mage-light or anything, have you?"

"No, sir."

"Well, then. Let's get ourselves cleaned up for supper. We're both travel-grimed. Your mother will have to change her apron."

Aris looked. Sure enough, a dirty face and tears had left marks on it. But she only tousled his hair and said, "Bathhouse for the pair of you. I'll send in clean clothes while you're bathing. You won't mind Juris's outgrown hunting clothes, will you, Aris? I'm sure you've grown into them, and your old things will be too small."

uris's old clothes fit him well enough and had the softness of long wear. Clean, with the tears eased and the old secret out, Aris came to the table hungry enough to eat for three. The familiar table, the familiar dishes, his mother's recipes, all eased the remaining tension.

"Is that your foal, Ari?" asked the sister two years older than he. "He looks good."

"He would," said another. "That's the best mare we have."

"The best *old* mare," said the first. "There's—"

"Girls!"

"Sorry, Mother."

"I held him within the first day," Aris said, glad to have the conversation on a topic all the Marrakai could agree on. "He has his name."

"Da, when Gwenno finishes her squire years, can I ask Duke Verrakai to take me?"

"What, are you going to be another knight-candidate?"

"Maybe . . . but I want to squire somewhere. So may I have a foal this year? Then it'd be old enough—"

"Later. Right now the topic is Aris's foal." He looked at Aris. "I was watching him on the way here, Ari. Very nice movement . . . might make a breeder. While you're here, we'll talk about that and I'll teach you the chants you'll need."

Aris almost choked on a redroot. He was going to be allowed to train a possible breeding stallion?

he next days were full of work in the garden, in the barns and, best of all, the daily sessions with his foal. His father watched, gave a few suggestions, and added to his knowledge of the secret horse-working language. Aris helped his father and the grooms with the other foals, giving them all the basic handling and training all Marrakai horses received. He had time to ride out on Marrakai lands alone as well as with his sisters.

"The situation in Fintha worries me," his father said. "I don't want the girls riding out in the woods alone this summer. We know some Finthans have come across; there could be more. We don't have any mail in their size, and you've had better arms training at the palace than they've had here. If I hadn't agreed to let Gwenno stay in Vérella, she could take them. But if you're along, I trust you'll all come to no harm. Wear a helmet and mail even when you're out alone."

Aris nodded. He now wore a sword, not just a boy's dirk, and had a mail shirt, hot and heavy as it was. Camwyn had been right about that—but Camwyn had persevered, and so would he. Soon the helmet and mail felt less awkward and heavy. He enjoyed his rides in the forest as much as those across open fields and stopped in farmsteads and vills to speak to Marrakai tenants. His sisters, both of whom had been on a horse since early childhood, did not slow him down, and their chatter helped keep his mind off Camwyn.

For several tendays he saw no one on Marrakai land who should not be there. But on one ride alone, following a woods trail near the western border, he spotted footprints of several people and some goats or sheep. Shortly after that, he found an obvious campsite. The animals had been penned with fallen branches; he could see the depressions where people had slept, padding the earth with leaves.

He dismounted to examine the pen. Goat and sheep tracks looked alike to him, but the tuft of wool caught on a twig defined it: sheep. He kicked drifts of leaves apart and found a pile of offal concealed under branches and leaves. They had butchered a sheep and eaten or carried away the meat. With continued searching, he found their water source and a fire-pit with cold, wet ashes. At least they had taken care not to start a wildfire, but the concealment of the offal and the fire proved they were intruders, not Marrakai herders who'd followed strays into the woods.

Mounting, he turned and followed the tracks back down the trail to the place they veered off it. He reined in there and thought what to do. The nearest farmsteads would take him south, farther away from home. The nearest border guards were south and a little west, even farther from home. The traces indicated several adults and perhaps a dozen sheep. The prudent thing to do was go directly home and tell his father.

He had never been known for prudence. If he could locate the group—if he could bring them in himself—he saw himself taking them up to the house, and the vision wavered. He wasn't even a squire yet. He wasn't wearing Marrakai colors. What if they—

The twang of a bowstring and the whirr of an arrow passing within a handspan of his head made the decision clear. He set heels to the horse and galloped away, not slowing until he was certain he was out of range. Then he took the most direct route home.

As he came out of the trees into the fields of Pickoak, the first vill on that route, he slowed to a walk. The tree for which the vill was named, the largest pickoak on Marrakai lands, stood alone in the barton's drill field. He asked women near the well where the yeoman-marshal was.

"They're all clearin' ditch in the field yonder." Two of the women pointed. "What's the need?"

"Strangers in the woods," he said. "They have sheep, and they're armed with bows. Willing to shoot without speaking."

"How far away? We should call in the childer."

"Are any out in the woods?"

"Not today, sir."

"Good. I'd keep them in sight. And keep your staves handy—are any of you archers?"

Two women raised their hands. One said, "I'll fetch my bow—and yours, Sela."

"I'll ride over and tell the yeoman-marshal and the others," Aris said. "And then I must ride home and tell my father."

Hadden, the yeoman-marshal, quickly sent a third of the men back to the vill to fetch their weapons and stay there. "You think they'll attack, then?" he asked Aris when the men had gone.

"They almost put an arrow into me," Aris said. "They might have

thought me a brigand, I suppose, but there was no word from them."
He described where he'd found the temporary camp; several of the
men nodded.

"They could be here by nightfall if they follow the main trail,"
one said. "No tracks of horses?"

"None but mine," Aris said. "I need to ride on, let my father
know. And I'll alert anyone else I see on the way."

"Gird's grace," they said, nodding to him.

He came into the home fields at a steady canter; far ahead, he saw
men lift their heads to look toward the sound of the hooves. His father came out of one of the barns as the hounds bayed, frowning.

"I know he's hot," he said to his father when he was close enough.
"But I had to hurry—there's strangers in the woods beyond Pickoak.
Several adults and some sheep—and they butchered one in a camp
they tried to hide."

"Did you see them?"

"No, sir. I saw the tracks and found the camp, then the fire-pit
they'd hidden—all cold and wet. I was thinking what best to do
when one shot at arrow at me from cover."

"Mallin—come take my son's horse and cool him off. I'll want
war saddles on the two freshest chargers and a spare packed for support. Aris, go tell your mother we need provisions for three days—at
once. And you find a Marrakai tabard and put that on over your
shirt. Get something to eat, too. We'll be leaving in a glass, no more.
I'm going to the Marshal."

They left the homestead as a cavalcade: he and his father, four of
the household men, mounted, the Marshal on his own horse, and a
tensquad from the grange marching behind, each with weapons to
hand and provisions in a pack. His father explained as they rode
along. "They can't get farther than Pickoak by dark even if they
move fast. And you roused Pickoak—Hadden's a good yeoman-
marshal, and they won't find the vill easy to take if that's their plan.
There's a chance they'll choose to go around it, or stay in the forest,
or even go back west."

"Do you think they're running from mage-hunters, or are mage-
hunters?"

"We can't know for certain until we find them," his father said. "But my guess is they're mage-hunters who assumed you were a magelord. Some of those people think all the nobles in Tsaia are, and though you wore no colors, the horse you were on would give you away. We don't want any mage-hunters bothering our people, and though I have sympathy for those fleeing mage-hunters, I have no right to displace my own people to make room for them."

"But if——"

"The Marshal-General should deal with it, Aris. Not saying it will be easy, but it's her job. She's head of the Fellowship, and the Fellowship rules Fintha."

"But suppose you saw someone being chased—hurt—and it wasn't safe for them to go back?"

No answer for several strides, then: "I don't know, Aris. Of course I would help them—stop the attack however I could—but—I have my own people to think of as well. I'm sure someone would say there's plenty of land for all, but if we clear more land, where will we get the wood we need? We've been managing the forest land for generations, providing wood for everyone to build with, wood for cooking . . . and it's been in good balance. I don't know—I don't know who would know, barring elves, and I can't see myself asking *them*— how much we could clear and still have that balance. And the same would be true for all the fief holders."

Another silence, longer. Then his father went on. "When the Lyonyan queen was here, she said something about the taig in Lyonya, about their forest and how Tsaia seemed to have only fragmented taig. She hadn't seen our forest, only those blocks of woodland near Vérella, but I could tell she disapproved. And she's half-elf. Full elves . . . I wonder if all would be woodland if they ruled."

"Is Chaya as big as Vérella?"

"No. Not from what Mahieran says. And fewer humans all around. There's no town between Riverwash and Chaya, for instance, and it's several days' ride at ordinary traveling pace. Only two or three farmsteads—quite small—not even a vill. He found the forest oppressive, he said. Too tall, too dark, too empty."

"The elves at Fin Panir didn't seem bothered by the lack of forests," Aris said.

"Did you have much speech with them?"

"No, sir. They said I was too young."

"Do you know if they were from the Ladysforest or another place?"

"Somewhere far to the west—the one I met was Ardhiel, who went with the expedition to Kolobia with Paks."

They arrived in Pickoak in the dusk to find that no strangers had shown themselves that afternoon or evening. Men were posted as watchers outside the vill, and all the livestock had been penned.

"Glad to see you, m'lord," Hadden said. "And you, Marshal. You'll need a place to stay . . ."

"We brought provisions," Marshal Nerrin said. "Don't trouble yourselves. A camp will be good training."

Night passed without incident. The next day, Aris waited in the village with two of the house guard while his father took the rest of the small force into the forest with a guide from the vill. "You'll be a help here," his father said. "In case they circle 'round—you're my logical representative."

He spent the day walking about the vill, learning everyone's name, down to the youngest, and collecting bits of information that one person after another thought his father should know . . . but would not bother his father by telling him directly. The vill had two wells, but one needed relining . . . and all the stone thereabouts was hard to shape into flats. Where could they trade for flats? There was a child showing mage-light, yes, but it was only one finger and "that Hadden, he says it's not worth tellin' the Marshal, but what if them mage-hunters come?" Widow Eskinsdotter had a rooster with a double comb, and one of them spotted black, and that was a bad omen, Granna Neslin said, along with "too many good years makes a bad one come double." It had been a dry winter and not enough rain in the spring; she predicted a bad harvest.

The troop did not return that night. Aris worried, wondering if he should ride out to find them in case they needed help, but decided to stay, as his father had bidden him. The next morning, he was up early, but that day was like the one before until late morning, when one of the village lads spotted someone running out of the forest edge and back in again. "Looky there, sir! I see 'em now, just there."

Aris, after a long look, could also see the occasional flicker of blue showing between the leaves . . . someone moving parallel to the forest edge, back and forth, as if looking for the best place to emerge . . . or as if waiting for others. The vill settled into midday somnolence, the sun's warmth having become heat in the last tenday. He and others watched the forest edge from inside the buildings.

Another boy was first to see a sheep emerge from the forest and drop its head to graze in the open. Then another and another. And finally an adult in a long blue shirt, gray trews, and a hat, with a shepherd's crook and a bow, stepped out and began moving the sheep along the grass, just outside the forest. In a few minutes, the shepherd turned, waved, and three obvious children came out of the woods and ran to the flock.

"What should we do, sir?"

Aris looked away from the window. "I don't know. If we go out, they may dive back into the woods, and I know my father will want to find them and talk to them."

"Think they're mage-hunters?"

"No . . . I think they're fleeing mage-hunters. Maybe that one shot at me thinking I was one."

"Or maybe mage-hunters was on their trail."

"That, too," Aris said, still watching. The children were now positioned along the woods side of the sheep, the adult nearest the vill. Then a thought occurred. "Do you think the Finthans know any Tsaian family sigils? Would they know this is Marrakai land and recognize this?" He touched the red horse on his green tabard. "I was wearing Juris's old hunting jerkin before."

"Might work," said one of his father's men. "But you should have someone with you."

"It would scare them," Aris said. Inspiration hit. "What about this? Two of the village children—not too big—and those sheep in the pen and one of the dogs. It will look like children and sheep—"

"You're getting tall for that."

"I'm the older brother." He liked that thought; he'd been the youngest brother for so long.

They started out along a lane that led between the village fields to southern grazing lands that stretched to where the forest curved around. Aris, who had not worked sheep before, had to be reminded how to position himself. He watched the dog, carefully not looking toward the forest to the west and remembering to hold the shepherd's crook so he wouldn't bang it with his sword.

"They're looking at us," one of the smaller boys said.

"Are they going into the forest?"

"No. Just looking at us."

"Good. Don't look, then look again in twenty paces. Then you can grab my arm and try to get me to look." Aris looked the other way, pointed to the child on that side as if giving him directions, and the boy ran off to the side, pretended to pick something up, and ran back. Then the other boy grabbed Aris's arm and shook it, pointing toward the intruders.

As if to assist, all the sheep stopped and looked, too. One baaed. Then another. The distant sheep baaed. Suddenly, all the sheep—both groups—started toward each other, the nearer flock turning off the lane and into a field of redroots. Aris said "No!" but the sheep had no intention of listening to him. He tried stopping one with the crook, and it lunged forward, yanking the crook out of his hand. He and the boys ran, trying to get ahead of the sheep; the dog ran faster, then started barking. Across the field, the people with the small flock were trying to stop theirs with the same lack of success.

The sheep won, the flocks flowing into each other before the humans, breathless and sweaty, could get to the scene. The dog, completely abandoning its supposed sheep-handling role, had thrown itself at the feet of the stranger children and rolled onto its back; one of them was petting it.

The adult had moved into the combined flock, trying to separate out some of the sheep, but without help or any place to pen them, the sheep moved right back into the mass of woolly backs.

"Why did you bring your sheep out when you didn't have enough dogs to control them?" the adult—now obviously an older woman—said to Aris. She had not run as far and was not out of breath.

"Me?" Aris said. "Why did you bring your sheep to our vill?"

"I could have passed your vill without a problem if only you—" She stopped and looked intently at his chest. "That's . . . is that a Marrakai mark?"

"Yes," Aris said. "It is. This is Marrakai land."

"Blessed Gird!" she said. Now she smiled. "We're safe, children. We made it."

"Made it?"

"The mage-hunters would have killed them," she said, waving at the children. "I brought them out—we were chased—there are mage-hunters after us—"

The dog leapt up, bristling, teeth bared. Aris looked where it did—and saw two men on horseback galloping toward them. For an instant he thought they were his father's men, but these men wore blue, not red and green, and both had crossbows spanned—one shot even as he watched. The bolt narrowly missed the woman and thunked into the ground, vibrating.

And he was out here alone, with no support and no helmet. "Get in the sheep and lie down," he said to the children. The woman already had her bow spanned; Aris drew his sword.

"You can't fight horsemen on foot with a sword," she said. "Take my crook . . . knock one off as he passes."

But the horsemen drew rein out of reach.

Aris drew himself up. "You are on Marrakai lands," he said. "You have no rights here. Go back where you came from."

"Marrakai! Magelords! All Tsaia's infested with magelord vermin. You don't need to die for a filthy magelord, boy! Free yourself from their tyranny."

He could think of nothing to say. Tell them he was Marrakaien himself? That would do nothing but get him killed. He tightened his grip on the sword in his right hand and the shepherd's crook in his left.

Then, from the forest, came the crashing sound of horses—many horses—forcing their way through undergrowth, and the first of his father's mounted men charged out, yelling. His father, riding flat-out, mouth open . . . his horse surging ahead of the others. Aris had never seen his father look like that. The intruders turned to face this challenge, raising their crossbows.

Aris ran forward, desperate to keep his father from being shot. Without thinking of the horses at all, he slashed the one to his right with the sword and jabbed the other in the flank with the shepherd's crook. Both jerked; one bolted, and the other bucked, bucked again, and its rider flew off. His father rode on to attack the fallen man as he stood up. His sword cut deep into the man's shoulder; the man screamed and fell. Aris stared as his father slid out of the saddle and finished the man, one thrust to the throat.

"Get them all back to the vill," he said to Aris, then mounted and rode off in pursuit of the other man, whose horse was throwing bucks as it ran.

Aris went back to the woman. "We've got to get to the vill," he said.

She didn't move at first. "Was that Marrakai himself?"

"Yes. My father. Come—he wants everyone safe in the vill."

With five children, an experienced shepherd, and a dog, it did not take long to move the sheep into the center of the vill. On the way he learned the names of the strangers and that the vill's sheepdog had been traded for across the border—it knew the shepherd and the children. Soon his father and the others rode in, all the horses lathered and two dead men lashed over the saddles of their mounts.

Aris looked at his father. The dark brows were up, the mouth tight.

"I'm sorry I cut the horse," he said. "But I thought I had to."

"You did right," his father said. He tapped his head. "Except . . . where is your helmet?"

"I thought it would scare them away," Aris said. "The newcomers, I mean, not the mage-hunters."

"Mmm. We'll discuss that later. Let's get the horses cared for, and then I need to talk to all the adults in the vill."

They stayed in Pickoak another night. The three children did indeed have mage-powers—or at least made light with a finger, as

Camwyn had before he gained other powers. The woman had a frightening tale to tell.

"They was up the vale, one vill at a time. Timos from our vill saw what happened—they burned Claybank to the ground for refusin' to let 'em in. Old Tower, they sent their children to us, but we saw smoke rise that day. I knew . . . my sister's grandchilder, all three, had it. Their mother's expectin', so I said I'd take 'em. Two childer from Old Tower. Esker took them. We left that night hidin' as best we could, and Esker went another way. We each took some sheep, hopin' from a distance someone would just think it was a shepherd.

"They had ridin' horses; we didn't. I thought we'd got away, but just as I was comin' to the forest, Peri said she saw horses behind us. I hoped they hadn't seen. We been hidin' in the trees, tryin' to get away from 'em. They shot one of the sheep and stopped to eat it . . . we been hungry awhile . . ."

Aris looked at his father, who looked back, then sighed heavily.

"You're welcome to stay, Sanits, but not in this vill. Come with us tomorrow; settle closer to the center of my land, where they're less likely to find you. We'll find you a home."

The children had been eating as fast as they could. Now they stopped, staring at Sanits. Her eyes filled with tears. "Gird's grace on you," she said. "I don't reckon you're Girdish—"

"But we are," Aris said. "Da's da's da, back in Gird's day, knew Gird."

"Then Gird's hand was in all this," she said. "But are there no mage-hunters here?"

"There've been those who tried," Marrakai said. "But the king's command is that no new-known mages be killed, unless they commit crimes, and no child under twelve winters, without his express command."

"Is your king Girdish?"

"Yes . . . Is that not known in Fintha?"

She looked down. "Folk says this, and folk says that, and how's a body from a vill a day's walk from another to know who says truth?"

"Tsaia is Girdish. You will find welcome here in the grange on my land or another. For now, though, do not worry about that."

"I worry about my sister's daughter . . . what if she . . ." She closed her eyes briefly, shook her head, and said, "Never mind that. What's done is done, whatever it is. You saved my life, you and your son, and you saved these childer, and we're all grateful."

In the morning, they rode back to the house, the children each riding with someone and the woman on the mage-hunter's uninjured horse. Aris, with the oldest child gripping his belt behind, had no thought of Camwyn that day.

CHAPTER TWENTY-THREE

"Aris, I need you."

Aris gave the foal's back a last gentle swipe with the soft brush and turned. "Yes, sir?"

His father nodded toward the foal. "Good job you're doing there, lad, and I'm sorry to have to take you from it, at least for long enough to ride to Vérella and back. I need to get word to the king and to your brother Juris, and though I trust my couriers to carry letters, there are things that should be transferred tongue to tongue by a family member, and that means you. I must stay here to supervise reinforcing the border."

"Yes, sir." The foal nibbled at his sleeve; he pushed it back a little and scratched the ear that fell under his hand.

"You will ride with an escort—and you will ride fully armed, in my livery." His father chewed his lip. "It's not—I don't think there will be trouble, Ari, but I'll admit the incursion from Fintha worries me. I lack the troops to watch every armslength of the border. If someone slipped through—if several have and combine once they're in Tsaia—well. Wear your mail. Wear your helmet, waking and sleeping, and sleep as little as you may on the road."

"Yes, sir."

"The letters are ready and sealed. Your escort has been told. Go change out of stable clothes; your mother has a pack ready for you and a meal. When you're ready, come to my study."

Bathing and changing took no time at all. Aris took a meat roll and two pastries from the pantry and went to his father's office. There both parents awaited him, faces solemn—and to one side his younger sister Istilin, looking scared. A candle on the table beside her burned brightly, though daylight streamed in from outside.

"You see," his father said, nodding toward the candle. "Night before last. And no magery on either side of the family since before Gird's time. Whatever this is . . ."

"I don't like it!" Istilin said. "I didn't *ask*—!"

"This the king must know. It's in his family. It's in our family. It's in the Verrakaien. It's only a matter of time until it's in every noble family and that makes us magelords in the old sense. You cannot assume, Aris, that you will not develop it; Beclan was older than you before he showed it. And we must not descend into that chaos again. I will not write this down: you tell him and tell Juris. No one else."

Aris could think of nothing to say. He nodded instead. His mother led Istilin out of the study. His father cleared his throat, then said, "Your foal."

"Yes, sir?"

"I know it is unfair, your having to leave. You know I have his name—if you want, I will talk to him while you're gone. We will need to bespeak him together."

"Yes, sir. Let's say goodbye to him."

In the small paddock, the foal lifted his head and came to Aris. His father leaned over to stroke the neck, run his hand down the foal's back. Into the foal's ear, Aris spoke the name of bonding. His father spoke it into the foal's other ear at the same time. Then, with a last caress for the foal, Aris walked out to the yard, where the men waited and a groom held one of the best horses, ready for him. He mounted, signaled his escort, and rode away.

Despite all concerns, nothing happened on the way to Vérella except the ordinary business of travel. He noticed that the trip was drier than usual, the grass already browning on the tips, the trees looking dusty and crops in the field not as full as they should be. The sky held no rain clouds he could see—but clear weather shortened the trip.

Aris could not be sure whether the tension he felt was entirely his or if the travelers they passed were in fact grimmer of face and more reserved than in previous years. They were certainly more sun-burned.

Once near Vérella, he saw more Royal Guard patrols, but with the threat of invasion from Aarenis, that made sense. His Marrakai pennon and livery passed him through with hardly a pause. "Errand for my father the Duke" satisfied those who bothered to ask.

They rode into the city through blustery winds and blowing dust that turned the sky beige. Aris felt coated with dust when he rode up to the Marrakai city residence. He had planned to go to the palace as soon as he arrived, but he was too grimy. The housewards took one look at his tabard and flung the doors wide.

"The kirgan spends most nights at the palace," the woman told him when he was inside and out of the wind, drinking the cup of sib she offered. "But the house is ready for the family any time. You may have the Duke's rooms if you want."

Aris could not imagine himself in his father's bedroom, in the bed his parents shared. "I don't expect to be here more than one or two nights. Which guest room is made up? I'll take that. And I've been riding through the dust—I need a bath before I take the Duke's letter to the palace."

Entering the palace gates as a duke's son with an urgent message from the Duke for the king was very different from entering as a page. Grooms came to hold his horse; he was addressed not as "Aris" or "lad" but as "Sagan Marrakai," "second heir." He was taken up-stairs at once and waited only moments before being announced as "Aris, Sagan Marrakai." Through the open door he saw his brother Juris, who had been at supper with the king, staring at him, wide-eyed.

"Not Father—" Juris said before the king could say anything.

"No, he's in health," Aris said. "Sir king, I carry messages from the Duke for you. In writing and by mouth."

"That serious?" The king raised his brows. He looked tired, as he had ever since the iynisin intrusion that had resulted in the prince's injuries.

"Yes, sir king."

"Does your father send you here to resume your duties at Court?"

"No, sir king; I am to return as soon as I have delivered messages to you and to my brother Juris."

"The same messages?"

A tricky point on which he wished his father could advise him, but the king's question could not wait.

"Sir king, the messages to you are from a duke to a king, and those to Juris are from a father to his son and heir."

"Ha!" The king grinned, and Aris relaxed a little. "This is not the scamp who first came here with a reputation as a blabmouth. You have learned courtiers' wiles while in the pages' hall, young Marrakai."

Aris said nothing, merely waited until the king finished.

"Let me see the written word first," the king said. Aris opened his pouch and handed it over; the king broke the seal and unrolled the letter. "Juris, why don't you let your brother give you whatever message he has for you while I read, and I will take the message by mouth when I'm done."

"Yes, sir king." Juris got up from the table and led the way out of the room. Once they were in the hall, he said, "What's going on, Aris? And I swear you've grown another inch."

"I have a letter for you." Aris handed it to him. "And word for your ear that must not be heard by anyone else."

"Not here, then. There's a safe chamber this way." A short distance away, Juris opened a door into a small storage room lined with shelves stacked with spare crockery, table linens, and cleaning tools. "Tell me now."

Aris told him first of their sister's magery and then of the presence of mage-hunters on Marrakai land, well inside Tsaia. "Father thinks he's killed them all—all of that band at least—but he expects trouble."

"Istilin? But she's—but we've never—and has he written the king about it? The king should know."

"It's the word for his ear. Not in the letter."

"Good. I'm the king's best friend as well as his oathsworn; I could not keep such important news from him." Juris shook his head as if to clear it. "What about those coming in from Fintha? Will Father let them stay or send them somewhere?"

"He was going to send them away until he saw them. He says now he will find room somehow for those who just came. I don't know how many. And he will need more soldiers to guard the border."

"Our border with Fintha is mostly thick forest. It would take an army—"

"We can't have the mage-hunters coming in and killing our people."

"No. We need to find some way—"

"Kirgan Marrakai!"

Juris opened the closet door. "Here I am, just chatting with my brother about things at home. Does the king want me?"

"Both of you."

Aris delivered his father's word to the king's ear. Mikeli nodded, looking no grimmer than he had before.

"It's everywhere now," he said. "Fintha, Tsaia, mage families, nonmage families. Whatever's started this seems determined to stir some magery into every family. I'll have an answer for your father by tomorrow, Aris. I'm sure he wants you to return immediately."

"Yes, sir king. He said no use to waste the time of a royal courier when I ride like one."

The king laughed. "You do have an escort, though—he's not sending you here and back alone—?"

"No, sir king. The escort is at Marrakai House, where I will stay this night."

"And I, if you'll permit," Juris said.

"Of course."

CHAPTER TWENTY-FOUR

Cortes Andres, Andressat

Ferran, Count Andressat, watched Aesil M'dierra ride across the inner courtyard to the foot of the palace steps. He had met her years before, when his father had contracted Golden Company for assistance during Siniava's War. She dismounted, handed the reins of her chestnut stallion to her squire, hung her helmet on the saddle hooks, and came up the stairs more light-footed than he expected given her age. There were threads of silver in her dark hair now, and her brows seemed thinner, but the look from under those brows was as penetrating as ever.

"M'lord Count," she said.

"Commander," he said. "Be welcome."

"I am sorry for your losses," she said. "Your brother, sister, and father, all in one year."

"Thank you," he said. "Andressat survives."

"As it has done, and we all hope will do, by Esea's Light."

That startled him. He had not realized anyone else maintained the Sunlord's tradition as well as Camwyn's worship.

"Light of the heart," he said, testing.

"Light of the mind," she said, answering. She smiled.

They walked inside, down the passage, and he led her to his father's—now his—office. On the desk lay the papers to be signed and the ritual gold coin, though the payment had already been made. Papers signed, coin transferred to her, he offered refreshments in the loggia, and she accepted.

Over a plate of spiced pastries and goblets of Andressat wine and after they discussed what little she had not already known about Andressat's military situation, using maps he had placed ready, Ferran changed the subject.

"You are a follower of Camwyn, aren't you?" Ferran asked M'dierra, ignoring her earlier mention of Esea.

She gave him a sharp look, one he hoped he did not deserve, and did not move her finger from the map they'd been discussing. "Yes, as are you. Is this pertinent to the situation around Cortes Cilwan?"

"Possibly not," Ferran said. No wonder the woman had never married, with a tongue as sharp as a blade. "I need to ask for your word of secrecy." Her brows went up; her lips thinned. "For more than the usual; I need to tell you something only my brothers and I know."

She folded her hands together and bowed. "My word on it; your secret remains with you alone."

"You know how my brother Filis died. I believe my father wrote you of the way Filis had sent us word that our enemy was one of those inhabited by a demon." She nodded, and Ferran went on. "Well, then. In the letter our enemy sent with the box made of Filis's scalp and some of his skin, he described what he'd done—did my father tell you all?"

"No . . . but rumors came that he had also flayed your sister and her husband."

"More than that," Ferran said, and told her. He could not keep rage from showing in his voice as he said "rugs to walk on." Her expression hardened, but she said nothing. "My father chose to commit what remains we had to the fire, to Camwyn, I thought. He asked Camwyn to burn with dragonfire any part of Filis left anywhere—"

M'dierra nodded, this time making the gesture of the Claw. "Did he end with 'By the Claw and the dragon who bore it, and by the power of Camwyn and the dragon together' . . . ?"

"Yes—do you know that chant? He said more—'I invoke—' "

She held up her hand, and he stopped short. "Never complete it for no reason," she said. "It's not a chant; it's a curse. The Curse of Camwyn's Claw. What happened then?"

"The flames shot up higher and higher, and then a streak of fire sped east and disappeared. And my father clutched at his chest and fell dead."

"It's a wonder Alured is still alive, if he is. Camwyn granted your father's wish—"

"But Father died."

"That is what happens. To invoke Camwyn's Curse is to use one's own death to cause another's woe." She looked thoughtful. "Or . . . that's what I was told and what I once saw done. That it always happens I know only by hearsay and not my own knowledge. So far you have told me nothing unknown to others. If that is your secret, then I fear it is no secret."

"There is more," Ferran said. "And it is . . . we think . . . somewhat of Esea as well as Camwyn. On the night before we buried my father, there is a family ritual. We believe the spirit knows where it would go, and we give it a chance to speak that wish. And my father, who I believed had no magery as the northerners speak of . . . his spirit spoke to me and said he had left me his magery. And I do not know what it is."

"You can recite the curse accurately?"

"Yes, but—"

"*That* is the magery, Count. With his title, you inherited the right—and the ability—to ask Camwyn one time to curse another. It is a thing passed down in ruling families—the old ruling families—from ruler to heir. If your father had other magery, I would not know, but I know that calling in the Curse of Camwyn's Claw is a form of magery and not worship. Whether Camwyn accepts or denies the petition, the one who speaks the curse dies. Choose your target with care: the dragon's breath speeds unerringly but only once."

"Does it always kill its target?"

M'dierra shrugged. "That I do not know. There may be worse things than a quick death by fire, and how the curse is formed—its details—will surely vary. But everything I've heard about it says it's a most efficacious curse, though not always instantaneous." She smiled, the slightly crooked smile that had turned his knees to jelly the first time he'd met her. "I think we may move boldly against Alured nonetheless and consider Camwyn more on our side than his. Some form of bad fortune will come to Alured, I suspect, before he comes near his aims, and this will be the campaign season to take advantage of it."

"I've heard nothing yet."

"No matter. A dragon flies in his own air but never flies far from Camwyn's Claw."

"They saw a dragon in the north—"

"So I heard, also. A dragon spoke to Lord Arcolin of Fox Company, who ended up with a tribe of gnomes moving into his land. A dragon—perhaps the same dragon—spoke to Kieri Phelan. It will be interesting to see what comes of that. A cohort of gnomish pikes is not beyond possibility, I suppose." She paused, then went on. "To seal the bond of secrecy . . . Jandelir Arcolin and I have been friends a very long time. Since before either of us was a soldier. Did you know he was from Horngard?"

Ferran thought about asking more, but her expression had hardened again. "Thank you," he said. "And if in fact our enemy is under such a curse, is this the time to move all our troops forward?"

She tapped the map. "Not all, I think, not yet. I believe it will be possible to retake Cortes Cilwan. Foss Council is leaning that way, using Fox Company as the core of an allied group. Arcolin and I shared some information in Valdaire before moving out. Kostandan in the north has interested itself in the matter, because a member of its royal house married the Duke of Fall's heir. That means Count Vladi— I'm sure you remember his company from Siniava's War—and some other reinforcements, by rumors coming down from Tsaia. I hope to hear more presently, when Foss Council makes up its mind." She paused long enough that Ferran cocked his head, inviting more. "Arcolin's junior captain," she said. "He is your son, I understand."

"Yes," Ferran said. "Acknowledged so by my father and by me."

"Is he staying with Fox Company, or will he return to his place here?"

"Fox Company, he says, where he has made a place for himself, and knowing I have younger sons who—he says—deserve the place they expect. But he says he will come if he's truly needed."

"A very sound young man," M'dierra said. "When I had him, he was overbold, as young men often are, but settled readily. I thought he had great promise and was delighted that Arcolin took him up for Fox Company. He will do well there. Will he at least take your family name?"

"I would not wish him to, after what happened to Filis, unless he would bide here, out of danger," Ferran said. "Let him be free of us all if it saves him that."

"Let him be free, always," M'dierra said. "Then if he comes back, it will be his heart calling and not fear. You will have the best of him then." She tapped the map, calling his attention back to immediate matters. "My advice is to place one of my cohorts forward in support of Fox Company but not all the way to Cortes Cilwan. If the alliance wants them, they may call on them; I will send a courier to Arcolin to tell him where and how to contact it. I have an experienced captain for that, someone Arcolin knows well."

"Do you need to hold your other cohorts here?"

"I think so, Count. There are two other routes by which Immer could attack you—coming upriver from Cha and coming overland from Pliuni. Immer's pirate bands are still active and could easily move troops along either route. My advice would be to reinforce Sibili with one of my cohorts, using your own for the western forts, allowing enough extra for swift couriers to be sent at need. That would preserve your own to hold the center, with ample time to move them."

"You do not usually disperse your company so," Ferran said.

"True . . . Your father preferred I keep them together, but I've seen the advantage, from Fox Company, of flexibility. As long as we maintain regular communication, we can move troops quickly where we need them—and it promises to be a dry summer."

"I see the sense of that, too," Ferran said.

The rest of their talk was of supplies: food for troops, forage for horses, bolts for crossbows. And when it was done, Commander M'dierra went down the stairs, replaced her helmet, mounted her chestnut stallion without assistance, and rode away.

Ferran wrote the requisite orders to his brothers, sent the couriers on their way, and then considered his father's last words and what M'dierra had told him. He certainly understood his father's use of the curse—but who else in the family had used it, and where else might it have been used? M'dierra knew of it . . . where? She had mentioned Horngard . . . but all he knew of Horngard was that it had some connection to Camwyn.

CHAPTER TWENTY-FIVE

Foss Council House, Foss, Aarenis

"I don't understand why there's been no further advance," Master-trader Vanchoch said. He was this year's Speaker and led all discussions. "Last year, the constant pressure, the sabotage, and this year . . . Immer hasn't moved so much as a pace toward the west. What is he up to?"

"He has other worries." That was one of the Cold Count's captains, a Kostandanyan named Piklûsh. "My commander tells you not to worry this year. Immer decided to conquer Fallo to protect his rear, and he has found it harder than he thought. We keep him busy, and you have time to retake Cilwan and run his agents out of Vonja."

Glances back and forth across the table.

"Did the other Kostandanyan cohorts reach you?" Arcolin asked Piklûsh. As Foss Council's mercenary support for the year, he had a seat at the table any time strategy was under discussion. Also new to the table was an Aldonfulk gnome, there because someone—Arcolin was sure it was Alured's men—had violated a gnome boundary somewhere along the Dwarfwatch foothills.

"Yes." He grinned at Arcolin. "But that is not all the Kostandanyans in Aarenis. We fooled that Alured. We brought in troops to Slavers' Bay. In winter. Troops from Valdaire now blocking his retreat on north road."

"One of my captains is Andressat's illegitimate son," Arcolin said. Both Ferran Andressat and Burek no longer hid their relationship. "I have good communications with Andressat, and of course he would like to see Cilwan freed."

"To turn over to a boy—how old is the boy now?"

"Not old enough, I agree," Arcolin said. "But you should talk to Andressat. He's not promoting the boy—though the boy's mother was his sister, after all—but he wants a strong ally there. He thinks it would not take much to dislodge the occupying force; Alured pulled some of them to use in the attack on Fallo. And if we need them, we can have a cohort of Golden Company as a reserve on the flank."

"We would need Vonja's permission to take troops through," another of the Foss Councilors said.

"And then we'd have to invite them." A long silence, as most of those present remembered several incidents from Siniava's War in which the Vonja militia's ineptitude—if not outright cowardice—had cost them a battle and many lives.

"It's in their interest," said Master-trader Vanchoch. "We vote."

In the end, the plan to retake Cortes Cilwan passed. Arcolin went out into the blinding sun—the sky was clear; it had not rained for two tendays—and rode back to Fox Company's campsite. There he told his captains to prepare for a march—he did not know yet how many cohorts, but he thought at least two.

"Good," Burek said. "We've had little to do this season, and the troops are stale."

Arcolin told them what he'd learned of the Kostandanyan actions in Fallo. "With luck," he said at the end, "Alured will fall off his horse and break his neck."

"Will that kill the thing inside him?" Burek asked.

"Not necessarily," Arcolin said. "Even as they die they can seize another body."

"And then we wouldn't know who had the thing in him," Burek said.

Arcolin considered leaving his squire Kaim behind—he could easily find tasks for him to do in Vérella, and he remembered the look on his father's face and how young Kaim was. But Kaim was fizzing with excitement, and leaving him behind could be as dangerous as taking him into battle.

Two hands of days later Fox Company packed up and marched

down the Guild League road with three cohorts of Foss Council militia and picked up two Vonja militia cohorts as it traveled on toward Cortes Cilwan. Once in Cilwan, they found the road almost deserted, with the few travelers hurrying away from the road as soon as they saw troops coming. Arcolin's scouts chased down one of them and found he was from Cilwan.

"They're fighting in the streets," he said. "Not so many of Immer's troops—but they have the palace and many more weapons. No more magic, though, not for tens of days."

"Why did you leave?"

"I don't want to die. My brother was killed, and he wasn't doing anything but going to the well for water. And if they catch you and you're not dead—you would not believe what they did to the Count and his lady."

"We heard," Arcolin said.

Recapturing Cilwan was easier than Arcolin expected because someone had poisoned the palace well; most of the occupying troops were sick or dying. Angry citizens milled around in the streets away from the palace, still afraid to come near. The sight of massed troops brought on a short fight with those in the palace, but it was over in less than a day.

"It's not always this easy," Arcolin told Kaim. "But for your first battle, it's ideal." Kaim had done well, following orders exactly. Arcolin had known squires who'd done much worse, including the fool who'd decided to prove his courage by galloping straight into the enemy lines by himself and getting killed as soon as he reached them. One fairly easy battle wasn't seasoning, but if Kaim continued as he'd begun, he would end up a good soldier.

Few of the Guild League traders who did not escape early had been left alive; they found one still hiding in a second basement. By default, he became the senior member of the Guild League Hall. Propping the broken door open with a table from inside, he declared Guild League trading active once more. Arcolin shook his head in amazement as he rode by. Where did the man think trade was coming from?

"Should we go on to Lûn?" The Foss Council militia commander bit into one of the early peaches from Cortes Cilwan's market and grimaced, then tossed it aside.

"Not without orders," Arcolin said. "I would, but my orders said to free Cortes Cilwan. Nothing about advancing."

"Umm." The man fished in one of his pockets. "They told me if it went well and if you thought we could, taking Lûn would give us a forward advantage point."

"It would—*if* we had the troops to hold it and were sure the food and water there were safe," Arcolin said. "But Cilwan's militia is mostly dead, though some escaped in disarray."

The Foss Council commander nodded his understanding. "So you think we shouldn't."

"Not without more resources. Cilwan's treasury's empty—Alured took it all away." Arcolin did a quick calculation of the cost to march their forces to Lûn and then occupy it. The total startled the other commander. "That much—no, I'm not authorized to spend that. It's not in your contract?"

"Nor in Vonja's, if you were thinking to ask them along. Operations outside Foss Council require more supplies and more risk, and you know how Vonja is about money." The man nodded. "At least there's spelt and wheat in the granary and harvest to come in the orchards and fields," Arcolin said. "No one will starve. But Alured may come back this way whether he wins or loses in Fallo. He will need Cilwan and its grain to feed his armies when he moves west again."

But Alured and his forces made no move for a time, and the half-cohort of Fox Company, cohort of Foss Council militia, and cohort of Vonja militia were enough to restore and maintain order. Trade slowly picked up again on the Guild Road between Vonja and Cilwan even as Arcolin marched the rest of Fox Company back to Foss Council, where he set up a new camp closer to the border of Vonja.

"Send word at once if you see any sign of troops gathering," he told Burek. "Have your scouts out every day. I expect both Vonja and Foss will recall part or all of their forces here."

Messages waited when Arcolin came back to Foss, brought by regular courier, not an Aldonfulk gnome. Calla and Arneson reported all well in his domain—the new recruit cohort had all arrived and were learning the basics, her pregnancy was coming along as it should, and Kolya was back to her usual routine of orchard work. But the letter from the king told of an iynisin attack in the palace itself—Prince Camwyn's injuries and the arrival of the dragon to take him away, the only hope for his survival.

Through the terse phrases that conveyed this, Arcolin could sense the king's grief. "For these reasons and not in anger, I have bade Duke Verrakai leave the realm with those things of which you know."

Arcolin wished he had been there; he knew he might never see Dorrin again. They had been friends more than half their lives. He understood why the king had sent her away and why she could not have come south, but her absence made his own responsibility for Tsaia's defense even greater. He read on: "For this reason I name you Constable of the Realm and, when your contract is up, urge your swift return that we may discuss matters. The unrest in Fintha is spilling over here, with those who would kill every mage coming across the border, both after fugitives and to kill mages in our territory."

Arcolin sent off an acknowledgment of this letter, offered a few quick suggestions, then wrote to the Aldonfulk prince.

"These Girdish who hate magery will not respect boundaries—and innocent fugitives may transgress by error. It is not one prince's right, in Law, to state the duty of another. If what I say transgresses Law, instruct me: my hesktak is not with me this year by my own request that he instruct my steward in the north.

"Here is what I know. These mage-haters are dangerous. They have transgressed boundaries between Fintha and Tsaia. They have killed people—even children—for being suspected of magery. They have acted against the command of the Marshal-General yet claim to be Girdish; they have acted against the command of the King of Tsaia and yet claim to be his subjects.

"If Lord Prince Aldonfulk has words of Law that would help me protect my people, human and gnome, I am listening."

That went off by gnome courier. Then he turned to matters of the Company itself.

The Sobanai soldiers Selfer had rescued from their captors had recovered their strength and had decided that they'd as soon be Fox Company soldiers as take their chances in the mercenaries' hiring hall. At least they'd be together—and since they were good horsemen and archers, they fitted well into Cracolnya's mixed cohort. Arcolin took their oaths for the season, with an option to renew them at Midwinter. Arcolin knew they would like to see their former companions rescued, but they also knew it was unlikely any were still alive.

Because of Burek's relationship and his location in Cilwan, Ferran, Count Andressat, sent regular messages to Arcolin about Cilwanese affairs. Cilwan's new Council appealed to the Count of Andressat for permission to consider "an arrangement" that would end the boy count's automatic right to rule when he came of age. Ferran pointed out that the palace and all its contents, including the archives—those not destroyed by Alured or his troops—were the personal property of the line of counts of Cilwan through the ages and must be preserved for him or—if he was not to rule when he came of age—be brought to Andressat for him or paid for. Ferran sent a group of Andressat militia to make that plain; Burek, as Ferran's acknowledged son, had almost Ferran's influence. The Council backed down.

So the archives remained where they were, and the Council's claim that the last count had not protected them and thus his son should not inherit died away. Burek set to work recruiting and training every interested citizen for Cilwan's own militia force. By the time the Vonja cohort pulled out and the Foss Council cohort announced they, too, would leave in another tenday, Cortes Cilwan looked to Burek for order and defense. Arcolin read over the reports from Burek and from the Foss Council commander with satisfaction. That young man was showing all the talent Arcolin had suspected.

Summer continued dry. He had seen other dry summers and knew the south saw less summer rain than the north, but still the heat was oppressive, and watching the river level drop and drop suggested water shortages to come.

CHAPTER TWENTY-SIX

Fin Panir, Fintha

Arvid recovered quickly from the blood loss as he threw himself into the new routine. One night in three he had night duty at the grange, walking the bounds, but some of the yeomen were also watching at night now, and though he slept near the main door, he got some sleep.

He learned to respond to "Yeoman-Marshal" instead of "Arvid." Most people, he could tell, admired what he'd done, but the families of the men he'd killed turned away when they saw him coming. It didn't bother him. Men who would kill children—they could hate him all they wanted.

For the rest of the quarter-year, though rumor spoke of unrest in the realm as a whole, the city had no more overt trouble. Some families moved away, true. But Fintha had always been an open city, with some moving back to their vills or one of the other towns as their fortunes changed and new people moving in. Gradually the yeomen of Hudder's grange settled back into their occupations, no longer guarding the entrance day and night. Arvid quickly mastered the accounting system common to all granges, and his earlier study with Deinar had taken him to all but a few of the articles of the Code of Gird.

"You're ready," Marshal Hudder said shortly before Midsummer. "Don't you think so, Nadin?"

Nadin nodded. "I'd say so, Marshal. An' if he stays here much longer, folk'll be thinkin' there's no hope for them as wants to work up. None of 'em comes close."

"Arvid, do you have an idea who might make a yeoman-marshal in your section?"

"Bodin," Arvid said promptly. "Melthar's as good in the basics, but he's slow to learn new things and I don't think he's ambitious. Bodin's quick. Best, he's committed to the Marshal-General's view about magery."

"Lost a niece, didn't he?"

"Yes. If she'd been his daughter, I'd worry about a thirst for revenge, but Bodin doesn't show it and I don't think he could hide it from me."

Hudder and Nadin exchanged a glance, then Hudder nodded. "He'd be my pick, too. You're definitely ready, Arvid, if you think about your people that way. Nadin, you'll take my note up to the Marshal-General this morning; Arvid, you'll take over the youngling classes."

It wasn't the first time he'd taken the classes; the children knew him now as more than the dark-clad stranger who'd rescued them. They bowed when he came into the barton, and the lessons went on as usual until the midday bell and dismissal. When Arvid went back into the grange, the Marshal-General was there, talking to Marshal Hudder.

"There's a Marshals class being confirmed Midsummer Eve," she said to Arvid. "You'll be confirmed then, too. Half of them are coming from outland grange work—I'll need to interview each one. I'll interview you now."

Her look was far less friendly than it had been; he wondered if her wound was paining her or if something else bad had happened. Since he no longer worked up on the hill, he'd heard only what everyone heard about how things were going.

"Come onto the platform," she said. Arvid stepped up; they faced each other across that space. "Marshal Hudder, fetch the relic."

The relic in Hudder's grange was a wooden belt buckle, said to have been worn by Gird in the wars. Hudder took the relic from its niche. "Open your hand, palm flat," he said to Arvid. Old wood almost as hard as iron, dark as iron with age, but much lighter than iron in his hand when Hudder laid it on his palm. It caught light, as the stick had in the grange at Valdaire, blazing out to light the entire grange, but it did not burn.

You are my Marshal.

"I heard that," the Marshal-General said. Her voice softened with awe. "The voice of Gird himself. And you do not flinch from it. That is well. Repeat for me the Ten Fingers, Arvid Semminson."

Arvid repeated them, this time flawlessly. The light dimmed, then brightened again.

"And now the Oath of the Marshalate."

That, too, he recited. This time the light held steady.

"Marshal Hudder, return the relic to its place."

As Hudder touched it, the light dimmed and slowly faded away. "Marshal-General—" Hudder began.

She silenced him with a gesture. "Later, Marshal. Let me complete this." Then, to Arvid: "Arvid Semminson, do you accept the task Gird has laid on you, to become a Marshal of Gird with all that means?"

"Yes, Marshal-General."

"Then so it will be, and you will be confirmed in the presence of the Marshalate in the High Lord's Hall on the first night of Midsummer. We will exchange blows at that time, but we will do so here as well."

The exchange was but a few touches with staves. Arvid thought the Marshal-General moved more slowly, with a stiffness she had not shown before. When they came down from the platform, he could not refrain from asking.

"No, Arvid . . . no Kuakgan has come yet. And as Paks described, the wound continues to pain me, sometimes more and sometimes less. I do not know how she bore it so long, and with none who understood it. But with her understanding, I will endure until a Kuakgan comes or Gird calls me home."

"I wish you well," Arvid said.

"And I you. You—" Against anything he expected, she put her hands to his face, pulled it toward her, and kissed him on the brow.

"If I had had children, I would have been glad to have you as a son. And your Arvi as a grandson."

In the next few days, Arvid worked even harder as he and Nadin began training Bodin and two others as potential yeoman-marshals. On the day before Midsummer Eve, Marshal Hudder released him from all duties. "Get yourself clean and rested and make sure they've the right clothes for you."

Late afternoon on the day, Arvid and Arvi sat downstairs at the Loaf, waiting for Marshal Hudder, who would present him. Marshal Cedlin and Marshal Hudder walked in together.

"Here he is," Marshal Cedlin said. "Cheer up, Arvid—you look like a man facing a drubbing."

"Am I not?" he said. "Do not all the Marshals get their chance?"

"Not anymore," Marshal Hudder said. "It would take far too long with this many Marshal-candidates and Marshals. No . . . you'll have one good bout with three different opponents. Neither of us; you'll get to surprise someone else."

"Time now," Marshal Cedlin said as bells began ringing throughout the city.

Arvid stood, feeling a little shaky in the knees, but that passed as they walked across the inn's common room. Outside, he was astonished to see yeomen from both granges arrayed in their ranks, carrying their hauks. They marched behind him and their Marshals on the way up to the citadel. Five others from the city were being confirmed that day; their granges also came in support of them. Those from outside had their supporters as well, usually two hands of yeomen.

The High Lord's Hall was almost full, evening light still coming through the windows. Arvid had noticed the Gird's Cow group around their stuffed cow outside and now saw them filing in. Arvid had been placed in the second rank, between a short dark fellow from a town on the South Trade Road and a wiry redhead from just north of the river. Once the Marshal-General had greeted the crowd, the candidates recited the Ten Fingers yet again and then the Marshal's Oath, not quite in unison.

Then the center space was cleared, and three candidates at a time faced an unfamiliar Marshal across the bare floor. Candidates and

Marshals both removed their shoes. The exchange was not nearly as simple as Arvid expected. Each pair fought with every standard weapon: hauk, staff, short sword, and then the Marshal's longsword. Those judging the length of each bout expected actual blows to be landed.

When it came Arvid's turn, his opponent was a dour black-bearded Marshal from near the eastern border. Arvid took a hard blow to the shoulder but gave one to the Marshal's hip. With staves he did better, landing several on the Marshal before the Marshal landed one on his ribs. They were both sweating heavily by then. In short sword and longsword, Arvid had the clear advantage; when the Marshal had not made a touch in the time a candle burned from mark to mark, he realized he would have to let the Marshal do so. He lowered his weapon looked the Marshal in the eye, and said, "I am not worthy. Mark me as you will." The Marshal smiled and drew the edge of the blade lightly down his forearm, drawing a thin bead of blood.

"Your blood honors my blade, for I had not the skill to take it. Alyanya bless you."

When his turn came around again, he had a different opponent, and then a last one who planted his stave hard on the floor and announced firmly that Arvid had proved himself enough. Those judging the bouts concurred.

In the final test, each had to kneel on the platform before the Marshal-General. She held the ancient sword said to have been Gird's and laid it to the neck of each. When it came Arvid's turn, he prayed silently, *Do not make a show of this. Please.*

His answer was a chuckle from within and a blaze of light around him as the sword touched him. He heard gasps from the others, then excited voices. He could not move for a long moment.

Get up. Now.

He stood up, tingling as if he'd been dipped in snow. Light shifted as he stood. Arianya still held the sword—and it was not the sword that gave light.

Someone cried out down the hall: "Magelord! Traitor! Kill him!"

Someone else said "No! It's Gird's light! He's a paladin!"

The only thought in the chaos of his mind was *Gird, you bastard.*

In his own light—but it wasn't his; it was Gird's or the High Lord's—he saw Paks, grinning at him. She winked and mouthed some greeting he could not, in his shock, understand. Beyond her, he saw the crowded hall as a mass of pale faces. Some . . . He stared at them. Some were touched with something he now felt was evil.

Yes. You will know. You have been where they are.

He shuddered even as he accepted that judgment. He had indeed been that angry, that vengeful, that willing to do harm. And he knew himself capable of harm still.

All are. It is a choice. And not always easy.

"I confirm you," the Marshal-General said loud enough to be heard. "Marshal Arvid, be true to your oath."

"I swear," he said. In his head, he felt Gird's response. He stepped aside to join the other confirmed Marshals, and the next, the fellow from the south, stepped forward. His light dimmed, but his awareness of those too fond of evil remained. Noise continued down the hall, rising and falling with each candidate confirmed.

When it was done, all the new Marshals were greeted first by Marshals, then knights and paladins, and then the other guests. Arvid noticed that aside from the Marshals and others from the citadel, the only people who came forward to greet him were from the two granges he knew best, those whose names he knew.

It was after the turn of night when the Hall emptied into the courtyard, very like the night of the riot back in autumn but for being barely cool, with a breeze smelling of the meadows to the west. From this point, the celebration reverted to the ancient rites of Midsummer. Arvid put his arm around Arvi's shoulders.

"Want to go out to the bonfire in the meadows?"

"Da—those men who think you're a magelord. You're not, are you?"

"No, of course not. You know what I am: both my parents thieves—"

"But I heard that in Tsaia some magelords were in the Thieves' Guild."

"Who told you that? I don't—" He stopped, remembering for the first time since he'd left Vérella the rumors about the Liartian who was supposed to be a noble . . . and a magelord. "I don't think so," he said more slowly. "All the thieves I knew were common as ashes. My parents—" If they were his parents. That thought came to him for the first time. His mother—a street singer, she said, before losing her looks to a jealous rival's knife. From her he'd gotten his voice, and she'd shaped it with exercises. His father—a thief from birth, from whom he'd learned knifework, wall climbing, silent movement, and poisons. He'd assumed all that was true. But . . . was it?

"I'm not a magelord," he said. "I have no magery in myself. That light came from Gird."

"That's what I said," Arvi said. "But the man next to me said Gird wouldn't give paladin's light to a dirty thief."

"Um. What else?"

"He said the Marshal-General's gone over to the magelords. He says you're proof."

Arvid felt a prickle down his back and turned. A few paces behind him, a man turned his back quickly.

"It's Midsummer Eve," he said. "Coming to dawn soon. Alyanya's most sacred day. However unhappy someone is, surely he'll have sense enough not to cause trouble today." He hoped. But after all, what better time to cause trouble than on a day no one expected it? He looked around, then overhead. Here in the courtyard, he could not see the horizon, but the sky seemed murky, the stars that had burned earlier now dimmed.

"Come," he said to Arvi. "Let's get you something to eat." And himself someone to tell, someone who could do something. He guided Arvi toward the side of the courtyard where tables were piled with food. Someone reached out as they passed and put a flower crown on Arvi's head. Arvid turned and caught a glimpse of a woman handing out flower crowns to other children.

Arvi started in on a pastry stuffed with berries; Arvid chose a meat roll. He saw no one he knew around him now. He felt off balance, uncertain. And then he saw Paks coming, a flower crown lopsided on her head. As in the fall, in the riot, she came directly to him, a broad smile on her face and the silver circle that still made his skin raise up in bumps.

"Everyone's told me about you and the children," she said. "I knew Gird had a plan for you."

"Did he tell you the plan?"

"No. That's between you two." She changed the subject abruptly. "I told the Marshal-General I found a Kuakgan, but he's not here . . . I thought he would be."

"I wish he were. I wish she'd go somewhere with more trees—they need trees, don't they?"

"Yes. He said he'd find a tree to bring with him. But come—let's go to the bonfire. We don't have much longer." She took his son's hand; he put an arm around the boy's shoulders, and they went out to the big field beyond the stable block. The scent of the night-blooming flowers starring the grass filled his nose. With the others they danced the old dances and sang the old songs . . . Arvid knew the thieves' words to those tunes better . . . and watched the sun rise red over the eastern end of the world before walking back to the city.

Another Marshal met them as they came into the main courtyard. "A Kuakgan's come," she said to Paks. She sounded excited. "He says his name's Sprucewind, and he asked for you. And he has a tree growing out of his arm."

"Good," Paks said. "I'll come with you." She turned to Arvid. "Good Midsummer to you, Marshal Arvid, and you, young Arvid. Gird's grace—I'll see you another time, I'm sure." She went off with the other Marshal.

"A tree?" Arvi said.

"That's what she said," Arvid said. "Growing out of his arm. Do you think we drank too much spring wine?" Arvi giggled; they walked back to the inn together.

❦

Marshal-General Arianya stared at the shutter pulled close in her window, wondering if it would not be better to die. No Kuakgan had come to help her, and she knew—hated knowing—that some iynisin magery still remained within her, sapping her strength and making her irritable. She was weakening—more and more she felt absent from herself, distant from everything. Marshals and paladins had tried to heal her, and at first—for a time varying from one day to five—she felt better. But she no longer believed any of them could heal her finally. Prayer led to resignation, but resignation, she knew, would not accomplish what Gird wanted her to accomplish. Nor, she was also sure, would the grim stubbornness it now took to hold on each day, to fend off the grief for mistakes she had made that hurt others, to bear the load of guilt.

Down the hall came a patter of rapid footsteps. No doubt one of the juniors with some problem. She struggled to sit straighter behind her desk, to banish from her mind, and she hoped from her face, the exhaustion and impatience she felt.

"Marshal-General—there's a Kuakgan come."

For a moment the word made no sense . . . then the meaning appeared. A Kuakgan. Who might be able to help her.

"Thank you," she said to the boy, who stood there, practically hopping from foot to foot with excitement. "See that he has refreshment, will you? When he has rested, I will seek him out."

"But he's here, Marshal-General! Right here!" The boy—she couldn't think of his name—turned, and a man in a long green robe came to her door. Youngish, she thought. And—her breath caught. Just below the elbow of his left arm, a small tree jutted out. A small fir tree . . . Her mind lurched sideways. How awkward it must be to have a tree as long as your forearm sticking out like that . . .

"Marshal-General?" His voice was quiet, gentle. He took two steps closer, and she caught the clean sharp scent of the fir tree. "You were attacked by kuaknomi, I am told. You are not well."

"Better . . . but not . . . well."

"I am sorry it took such time to come here, but . . . there are so few trees." He had stepped past her to the window and opened the shutter. "It took long to find one willing to share and near enough here."

Arianya turned her head from the light pouring through the window; it felt abrasive, like blown sand. "Too bright," she said.

"A tree needs light," he said. "And you need a tree." To the boy he said, "Can you find a pot, so high and so wide, and have someone help you fill it with good soil?" The boy nodded and left at a run. "All my healing is from the taig," he said to Arianya. "The life within all living things. You had a dream—a dream of a forest—"

"How did you know?"

"Dreams . . . wander. Your dream sought my aid before word came to me, but I did not know where you were." He hummed a moment. To Arianya's astonishment, a butterfly, scarlet and black, floated in the window and landed on the tree on his arm. "With your permission, I would touch your head."

"Yes," Arianya said, staring at the butterfly.

"Your healing will not be like Paksenarrion's, for her injuries, and Master Oakhallow's resources, in his own Grove, were both greater. Let me see . . ."

The scent of fir grew stronger; his hands—dry as bark—lay on her head without heat and stroked down to the back of her neck, to her shoulders. She closed her eyes.

When she opened them again, morning light no longer came through the window, and a great pot stood in the corner of her office, and Paksenarrion was there as well as the Kuakgan. "I must move this tree," Sprucewind said. "At least for a time, it must live in the pot. Are you feeling better?"

"Yes," Arianya said. Her office smelled fresh as a mountain grove.

"Good. This may be distressing to watch, but do not fear. This young fir and I are not . . . entirely . . . one yet." As he spoke, he changed . . . The robe he wore seemed more and more like actual moss, and his arm, now draped in moss, more like a gnarled branch, in the hollow of which the smaller tree had taken root. He looked at Paks. "You, having been healed by the Tree, may hold this tree: have a care and do not tug. Like that—yes—and invite it to leave a small home for a larger one. I will urge the separation from within."

Arianya was certain now that bark covered his arm . . . and his face had turned the exact brown she remembered from the spruce trees she had seen on her travels. Slowly, his arm lowered a little, even as needles sprang out of his fingertips . . . and as slowly, the seedling's roots slid free of his arm, pale and glistening slightly. Arianya gulped and glanced at Paks. Her gaze was on the little tree, her expression serious but serene. Had she known the tree was literally growing out of the man's arm ... or his limb? But now the last rootlets—spread wider than Arianya had imagined—hung loose in the air.

Sprucewind hummed; the rootlets quivered. "Now, hold it above the pot," he said to Paks. "I will sing it in." She did so. Arianya watched as the Kuakgan hummed and murmured words she did not know. The little tree's rootlets reached for the soil and then sank into it, spreading, she could tell by the crumbs of soil displaced by the roots. Finally the seedling stood upright in the center of the pot. When Arianya looked at Sprucewind, his hands bore no needles, and his robe—the sleeve once more covering his arm—looked like dark green cloth. His face looked completely human once more.

The next hours confused Arianya at first. Sprucewind watered the tree, leaned out the window, and hummed. He touched her hands, her head. Meanwhile, the butterfly that had come first was joined by two others, small, with green wings and a few orange spots. A beetle flew in and landed on the tree's tip. Sprucewind addressed a hiss at it, and it flew away. A bird—an ordinary little brown bird, Arianya thought—landed on the windowsill, then hopped down to the soil, lifted its tail, and deposited a dab of birdlime. Sprucewind held out a finger; the bird hopped on and—when Sprucewind lifted his hand—plucked a hair from his head and then flew away.

Finally, Sprucewind sat down in the room's other chair. "You will forgive, I hope, my planting the fir and making it comfortable. It had traveled a long way with me, and we were not, as I said, wholly compatible. Spruce and fir are both conifers but distant cousins, not siblings."

Arian had never thought of trees as having family relationships. "Where did you find a fir?" she asked. "We have none near here."

"True, and that's why it took me so long to come. I cannot sustain junipers—such as grow nearby—for even a few days' travel. I had to find a tree I could carry close enough that I had sufficient sustenance for it. This one came from a speck of a vill northeast of here, across the river. It is near where Paksenarrion came from and is called Three Firs. That was nearest." He cocked his head. "You offered me refreshment before—would it be convenient to have bread, perhaps cheese—?"

With the tray of bread, cheese, hard sausage, and pickled redroots, the kitchen sent up both sib and water. Sprucewind took water. "And I advise you to drink the same while we discuss your healing. I will be using what this young tree provides, and it is not compatible with the tree foods usually used in sib."

Arianya put down her mug of sib and poured water instead.

When he had eaten, he leaned back and touched the tree; it shivered, then settled. "We come now to your problem. You do not have any remnant of a kuaknomi weapon still in your body, but you do have that poison still keeping your body from healing itself. Both my tree, the spruce, and this fir are apt for dealing with such toxins; both are clean trees, as most conifers are. Close your eyes and breathe deeply."

Arianya did so; the fragrance of conifer forest filled the room and her head. When she woke—she had not noticed falling asleep—night had come outside. Across the room, Sprucewind, eyes closed, lay back in a chair with one hand holding a limb of the little seedling . . . a little seedling surely taller than it had been. Sprucewind's arm had silvery green needles on it again. And the desk was piled with empty bowls.

Sprucewind woke as she watched; he withdrew his hand from the tree, and the tree shivered as if he'd shaken it by the trunk. The needles sank back into his arm; the skin smoothed out, changing texture and color. He blinked a few times, then his gaze sharpened. "Ah . . . we have made some progress."

"What did you do?" Arianya asked.

"I am not sure I can explain," he said. He hummed; a large moth flew in the window, landed on his hand, then flew out again. "Iynisin poison is distilled of their hate for all living things. They began with trees, but hatred grows, and they came to hate all green life—and all who love it—and then all other life. Their poison affects different kinds of life differently and kills slowly, so as to warp and ruin whatever the high gods intended before death comes. To the Sinyi, their closest kin, it brings a quicker death than to humans. In humans, in whom awareness of self is strong, it attacks that awareness, so they are not as aware of themselves and it makes them irritable, even angry."

Arianya shifted in her chair. She had, she knew, been irritable.

"So first I had to find your heartwood—your real self—and begin . . . filtering? . . . yes, that is the word . . . the poison from you. I think it is not a thing that wound healing, the kind you know about, can do. For me it takes myself and a tree of reasonably close kindred. I let the poison pass through me—"

"Doesn't it hurt you?"

"Yes, but not as much. In a forest it would be easier; I could have the aid of all the trees of my tribe and some of the others as well. But you see—it went from me to the tree, and the tree, small as it is, transformed it to nourishment."

Arianya blinked, trying to think her way through that. "How?" she said finally.

"I am not sure." He spread his hands. "Too much will sicken us— both the tree and me—and at some point would kill us. But in small amounts—a drop at a time—it can be done without more than effort and a little discomfort." He tipped his head and gazed toward the pile of bowls. "I do need to eat a lot."

"All you want," she said.

"And you need to eat a lot, too. I will call on your kitchens again, and then I must sleep for a while. You must sleep in here, with the tree to guard your sleep. Tomorrow we begin again. Healing of iynisin poison cannot be rushed, but I think a few days will be sufficient."

Not until the last day was Arianya able to stay awake during the treatments. The Kuakan kept his hand on hers; she watched it stiffen, the skin drying, turning greenish gray before the fine needles of a spruce came up, furring the back of his hand, even as his fingers took on the appearance of twigs. On his arms, the bark was browner . . . and his face, too, seemed drier, more like bark. She felt a peculiar sensation along her bones, where the ache had been, and then—a sick orange-brown color shriveled the needles of his hand on hers, leaving the barklike skin exposed, then moved up his arm, even as fresh needles sprang from below the others.

Where he touched the young fir, one branchlet's needles turned the same sick orange-brown and fell off; the branchlet darkened as if scorched . . . then recovered, even as the Kuakgan's hand recovered. One small pulse at a time, each perhaps half the length of his hand long.

Arianya wanted to stop, but his grip on her hand was firm as a tree's root. She watched . . . and his hand abruptly turned a brighter green than before and a green streak ran up her own arm. Her mouth tasted of green—of fir and spruce needles she had nibbled as a child, of every herb in the garden—and for a moment she felt alive in a way she never had. Then it faded as he released her and sat back, his eyes gleaming.

"It is finished," he said. "All the poison is gone. Look at the tree."

The tree now stood as tall as the pot, every needle crisp and full. Sprucewind's expression was rueful. "It needs the earth and the root touch of others," he said. "You will need to find a wagon to haul it somewhere firs grow. It must not die . . . for then the poison will be released again."

"Did any of your—any Kuakgan—know Gird?"

He tipped his head to one side. "I don't know, Marshal-General. I doubt it; we avoid conflict if we can. And this was magelord country, wasn't it? They weren't fond of us, though less hostile than elves."

Arianya felt a nudge—more like a buffet—on her shoulder. "Then I think it is past time we met the people who prefer avoiding conflict to starting it. Not like the elves, who withdrew completely, but . . . like trees in a grove, touching branch to branch and root to root."

"There is some jostling for power," Sprucewind said. "Trees may be slow, but they do have territorial ambitions." He smiled.

"We have a common enemy," Arianya said. "We ought to make common cause where we can."

New Marshals usually had time between being confirmed in their new rank and being assigned to a grange. Arvid reverted to his earlier schedule, going up the hill every day to help out in the archives, where piles of new material had come in from Kolobia as fast as those in Kolobia could bring it.

All the magelords had been literate, and those in the main stronghold had produced far more writing than anyone realized until they brought it back. Recipes from the kitchen, lists of supplies, little sketch maps, a list of words in a language no one had seen before, recipes for herbal remedies, records of projects begun and finished, with dates referring to a calendar they didn't know . . . all in a jumble, large and small pieces of paper, cloth, skin, bundled together, as much as those obeying the elves' orders to leave could manage.

Arvid intended to sort out anything having to do with legal matters, since he was still studying the Code with Deinar, but he was fascinated by the hints at the individuals who had lived there as shown by their writings. A cook's notes on edible local plants, how to recognize them and how to use them. "NOT this" with a drawing of something with three slender pointed leaflets and "THIS" underlined twice with a plant having two slender pointed leaflets, with a sketch of someone bent over and throwing up by the three-leaflet image.

A little book, pages sewn together with linen thread, detailing the watch-list for—he riffled through it—more than a year. So they had a militia? They were guarding against . . . what? And how, then, had they been surprised? Each line was initialed . . . A, S, or RM. He looked more carefully. A must be Aris . . . no other name given. S would be Seri. RM? He found a page with a line through it and a scrawled "Rosemage" at the bottom with a stylized drawing of a rose, very like the Tsaian Rose.

In the pile in front of him, he spotted another, similar book and pulled it out; half the pile slid off the desk where he worked and scattered itself on the floor. Sighing, he picked it up and put it back on the desk before opening the book.

The stylized rose, drawn larger, was on the first page. On the next page, the fine, dense writing began.

I came to him a woman deeply wounded and a killer.

He blinked. Was this a tale or something real?

He was as I had been told, a peasant. Lean from hunger but
broad in frame; if a horse, he would have been bred for draft.
I did not please him, being mageborn. But this matters noth-
ing for what I have to tell. Let my past be gone, my killings
and my savings. For only those who were there know how Gird
died, since the tale has grown wings and flown away from the
truth. And of us, one has lied.

Arvid looked around the room. Others were busy on other piles,
sorting steadily by some rule of their own. He went back to reading.
For all the dramatic language of the first page, once the writer got
into it, the story of Gird's last day was told plainly, baldly, with only
a few interpolations from the past. It resembled the official version
only in that Gird was alive at the beginning, did something heroic,
and died.

No demon. No monster. No valiant defense with a cudgel. A
quarrel that began with a mageborn girl and a peasant-born bully, a
quarrel that gathered a mob, that would have ended with the girl
dead and the mob hunting more mageborn prey, as they had in the
last days of the war. This "Rosemage"—the woman who wrote the
book—and Luap trying to calm the mob without success. Gird's arrival; the crowd for once not listening to him.

A sultry day, threatening storm, the woman had written.
"The city stank; the crowd stank; such weather brings out bad
smells. And their anger, like a storm gathering. Mine as well,
for their stupidity and malice."

Gird had said words the woman had not written down—

Words I never heard before, words that might have made the
world itself. From his face, Gird himself did not know what
they were, only that he must say them. Then the rage to kill
lifted, the evil thoughts; I felt this in my own heart, for I had

been angry with those peasants. I could almost see it, the mob's
thoughts in a dark cloud hovering over us all. It seemed Gird
saw it, too, for he looked up, not at the mob, as he spoke. They
did not see; I asked witnesses later, and they did not see. Then
the cloud thickened, and Gird took it in . . . I saw it happen,
though none other has written it. I saw fear on his face, then
duty accepted, and his mouth stayed open and the darkness
went in, all of it. How he did so I do not know. The gods aided
him, Arranha the priest says, but even he cannot explain. Only
when the dark cloud was gone and Gird had fallen, having
taken the evil into himself and then died, the day freshened and
the mob's anger was gone. We felt sorrow but also relief.

I do not know the words. I do not know how it was done.
But I know Gird's own Luap lied about it in the story he wrote,
as he has lied about many things. Gird knew he could not stay
true, but no one else believes. He has that much of the royal
magery of his father to charm those around him, yet without
truth there is no authority. Gird did not want this division
between the peoples; he had seen the far land and chose to
remain here. I cannot trust his Luap, but yet none of the
peasant-born trust me, and I cannot say they should. Perhaps,
lacking the man who most believed that peace was possible
between us, it is best to withdraw while Gird's peace lasts. It
will not last forever.

Arvid chewed his lip. *That* was going to upset people if this became the official version. Mob violence in Gird's day? The people
refusing his guidance in an era when everyone thought no one questioned him? And some sort of "cloud" instead of a demon?

He read beyond that part of the book to see what he thought of
the writer's character. A blank page, then writing in a slightly different ink, this time reporting on a meeting of magelords planning to
relocate to Kolobia. The same plain, terse writing: who said what,
what the plan was, followed by a list: clothes, weapons, tools. The
book continued to a point after the move to Kolobia, where the old
priest of Esea died. The woman had suspected treachery but could

not prove it and ended the little book with "Something is very wrong, but I cannot understand what it might be. A's power of healing weakens. Were we brought to this place only to fail and die? Then I shall die well, in memory of the old man."

Did she mean the old priest or Gird? Arvid read the passages again and still was not sure.

He thought about showing it to the senior scribe, but really—it was a matter for Marshals. Even High Marshals. Even the Marshal-General, who was recovering now from whatever the Kuakgan had done. The Kuakgan was still in Fin Panir, wandering out to the few scrubby trees on the north sides of hills and coming back to talk to the Marshal-General. But the Marshal-General looked much better, more relaxed even in the midst of all the furor about mages.

With the books in hand, he gave the watch list record to the senior scribe and suggested that others might be found. "I found something of interest to the Marshal-General," he said, "and I'm taking it to her."

"Has it been cataloged?" the scribe said. "If not, let me put it on the list."

It went on the list as 765-B, and the scribe wrote that on the goatskin cover.

"There, Marshal. Now we'll know how it fits in." Arvid thanked him and took the book upstairs.

He had seen the Marshal-General only in passing since the night of his confirmation; she had looked healthier and more relaxed, but he did not expect her to get up from her desk and give him a strong hug. "Marshal Semminson," she said. "Or do you prefer Marshal Arvid?"

"Arvid, Marshal-General. Just Arvid."

"You've been staying away."

"I've been busy. And I found something. This is a contemporary's account of Gird's last day. And it's not like Luap's." He handed her the book.

She took it and read the passage, then turned back and reread it. "Well," she said at last. "That is . . . very different. The first bit is strange, but then it reads like someone who was there."

"That's what I thought, Marshal-General. And it's different enough that it's going to cause a stir, but if this is the real story, then . . ."

"Then we must start teaching it. I must say I will miss the leering demon twice the height of a man with red eyes and claws as long as a man's thigh."

"And the hideous breath," Arvid said, grinning. "And Gird declaiming the Ten Fingers at it was a nice touch."

"It will have to go to the Marshalate," she said. "And you'll have to bear witness you found it and didn't alter it. Give it to Deinar; he's a good man for recognizing altered texts. It will be useful to my side of the mage argument but for that very reason suspect. At least it has a catalog number on it. And how's your son?"

"Growing," Arvid said. "Marshal Cedlin says he's caught up with the children who've been in school all along. Easier when they're this young, he says."

"That's good. Because soon we'll need you to take over a grange from one of those I'm replacing—the mage-haters. You need to think about whether to leave Arvi here with another family or take him with you into what might be a hostile situation."

Arvid hadn't considered that at all. "He won't like being left," he said.

"And you won't like it if the local people take against him. Think about it. It won't be until after the fair at Hoorlow, anyway, unless there's a crisis somewhere."

"The fair at Hoorlow?"

"Every fall. If you're not needed elsewhere, you're coming with me this year. It's in the depths of Old Girdish country, where the first battles were fought. I'll tell you about it later; I've got to get back to another project."

Arvid delivered the book to Deinar and told the chief scribe who had it, then went back to the pile of writings on his desk. Someone had taken away part, and someone else had added more. By dinnertime, he was looking forward to the fair at Hoorlow, wherever that was.

CHAPTER TWENTY-SEVEN

Fox Company Camp, Foss Council, Aarenis

Arcolin opened the message from Burek and frowned. "So . . . Alured's on the march, is he? He'll find Cilwan a harder nut to crack this time." He turned to his squire, Kaim, busy cleaning Arcolin's tack after the morning's ride. "Kaim, go find the captains. Meeting here as soon as they can."

"Yes, my lord." Kaim took a moment to put the rags and brushes away before leaving. Arcolin smiled. Kaim had proven every bit as diligent and steady as Arneson and the boy's father had said. Not a complaint out of him all the hot dusty summer so far. He made himself useful in every situation, never wandered off, never did any of the things that Arcolin, after the years of Kieri's various squires, expected from a youngster in a first campaign season.

Soon enough the other captains came in: Cracolnya and his junior, Versin; Selfer and his junior, Garralt. Kaim followed them in and retreated to the corner of the tent where the tack hung.

"Has that devil Alured moved?" Cracolnya asked as he came in.

"Yes. Burek put scouts down around Lûn," Arcolin said. "There's a force come into Lûn from downriver, in Immer's colors."

"So either he took Fallo or he got his shins kicked," Cracolnya said, dropping into one of the folding chairs. "Good thing you moved our camp down here, then."

"My lord?" Kaim gestured to the table. Arcolin nodded.

"And bring the dried plums," Cracolnya said over his shoulder. Then to Arcolin, "Have you heard more from the Kostandanyans?"

"Only the message two hands of days ago. Fighting around Fall's great house, wherever that is. I've never been that far into Fallo."

"If he hasn't defeated Fall, then why would he take his troops west?" Garralt asked. "He's leaving his rear open."

"We don't know how many troops he has," Arcolin said. "Siniava seemed to pull them out of the ground like redroots—always more left behind."

"If he takes men from the cities down on the coast . . ." Selfer let out a long whistle.

"I told Foss Council Alured might move back into the main river area before summer's end," Arcolin said. "They've agreed Cortes Cilwan must not fall again. Andressat has moved a cohort of Golden Company to its eastern boundary, and Aesil M'dierra has agreed that I can command them."

Cracolnya sat up straight. "Has she now!"

"Yes. I know the captain of that cohort, Sarnol; we get along well. Foss Council would rather risk its hirelings than its own militia—and I cannot blame them. Vonja claims it can't spare anyone, not surprisingly. But Sorellin will send a half-hundred of its pikes. So, Captains: How soon can we march?"

Cracolnya blinked twice. "Not this evening, m'lord. The farrier's here now and not done. If he works through the night . . . in the morning. Can Burek hold until we arrive?"

"Yes," Arcolin said. "He's confident of that; he's been drilling the entire populace since we took the city."

"My cohort's ready," Selfer said. "Strike tents tonight?"

"No, dawn. No sense letting spies have that much lead on us. No one leaves the camp tonight. Pack the wagons after dark. Alured has to know we would have scouts out; he has to know we'll be coming. He will want Cortes Cilwan back, but he may divert and strike elsewhere. Sorellin, for instance."

Until dark, Fox Company's camp appeared no busier than usual, following the routine of each day during campaign. Sentries went out as usual and walked the bounds until the last to the jacks filled them in . . . a little more than usual. And in the near-dark, all that had been packed earlier, in the guise of straightening up the camp, went into the wagons. The tents remained: the Duke's tent, with its several rooms lit, and officers coming to make the final report of the day. All as usual.

Arcolin slept sound, as he always did when a plan had been set. He dressed in the dark, by feel, and woke Kaim, who did the same. Outside, there was scarcely light to see, the tents vague blurs against the dark. One by one they came down with no more sound than air whooshing from the canvas as it collapsed. Smoke from the cook fire rose straight up, paler than the dark—something anyone watching from a distance would expect to see. Fox Company did not lie abed of a morning; everyone knew that.

They ate breakfast on the flattened turf that had been rows of tents the day before—anyone watching could see now that the camp had changed, but Fox Company had moved every tenday, if only to fresh ground. Wagon teams were hitched and ready, the last of the camp tidied. Arcolin finished a mug of sib and grinned at his captains. "Well done, all. No way to hide the Company, but if someone moves ahead of us now, we'll know it."

Cracolnya stood up. "Scouts out," he said to the cluster of men nearby. "Keep just in touch." They nodded and moved off to collect their horses.

Arcolin stood, and everyone scrambled up. Cooks poured water on the last of the fire and raked it over. Clouds of steam rose. Low-voiced, the sergeants of each cohort got them all in order of march. Kaim led up Arcolin's horse and his own. They mounted; Arcolin started down the road, and his cohort lined out behind him, the steady tramp of their feet as familiar and reassuring as the beat of his own heart. He heard the others join them, heard, behind all that, the jingle of harness and crunch and grind of wagon wheels moving from turf to the road.

Fox Company marched around Vonja, avoiding the congestion of the city's center, then back to the Guild League road. Once past Vonja, traffic was light, only foot travelers and the occasional two-wheeled cart. Other travelers moved off the road to let them pass, and they made good time. Scouts rotated in and out, bringing word.

"Where is Golden Company's cohort?" Selfer asked.

"Coming cross-country from Andressat," Arcolin said. "I don't expect to see them before we reach Cortes Cilwan. They're mounted; they'll make good time. It hasn't been wet."

Indeed, it had been dry, and the river was low, long strings of green weed in the murky, stale-smelling water. They watered the horses in it but took their own water from the little vills they passed.

Another messenger from Burek met them the day before they expected to reach the city. Alured's troops had made one attempt on the east gate of Cortes Cilwan but had been driven back. Burek estimated five hundreds in all had come from Lûn; the half-hundred from Sorellin had arrived before them, strengthening the defenders. The city had ample water in its wells.

The next morning saw smoke in the air to the east; Arcolin recognized the smoke of burning fields, not a burning city. By midday, they were in sight of Cilwan and the invaders.

Arcolin's forward scouts reported that the invaders, having made another unsuccessful assault on the east gate, had encircled the city and set nearby fields afire. Now, having spotted Arcolin's force, they were gathering on the west side.

"Is Alured commanding them?"

"I'm not sure," one scout said.

"Do the troops seem strange in any way—under a compulsion?"

"No, my lord. They seem . . . vague, I'd say. Not as organized as I expected."

"Alured was never vague for the flick of a finger that I knew him," Arcolin said. "If they're uncertain . . . he's not there." He dismounted. "Kaim, stay mounted—let me know if they start moving fast. The way they're milling about, they won't be here for another three turns of the glass. Feed the troops—a light meal, plenty of water."

"Yes, my lord."

Slowly the mass of enemy troops near the city's walls thickened.

"What's taking so long?" asked Versin.

"Moving them around the city," Arcolin said. "Kaim, you can dismount, get something to eat." To Versin he said, "Whoever's commanding over there wants to leave enough—whatever he thinks is enough—by the east gate and some by the north gate and some to

guard the bridge. He's uncertain. He might be waiting for reinforcements from Lûn, but I don't think so. He should have come on at
once; his situation will worsen now."

"Why?" Versin asked.

"The sun," Arcolin said, and pointed to the shadow at his feet,
stretching now an armslength toward Cortes Cilwan. "Yes, we're past
midsummer and the days are shorter . . . but the sun will be in their
face all afternoon and not in ours. Unless he waits until after sundown. Which will give him other problems."

The mass finally began to move their way, widening as it moved.
Arcolin mounted again. At the back of the mass a few were on
horseback—the commander, perhaps messengers or subordinate
commanders. Off to the south, he saw something moving . . . a glitter
in the afternoon sun, a low dust cloud. He squinted. One cohort
should be about that long . . . and this was longer. They must have
sent another. He grinned and looked down at his captains. "This will
be interesting," he said. "Golden Company's heading for the bridge."

"All of them?" Cracolnya asked.

"Can't tell. Maybe. More than one cohort, anyway."

Ahead of them, the enemy had formed a wide shallow front. They
knew he had left troops in the city earlier in the season . . . but perhaps they thought he'd left most of them. At any rate, they seemed to
be attempting to outflank Fox Company on both flanks at once.

"Time," he said, and named the formation he wanted. On an open
plain like this, a hidden reserve was impossible. His half-cohort and
Selfer's whole one would be narrow and deep, Cracolnya's split into
two mounted units. He turned to Kaim. "Stay close and do not attack:
understand?"

"Yes, my lord."

"You have my second sword; we'll hope I don't need it."

The larger enemy formation came on; though most of the troops
carried sword and shield, clumps of pikes were spaced along it. A
gap now opened between the city walls and the enemy. He looked
south again. Golden Company was close enough now to see the colors
of the second and third units . . . Clarts. They'd brought Clart Cavalry
along.

Wide on his own flanks, Cracolnya's archers put a flight into each end of the enemy formation, then whirled and galloped away. No arrows came in response, and the outer ends of the enemy formation edged inward. Arcolin looked toward the city. Surely they also had cavalry hidden around the city walls, and at some point it would come out and try to engage Cracolnya's cohort, but nothing happened.

"They do have a lot of troops, don't they, my lord?" Kaim said. His voice was unnaturally calm.

"They outnumber us, yes," Arcolin said. "Twice our number. Not, Gird be thanked, twice our tactical skill." He waved the pennant he carried, and the central formation marched forward. The enemy, as he expected, began to curve inward.

Then horn calls, more frantic than melodic, rang out from near the city. One of the horsemen turned and galloped back toward the city, mouth open. Soldiers near him in the rear turned around, slowed, and the wide front softened in the center.

"It could not be better . . ." Arcolin muttered.

"My lord?"

"Kaim, see that—see how their ranks are opening up? Right where we want to go . . ." He waved his pennant, caught the sergeants' attention. "Advance! Fast! Now!"

Fox Company's central formation hit the center of the arc; when the enemy's front rank gave back, they felt no support behind them. Arcolin could see the mounted men yelling at them, but too late; his formation punched through, and the ends of the arc came together with nothing between them and Cracolnya's archers shooting into their backs. Even before that, a quarter of the last rank on the south end of the arc had peeled off to stare as Golden Company's lead cohort and Clart Company took the bridge and then came around the city like a scythe, cutting down the troops left to guard the wall and clearing the west gate, which promptly opened to let Burek, his half-cohort, and an oversized formation of Cilwan militia out and then closed again.

The enemy troops did not yield easily, even so. They still outnumbered Arcolin's formations, and Burek wasn't in contact yet.

However disorganized they'd seemed at first, they fought hard once they were close. A lucky shot by one of Cracolnya's archers took one of their mounted officers, and one of the former Sobanai charged right into their formation and hacked his way—wounded and dying—to hamstring another's horse. Even when Golden Company and the Clarts arrived, even with Burek's troops on the scene, it was almost sundown when the last of Alured's soldiers fell.

Carrion birds had gathered by then, and the stench of death, the cries of the wounded, turned Kaim pale. Arcolin said nothing about it. This was war, and if Kaim wanted to be a soldier, he would have to learn to live with it.

It was full dark, a hot, sultry night, by the time the last Fox Company wagons rolled into the city and the gates closed behind them. Ahead the streets were crowded and noisy; torches burned at every door. In the large market square near the palace, Nasimir Clart raised a cheer as Arcolin rode up, and Sarnol, Golden Company's senior captain, joined in.

"I didn't expect you," Arcolin said to Clart, who grinned.

"Aesil wanted to surprise you," he said. "And Andressat wanted to be sure there was no more looting in Cortes Cilwan."

"Also," Sarnol said, "we have the cub along." He jerked his head a little, and Arcolin looked that way to see Poldin M'dierra.

"She let him come?"

"She did. Said the lad had to be blooded sometime. Who's your squire?"

"Kaim, son of the count whose holding is south of mine in Tsaia." Arcolin eased his back. "You certainly came at the right moment."

"The luck was with us," Clart said.

"Camwyn's Claw," Sarnol said. "And Esea's Fire."

"And as neat a trap as ever we sprung," Arcolin said. "You're coming up to the palace later to talk?"

"Of course."

"Then I'd best get on."

Kaim said little on the ride to the city, but he dismounted when Arcolin stopped in the palace courtyard and stood ready to hold Arcolin's mount. "You've done well, Kaim," Arcolin said. "A hard-fought battle, and you stood firm. When you've put the horses away, get a meal and some rest."

"Yes, my lord." Kaim led the horses away, and Arcolin saw Burek waiting for him on the palace step.

"My lord, I was never so glad to see you in my life," Burek said. "I did not doubt you were coming, but some of the new militia were on the point of panic. They'd seen what Immer's men could do when they held the city before."

"You held them together very well," Arcolin said.

Arcolin half expected another attack from downriver, but none came. The few prisoners they'd captured at the end of the battle—all wounded, some fatally—could tell them nothing about Alured's plans, only insisting that his name was Visli Vaskronin, Duke Immer, not Alured. Where he was or why he had not come to command in person, they did not know.

"I don't believe he's dead," Nasimir Clart said, leaning his elbows on the table. "If he was, you'd have people dancing for joy all the way down the Immer."

"Except his pirate friends," Soldan said. "But I do wish we knew what had happened in Fallo."

The answer came three days later in the person of Count Vladi himself with an escort of four hands of Kostandanyans rather than his own polearm company.

"So, you took Cortes Cilwan back," he said to Arcolin. "That is good. That man is demon-ridden."

Arcolin knew he meant Alured. "So Andressat's son managed to convey," he said. "Did you know about that?"

"Not until later." Vladi accepted a seat under the awning of Arcolin's tent. "I was over there since middle of last campaign season, trying to get Sofi Ganarrion and his daughter out of there, but she was pregnant. I would not say this to everyone, but Fall's son is useless save for tupping girls."

"Is he back in Kostandan, then?" Cracolnya asked.

"Sofi? No. And the Duke of Fall and his worthless son are still alive as well, no thanks to the son. No warrior, that one. Fall should disown him and declare one of his nephews his heir. Sofi says he will not go north without the promise of some position in the court and forgiveness for all that happened."

"I've always wondered," Cracolnya said.

"You will continue so," Vladi said in a tone that created a long pause in the conversation. Then he heaved a sigh, stroked his pointed beard, now snowy white, and said, "I tell you what I can tell you. *Our* king—" The emphasis was clear. "—he sent shiploads of troops from up north, around the Eastbight in winter, when pirates and spies are few. Though . . . we killed some."

"And Alured—Immer—didn't find out?"

"Not until too late. I had no duty to invade his land; my duty is to protect Ganarrion for his father's blood's sake. Immer thought Fallo weak—which it is, or was—and planned to take it to secure his flank. He will not try that again, or not for a long time."

"Did you kill him?"

"Oh, no. Demon-ridden, as I said. Hard to kill as long as the demon has him. But he took a wound or two and doubtless needed some time in a bed." Vladi took out a flask and poured three fingers of a clear liquid into a glass. "Let us drink, Captains, to the defeat of enemies and the safety of allies."

The others poured ale or water as they chose and drank the toast. Vladi stayed until all but Arcolin had gone to bed that night, then spoke. "What is this I hear of demons in the north?"

"Iynisin," Arcolin said. "Kuaknomi, we call them in Tsaia, or blackcloaks. They attacked."

"Ah. Very old trouble. Very bad. I hear the silverbloods want to war with them again."

"Silverbloods?"

Vladi spit. "Those so-called Elders, the tree singers. They would not let us south of the river up there, wanted all for themselves. You know the demons are their cousins—"

Arcolin had never known the Kostandanyans' opinions about elves were so different from his own. He could not think what to say; Vladi started again.

"They call them dark cousins when they admit their existence at all. That woman silverblood, the Lady you people call her: she drove all the Seafolk out when all we wanted was a little land to farm and the river to fish in. I heard she died last year; one of her own killed her . . . maybe not a close cousin but a dark one. Good riddance. Phelan the Fox is king now, eh?"

"She was killed by iynisin, yes," Arcolin said.

Vladi poured himself more of whatever was in his flask. Arcolin was sure it wasn't water. "I thought, when Kieri Phelan was young, just Halveric's squire, that he had the look of royalty, but later just a good soldier. That can be enough for a man. And now he's king up there. I would visit him and toast his success if not that my king tells me to keep watch on Ganarrion."

Arcolin realized that Vladi was working his way to something. "Do you have a message for him?" he asked, hoping to shorten the ordeal.

"Perhaps," Vladi said, stiffening again. "I hear he is part silverblood and that deplorable Lady his grandmother . . . Is that true?"

"Yes," Arcolin said. "Apparently."

"What Aliam Halveric told me, years ago . . . he took the boy in, and the boy had come through the woods from the east."

"Yes," Arcolin said again.

"So . . . then . . . when I was young, a boy, all our boys go to sea for two winters. And I went to sea as I was bid, and we sailed far out in the eastern ocean and came to land on the other side. And then we sailed back." He paused to pour and drink another glass. "And there was a man, a magelord of Aare, he said he was, at the port where we landed to sell the fish we had caught, and he questioned the captain of the ship closely about a boy who had run away."

Arcolin's skin rose up in gooseflesh. "Did he give his name?" he said.

Vladi looked hard at him, his eyes cold. "Would you know the name if I said it?"

"I might," Arcolin said.

"That man was demon-ridden, too," Vladi said. "He looked at me, and I felt fear for the first time. Our captain saw it and sent me below, and they gave me the drink so I vomited out the fear the demon had put in me. Still I don't forget. Kieri should be very careful. It was long ago, but the demon-ridden do not die easily. And it comes to me that when Alured the Black was a pirate, it is said he sailed from across the eastern ocean, and . . . he is demon-ridden."

"You think it is the same?"

Vladi shrugged. "Who am I to know the ways of demons or which one is which? There is more than one kind, that I know. Very long ago, I think, the Elder demons taught some men how to become demons themselves and how to take the bodies of others and use them so they need not die of age. If Kieri the Fox was ever a demon's plaything, then despite the years between he might become so again if the demon found him."

"No!" Arcolin could not help himself. "He would never—not now. He has his own magery."

"The demon has a magic stone," Vladi said. His chin was sunk on his chest now, his eyes half closed. "I saw it when I was a lad on our ship, and I saw just such a stone in the hand of that Alured when he invaded Fallo. Red as ruby, but not ruby. A demon stone." His voice softened. "Might be same stone. Might not. But . . . I would tell Kieri to be wary." He was silent a long time; Arcolin waited for him to speak, but then, in one long noisy breath, Vladi started snoring.

In the morning, Vladi swore he remembered nothing of what he'd said and would confirm none of it. "I was drinking spruce," he said. "I was drunk. Gods only know what I said or what I meant by it. And my head splits with the sunlight and the heat. That is what comes of drinking spruce and talking of demons. I will go back to my work."

CHAPTER TWENTY-EIGHT

Cave, Southern Waste

The boy woke. In the dark, he had no idea what time it was, or where, and his head . . . his head was a strange place, full of empty shelves, shattered boxes, torn fragments of cloth. He reached out his hands . . . one glowed red as a firecoal, but he could see nothing beyond the dark.

Sense departed; he fell again into heavy sleep and did not know it when a vast shape crept near him, wrapped a long, fiery tongue around him, and drew him once more inside. For a time he dreamed . . . dreamed of staring into a fire, the flames dancing and writhing, the colors beyond any colors he had seen. He dreamed of melting, of being poured, twisted, and stretched, molded . . . he dreamed of every good scent a bakery could produce—spices toasted on hot iron, then baked in bread and pastries . . . he dreamed of lying on a roof somewhere, the sun warming his back.

And he woke to darkness solid as stone. Warm. Comfortable. Where was he? He put out his hands, and one glowed red as a fire-coal, and he could see nothing more in the light of that hand. He wasn't afraid, and that brought him the first flicker of real thought: Why wasn't he afraid? He felt himself, rediscovered his arms, his hands, his head, his neck, his chest and belly, and . . . What was that? Something tangled over him, something flexible . . . but soft. He pulled it up, sniffed it, rubbed his face in it, then put it aside. He had no more name for it than he had for himself. For a moment that woke fear, fear that threatened to pull him down to nothing again.

Had he always been in the dark alone? He tried to answer that question, and a vague sense of light came to him . . . of space illuminated. Of . . . rooms? Of knowing what was over there, or over here, knowing what he could touch from where he lay and what was out of reach.

As he lay wondering about this, a sound moved in the darkness, a sound for which—like everything else—he had no name. A long streak of red, edged with flickering blue, appeared. He shrank back, frightened by what he could not understand. The red shortened, disappeared.

"You're awake," a voice said.

The words, he knew, referred to himself. He should know them.

"I will touch your head," the voice said.

He was still puzzling out the meaning from the sounds when something warm brushed his face and settled—not uncomfortably—around the left side of his face. The something grew warmer; a smell came with it, a smell that brought with it a memory of red, yellow, heat, and loud noise. Darkness swept across the remembered fire, then his memory jerked aside and he saw a figure hitting . . . hammering . . . the word came to him . . . on something . . . the noise hurt.

"Better," the nearby voice said. "Drink."

He had not thought of his face, but when a rim touched his lips, he opened them and drank whatever it was that flowed down his throat. He felt different after. Thoughts moved in his head, separate as beads on a string. He could imagine beads and string-wire-thong-rope.

"I will take you," the voice said.

Before he could realize what would happen, he was wrapped down his length in that warm touch and moving—he could feel it under him, a quiver. The noise returned—a noise like the sound of hammering but much fainter and less regular. A distant clang and clatter. He slept.

At next waking, darkness had been replaced by light. He could see no source for it, could not name it, but he could see across a space to a solid wall of rock and see the surface of rock between himself and that wall. That way—the light dimmed. That other way—the light seemed stronger. He looked down at himself: a body he recognized as . . . human. He lifted his hands, stared at them a long time in puzzled wonder. Slowly words came: "finger," "thumb," the numbers to count fingers with, the name "hand" for the whole. He had time alone to consider the rest, to recover the names: wrist, arm, elbow, shoulder, head and neck and chest . . . to remember that what he saw with were eyes, what he smelled with—still a smell he could not name—was a nose, and his mouth—his lips—his teeth . . .

He made a sound himself and remembered that he heard himself with ears. The sounds he made . . . were not words, though he did not have a word for words; he only knew the sounds meant nothing to him. Abruptly, his body made demands; he sat up and looked around. Without naming it, without knowing what he would do, he stood and, stumbling, one hand against the rock wall nearest, made his way toward dimness and found there a pot that smelled . . . right. Fluid emerged; he knew it should go into the pot and aimed it. Most did.

He turned, steadier now on his feet, and moved toward more light. He had lain . . . there on something soft. He did not want to lie down. He wanted to move; he wanted to see. An angle of wall blocked him; he moved along it and found between that and the other wall an opening half the width of the chamber he'd been in.

Beyond a turn of the wall, brightness stabbed his eyes; he squinted, blinked away the instant tears, and ventured closer, very slowly. A gust of air brought him more smells, smells he now thought he should know. He went on carefully, one step at a time, one hand always on the rock, until the rock fell away before him and he was looking out over shapes and colors, smelling too many things to count, seeing distance after distance melting away into haze. Colors . . . his mind dredged up only a few names, and none that quite fit but for "blue" of the sky . . . another word he remembered . . . and "green" for a small plant growing in another pot, just inside the opening.

He sat down, his legs failing him suddenly, and stared out at the vastness, his eyes watering, the water running down his face, and tasting . . . salty, he remembered as he licked his lips. Salty. The light shifted as time passed; he did not think about that but merely noticed more light, a paler sky. The wind continued to blow across his face, bringing more strange scents.

"It is good to see you in the light," said the same voice he had heard before.

He turned and saw a . . . human? Dark skin, unlike his, and fire-gold eyes. The human—if it was a human—wore dark clothes that rippled in the wind like . . . like . . . flames, only flames . . . were not . . . dark. The man held a pot, a pot he recognized, and carried it to the opening, closer than he himself had gone, and threw its contents outward, even as a long red tongue emerged from the man's mouth and in a gout of flame incinerated those same contents and then—aimed at the pot's interior, scoured the pot, and set it down.

"You are not human." His own voice startled him. It spoke words, and he knew the meaning of the words, and more words rose in his mind, a chattering swarm of them. "Too many words," he said then, and shut his eyes.

"You see truly," the other said, and this time he knew the meaning of those words as well. "I am Dragon, and we share a name, you and I. Do you know it?"

He shook his head, unable to speak for the clamor of all the words. Something warm touched the heart-hand side of his face, and the words settled as blown leaves settle to the ground when the wind passes. He opened his eyes. "Dragon," he said.

"Your name is Camwyn," the dragon said. "Camwyn . . . dragon-friend."

The words lay still in his mind, ready for his use, and now he knew the use. "I . . . am not at home," he said.

"Where is your home?" the dragon asked.

He looked out into the blues and grays and tans for which he now had names and at colors for which he had no names because he had never seen them before. Now he knew the wind felt dry and hotter than it had. Now he knew the land below had no forests, nor farmers' fields, nor pastures for beasts, for there was nothing green there and no water that he could see.

"I don't know," he said. "It was . . ." He felt around for direction and found none. "There were trees outside the city," he said.

"Yes," the dragon said. "There were trees and fields. Do you miss them?"

He thought about that. Between the vague memory of another place and time and this place now lay a thick curtain of nothing.

The dragon cocked his head. "Well. This has been a safe place for you, in this time, but you are correct: it is not your home. If you do not know where your home is, perhaps a new home will do."

"Is there any water?"

"I brought water for you," the dragon said. "A moment." The dragon walked back down the passage, into the dark, carrying the pot, and returned shortly with a different-shaped pot and a mug.

Water. Cool, fresh, cleaning the last taint of salt from his . . . tears. "My name is Camwyn," he said. "Has it always been Camwyn?"

"Yes," the dragon said. "And you were a prince, and you will be a king."

"I don't remember," he said. "I am Camwyn. Camwyn is my name . . . and my . . . myself." He looked down at his legs, bare to the wind. Scars marked them. "I am not a child."

"No," said the dragon. "You are a young man. Do you want the tale of your coming here?"

Tale . . . the word meant story, a kind of story sometimes not real but also a story that could be real.

"Yes," he said.

"You were beset by evil enemies," the dragon said. "You fought them; they were many, and you were but one. You were wounded—those scars you can see, and also inside your head, where you cannot see. So you have no memory of that, but . . . you are alive, and now awake, and you have words."

"Evil enemies" had a familiar sound, a sound that belonged in tales. "If I have words," he said, "then . . . I can think."

The dragon made a strange noise, almost like a kettle hissing. He remembered hearing a kettle hissing. "Words alone do not make thought," the dragon said. "Good thought makes good words." Again that cock of the head and a flicker of red tongue. "Tell me, Prince . . . are you wise?"

Almost, the question made no sense. Wise . . . slowly his mind retrieved the concept. He stared at the scars on his bare legs. "Was it wise to fight one against many?" he asked.

"It depends," the dragon said, "for what reason you fought."

"I do not remember."

"You were trying to save a treasure from being stolen when everyone else was enchanted and could not respond. And you were afraid your brother might be hurt."

"My brother—" He scowled, struggling to remember. "I have a brother? Where is he?"

The dragon sighed. "He is far from here; the people there had no way to save your life. So he let me take you away, since I have skills in healing they do not."

"I should go—?"

"No. Not as you are. Let us see what wisdom comes to you, Camwyn. Consider a king—your brother—who loves you well and has seen you sinking near to death. He is offered a chance to save your life—and possibly but not certainly your mind—at the cost of sending you away with a stranger and very likely never seeing you again. Was that wise?"

Camwyn looked a long moment at that dark face and then down at his own hands. "If I loved a brother . . . if it was his death . . . but it would be hard."

"It was hard. But was it wise?"

"It was love," Camwyn said. His eyes watered; he did not try to brush the tears away. "I don't know about wise."

"A good answer. Now, imagine that king again: his brother is away, he hopes finding healing. His kingdom is in peril, and to save his people he must not sit worrying about his absent brother but act—act quickly—to save them."

"Yes . . ." Camwyn looked at the dragon again. "Is that what is happening?"

"I am here, not there," the dragon said. "But he expected trouble to come. Let me go on. That king, say, in that time—when perhaps trouble has come or perhaps is only nearing—what will it mean to him if his brother comes back, still weak, still with no memory? What will it mean to the kingdom?"

"He will be happy," Camwyn said. "But . . . he will want to be with his brother and think only of his brother." He scowled, thinking hard. "And . . . a king . . . he should think of his kingdom." In his mind, a vague shape appeared . . . a crown, he finally realized. "My brother . . . you said he is a king. And loves me. But . . . I cannot see his face. I cannot . . . I do not know . . . his name."

"No," the dragon said. The dragon's voice was soft.

"He would worry about that," Camwyn said. "About me. And if there is danger . . . he might not be fast enough. He might . . . he might die. And the people." He scuffed his feet—bare, pale—and looked down his thin scarred legs at them. "It would be . . . wise . . . not to go. Until I remember." He looked back at the dragon. "Will I remember?"

"I do not know, Prince Camwyn Dragonfriend," the dragon said. "But I know you just said a wise thing. And you still have a good heart. And you will be a fine king."

"I don't want my brother to die!" Camwyn said. "I can't be king until—and I don't want him to die!"

"That throne is not the only one in the world," the dragon said. "I know a throne that needs a wise prince—yes, even a prince who cannot remember all his former life. No one need die for you to sit on it."

Camwyn scowled. "Wasn't there a king before?"

"Yes. An unlucky and not well-loved king and a Chancellor who broke faith with his oath." The dragon tilted its head. "You are young, but you are not a liar nor a fool."

"I hope not," Camwyn said. He touched the heart-side of his head. Under his hair, he felt a ridge.

"You have a scar there," the dragon said. "From a wound you took and the treatment that healed it. It is why your memory is gone, and it is why your healing took so long."

"How long?"

"A full season," the dragon said. "But now, it is time for you to strengthen your body more than you could do walking the bounds of this cave. We must go elsewhere."

He wanted to ask where, but astonishment took him instead as the dragon stepped out into the air and changed before his eyes, then uncoiled a long red tongue back into the cave. "Stand on it," said the voice in his mind. "You have ridden this way before."

Camwyn did so, and the tongue drew him in.

"Sit down and face the outer world," the voice said.

He had a vague memory of some previous ride, when he stood up with . . . with someone else beside him . . . but he sat down on the warm dry tongue, solid as a plank, and gazed out. The cave entrance shrank—was distant—he could see the entire mountain and the small dark mouth of the cave, and then the dragon turned, and he was looking along the side of a mountain range larger than he had ever imagined.

"Is this the Dwarfmounts?" he asked.

"No. They are sunrising of here. We go north."

North. He was unsure of that word and its meaning, but as the dragon flew along the line of mountains, he breathed in the crisp air that came into the dragon's mouth. To his heart-hand, the land fell away into the pale tones he had first seen from the cave—another, smaller, line of mountains rose from beside a salt-white plain, and in the distance yet another. Rows of mountains, with nothing green between them. A streak of white fire moved across his vision.

"What was that?"

"A young dragon," the dragon said. "They are all fire and no wisdom."

Another streak, another—and this one came nearer.

"Will it hurt you?"

The tongue beneath him trembled; the dragon sounded amused as he said, "No. I am elder."

From the safety of the dragon's mouth, he watched as the fiery being came nearer yet; he could just see the outline of what might be bones within it as it matched speed with the dragon for a short time; then the dragon pulled ahead.

Camwyn did not mean to sleep, but he fell asleep on the dragon's tongue, and when he woke, the dragon's tongue was sliding out of its mouth onto grass. "Rise," the dragon said.

He stood a little unsteadily and walked along the tongue until he could step off. The ground was firm under the grass; all around were great rounded hills with outcrops of red rock. Most had clumps of trees here and there. He could just see the jagged tops of mountains beyond one hill. When he looked more carefully, he saw animals . . . large animals . . . grazing some distance away. One lifted its head, then another. Several moved toward him.

He thought he should know what they were . . . but he couldn't think of the word until one of the animals whinnied and another broke into a trot. Horses. These were horses.

When he turned around again, the dragon had transformed once more into a human shape. "Come," the dragon said, holding out his hand. "There is a place for you."

They walked some distance; Camwyn had never been so far from a city and had no idea how far away things were. Around an arm of the nearest hill, the dragon led him along a path beside a creek, into a grove of trees, and finally to a low house built of stone. "Who lives here?" Camwyn asked.

"At this time, you do," the dragon said. "You need to regain your strength. Here you have space and time to finish healing."

"Alone?"

"Not . . . entirely. We will go inside."

The small house seemed larger inside than it had looked outside. One large room with a table, a bench, several chairs. On the table, a cluster of dishes, pots, cooking tools . . . and a stack of papers and books. A fireplace at one end, and beside it a door into another, smaller room. In that room a narrow bed, and beneath it a pot.

"Sit here," the dragon said. Camwyn sat down, glad to be off his aching legs. The dragon sat as well in his guise as man. "You will live here awhile, Camwyn, with no duties but to grow stronger and wiser. You will have food and water, and you will have instruction from those I send. For the first, eat well, drink deep of this water, which is pure and healthful, and walk about daily until your legs bear you without effort. Will you do these things?"

"Yes," Camwyn said. He felt dazed and uncertain, but his mind had grasped the use and names of table, bench, chair, bed, dishes, and pots.

"Good." The dragon stood, but when Camwyn stirred to rise, he put out a hand. "Wait here. I will return shortly with someone who will help you."

The room was cool and dim when the dragon left; Camwyn tried to order his thoughts, but they ran through his mind like . . . like sheep, he thought finally, with a vision of woolly backs flowing down a slope like water.

"Well, lad!"

A different voice. Camwyn jerked, having dozed off without realizing it. Before him stood an old man, one arm crooked, withered, the hand clenched into a nest of sticks, but with bright, unclouded eyes of green. "Sir," he said out of a dry mouth.

"You're my new neighbor," the man said. "And hungry, I'll wager." He turned away and set something on the table with a thump. "I've bread, cheese, onions, sausages—enough for a start." He looked back at Camwyn. "Been injured and sick, I hear. Need feeding up, the dragon said, and so you do. I'm Mathor—not a common name where you're from, so dragon said. Never mind, it's the name I came with. A fire, that's what we need. A hot drink will do you good."

Camwyn sat watching as the man bustled about, building a fire, fetching water in a pot, setting it to boil. From a leather pouch, the man took a handful of dried leaves and twigs and dropped them into the water as it heated. Camwyn's nose remembered the smell as it steeped but not the name.

"Sib," Mathor said, as if he knew Camwyn's confusion. "Sib and a touch of something my gran knew." He handed Camwyn a mug whose contents steamed.

Camwyn sipped; the flavor startled his tongue and seemed to clear his mind. "Sir," he said. "Thank you."

"There's no sirring or lording between us," Mathor said, but without heat. "You're Camwyn, I'm told, and I'm Mathor."

"Thank you . . . Mathor," Camwyn said. The unspoken "sir" sat on the end of his tongue like a bur. He could assign it no meaning but custom.

"You finish that and I'll have some food ready for you. Take a stroll outside if you like."

He was outside with a mug in his hand before he knew it. Behind him the door closed, but he could hear Mathor humming to himself inside. He looked around. Under the trees, wildflowers sprinkled the ground; the sound of the creek gurgling and splashing soothed his ears. A bench—he did not remember that bench—sat beside the house. He did not sit but moved toward the water, drawn by the sound.

Stones had been piled to make a low dam; behind it was a pool just larger than a bathing tub. Camwyn walked upstream to the dam and looked at the pool. Where it was not edged by rock, a fringe of mint and flowers surrounded it. As he watched, something wet and glistening threw itself off the dam into the water . . . his mind groped and came up with *frog.*

When Mathor called him back to a room filled with the smells of delicious food, Camwyn sat across the table from the man and ate eagerly. Mathor had opened shutters Camwyn hadn't noticed before, letting light and air into both rooms. He showed Camwyn where the jacks was.

"The pool," Camwyn said. "There's a dam, and—"

"Oh, that pool." Mathor nodded. "Looks the right size for a splash, doesn't it? But that's where I get the water. Splash there and you'll have grit in your teeth when you drink. I'll show you a place you can splash later—tomorrow maybe—but meantime, you'll bathe from a tub." He nodded across the room, and there was a wooden tub hanging from a spike in the wall. Camwyn didn't remember it from before. "There's water heating in the fire—" A tall ewer and buckets to fill the tub. Camwyn didn't remember those, either.

He slept that night under blankets that had not been on the narrow bed when he first saw it, windows he had not seen either stood open to the night air, which Mathor pronounced healing. "This is a safe place," he said as he left for his own place, one Camwyn had not seen. "Nothing here will harm you."

Next morning Camwyn woke when something tickled his face. He opened his eyes to find a horse's head hanging over his bed . . . a long milk-colored forelock and mane, bristly whiskers, a soft muzzle. After the first startled jerk, he lay still, fascinated. Was it a wild horse, like the others, or Mathor's? It seemed to wink at him, stiff golden lashes coming down across a deep brown eye, then pulled its head back out of the window. Camwyn sat up just as he heard the sound of ripping grass. Out the window were three horses: the cream and gold one that had wakened him, a red chestnut mare, and a foal whose spindly legs were spread wide as it sniffed at something in the grass.

Camwyn got up, not surprised to find a chest in the room that had not been there before and clothes hanging on pegs. He dressed, took the pot from beneath the bed, and took it out to the jacks, where he emptied it and filled in that section of trench.

"Well met, Camwyn." Mathor was coming down the path, carrying a basket. "We have eggs this day. And some greens."

After breakfast, Mathor urged Camwyn to take a short walk. "Here's bread and cheese and a jug of sib. Go where you please for a time. Nothing here will harm you."

That set the pattern for the first hands of days. Waking early, usually with a horse face in his window, breakfast with Mathor, then walking—slowly and in brief stretches at first, then longer ones. He ate whatever Mathor prepared with good appetite and slept without dreams he remembered. Mathor gave him the names of local plants, and his own mind restored many words for his thoughts, though try as he might, he could not remember much of his past. Was that face a brother? A father? An uncle? A friend? Was that other room—so different from this—a place he had lived or only visited?

One morning he made it back down to the main valley, where he found more of the horses grazing at the near end. They all raised heads and looked at him. Several approached, including the one with the milk-white mane. He put out his hand, and a muzzle brushed it; he could not resist stroking that golden neck, that silky white mane. The horse gave a soft sound, welcoming, and he kept stroking. His fingers caught in the mane—and the horse moved away, pulling gently. He walked with it, through the herd, out the other side.

When the horse dropped to its knees, Camwyn stared. What did that mean? Did it want to roll? He stepped back. The horse snorted. Camwyn had the impulse to climb onto that sloped back . . . but he had no saddle, no bridle—those names came to him, but so did the memory of riding. He had ridden. If the horse didn't mind . . . the horse snorted again, expressing, he was sure, impatience.

He came forward and gingerly—feeling the stretch in his muscles—clambered onto the horse's back, clutching a double handful of mane. A lurch that nearly cost him his seat, and another, and the horse stood. He felt dizzy for a moment, then his head cleared. He was riding—or sitting, he corrected himself—on a horse. A tall horse, for the ground seemed impossibly far away. The horse took one step. Camwyn tilted but recovered. Another step; this time Camwyn was able to stay upright. The horse walked off, and Camwyn first struggled to adjust to the back and forth, the sideways sway, and then found it no effort. The horse walked around the herd—all watching, as if to critique his riding—and then stopped again and shook its head.

Dismounting was harder than he'd thought it would be, but the horse stood patiently as he squirmed his way off, landing off balance and falling. The horse pivoted neatly and leaned down to blow gently in his hair. Camwyn sat up and put a hand behind its head. "Thank you," he said. He took a handful of mane; the horse lifted its head, helping him up. When he let go of the mane, the horse walked off. Camwyn stood for a time watching the horses, then trudged back up the hill to his house.

Every day after that included a ride. Usually it was that horse, but sometimes one of the others. Often he had to walk half the length of the valley to find them, though they usually ended the ride closer to the house. As he grew stronger, the horses quit kneeling for him to mount, at first standing near a rock or stump on which he could climb but then on lower ones, and lower ones, until he was finally mounting from the ground. Their behavior once he mounted changed, too—from a slow walk to a faster one, to a comfortable gait for which he had no name but fast enough to put a breeze in his face, then a trot. He fell from time to time; the horse from which he'd fallen always stopped while he got up and mounted again.

One day when he returned to the house, he found two others with Mathor. The man was taller than Mathor, with long-fingered, ink-stained hands, and the other was a woman, yellow-haired and gray-eyed, with a merry grin. She had a ring of silver on her brow.

"Dragon says you're well enough to start learning wisdom," Mathor said. "And you won't learn that from me." He laughed. "Master Kielson is a scholar and judicar; he'll help you with this—" Mathor gestured to the pile of papers and books on the table. "And this paladin will help you regain your fighting skills."

Camwyn's memory nudged him. At one time—he thought—he had been able to read and fight. The scars on his legs and what Dragon had told him proved the latter. He nodded to them; Mathor had a meal ready, and they all sat down to eat.

Reading came back to him quickly—the papers and books taught him about something called "House of the Dragon"—a bard's tale, he would have thought, tracing the story of that house from "Camwyn Dragonfriend" to a time when the king and his sons all died and left the Dragon Throne empty, in the care of a man who proved a fool.

"Dragon does not like fools," Master Kielson said.

"Some of the others were fools, too," Camwyn said. They had discussed the actions of a line of kings over the long years—some wiser and some more foolish.

"The question is, Camwyn, are you wise or a fool? You yourself?"

He glanced aside. The paladin sat at the end of the table, rubbing wool fat into a strip of leather. She looked up with a smile but said nothing. "I think . . . I think it is being a fool to claim wisdom, like claiming a sword or a boot as one's own. For no one is perfectly wise but the gods—or maybe Dragon, if Dragon is not a god. But I know some things accounted wise, and I try to see ahead to the flowers of a seed, and the fruit of that flower, and the seeds it leaves. I could not do that when I woke, but I am learning."

Master Kielson nodded. "And what must a man do to remain as wise as he is?"

"Learn more," Camwyn said. "Become wiser. But learning means mistakes, and mistakes are not wise." He paused, scratched his nose, and went on. "I think . . . if I could see more ahead . . . I would make fewer mistakes. But sometimes you can't wait to think to the end of time."

"True, and well said. We have discussed all the past kings in the House of the Dragon: Which do you think was wisest?"

"Camwyn III," Camwyn said. He listed his reasons.

"And which the most foolish?"

"Pelyan. He was not only lazy, mean, and a drunk, he drove out that other one, the bastard."

"Do you know what became of the bastard?"

"No—do you?"

"Indeed yes. In another land he became a peer of the realm; he is a notable military commander and has met Dragon, who considers him somewhat wise."

"As wise as Camwyn III?"

"No . . . but wiser than Pelyan or the one who became Chancellor." Master Kielson stood up and stretched. "Well, Camwyn, my work here is done, I believe. You are competent in reading; you have learned the language of the house, and from here, I believe you can educate yourself."

"Alone?" Camwyn stared. "Sir—what I learned is that I need help."

"And you will find the help you need, I'm certain, but for now, it is time for me to go to another student who needs me more now than you do." He nodded toward Paks. "And you still have work to do with this lady before Dragon returns."

Camwyn bowed, and Master Kielson bowed in return, then left and—when Camwyn looked—walked up the path that led past Mathor's house to . . . where? Camwyn had never gone to the top of the slope . . . Was there a town beyond? Why had he not wondered that before? And why had he not wondered that the season seemed, as it had when he first came, late spring. The spindly-legged foals were now much larger, able to gallop with the herd . . . but nothing had changed in the land itself. Day after day had slipped past; he had no count of how long he had been there.

"Well, Camwyn, are you ready for a ride?" Paks grinned at him.

What could he say but yes? He nodded, said the word, and followed his last teacher out of the house, down the path along the creek.

Two horses waited there. Paks always rode the same horse, a red chestnut. Today a dark horse, almost black, waited for him. Both were saddled.

"They have saddles," Camwyn said, then felt stupid.

"Your balance is better, but now you need a different exercise," Paks said as she mounted. "Do you remember how to use stirrups?"

Camwyn did not. The saddle looked higher—no way to jump and throw himself across it. The stirrups—what was he to do with them? Paks coached him; the horse stood patiently, and finally he was up. It felt unnatural—he couldn't feel the horse's muscles moving under him.

"You can fight riding bareback," Paks said. "But it's a lot easier to fall off or be pulled off."

In a few days, Camwyn rode confidently in the saddle, though he still rode bareback at times. He knew he was stronger. Though he did not remember where he had learned it, his muscles seemed to know sword work, and Paks taught him new things as well. She also had him run on the hills, up and down and across the slopes, and through the woods until he no longer stumbled and fell or had any fear of heights whether he stood on a tree's limb or at the edge of a cliff many times his height.

"Did you know me before?" he asked her once. "Do you know where I came from?"

"I know what the gods show me," Paks said. Her gray eyes seemed to see far beyond his vision, into another world, perhaps. "And I know what you are now, because you have shown me."

It was not the answer he wanted—not really an answer at all when he thought about it—but he knew it was the only answer she would give.

CHAPTER TWENTY-NINE

Bannerlíth, Prealíth

Coming from the elvenhome to Prealíth's ordinary forest had been a shock, like a dip in cold water. Almost, Dorrin wanted to turn back, reenter the elvenhome, and stay there forever. But with the outside world had come that sense of urgency again. In Prealíth, the trees showed autumn colors, though still mixed with green. If she was to sail this season—and she must—they should make haste to the coast before it ended.

Days more travel lay before them even though they picked up the pace, riding more swiftly. Forest frayed into farmland with scattered patches of woods, and they had dirt lanes to ride on and farmsteads and villages where a coin would buy a night's lodging and dinner. Finally, from a hill, Dorrin caught her first sight of the Eastern Ocean, a dark blue line against the lighter sky.

As Dorrin and her escort neared the coast, the land descended; the city of Bannerlíth seemed to flow down the last hills in a torrent of white and red to encircle its harbor. Dorrin reined in and looked down at the city and then out to sea. The ocean looked much bigger this close. She had only the vaguest notion how far it was from this shore to the distant continent from which the Seafolk had come, from which Kieri had escaped. On this afternoon the sea looked almost black-blue in the distance, but nearer to shore it had a cold green cast. Rocks and larger islands lay offshore to the north; to the south she could just see the loom of the Eastbight, a vague line in the haze.

Her stomach tightened. Now the real journey began. All across Lyonya she had been safe in the bubble of the elvenhome, guarded from any harm by the King's Squires who escorted her. Even in western Prealíth, she had felt safer than here, where her world as she knew it ended and the unknown began. From Bannerlíth, she must go on alone.

She shook herself out of that mood and reviewed her resources. The loose jewels were well hidden, sewn into the lining of her doublet. Kieri had provided the kind of small box he said sea passengers usually carried, and the regalia fit into it underneath her spare clothes. She had a letter from him to the Sea-Prince, and this was the right season to sail from Bannerlíth to the Immerhoft Sea.

She lifted her reins. "It's a lovely city," she said. "At least, seen from here."

"It is indeed," said Berne.

The city gate was nothing more than an arch with a pole across the track and two men in green and blue lounging in the shade of a tree.

"You're from Lyonya!" one of them said. "I remember you. Message for the Sea-Prince?"

"Yes," said Berne.

"And who's that?" He pointed at Dorrin.

"Someone the Sea-Prince wants to meet," Varne said.

"Go on, then." The two men lifted the pole from its brackets, and they rode through.

The track steepened as they went on, finally turning into paved streets that wound back and forth across the slope between whitewashed buildings: houses, shops, and—below—obvious warehouses on the same level as the harbor. Finally they came to the Sea-Prince's palace. Built of white stone, it stood nearer the harbor than the top of the hill, with a colonnaded front and a broad terrace of stones set in a pattern of fish and birds. The King's Squires knew the way to the entrance and were recognized; they introduced Dorrin as "a close friend of our king's."

Dorrin spent that night in a palace guest suite as lavish as any in Vérella but very differently styled—uncluttered, with a small balcony giving a view of the sea. She had eaten dinner with the Sea-Prince and his family—his shy young wife and a small boy. The service was simple: a fish on a platter, some steamed grain, and a deep dish of strange-looking things, strings and bag-like bits and—a moment of horror—*eyes*.

"What is that?" she asked.

"A treat," the Sea-Prince said. "Only at this season can we get the small ones. Look—" He picked up something that looked both impossible and disgusting to Dorrin. "Cut it into small pieces, like this, and dip it in the green sauce. Or the yellow."

Dorrin would rather have kept to the fish and the grain, but he looked at her with such enthusiasm that she accepted the horror on her plate and cut off chunks the size he recommended. Dipped into the sauce, it tasted vaguely charred, but the sauce was delicious.

The child, she was astonished to see, ate another of the things, biting off pieces of the stringy parts with obvious pleasure.

"What do you call it?" Dorrin asked.

"Two-hander," her host said. "Because we have ten fingers on two hands, and it has ten legs. They aren't like our legs, but it moves with them."

After dinner, she asked the Sea-Prince about taking passage on a ship to the Immerhoft ports.

"Which ones?" he asked.

"The western ones," she said.

The Sea-Prince did not ask why but stared out at the sea for a long moment. "Only a few ships will go this time of year," he said. "Early autumn is the season of the best winds, yes, but also the season of great storms. You are not experienced with ships?"

"Not at all," Dorrin said.

"You will need a very good ship and a very good captain. And you have no attendants. That is easier in some ways, but—there are no women sailors on the ship I am thinking of."

"I have been a mercenary," Dorrin said. "Being the only woman will not bother me."

"Well, then. Tomorrow I will introduce you."

The ship the Sea-Prince took her to—*Blessing,* a regular on the route between Bannerlíth and the southern ports—was sailing the next day. Dorrin had seen ships like it in the Immer ports: the high front and rear, the bluff bows. Its gray-bearded captain, introduced as Captain Royan, nodded to the Sea-Prince then stared at Dorrin. "Is you dress like that all time?"

"She's from Tsaia," the Sea-Prince said, as if that explained everything.

"But is man wears such and a sword."

"There, some women do."

The captain shrugged. "May be better. Come aboard. See cabin." Dorrin walked around things like tree stumps with ropes wrapped around them, past boxes, barrels, clay pots, and a stack of furs, carefully stepping where the captain stepped. The cabin, in the high aft section, was small but had a window. Under the bunk—a plank shelf with a rim—was a chamber pot fitted into a niche and a space big enough for her box, with a removable board across the front. At the head of the bunk was a niche with a jug; it, too, had a wooden slat that held it in place. On the opposite wall were cubbyholes behind a sliding door.

The Sea-Prince asked questions she had not known to ask: the length of the voyage (at least three tendays, maybe more in bad weather), whether she needed to supply her own bedding (yes), and rations (optional, affecting the price of passage). Dorrin agreed to the price and—at the Sea-Prince's advice—chose to provide her own rations.

Food and bedding were available in a chandler's across the wide stone dock. Before midday, she had seen her new bedding and stores taken aboard *Blessing* and gone back to the Sea-Prince's palace to retrieve her baggage. She ate a leisurely luncheon with the Sea-Prince's wife and child, as he was meeting with others.

"I wish you fair voyage," that lady said. "And as this is your first, here is a remedy for seasickness." She handed Dorrin a small round box. "Dried leaves of a seaside plant, taken in sib, should help. Laran never gets seasick, so I'm certain he didn't mention it."

Dorrin opened the box and looked; the furry gray leaves smelled strongly, though they did not look attractive. "Thank you," she said. "Thank you both for all your help."

One of the servants carried her baggage down to the harbor for her. More people crowded the dock, both bringing cargo to the ship and unloading another that had just arrived. Dorrin edged through the crowd, avoiding piles of cargo waiting to go aboard—bales of wool, bundles of cloth, boxes. At the gangway, the captain waited, a clerk beside him with a tally board.

"Ready to board, then?" he said. "Is that all you're bringing? Good . . . Gith . . . come take the passenger's box to the cabin. Come on, now, over you come." Once she was aboard with her bundle and the sailor had picked up the box, he said, "To your cabin now, if you please, and stay out of the way until we've got this lot stowed. Things will quiet down later. We will eat together this evening."

Dorrin followed Gith to her cabin, where a thin mattress and folded blanket now lay on her bunk and boxes of her provisions took up half the meager floor space. He pushed her box under the bunk and slid the plank through slots to secure it there. Then he pointed to the roll of netting along the side of the bunk.

"You know how to put that up?"

She had no idea what the netting was for and said so.

"Storms," Gith said. "Hooks here." He showed her. "And here, on the bulkhead." He gave her a gap-toothed grin.

"Thank you," Dorrin said. Surely she wouldn't need a net.

"Your meat's in the galley already," Gith said. "And when Cap'n says it's clear, Cook wants to talk to you about your meals. Maybe move some of these boxes later."

Dorrin thanked him, slid the cabin door closed, then looked out the window above her bunk. Her cabin was on the water side of the ship; she looked across the harbor, then down at the green water below. Down there, someone rowed a small boat, about the size she'd seen on rivers, back and forth along the side of the ship. The cabin felt stuffy; she left the window open and opened the door again. A short narrow passage led to the deck outside, from which came the noise of men at work. She took off her doublet—far too warm—

folded her cloak for a pillow, and lay down on the bunk to wait out the time until the captain came.

***

"We've another passenger," the captain said at dinner. The captain's cabin, much bigger than her own, took up the entire width of the ship at the rear, with room for a dining table that would seat six. He leaned back in his chair and smiled at Dorrin.

"He ate ashore?" Dorrin asked.

"Oh, no. Not in your class. He's working his passage back south. Missed his ship, he says, being ashore with a toothache, but he's a sailor right enough. Hands like shoe leather; feet, too. I made him run up the rigging and throw a few knots to be sure he could. I don't expect you'll notice him, and as he's crew, he's not supposed to speak to you." He set his hands flat on the table. "Now, about that—ship has rules, and even paying passengers must follow them."

"Certainly," Dorrin said.

"You're welcome on deck, but there's a dark line—blackwood—you must not cross unless I give permission aft of the mainmast. Between that line and the cabins back here, you can walk back and forth for exercise or sit on the deck or a coil of rope if there is one. But if I tell you to go below, that means into your cabin, and it will be for a reason. You've never sailed, you said, and it's all too easy for a land-legs to fall or get in the way."

"I understand," Dorrin said. "Stay on this side of the black line."

"I may invite you to the upper deck, but you must not come up without my invitation. You may come into the passage between the cabins, but you may not come into my cabin without invitation." Dorrin nodded, and he went on. "Even if a hatch is opened, you're not to go down in the hold without permission. It's not for trash or the spill of your pot. Gith will empty that, but otherwise you're to keep your compartment tidy so that when the ship rolls, everything stays in place. And don't leave things about, outside your cabin. Gith will tap on your door at mealtimes if you're in your cabin; you can ignore the bells and other signals the crew needs."

Dorrin discovered that everything on the ship had a different name than it would have had on land. Doors were hatches, walls were bulkheads, floors were decks—all of them, not just the top one, as she'd thought. Windows were ports, confusing because instead of heart-hand and sword-hand, the ship's sides were port and starboard. What she called ropes were lines or cables or halyards or—in a few cases—ropes, and most of them had another specific name as well. Every sail had its own name. Every mast had its own name, and so did other parts of the ship. Days after they left Bannerlíth, she was still struggling to remember which was which.

The ship moved not just through the water but *on* the water. Dorrin had heard of ships "rocking" and had thought of them as like a seagoing rocking chair, but it was more complicated than that. The ship could, at any time, lean one way or the other or a combination of the two, and it was never completely still and level. Nor was it quiet. She had imagined, seeing the ships on the Immerhoft Sea from shore, that they glided along without a sound. But there was one noise or another all the time, in rhythms it took her days to understand. Shouted commands, shrill whistles, the thud of bare feet on the deck as sailors obeyed, the creaking of wood as the ship tilted this way and that, the flap of sails when they changed direction or the wind did, the splash and gurgle of water along the ship's sides, the bell that rang the turning of the glass, the louder gong that called crew and passengers to meals. At first Dorrin alerted to every shout—shouts ashore meant some emergency—but here they meant nothing to a passenger.

When Captain Royan invited her to come to the upper deck, she could easily see the Eastbight, its mountainous mass jutting into the ocean on the sword—no, the starboard—side. The ship kept well away from it, so she could not see any details.

Royan spent most of his time on that deck, keeping watch on the sea, the ship, the sailors, and any other ships they met. Ships came to Bannerlíth from the far Eastern Continent as well as from Aarenis, so on most days they saw at least one. Royan explained what cargo they likely carried, from where, and for what market.

The first days, she later realized, were easy. They had left in fair weather, and it continued for a hand of days. By then, Dorrin could keep her balance on the open deck as she walked to and fro. On the sixth day, when she came out on deck, Royan shouted down to her from the upper one.

"Look at the sky: we've weather ahead."

Dorrin looked up into a sky with a pattern of clouds like fish bones, pale against the blue. They looked harmless to her, nothing like the thunderheads of summer storms inland or an approaching blizzard in winter. The wind continued to blow as it had; the sea was no rougher. But all the morning, a faint haze dimmed the blue between the fish bone clouds, and they thickened until they looked more like the curds in buttermilk than fish bones.

Royan came down for lunch and said, "We'll be fine as long as we're this side of the Eastbight, but tomorrow we'll be past it. There's storm coming—not unusual this time of year. Can't tell how bad yet."

"What should I do?"

"Stay in your cabin as soon as you can't keep your feet, or if I say so. Don't eat much; you'll heave it up, and the smell will make you sicker. Dry bread and water is best. Always have a hand for the ship—a hand on something fastened down. If it's a bad storm we'll go around it—out to the middle of the ocean if need be."

In the afternoon, the wind freshened a little, with occasional stronger gusts. Dorrin could just see where the dark ridge of the Eastbight dropped sharply to the sea and disappeared. Far ahead, the water looked different, with short lines of white drawn on it. The ship had developed a stronger movement, so the lamp hanging from the ceiling—overhead, she reminded herself—at dinner swung noticeably, but she did not feel sick. She sat down with a good appetite and ate as she normally would.

"Best get in your bunk," Royan said when they had finished. "Latch everything in; hook the netting up. Best leave the jug in its niche until you need it, but don't wait too long. Try to heave into that and not on the bunk or the floor."

"I don't feel sick," Dorrin said. The fresher wind had cleared her head, and she felt more excited than scared.

"You will," he said. "Everyone does, first storm. Especially in the dark. Do what you need to now and then stay in."

"Yes, Captain," she said.

This time he smiled. "That's the way. You'll be a sailor by the end of this trip."

She finished in the ship's peculiar arrangement for personal needs, latched the chamber pot into its compartment under the bunk, then lifted and replaced the slat that secured the jug into its niche at the head of the bunk so she could be sure of finding it in the dark. She was sure she would not need it. She was ready for whatever might come, she decided, and lay down, leaving the window open for the fresh air and light. The light dimmed quickly; the ship moved and creaked a little more. She might as well sleep, she thought, and—unconvinced it was necessary—hooked the netting onto the bulkhead.

She was dozing off when the ship suddenly heeled. She rolled into the netting and then back onto her bunk as it righted. A blast of wind came in, smelling of fish, then a spatter of either spray or rain. She could hear the wind whining through the rigging and the loud crack of sails. She struggled to find the bar by which she could pull the window shut, but while she was half-sitting, the ship tipped down and heeled again. She lost her grip on the window as she rolled into the netting again, then banged her arm into the bulkhead when she rolled back; the ship tipped up next, so she slid backward, her head bumping the end of the bunk.

When she finally got the window closed, she had an uneasy feeling she did not want to admit was seasickness, but as the ship continued to pitch and roll, she soon had no doubt. She had thought the jug unnecessary, far larger than anyone would ever need, but she was soon grateful for it and its large cork. Finally, her stomach was empty and she wedged the jug between one of the provisions boxes and the bunk.

Though she had nothing left to throw up, she still felt every lurch and sway of the ship. If only it would stop, even for a moment . . . but it did not stop. Instead, the movement intensified with the howling wind. She thought her body would come apart, but all she could do was lie there, hands fisted in the netting to keep from being flung from side to side as violently.

The night seemed to last forever. When at last a little gray light seeped into her cabin, the ship still lurched in what felt like all directions at once. Her window was only a gray blur, water streaming down it. She heard footsteps, but no one came until the ship's movement eased a little. Then someone knocked on her door, and the cook appeared.

"Here for your jug," he said, and walked—unsteadily but moving upright, which Dorrin could scarce believe—to take the jug from where she'd wedged it. "I'll be back shortly," he said, and went out.

Dorrin tried to convince her stomach that the lurching wasn't nearly as bad. Very soon the cook returned with the jug, now empty, and put it back in its niche.

"You have anything for the sickness?" he asked.

She had forgotten about the Sea-Prince's wife's gift. "Someone gave me . . ." she said, and then her stomach turned. She clenched her teeth and managed not to heave. Instead she pointed to the cubby where she had put her kit. "Round box," she said.

He took the box, bracing one leg against the base of the bunk, and opened it and sniffed. "Good," he said. "I'll fix this."

Dorrin closed her eyes. She had never felt this sick in her life. She had heaved before, yes, from bad food in Aarenis, but always once or twice had been enough, and then the empty feeling and then it was over. This went on and on.

Eventually the cook came back with a mug that smelled of sib and the herb in the box. Her stomach roiled. "You drink this, tiny sips," he said. He unhooked one corner of the netting, put an arm behind her shoulders, and lifted her a little. "Tiny sip," he said, putting the mug to her lips.

She didn't want anything, but she sipped. Once . . . twice . . . a third sip.

"Two more," he said. "Then rest, then I come again."

Two more sips. He took the mug from her lips, let her back down slowly, rehooked the netting, and went away with the mug. Dorrin closed her eyes again. The nausea lessened, though the ship continued its uneven motion.

When next someone tapped at her door, Dorrin woke from a doze. Captain Royan looked in.

"You'll do," he said. "The herb helps, doesn't it? Nice couple of squalls we had. You might get up and use the pot now, while you can."

"Squalls?" Dorrin said. Surely that had been a huge storm and they were lucky to be still afloat.

"Yes. Not the main storm. As I said, we're going farther out, around it. We should have a half-glass, maybe, before the next squall. Can you stand?"

She was sure she could not, but he unhooked the netting and helped her sit up. "Put your pot in the niche just outside the door when you're done. I don't want you out in the passage or on the ladders; someone will take it for you. Don't forget the lid." He left.

Sitting up was worse than lying down, but Dorrin managed to retrieve the chamber pot, use it, and push it along the deck with her foot, then get it latched into place in the niche beside the door. It occurred to her that a ship carrying passengers on a regular basis must be familiar with seasick passengers and their needs.

She had made it back to her bunk and rehooked half the netting when the cook reappeared with the mug of sib and a piece of dry bread. At his direction, she drank more this time—ten sips—and ate half the bread. Then he said, "Squall coming," and she lay down while he hooked up the rest of the netting and left her.

This time was not quite as bad. Though she threw up the bread, she had no dry heaves after. The movement of the ship, the noises of the ship itself, the wind, and the water were still distressing, but she no longer felt she was at the edge of endurance. As soon as the ship's motion eased again, she fell asleep and slept (she later heard) through another squall. This time when she woke, she was actually thirsty and hungry when the cook appeared. She was able to sit up and drink a half mug of sib and eat a whole piece of dry bread.

The next dawn brought brighter light. Dorrin looked out the window—coated with what looked like frost-fur—and opened it a little and breathed in the fresh air. She put a hand through the opening and felt the outside of the window, then tasted her finger. Salt. She pushed the window wider. The ship moved up and down over deep green water with white at the top of every wave. She could not see ahead or behind, but in the direction she could see, no land showed, only a vast expanse of water, all of it shaped into the hills and hollows of waves.

"Past the worst of it," the cook said when he appeared with a mug of sib and another piece of bread. "How sick?"

"No more in the jug," Dorrin said.

"Good," he said.

She drank the sib in small swallows and ate the bread in careful bites. The ship's motion, as it slid down into the hollows between waves and tipped up to climb over the crests, no longer bothered her while she was sitting in her bunk, mug in hand. After one slop of sib over the top, she learned to let her hand stay in place while she and the ship moved. Much like drinking from a flask while riding, she realized.

By midday she was able to eat more than dry bread, and though they passed through another squall in the afternoon, she felt no sickness. The captain explained that they had turned south while the storm moved north.

"We go behind it," he said. "Come on deck—you should see."

She wasn't at all sure she could walk, with the ship falling out from under her and then shoving upward, but the captain helped her down the passage. "Loosen your knees," he said. "Go with the ship." She tried and at once felt steadier. It was like riding a horse, where stiff joints made balance more difficult.

Once outside, on deck, she held on to the rail of the ladder to the upper deck and looked around. The wider view showed no land at all. Dorrin had no idea how far away land might be or in which direction. Clouds obscured the sky, but here and there a ray of sunlight stabbed through.

The next day they sailed under a blue sky spotted with puffy white clouds over smaller waves.

CHAPTER THIRTY

"**W**e've got to bear west again," the captain said. "The way the wind is, we'll miss the Immerhoft if we don't."

Dorrin listened without commenting. Her stomach had settled in the better weather, and she was able to exercise on the deck, not just in her cabin.

"Not all the way to the Eastbight—" the first mate said.

"Yes, unless the wind changes. We'll need the backflow off the mountains there."

"I'll start drilling the men, then," the mate said.

Dorrin looked up at that. "Drilling?"

"Come in too close and Slavers' Bay pirates will come out and look us over. Best to be ready to fight. We may need you, too." That last in a tone that was almost a question.

"Certainly," Dorrin said. She watched as the mate used the captain's keys to open a storage locker in the passage just outside his cabin—javelins, crossbows, heavy wide-bladed swords she remembered seeing in Aarenis. Every day the crew practiced maneuvers she had not imagined, running up the rigging with a quiver of javelins, tossing rings of rope two handspans across to land over a man's head, grappling with one another on the deck . . . nothing like the drills her own troops had used, yet—on a ship moving in the water—it made sense. She herself practiced her footwork, her point control, all the movements that could be performed on the ship. The captain even supervised her first attempt to climb the rigging, and the next day she made it up to the basket lookout on the mainmast.

Two hands of days later, a smudge on the horizon caught the morning light.

"The Eastbight's prow," the captain said. "A little north of where I hoped we'd find it."

"How close do we come?" Dorrin asked.

"No closer than this, I hope," he said, looking aloft to the streamer she now knew showed wind direction whichever way the ship turned. "And the wind's fair for us." He turned away from her and began giving orders she now half understood. Sailors hurried to obey, and the ship swung to heartward—port, as he called it.

By midday they were closer to the Eastbight but not much, and the peak she had first seen now lay off the sword—starboard—side, a little aft of the ship. She could not see where the mountains met the sea, only the loom of their tops.

To her surprise, the captain ordered some sails furled; the ship slowed. She looked; he looked off to the southwest, then ordered more sails brought in. "If we sail past the Elbow in the afternoon light, they'll pick us up from the lookout they keep on the summer side of the Eastbight and maybe attack by night. Don't want to clear the Elbow in afternoon light. We'll bide here until sundown, then raise all sail and try to get past the worst of 'em by night . . . They'll spot us in the morning, but it'll be a stern chase and they probably won't bother."

The ship lurched about in the seas with so little way on, but Dorrin felt no nausea. Instead, as the afternoon wore on, she leaned against a coil of rope, watching the sailors on the deck. Some hauled heavy, odd-shaped metal pots from the hold, setting a row of them down the centerline of the ship. One flaring side rose above the rest of the rim to the height of a man's chest. Dorrin had no idea what they were for. A few slept—those on watch the previous night, she supposed. Two were mending—one a sail and the other a pair of the short trousers they wore. The one who had joined the ship in Bannerlíth to work his passage, recognizable by the long strip of red cloth he wore wrapped around his waist so often, climbed the mainmast. She had wondered whether the red meant he was Falkian, but the captain had told her so firmly not to waste his crew's time that she had said nothing.

Now she wondered what he was doing up there. He had his knife out—she could see the flash of it moving in the light. Repairing something? The captain had explained that lines needed constant repair.

A bellow from the deck above interrupted her musing, immediately joined by a bellow from the main deck, the man the captain had introduced as his mate. The man on the mast came down quickly, the knife tucked into his sash; she could see the bone handle sticking out. Now they talked, low-voiced. She couldn't hear the words and thought she probably wouldn't understand anyway if it was all about the ship. But from the postures and expressions, the man had done something he shouldn't have and was getting an earful. Dorrin looked away. No one liked to be stared at while that was going on.

She was surprised, therefore, when a little later the man came aft and sat on another coil of rope nearby. The glance he gave her was so calculating, so intent, that she frowned before she caught herself. He smiled then, a sly twist of the lips, got up, and walked back 'midships.

As the afternoon waned into evening, a haze spread over the water—not as thick as fog but chilly nonetheless. The captain came down for supper before dark, shaking his head. "Wind change," he said. "It may help us, but we'll have to look sharp to our steering." He did not explain more. Dorrin addressed herself to her meal and asked no questions.

With the last of the light, the captain ordered sails spread, and the ship headed south once more, all lights onboard shuttered. Because Dorrin's cabin was on the seaward side, the captain had told her she could have a candle if she wanted but to close the window and curtain. She preferred fresh air and came out on deck, looking up at the stars. She had learned enough to know they were sailing south. Over the side, the ship seemed to move through thin veils of mist, though it did not rise to the level of the deck.

Far off toward the land, she saw a light, lower than a star and yellower. She squinted. It must be somewhere on the Eastbight, but . . . the captain had said the sunrising face was cliffs dropping sheer into the sea, uninhabited. She looked around the deck in the dim starlight; sailors moved about, hardly visible. Then, high overhead, a light sputtered and flared at the top of the mainmast, a peculiar greenish yellow Dorrin associated with wizards' tricks.

The captain roared from the quarterdeck. Instantly, the thud of bare feet running on the deck—Dorrin could not tell how many. The mate snapped out orders; Dorrin backed into the cabin passage to be out of the way. The light above cast shadows and dim flickers of light onto the deck, making it impossible to see all that was going on. In that stuttering light, Dorrin saw one sailor leap for the foot of the mainmast and start up while two more raced up the rigging, each with a bucket hanging from his belt.

"One missin', Captain," called the mate from 'midship.

"Our working passenger?" the captain asked.

"Aye, sir. Not on deck; might be below or overboard."

"Arm the known crew. Send a detail below to guard the rudder cables." A pause, then: "Passenger: arm yourself. You will be needed."

Dorrin had changed as soon as supper was over, arming shirt, mail, and doublet, and had laid out gorget, bracers, and the rest of her gear on her bunk. Dagger drawn, she moved warily down the passage and into her cabin. She heard nothing, smelled nothing, but the usual. She closed the cabin door by feel, then covered the window and lit a candle to make finishing her preparations easier. On with padded cap that went under the simple helmet, on with the gorget, the bracers, the boots. She looked again at her sword—but the captain had given her a cutlass, better for fighting aboard. She grinned; she felt happier than she had since she'd boarded. This was her world, the world of blades. Ahorse, afoot—and now on board a ship. She blew out the candle, pinched the hot wick to be sure it was safe, and eased back out onto the deck. Now the light at the masthead was gone, but off to the west, where land loomed, another light showed.

In the dim starlight she saw that the gridwork over the main hatch was open and heard voices from below. They grew louder until one of them yelled, "Captain! Found the fishbait sawing at a rudder line."

"Bring him up," Royan called. "Rig the spare line. And mount the bells in place."

Bells? Dorrin hadn't heard or seen any but the one ship's bell that marked the watches. Now she saw shadowy figures pulling the strange pots from the center of the ship to the rails, where they clanked on something. Meanwhile, two sailors ran up the ladder from the hold, then hauled up the man they'd captured and bound. The captain came down to the main deck.

As Dorrin watched, the mate and two crewmen forced the man's arms across the rail. "You would leave my ship rudderless in the ocean, helpless when your friends come," Royan said. "I will leave you armless, helpless when the fish come." The man screamed for mercy, but two quick strokes with the captain's cutlass and his hands and forearms fell overboard as his blood spurted out. "May your blood call Barrandowea to my aid," Royan said. Then to the mate, "Overboard with him." They threw the man overboard. Dorrin heard only one splash and could see nothing of him.

Dorrin's stomach turned, but she clenched her jaw and said nothing. The man had betrayed them to pirates and intended evil to everyone on board. They sailed on through the night, and the captain explained the use of the "bells," the great bronze pots now fueled with sap from the forests of Kostandan.

❦

D orrin had become used to the ship's noises—the flapping of sails, the creaking and groaning of the ship as it rolled, the slap and thud of bare feet on the deck, the wind whirring or whistling through the rigging, all the sounds water made against the hull. Now she heard something else—but before she could react to it, a hideous howling arose from all around the ship. Then a score or more of grapples trailing ropes flew up over both sides of the ship, smashing into the less cautious sailors who rushed to the rails at the noise. Some caught in the rigging, some scraped across the deck to lodge under the rail.

But *Blessing*'s crew had been through pirate attacks before. Lights appeared on the deck, set into the polished bronze bells Dorrin had puzzled over. Though dim, they made it possible to tell sailors from pirates. "Cut the ropes—the grapples—" the captain told her. Sailors were already doing that, cutlasses thudding into the rails, slashing lines hanging from grapples in the rigging. From high above, the first fire-tipped bolts flew down, aimed at the pirates' sails. Dorrin slashed at lines she was sure weren't the ship's own rigging and at the arms of a pirate about to climb over the rail. Blood spurted; he fell backward with a cry. She ducked as another grapple sailed past her head, skidded on the deck, and snapped into place under the rail.

Shouts and screams forward—Dorrin chanced a glance that way and saw a confused mass of men, pirates pouring over the bow railing, pushing defending sailors back and off the foredeck. "Stay back," the captain called. "Keep them off the port side, away from the ladder up here. Use the fire-rings!"

Dorrin picked up one of the pitch-soaked rope rings, lit it at the nearest bell, and hurled it at the pirate sail that had come alongside; flames wreathed it as it flew, and it hit, clinging. The sail caught; flames rose, giving more light to see two pirates just coming over the rail. Dorrin struck one with her cutlass and pushed a lit fire-ring onto the other. Screaming, he dropped his cutlass and jumped back over the rail, but instead of water, he landed on the pirate ship's deck. Dorrin scooped up his cutlass but had no time to see what happened to him, as more pirates had come over the opposite side.

The fight raged over the deck, but gradually the crew prevailed, as their use of fire had set three of the pirate galleys aflame. Dorrin wondered at first that the pirates did not use fire against *Blessing* but then realized they wanted the ship and its cargo. The last few pirates on the main deck were backed against the starboard rail, fighting for their lives, when she heard a yell from the upper deck. She ran up the ladder to see a clump of pirates, the steersman lying in a pool of blood, and the captain fighting for his life.

Dorrin charged into the pirates, both cutlasses at work; she and the captain together took down those then the next who tried to climb over the stern rail. Finally, it was over . . . the ship sailing on, the dead pirates thrown overboard without ceremony, the dead crew—only four, Royan said, after he had committed each to the sea with a prayer to Barrandowea to give them a fair voyage to their next home. The steersman was alive but injured and in bed in the other passenger cabin. In the dawn light, the crew cleaned the decks of blood and other debris from the fight, cleaned out the great pots, and lowered them into the hold again.

"In the end, we sank 'em all," Royan said at breakfast. They ate on the upper deck; the sailor steering now had less experience, and Royan watched him closely. "Better than most sea fights, and it'll be a lesson to them. Other ships will have an easier time for the rest of the season, I expect."

"How will those ashore know these lost?" Dorrin asked.

"The fires. Those flames would be seen ashore, and they know what that means."

"So you don't expect another attack?"

"No. Those ashore won't see any gain in it."

They sailed down the eastern coast of Aarenis, land just visible from the upper deck, with someone on the masthead watching for landmarks. Day after day of careful sailing; Royan had explained that shifting shoals reached well out to sea from this sandy coast. Finally, the lookout spotted the higher rocky point that marked the opening of the Immerhoft Sea. As the ship heeled, making the turn into that bright blue water, Dorrin felt a surge of joy from the crown. "Patience," she murmured, looking south to see a similar rocky point that was her first view of Aare itself.

Ahead, islands showed against the blue. They would, she thought, be turning again to be well outside those guarding the entrance to the Immerhoft ports and Alured the Black's pirate associates who watched every ship that passed into that vast bay.

But instead of turning away from the shore, the captain steered along it.

"We must go in for water," he explained when she asked. "We lost days in the storm; we're low, and what water we have is foul. I know the Sea-Prince told you we would not stop here, but do not worry, lady—we sail in and out of this port every year."

"I was here during Siniava's War," Dorrin said. "My unit was allied with Alured's . . . some people here may remember me. And . . . the unit I used to be with is now under hire to oppose him."

"Politics." He scowled for a moment. "You do not want to be seen as yourself, eh? You might be in trouble either way? But we will not go to Immerdzan, only to Ka-Immer. Were you there?"

Dorrin nodded. "Not for long, though. I would worry more about Immerdzan."

"That delays too much when we sail all the way to the western ports. But even at Ka-Immer, it is true, officials come and look over the ship. You will be crew."

"But I don't know how—"

"You were soldier; you can use crossbow, yes?" At her nod, he smiled. "Yes. We have a day or more. You learned how to climb up—you will go up mast as high guard. Lucky you spent time on deck—tanned feet, tough on bottom. Lucky your hands are callused, too. I give you new name. Braid your hair like a sailor. Wear sailor clothes—we have. We clear out your cabin—no passenger aboard, just crew."

"I'll take my box down," Dorrin said. He did not believe at first that no one else could move it, but when he couldn't move it even a fingerwidth, he shrugged and showed her where to stow it.

By the time they came into Ka-Immer's harbor, Dorrin had practiced that trip up and down the mast; she was able to do it as quickly as most sailors, even with a crossbow hung from her belt.

The port officers who came aboard at Ka-Immer glanced up at the guards above, but no more. Dorrin was in the mainmast's basket, paired with another sailor. Her task was to watch the side of the ship away from the dock, where thieves in small boats or even swimming might try to climb the anchor cable to come aboard. Once more the small boat on deck was being rowed up and down by two of *Blessing*'s sailors.

Facing the other way, her partner kept up a stream of chatter about what was going on dockside. Water barrels going out, water barrels coming aboard. Cargo—furs, northern woods, dried fish—unloaded and sold. Other cargo—loaded and stowed. All day the traffic came and went dockside while she warned off five or six small boats that came too close on the other, always when their own boat was changing crew or out of sight at one end or the other.

Late in the afternoon, her partner said, "There's something—the pirate himself just arrived."

Dorrin almost turned around to look; instead she said, "What? Where?"

"At his palace. His banner went up. He claims he's a duke now, but he's only a pirate really. Used to sail out of Whiteskull, and he's still running that pirate fleet and another up at Slavers' Bay. He doesn't come here much. Lives somewhere upriver. Likely he won't come down to the dock before we leave tomorrow. Banner goes up this late, he's bound to have dinner tonight, and captain wants to leave at dawn."

At dusk, trading closed on dockside. The last visitors to the ship left; sailors hauled in the gangplank. Those assigned as night guards climbed up the masts; Dorrin and her partner climbed down and went forward with the other sailors clustered near the foredeck. A different cook handed out fresh bread bought onshore and a bowl of fish soup. Two baskets of fresh fruit from the market were set out for anyone to take. Torches flared at intervals along the waterfront; the ship's lanterns were lit. After a long day in the cramped top basket, Dorrin was glad to stretch out on the deck with the others.

CHAPTER THIRTY-ONE

Cortes Immer, Aarenis

The Duke of Immer lay on his bed in Cortes Immer sweating and cursing. Despite what his surgeons said about his wounds, he was sure they should have healed by now. He had lost too many troops in the unsuccessful attempt to conquer Fallo. How had so many Kostandanyan troops filtered in without any of his spies noticing? How had they made it so far west, coming out of nowhere, it seemed, to outflank and attack his own flanking force from Rotengre? He needed more troops, and he needed to be seen as a strong leader again, not a weak man lying around in bed. Men followed strong leaders, not . . . He looked down at himself, still heavily bandaged, still lame.

His advisor was silent. He himself was determined to go down the river to the Immer ports, where he had the largest population and could draw on the pirates based at Whiteskull. His advisor had disagreed, insisting that the most important prizes were all in the north and could be taken by stealth as well as by mass of arms. They had quarreled; his advisor had withdrawn into whatever part of himself the advisor alone could enter until, his advisor said, he showed sense.

He knew better. His spies had told him Mikeli of Tsaia had sent the regalia away, almost certainly with Duke Verrakai . . . and Duke Verrakai had next been seen on Bannerlíth dockside, accompanied by the Sea-Prince, taking passage on *Blessing* with Captain Royan in command. Immer spared a curse for the Sea-Prince, once an ally.

Immer's own agent, arriving in Bannerlíth that day, had realized he could not hire a ship likely to arrive in the south before *Blessing*. Instead, he had put a disguised pirate aboard *Blessing* and followed his original plan, going on up the Honnorgat to enter Tsaia through Lyonya. Once in Tsaia, he had passed the word to another agent, who brought it across Aarenis.

Weather was brewing behind us, his letter said.

Royan is a good captain, and Blessing *a sound ship, but he will veer far out to sea and lose time when the storm reaches him. Best of Simyits's luck, the man aboard will bring down a pirate attack on the ship, though that depends on where the storm leaves them. If the pirates cannot find the ship, they will run short of provisions and have to stop at Immerdzan; if not, he will still be days later passing Whiteskull than planned. Interception should be possible.*

Interception could be possible—but only if he himself could be in Immerdzan so the necklace could show him if indeed the Verrakai and the crown were on the ship. He needed to heal faster . . . and for that he needed the aid of his advisor, who had helped him heal quickly before . . . but his advisor refused to come forth. Only blood magery would give him the power to use another's death to heal his own wounds, and he did not know how to do it. His advisor did.

He had sent word downriver to hold *Blessing* on some pretext until he arrived—but what if the ship stopped at one of the other Immer ports instead? Immerdzan was the obvious choice, the largest and the most sheltered harbor—*Blessing* had traded there before, but also had stopped in Ka-Immer.

Immer struggled to sit up. The broken ribs hurt with every breath and more with movement—damn that thief horse. He could neither ride nor walk far, but he could lie abed in a boat as easily as in his fortress. Days had passed, tens of days, since Dorrin Verrakai had stepped aboard the ship. Where was she now? And did she really have the crown with her? He must not take the chance—he must head south now. Once up, gasping with the pain, he hobbled to his jewel case, leaning on a chair. The necklace sparkled at him . . . light rippled around the room, as if from dancing water. He stood watching it . . . and slowly, very slowly, it began to move, edging toward the corner of the box facing southeast, the opposite corner to the one it had favored before he left for Fallo.

He put his hand on it, felt the smooth, cool stones slipping, ever so slowly, across the calluses of his hand. He didn't need his advisor . . . He had his own magery, and this necklace would lead him to the crown. The crown and the throne. King of all.

He put the necklace on. It felt cool against his hot skin, and an old memory of the years he thought lost returned. When he was a boy, flushed after dancing for his master, his master had draped a chain of gold coins and another of rubies around his neck. The smooth chill of gold coins and rubies pulled from a carved box had made his skin prickle, and he had danced again, as he was bidden, enjoying the feel of them sliding on his body.

He hobbled back to the bed and rang the bell there, summoning servants and physicans alike. "Bathe me," he said to the servants. As they scurried away to fetch water and build up a fire, he turned to the physicians. "Prepare a litter for me," he said. "See that a boat is provisioned; I will go downriver that way. The business is urgent."

Being on the river eased him. Though the stone walls of Cortes Immer kept out the summer heat, they also held in the smells and sounds of the fortress. Here on the river, as the current carried his boat down, fresher air blew through the cabin and the gurgle of water soothed his ears. He remembered being Alured and how he had loved to play in water, splashing in shallows, swimming in the pools of a river . . . he could not remember where. His leg, which had been swollen and hot for so long, so painful he could not put weight on it, now shrank a little day by day. His broken ribs eased a little, though any sudden jar sent a spike of pain through his side.

Though he reminded himself daily that he was Visli Vaskronin, Duke of Immer, and all on the boat called him by his title, the water gave him back Alured, one fragile memory at a time.

He was entirely Immer, however, when he thought ahead to the port cities, for there he had come to his title and his rule for the first time. As Immer, on the advice of the one who shared his body, he had defied Kieri Phelan and flogged and tortured those who had opposed him. He had learned to despise Phelan for his weakness, for his refusal to use torture against enemies. Phelan had finally left him alone, withdrawn his troops, and he, the new Duke of Immer, had had to finish his conquest by himself. And he had done it.

He knew more about Kieri Phelan than Phelan knew about him, thanks to his advisor. More about Phelan than other people knew. Phelan also had served his master but had not been worthy of the choice given to young Alured. He had run away, weakling that he was, and though others had saved him, brought him to power, *that* was his flaw. That weakness would bring him down in the end.

All through one afternoon on the river, he thought about that. No one feared Kieri Phelan as they feared Immer. And because they feared him more, he could command more. When he came to power, when he ruled Tsaia and Fintha . . . he would confront Phelan and defeat him. Army to army, commander to commander, he would prove he was worthy to be king of all. To wear the crown, any crown he wanted, all the crowns at once, if he chose.

The sun went down, and the boat, now tied to trees by the river's edge, tugged only lightly at its mooring. With the dark and the smell of the river and the little gurgle of the water moving by . . . he slid back into Alured, the Alured before . . . the Alured before hunger and thirst and exhaustion and pain. Slowly, the memories his advisor did not want him to have, memories that had frayed, been torn away one time or another . . . those memories touched at the edges, giving him back a whole sequence. Alured almost remembered parents . . . but the faces would not come clear. He slept and dreamed of towers and gold and trumpets blowing and his name shouted by crowds as he rode by.

A lured-Visli Vaskronin, Duke of Immer and future king of everything, arrived at Immerdzan in the evening. He was able to stand, though the steps up from the river dock to the street exhausted him even with the help of his physicians. He was glad to ride in a carriage the rest of the way to his palace and glad that—as the night thickened—no one seemed to recognize him. The harbormaster reported that his messenger had arrived, but *Blessing* had not sailed to Immerdzan. He felt the stones of the necklace shift across his chest. East . . . that would be Ka-Immer. His messenger had reached Immerdzan and undoubtedly Ka-Immer as well. If *Blessing* was there, the harbormaster would detain the ship. If it had not arrived yet, all the better. Tomorrow he would go to Ka-Immer. He would recognize Dorrin Verrakai if the harbormaster did not; he remembered the tall, narrow-faced woman who had treated him with cool and distant courtesy edged with contempt.

What did I tell you about enemies?

His advisor was back.

She scorned you; when you take the crown, destroy her.

Ways to do that ran through his mind, vivid instructions from his advisor. He argued. The woman was old, not attractive. Why bother when she would die soon enough anyway? All he wanted was the crown and the other jewels, the power to rule everything.

That is not enough. Everyone must fear you, not just admire you. You will never be safe until they do. The strong never leave an enemy unbroken. Vengeance, always vengeance. And this will add to Phelan's anguish when . . .

He shifted in his bed, and his ribs stabbed again. If his advisor kept talking, he did not hear it. One of his physicians came in then.

"My lord, you must rest if you are to travel tomorrow safely. Your leg is seeping again. You must have numbweed for the pain so you sleep soundly."

He hated numbwine; a strong man should not need it. But now his leg throbbed, and the night was hot, the humid coastal air scarcely moving through the windows. He nodded and drank off the goblet of the stuff once it was mixed. The drug took effect; he sank into a soft, dark cloud and neither dreamed nor heard his advisor the rest of that night.

CHAPTER THIRTY-TWO

Ka-Immer, Aarenis

Dorrin woke in the dark, stiff and chilled from sleeping in the open, to the sound of a high whistle and bare feet running on the deck. Stars had faded; the sky gave enough light to see the masts and rigging black against the eastern sky. Someone grabbed her arm and pulled her into a line of sailors hauling on a rope. She took hold, pulling when the others pulled without knowing why. The rattling of blocks and the rising line of sails made it clear.

"Heyyyy . . . HO! Heyyyy . . . HO!" She pulled on "HO!" along with the others.

"Freeeeee—ALL."

Something thumped loudly on the deck on the dock side of the ship. Another something. The ship jerked a little, and the bow came away from the dock. From ahead and below, Dorrin heard a low chant, counterpoint to the one on deck. She wanted to go look, but if she was being crew, then she should do exactly what crew did.

"Heyyyy . . . HO! Heyyyyy . . . . HO!" Other sails were rising now, ever clearer against the brightening sky. The ship did not seem to be moving even as fast as a walk until the sail made a noise, then filled, no longer hanging straight down. *FLUP.* Another sail . . . *FLUP.* The deck shivered under Dorrin's feet.

"Waaaaay . . . ON!" someone shouted. She could see the shapes of the sailors now and feel a touch of wind on her cheek. They were pointed almost straight away from the dock.

"Come along," said a voice she recognized as the cook from the storm. "You'll be in the way out here."

She let go the rope and followed him, noticing others now moving quickly about the deck in patterns—a dance she did not know. Half the sails were up, and the one the captain had told her was the steering sail jutted out at an angle to the others. Away from the dock and the city buildings, away from the rise of ground behind the city, the breeze strengthened. The ship glided on, gaining speed as it went, until they were out beyond the harbor, when a still stronger breeze filled all the sails and the ship tilted gently over the first swells.

Everything was back in Dorrin's cabin but the box. When she went down in the hold, it came to her hands before she touched it. She did not need to open it to know the crown and jewels were still there; the crown murmured its contentment. Back in her cabin, she slid it under the bunk again. From her window, she could see the shore of Aarenis angle away to the northwest, one side of the funnel-shaped bay into which the Immer emptied, with Immerdzan at its mouth.

She ate breakfast in the main cabin with the captain, Sun poured in the windows at the stern. The cook had made stirred eggs, and a southern hot sauce was on the table, along with a dish of oilberries.

"We're sailing west across the bay," he said. "We'll head south between Seafang and Whiteskull, into the Immerhoft itself, and then, barring weather, it's easy sailing to the western ports." He shoveled in another mouthful of eggs, followed it with oilberries, then bread and honey, and gave a satisfied sigh. "I don't expect any trouble. We're a known ship; I pay the bribes in whatever Immer port I dock—did that yesterday while you were up the mast—and there's nothing in this cargo that would interest them." He belched, then went on. "They always look at the cabins—but yours was bare as an eggshell, and your things stowed where they wouldn't bother. They saw crew, and cargo I'd paid the toll for, and nothing more."

"Immer was there. In Ka-Immer."

"Yes, flat on his back in his palace, is what I heard, gossip before I came back to the ship at close of trading and pulled the plank. Took a wound or two in a battle, is what they said, but I don't know for sure. By the time he's up to see or ask questions, we'll be out of sight and any gossipers on shore will have nothing to say about a woman aboard old *Blessing*."

Dorrin hoped he was right. What he said made sense, but years as a mercenary had taught her that careful planning did not ensure anything. An enemy might not—too often did not—do what seemed logical.

"Come up top with me," the captain said after breakfast. "The bay's a busy place, lots of ships."

Dorrin followed him up the ladder. The deck up here seemed to magnify every slightest movement of the ship, but the swells were not very big. She had no trouble keeping her feet. The morning sun made sails visible even when ships were far away. Behind them, the coastline they had left seemed lower, flatter.

"Those are fishers," the captain said, pointing to a group of three small boats, low to the water but with upturned bows. "More over there. And there's one like *Blessing*, heading out from Immerdzan. Could be *Bountiful*."

"What's that one?" Dorrin asked, pointing to another long low ship with one square sail, angling well away from them.

"Galley. Men row it as well as depend on the sail. They can move faster than a ship like this. Shallow draft, too; they can go right up a river or land on a shore. That one . . ." He squinted at it. "Headed for one of the fishing villages along the shore or maybe Immerdzan. Ah, now. Look there . . . see the different color to the water?"

Dorrin saw it ahead, a broad streak of brownish green.

"That's the Immer . . . pushes its water out this far and farther, too. We have to cross it, and it'll push us south even as we're sailing west. Help us on our way to the sea beyond Seafang."

Ka-Immer

Alured awoke late in Immerdzan from the heavy dose of numb-wine. His ribs hurt him less when he woke, but his leg throbbed under its bandages, and when his physician unwrapped it, the wound had opened again. His foot was swollen, red, and the swelling extended up his leg.

"You must rest, my lord, with the leg elevated. I will poultice it and draw out the heat—"

"No! I must go to Ka-Immer today."

"My lord Duke, you are fevered—"

The necklace, hidden under his nightshirt, slid across his chest, tugging at his neck. "I must go," he said. "I *will* go." To the servants standing by, he said, "Order the carriage at once."

No. Fool. Forget that crown.

He struggled to sit up, fighting the physician, his servants, everyone.

Take off the necklace. Lie down. You are sick. You should not have come. I told you. You are a fool—

"I am strong," he said aloud. "I will go." He felt the other's magery pushing against his will, demanding mastery. Cold malice now, as he had seen when he was a boy and the master had been tormenting someone else . . . no praise, no encouragement, only contempt.

I thought you were worthy, but you are nothing . . . a stupid fool, just a pretty face who will not listen . . . you think more of that bauble than you do of me.

"Let me alone! Get *out* . . . I don't need you—!" He squeezed his eyes shut, ignoring the others in the room, fighting the pressure, murmuring his own name, his real name, over and over. "Alured, Alured, Alured . . . I am *Alured* . . ."

The pressure ceased. He opened his eyes to see the others staring at him, some frightened, some worried, and one . . . looking back at him with eyes he knew very well.

"He's very sick," the harbormaster said. "We must all hope he does not die. He thinks he does not need us, but . . . without us, he will certainly die." That suggestion of a drawl, that insinuating tone . . . His advisor, he realized, had deserted him for another.

He felt both terror and relief. With all his strength he said, "I will *not* die. And I will gain what I seek." He looked at his physician. "Something must be in the wound. Cut it open, find it, clean it—or cut it off if you must."

Four days later, he arrived in Ka-Immer, weak from blood loss but the wound now draining only clear fluid. It had been a fragment of metal the original physician had not found, and now, he was sure, he was healing. All the way the necklace had shifted on his chest with every change of direction, and once in Ka-Immer it pointed at the harbor. He would wait until morning, he decided, before talking to the harbormaster here; it had been a difficult journey. He accepted a dose of numbwine without protest and slid into dreamless sleep.

When he woke, the sun was well up, shining through the window, and the necklace no longer pointed to the harbor. The harbormaster, summoned, told him his messenger had never arrived . . . and *Blessing* had sailed that very day on the dawn breeze.

D orrin was asleep, making up for the previous night, when the captain woke her. "Come up; you need to see this." The tone of his voice told her it was nothing good.

Once on the upper deck, she saw the sea was now a darker blue, with the sun highlighting sails in the distance.

"That one," he said. "Big square sail. It's on our track and has been since midmorning. Top basket saw it first, sure it came out of Ka-Immer. Not a merchanter. Closer now than it was, though it'll be dark before it catches us. And there's one just come out of Whiteskull— see there? Anything out of Whiteskull is a pirate."

"It could be someone headed for the western ports like us."

"Not likely." He was silent a long moment. "If they're after you . . . All I know of you is the Sea-Prince asked me to take a passenger and ask no questions. And I haven't."

"You haven't," Dorrin agreed.

"But now . . . you told me you were in Aarenis before, even in the Immer ports. Fighting, you said: that would be Siniava's War, eh?"

"Yes."

"And you might have enemies, you said. Even the Duke of Immer. You should've been safe enough aboard, up there in the basket . . . but someone's on our track, with a way to call in help. What did you do, steal from the Duke? Summat of great value? Is that what's in your box that only you can move?"

"I stole nothing," Dorrin said. "Something was stolen from my family, long ago. Stolen again in Fin Panir before I even knew it had been lost to us. And from that theft it came to Aarenis and the Duke of Immer; that much is known."

"So . . . you are hunting it back?"

"No," Dorrin said. "I have the rest . . . what it belongs to . . . and Immer wants it. He thinks it will give him mastery of the whole world."

The captain stared at her a moment, then burst out laughing. "Mastery of the world! The man is crazy! And why would he think that?"

Dorrin shrugged.

"It must be magic, whatever it is . . . if he thinks that."

Dorrin said nothing.

"And you have it. Here, on my ship?" He looked around as if it might be up on the top deck with them. "No—you have it on your person? Or in that box." He came close to her. "What is it?"

"I must not tell you."

"Not tell me? When my ship is in danger, you think you will not tell me what that danger is?"

"The danger is in those ships," Dorrin said. "Not in what I have or do not have."

"Do not chop words," he said. "This is *my* ship—my life. My people. We carried you safely from Bannerlíth, through storm and good sailing both, and gave you cover in Ka-Immer. Yes, I know you fought with us against the pirates, but that saved your skin as well as mine. I will not risk my ship and my people for some . . . some . . ." He turned aside and spat. "You will tell me or you will go over the side, and may the fish demons gnaw your bones to sand."

"If you throw me to the sea," Dorrin said, "and Immer finds what I left aboard, he will rule everything and great trouble will come of it. Do you think he will treat you courteously when he finds it? No: he will kill you and everyone aboard to hide what he has taken and keep it secret, and all Aarenis will come to be as Aare is now, a barren land."

"You speak nonsense," he said, breathing hard.

"I speak truth," Dorrin said, touching her ruby.

"So . . . what do you plan to do, *truth speaker,* when they catch up with us? Will you hide in the basket again and pretend to be a sailor? Hide in the hold and be dragged out like a rat? Or fight? I tell you, though we carry crossbows and cutlasses, if it comes to it before we are out in the open sea again, we will not fight free before more ships come from Whiteskull and Seafang both." He took a breath or two, looking again at the distant sail behind them. "I am not willing to lose my ship for you. I do not hate you, but . . ."

"Will they be here before it's dark?" Dorrin asked.

"What? No . . . no, not if the wind holds, but they can follow us in the dark. We will show against the sky as long as it is light, and they will be close . . . Why?"

"Put me and my box in your rowboat. I will row away. When they stop you, I will not be there."

"You know how to use oars?"

"No . . . but it can't be that hard. I watched the boats in the harbor."

His eyebrows went up, and a snort of amusement came. "Cannot be that hard? If this were not a serious matter, I would do it now and let you find out how hard it is not."

"I do not want you to lose your ship or be hurt or your crew to suffer because of me," Dorrin said. "If I leave the ship with my box, you will be safe."

She could tell he was considering that, though he was shaking his head slowly. "You will be killed. It will be my fault. The Sea-Prince will ask when I come again if you made it safely to Marley."

"If we are close enough to the western shore I can row to shore, and hide . . . make my way west on land . . ."

"But you want to go to Aare—"

"Yes."

"Why?"

"What you do not know, you cannot be made to tell," Dorrin said.

"You'll never make it to shore," he said. "I just wish I knew how someone found out you were on this ship."

"Someone in Bannerlíth," Dorrin said. "Or . . . the thing stolen from my family was a magical item. Perhaps it guides him." She was sure of that.

The other ships drew nearer. Now Dorrin could see the black and green design on the sails of both: a sea-monster, with arms, claws, a serpent body, and a fish's tail. She went back to her cabin, put on her mail, belted on the sword, and pulled the box out from under the bunk. She at least would fight. She felt the ship slow . . . heard flapping as the sails came down. When she came on deck, sailors were in a row across the deck, armed with wooden staves and cutlasses, watching her, and the captain was leaning over the railing of the upper deck. She looked up; two sailors in the top basket had crossbows aimed at her.

"Here's what it is," he said. "You admit you, or what you've got in that box—or both—are what they want. Those are all Immer's ships. I paid the fees—nothing held back, and they know that. If we make it easy, they'll take you and won't harm my ship or my crew. If you want to fight them, do it somewhere else, not on my ship. If you were willing to be cast off in a rowboat, you should be willing to do that."

"And if I'm not?"

"If you think you can take down my crew, that's near four hands altogether, including the cook behind you now with a carving knife, you're welcome to try, and we'll hand you over to them bound and bloody and probably dying."

Dorrin glanced back. The cook grinned at her, not a friendly grin.

Free me. Open the box.

She let the box slide out of her arm and set it on the deck, then bent to the clasp.

"Stop!" the captain said. "Don't open it. I'm not letting you throw it overboard or loose whatever magery is inside. Just stand there until they come, and then get off my ship."

"Later," she said quietly to the crown. It did not reply.

The ship rocked gently in the waves as the other ships came nearer. All were galleys, one of them rowed by men in green and black uniforms and the others by crews of what looked like brigands, but with green and black badges to match the pennants flapping from the mastheads. Two slid alongside, one on either side; the others waited at a little distance. One hailed the captain; its crews wore the uniforms.

"You have a passenger."

"Aye, so I do. Standing there on deck."

"We take."

"Go ahead." The captain nodded to his crew, and two of them tossed a bundle of netting over the side.

Men with cutlasses and crossbows swarmed aboard from both sides; one of those in green and black wore a helmet with a green plume. *Blessing*'s crew retreated to the bow, offering no resistance.

"You didn't say at Ka-Immer," the man with the helmet said to the captain.

The captain shrugged. "Nobody asked."

The man looked at Dorrin. "Put sword down."

"No," Dorrin said.

"Or we kill." He half drew his own sword.

Dorrin shrugged. "If you kill me, you will not be able to move the box."

He laughed and said something she did not understand. Two of the men in black and green came toward her and took hold of the box. They tugged; it did not move. Tugged harder . . . still no movement. They looked at her, then at their commander.

"You cannot move it without me," Dorrin said. She murmured nonsense, hoping they would take it for a command, and touched the box with her boot. It rose in the air and settled into her arm. Their eyes widened.

"You bring, then," their commander said.

From the foredeck of the galley, Dorrin looked up at *Blessing*. Sails lifted; the ship moved through the water, away from the galley. The other galleys were already rowing back toward Whiteskull.

"You come," said the man with the helmet. Half the oarsmen were back at their benches, working their oars to turn the galley around; the rest, weapons still in hand, formed a guard around Dorrin as she moved aft between the rowers. She had no idea what would happen, though she suspected it would end with her death when they reached shore.

When the black-haired man hobbled out of the aft cabin and faced her, she did not recognize him until the man with the helmet addressed him as "my lord Duke." The Alured she remembered— young, handsome, arrogant, and oddly appealing—had aged and now looked desperately ill, his face lined with pain, fever patching his cheeks an unnatural red, his lips pale as if he had lost blood. One leg was bandaged, the bandages stained as if the wound drained. Yet the determination he had always shown was still there. And a glint of blue showed at his throat, where his hand clutched at his shirt. He stared at her then spoke to his commander.

"Take the box; open it."

The man reached for the box; Dorrin did not try to hold onto it, and it jerked from the man's hand, crashing to the deck as if it were heavy with gold.

"Open it!" Alured said again; Dorrin could hear the strain in his voice. Once more, the men tried and could not open the box.

"*You*, Captain Dorrin. Open it."

"No," said Dorrin. "And you will not open it without me."

He laughed a little. "So you think. I have the key to that lock." He reached into his shirt and pulled out the necklace. Dorrin caught her breath. It was larger than she had imagined, the stones glittering in the afternoon sun. And it leaned away from Alured's hand toward the box like a pennant in the wind. Dorrin heard indrawn breaths from some of those watching.

"Bring it to me," Alured said, looking at the necklace. "Open, now . . ."

Dorrin had been sure the crown would command the necklace, that the box would not open for anyone but her. When the box flew open and the regalia lifted out from beneath her spare clothes, her heart sank.

"Yes," Alured said. "There it is—there is my crown!"

The crown hung a moment in the air, revolving, sending watery patterns of refracted light over them all, the galley, the water around, until Dorrin was dizzy with it. And then the crown settled on her head, a definite weight.

Queen. At last. Together.

The necklace lifted from Alured's neck and slid over his head as if weightless.

"No!" Alured said, grabbing it before it could escape. "You're wrong . . . it's not hers! It's mine! *I'm* the king! She's just an old woman. I'm strong. *I'm* the one!" He hobbled toward her. "Give it to me!" Then to the others, "Make her give it to me! Get it—"

Quick as a striking snake, the necklace recoiled and wrapped around Alured's neck, tightening like a noose. Two of the loose stones from the box flew straight at his face, striking his eyes. He shrieked, clawed at his throat, staggered onto his bandaged leg, and fell.

And at that moment, Dorrin felt a crushing blow on her back that drove her over the side of the galley, face-first into the water.

CHAPTER THIRTY-THREE

Foss Council, Aarenis

Arcolin watched dust rising from a fast-moving horseman on the path beside the Guild League road's paved center section.

"One of ours?" Cracolnya said.

"We'll know soon enough," Arcolin said. As the rider neared, Arcolin could see the rose of his tabard under a coating of yellow dust.

"My lord Duke," the rider said, barely able to talk. "King's word." He dismounted and quickly removed a velvet pouch from the near saddlebag and handed it to Arcolin.

"Come," Arcolin said. "We'll see to your horse." Cracolnya had already called one of his soldiers over, and he led the horse away. The courier slapped at his dusty clothes as he followed Arcolin into the tent.

Cracolnya dipped water into a mug and handed it to the courier while Arcolin pulled out the message tube, untied it, pulled out the rolled message, and untied the ribbons around that. He expected the news to be bad—why else send a royal courier here at top speed rather than using Fox Company's own courier?

Mikeli had written in haste but with great formality. He wanted his Constable back in the kingdom, with his troops, to defend Tsaia's western boundary from invasion by Finthans and part of the south boundary from invasion by gnomes. Gnomes? That made no sense . . . Why would they—

We know this risks breach of your contract with Foss Coun-
cil, and we would not ask if it were not vital to the realm.
You informed us that invasion from Aarenis was not likely,
that the Duke of Immer had not advanced west this entire
season. What we face here is not mere threat but actual inva-
sion. Finthans have crossed the border, some claiming to flee
mage-hunters, and mage-hunters pursuing them. Some have
transgressed a gnomish boundary near Duke Elorran's lands,
and the gnomes—Gnarrinfulk, I understand—blame us and
threaten retaliation. Come at once with as many troops as you
can swiftly collect.

"Trouble?" Cracolnya said, glancing at him.

"Always," Arcolin said. "Your cohort's ready to march, isn't it?"

"We can start tomorrow at dawn," Cracolnya said.

"How about tonight?"

Cracolnya's brows rose. "That much trouble?"

"It will be if the gnomes attack," Arcolin said. His mind raced as he thought of all he must do and in what order. "I'm riding to Foss immediately; I should be back here before dark. Start packing now and read this when you have time." He handed over the king's letter.

"Sir—my lord—the king needs an answer—"

"You'll come with us," Arcolin said. "We have no fast horse for you to ride back; you can find one in Valdaire."

Once he reached Foss, he went to the head of the council. "My king commands my return earlier than planned; I leave you both infantry cohorts."

"But—"

"But you hired all three. I know. And I know we have marched long and fought two battles for you this season. My king has urgent need; I'm taking the mixed cohort, and there is no sign that Immer is active. You've heard the same rumors I have."

"That he died in Ka-Immer or at sea? Yes, but there's no proof."

"No, but the fact is that he did not capture Fallo, there are Kostandanyan troops allied with you, and a solid garrison of friendly troops in Cortes Cilwan. Wherever he is, alive or dead, he is not on the march here."

"What's happening in Tsaia?"

"Fintha," Arcolin said. "You've heard about the split among Girdsmen, haven't you?"

The councilman waved his hand. "Something religious; I'm not Girdish. I didn't understand it."

Arcolin explained as quickly as he could. "And so," he said, "some people are running from the mage-hunters, and the mage-hunters are chasing them, and they're not paying attention to borders. Including gnome borders."

"Ahhh."

"Yes. And the gnomes are . . . very angry that their borders have been transgressed, and they blame the king. Now, the king knows that I speak gnomish—"

"I see. Well. I see it is in your contract that you personally will have to leave if your king commands. And you usually do rotate a half-cohort to a cohort out in winter . . . but this is early . . . so let us say . . ."

The bargaining lasted only the turn of a glass, and Arcolin rode back to camp satisfied with the arrangement. Cracolnya had his cohort packed and ready to leave, wagon teams hitched. Couriers were on the way to the other two cohorts; Kaim had seen to Arcolin's own gear and his other horse's readiness. Arcolin rode to the head of the column, and they started off.

By traveling through the night, they had a clear road, and had almost reached Valdaire when morning traffic began to slow things down again. Still, they were in Fox Company's winter quarters in Valdaire by early afternoon. The royal courier changed to the mount he'd left there on the way to Arcolin and rode away. Arcolin rode into the city to find the workshop where Dattur had worked.

In gnomish, with his stole visible, he said, "I seek a kapristin who would carry a message to Lord Prince Aldonfulk. I have price of Law for service."

All the gnomes in the room stared at him before one said, "It is that no Aldonfulk is in this place today, Lord Prince Arcolinfulk. Is it that the Lord Prince will send message by outclan?"

"Yes," Arcolin said. He laid down the coins on the nearest worktable: the price Law set for such a message.

Another gnome pushed aside a curtain between that room and another. "It is that it is urgent?"

"It is," Arcolin said. He pulled out the letter he had written and his gnomish seal and ink. "Law requires witness for what I have written."

Two gnomes stepped forward, including the one who had come from a back room; the others moved to the far side of the room. When Arcolin had properly signed and sealed the letter, finishing with a carefully placed drop of his own blood, the two gnomes added their names and marks. "It is done," one of them said. They bowed; he inclined his head.

A detachment of Royal Guards met Arcolin and his cohort in Five-way. Arcolin introduced himself to their captain, a young man not, Arcolin was certain, over thirty winters. At least he had expected Arcolin, though he seemed to have no idea why Arcolin had come.

"The king recalled me from Aarenis to take command of the defense," Arcolin said. "We will leave immediately for the border."

"But I thought you would stay at least a night—"

"In Fiveway? Find lodging for a hundred men, mounts, and supply wagons in trade season? No. It's not even midday yet. We're not stopping."

The captain stared at the gnomes now riding in the first supply wagon. "Are those . . . ?"

"Aldonfulk," Arcolin said. "Envoys from the Aldonfulk prince and also my escort to Lord Prince Gnarrinfulk."

"You're going to . . . but you can't!"

"Of course I can," Arcolin said. "I'm the Constable, and the king expects me to deal with threats to the realm."

"But—but you can't represent the king as a mercenary commander!"

Arcolin repressed a sigh. "No, of course not. I will meet with Lord Prince Gnarrinfulk as a fellow prince."

The man gaped; Arcolin signaled, and his cohort turned onto the South Trade Road.

"What am *I* supposed to do?" the man said as the column started past him.

"Fall in behind. I'll need you to deal with Finthans fleeing the mage-hunters." Arcolin glanced at Cracolnya, who grinned at him.

Arcolin considered going to Duke Elorran's house, for he needed to cross Elorran land to reach Gnarrinfulk's nearest border, but talking to Gnarrinfulk's prince was more urgent than anything else. His gnomish guides told him where to turn off the road, pointing up the slope.

"Cracolnya, you and the royal troop continue on the road and camp before dark. If I'm not back this evening, continue tomorrow but don't go beyond the border."

The Aldonfulk gnomes led the way on foot; he rode behind them, as always amazed at how fast they could cover the ground with their short legs. By early afternoon, when Arcolin glanced back, he could see the road as a dusty scar on the land, but his cohort was out of sight behind the shoulder of a hill.

The line in the grass, when they came to it, ran perfectly straight along the front of the hills, rising and falling with the terrain. A stone set an armslength on this side bore a carved message: GNARRIN-FULK. STOP.

Arcolin dismounted. The land seemed empty and silent, the only sound the wind in the sunburnt grass. One of the gnomes with him picked up a rock from the ground and tapped on the marker stone. They waited. Arcolin straightened his scarf of office. Then, as if rising straight out of the stone, a line of gnomes appeared, all armed with pikes.

"Law is," said one of them.

"Law is," Arcolin replied in gnomish. "Lord Prince Arcolinfulk would speak to Lord Prince Gnarrinfulk."

"It is that this *human* is gnomish prince?"

"It is so. Lord Prince Aldonfulk has said," one of the gnome guides said.

"It is that *human* gave stone-right? Lord Prince Arcolinfulk?"

"It is," Arcolin said.

"It is that Lord Prince Arcolinfulk come with us."

Arcolin and his Aldonfulk escort followed the gnomes. Gnarrinfulk, he knew, was the gnome princedom that had tutored Gird himself in organized warfare. Once inside, and facing the Gnarrinfulk prince, he bowed and introduced himself with formality. The prince bowed in return and responded in Common, to Arcolin's surprise.

"It is Gnarrinfulk speak Common from Gird. Gird slow to learn words of gnomish."

Arcolin managed not to gape. Was the Gnarrinfulk prince claiming to have known Gird? He did not ask; instead, he moved on to the reasons for his visit. "My king says you have problem with humans here and in Fintha trespassing on Gnarrinfulk lands."

"Yes. Breach of contract. Gird promised no trespassing. Only few—children now and then—since Gird. Kapristi not harm children. Hurt children is not Law."

"And now?" Arcolin asked.

The trouble had gone on for more than a year, the gnome prince said. Time and again humans—even humans wearing Girdish symbols—crossed the trimmed line, ignored the boundary stones. Not just single humans but groups, and sometimes the groups fought and shed human blood on Gnarrinfulk stone-right. Worst of all a child or children had been killed on Gnarrinfulk stone-right.

"Is not Law. Not Law, nor Code of Gird," the prince said. "Sent message to Marshal-General and to king in Tsaia. Both say cannot stop. Some quarrel of humans. Human quarrel not Law."

"Did the Marshal-General or the king say why the quarrel?"

"Why is not matter. Law is Law. Contract broken is un-Law. Contract broken is . . . is broken both parties."

"Law is Law," Arcolin agreed. "Hurt children is not Law."

"Kapristi not hurt children."

"Some men wear Girdish symbols wrong," Arcolin said. "Not Girdish. Not in Law. Not obeying Marshal-General. Not obeying king. They hurt children. They kill children. Parents take children and run—"

"Why kill children?"

"Children have magery. Girdish law—Code of Gird—says no magery is good."

"Gird not say that."

He had to ask. "Lord Prince Gnarrinfulk knew Gird?"

A nod. "Gird here. Learn from Warmaster. Gird . . ." A long pause, then a mutter in gnomish Arcolin could not quite hear. "Gird want Law, but no human can . . . even human gnome prince. We teach—taught. Gird learn what Gird could. But already knew, it is not magery but it is that mages used magery wrong."

"So Marshal-General thinks," Arcolin said. "But some Girdish think all magery evil. Those turn against Marshal-General."

"Marshal-General is prince of Girdish," the prince said. "Turn against prince is not Law. Is make *kteknik*."

"These *kteknik*—" Arcolin chose to use the gnomish word. "—they have killed children and adults who they think have magery. Without reason. Against Marshal-General's commands. Those accused flee to save children."

"So . . . it is that the quarrel is those in Law against those *kteknik*?"

"It is."

The prince said nothing; Arcolin waited. And waited. Finally, the Gnarrinfulk prince nodded again. "It is not known before. Law is that only some Girdish break contract by intent. Other Girdish wrong—boundary is boundary—but save children is not wrong." He tilted his head to the side. "Lord Prince Aldonfulk wrote, said you saved kapristinya and children. After Dragon said all *kteknik*."

Arcolin nodded rather than argue what Dragon had actually said. "Law to save children."

"No kapristin would have known if all died."

"It is not for being known," Arcolin said. "Law required."

"Ah. Lord Prince Aldonfulk wrote you have hesktak who was once *kteknik*."

"Yes." Where was this leading?

"Hesktak teach you well. You speak Law. Your tribe prosper. You have scent of Dragon. You met Dragon?"

"Yes," Arcolin said. "More than once."

The faintest hint of a smile on the prince's face. "Dragon ask are you wise?"

"Yes. No man wise compared to Dragon."

The prince nodded. "What help needs Marshal-General and king?"

Arcolin had not expected that offer; he had hoped merely to keep the gnomes from attacking humans in retaliation for border violations. He suggested that the prince let those fleeing mage-hunters across the border long enough to escape but stop the mage-hunters.

"Is not enough," the prince said. "Is need help Marshal-General restore order. Order is Law. No order is *kteknik*. *Kteknik* humans is trouble."

From that moment, things moved rapidly. The gnomish Warmaster appeared at the prince's call, bringing maps. The gnomes' information on the situation in southern Fintha was more recent than Arcolin's. They knew a force from Fin Panir had come south . . . they had assumed it was to attack the Gnarrinfulk.

"I believe they are after the mage-hunters," Arcolin said. "Do you know of a force of them?"

The Warmaster knew of other gatherings of humans but had not distinguished among them. "Only that some chase some."

The Gnarrinfulk prince, in rapid gnomish, explained to the Warmaster what Arcolin had explained to him. Then he turned back to Arcolin. "It is that Lord Prince Arcolin prevented Gnarrinfulk error of Law. It is Gnarrinfulk say Law is those hunt magefolk *kteknik*. Gnarrinfulk for Law and contract with true Girdfulk. Warmaster go with you. Law is Law." He stood and bowed.

"Law is Law," Arcolin said, bowing in return.

T he Aldonfulk gnomes did not reappear; Gnarrinfulk gnomes took Arcolin and his horse "by the stone," as they put it. He emerged in morning sunlight from the side of a hill that closed behind him, and there below, on the South Trade Road, was his cohort and the Royal Guard troop.

"Well?" Cracolnya asked.

"Allies," Arcolin said. "They are mustering in support of the Marshal-General; the gnome prince has decided that only the mage-hunters, not those fleeing them, have breached the old contract between Gird and gnomes."

The Royal Guard captain stared. "How did you convince a gnome? We tried; gnomes don't listen. Just said law, law, law all the time."

Arcolin looked around. He could not see any gnomes. That did not mean no gnomes were there, listening. Whatever he said must work for both peoples. "Gnomes live by Law. They value Law. They value contracts, which are the word of Law and set the equality, the balance, between parties to the contract. Trespass breached Gird's contract, the basis of peace between gnomes and humans."

"Yes, but—"

Arcolin held up his hand. "In Law, few things—many fewer than for us—allow one party to a contract to break its terms without freeing the other completely. In this case, breaking a contract of peace would have meant war. The prince did not know that one of the very few conditions that alter contracts existed."

"And what is that? Some gnomish silliness?" The captain was clearly still annoyed, and worse than that, loud, and worse than both, showing contempt.

Arcolin could not ignore that, not with the feeling that hundreds of beady black eyes were watching him from behind every rock on the slope. He glared at the man until the captain wilted a little. "I am telling you, as the Constable of this kingdom, Duke of the North Marches, member of the Royal Council, and the king's representative in this place, that this is no way to speak of our allies. Since Gird's day, Gnarrinfulk has honored Gird's contract. No human has come to harm from them; they have never taken so much as a rabbit from the other side of their boundary. Moreover, they have shown mercy to those who broke it without intent, such as shepherds whose sheep strayed. Yet you speak of them as if they were fools. These are the gnomes who taught Gird warfare and the reason you and I are both Girdish. Show respect for Elders."

The captain reddened and looked down. "Sorry, my lord," he said.

"Remember it," Arcolin said. "We are honored and very fortunate to have gnomes offer to help our king and the Marshal-General. Now, you asked what condition made it possible, in Law, for the prince to regard the situation differently. It was children: the children the mage-hunters have killed and tried to kill. Under Law, attacking innocents for what they are, rather than what they have done, is against Law."

"They changed their minds for *children*?" At least that was in a low voice.

"Wouldn't you?" Arcolin said. Without waiting an answer, he signaled Cracolnya, and the cohort started forward.

"That was an impressive list of titles," Cracolnya said, keeping his voice low. "But I notice you did not say 'Commander of Fox Company.'"

"I didn't think it would have the right effect," Arcolin said. "Besides, here and now Fox Company outnumbers his. He got the point."

"Just want to be sure you still consider us important," Cracolnya said.

Arcolin turned to look at him. "Important? Of course the Company's important. None of the rest would exist without the Company."

"Good. I'm too old to be finding another place if you had changed your mind."

The closer they came to the Finthan border, the more signs of struggle appeared on the road. Carrion eaters lifting from the ground revealed bodies . . . first one, then another, then three together. The road itself was empty; with word of unrest, many traders had chosen not to go to Fintha this year.

At the border itself, they saw no one at first.

"Do we go on?" Cracolnya asked.

"I'm not sure—" Arcolin looked around, hoping to spot a gnome. Instead, he saw a group of people north of the road, already on the Tsaian side of the border. Perhaps three or four hands of them, adults and children both, hurried along the brushy side of what might be a creek. That low ground led toward the road; his troop had crossed a dry wash only a short time ago. Farther away, still in Fintha, he saw another, larger group, on horseback, riders on either side of the brush cover as it broadened farther down the slope. They moved steadily up the slope a little faster than the fugitives as they searched clumps of brush. "There's trouble," he said. "Mage-hunters after those—" He pointed to each group in turn.

"What do we do?" the Royal Guard captain said.

"Save the children," Arcolin said. "And their parents, of course."

Cracolnya needed no direction; he led the cohort off the road and down the slope, aiming to cut between the pursued and their pursuers. The pursuers, instead of turning back at the sight of a military unit marching toward them, kicked their horses into a gallop and yelled something Arcolin could not distinguish. The pursued stopped short, staring, then tried to run straight up the slope to the road.

"Captain—charge them!" Arcolin looked at the Royal Guard captain and pointed his sword at the pursuers.

"But they're still in Fintha!"

"Not in another twenty strides," Arcolin said. "Go! Now!"

"I can't cross the border without the king—"

"Shall I tell the king you disobeyed me? GO!" He smacked the captain's horse on the rump with the flat of his sword; it bolted after Cracolnya and the cohort, and the troop followed. Arcolin put spurs to his own mount and caught up.

The pursuing party split, trying to swing wide around both the cohort and the cavalry troop. Arcolin grinned. Cracolnya would be happy about that . . . The crossbowmen of the mixed cohort turned smoothly and shot into the flanks of the pursuers, dropping almost half of them.

The rest, seeing this, peeled off and galloped away full speed as another flight of bolts took three of the hindmost. Arcolin pulled up. The Royal Guard captain wrestled his horse to a stop and turned back to Arcolin, yanking his sword out of its scabbard.

"How dare you!"

"You disobeyed an order. Would you rather I'd killed you?"

"You—"

"Sir!" That was one of his troopers. "Sir—no—!"

"Problem, my lord?" Cracolnya's voice was smooth as butter, but he held a crossbow steady, the bolt aimed at the captain's back.

"No," Arcolin said. "The captain has misunderstood the situation." He looked at the troopers loosely clustered nearby. "See if you can collect the loose horses those brigands were riding. We'll need them later." They hesitated but finally turned and rode off. Then to the captain, "Put that sword away and think about why you didn't manage to draw it in the face of the enemy but only when confronting your commander."

"You—!"

"Yes. As Constable and as Duke Arcolin, I am your commander in this place. I told you that before. Put up your sword."

Red-faced, beginning to shake—was it anger or reaction, realization of what he had done?—the captain finally got his sword back in the scabbard after a couple of tries. Arcolin sheathed his own in one practiced motion and nudged his mount closer to the captain's. Cracolnya's cohort was now between him and the rest of the Royal Guard contingent, alert and ready for anything.

Arcolin went on. "If you cannot, or will not, follow my orders, I will send you away. As you are, you are a danger to my people and yours. Do you understand?"

"I—I—you can't do that."

"I can. I will. One more time: Will you do what I tell you, at once and without question, or will you go back to Fiveway on foot, unarmed, and try to explain yourself to your senior in the Royal Guard and the king?"

"On *foot*? *Unarmed*?"

"Of course. Why would I leave someone like you on a valuable charger? With a sword? Either you accept me here and now as your commander and give me the loyalty owed, or you go home in disgrace. *If* you make it that far." Arcolin made his tone conversational. "Now: give me your answer."

The shoulders drooped. "I—I accept you . . ."

"Good. I am pleased to hear it. Go back to the wagons and tell the drivers to start setting up camp. The people running from the mage-hunters will need care."

The captain opened his mouth, shut it, finally bit off a "Sir," and turned his horse back up the slope.

"He wouldn't have lasted long in Aarenis," Cracolnya said after he'd ridden off. He took the bolt from his crossbow and eased the string.

"Young, inexperienced," Arcolin said.

"Dead," Cracolnya said.

"True enough. Let's go meet our travelers."

Cracolnya said "Camp" to his sergeants and followed Arcolin to the group now huddled in the dry wash near the road.

They were, as Arcolin had thought, Girdish families from a vill near the Finthan border.

"We hear Tsaia doesn't kill mages," one said.

"Or them as aren't mages but someone says they is to steal their cows," another said.

"The king said no killing mages," Arcolin said. "You are safe for now. What about your supplies?"

The first one—he gave his name as Dorthan—shook his head. "They almost caught us in camp two nights ago—we had to run, leave everything."

"We have water and food up on the road," Arcolin said.

Soon the cohort had laid out a proper camp, and the fugitives, now under canvas, had eaten and drunk their fill. Of the nineteen, five confessed to being mages, four of them children who could do no more than make light with a finger. The fifth, a woman, had a parrion of healing. "Had it all my life," she said. "So I thought this was just somethin' else I'd picked up. Only they said it was magery." All the rest were relatives of the mages or those afraid of being killed even if they weren't.

"No better'n brigands," Dorthan said. "They got our sheep, our goats, our cows, our houses . . . It's not right, but we're not enough to fight 'em."

"What about the grange?" Arcolin asked.

Dorthan hooked his forefingers together. "Tight as that with the mage-hunters, Marshal is. Him and his snuck around the bartons, takin' weapons. Not that we had much."

"Took my fightin' staff that I made myself," said another, who'd given his name as Tamis. "Walked two days there and back to get wood for that, I did. Had it up dryin' all one winter."

"How many of you being hunted by the mage-haters are in this area?"

This provoked a lively argument and much counting on fingers. While that continued, the Royal Guard troop came back to camp with eighteen horses, all with saddles, and three captives, all injured. The others, they said, were dead where they lay.

That night, mage-hunters tried to sneak into the camp. Two were caught, and one killed.

"We can't deal with this from here," Arcolin said. "We're going to have to go into Fintha and link up with the Marshal-General's people . . . For one thing, that's who the gnomes want to work with."

"Gnomes!"

Arcolin looked at the Royal Guard captain, and he subsided. "We didn't need them yesterday. We outnumbered the mage-hunters, and as you noticed, we outnumber them more now. But we need to clear a defensible area where the fugitives—these and any others we find—can live in some safety. Ideally, we'd start with vills that border Tsaia—as a buffer—and then work toward the west. And we don't have an idea how many of the people are in which camp, for that matter. I wonder if the Marshal-General does."

Blank looks from the others.

"Never mind. We're going to take these people home and see what we have to work with."

"Home?"

"Their vill. Where their houses are. And we're going to get their livestock back, and their other possessions if we can."

Two days later, the villagers were back in their homes and the mixed cohort was camped in one of the fields. Stray sheep and goats had been brought back in.

"They'll come again," Dorthan said.

"I hope so," Arcolin told him. "We will be here."

On the fourth day, a large group of mage-hunters appeared, perhaps a third of them mounted, led by a man in a Marshal's tabard.

"Your Marshal?"

"He was," Dorthan said. "He's not my Marshal now."

"What's his name?"

"Coben," Tamis said.

Arcolin rode out toward the approaching mob.

"You there!" the Marshal said. "Magelord of Tsaia—you don't belong here!"

Arcolin laughed. "Marshal Coben," he said. "The one who does not belong here is a traitor to Gird, an oathbreaker."

"I'm not the oathbreaker. That woman in Fin Panir—"

"You mean the Marshal-General?"

"That *woman* in Fin Panir, who should never have been a Marshal, let alone Marshal-General—*she* is the oathbreaker."

"Not according to Gnarrinfulk," Arcolin said. "The Gnarrinfulk prince believes she has broken no oaths but your kind has . . . you have trespassed on gnomish lands—"

"Only to kill mages. We haven't hurt anything."

"You spilled human blood on gnome land. You broke Gird's own oath to Gnarrinfulk, that humans would never trespass. To Gnarrinfulk, you are *kteknik*—outlaws—for breaking that old contract."

"It was hundreds of winters ago! We cannot be bound by something we never swore to."

"You are bound by your Marshal-General's word, which she and every other Marshal-General since Gird swore to," Arcolin said. Some of the others in the mob were listening now, then murmuring to those behind them. "Gnarrinfulk has no patience with *kteknik* humans: for gnomes, to be outside Law is to be outside life."

"*You* are outside law," the Marshal said. "You are a mage, and in the Code of Gird—"

"I am not a mage, and the Code of Gird does not support killing children."

"They're mages! Evil!"

Arcolin heard hoofbeats behind him. He hoped it was not the captain again.

"Sir." A quiet young voice. Not the captain, then. Kaim.

"Yes?"

"Captain Cracolnya says the mule has foaled a cow." A pause. "A three-legged cow with one left horn."

Another force, not quite as large as this, approaching from the west.

"How interesting," Arcolin said. He could not be sure Marshal Coben had heard. In the interest of greater confusion, he raised his voice. "Well, Marshal, did you hear? The mule has foaled a cow."

The Marshal paled. "A . . . *cow*?"

What was that about? He'd never heard of a Marshal afraid of cows. "A cow, yes."

"What color cow?"

The Company had never used cow colors in their code, only the number of cows, legs, and horns. What color cow would most confuse this Marshal? Arcolin took a guess. "Dun," he said.

"You lie! *You* have never seen Gird's Cow! You are not a true yeoman of Gird!"

Gird's Cow? Was the man wit-wandering? But if it distracted him . . . "Yes, dun," Arcolin said cheerfully. "A very nice cow, in fact." He didn't mention the three legs or one horn.

"If you were really Girdish and Gird supported you, then an army of Gird would march over that hill—" Marshal Coben flung out his right hand, pointing to the west. "But since you are not . . ."

"Look at the hill," Arcolin said. Out of the corner of his eye, he had seen movement there, and now, rising above the crest, was a Girdish blue banner with a device he did not recognize at first. Not the "G" for Gird or the entwined "GL" for Gird/Luap. It looked more and more like . . . a cow.

CHAPTER THIRTY-FOUR

s the force carrying the banner crested the hill, Arcolin could see that several were Girdish knights and more were Marshals, with ranks of yeomen behind them.

"That's hers—the mage-lover's!" Coben turned in his saddle, yelling at his followers. "Get ready to fight."

The approaching force halted partway down the slope. One of the riders, a Marshal, trotted toward the vill; Arcolin did not turn to watch. That would be someone sent to find out who the soldiers in maroon and white were and reassure the villagers that the newcomers were not mage-hunters. He backed his mount a few paces; no use getting caught in the melee or mistaken for one of these.

When he heard hoofbeats behind him again, he thought it must be Kaim with another message from Cracolnya, but instead he heard a voice from the previous year.

"My lord Duke . . . I did not expect to find *you* here."

"Arvid!" He had to look. Arvid indeed, only instead of a merchant's garb, he wore a Marshal's tabard and insignia. "You're a *Marshal*?"

"I also find it hard to believe," Arvid said. "You should hear the rest of it, but I have a message to deliver." He turned to Marshal Coben, who was staring at him.

"Coben, you have broken your oath to the Marshal-General; you are summoned to the Marshalate for judgment." Arvid's voice rang out over the murmuring of Coben's followers.

"That mage-loving viper—"

"Should you refuse to appear, your name will be summarily struck from the rolls of Marshals, and you will be declared outlaw in all Fintha, bait for any man's sword. In the meantime, you are no longer Marshal of Norwalk Grange; another Marshal will take over."

"Who?"

"Me." The faintest hint of amusement in that, then Arvid's tone hardened again. "By order of the Marshal-General of Gird and the Judicar-General. You will hand over your medallion and your tabard—"

"I will *not*!"

"—or it will be confiscated." A long pause during which Coben turned purple. "Also by me."

"You would not dare!"

"Oh, Coben . . ." Arvid's voice had gone honey-sweet. "You have no idea what I would dare." His gaze swept over Coben's followers. "Nor have they." Several of them moved back, bumping into those behind them.

Arcolin grinned. He had wondered from time to time how the former thief-enforcer was getting along in Fin Panir—would he really stay in the Fellowship? And if he did, what would that do to the Fellowship? And here he was, confronting a bad Marshal and . . .

"So you have a choice, Coben. Hand over medallion and tabard—and the keys to the grange if you have them on you—and be escorted to Fin Panir for judgment. Or do not and end the day with your guts strewn on the ground like a wolf-killed sheep."

"I'm not giving up anything to *you*," Coben said. "You don't scare me, mage-lover."

"Good," Arvid said. "I was hoping for that." He looked past Coben again. "And what about you lot? Going to give up or fight with Coben?"

"Fight," said a number of them, but not, Arcolin noticed, all. Some toward the back were already edging away, watching the Girdish formation on the hill.

"Perfect," Arvid said. He raised his arm twice. The Girdish formation started forward. Then he spurred his horse so it leapt toward Coben's and sliced Coben's throat side to side with a blade like a small sickle. Blood gushed out, turning Coben's blue tabard garish red. Arvid stiff-armed him, and Coben slid sideways from the saddle, one hand still clutching the rein, the other the hilt of a sword he had not yet drawn, his feet caught in the stirrups.

Before Coben's men reacted, Arvid's horse had spun, kicked out behind, and leapt out of reach of their sticks and hauks. Coben's horse, ears flat and nostrils flared, kicked out at anyone who approached, shying and whirling as Coben's weight dragged at the saddle and his blood soaked the ground. In the same pleasant tone, Arvid said, "I'm glad you made it so easy, Coben. And the rest of you . . . You want a fight—you've got one."

The Girdish formation on the hill moved with perfect discipline, weapons ready. The mob Coben had led did not. Some rushed at the Girdish, some hung back, some tried to run away.

"Do you plan to kill them all?" Arcolin asked Arvid. His breath came short. He had not expected Arvid's instant attack on Coben or the way he'd killed the man. Surely that blade was more thieflike than Girdish.

"This mob, all in one or in pieces, has terrorized a quarter of the realm, killing more than a hundred sixty," Arvid said, his voice cold as winter. "Men, women, children, they didn't care. Yesterday they wiped out an entire village. And they've caused trouble with the gnomes and with Tsaia—which I suppose is why you're here and not in Valdaire."

"Yes," Arcolin said. "The king's worried."

Arvid nodded. "So I thought. And so, yes, I plan to kill them all. The Marshal-General has tried reasoning with them, but it does no good."

"It may cause trouble after."

"She knows that. But it leaves the innocents like the people in this vill alive."

The battle once joined was short and brutal, the outcome inevitable. Afterward, as the sun set, Arcolin, Arvid, and a High Marshal named Donag sat in Arcolin's tent. Arvid had spent most of his time with the villagers, reassuring them and explaining the Marshal-General's intentions. Now he explained them to Arcolin.

"She's made progress in the northwest," he said. "Fin Panir and the land around it. Also most of the land north of the Honnorgat, downriver almost to Hoorlow."

"They were never as fervent about Gird up there," Donag put in. "That's why there's trouble on the Tsaian border—those mage-hunters moved east, found allies there."

"And south," Arcolin said. "The Gnarrinfulk gnomes have seen too many people coming across their boundary, including mage-hunters killing people on their land."

"Marshal-General was worried about that," Donag said. "That's one reason she chose him." He pointed his elbow at Arvid. "Saw you knew him. Proof things change. Never had a Thieves' Guild enforcer as a Marshal before."

"Never needed one before," Arvid said, just loud enough to be heard.

"What he won't tell you," Donag went on, "is how he saved nearly all the children of a grange in Fin Panir from mage-hunters who'd taken them and hidden out in a wool warehouse."

"Short version: I came too late for three," Arvid said, red to the ears.

"*And* had already been learning so much so fast, it spooked people. *And* when he took his Marshalate oath, he lit up the whole High Lord's Hall, convincing some he was a mage himself." Donag was grinning at Arvid.

"It was Gird," Arvid said.

"Of course it was Gird. Wanted us to notice the mage-haters in the group, no doubt."

"How's your son?" Arcolin asked, changing the subject for Arvid's sake. "Is he coming to stay here now that you're Marshal?"

"No, he's in Fin Panir. Good people are taking care of him. I don't expect I'll be here long, but as High Marshal Donag said, the Marshal-General wanted me here because of the Gnarrinfulk, because Dattur and I were friends and I speak a fair bit of gnomish."

"You should talk to them," Arcolin said. "I'll introduce you."

"You know them?"

"Hmm. Yes. Remember what Dattur said about me being a gnome

prince? I didn't really—it was hard to believe—until I had a message from the Aldonfulk prince, and he gave me this stole—" Arcolin pulled it out. "Dattur is now my hesktak—my advisor in legal matters that a prince must know. Lord Prince Aldonfulk and I communicate by regular courier, and when my king told me the Gnarrinfulk were threatening to invade Tsaia and Fintha both, Aldonfulk provided me guides and envoys to the Gnarrinfulk prince."

"What did he say? Are they going to invade?" Donag asked.

"They accept the Marshal-General as the legal ruler of Fintha," Arcolin said. "They understand now that the mage-hunters alone have breached the old contract between Gird and Gnarrinfulk, and they consider mage-hunters *kteknik*, outlaws. The main reason for that is the child killing. They found a child's hacked corpse on their land, and that's what really set them off. They have offered help to the Marshal-General and to my king. Since I have met you, High Marshal, and you, Marshal Arvid, I assume I have made the required contact with the Marshal-General's forces and can now go tell my king where the situation stands."

Donag nodded. "After today, we should be able to get back through to Fin Panir with no difficulty. I may be able to attend the fair at Hoorlow after all. You, Arvid, will have to miss it this year."

"The fair at Hoorlow?" Arcolin had never heard of Hoorlow.

"Annual celebration," Donag said. "You're Girdish; you must remember the Battle of Grahlin."

"When the Sier took the water out of a river, forced it up a well, melted a fort, and Gird lost the battle."

"Yes, that one. Well, after the war, that Sier was dead, like most of them, and people moved in. Found Grahlin itself full of dangerous things, especially the Sier's old palace, so they tore most of it down and rebuilt it on the outskirts, nearer the river. That's Hoorlow, lower and near the Hoor. It's grown, of course, some of it back up the rise into what was Grahlin."

"And they have a fair," Arcolin prompted.

"Yes. Where they reenact the Battle of Greenfields every year. The one Gird won, the last big battle of the war." Donag had a straight face, but his eyes twinkled.

Arcolin laughed. "I suppose that makes sense. Nobody's going to reenact a battle they lost, and without mages, nobody could reproduce the spouting well anyway."

"Exactly. I doubt they did that in Gird's day, but sometime after that whoever was Marshal-General started coming to Hoorlow's fair and presiding over the mock battle. It's a great time . . . three times the population or more for the week of the fair. Inns and taverns make most of their year's income. Competitions for everything you can imagine. Marshals and High Marshals in Fin Panir vie for the honor of escorting the Marshal-General. We get to command the enemy, you see. Stand around in plumed helmets and wear what's left of the ancient robes found in magelord palaces. Of course, then we have to die ingloriously, but . . . I've always enjoyed it."

"Die ingloriously? She didn't tell me *that* when she invited me to this year's," Arvid said, putting on a look of horror.

"She never does, the first time," Donag said. "That's part of the fun for the rest of us. Anyway, you're not going; *you'll* be here trying to talk 'it is that' and 'is it that it is' with a lot of sober, industrious gnomes and learn the local peasant dialect, perfectly safe from inglorious fake death while exposed to the real thing. Life of a Marshal. Whatever Gird wants."

"Why do you have a cow on your banner?" Arcolin asked. "Is it that rumor I heard about a cowhide on sticks someone was calling Gird's Cow last spring?"

"That story made it to Tsaia? Yes, that happened. It stank." Donag finished off his mug of sib. "They're very earnest, the Gird's Cow people. They sing songs about Gird's Cow. Badly. But Marshal-General, she thought it was a good idea, says Gird did, too, and they've got a man whittles these little cows—" He pulled a cow-shaped piece of wood out of his shirt. "Arvid's got one, too, and Marshal-General . . . most of us. Mage-hunters hate 'em. So now Salis and his crew are trying to carve a cow-size cow. They were draggin' that other all over, and people started cuttin' bits off the hide to take home and tack up. And then some mage-hunters poured oil on it and set fire to it. This way it'll be solid, Marshal-General says."

"Do they sing about what color cow?" Arcolin asked, thinking of the dead man's reaction to what he'd said.

"Yes, indeed: dun. Gird's favorite cow color. Least important thing about Gird, if you ask me, is what color cow he liked. We've never taught that in the granges. A cow is a cow." He poured himself another mug of sib. " 'Course, where I grew up we milked goats."

"When do we meet the Gnarrinfulk gnomes?" Arvid asked, ignoring Donag.

"Soon," Arcolin said. "Tomorrow I'll take you—"

"Excuse me, my lord." Kaim stuck his head in the tent. "There's a gnome to see you."

"Timing," murmured Arvid, "is everything."

A rcolin and his squire Kaim rode into Vérella before Autumn Court, having left his mixed cohort on Duke Elorran's lands to bolster that duke's almost nonexistent local militia and patrol the western border. He had sent word ahead that the Gnarrinfulk threat no longer existed and that the gnomes were acting in support of the Marshal-General, so felt free to visit Calla's parents before going to the palace.

"Had a letter just yesterday," her father said. "She's in good health. Jamis, too, though he took a tumble off a horse. Wanted to ride a real horse, down in the village, apparently. No harm done."

"You're back early, aren't you? It's a full tenday to the Evener," her mother said. "And who's this with you?"

"Yes, I'm early," Arcolin said. "And this is Kaim, my squire. Count Halar's son."

"Surely you're hungry, a tall lad like you," she said to Kaim. "I've baking fresh from this morning."

Kaim looked at Arcolin. "Go ahead," Arcolin said. "I should go to the palace now, but I won't need you—bring your horse along later." To Calla's father: "They'll take them at the palace—no need for them to be eating your fodder."

At the palace, he met Duke Marrakai in the courtyard. "Did you hear the news?"

"I sent some news—is this about the Gnarrinfulk gnomes?"

"No . . . the dragon. The dragon came to Mikeli and told him

Camwyn is still alive but has no memory of his past. Mikeli . . . Well, you were not here all summer; you do not know how it's been. He blamed himself, though we all knew it was not his fault. He was sure Camwyn had died and the dragon had chosen not to tell him. Now . . . he is grieved, of course, that his brother has no memory but rejoices that he lives."

"Where is Camwyn? Here?"

"No. Somewhere in the dragon's care. The dragon said it would be a long, slow process—that Camwyn can now walk a little but must relearn everything he learned as a child. Mikeli agreed not to search for him; the dragon promises a good future."

"Any more iynisin problems?"

"None. Thank Gird and Falk and all the gods there are. Of course we have other problems, magery not least among them. Mikeli let us read your courier's letter . . . Did you get to see Elorran?"

"Yes. And he does have the scars you mentioned all over the side of his head, and one eye's gone. The other's blind now. A sad case. They keep him tied upright in a chair by day and locked in at night. His steward's done his best, but with no help from Elorran—not even a sensible word from day to day—he's struggled to keep the holding together."

"Do you think it was magery?"

"How could it be magery?"

"I don't mean an injury made by magery—but an attack by someone who thought he had magery. Or maybe he did and they wanted to destroy it."

"But who?"

"Someone in the family. Afraid of having it known."

Arcolin shuddered. "That kind of fear . . . that hatred . . . it hasn't saved us from real dangers, like iynisin or blood mages. It's just made people kill and hurt those who have done nothing wrong."

"Indeed. Come to us for dinner while you're in the city. Oh—and Gwenno's now in the Bells and wildly happy about it. Now the older of the Mahieran girls at home is clamoring to train there. I don't suppose you want a girl squire . . . ?"

"No," Arcolin said. "Not one in the royal family, anyway."

When he reached the king's office, the king did look less strained than he had before. "You sent good news, Duke Arcolin."

"I just heard better news from Duke Marrakai," Arcolin said. "Prince Camwyn alive—"

"Yes. Though not likely to return. However, at Midsummer Court, the Council—in your absence but with, I told them, your concurrence—agreed to Rothlin's marriage to Ganlin of Kostandan when she has finished her training. Roth is happy, and I am momentarily off the hook where marriage is concerned, though I expect the nudging and winking will start again soon."

"Do you want to marry?"

Mikeli sighed. "Yes, but not with all the trouble it takes, on top of other troubles. You didn't marry for years, possibly for some of the same reasons. When Queen Arian was visiting . . . well . . . a queen like that would brighten the whole palace. But she was not happy here, though she was courteous about it. So there's a tangle: if the kind of woman I feel attracted to dislikes the life I must lead—and she must lead—then by marrying her I make her unhappy. I don't want to do that." He shook his head.

"I hope you don't have to wait as long as I did," Arcolin said.

"At least you didn't have people nagging you about it from the moment your mother died," Mikeli said.

CHAPTER THIRTY-FIVE

Dorrin roused to the feel of hot sun on her back and legs and uncomfortably hard lumps under her. She opened salt-crusted eyes—they stung, and she blinked repeatedly—to see in front of her a glare of sunlit sand and . . . under and immediately around her body . . . a dazzle of jewels, most blue and white. More jewels than she had carried with her, more jewels than she had imagined existed.

She lay blinking for some moments, then shifted stiff limbs and aching back—why aching?—only then remembering the blow that might have severed her spine if it had landed with all its force. She had fallen into the sea, tried to swim, but her legs would not respond. She remembered sinking . . . looking up to see the water's surface from underneath, a long narrow shadow that must have been the galley, then deeper and deeper. Vague memories then of the light fading, fish flashing past in silver and blue, and other sea creatures staring at her. Then, in the dim green-blue light, a time of rest on soft mud. She could not have been breathing . . . but she did not recall feeling any distress.

What, then? Swimming? Walking? No, being pushed or pulled or carried or otherwise moved through the water.

Surely it had been too long for a human to stay alive underwater. But past the initial moments, she remembered no fear, no struggle not to breathe, no helpless gasp for air that filled her mouth with bitter saltwater. Just peace and strange noises—squeaks and clicks—she had never suspected lay beneath the waves.

Perhaps a dream? But the pain in her back proved—when she put her hand back to feel it—a definite bruise. Surely she couldn't dream so realistic a bruise. She sat up finally, the jewels she had lain on shifting beneath her, coalescing into a narrower and taller heap until she sat on a sort of chair. She felt weight pressing on her head, a rim on her brow, and, lifting her hands, met a familiar shape—the crown she had first seen in the hidden niche of her study.

"You," she said aloud, her voice hoarse.

No words this time but a sense of joy.

From her seat, she looked up and down the shore. Sand nearby, a long stretch of it, but in the distance a headland of dark rock. Aside from the strange seat on which she rested, no sign of humans—no footprints on the sand, no sails on the sea. Inland, the sand rose to dunes, and behind that more dunes, and some distance away—she could not tell how far—rough rocky hills backed by higher mountains. No grass, no trees. Rock and sand alone and the jewels that now gave back the sun's light.

"This is Aare," Dorrin said. "And this is where you wanted to come. Give back your water, then, and restore the land."

You. Your magery.

"I don't know how." Looking around again, Dorrin saw no sign at all of fresh water or anything that might be food. Though the sea might be full of creatures, she had no idea which were edible or how to find and catch them. For a moment that was funny—a woman brought up inland, in forested country, skilled with bow and sword, now alone on a sandy shore where none of her skills—or for that matter the bow and sword, if she'd had them—had use.

You go here.

Into her mind came a vision of a place and a sense of direction: inland, past those mountains, a void in the land wider than she could see across . . . rocky cliffs in different colored rock down to a lumpy, unlevel bottom . . . what a huge lake or inland sea might look like, she realized, without its water. Near the rim of it, the ruins of three towers and a tumble of fallen white stones around them. A thread of trail down, a flat place, a circle of something flat and pale. Sand? Dried mud? She could not tell.

The vision faded, but the sense of direction did not.

Queen of Water . . . bring us there.

While she sat there, the sun and breeze had dried her; her boots and her leather jerkin were still damp. But she had nothing in which to carry the jewels that made up her seat . . . and though a shirt had held the bones from the well, it would not hold these. And besides— she had no water, no food, nothing but the clothes she wore and the crown on her head.

Then the goblet from the set of regalia rose in front of her as the crown had done before.

Drink.

The goblet moved closer. She reached out, took it, brought it to her lips. Cool water eased her salty lips, ran down her throat . . . she only then remembered the frightening verse engraved in its rim. But nothing bad happened.

You are the Queen of Water.

Dorrin stood; the stones slithered down from the seat shape into a pavement beneath her feet that extended perhaps ten strides in front of her in the direction she felt sure was right. Well, then . . . she took a step; the jewels supported her in the sand.

"Won't that damage you?" she asked, not entirely sure whom she meant.

You are the Queen of Water; you cannot hurt your element.

Dorrin walked forward; the jewels rustled along the sand on either side of her, moving to the front of the strip as fast as she walked. It was easier to walk on than loose sand. The regalia that had not attached itself to her—the crown to her head, the rings to her fingers, the necklace now draped around her neck—floated along on either side.

Once on top of the first dunes, she turned and looked back to shore. Far out, sun caught the curve of a sail, but the rest of the water lay empty of ships. She could not see land beyond it. She walked on that afternoon, first down the back side of the first dunes, then between two of the next, coming to higher, firmer ground inland as skeins of cloud to the west took color from the sun as it set. Behind her now the sea seemed a glistening sheet of darker blue; off in the distance she could see an island jutting up, white cliffs catching the sun. Was that Whiteskull, the island the captain had warned of as a pirate lair? Or another? East along the coast, the dark headland showed that it ran back to the mountains still distant from her.

Here the ground was hard and lumpy, mixed gravel and rock; she thought briefly of turning back to the dunes for a more comfortable place to sleep, but the jewels still moved before her, smoothing her way. Only when it was completely dark did movement stop. Then, as her legs failed her and she stumbled and nearly fell, the jewels once more rose, this time shaping a hollowed surface long enough to lie down in.

Rest. You are safe.

After all that had happened, that seemed foolish, but she saw nothing around for brigands to live on. She lay down on the jeweled couch rather than the stony ground, wondering how cold it would be . . . but the jewels shifted around her, and soon she was comfortable and warm.

When she woke the next morning, the first thing she saw were white-robed figures standing in a circle around her couch. She sat up, the jewels rearranging themselves, slithering quickly to make her seat.

"It is the One," one of them said. She saw no sign of rank, but they all bowed to her when that one moved his hand.

"Who do you think I am?" Dorrin asked.

"The One who was to come, the Healer for the land."

"And who are you?"

"Those who watch for the One." Not the same speaker but another. "It is time. Will you have food before we go?"

Her stomach rumbled. "Yes, thank you."

Food was a dry, nearly tasteless slab of what Dorrin guessed was unleavened bread and a piece of dried meat, hard as wood. "Suck on it," one of them said. "It will soften."

Dorrin took a couple of bites of the breadlike slab, then stood. The jewels shimmered as they rearranged into a path again. The watchers bowed.

"So it is true, as we were told. It is all true, and the end will come."

That sounded ominous, but the crown gave no warning. Dorrin took a step on her jeweled path; the goblet floated to a convenient height, and she sipped from it.

"My name is Dorrin," she said. "May I hear yours?"

Quick glances around the group, and one finally bowed and said, "As the Queen of Water wishes. I am Silig and bear within me two hands of those who came before."

The next in line bowed. "I am Cebrig and bear within me two hands and one of those who came before."

"Wait—" Dorrin interrupted the recitation, suddenly revolted. "Do you mean you . . . you kill a younger to transfer your . . . your essence—?"

"No! That is abomination!" said Silig, dark eyes flashing. "I am this-born, youngest of my heritage, and came to watcher at twenty, when Herrin died, who came to watcher when Orig died, who came to watcher when Ilfin died, who came to watcher—" he went on, all ten of them. "They live in me, my elders, for only thus can humans approach the wisdom of the Elder Kin, whom surely you know, for they departed to the lands you came from."

"It was done willingly, then?"

"Of course. It is the greatest gift and honor one of us can have, to cradle those who cradled us and let them see the end of their long waiting, which now has come. Should we let them die wholly, with their hopes yet unfulfilled?"

"Er . . . no. But—do you know of the other, of killing someone to transfer one's own mind?"

Now they all glared at her. "Did you such a thing?"

"No. But I knew those who did. That is how it was done in the north. I had not heard of . . . of cradling elders down the generations."

"Your elders died wholly?"

"*My* elders did what you call abomination," Dorrin said. The harshness in her voice surprised her. "They used blood—" She stopped as all the watchers turned their backs.

Silig turned around finally. "To make these—" He pointed at the jewels. "—of blood, that is the worst of all. We cannot . . . we cannot hear it."

"I will not tell it," Dorrin said.

"And you did no such thing?"

"Never."

"And you bear the crown, the necklace, the rings: none of evil can handle them. Tell me, Queen of Water, does the crown speak to you?"

"Yes, it does. It told me to come here."

"Then please come with us and do not speak of that other again."

They began again, climbing steadily up the barren slopes of stony hills, heat rising from the rock in waves . . . but the path of jewels was cool beneath Dorrin's feet and smoothed her way. The watchers did not attempt to step onto it. Finally Dorrin asked them why they did not.

"Only the One may set foot upon the sacred," said Qaraf. "It is not for us. It is for you and because you are bringing it home."

That day and the next they worked their way to the foot of the mountains. Dorrin looked back now and then to the shimmer of the water behind. The view widened as they climbed; she could now see distant islands and a smudge that might be another island or the nearest part of the shore of Aarenis.

When she was thirsty, the goblet came near and gave her water. None of the others would drink of it but sipped now and then from waterskins.

As they neared the mountains, Dorrin saw shattered rock, red and black spires of it, and nothing more. Higher up the slopes—no trees, no bushes. Her guides led her straight toward a cliff; she wondered how they would climb it, for she could see no trail. Then one vanished into the rock, and she followed into a narrow cleft, as if someone had cut the rock with a sword . . . but not a straight cut. The cleft twisted, divided, rejoined, climbing up stone steps that looked as if water had once flowed down them . . . then leveled again, twisted, climbed.

Traversing the mountains took days; Dorrin lost count of them. Her guides knew of a few scant sources of water. "For sometimes a rain comes from the sea, and the rock holds it." The watchers had, over the years, enlarged sheltered basins to store this rainwater. They had also tunneled out from these—over how many years, Dorrin could not imagine—to create lookout points from which they could observe long stretches of the shore.

"We knew the One would come," Silig said. "And as the years passed and the life of the land failed, those we now cradle prepared for the years of duty ahead. From here we see all that come to these shores . . . though . . . in my lifetime . . . not all these watch stands were watched. Not all still hold water enough."

Dorrin looked out the hole in the rock, down across the barren hills to the barren dunes, and then to the sea. The sails of three ships caught the light; more islands than shc had known of studded the sea, though she could not tell if people dwelt there.

"How are so many of you here, then? Is the place the crown told me of nearby?"

"No, Queen of Water. It is many days' journey inland. But three or four winters ago, the Guardians had received a sign and said the veil had been drawn aside and the One would come in the lifetime of those young enough. We were sent, all the watchers, to be sure that the One would find welcome and guides. We were in each of the watch places, all along the coast, and when one of us saw you wash ashore with those—" He pointed to the jewels. "—word passed to the others. As many of us as could went down to meet you."

She could have died before they arrived. But perhaps not; she'd had pure water to drink, and a few days' fast would not have been fatal. The watchers themselves needed water and food . . . they could not have gone from shore to the water basins even every other day.

For several days more they followed steep trails up and steep trails down, sleeping each night near one of the water sources. Dorrin lost track of the days, for the crown had begun to sing, and the song in her head distracted her from anything as mundane as counting the days that passed. The song sounded of water now . . . drips at first, then trickles, then the chuckling of a small stream. What words she could discern were few, "almost" and "soon" and "closer." The jewels that laid a path for her feet made a couch each night for her rest and a seat whenever she needed one.

Finally they came out of yet another narrow cleft to look down a slope to barren country below. Far off, a lighter color might be dunes, Dorrin thought, but nearer, it was clear the land was mostly rock and gravel, undulating toward the south. Waves of hot air shimmered in the sun, and a hot breeze flowed up to touch her face. Dorrin squinted through the heat haze and thought she saw a huge lake shining in the distance.

"Is that water salt?" she asked, pointing.

"It is not water at all," Silig said. "It is the lure that the Liar puts out to tempt the wanderer away from what little water there is. We will spend the day in this shade and start at dusk, for the plain is hotter than the mountains."

Dorrin slept poorly in the afternoon; heat radiated from the rocks, and despite the cool of the jewels beneath her, the hot air from below seemed to scorch her face.

At dusk, her guides offered her a white robe like theirs. "The night will be cold, and tomorrow we can offer no shelter from the day's sun. In this you may rest."

The robe felt strange over her clothes—not as harsh as most wool nor yet as smooth as silk. They walked through the night under brilliant stars, pausing once to eat. As the stars faded near dawn, Dorrin looked back; the mountain range stood dark against the paling sky, but as she watched, sunlight picked out one peak after another as if a flame were skipping along the crest.

They walked on until the stifling heat slowed them. Dorrin had water to drink, but the glare and heat made her dizzy. They crouched in the meager shade of waist-high rocks scattered across the slope, each with the robe's hood pulled across the face. Dorrin tried to doze but found it impossible.

As soon as the sun was down, the air cooled again, and once more they set out. Day after day the same routine—walk at night, try to sleep by day. The mountains receded behind them to a line on the sky visible only at dawn and dusk.

Finally, she saw ahead of them a cluster of white stone huts and three broken towers surrounded by looming dunes of red sand, the place of her earlier vision. When they came to it, more white-robed figures came out, bowing to her and gesturing that she should enter one of the huts. Inside it was cooler, and she slept awhile, grateful for the protection of the walls and roof. In early morning, they took her from the village to see the rim of a vast bowl.

"Here," said one who named himself a Guardian. "Here is where it will be. We will guide you."

For the rest of that day she stayed in the hut, out of the burning sun, while the people made some preparation she did not understand, chanting in a strange tongue near one of the broken towers. She felt no anxiety, as she had felt none since she had come to the deck of the galley. Whatever was meant to happen would happen.

Before dawn, the white-robed Guardians woke her. Overhead the stars were bright, giving enough light so that the Guardians made vague shadows. The trail the Guardians led her on was steep and rough, but the jewels fashioned steps for her and she did not slip. Nor did she peer over the side into the darkness below. What she had seen from the rim was frightening enough. If she slipped—

You are safe.

For now. As they descended, the night seemed darker, with the dark walls rising around and cutting off most of the starry sky. Then a soft glow rose from beneath her, as if water reflected the starlight. One of the Guardians muttered; the two in front turned to look. Both bowed low but said nothing and turned away from that glow, tapping with their sticks as they had before.

Through the rest of the night, Dorrin walked in that light, never slipping.

As night faded into predawn, they were on the last slope down to the floor of the vast bowl, its rim black against the lightening sky. Here the path's zigzag way showed pale, worn by many years of travel, less rough than on the harder rocks above. By the time the sky was a clear blue and sun touched the rim behind them, they had reached the floor—not a level plain, as it had looked from above, but humped and hummocked with drifts of sand caught in heaps of fallen rock, threaded by ancient channels of running water.

But shortly before midday, with the sun beating down and glaring off the white sand and clay, they came to the place the Guardians insisted was ordained: a circle of bare white clay, hard as bone. Now the Guardians formed their own circle around it and motioned to Dorrin where she should stand. They began a low chant; she could not understand the words.

The Guardian of Guardians stepped forward, followed by two who each held small stone jars. He held out his hand; one poured something into it. He crouched, holding his hand low over the center of the circle.

Dorrin watched carefully. Whatever it was flowed like water or . . . sand, she realized, as with a movement of his hand he drew on the flat white surface with a line of color, rust-red. Moment by moment, the design grew, forming a pattern she had never seen but that throbbed with power long before it was complete. Other colors joined the red: blue, yellow, green, black, white, each from its own jar one of the helpers held out to him.

She recognized some of the symbols—the image of the Sunlord, Esea, the Stormlord, Rainbringer, Barrandowea, the familiar wheat sheaf of Alyanya, the circle of the High Lord. But the rest, though it teased her vision as the elven patterns had, she did not understand.

At times it seemed the design drew itself, but Dorrin saw the tension in the man's hand, the care with which he worked from the center outward. The center itself he left bare, perhaps a handspan across. He stepped back as the sun reached its zenith.

Wind died; the sun beat down. With a gesture, the Guardian of Guardians halted the chant.

"The One's seat is there," said one Guardian to Dorrin. He pointed not to her but to the empty center of the pattern.

Now, O Queen.

"How can I—I cannot walk on that—" The design would be ruined.

Let me go. Set me free.

"Be what you are," Dorrin said. Where the words had come from she could not have said. "Be what you are and where you should be . . . I set you free."

Familiar weight lifted from her head; the crown rose and floated above the pattern, then settled on the empty center. Within its brilliant circle, the bare clay showed white.

"Your water there," the Guardian of Guardians said.

The goblet hung in the air at her heart-hand. She took it, reached far out over the design, and poured. Water fell in a silvery ribbon, sparkling as it fell, into that circle . . . and rose, contained by the frame of the crown, to reach the jewels.

One by one, they burst, exploding with water, a river from each jewel, it seemed, water rising so fast that Dorrin and the Guardians were knee deep in a moment, the careful design on the sand covered . . . but still shimmering beneath the water, undisturbed. The jewels she had walked on, sat on, lain on, dissolved into more water; the water rose steadily, thigh-deep, waist-deep, still clear as crystal.

The light dimmed; Dorrin looked up to see clouds gathering overhead, blotting out the sun, dark as the summer rainstorms in the north, and in the next moment rain roared down to join the water rising up.

The water had motion now, tugging at her white robe; she struggled with it and got it off, the better to stand, to try to wade back to the distant wall of rock, but the current strengthened, pulling her into deeper water, and the rain fell so heavily she could not tell which direction to go. It pounded her head, her shoulders; she was soaked to the skin in the first moments; she could scarcely breathe. She would drown if she fell; she might drown standing up.

When the rain ceased to fall on her, she looked up to see a vast dark shape hovering over her like the roof of a house hanging in the air . . . beyond its protection, rain lashed the water, but here not even a drip fell from the creature above her. Staring at her was one large flame-colored eye; she realized, blinking water out of her eyes, that its sinuous neck had twisted around to watch her even as she sheltered under it.

"Are you wise, Dorrin Verrakai?"

The same question a dragon had asked Kieri, Arian, Mikeli, Arcolin. The same dragon? Who could tell?

"I have tried to learn wisdom," she said. "But I would not call myself wise."

"Did you know what you were bringing to this place? What would happen?"

"I knew the jewels were water enchanted into stone, the water that once nourished the land. I thought—the jewels told me, and I believed—that here they could restore the land, make it beautiful."

"And is dry land always ugly?"

This was ridiculous. The water was up to her chest now, her feet almost lifting off the ground beneath, and she was discussing beauty with a . . . a dragon? But under the gaze of that eye, half the height of her body at least, she could only go on, ignoring the chill tugging of the water, the sound of the rain beyond.

"It may be beautiful," Dorrin said, "if it was made by the gods to be dry. And such land may exist. But this land was made dry by error, by stealing its water to make jewels, baubles to decorate a crown or a box or a goblet. To make bracelets and rings and other decorations. That, I believe, was wrong."

"I have heard of you," the dragon said. "I have heard of you from those you know: Half-Song and Sorrow-King and two other kings. Have you heard of me?"

"You are the dragon," Dorrin said.

"Yes, I am Dragon. Do you know what dragons are?"

"Elders," Dorrin said.

"Transformation," the dragon said. "A dragon changes what it touches; it is our nature to change . . . and that nature requires wisdom not to ruin the world. Those jewels were transformed from water to stone by magery—the magery of your ancestors. You say it was wrong. I say it was not wise. But did you think what would happen to this land? Touch my tongue with yours and I will show you."

The dragon opened a vast maw edged with gleaming teeth longer than swords, and out came a tongue shimmering with heat. It came toward her a few fingerwidths above the water. The heat of it dried the water on her face, her hair. Touch *that* with her tongue? But Kieri had. Arian had. She opened her mouth and touched.

Warmth, no more. The fragrance and flavor of spiced bread. The tongue withdrew an armslength.

"You should see. Come onto my tongue and I will show you."

Dorrin reached, and the tongue advanced again, this time sliding under her arms, curling around them, and drawing her into the dragon's mouth, into that dry warm space like a small cave. The tongue she sat on now felt as firm as a plank, warm as wood in the sun. She looked out the dragon's mouth, past the teeth, into the maelstrom.

"I will rise," the dragon said.

Dorrin's view expanded; her breath caught as the dragon lifted higher and higher, then moved toward one rim of rock. What had been a vast empty bowl—too wide to see more than part of its rim—was now a lake, rising visibly. At the rim, streams of water poured down, brown torrents full of sand and rocks. Muddy water swirled into the clear that had risen from below.

"It is a great transformation," the dragon said. "This place was once a lake and is a lake again, and this lake had an outlet to the sea, a mighty river . . . and that river will flow again, and the sea itself may rise higher."

"That much water?" Dorrin asked. She could not imagine it.

"It might be. If every water stone the magelords made transformed at once . . . it might be that much water." The dragon sounded more thoughtful than alarmed. "It has been a long quiet time while the magelords slept and the transformations ceased. Now it is more interesting. It might even be more wise."

Dorrin stared out at the falling water, the flowing water, for what seemed days long, watching the water rip at the edge of the cliffs and rocks crumble. The dragon moved from time to time, giving her different views of the deluge . . . the ruins where she had stayed falling, sliding, dragged over the receding cliff to disintegrate in the churning waters of the great bowl. She hoped the people had escaped. Another side of the bowl, where black cliffs did not crumble as the waters climbed higher, so that a sheer black wall rose above the floor. The far side, where the rising water tore at and finally destroyed a natural dam of tumbled rock and went racing along four men high at the front, seeking the sea.

How long it rained and how long she watched, Dorrin could not tell. She slept and woke again; the sound of the water, the sight of it falling and falling, flowing and flowing, numbed her senses. Eventually she became aware that the rain had stopped and that it had been stopped for some time. She was standing on wet ground, with the dragon's snout not two strides away and one of its eyes staring at her.

"Did you expect to live through your adventure?" the dragon asked.

"No," Dorrin said.

"You did not think the waters of life would save you?"

"Not once they were nearly drowning me," Dorrin said. "But you came."

"Yes, but I am not a tool for humans to wield," the dragon said. "Your judgment was wise—no one could live through all your tasks. Wisdom is rewarded with wisdom's gifts, which are not what the recipient expects."

"Am I dead, then?" Dorrin asked.

"Not a wise question," the dragon said. "But no, you are not dead yet." Then the mouth opened, and Dorrin saw the true dragonfire and knew she would be consumed.

CHAPTER THIRTY-SIX

Hoorlow, Fintha

Marshal-General Arianya and her escort rode through the hot, dusty forest, its shade frayed by drought, leaves turning brown instead of yellow or orange. Usually it was cooler this time of year, making the trek to the Hoorlow Fair a pleasant diversion. That, it still was, especially with the good news from the south that the Gnarrinfulk gnomes did not blame her for the mage-hunters' behavior. Donag's report of Arvid dealing with the rogue Marshal startled her—the weapon was not standard Girdish issue—but after all, he was what he was, and now he was using his talents for Gird.

As she rode out of the forest, she saw Farfields Grange in the near distance, with the flags marking the "battlefield" already up and shifting in the light breeze. To her surprise, no delegation from the grange appeared to meet her.

Nearer, she saw that grange and barton empty, gates and doors open, despite the pole flying a blue flag that should have indicated its Marshal's presence. Beyond, in the city itself, streets were also empty. The merchants' wagons that should have been parked in the field set aside for them during the fair weren't there, and as she and the others rode toward the bridge, no one came out to see who had arrived.

Her skin prickled. Something was not at all right.

The bridge arched over the Hoor, and as she reached the higher point of the arch, she saw that only a trickle of water ran in it. The drought. Would rain come again? Nothing in the blank blue sky, dust-colored around the edges, promised rain. Ahead, down the main street that led to the larger market square, a crowd of people blocked her view of Grainmarket Grange, though she could see the roof with its blue banner. More people were pouring into the crowd from side streets, and whatever was going on looked too much like the mobs in Fin Panir.

"Trouble?" asked High Marshal Donag.

"Undoubtedly," Arianya said. "Let's hope it's not children in peril again. Though if it is, I hope Farfields being empty means they've gone to help protect them." She glanced at Sir Piter, who commanded the knights. "What do you think?"

"Trouble, definitely," he said. "And the most likely thing is someone's shown mage-powers. Another lynching wouldn't surprise me. Isn't this area known for—" He paused, clearly trying to find a polite way to say it.

"Stubborn refusal to admit things may have changed? Age-old superstitions? A firm belief in their own righteousness?" Arianya said. "Yes. I never had acknowledgment from the Marshal of Wetfoot Grange when I sent out my last letter on the topic." She sighed. "Well, whatever it is, we're here to deal with it. Let's go."

"We could work our way around, come at them from the far side," one of the other knights suggested.

"The Marshal-General does not sneak into cities or 'come at' fellow Girdsmen," Arianya said. Militarily it might make sense, but experience told her a straightforward approach would appeal to at least some of the crowd ahead.

They rode on, past side streets where those who had been hurrying toward the market square stopped abruptly, staring openmouthed at the mounted troop, until they neared the rear of the mob. When those at the back of the crowd heard the horses' hooves, they turned to look. Then, as she'd expected, they moved aside, making a passage. Gird's banner, the blue surcoats, all the symbols of the Fellowship on the riders and the horses' tack, had their effect.

"When did you hear?" someone shouted.

Arianya turned toward the voice; a man waved his hand.

"Hear what?" she said. "I came as I come every year for the fair and the battle. Is there more?"

A mutter ran through the crowd in which she heard her name and "magelords" before someone nearby said, "It's magery, that's what it is. Them magelords coming back. Want to rule us again. We're not having that."

"What's happened, then? No, wait—I'll want to speak to Marshal Pelis at Grainmarket—he's at the grange, I see."

"He's turned on Gird!" That angry voice was a woman's. "He's not Girdish, not really—he says we have to let 'em bide."

"I'll talk to him," Arianya said, and nudged her horse forward. The crowd opened just enough to let the riders through and closed behind them.

Marshal Pelis, square-built as a block of stone, stood in front of his closed grange door with two of his yeomen, all with hauks in hand. Arianya reined in. "Marshal—Gird's grace to you and your grange. I came for the fair—what is this?"

"It's trouble, Marshal-General."

"It's magelords!" screamed a woman in the crowd.

"It's damn fools workin' themselves up to mischief!" Pelis's bellow could have been heard at Farfields, Arianya thought.

"You're a coward, Pelis!" That was a man's voice, a sneering voice. "You just don't want to risk your own hide."

"Come face to face with me and say that," Pelis said. "I know you, Jenits Forgusson. You've not been at drill for a year, you drink too much, and the only time you make a fist is to hit your wife and childer. Man beats childer is the coward, I say. Gird didn't beat his."

Some in the crowd laughed; others stood stony-faced, silent. Not a good sign. Arianya smiled at Pelis, who gave her a short nod. "Let's see if the Marshal-General can straighten this out," she said, loud enough to be heard though not as loud as Pelis. "You all know me; I've been here year after year for the fair and the battle. You know the vill I came from, not two days' walk from here. Will you hear me?"

"Aye," came from most, though there were mutters as well.

"Well, then. I will hear what Marshal Pelis has to say, and then I will hear from Hoorlow Council. Then I will tell you what I think. In the meantime——" She glanced at the sun's angle. "——I think it's near nooning, isn't it? Time to have summat to eat. It'll take me a glass or so to hear everyone out."

Across the square, she saw people drifting away from the edge of the crowd. Those nearer, however, stood their ground, obviously intent on waiting it out. She smiled at them; they did not smile back. "It is market day, isn't it? We've traveled far; we're hungry. Donag, see to everyone's needs——I'm partial to a bit of old cheese and a garlic sausage."

She dismounted and turned to Marshal Pelis. "Let's go inside, Marshal. My head's had enough of this sun."

"Yes, Marshal-General." He led the way to the door. Arianya glanced back; the stubborn part of the crowd had taken a step nearer but been blocked by the mounted knights. She hoped everyone would have sense. She was sure someone wouldn't.

Grainmarket's interior held the group of accused mages: men, women, youths, children, one a babe in arms. Arianya ignored them for the moment, following Pelis to the platform, where she bowed to the relic in its niche.

"Gird's grace on this grange and all who enter," she said, turning to look at the group. She recognized a woman she'd seen the previous year selling dyed yarn, evenly spun. "I remember you," she said, approaching; the woman shrank back a little, pushing a child only hip-high behind her. "You're a spinner and dyer, aren't you?"

"Yes," the woman said, looking down. "Please . . . don't hurt 'im."

"I'm hoping no one will be hurt," Arianya said. She looked at the others, sure she must have seen some of them at the fair in previous years. Yes——that man——he'd brought a lathe and turned legs for chairs and smooth rounds for other uses. And that one, who'd had furls of cloth. "Are you all from Hoorlow?"

"Not all of them," Marshal Pelis said. "Some are from the vills about. Came here for sanctuary, some." He cleared his throat. "See here, Marshal-General, I know what you've wrote——you don't want childer killed, and I'm with that, but what about adults?"

"Adults?"

"Felis over there. Seen using magery to lift a stone."

Felis, skinny and tall, hunched his shoulders as Arianya looked at him. "You have the lifting magery?" she asked him. "When did it come?"

"Just after last year's fair, Marshal-General. I'd gone down in the back, couldn't work, and my old mother, she'd gone blind; she couldn't do much. So one night I said, like anyone might, too bad I'm not a mage, so's to lift stone another way, and next mornin' a half loaf of bread come to m'hand. I dropped it, bein' so startled, but then . . . I tried it again and it worked. Could move stone up to this size—" He held his hands apart. "And anything else that weight. Went back to work that day, and no trouble to anyone until a mage-hunter spied on our vill."

"It was that Haran," a woman said, and two others nodded. "Said she was on the way to see her sister's youngest, who'd just had a babe and sprained her ankle. Doby took her in, let her stay a day or so . . ."

"Haran?" Arianya said. "Where did she say she was from?" Haran, the Marshal who had been angry with Paks for "weakness" and whose relative had defended killing children with mage-powers and died in the trial of arms he demanded.

Shrugs, glances back and forth. Finally the first woman said, "Somewhere sunsetting or summerwards, I think, but I don't recall she gave a name."

"She's here," another said. "She and the other mage-hunters. It's them yelling for stoning and burning."

Marshal Pelis held up a hand, and the group fell silent.

"I don't think Gird wants anyone killed who hasn't done wrong," Arianya said. "I don't see that using magery is any more wrong than using a tool to make work easier. So, Marshal Pelis, you did right to bring these people into the grange and give them sanctuary. But we still have to convince the people outside."

"You know this area holds by traditions," he said. "They don't like change, and they believe magery is evil."

"It's not as evil as murder," Arianya said. "Unless it's used to murder. And I'm sure you'd have told me if any of these had used theirs to murder."

"Indeed I would. And they haven't. But I don't know how you're going to convince that mob in the square. They're convinced it's magery that's kept the rain from falling and the river from running. Made the marshes dry enough to walk across dry-shod."

"I must hope Gird gives me the words," Arianya said. "Perhaps he'll send rain—that might help."

"I doubt it," Pelis said. He sighed. "I reckon this is the day we'll all get our heads bashed in, but better that than giving up."

The people outside probably felt the same way, Arianya thought. "Is there a way out the back?" she asked. "Can these escape while we talk to the crowd out front?"

He shook his head. "They're already back there with weapons, lookin' to cut anyone down who comes out. I put yeomen there, but I don't know how long they can hold out."

"Then I must pray for Gird's aid and face whatever comes if it is not his will to grant it," Arianya said. She felt heavy and cold even though the day was, like all the days for too long, hot and bright. This might well be—probably was—the day she would die, and she could not argue that she deserved better. It was her leadership that had failed, as she had failed Haran in not noticing how the woman slid into arrogance and hatred. Her prayers as she and Pelis stood there were for the mages and the mage-hunters both, that they would come to find peace with one another. *No more hating,* she prayed. *No more killing.* Peace washed over her, and a fragrance of roses. Alyanya, at least, accepted that prayer.

At the door, High Marshal Donag tried to talk her out of going back outside. "You could let me talk to them—what if they kill you?"

"Gird died to prevent the killing of one innocent child," Arianya said. "Should I flinch from dying to prevent the massacre of a dozen?"

"It's not necessary—"

"It is very necessary. Not just that I'm the Marshal-General but that I'm the Marshal-General they've decided to hate. I must be the one in front."

"In armor, then."

"I'm crazy, perhaps," Arianya said. "But not stupid."

She moved toward the door; the others moved away, letting her through this time. She felt very unlike the way she had expected to feel . . . not heroic, not scared, not much of anything but determined. The children were innocent: that much she knew for sure.

Jeers from the crowd as she came into view. "You will not kill those children," she said. She spotted Haran wearing a Marshal's tabard, to which she was no longer entitled. Haran's expression mingled contempt and anger.

"They're mages! They're evil!" came from several sides.

"They're *children*. Gird wouldn't let you kill one child . . . I won't let you kill these!"

"Then we'll kill you." That was Haran's voice; others chanted their support. "Kill her! Kill her!"

"You can certainly try," Arianya said. "But you won't get to them until I'm dead. And I am not going down without a fight." She drew her sword.

Those in front of the mob, armed with hauks and ordinary sticks, stopped their advance at the sight of drawn swords. Five—she and four of Knights of Gird—were outside—enough to block the door. The children and the rest of the loyal Girdish were inside the grange.

The first arrow bounced off her chest plate, not even scratching it. A homemade bow, she judged, and not a good one. Or a good archer.

"Gird would not kill these children," she said, keeping her voice calm.

Growls and mutters from the crowd. Someone in the back began another chant: "Kill . . . kill . . . kill the demons." Voices joined until it made one roar, bouncing from wall to wall: "KILL! . . . KILL! . . . KILL! . . ." Another arrow struck, bounced away. One hit her helmet, hard enough to feel. Other arrows followed, aimed at the Girdish knights, but none penetrated. The first stone flew past, missing her head by a handwidth. Then one hit her helmet. Her vision blurred and darkened for an instant.

The very air thickened with malice, and she remembered the account one of the magelords in Kolobia had written of Gird's death— the thickened air, the way Gird had spoken words that seemed to condense all that anger and hatred into a darkness—a cloud?—that he then took in and swallowed and fell dead.

She needed those words, and she did not know them. The writer had not written them down. Possibly no one could write them down. She glanced up in time to see another shower of stones and beyond them, above the buildings, just such a darkness. Boiling, churning darkness like the most dangerous of summer storms, but silent . . . and under it a pallid sickly light that no one else seemed to notice felt completely and utterly wrong.

Words—I need the words—She sent the prayer as strongly as she could even as two stones hit her, shoulder and thigh, and one of the men beside her staggered and almost fell.

Nothing happens the same way twice. She did not recognize that voice.

The mage-hunters screamed at the crowd, the crowd roared, surged forward . . . and with a resonant thrum as if the heartstring of the world had been plucked, a blaze of light stabbed down, followed by a CRACK and then boom of thunder so loud Arianya was sure her ears were broken. She had an instant to see a line of black, blasted bodies between her and the rest of the crowd, with others fallen just behind them, when the water came.

It was not rain like any rain she'd been in before. Not individual drops at all, but water in a mass like tipping a barrel onto a fire: solid water, cold, heavy, drenching her in an instant. She couldn't see; she couldn't hear anything but a vast roar; she couldn't breathe. She bent over, trying to make an air space in front of her face; water bounced back up from the paving stones and splashed her face, but she could breathe in short gasps. Water pounded her back, soaking through the surcoat, the mail, the arming shirt. She was wet through in seconds; water ran down her drenched legs, filling her boots; it ran under the back of her helmet and around her head inside it, dripping out of the front, slightly warmer than the rest.

Despite the roar of the water, she heard the clatter of wood and the splat of wet cloth as market stalls collapsed under the pounding rain and the cries of those pushed to their knees by the force of the rain. Water rose on the stones of the street, flowing back down toward the Hoor; bits of trash floated by, fruit from the market, a basket, someone's head scarf, a stick long enough to have held up an awning. The city smells, the dirt, the trash, the jacks, combined with the fresh smell of the rain. She tried to look up; she could just see that the men beside her were down on their knees . . . and so was as much of the crowd as she could see before she ducked her head again to breathe.

A roof gave way somewhere nearby, with timbers cracking and a different tone of falling water added to the din. Her back was sore from being pounded; she felt she'd been beaten. The water ran clear over the stones now, all the dust and filth of a city street carried away. A frog swam by, then a small fish of the kind found in some wells. Still the water came down, as if the gods were filling the whole world with water. Now all she could smell was the water itself, the smell that rises from clean wells of pure water on a hot day.

As suddenly as it had started, the rain stopped. A ray of sunlight pierced the clouds. Arianya pushed herself to kneel upright, blinked, swiped the water from her eyes.

And there, in the sunlight, in a patch just large enough for it, stood a cow. A dun cow. A dun cow whose dry glossy coat gleamed in the sunlight. A cow with a garland of fresh flowers around its neck, roses and bluebells and snow-daisies. The cow looked around the square, then walked over to her as others also looked up and struggled to rise. Arianya could not move. A perfectly dry dun cow with a garland of flowers around its neck appearing suddenly in the street after such a rain? It could be only one cow.

The cow looked her in the eye with its mild gaze, then reached out and swiped her face with its rough tongue—part caress, part correction. Its breath smelled of mint and green grass and roses.

"Gird," Arianya said.

The cow swiped her with its tongue again. Arianya reached up and grasped the shiny horns, and the cow lifted its head, helping her stand. Joy burst through her; all doubt and guilt fled. Around her others were rising now, their faces filled with astonishment and joy instead of hatred and anger. They were alive. She was alive.

She stood with her hand on the neck of Gird's Cow, and the people stared.

"The cow's not wet," someone said.

"It's got flowers—they aren't wet!"

"It's Gird's Cow," Arianya said.

"But—"

And someone else interrupted. "Gird's Cow—I heared of that. But it was just a cow's hide over sticks, they said."

"Is anyone hurt?" Arianya asked. "We need to help them."

One of the knights walked over to the sodden, blackened bodies of the mage-hunters. "Naught we can do for these."

"We can bury them," Arianya said. "And mourn the hatred that brought them to this."

A fresh breeze sprang up, bringing more scents of wet grass, fresh flowers, hope. Now the clouds shifted apart, the sun gleaming on wet cobbles, the stones and bricks of houses, the wet clothes. Steam rose from the street as it dried.

The angry mob had dissolved into individuals—family members checking on one another, neighbors teasing neighbors about how they looked as if they'd gone swimming in the river, merchants too happy to have survived to complain about the collapsed stalls, the missing wares.

"Reckon we needed a good washin' out and coolin' off," one man said to Arianya. "We was all that hot and bothered."

"Reckon we all did," she said, wringing out her surcoat.

One by one people came up to pat Gird's Cow, who stood quietly, tail swinging gently back and forth. The wet caresses left no mark on the cow's shining coat. Occasionally, the cow would swipe her tongue onto someone's hand or someone's face, but that was all.

The grange door opened with a scrape and splash. Gird's Cow turned and walked into the grange, with Arianya beside it. Inside the grange, the smell of cow was strong enough to notice but not unpleasant. The cow walked up to Marshal Pelis first. He put out a hand, and the cow wrapped its tongue around it, a double swipe. His brows went up.

"Well. Gird's Cow indeed."

Then it licked every one of the mages, child and adult both, and walked up to the platform. It put one hoof on the platform and then—a little clumsily—lurched up onto it. It stood there a long moment, then let out a sonorous *Mooooah!* And vanished. The flower garland dropped onto the platform.

Within the glass, reports came back that the Hoor had risen to bank-full and flowed clear as glass. Every well in town was full or overflowing, every trash heap or muck pile had been washed away, and the only building whose roof had collapsed (though many had leaked) was the one in which the mage-hunters had gathered. The field where the mock battle took place every year was a sodden mess of knee-deep mud, so a much smaller fair replaced it, with competitions for individual skills instead. Arianya spent the next two days handing out prizes for Best Lacework, Best Cherry Pie, Fastest Leg Turner, and the like. The accused mages, child and adult, participated without comment . . . it was as if people forgot that they knew mage from nonmage.

As the cavalcade rode away from Hoorlow back to Fin Panir, it was clear that the rain had not been local . . . all the land they rode over had been refreshed. New-sprouted grass and flowers out of season grew on every side; the trees no longer looked dusty and tattered but full and healthy. In all the vills and towns, the people had the same look as those in Hoorlow: free for a time from anxieties and sorrow, anger and hatred. Here and there, people told of seeing a dun cow appearing immediately after the rain, a cow that swiped people with a rough tongue, mostly those who had been deep in sorrow about something.

Fin Panir itself had been drenched with the same healing rain. The Company of Gird's Cow, who had been struggling to carve a wooden cow, had been stunned to see their incomplete carving come alive. "The right color, even!" Salis said. "We was all workin' on it, y'know, and then come the rain, and we couldn't even stand upright, let alone see anything . . . and when it stopped, there was Gird's Cow, the real one, just like I imagined it."

Arianya had a momentary vision of Gird's Herd, an infinite number of identical dun cows, and pushed it down. "What did it do?" she asked.

"Walked up to me and gave me a lick of that rough tongue like I've never had before," he said, grinning. "Like a big dog, only the tongue's that rough, you know. Bein' slapped with a bit o' coarse sackin'. But I knew what it meant. Hugged that cow's neck, and it gave me another one on the shoulder. We walked 'er around the city, then back up here, and she's in the meadow now, sleek as you please."

"She's still here?"

"What! You don't think I'd send Gird's Cow away, do you?"

"No, but . . ." She explained about the many sightings of Gird's Cow, including the cow that had licked her in front of the grange in Hoorlow.

"Well." Salis scratched his head. "Well, I dunno about that. Maybe Gird has all the cows he wants now, or maybe the cow . . . just is where she needs to be, wherever that is."

CHAPTER THIRTY-SEVEN

Chaya, Lyonya

With Dorrin and most of the magelords gone, Chaya settled into its usual summer routine. The handful of remaining magelords adopted modern dress and Common tongue. High Marshal Seklis left. A courier came from the Sea-Prince, reporting that Dorrin had been taken safely aboard a trader known to the Sea-Prince and should reach Aarenis—Barrandowea-Stormlord willing—well before the end of the trading season. Kieri already knew from the King's Squires who had escorted her what ship she had taken, but the Sea-Prince also sent a chart of the probable route. Kieri sent back a note of thanks.

Kieri expected the western elves to return to their elvenhome after the magelords were out of Kolobia, but they didn't.

"Your queen is our king's granddaughter," Caernith said. "Your children are his great-grandchildren—"

"But only half-elf," Kieri said. "From what the Lady said, Dameroth fathered many half-elven children."

"In different times. Your queen is the only one of Dameroth's children alive in this time. And the only one who ever came to such prominence; married a half-elven ruler and thus had children also half-elven, carrying the elvenhome gift from both parents. He wants to know how they get on."

"He could visit," Arian said a bit tartly. Kieri glanced at her. Tilla had a handful of Arian's hair. She reached up and patiently unhooked the tiny fingers. "I wonder if I was as active at this age. I see others born within the same fiveday who are not yet sitting up so strongly. Tell me, Caernith, are elven babies faster to learn skills than human babies? I'd have thought, with such long lives and a longer pregnancy, they'd be slower."

Caernith smiled, a surprisingly sweet smile. "They learn many things faster, milady. These two in particular; I suspect it's having elven blood on both sides. You've noticed their babbling often sounds like singing."

"Yes, I have," Arian said. "And my mother said I started singing very young."

"They will learn speech early and then sing in earnest. It would be well to have musicians play here every day or so to educate their ear. And they may be on their feet, though still a little unsteady, well before they're a year old. Elven children are not babies long—they grow and learn quickly for the first two years, outstripping human children. Later, however, they will seem to stay the same for a long time—an elf child of thirty winters may be no more than chest-high on an adult and far from adult in other ways. They need more years to learn elven lore and history, you see."

"And half-elves?" Kieri asked.

"Their pattern is more like the human but faster in the early years. You, lord king, began standing at just half a year and speaking words perhaps three tendays later, according to the elves who knew you then. When you were lost, you had both elven speech and human, as if a much older child, though not excessively tall. And you, my lady, were much the same. These two—" Caernith reached out to ruffle Falki's hair. "These two bid fair to exceed either of you. I will be surprised if by the end of the next quarter-year they are not on their feet and speaking."

Though Kieri still had many duties as king and lord of his elven-home, he and Arian found time to play with their children. And on Midsummer, when he went to the King's Grove to sing the sun into harmony, he presented his children to the Old One in the bone-house as well.

Paran Oathkeeper, the Tribe rejoices in the birth of your children. Put their hands on my head.

Kieri put each of the children's hands on the old skull for a moment.

We know them. They are ours. Bring them again when they can stand on their own.

Regular news from Tsaia reported continued unrest in Fintha, often spilling over the border, but no more iynisin attacks. King Mikeli had decided to recall Arcolin from Aarenis, in light of Arcolin's report, to undertake a stronger defense of Tsaia's border with Fintha. In Aarenis, Arcolin had reported to Mikeli that the danger was less: the Kostandanyan troops had held off Immer's in Fallo, and Cortes Cilwan had been retaken. Arcolin's letter to Kieri mentioned Count Vladi's warning, along with the circumstances:

> *He had been drinking, and I am not sure what he meant by "demon-ridden." Perhaps what Dorrin told us of—what almost happened to Stammel, another being in the same body. That is what Andressat thinks the code his son pricked on his own body means. But rumors have multiplied—that Alured has died of wound fever or has lost a leg or was deposed after the defeat by his own commanders. No one I trust has certain word about him other than he was injured in Fallo, thrown from his horse in the midst of battle. Sorellin reports no more trouble from Rotengre; trade is beginning to return up the Immer from the coast.*

Ganlin of Kostandan, Mikeli wrote, was going to marry Rothlin Mahieran, but not until she had finished her training at Falk's Hall. That surprised Kieri; he'd been sure she would marry sooner.

The Kostandanyan ambassador explained: "They wanted a Girdish woman at first, but with more Girdish troubles, Royal Council thought better Falkian knight. Our king has no care either way, just wants Ganlin married to good rank."

So the summer wore on, drier than most but yielding good crops of the summer grains. Kieri's days were full, dawn to dusk, but nothing seemed as perilous as the year before. Arcolin came back to Tsaia well before Autumn Court, having negotiated with Foss Council to bring along one cohort of the Company. He sent Kieri a fuller account of the state of Aarenis, including a new rumor that Alured had died on a voyage to the pirate base at Whiteskull.

As Caernith predicted, the twins grew and learned rapidly, their first infant sounds quickly coming to resemble near-speech, and musical speech at that. The elves of Kieri's elvenhome seemed almost as fascinated by the babies as he and Arian, but they were not alone. Kieri's human subjects also came to see them, bringing gifts. By the Autumn Evener they were both standing, even lurching from one parent to another, not quite walking. Both could say a few words clearly enough to be understood.

Though Kieri wondered where Dorrin was and whether she had completed her task and about the future of Aarenis and whether a new ruler like Alured would rise to menace everyone again, the twins' progress distracted him again and again. What would they do next? When would they speak whole sentences?

Then, in one tremendous downpour, the rains returned and continued for three days. The usually placid river near Chaya rose above its banks, flooding the water meadows. Every well in Chaya overflowed.

"She did it," Arian said as they stood by the windows watching rain stream down.

"We don't know that for certain," Kieri said. "We've had dry years and wet years before."

"The taig says this is different."

Arian was right; he could feel that himself. Late as it was in the year, the rose garden burst into early-summer bloom. In the Royal Ride, wildflowers spangled the grass even as the rain continued. Then it vanished, leaving a blue sky and bright sun. The little river's floodwaters went down with unnatural speed, leaving it bank-full of clear water. Days later, a courier arrived from Tsaia to report the same rain there, everywhere it seemed.

"Will she come back?" Arian asked.

"If she lived through whatever she did . . . maybe."

Winter came with its usual snows, and in the spring the new growth returned. The twins were not just walking but running, busy, curious, and endlessly chattering. Tilla's red hair had continued curly; Falki's dark hair now waved a little. The first ships into the river port brought word that Alured's domain had fragmented. The Immer ports formed their own alliance, based on the Guild League, and one of Alured's captains ruled in Cortes Immer, apparently with no ambitions to extend his realm. Lûn and Rotengre were free cities again, though Rotengre retained a bad reputation.

Traders moved through Lyonya, along the River Road in the north, across the middle road through Verrakai territory, and even south from Chaya to pick up the South Trade Road near Halveric's steading.

"We had to build an inn," Aliam said one morning in Kieri's office. "Otherwise they were camping anywhere and cutting down trees without noticing which were which. Though I suspect some intended to steal blackwood."

"What about the road west?"

"That's their problem," Aliam said. "We talked to the gnomes, as you suggested, and they let us use what they call nedross rock. Good for roads. I told the merchants they were welcome to break it up themselves." He set his mug of sib down on the table. "I am not turning road builder at my age. If my sons choose, they can, but being your military commander is more than enough for me."

"Does it bother you to have that traffic there?"

"Not at all, so long as they don't steal or make a mess of my groves. Remember, I left home to go fight wars in Aarenis. The elvenhome forest was a trap for the likes of me. I wanted more. Now Estil and I are back in the bigger world. Some don't like it, of course, but not many. Sier Davonin, perhaps."

"She complains about some things, but actually she likes the trade coming in, she told me," Kieri said.

"What about the elves?"

"They're adapting. And I've told them that I will never grant the deep forest to humans. They have almost as much land as before, and I'm enforcing some of the same rules, though not all of them. Outlanders can come through but not settle. Lyonya will always be different."

"Good," Aliam said. He stretched. "I'd best get back to work before the king decides I'm too old for my job."

Kieri laughed. "Don't start that, Aliam. You will be my military commander as long as you live—no one else here has the experience."

Several days later, Kieri came into his office to find a man seated in a chair, with Falki standing between his knees. He stopped, startled: Who was this man, and how had he reached the office without being announced? He had never seen the man before in his life, he was sure of it. He looked foreign—perhaps someone who had come to Lyonya seeking work. Or a sailor come from the river port. Someone used to outdoor work, heavy-shouldered, in rough clothes. And why was Falki here? Where were the nursery maids who were supposed to be with the children at all times?

"I have waited a long time for this," the man said. He smiled. When Kieri said nothing, he went on. "You do not know who I am?" The man held Falki firmly but apparently not harming him. Then he ran his hand over the child's hair, stroked the side of his face idly, as one might stroke a favorite statue, while watching Kieri. Falki shivered, lips pressed together.

Kieri's stomach twisted; dark memories stirred deep in his mind. "I do not," he said past clenched teeth. "What are you doing here?" His hand moved to his sword.

The man ran his hand under Falki's chin, lifting it a little, and slipped his fingers into the neck of the child's shirt and ripped the light fabric, baring his chest. "I have missed this," he said. Falki twisted, distress on his face. The man leaned a little forward and pressed his lips to the boy's hair. "Shhh . . ." he said. "Be still, child." Kieri could feel the power in the man's voice. Tears welled in Falki's eyes.

"Get away from him," Kieri said. The memories rose to the surface—what he and Arian had talked of—what he had most feared. He pushed them back. It could not be . . . it must not be.

"Would you rather I petted *you*?" the man asked. Then, in a voice Kieri had never forgotten, "Kneel to me!"

Kieri's knees loosened for a moment, then rage swamped all fear as he knew without a doubt what mind lay behind that unfamiliar weathered face. "You . . ." he breathed. "Sekkady."

"Ah, yes. I knew you would remember soon enough. You thought you had escaped me, didn't you? And so you did, for a while . . . but I knew the time would come." The man who had been many men, including the Duke of Immer, and was now once more Edigone Baron Sekkady smiled a too-familiar smile. "A long wait makes the feast sweeter. Kneel to me, vas'tanho."

"No," Kieri said. He could scarcely breathe for the mix of horror and rage. He struggled to remember what of his magery might work against Sekkady.

"No? Do you not care for your child? Have you forgotten so much?" The hands moved, one finger stiffening—Falki flinched, eyes wide, but still silent.

The words came into Kieri's mind and out his mouth in a long flow of power; Sekkady's arms flew wide, strained back. Kieri took the three strides to Falki, picked him up and cradled him, then stepped back.

"You—you—I took that from you—" Sekkady said. "You have no powers."

"No," Kieri said again. As the man tried to stand, Kieri spoke another word of power and knocked him flat. "How many have you destroyed, Sekkady, outliving your own body to seek me? And why? You had other slaves." Falki whimpered softly. He spoke to his son. "There, lad. It's over."

"It's not! You *will* kneel—you will see your child as you were—"

"Be silent," Kieri said with a flick of his fingers. The man's mouth moved, but no sound came out. "You silenced others: now I silence you. You will speak only to answer my questions . . . and you *will* answer." Deep in his mind he felt the touch of Sekkady's power and tossed it away. "How many lives?"

"Hundreds—thousands—what does it matter? Not all were spent hunting you . . ." Now the voice was harsh, strained.

"And you pulled their power, their life, into your bloodstone," Kieri said. "You still have it, I'm sure."

The man's eyes shifted, a quick glance that told Kieri where. That pocket, of all the pockets in his shabby clothes, or in a pouch beneath.

Kieri heard a sound behind him. He turned and saw Arian behind him, face white as salt, eyes blazing, her sword drawn, and with her two of her Squires, one of them holding Tilla. How long had she been there? What had she heard? "I will deal with this," he said to them. "Arian, take Falki and Tilla out of this."

"I want to kill him," Arian said a little breathlessly. Kieri had never seen that expression on her face before.

"No, love," he said. "You could, of course—but you must not. It would hurt you in the end."

"No one came for you," she said, "but I have come—why should you bear it all?"

"Someone did come in the end. And as for why: I am the king."

Her expression softened a little.

"Yes," he said, as if she'd spoken. "Put up your sword and take our son. Our very brave son," he said, nuzzling Falki's neck. "You were brave and good," he said to the boy as Arian sheathed her sword and moved to his side. "And you will remember that and little else."

"Kieri—"

"Do not fear," he said. He did not fear. He had passed through his greatest fear and lived; he had saved his son before his son had been hurt as he had been. Sekkady no longer controlled him; that threat about the bloodstone had been a lie. He felt calm then, neither enraged nor terrified . . . that had passed. Falk, he thought, had taken it away, leaving him the power to think, to make decisions.

He looked at the wretched thing on the floor . . . the last of many men Sekkady had ruined. Pity for the man, whoever he had been, whatever he had been of good or evil, brave or craven, rested on him lightly as a flower's petals: that man was dead, his story ended. The spirit that had stolen his life and now animated his body, the spirit that had stolen Kieri's childhood and tormented so many more as well, that spirit still alive, powerful, and malign, must be dealt with.

When the others had left the room, Kieri released the lock on the man's speech. Sekkady began with curses—curses he clearly thought potent, though Kieri felt them as little as grains of sand. Finally, gasping for breath as if he had been running, Sekkady slowed. "You will become me," he said then. "When you kill me, that will free me to invade you as I did this body—"

"You cannot," Kieri said. He was sure of that.

"If you torture me—you want to, I am sure—" Sekkady smiled, that cruel smile Kieri knew so well.

"No," Kieri said. "*You* delight in others' pain. I do not."

"Then why have you not killed me already?"

"To learn pity," Kieri said. "I pity already the man—all the men— whose bodies you stole. But I do not yet pity you—I do not yet understand what made you what you are."

A smile—a smug smile this time—settled on that face. "Well. Then you will surely become like me in your own time, and that will give my death savor. For to understand me—even more to pity me— is to become me. You cannot understand without realizing how much more I have than you, and you will want it for yourself."

"No. But tell me: What made you what you are?"

"What made me the greatest mage since the fall of Aare?" The smile widened, gleeful and feral at once. "Power. Strength. Will. I never flinched from what I had to do to become that, whatever it was."

Despite himself, Kieri shivered. In Luap he had sensed some good eaten out by evil, a weak man who might have been good if he had not been tempted beyond his strength. But here . . . here was strength, not weakness, and one who had chosen evil freely. He sensed nothing good, if ever there had been.

"The iynisin are right," Sekkady said. "When the First Tree turned traitor, when it revealed weakness and could not resist a human's song, all creation was contaminated. Love is weak. In every love song, every tale of love, the lover is weakened until he cannot resist the beloved. Your weakness, too—you would not let those you love kill me lest they be harmed. That is folly. You should have learned better from me. All that matters is power, and power means the power to kill, to destroy. If you can destroy, you can control anything. So I learned when they taught me how to create the most powerful of all the jewels of power—the bloodstone. You must care only for power, they said. You must kill any you love first and always. Their blood is in the stone. That proved my worth to them—"

"You are in league with the iynisin? They taught you, didn't they?" Kieri glanced around the room, looking for any sign of an iynisin's arrival.

"I am Gitres's servant, as are they. Together we will unmake this flawed world riddled with weakness. That silly woman who thinks Falk can protect her, who intends to restore water to Aare—she will not succeed. She was thrown overboard with a broken back and sank like a rock. Even if some power aids her—and it won't—and even if she succeeds in her quest, I can undo what she has done. No one can destroy the bloodstone, and any who holds it will use it."

"She has succeeded," Kieri said. "Rivers flow where only sand blew; the drought here in the north has ended."

"You lie!" The voice was nearer. Sekkady had moved in spite of the power Kieri had used. He was only an armslength away now, and he held the great red jewel Kieri remembered. Its power had clouded his mind despite his own defenses.

"You see," Sekkady said. "I still have more power than you. *Your* blood is in this stone, too—blood from the wounds I dealt you. Your blood gave me power over elves as well as humans. Either your blood in the stone will force you to submit and you will be my slave again, you and your queen and your children—or you will take it from my hand and—join me."

A flicker of light from his own heart-hand caught Kieri's attention: the dragon figure deep in his ring writhed, glowed. Simultaneously the torc around his neck loosened, straightening, sliding down his arm toward the ring, its gold covering uncurling to reveal the spiraling whiteness Kieri had briefly glimpsed before, this time clearly a long white horn.

Hardly thinking, he grasped it when it slid into the palm of his heart-hand; the dragon figure flowed out of the ring and into the horn, lighting it from within until it reached the tip, and extended a fiery tongue the pure white of starlight. Sekkady's eyes widened. "That! How did you—it was lost!" He lunged, reaching for Kieri with the bloodstone.

The horn twisted in Kieri's hand like a live thing, faster than Kieri could have moved it himself, and the dragon's tongue touched the bloodstone, pierced it.

A roar burst from the stone, loud as the battle cry of an army. Blood spurted out, wave after wave that never touched the horn's purity nor Kieri himself but splashed back on Sekkady. The thick metallic tang of blood filled the chamber, choking-strong. Then the bloodstone shrank, and the blood lifted in red mist that coiled about Sekkady. Thicker . . . thicker . . . Kieri could no longer see the man's shape within it.

When it dispersed, Sekkady was gone. Where he had been, nothing remained but the clean floor. No blood, no mist of red, no stench, no body, nothing.

Kieri looked around the room. Silence. Peace. No danger that his senses, human or elven, could detect. More, a feeling of joy that came not only from his own heart but filled the air around him. Could that be the spirits released from the bloodstone? It faded, and as it did, Kieri was aware of movement in what he held. He watched as the straight horn curled slowly and the little dragon figure flowed back up the length, leaving the tip once more shiny white as a child's tooth. "Thank you," he heard himself say, and repeated it in elven and the old tongue of magery. "I don't understand."

The dragon paused in its way, and the tiny tongue of fire extended again. Waited. Kieri bent his head and touched his tongue to it. Hot . . . with a flavor of the dragon he'd met. It disappeared—reappeared for an instant in his ring, and then sank into the green again. The horn continued to curl toward its former shape. He wanted to touch it with his other hand, to feel that smooth surface, the coils of its spiral, but he could not—and even as he watched, gold wrapped it round once more, until it was, as it had seemed, a simple torc for his neck. He put it on again.

Well done. More than one voice, but Falk, he was sure, was among them.

Then a blast of enmity came out of the air, cold, implacable hatred. He turned. Iynisin.

"You are even more foolish than your grandmother," said the one in the center. "We cannot be undone by mortals. That one was only mortal—"

"And so am I," Kieri said. "But you can be undone by those of steady purpose."

"You think so?"

"And by Elders older than you," Kieri said. "Dragon destroyed your western hold, did he not?"

"Dragon!" They spat, all of them, vile stuff that hissed on the floor like acid. "Dragon killed many of us, but Dragon cannot be everywhere at once. Dragon is busy elsewhere, and you are here, little king. We will unmake you."

Swords appeared in their hands, and they moved to encircle him. Their malice battered him before they were close enough to strike. Power he recognized as greater than his own—but not beyond what he could resist. He drew his sword; they would not kill him easily.

Even as the first one struck, Amrothlin ran into the room, sword drawn and calling for aid. Then other elves, then his Squires.

When it was done, five iynisin lay dead, and Amrothlin, badly wounded, lay with his head in Kieri's lap. "I was wrong," he said, gasping. "I should have—I didn't believe—and I could not let you die—"

"Uncle," Kieri said, "I honor you, whatever lies in the past."

"Take me where my mother lies—please—others can show you. And remember me as one who saved a king's life."

"You are not dead yet—"

"No, but I will die of this wound. It is not the first iynisin wound I have taken."

That night Arian and Kieri lay in the king's bed with the twins between them. Falki slept peacefully; Tilla seemed to be dreaming, twitching and muttering.

"Is it over?" Arian asked when Kieri had told her everything that had happened.

"Is anything ever over? I'm sure there's still evil in the world and it will seek destruction. But if the rains come, and the sun, to refresh the taig, I think we can deal with the rest—"

"Listen," she said.

From outside came a faint sound. Kieri rolled out of bed and went to the window, pulling the curtains back. Damp air wafted in; he touched the sill outside and felt drops touch the back of his hand.

"What Dorrin did will last," Arian said. "The taig will have the rain it needs, and farmers in all lands, as well." She sounded completely confident. "Gitres Undoer will not prevail, not in our lifetimes or our children's."

"Well," Kieri said, surprised by her vehemence. "If that is so, then my worries are over. And it feels like it's going to rain all night. Now I can sleep."

"If that's what you want to do."

"Oho. You have something else in mind?"

"You are the last of your grandmother's line. I am the last of my father's. Now my grandfather thinks elf-lords should have more heirs . . . and I agree."

"Every child," Kieri said, "can be hurt."

"Is that really your concern? Everyone can be hurt. Every living thing—even stone—can be hurt. But you and I are on the side of life, of beauty, of honor . . . and so you risk, as that man who set you free from Sekkady risked his life for you, and I risk, as my father risked for the Lady."

"Then let us move these two back into the nursery—without waking them if possible—and risk what pleasure we can find."

All that night the rain fell steadily.

T he next day, Falki came to Kieri and hugged him. "Father—that was a bad man."

"Yes, he was."

"You said I was brave."

"You were."

"Did you kill the bad man? Will you dig up his bones and put them in the bone place?"

"His bones will not be here," Kieri said. "And as for killing—I am not sure what happened. But we have friends, Falki, who are stronger than either of us, and they helped me. I think they killed him, and his own evil made him . . . disappear."

"Was Tilla brave?"

"Yes. She was quiet, remember?"

"He didn't touch her."

"No, he did not. But you are both brave children; I have seen that before. And now—" Kieri had seen the arrival of the Council members. "And now it is time for you and Tilla to have a run in the gardens in case it rains again. Lieth will take you. If it starts raining again, you can visit the stables." A rare treat he hoped would put the recent past out of mind.

"Grown-up talk?"

"Grown-up talk. We will meet at dinner."

"Thank the gods for the spring rains," Sier Halveric said.

"As long as it doesn't delay planting." Sier Belvarin looked out the window. "We don't need another flood."

Sier Davonin ignored them. "Why did all the elves come running this way yesterday?"

"We had a little problem with iynisin," Kieri said. "It's over."

She gave him a long look, then shrugged. "As the king says."

"It is a time to rejoice," Kieri said. "Yesterday a great evil was defeated, though at great cost. Let me tell you." They listened, shock and horror at first on every face, fear passing to relief, even as he had felt it when those things happened. "The bane of my life that I thought long dead . . . is now finally certainly gone. Falki lives, unharmed, and—judging by this morning—has taken no lasting hurt. Tilla had a restless sleep at first but woke happy. There may be more iynisin, but we have elves now who do not dispute their existence and are ready to fight with us, to defend us."

"Perhaps we need not consider those things we came to discuss,"

Sier Davonin said. "At least until tomorrow. By the king's leave, I would suggest a day of thankfulness."

Others nodded.

"Then," Kieri said, "let us do exactly that, Sier Davonin. With my thanks for your good sense. Unless someone has urgent need . . ." None did. "Let us be as extravagant as the good fortune shown us," Kieri said. "We will meet three days hence, and in the meantime— feast and be merry."

"Three days," the others said, and dispersed.

Kieri went in search of the twins and found them in the kitchen gardens, wet to the knees and not a little muddy, trailed by a half dozen hens. Lieth stood at the end of a row, grinning.

"They're turning gardener?" he asked her.

"Not exactly, though they are picking caterpillars off the vegetables and feeding the hens. The hens were already doing that, but—"

"Da!" That was Tilla. "Caterpillars come out of eggs, Lieth says."

Kieri cocked an eyebrow at Lieth.

"They do," she said. "My gran showed me. Moths and butterflies lay eggs; caterpillars come out of them."

"Lieth knows," Kieri said.

"So . . . if a hen eats a caterpillar, will the hen's egg hatch caterpillars and not chickies?"

"No," Kieri said. "Only chicks come out of hens' eggs."

"Good." Tilla plucked a caterpillar from a leaf and handed it to a speckled hen. "I like eggs, but I don't want to eat caterpillars."

"Nor do I," Kieri said.

"I ate one," Falki said. "It tasted like the leaf."

Kieri glanced at Lieth again. She spread her hands. "Before I could catch him. Just grabbed it and put it in his mouth. Luckily, one of the smooth ones, not the hairy ones."

"We should go inside now," Kieri said. The twins looked at each other, then at him.

"No more, hens," Tilla said to the line of chickens. "Da says no more. You have to find your own."

"We'll go in through the scullery and get some of that mud off you," Lieth said to them.

"How were they?" Kieri asked quietly when the children ran ahead.

"Fine, I think. Though Tilla said something about Falki being afraid and holding—I think that was the word—his fear so he could sleep."

"That's . . . not supposed to be possible," Kieri said. Then he laughed. "But with these two, who really knows?"

CHAPTER THIRTY-EIGHT

Dorrin came to herself again lying on fragrant but prickly herbs, the midday sun beating down on her. She pushed herself up. The land around looked nothing like anything she had seen in Aare. She was on the slope of a hill, and beyond another hill she could see a straight line of darker blue against light blue sky. It must be the sea. But which sea, and which direction should she go? She wore the sea-stained and torn clothes she'd had on under the white gown the Guardians insisted on; she had nothing else. No water and nothing to put water in. No food.

She had not expected to wake at all. She had seen dragonfire coming toward her and . . . and nothing. She felt no pain; she had no blisters. Was this a dream to ease her dying? Or had the dragon been a dream before?

A shadow passed over her; she glanced up. Not a dragon. A bird—another bird—circling lower. Corpse eaters that must have wondered if she was dead. "HAI!" she yelled at them, waving her arms . . . the lowest tipped a wing, caught air from the hillside, and rose back up and away. Surely a dream would not include such birds behaving so naturally like birds.

Hilltops gave better views. Dorrin turned to climb upward and only then realized her boots were still wet enough to squelch and the left had a long gash down the side; the upper flopped over. She felt at her belt. No dagger. Her hair—she found the leather thong still entangled in it, worked it free, and tied the boot to her shin with it. Her hair blew into her face. She ignored that and climbed.

From the top of the hill, she saw more of the water—blue, sparkling, stretching out on either hand—but the coast itself was hidden by the lower hills except in the hazy distance, where a headland of some sort jutted out. Between her hill and the next one seaward she saw nothing but low scrub and patches of grass. Off to her sword-side, an island poked out of the sea, mountainous, cone-shaped.

She looked all around. More hills, and in the distance away from the sea, a suggestion of higher ground. She squinted. Farther—right at the edge to her heart-side—dim purple shapes against the lighter blue. Mountains. But which mountains? Mountains she had seen before or mountains in some land where she had never been? If this was Aarenis, for instance, the sea would be to the south and those mountains in the west.

The hill had a grassy top, showing gray-white stone between the clumps; the sea side, where she'd woken, was patched with more of the fragrant plant she'd been lying on. She didn't know the name, but she knew it grew in southern Aarenis. Was she in southern Aarenis? She had no way to be sure. The far side of the hill, down at the crease between it and the next hill, had a line of scrubby trees. The slope down was a little steeper than the slope she had climbed. A faint game trail led downward in zigzags.

With a last look around, Dorrin decided that the game trail and trees offered the best chance of water. She started down, watching her footing carefully. The trail, scarcely a foot's width, twisted and turned around clumps of tough grass and mounds of aromatic scrub. She came to a steeper part and braced one hand on a rock outcrop to edge around it.

And found herself face to face with a man a little below her height. She straightened up and stared. He stood scarce an armspan away . . . a man who might have been her height had he stood straight, but he was a little stooped. Rough-cut hair, mostly gray . . . brown eyes . . . a scar across his face from some blow that had misshapen his nose. He wore a brown tunic over brown trews, and his feet were bare, brown as his trews. He looked back at her and smiled, goodwill radiating from him like the sun's heat from the rocks.

"Well met, Daughter," he said. "I am glad to find you so far advanced."

Dorrin frowned; that made no sense. "I do not think I know you," she said. "My name is Dorrin—"

"Verrakai, yes." His smile widened. "And you know me better than you think. As I know you and have long known you."

Dorrin searched her memory but found nothing. "Do you know where I am?" she asked.

"Here with me," he said at once, as if that were a full explanation. "Do you know where you are?"

"No," Dorrin said. "And—forgive me, ser—I have no memory of you."

"Do you not?" Amusement danced in his eyes, lighting them from dark brown to amber. "Then tell me, Daughter, what is it you lack?"

Lack? Everything . . . or . . . she was alive, so not lacking life. What she lacked was knowledge. "I do not know where I am," she said. "Or which way to go to find my home. Or where to find water, or food, or—" She pointed at her ripped boot. "—a cobbler or anything to pay the cobbler."

"It is knowledge you lack," he said. "And perhaps I can aid you. Where you are—as I said—is with me. For the time being, that is all you need to know. To guide you to your way home will require some time and conversation. But as for water . . . consider where you stand."

Dorrin looked. The outcrop she had come around . . . another two or three boulders as tall as she. Here on the side of the slope, more than halfway down, they formed a cleft. She would not have been surprised to see a trickle of water coming out from under one of them—a spring made sense here. But there was no spring, only a fringe of dry, brown fern leaves.

"A spring was there," she said. "But it's not there now." She looked back at the man. He nodded, saying nothing. "It's dry," she said. He still said nothing. What he might mean seeped into her mind.

If he knew—but how could he know?—that she had once had water magery— "I'm not the same," she said. "That's all gone."

"Is it?" he asked. "Do you not think the land honors those who heal it?"

Dorrin frowned again. "I was certain . . ."

This time he laughed aloud, and a breeze sprang up, shaking the leaves of trees and shrubs alike, as if they also laughed. "Daughter," he said, his voice still amused, "you might at least ask the water's grace."

Moved by an impulse she did not understand, Dorrin turned, found a sprig of pale blue flowers on the aromatic shrub, and stooped to lay it in the mouth of the opening below the higher stone. She put her hand on the rock. "May the gods bless this spring," she said, "and may water nourish the land."

"*Eshea valush*," the man said.

Dorrin stared. A tongue of clear water flowed from beneath the rock; as it moistened the fern fronds, they lifted, greening even as she watched. It spread, wetting the soil outside the rock's shade, overflowing the lip of the ferns. More water emerged from under the other rocks; the trickles joined, and the little stream ran off downhill.

"Thank you," Dorrin said.

"*Eshea valush*," the man said again. Then, to Dorrin, "You are thirsty, Daughter. Drink."

"You are my elder," Dorrin said. "Please—drink first."

The man bowed, as one who has been taught grace, and knelt by the little stream now running clear between them. He put his hand down, let the water fill it, and lifted it to his mouth. Twice he drank as Dorrin watched—noting the scarred, callused hands, the signs of age and poverty on his feet as well. "And now you," the man said, rising.

Dorrin knelt and let the water fill her hand. It tingled with life, as Arian had taught her to feel it, as her own magery felt it. She drank one handful and then another. Cold, clean . . . joy filled her with the water, as if it sparkled in her veins. She looked up at the man, who stood watching her with a mix of pride and amusement.

All at once she knew who this was. "Lord Falk," Dorrin said. Her voice failed for awe; she could say nothing more.

He nodded. "Yes, Daughter : . . you are correct in your surmise. This is the form in which I choose to appear." He reached across the rivulet, offering her his hand. "Come, now. You and I should walk together this day; there are questions to be asked and answered."

Dorrin stood and took his hand. Warm, dry, the strength of his grip no more than companionable . . . and she was on the other side of the rivulet, where the game path ran on downhill into the shade of the trees. "I didn't know . . ." she managed to say.

He shrugged. "It is no matter. Now you do."

When they reached the trees, the path led in among them to a glade near a tumble of rocks with puddles between them.

"It will take some little time for the stream to rise again," Falk said. "All the springs hereabout are small."

"Are they all rising?" Dorrin asked. "Just from one—"

Falk chuckled, folding himself down onto a rock and gesturing to her to sit on another. "Daughter, you do not know your own power even after what you have done. Do you remember what that was?"

She had not thought about it, she realized, since she found herself on the hillside. Now, as if through thinning mist, she regained a memory of herself . . . herself on a ship . . . in the water . . . on a barren sandy beach . . . walking somewhere through red and black rocks rising from the sand. A weight on her head, a box she must carry, no matter how tired she was. Smooth stones beneath her feet, forming a path. Figures in white robes, walking nearby, urging her on. Clearer and clearer . . . the heat, the dry mountains, the dry plain beyond, three white towers piercing a heat-hazed sky . . . and the great empty bowl of rock near it. Designs . . . water. Water and water and something . . . a dark shape . . .

He went on. "What you did, returning Aare's water . . . that was more than well done. So you and I have been granted this space, this time, for your rest and recovery and for you to think how to live the rest of your life."

"I did not expect to live," Dorrin said. "Not when I went into the sea and not when the water rose around me. And not when the dragon showed me the fire."

"I know," Falk said. "I did not expect to live when I saw the look on that man's face as my brothers walked out free. And yet—" He grinned at her. "I lived a long time after that, you know. And here I am, still meddling in the world's affairs."

"I . . . should go back," she said.

"Back to Tsaia?" he asked. She nodded. "You have no oath to the king now," he said. "He released you."

"But my people—"

"Do not expect your return," he said. "You told them so, if you do not remember. A desperate chance, you told them. Your heir, young Beclan . . . I am not sure he is mine, in the end. With all the turmoil in Tsaia, he may go to Gird . . . but either of us will be glad to claim him."

"You . . . know Gird?"

Another chuckle. "In a way. Yes. The way the high gods chose. We do not walk together, exactly, but we know . . . I am sorry, Daughter, but this is not possible to make clear to you. Gird has taught me; I think I have taught him. Camwyn and Torre have given us both lessons we needed."

"Torre . . . of the Necklace?"

"Yes, of course. Did you think she was legend only, while I once walked on earth? We are all people who once lived and also aspects of the gods' will."

Dorrin wanted to ask which gods but thought better of it.

"Even now," Falk said, "I cannot comprehend the high gods. I know names—names used in this place and that, each people trimming the gods to their own measure, to their own understanding. Esea Sunlord and Barrandowea Lord of the Sea and Alyanya of the Flowers: those my father taught me when I was a child. But Adyan Namer, Sertig Maker, High Judge, First Singer . . . these are names for powers far beyond me."

Dorrin thought of the night she had lain on sand in the desert, staring up at stars that seemed to recede—layer after layer of patterns, endless, beyond comprehension, into the darkness.

"Exactly so," Falk said, once more recognizing her thought. "Is there but one power above all, or do they share equally? No one can be sure. What we can know is that we—you and I and all others who have walked the earth—are not the high gods. And yet we are more than grains of sand or drops of water." He reached out and touched her knee with one finger. "As you have shown, Daughter."

Dorrin said nothing. She heard water dripping now, saw rings spread across the surface of the puddle she'd been watching. Then, long before the drip could have filled it, the water's surface lifted, overflowed its rock lip, and ran down into the next puddle. Upstream, more water sounds approached—the chuckle of water over rocks, the gurgle of water along a creek bank. Had she really started this?

"Will it do harm?" she finally said. "Bringing water in a dry season if it's supposed to be dry?"

"No," Falk said. "Once these springs ran in wet season and dry. Like your well, they were dried by a curse, and you have lifted that curse." He looked around. "Are you hungry, Daughter?"

She was, suddenly. Her stomach cramped with hunger. How long had it been?

"We have only a short way to walk," Falk said. "Come." Once more he held out his hand, and once more she took it. He led her upslope beside the stream, with its laughing waters, and after a time they came out of the trees to a grassy bowl centered by a pond. "There," he said. "Walk into the water, my daughter, just as you are, and bring back what you find."

Dorrin looked at the water—limpid, crystalline. She could see all the way to the bottom . . . see water plants waving in the current from the springs there, the sand disturbed by the uprising water. She looked at Falk, who said nothing, waiting for her response.

Well. He was her patron; she wore—she had worn—his ruby. She walked to the edge and took a step into the pool, then another. The water drew her in; she sank into it, and as she did, she felt its life enfolding her. Down, down . . . she looked up for a moment at the silvery wavering surface and then down again. What was she supposed to bring back? Her feet touched the sand, tickled by the water plants . . . Her boots had disappeared, and as she realized that, she knew her clothes had disappeared as well. A box lay at her feet that had not been there a moment before. She crouched to look at it, picked it up, and the water lifted her to the surface, to the pool's very margin.

She stepped out, holding the box, and almost stumbled as she discovered that she was dry, clothed in brown like Falk, with comfortable boots on her feet. Falk smiled at her. "Let me have the box, Daughter."

She handed him the box and stepped back; it opened in his hands, expanding as it did, and he took from it a red belt, a red length of ribbon, and a stone that flashed in the sunlight.

"Come here, Daughter."

Dorrin took a step toward him; he took the ruby and pressed it to her forehead. "No one can take it from you," he said. "And now—let us eat." He sat down and took from the box a loaf of bread, a round of cheese, an onion, a length of sausage, and a plain-hilted dagger in its sheath. "Every wanderer needs a knife," he said, handing it to her. Then he took out a mug, heavy pottery glazed green, and set it between them. By this time Dorrin was not surprised to see that it held liquid.

She cut rounds from the sausage and wedges from the cheese while he broke the loaf of bread. They ate, sharing the watered wine in the mug, passing it back and forth. As they did, the shadows lengthened; though midday had seemed to last a long time, now the sun moved quickly. Falk pulled a blanket from the box. Dorrin was past wondering what else the box might yield—a sword and full suit of armor? a horse?—and took the blanket he handed her.

"It is safe to sleep here, Daughter, and you are tired. Take your rest."

Darkness fell even as she wrapped herself in the blanket, and she slid into sleep. In the morning, she woke refreshed to find the green mug full of water beside her, along with a fresh loaf of bread. Falk was nowhere to be seen, but she heard a deep voice singing over in the trees.

That day they talked again. "You might have died," Falk said, "but you did not. I might have died, and I did not. What I did changed me, as you are changed, and I had to find a way to live different than both my lives before, my early life as a prince and my life as a slave. So you must find a way to live that fits who you are now, not who you were."

"You think I should not go back to Verrakai domain? Even to Tsaia?"

He shrugged. "Maybe . . . or maybe not. What matters now is that you are true to your real self, the self you are now, that grew out of the self you were. Can a gold ring go back to being specks of gold in ore?"

"It can be melted into a lump."

He laughed. "So it can, Daughter, so it can. And one thing the same with you is that sharp mind. But can it put itself as a vein or as specks back into the mountain from which it came?"

"No," Dorrin said. "I see . . . but I am no gold ring, all one kind of stuff."

"You are human stuff," Falk said. "Not half elf or half dwarf or half anything. All human."

"And human stuff is . . . ?" she asked, grinning now herself.

"Capable of choice," he said. "For among humans is the greatest diversity. The Elders were made each for mastery of one suite of arts, but among humans are minstrels and bards for song, smiths for working metal, masons for working rock, farmers for nurturing plants and animals." He smiled at her. "And that, Daughter, is why I offer you choice—the gift given humans of which arts to choose. You may choose to go back to the life you had—or as much as you can salvage after your time away—or choose a different one. I am here, among other reasons, to help you find the choice you want most."

Dorrin nodded, staring at the grass. What she wanted . . . she wanted to hear children laughing again. She wanted to come into Farin Cook's kitchen and see that formidable woman kneading dough. She wanted to see Kieri again, and Arian, and the twins. She wanted to see King Mikeli when he was not frightened and worried. But . . . she also wanted no more of those sidelong looks, those tightly clamped mouths when she walked in the palace in Vérella. She could do without the court dress, without the women staring at her in the short puffed trews and stockings . . . not that she wanted to wear their dresses, but that was the problem.

"What I want," she said finally, "is not possible."

"Not as you now think, perhaps. But you are still young, Daughter—"

"Young! My hair is gray now, and I am past fifty winters!"

"And my hair is gray and has been for twenty times fifty winters, yet here I am. Still young."

Dorrin blinked. Young? He didn't look young . . . but he did sound and act like someone who had plenty of time left for . . . whatever it was embodied saints did. Which brought up another thought.

"Are you sure I'm not dead? And . . . just embodied?"

"You're not dead," Falk said. "Or I would not have said you had the choice of returning to Tsaia. When you leave this place, you will be as you were: alive, in your own form. Though with gray hair which may—or may not—grow in dark again. At your age gray hair suits. So, let us consider your future. What is the one thing, or one person, you would most like to see again?"

Images flickered through her mind: the front of Verrakai House, Farin, Mikeli, the children, Beclan her heir, Daryan and Gwenno, her squires, and most of all . . . Kieri and Arcolin, so long her companions and friends. She let herself imagine not seeing them ever, one by one, and one by one the images faded until only those two were left. Kieri, her commander and oath-holder. Arcolin, fellow captain and faithful friend. She said their names.

Falk nodded. "I think you may see them again whatever path you choose though it may be later. Even much later. And the others . . . will go their own ways, remembering their time with you, and it may be one or another will cross paths. You have helped shape them into what they become. And you have shaped yourself, but, Daughter, you do not know who you are. You know your name and your family but not yourself. And until you do, your choices will turn you aside from your own path."

"I am Dorrin Verrakai," Dorrin said. "Outcast of the family.

Knight of Falk. Mercenary. Duke by appointment of a king too young to understand why that may have been a bad decision."

"Was it? I disagree. You saved his life, risking your own and your honor to do so. You saved his cousin. You exposed, by your right use of magery, the depth of suspicion against it that could have ruined his realm. Do you not realize that your use of magery—though it frightened and confused him, though he was swayed by others for a time—prepared him to fight for justice for those who later developed it?"

"I . . . am afraid it was my use of magery that caused more to emerge."

"No. Not that. Though your freeing the regalia from the evil captivity your ancestors created was part of it. Magery in humans is a talent, like singing or weaving or farming: it must be used, and used rightly, or it vanishes. The regalia, freed, sought their necessary use, to which you finally brought them."

"If I had known earlier—if I had gone earlier—then would magery have come again?"

"Yes. Other forces also acted to restore it, and not all were bad. There may be worlds where humans do not have and do not need magery, but here . . . they do. So many things brought it back, and you made it more likely that children would not die for having a hand light up."

Dorrin thought about that. "Then it was not my fault."

"No, it was not your fault. Any more than your family was your fault. Now, free your mind from that . . . You worked hard to redeem your family's name, both when estranged and later as duke, but their name is their name—it was not your life's work to redeem it."

"I thought it was," Dorrin said. "The Knight-Commander said—"

"Even Knight-Commanders can make mistakes, though new-made knights may not recognize it. Did you not learn, in my Hall, that each cleans his own shield?"

"Yes, though—"

"Though you also help one another. Yes. But the shield, representing your honor: that is yours to clean. Those members of your family who did dishonorable things—their shields are theirs to clean."

Dorrin started to say, "But they're dead," but stopped.

Falk nodded as if she'd said it. "You understand," he said. "It is not your task; it is not your honor. Your honor is unstained—whatever others think, I know—and the High Lord knows, by whatever name the high gods are called—that your honor is unstained. And that is all you need. Except . . . what do you really want?"

A quiet life. At least not a life where—though Falk said her honor was unstained—others still doubted her.

"So you need to start again. A new name—are you willing to give up Verrakai?"

She had been willing to give up Verrakai at fourteen, when she ran away; she had not used it for years. But she had begun to make it honorable . . . but Beclan could do that. She could—maybe—shed Verrakai and its associations like taking off a dirty cloak. "Yes," she said to Falk's patient face. "Yes. But what name would I have? Dorrin . . . something . . . ?"

"Dorrin was enough for you once. Falk has been enough for me. Or you may find another name you like better."

That night she slept again under the stars and, if she dreamed, did not remember it when she got up. She woke to the clonking of sheep bells and the smell of sheep. She rolled over, unwrapping the blanket, and two sheep shied away, baaing. Half the flock was already at the water, drinking, along with a shaggy dog. Staring at her from the other side of the flock was someone in a long shirt with a patched cape over it, bare-legged. Falk was nowhere in sight, and she knew he would not return. The box she had fetched from the bottom of the pool lay beside her, tied with three leather thongs.

Dorrin rolled her blanket, tied it, and picked up the box; it felt heavy again. She hung the blanket over her shoulder and moved slowly through the sheep; the dog, she saw, had returned to the shepherd. Half the pool's margin had no sheep near it; Dorrin dipped her mug into the clear water, then walked a distance from the pool and sat again. She opened the box. Bread, cheese, sausage.

"I have food," she said in Common, hoping the shepherd knew it. "Will you come?" She made the gesture she knew. The other stared for what seemed a long time, then spoke to the dog, which moved off toward the flock. Then the other—Dorrin still wasn't sure if man or woman—came closer, slowly.

"Thought you dead." The voice was high for a man, heavily accented, and closer Dorrin could see a vague female shape under the big loose shirt. Her face was tanned and grimy, smeared with what looked like charcoal. "Share." The woman—or girl?—pulled a small leather bag from somewhere in the cloak. "Salt."

"Share," Dorrin said, setting out the loaf, the cheese, the sausage.

"Meat!" A sudden grin flashed white in that dirty face, and by the teeth Dorrin decided she was young, no more than fifteen summers. "You share *meat*?"

"Share," Dorrin said again. She sliced off a hunk of sausage, a thick slab of bread, and set the sausage on the bread.

The girl sat down; this close Dorrin could see the smooth skin of youth under the dirt. Dorrin set the bread and sausage between them and cut a serving for herself. The girl held out the leather bag. "Salt," she said again. "You put." She pointed at the bread.

Dorrin took the leather bag—greasy and smelling of sheep and dirt—and opened it. Grainy, gray, but—probably—salt. She took a pinch and sprinkled it on her bread and sausage. The girl nodded, snatched up the bread and sausage as if afraid Dorrin would take them back, and bit into the sausage, watching Dorrin closely.

Dorrin ate her own too-salty bread and sausage more slowly, then pointed to the cheese. "Share?"

The girl shook her head and pointed to the sheep. "No need." She looked around. "Much water. No water last time come. You bring?"

"Water came," Dorrin said.

The girl peered at Dorrin's face, leaning close. "You . . . strange."

That was probably true, Dorrin thought, suppressing a desire to laugh. This girl, living in this remote wherever it was—might never have seen a woman soldier—though at the moment she wasn't a woman soldier.

"Red. There." The girl's dirty finger pointed at Dorrin's forehead.

"Bumped head," Dorrin said, though she didn't remember bumping her head.

"Not hit. Thing. Red thing face."

Before Dorrin could answer, the dog barked and charged back up
the slope across the pool: barking and barking. Dorrin looked . . .
four riders on small rough-coated horses coming down the slope. One
of the riders yelled something Dorrin couldn't understand; the girl
waved. "Friend," she said to Dorrin. Dorrin stood up; the riders
reined their mounts to a halt, staring at her.

"Water," said one.

In that other language, whatever it was, they spoke to the girl;
she whistled to the dog, and soon the sheep, the girl, and the men
started up the slope, away from the water.

"Come. Come we!" the girl called. Dorrin took a step, then
stopped. Falk had said she could be what she wanted. Did she want
to be a curiosity to a herd girl and some strangers with flocks of
sheep? No. She had—she knew she had—helped bring water here.
She owed them no more.

She turned, gesturing another way, and began her own trek
toward the unknown.

꧁꧂

For days, Dorrin walked alone in a land apparently empty of people or their works. She had seen no one since leaving the sheep
and the girl behind and for the last two days had seen no signs of
familiar animals—no tracks of sheep, cattle, or horses. The hills
among which she walked were covered with short grass and scrubby
bushes. She had found water easily—dry as the hills looked, every
hollow in them held at least a spring and a pool. In the first pool, she
had looked at the reflection of her own face: there in the center of her
forehead was a gleaming drop of red: Falk's ruby. Part of her now,
just like Paks's silver ring . . . but it couldn't mean the same thing.
She didn't want to think about what it could mean, but she had little
else to think about. Her memory of the flight to Aare and what she
had done returned, one scene after another. Her memory of Falk—
she had seen Falk himself, the Falk of legend, and he himself had
pressed that ruby into her forehead. She felt it: a smooth bump to her
fingers, as if it had grown there all her life. And Falk had told her to

think about who she was now . . . what life she wanted as she was now and not as she had been.

She found the walking easy enough. She went whatever way seemed most interesting and did not hurry, taking time to notice flowers and interesting stones in the clear little creeks, to listen to the birds, to watch lizards panting on a rock in the sun and interesting beetles scurrying across game trails. So many things she had not really seen before, not heard or smelled, focused as she had been on her duties. Arian had taught her about the taig, but she had still thought of everything in terms of threat or not-threat, her duty to protect.

What Falk had said about humans came back to her: what she had been—a soldier, a duke—did not determine what else she could be. Yet she did not want to forget what she had been or the people she had known. She wanted . . . she wanted to find another use for those skills she had already, and she wanted to try out new things, including this careful attention to what she had ignored so long, from beetles to birds.

On the eighth day, she decided to spend the hot afternoon in the shade of a clump of small trees circling a spring-fed pool rather than walk through the hot afternoon facing into the sun, at least until the sun dipped behind the shoulder of the next hill sunsetting. With no idea where she was going and no duties to perform, she need not, she decided, force herself to endure the heat. She could rest if she wanted to. She had eaten a hunk of sausage and bread when she heard the hoofbeats.

Looking out between the trees, she saw across the little valley a black horse trotting—head high and proud, mane and tail flowing like dark water. She felt an instant stab of longing. She had ridden many horses in her life—good military horses trained to war, the Marrakai-bred mare she'd taken to Kieri—but she had never ridden or even seen a horse like this. It looked like a smaller, more agile version of a Pargunese Black—nothing ponderous about it as it seemed to float two handspans above the ground.

As if the horse heard a command in her thought, it stopped short. Ears pricked, head turned to her. Then an echoing whinny, and the horse broke into a gallop, running straight toward her clump of trees. Dorrin scrambled to her feet and moved out into the open. If the horse ran at her, she could dodge . . . but she didn't want to dodge.

Nearer. Nearer still . . . and it slowed to that same high-stepping, airy trot and finally halted just out of her reach. Nostrils flared; it uttered a sound more like a human mutter than a horse. Dorrin took a step forward. "You . . ." she said. Her voice sounded strange after the days of silence. "You are beautiful," she said. "Where are you from? Whose are you?"

The horse yawned, showing a mouthful of big yellowish teeth, then walked the rest of the way to her and put its head against her chest. Her hands moved naturally to caress the cheeks, rub the poll, scratch behind those alert ears. The horse pulled its head from between her hands and reached over her shoulder, then pulled—a hug, she realized. It sighed, a big gusty horse sigh. Then it released her, walked around her, and went to drink at the pool. Dorrin followed, her mind in a whirl of confusion.

When the horse had drunk its fill, it pushed among the trees to where she'd left the box, picked it up in that very large mouth, and came back to her. She reached out; it bumped her hand with its nose and—as suddenly as it had appeared—dropped the box, bent the near foreleg, and bowed. Did she want to mount? Of course . . . but the box? She picked up the box; the horse turned to look at her and snorted. She put it back down; she could come back for it later. Maybe.

She clambered on, awkward without the familiar aid of a stirrup. The horse stood, then reached down to nose the box. It disappeared in that instant, and Dorrin found herself sitting in a saddle, saddle-bags behind her and her rolled blanket tied in front of them, her boots resting in stirrups. "Falk?" she said. No answer but a toss of the horse's head, and then it set off at a trot, angling across the sun's light . . . north, she thought. It must be Falk.

"You know where we are going," she said to the horse. An ear flicked back at her. She knew it meant yes. "Do I—is there something I need to do there?"

Another ear flick. Dorrin's heart lifted. Here was the change she wanted, a new adventure, a challenge—and as if the horse understood that, it surged into a gallop.

Acknowledgments

It may seem odd to thank a bicycle shop for help on a book that has
no bicycles in it (not even one!), but sustaining the writer is part of
the help needed to keep a series going. In this case, the good advice
and service of University Cyclery in Austin, Texas, enabled this
writer to recover physically and regain the endurance necessary for
those weeks of very long days at the computer. So thanks, guys. As
usual, David R. Watson supplied important information and suggestions for more sources on ships and sailing appropriate to this world
and period. The fellowship of musicians in St. David's music program
provided more musical and spiritual support. Jenny Meadows helped
me untangle a particularly knotted section with wise advice. The
denizens of the Paksworld blog (www.paksworld.com/blog) helped
out repeatedly by looking up minor details in previous books for me
and making very interesting comments that pushed me to think twice
(or more) about situations and characters. Both my agent, Joshua
Bilmes, and my editor, Anne Groell, offered sound advice and assistance in the last revision process. And, of course, this book rests on
the help of all who helped with previous books in this story-universe,
all the way back to those first months in 1982 when I started *Sheep-
farmer's Daughter* and a few friends clamored for more. Thank you all
(and as always, mistakes are all my fault, not that of any helpers).

extras

www.orbitbooks.net

about the author

Former Marine **Elizabeth Moon** is the author of many novels, including *Echoes of Betrayal*, *Kings of the North*, *Oath of Fealty*, the Deed of Paksenarrion trilogy, *Victory Conditions*, *Command Decision*, *Engaging the Enemy*, *Marque and Reprisal*, *Trading in Danger*, the Nebula Award winner *The Speed of Dark and Remnant Population*, a Hugo Award finalist. After earning a degree in history from Rice University, Moon went on to obtain a degree in biology from the University of Texas, Austin. She lives in Florence, Texas. You can visit her website at www.elizabethmoon.com.

Find out more about Elizabeth Moon and other Orbit authors by registering for the free monthly newsletter at www.orbitbooks.net.

if you enjoyed

CROWN OF RENEWAL

look out for

ICE FORGED

Ascendant Kingdoms: Book One

by

Gail Z. Martin

Prologue

This has to end." blaine mcfadden looked at his sister mari huddled in the bed, covers drawn up to her chin. She was sobbing hard enough that it nearly robbed her of breath and was leaning against Aunt Judith, who murmured consolations. Just sixteen, Mari looked small and lost. A vivid bruise marked one cheek. She struggled to hold her nightgown together where it had been ripped down the front.

"You're upsetting her more." Judith cast a reproving glance his way.

"I'm upsetting her? Father's the one to blame for this. That drunken son of a bitch..." Blaine's right hand opened and closed, itching for the pommel of his sword.

"Blaine..." Judith's voice warned him off.

"After what he did... you stand up for him?"

Judith McFadden Ainsworth raised her head to meet his gaze. She was a thin, handsome woman in her middle years; and when she dressed for court, it was still possible to see a glimpse of the beauty she had been in her youth. Tonight, she looked worn. "Of course not."

"I'm sick of his rages. Sick of being beaten when he's on one of his binges..."

Judith's lips quirked. "You've been too tall for him to beat for years now."

At twenty years old and a few inches over six feet tall, Blaine stood a hand's breadth taller than Lord McFadden. While he had his mother's dark chestnut hair, his blue eyes were a match in color and determination to his father's. Blaine had always been secretly pleased that while he resembled his father enough to avoid questions of paternity, in build and features he took after his mother's side of the family. Where his father was short and round, Blaine was tall and rangy. Ian McFadden's features had the smashed look of a brawler; Blaine's were more regular, and if not quite handsome, better than passable. He was honest enough to know that though he might not be the first man in a room to catch a lady's eye, he was pleasant enough in face and manner to attract the attention of at least one female by the end of the evening. The work he did around the manor and its lands had filled out his chest and arms. He was no longer the small, thin boy his father caned for the slightest infraction.

"He killed our mother when she got between him and me. He took his temper out on my hide until I was tall enough to fight back. He started beating Carr when I got too big to thrash. I had to put his horse down after he'd beaten it and broken its legs. Now this…it has to stop!"

"Blaine, please." Judith turned, and Blaine could see tears in her eyes. "Anything you do will only make it worse. I know my brother's tempers better than anyone." Absently, she stroked Mari's hair.

"By the gods…did he…" But the shamed look on Judith's face as she turned away answered Blaine's question.

"I'll kill that son of a bitch," Blaine muttered, turning away and sprinting down the hall.

"Blaine, don't. Blaine—"

He took the stairs at a run. Above the fireplace in the parlor hung two broadswords, weapons that had once belonged to his grandfather. Blaine snatched down the lowest broadsword. Its grip felt heavy and familiar in his hand.

"Master Blaine..." Edward followed him into the room. The elderly man was alarmed as his gaze fell from Blaine's face to the weapon in his hand. Edward had been Glenreith's seneschal for longer than Blaine had been alive. Edward: the expert manager, the budget master, and the family's secret-keeper.

"Where is he?"

"Who, m'lord?"

Blaine caught Edward by the arm and Edward shrank back from his gaze. "My whore-spawned father, that's who. Where is he?"

"Master Blaine, I beg you..."

"Where is he?"

"He headed for the gardens. He had his pipe with him."

Blaine headed for the manor's front entrance at a dead run. Judith was halfway down the stairs. "Blaine, think about this. Blaine—"

He flung open the door so hard that it crashed against the wall. Blaine ran down the manor's sweeping stone steps. A full moon lit the sloping lawn well enough for Blaine to make out the figure of a man in the distance, strolling down the carriage lane. The smell of his father's pipe smoke wafted back to him, as hated as the odor of camphor that always clung to Lord McFadden's clothing.

The older man turned at the sound of Blaine's running footsteps. "You bastard! You bloody bastard!" Blaine shouted.

Lord Ian McFadden's eyes narrowed as he saw the sword in Blaine's hand. Dropping his pipe, the man grabbed a rake that leaned against the stone fence edging the carriageway. He held its thick oak handle across his body like a staff. Lord McFadden might be well into his fifth decade, but in his youth he had been an officer in the king's army, where he had earned King Merrill's notice and his gratitude. "Go back inside, boy. Don't make me hurt you."

Blaine did not slow down or lower his sword. "Why? Why Mari? There's no shortage of court whores. Why Mari?"

Lord McFadden's face reddened. "Because I can. Now drop that sword if you know what's good for you."

Blaine's blood thundered in his ears. In the distance, he could hear Judith screaming his name.

"I guess this cur needs to be taught a lesson." Lord McFadden swung at Blaine with enough force to have shattered his skull if Blaine had not ducked the heavy rake. McFadden gave a roar and swung again, but Blaine lurched forward, taking the blow on his shoulder to get inside McFadden's guard. The broadsword sank hilt-deep into the man's chest, slicing through his waistcoat.

Lord McFadden's body shuddered, and he dropped the rake. He met Blaine's gaze, his eyes wide with surprise. "Didn't think you had it in you," he gasped.

Behind him, Blaine could hear footsteps pounding on the cobblestones; he heard panicked shouts and Judith's scream. Nothing mattered to him, nothing at all except for the ashen face of his father. Blood soaked Lord McFadden's clothing, and gobbets of it splashed Blaine's hand and shirt. He gasped for breath, his mouth working like a hooked fish out of water. Blaine let him slide from the sword, watched numbly as his father fell backward onto the carriageway in a spreading pool of blood.

"Master Blaine, what have you done?" Selden, the groundskeeper, was the first to reach the scene. He gazed in horror at Lord McFadden, who lay twitching on the ground, breathing in labored, slow gasps.

Blaine's grip tightened on the sword in his hand. "Something someone should have done years ago."

A crowd of servants was gathering; Blaine could hear their whispers and the sound of their steps on the cobblestones. "Blaine! Blaine!" He barely recognized Judith's voice. Raw from screaming, choked with tears, his aunt must have gathered her skirts like a milkmaid to run from the house this quickly. "Let me through!"

Heaving for breath, Judith pushed past Selden and grabbed Blaine's left arm to steady herself. "Oh, by the gods, Blaine, what will become of us now?"

Lord McFadden wheezed painfully and went still.

Shock replaced numbness as the rage drained from Blaine's body. *It's actually over. He's finally dead.*

"Blaine, can you hear me?" Judith was shaking his left arm. Her tone had regained control, alarmed but no longer panicked.

"He swung first," Blaine replied distantly. "I don't think he realized, until the end, that I actually meant to do it."

"When the king hears—"

Blaine snapped back to himself and turned toward Judith. "Say nothing about Mari to anyone," he growled in a voice low enough that only she could hear. "I'll pay the consequences. But it's for naught if she's shamed. I've thrown my life away for nothing if she's dishonored." He dropped the bloody sword, gripping Judith by the forearm. "Swear to it."

Judith's eyes were wide, but Blaine could see she was calm. "I swear."

Selden and several of the other servants moved around them, giving Blaine a wary glance as they bent to carry Lord McFadden's body back to the manor.

"The king will find out. He'll take your title…Oh, Blaine, you'll hang for this."

Blaine swallowed hard. A knot of fear tightened in his stomach as he stared at the blood on his hand and the darkening stain on the cobblestones. *Better to die avenged than crouch like a beaten dog*. He met Judith's eyes and a wave of cold resignation washed over him.

"He won't hurt Mari or Carr again. Ever. Carr will inherit when he's old enough. Odds are the king will name you guardian until then. Nothing will change—"

"Except that you'll hang for murder," Judith said miserably.

"Yes," Blaine replied, folding his aunt against his chest as she sobbed. "Except for that."

"You have been charged with murder. Murder of a lord, and murder of your own father." King Merrill's voice thundered through the judgment hall. "How do you plead?" A muted buzz of whispered conversation hummed from the packed audience in the galleries. Blaine McFadden knelt where the guards had forced him down, shackled at the wrists and ankles, his long brown hair hanging loose around his face. Unshaven and filthy from more than a week in the king's dungeon, he lifted his head to look at the king defiantly.

"Guilty as charged, Your Majesty. He was a murdering son of a bitch—"

"Silence!"

The guard at Blaine's right shoulder cuffed him hard. Blaine straightened, and lifted his head once more. *I'm not sorry and I'll be damned if I'll apologize, even to the king. Let's get this over with*. He avoided the curious stares of the courtiers and nobles in the gallery, those for whom death and punishment were nothing more than gossip and entertainment.

Only two faces caught his eye. Judith sat stiffly, her face unreadable although her eyes glinted angrily. Beside her sat Carensa, daughter of the Earl of Rhystorp. He and Carensa had been betrothed to wed later that spring. Carensa was dressed in mourning clothes; her face was ashen and her eyes were red-rimmed. Blaine could not meet her gaze. Of all that his actions cost him—title, lands, fortune, and life—losing Carensa was the only loss that mattered.

The king turned his attention back to Blaine. "The penalty for common murder is hanging. For killing a noble—not to mention your own father—the penalty is beheading."

A gasp went up from the crowd. Carensa swayed in her seat as if she might faint, and Judith reached out to steady her.

"Lord Ian McFadden was a loyal member of my Council. I valued his presence beside me whether we rode to war or in the hunt." The king's voice dropped, and Blaine doubted that few aside from the guards could hear his next words. "Yet I was not blind to his faults.

"For that reason," the king said, raising his voice once more, "I will show mercy."

It seemed as if the entire crowd held its breath. Blaine steeled himself, willing his expression to show nothing of his fear.

"Blaine McFadden, I strip from you the title of Lord of Glenreith, and give that title in trust to your brother, Carr, when he reaches his majority. Your lands and your holdings are likewise no longer your own. For your crime, I sentence you to transportation to the penal colony on Velant, where you will live out the rest of your days. So be it."

The king rose and swept from the room in a blur of crimson and ermine, followed by a brace of guards. A stunned silence hung over the crowd, broken only by Carensa's sobbing. As the guards wrestled Blaine to his feet, he dared to look back. Judith's face was drawn and her eyes held a hopelessness that made Blaine wince. Carensa's face was buried in her hands, and although Judith placed an arm around her, Carensa would not be comforted.

The soldiers shoved him hard enough that he stumbled, and the gallery crowd awoke from its momentary silence. Jeers and cat-calls followed him until the huge mahogany doors of the judgment chamber slammed shut.

Blaine sat on the floor of his cell, head back and eyes closed. Not too far away, he heard the squeal of a rat. His cell had a small barred window too high for him to peer out, barely enough to allow for a dim shaft of light to enter. The floor was covered with filthy straw. The far corner of the room had a small drain for him to relieve himself. Like the rest of the dungeon, it stank. Near the iron-bound door was a bucket of brackish water and an empty tin tray that had held a heel of stale bread and chunk of spoiled cheese.

For lesser crimes, noble-born prisoners were accorded the dignity of confinement in one of the rooms in the tower, away from the filth of the dungeon and its common criminals. Blaine guessed that his crime had caused scandal enough that Merrill felt the need to make an example, after the leniency of Blaine's sentencing.

I'd much prefer death to banishment. If the executioner's blade is sharp, it would be over in a moment. I've heard tales of Velant. A frozen wasteland at the top of the world. Guards that are the dregs of His Majesty's service, sent to Velant because no one else will have them. Forced labor in the mines, or the chance to drown on board one of the fishing boats. How long will it take to die there? Will I freeze in my sleep or starve, or will one of my fellow inmates do me a real mercy and slip a shiv between my ribs?

The clatter of the key in the heavy iron lock made Blaine open his eyes, though he did not stir from where he sat. *Are the guards come early to take me to the ship? I didn't think we sailed until tomorrow.* Another, darker possibility occurred to him. *Perhaps Merrill's "mercy" was for show. If the guards were to take me to the wharves by night, who would ever know if I didn't make it onto the ship? Merrill would be blameless, and no one would be the wiser.* Blaine let out a long breath. *Let it come. I did what I had to do.*

The door squealed on its hinges to frame a guard whose broad shoulders barely fit between the doorposts. To Blaine's astonishment, the guard did not move to come into the room. "I can only give you a few minutes. Even for another coin, I don't dare do more. Say what you must and leave."

The guard stood back, and a hooded figure in a gray cloak rushed into the room. Edward, Glenreith's seneschal, entered behind the figure, but stayed just inside the doorway, shaking his head to prevent Blaine from saying anything. The hooded visitor slipped across the small cell to kneel beside Blaine. The hood fell back, revealing Carensa's face.

"How did you get in?" Blaine whispered. "You shouldn't have come. Bad enough that I've shamed you—"

Carensa grasped him by the shoulders and kissed him hard on the lips. He could taste the salt of her tears. She let go, moving away just far enough that he got a good look at her face. Her eyes were red and puffy, with dark circles. Though barely twenty summers old, she looked careworn and haggard. She was a shadow of the vibrant, glowing girl who had led all the young men at court on a merry chase before accepting Blaine's proposal, as everyone knew she had intended all along.

"Oh, Blaine," she whispered. "Your father deserved what he got. I don't know what he did to push you this far." Her voice caught.

"Carensa," Blaine said softly, savoring the sound of her name, knowing it was the last time they would be together. "It'll be worse for you if someone finds you here."

Carensa straightened her shoulders and swallowed back her tears. "I bribed the guards. But I had to come."

Blaine shifted, trying to minimize the noise as his heavy wrist shackles clinked with the movement. He took her hand in both of his. "Forget me. I release you. No one ever comes back from Velant. Give me the comfort of knowing that you'll find someone else who'll take good care of you."

"And will you forget me?" She lifted her chin, and her blue eyes sparked in challenge.

Blaine looked down. "No. But I'm a dead man. If the voyage doesn't kill me, the winter will. Say a prayer to the gods for me and light a candle for my soul. Please, Carensa, just because I'm going to die doesn't mean that you can't live."

Carensa's long red hair veiled her face as she looked down, trying to collect herself. "I can't promise that, Blaine. Please, don't make me. Not now. Maybe not ever." She looked up again. "I'll be there at the wharf when your ship leaves. You may not see me, but I'll be there."

Blaine reached up to stroke her cheek. "Save your reputation. Renounce me. I won't mind."

Carensa's eyes took on a determined glint. "As if no one knew we were betrothed? As if the whole court didn't guess that we were lovers? No, the only thing I'm sorry about is that we didn't make a handfasting before the guards took you. I don't regret a single thing, Blaine McFadden. I love you and I always will."

Blaine squeezed his eyes shut, willing himself to maintain control. He pulled her gently to him for another kiss, long and lingering, in lieu of everything he could not find the words to say.

The footsteps of the guard in the doorway made Carensa draw back and pull up her hood. She gave his hand one last squeeze and then walked to the door. She looked back, just for a moment, but neither one of them spoke. She followed the guard out the door.

Edward paused, and sadly shook his head. "Gods be with you, Master Blaine. I'll pray that your ship sails safely."

"Pray it sinks, Edward. If you ever cared at all for me, pray it sinks."

Edward nodded. "As you wish, Master Blaine." He turned and followed Carensa, leaving the guard to pull the door shut behind them.

"Get on your feet. Time to go."

The guard's voice woke Blaine from uneasy sleep. He staggered to his feet, hobbled by the ankle chains, and managed to make it to the door without falling. Outside, it was barely dawn. Several hundred men and a few dozen women, all shackled at the wrists and ankles, stood nervously as the guards rounded up the group for the walk to the wharves where the transport ship waited.

Early as it was, jeers greeted them as they stumbled down the narrow lanes. Blaine was glad to be in the center of the group. More than once, women in the upper floors of the hard-used buildings that crowded the twisting streets laughed as they poured out their chamber pots on the prisoners below. Young boys pelted them from the alleyways with rotting produce. Once in a while, the boys' aim went astray, hitting a guard, who gave chase for a block or two, shouting curses.

Blaine knew that the distance from the castle to the wharves was less than a mile, but the walk seemed to take forever. He kept his head down, intent on trying to walk without stumbling as the manacles bit into his ankles and the short chain hobbled his stride. They walked five abreast with guards every few rows, shoulder to shoulder.

"There it is—your new home for the next forty days," one of the guards announced as they reached the end of the street at the waterfront. A large carrack sat in the harbor with sails furled. In groups of ten, the prisoners queued up to be loaded into flat-bottomed rowboats and taken out to the waiting ship.

"Rather a dead man in Donderath's ocean than a slave on Velant's ice!" One of the prisoners in the front wrested free from the guard who was attempting to load him onto the boat. He twisted, needing only a few inches to gain his freedom, falling from the dock into the water where his heavy chains dragged him under.

"It's all the same to me whether you drown or get aboard the boat," shouted the captain of the guards, breaking the silence as the prisoners stared into the water where the man had disappeared. "If you're of a mind to do it, there'll be more food for the rest."

"Bloody bastard!" A big man threw his weight against the nearest guard, shoving him out of the way, and hurtled toward the captain. "Let's see how well you swim!" He bent over and butted the captain in the gut, and the momentum took them both over the side. The captain flailed, trying to keep his head above water while the prisoner's manacled hands closed around his neck, forcing him under. Two soldiers aboard the rowboat beat with their oars at the spot where the burly man had gone down. Four soldiers, cursing under their breath, jumped in after the captain.

After considerable splashing, the captain was hauled onto the deck, sputtering water and coughing. Two of the other soldiers had a grip on the big man by the shoulders, keeping his head above the water. One of the soldiers held a knife under the man's chin. The captain dragged himself to his feet and stood on the dock for a moment, looking down at them.

"What do we do with him, sir?"

The captain's expression hardened. "Give him gills, lad, to help him on his way."

The soldier's knife made a swift slash, cutting the big man's throat from ear to ear. Blood tinged the water crimson as the soldiers let go of the man's body, and it sank beneath the waves. When the soldiers had been dragged onto the deck, the captain glared at the prisoners.

"Any further disturbances and I'll see to it that you're all put on half rations for the duration." His smile was unpleasant. "And I assure you, full rations are little enough." He turned to his second in command. "Load the boats, and be quick about it."

The group fell silent as the guards prodded them into boats. From the other wharf, Blaine could hear women's voices and the muffled sobbing of children. He looked to the edge of the wharf crowded with women. Most had the look of scullery maids, with tattered dresses, and shawls pulled tight around their shoulders. A few wore the garish colors and low-cut gowns of seaport whores. They shouted a babble of names, calling to the men who crawled into the boats.

One figure stood apart from the others, near the end of the wharf. A gray cloak fluttered in the wind, and as Blaine watched, the hood fell back, freeing long red hair to tangle on the cold breeze. Carensa did not shout to him. She did not move at all, but he felt her gaze, as if she could pick him out of the crowded mass of prisoners. Not a word, not a gesture, just a mute witness to his banishment. Blaine never took his eyes off her as he stumbled into the boat, earning a cuff on the ear for his clumsiness from the guard. He twisted as far as he dared in his seat to keep her in sight as the boat rowed toward the transport ship.

When they reached the side of the *Cutlass*, rope ladders hung from its deck.

"Climb," ordered the soldier behind Blaine, giving him a poke in the ribs for good measure. A few of the prisoners lost their footing, screaming as they fell into the black water of the bay. The guards glanced at each other and shrugged. Blaine began to climb, and only the knowledge that Carensa would be witness to his suicide kept him from letting himself fall backward into the waves.

Shoved and prodded by the guards' batons, Blaine and the

other prisoners shambled down the narrow steps into the hold of the ship. It stank of cabbage and bilgewater. Hammocks were strung side by side, three high, nearly floor to ceiling. A row of portholes, too small for a man to crawl through, provided the only light, save for the wooden ceiling grates that opened to the deck above. Some of the prisoners collapsed onto hammocks or sank to the floor in despair. Blaine shouldered his way to a porthole on the side facing the wharves. In the distance, he could see figures crowded there, though it was too far away to know whether Carensa was among them.

"How long you figure they'll stay?" a thin man asked as Blaine stood on tiptoe to see out. The man had dirty blond hair that stuck out at angles like straw on a scarecrow.

"Until we set sail, I guess," Blaine answered.

"One of them yours?"

"Used to be," Blaine replied.

"I told my sister not to come, told her it wouldn't make it any easier on her," the thin man said. "Didn't want her to see me, chained like this." He sighed. "She came anyhow." He looked Blaine over from head to toe. "What'd they send you away for?"

Blaine turned so that the seeping new brand of an "M" on his forearm showed. "Murder. You?"

The thin man shrugged. "I could say it was for singing off-key, or for the coins I pinched from the last inn where I played for my supper. But the truth is I slept with the wrong man's wife, and he accused me of stealing his silver." He gave a wan smile, exposing gapped teeth. "Verran Danning's my name. Petty thief and wandering minstrel. How 'bout you?"

Blaine looked back at the distant figures on the wharf. Stripped of his title, lands, and position, lost to Carensa, he felt as dead inside as if the executioner had done his work. *Blaine McFadden is dead*, he thought. "Mick," he replied. "Just call me Mick."

"I'll make you a deal, Mick. You watch my back, and I'll watch yours," Verran said with a sly grin. "I'll make sure you get more than your share of food, and as much of the grog as I can pinch. In return," he said, dropping his voice, "I'd like to count on some protection, to spare my so‑called virtue, in case any of our bunkmates get too friendly." He held out a hand, manacles clinking. "Deal?"

With a sigh, Blaine forced himself to turn away from the porthole. He shook Verran's outstretched hand. "Deal."